FLORA
FYRDRAACA

FLORA
FYRDRAACA

YSABEAU S. WILCE

Cierra Califa

SF
BC

FANTASY

FLORA SEGUNDA Copyright © 2007 by Ysabeau S. Wilce
Publication History: Harcourt, Inc. hardcover, January 2007
                        Magic Carpet Books mass market paperback, May 2008

FLORA'S DARE Copyright © 2008 by Ysabeau S. Wilce
Publication History: Harcourt, Inc. hardcover, September 2008

First SFBC Science Fiction Printing: June 2009

Published by arrangement with
Houghton Mifflin Harcourt Publishing Company
6277 Sea Harbor Drive
Orlando, Florida 32887-6777

Visit The SFBC online at http://www.sfbc.com

ISBN # 978-1-61523-177-5

Printed in the United States of America.

FLORA
FYRDRAACA

Contents

Contents

FLORA SEGUNDA

Being the Magickal Mishaps
of a Girl of Spirit,
Her Glass-Gazing Sidekick,
Two Ominous Butlers
(One Blue), a House with
Eleven Thousand Rooms,
and a Red Dog

For Two Furies, Ooo & My

The Maiden caught me in the Wild
Where I was dancing merrily;
She put me into her Cabinet,
And Lock'd me up with a golden Key.

—WILLIAM BLAKE

Crackpot Hall:
The Fyrdraaca Family at Home

A Speech by Flora Nemain Fyrdraaca ov Fyrdraaca
on the Occasion of her Fourteenth Birthday

Crackpot Hall has eleven thousand rooms,
but only one potty.
The Warlord freed all the slaves, but he
forgot to free me.
Like Crackpot Hall, the Fyrdraaca family used
to be glorious, but has now fallen on hard times.

BLASTED HECK, I'm supposed to be writing my Catorcena speech, where I am supposed to be celebrating the fabulousness of my House, the glory of my family, the fantasticness of my future. But I can't think of what to write because Crackpot Hall isn't fabulous, and the Fyrdraaca family is not much glorious anymore, and my future is hardly going to be fantastic. In my speech, I'm supposed to write the truth.

Well, here's some truth.

Let's start with the fabulousness of my House. So there are four great Houses in the City of Califa, and every one of them but Crackpot Hall has a magickal Butler. At Saeta House, your hat is taken by Furfur's floaty hands. At Sanctuary School, Archangel Bob wafts through the hallways, his red wings fluttering blanketlike behind him, and not one mote of dust or one smudge of dirt escapes his eye. Bilskinir House is closed now, since the Haðraaða family died out years ago, but they say Paimon is there still, waiting for a family that will never come home again.

And then there is our House, Crackpot Hall.

At Crackpot Hall I take your hat, and I try (mostly unsuccessfully) to watch out for dust motes, and I make sure the lamps are lit at night. No Butler, just me, Flora Nemain Fyrdraaca ov Fyrdraaca, last on the Fyrdraaca family list, slaving away at endless chores that should be done by our Butler. But thanks to Mamma, we don't have a Butler anymore.

They don't call my mamma the Rock of Califa for nothing. Mamma doesn't like swirling décor and shifty rooms any more than she likes swirling clothes and shifty people. Mamma prefers things that do not change, and a House with a mind of its own often does just that. Also Mamma hates magick; it's a trick, she says, a cheat, an easy way to do hard things. Mamma is *all about* the hard things. So she banished our Butler, and now Crackpot Hall is quiet and still.

Quiet and still and falling apart.

Ayah so, this quietness is good for Mamma's peace of mind, but it's awful for the rest of us. When it rains, water leaks through the windows and puddles on the floor. Crackpot's fancy front gates are too heavy to open, so we have to use the delivery gate, like servants, and our garden is an overgrown jungle. Most of the House we can't even get to—doors do not open, stairs stop on the first step, hallways end in darkness. Crackpot Hall has eleven thousand rooms, and my family lives like squatters in just a few of them. The toilet in the one potty we *can* get to is always overflowing, and when it does, we have to go outside to the bog, where it is dark and cold, and the wooden seat is splintery.

The Butler was banished before I was born, so I don't remember Crackpot Hall's glory, but my sister Idden does. According to Idden, before, when you entered a room, the lights flickered on and the fire rose up to greet you. Before, when you reached for a towel, it was clean and fluffy and smelled of lemony sunshine. Before, delicious dinners appeared on command and dirty dishes disappeared. Before, rooms shifted with your desire, so it was only ever a short step away to the potty, and you had *dozens* of potties to choose from. Now, all gone. That's the truth about Crackpot Hall.

The truth about the glory of my family. From the outside, I guess the Fyrdraacas look pretty glorious still—some of the Fyrdraacas, anyway. There used to be many more Fyrdraacas, but like the House itself, we've dwindled. Now we are just four.

Mamma is Juliet Buchanan Fyrdraaca ov Fyrdraaca, the Warlord's Commanding General. She helped broker the peace with the Huitzil Empire, thus saving the Republic from certain defeat and ruin. That was almost fourteen years ago, just after I was born, but crowds still cheer Mamma in the street, and she hasn't paid for a drink since. The Warlord is really old now and has only one leg, so he relies on Mamma for everything.

Idden graduated with honors from Benica Barracks, joined the Enthusiastics, the most prestigious regiment in the Army of Califa, and has already been promoted to captain. She has perfectly straight teeth, can rhyme sonnets on the fly, and will probably make colonel before she's thirty.

Of our five gazehounds, two (Flashingly Fine and Dashingly Handsome) have won the Warlord's Cup at the Saeta Kennel Club Dog Show. Two others (Lashings in Wine and Crash Worship) are champion hunters and once brought down a bear.

And then there is Flynn.

Flynn is the youngest gazehound pup. He is as burnished red as his siblings and has the same caramel-colored eyes. But as the runt, he did not come out right. He's prone to overheating and falling over, piddling when he gets excited, and yapping like a little poodle.

And then there is Poppy.

Poppy is Reverdy Anacreon Fyrdraaca ov Fyrdraaca, and he used to be the glory of the Fyrdraaca family. He was a champion shot and a champion steeplechase rider. No man in the Republic could fight harder, shoot straighter, dance longer, or bust heads harder than my father. He was renowned for spirit and devilry, a real Hotspur, and so he was dubbed by the press, and so everyone calls him. But during the Huitzil War, he got captured, and the Virreina of Huitzil convicted him of war crimes. He spent three years in a Huitzil prison, and when Mamma finally ransomed him, he was broken.

Once my family had another Flora Fyrdraaca, and by all accounts she was fabulous. This was before I was born, so I never knew her. When she was lost, Mamma destroyed everything in the House she had ever touched; now no trace of her remains at Crackpot. But Idden managed to hide one of Flora's images from Mamma's purge, and in this portrait, Flora has golden curls and pink rosebud lips, the spitting image of Mamma. Even Idden, who can be pretty sour, allows that the First Flora was supercute, a real doll, sunshiny and happy all the day long. Adorable.

But the First Flora is gone now, lost in the War, and I'm hardly a replacement. I'm only the Second Flora. Flora Segunda. I don't have golden curls or rosebud lips, nor do I look the slightest bit like Mamma. I'm not adorable, and I'm certainly not sunshiny, and I don't see there is much in life to be happy about. Particularly not now. That's the truth about the glory of the Fyrdraaca family.

And that brings me to the truth about the fantasticness of my future. *Fyrdraacas are soldiers,* Mamma says. We are born to the gun. So when Fyrdraacas turn fourteen and celebrate their Catorcena, and are then adults in the eyes of the Warlord, off we go to Benica Barracks to learn to march, to learn to ride, to learn to shoot, to learn to die.

But I do not want to go to the Barracks and learn to be a killer, a servant, a slave. To learn to follow orders, like Idden, and to learn to kill, like Poppy, and to learn to give everything for my country, like Mamma. Not me!

I want to be a ranger, a scout, a spy. Rangers don't follow

orders; they slide around the rules, scoot around the edges of the law. They hide and they listen and they uncover things that are concealed. They discover the truth though it be surrounded by a bodyguard of lies.

Rangers act with cunning and with clarity of Will, and absolute focus—and magick. Nyana Keegan, the greatest ranger who ever lived, could turn her thoughts outside in, and when she turned her thoughts inside out again, she was someone else entirely. Nini Mo, as everyone called her, could read sign on the air, smell someone's thoughts, and twist broken glass into fire. She was a great adept who turned the Current to her Will and used magick to further her aims.

When the War started, Nini Mo organized the Ranger Corps to act as the eyes and ears of the Army, to go where no soldier could go, and to use cunning and cleverness—and magick—to win the kinds of battles that are not fought with guns and swords. No one but Nini knew who the rangers were, and this secrecy made them deadly. But as part of the peace accord with the Huitzil Empire, the Ranger Corps was disbanded, its rangers dispersed, some arrested, some killed. They say there are no rangers anymore, although I don't believe that. Rangers are sly and hard to catch, like coyotes, and I am sure that some of them got away.

So I can't join the Ranger Corps on my own, but I could be a ranger alone, as rangers really prefer to be. Then, why not satisfy Mamma, satisfy family tradition, and go to Benica Barracks, anyway? Be a soldier publicly and a ranger in private?

Because soldiers cannot practice magick, of course. Adepts have one foot in the Waking World and one foot Elsewhere, and that's hardly conducive to military discipline. Adepts are loyal to their Art first, the Warlord second—if at all. There's no honor in magick, and a soldier, says Mamma, is nothing without honor. A soldier caught meddling in the Current would be shot.

I can't be a soldier and a ranger, too. But I don't dare tell Mamma that I will not go to the Barracks. Mamma never raises her voice or threatens, but her disapproval *hurts,* and she expects so much to be obeyed that everyone obeys her. Every Fyrdraaca for generations has gone to the Barracks, even the dogs. For my whole life, Mamma has spoken of duty and how important it is to be true to your family honor and to your country.

Even if this means being untrue to yourself.

ONE

Mamma. Sleeping Late.
An Overdue Library Book.
The Elevator.

As COMMANDING GENERAL of the Army of Califa, Mamma
is in charge of just about everything, so she is not much home—
she's always off on an inspection, or maneuvers, or at a grand
council somewhere, or just working late. Thus, Crackpot's crumbling is no particular bother to her. Idden, too, is nicely out of
it, even if her current post, Fort Jones, is the back end of Nowhere. At least she can count on having someone else do her
laundry and cook her supper.

Mostly just Poppy and I are stuck home alone, which really
works out to just me alone, because Poppy only comes out of his
Eyrie when the booze and cigarillos run out. Then he's just a
thin shadow in a worn cadet shawl and bloodstained frock coat
creeping out the back door, off to buy more booze, so he hardly
counts at all. Thus, it is me who reaps all the inconvenience.

When Mamma *is* home, she gets up at oh-dark-thirty and
makes me get up with her, so that we can have family time at
breakfast. This, of course, is not really family time, since Poppy
isn't there, and Idden isn't there, and the First Flora isn't there.
On these occasions, it's just Mamma and me, half a family, having half-a-family time. And since that's all we are ever going to
have, that's what we have to learn to like.

It makes Mamma happy to pretend we are a happy family,
so I sit and suffer through warmed-over takeaway and café au

lait, and she asks me about school, and I ask her about work, and this morning time makes up for the fact that she stays at the War Department every night until ten and I usually eat supper alone.

But when Mamma is off on one of her trips, I sleep until the very last minute and rush off to Sanctuary School without my breakfast, but with an extra half hour of snore.

Now, the Butler may be banished, but that doesn't mean that the House is entirely dead. Occasionally it groans and thrashes a bit, like a sleeping person whose body moves though her mind drifts far away. But it never moves like you would want it to, like before, when the potty would be next to your bedroom in the middle of the night, but tucked Elsewhere otherwise. Sometimes the long way is the short way and the short way is the long way, and occasionally there is no way at all.

This does not happen too often, because Mamma is strict that it should not. Before, the Butler kept Crackpot in order, but now it's Mamma's Will alone that keeps the House in line. She likes to be in control of things and usually is. But when Mamma is gone, her grip slips a bit, and then so does the way downstairs, or to the back door, or maybe even to the potty. The House moves not in a good and useful way, but in a horribly inconveniently annoying way. Sometimes you have to be careful.

Like the Elevator. Our rooms are spread along three floors, and it's a bit of a hike to get from the kitchen in the basement up to my second-floor bedroom. The Elevator would be much quicker, but we aren't supposed to use it without Mamma. Once, when I was just a tot, Poppy tried to take the Elevator back to his Eyrie. Mamma warned him not to, but he was drunk, and he roared that he would see her in hell before he'd take another order from her, General Fyrdraaca, *sir*! When he staggered onto the Elevator, the iron grille slammed just like an eyelid snapping shut in fear, with Poppy still cursing blue as the cage moved upward.

The Elevator came back empty a few minutes later, and for a

full week, we could hear distant howling and shouting drifting around us, but always out of our reach. Poppy finally staggered out of the Door of Delectable Desires, disheveled and pale, and, without a word, started the long climb up the Stairs of Exuberance to his Eyrie, from which he did not stir for the next six months.

After that, Mamma made Idden and me swear not to use the Elevator without her. With her, the Elevator goes where it should: It wouldn't dare do anything else. But she doesn't trust it with the rest of us, and so I have to climb up and down a zillion stairs, which is a chore, particularly when you are loaded down with laundry.

And that's where everything started—with the Elevator.

Mamma was gone on an inspection of Angeles Barracks, and I woke up on the sharp edge of running extremely late. I had been up until nearly three trying to write my stupid Catorcena speech—a total waste of time, for the speech is supposed to celebrate your family and future, and what about my family and future is there to celebrate? But I had stayed up half the night trying, and here was the result: I had overslept.

Tardiness is not encouraged at Sanctuary School. Most of the kids sleep there, and that I do not is a benefit Mamma arranged due to the need for someone to keep an eye on Poppy during her frequent absences. Of course, I'd rather sleep at Sanctuary, for Poppy is not someone you want to get stuck keeping an eye on. When he is good, there's nothing to see, for he keeps to the Eyrie and is silent. When he is bad, he screams like a banshee and crashes furniture. But there are the dogs to consider, as well. If Poppy were left alone to feed them, they'd starve.

But anyway, I still have to be at Sanctuary on time, so I was in a tearing hurry. I'd already been late three times in the past month, which had gotten me only detention. But a fourth strike meant more than just detention. First, it meant a trip to the Holy Headmistress's office, where Madama would sit me down and look at me sorrowfully, and tell me I must be mindful of my time because I was all that my mamma had left now that Idden had gone, and she *relied* on me. That would make me feel guilty, and I hate feeling guilty.

But even worse, then Madama would write Mamma a letter. And Mamma would come home and get that letter, and she would be superannoyed. Mamma superannoyed is fearsome. She doesn't scream or whack, but she would give me the Look that has reduced colonels to tears, and then she would remind me about duty, honor, and responsibility. I would feel worse than guilty—I would feel ashamed. Having Mamma give you the Look is about the worst thing in the world. It means you've failed her. And she was sure to mention, too, how sad it was that I had failed her so close to my Catorcena.

My Catorcena was only a week off. It's a big deal, turning fourteen, age of majority, legally an adult, wah-wah, suitable now to be received by the Warlord, wah-wah, and so it's celebrated in big-deal style. There's an assembly where you have to make a public speech about your family's history and obligations and the responsibility of adulthood. There's a reception where the Warlord greets you by name, thus acknowledging you as his loyal subject. It's all very tedious, overwrought, and complicated—a big whoop-de-do.

For some kids, this is the highlight of their lives, maybe the only time they get to see the Warlord in his courtly glory (you can see the Warlord propping up a bar South of the Slot any old time you care to look), the only time they have a fancy party at which no one looks anywhere but at them, the only time they get huge gifties. But I don't care about the Warlord in his courtly or noncourtly glory, and I don't care about huge gifties, and I don't care about fancy parties. And I certainly don't care about making a stupid speech about the history of my horrible, sad, decaying family.

Most kids want to be adults; then they are in charge of themselves. But not Fyrdraacas. Mamma is always in charge of Fyrdraacas, no matter how old they are, and for me, being an adult means only that I will be old enough to go to the Barracks next semester, whether I want to or not. And I certainly do not, although I have not yet gotten up the nerve to tell Mamma so.

So, I dreaded my birthday, and because of dreading was avoiding, and because of avoiding was nowhere near ready. My dress was still in pieces, my speech was still idle scribbles, and my invitations were still mostly uninvited. Instead of getting ready, I'd been avoiding, but now I was going to have to get cracking. Mamma was coming back in two days and if I wasn't ready, and there was a sorrowful letter from Madama tattling my tardiness, I would be in what Nini Mo, the Coyote Queen, called A World of Hurt.

So, when I opened my eyes and realized the sun on the wall was the wrong angle to be *early,* I flew out of bed, flew through the bathroom, squeezed into my stays, threw on my kilt and pinafore, flew to the kitchen, and chucked the sleepy dogs out into the garden. I paused at the foot of the Stairs of Exuberance, but all was quiet in the Eyrie above. Perhaps Poppy was actually sleeping for once.

I grabbed a stale bun for breakfast, yanked my boots and redingote on, snatched up the dispatch case I use for a book bag, gave the dogs their biscuits, herded them into the mudroom, then flew to the stables. (Guess who mucks those out?) I fed Bonzo and Mouse and was about to pound toward the back gate when I remembered I had forgotten the overdue library book that I had sworn to Arch-Librarian Naberius I would return that very day. Not just any old library book, either, but a very rare copy of Nini Mo's autobiography from Sanctuary's special collections. If I didn't get it back, he wasn't going to let me borrow volume 2, and I'd never find out how she escaped from the Flayed Riders of Huitzil. The book still lay on the settee in my bedroom, where I'd been reading it after I gave up on the stupid speech.

So I turned and flew back to the House. And in my hurry, I decided that rather than go the long way back through the mudroom, into the Below Kitchen, up the Below Stairs, down the Upper Hall, up the Second Stairs, down the Hallway of Laborious Desire, by Mamma's bedroom, by the potty, and finally to my room, I would take the Elevator. The long way is more certain, but it's not called the long way because it is short.

If Idden had kept her promise to not use the Elevator, I don't know, though she has always been a good one for doing what she is supposed to. But I don't believe in following orders. If Idden hadn't followed orders, she wouldn't be rotting away in the back end of Nowhere, getting shot at by people hiding behind bushes. If Poppy hadn't followed orders, he wouldn't today be locked in his Eyrie, drunk as a hatter and twice as mad.

There's a whole series of illustrated yellowback novels about Nini Mo called Nini Mo, Coyote Queen, and I've read every one more than once. The novels are a bit trashy and, of course, probably exaggerated for some effect, but not entirely untrue, for Nini Mo did have an exciting life. She was always having adventures and excitement and narrow escapes. I wouldn't mind having adventures and excitement and narrow escapes, and you certainly don't have those by following orders. Nini Mo didn't follow orders.

So I don't, either. When Mamma is not around, I use the Elevator all the time, and never have I had the tiniest lick of trouble. In fact, I wouldn't mind if the Elevator showed me something new, but annoyingly it only ever goes two floors up. Poppy had been gone for a week—where did he go? How did he get back? What did he see? The part of Crackpot I can reach is small, but I know the House is much bigger, because from the stable roof, you see a wide spread of gables and buttresses, which I have never been able to reach.

What Mamma doesn't know can't hurt me, I thought. I was going to be late, but I didn't dare go without that book, because Naberius is death to those who don't bring his books back on time. I rushed back into the House, through the Below Kitchen, and up the Below Stairs.

I had forgotten the First Rule of Rangering: *Never let down your guard.*

TWO

Lost. Many Empty Rooms. Very Dusty Towels.

IF THE ELEVATOR HAD let me off where it was supposed to, at the Hallway of Laborious Desire, I would have been able to nip right into my bedroom, grab the book, and still make the 7:45 horsecar, and, hopefully, Archangel Bob wouldn't even notice me creeping into morning assembly late. I am very good at creeping, although it's quite a challenge to sneak by an eternally vigilant denizen.

But the stupid Elevator did not let me off at the Hallway of Laborious Desire. No, the stupid Elevator had slowly and silently borne me upward, gently floating as on a summer swell, and though I banged and shouted, the Elevator did not slow or stop. Past the second floor it went, past a third floor—we'd never had a third floor before—upward and upward it went, smooth and steady, until, with a grinding whine, it stopped. The golden outer doors opened to a thick darkness.

I had matches in my dispatch bag (among other useful things). *Be prepared,* says Nini Mo, but why use a trigger when there are other, more clever methods of gaining light?

"⚜⊗〒 ⊕⊜〒⟋," I said. The Ignite Sigil was the only Gramatica Invocation I had mastered, but I had mastered it well, and now a spurt of magickal coldfire flowered in the darkness like a sparkler and illuminated the blackness beyond the closed grille of the Elevator. The wan light showed the hollow shadows of bulky furniture, abandoned and forlorn.

"This is not the Hallway of Laborious Desire," I said crossly.

The Elevator did not answer.

Act as though you mean it, and you will, Nini Mo says. I said firmly, "I want to go to the Hallway of Laborious Desire. And I am in a hurry, so let's be snappy."

No response.

"I'm going to tell Mamma."

Idle words, really, because it would be my hide tacked up on the wall of Mamma's study if she found out that I had disobeyed her. But bluff is always worth a try. The threat made no impact upon the Elevator's smug silence.

"Well, if you are going to leave me here, at least give me more light." *Sweetness is its own sticky trap,* says Nini Mo, so I added sweetly, "Please. Very pretty please, beautiful Elevator."

Nada. So much for good manners. I gave the golden grille a good kick, then pulled it open, stepping out onto the creaky wooden floors into a cloying darkness smelling of dust, decay, and the distant sea. The pouty Elevator snapped its grille shut behind me. I turned and grabbed, but it yanked out of my grip and vanished into the murk. Now I was stuck.

I held my hand underneath the coldfire spark and focused all my Will upon its hazy gelid glow. A tiny pinpoint of pain tingled above my right eye, but the light winked and brightened. Now I could see hulking furniture draped in tattered dustcovers, floating whitely in the darkness like ancient ignored ghosts.

There's no way out but through, Nini Mo said when she was lost in the Maze of Woefulness and Gloom in the yellowback novel *Nini Mo vs. the Flesh-Eating Fir Trees.*

I cautiously stepped forward. Somewhere there had to be stairs down and out—I just had to find them. My feet stirred up a haze of mold and frothy dirt, which glittered in the coldfire light that I now carried before me, floating above my open palm.

And I thought *our* rooms were a mess! Mamma is too busy or too gone to pay much attention to housekeeping, and though I usually manage to keep the actual filth at bay, it's hard to keep after the dust and spiders and all those dogs. Between laundry, cooking, cleaning, and homework, I can only do so much, and so our rooms are always dreadfully untidy. Judging just by our rooms, you might think Crackpot was only lazy.

But here it was obvious that the House was worse than lazy. Here, there were cracks in the walls, and the floor beneath my feet felt dangerously creaky, as though it might splinter and give way, plunging me down, down—to where? I wandered in the darkness, through room after room, and saw nothing but decay and dirt. Piled furniture and cobwebby chandeliers. Wallpaper peeling off in long curling strips. Parquet floors so dirty that the dust was as thick as a rug.

Sometimes there was evidence of earlier grandeur: an orangery, though the stunted orange trees were all spindly and gray, their fruit withered to dry husks that crunched under my feet. The glass ceiling above was black with dirt and let no daylight in, for want of which, I guess, the poor trees had slowly died. A long echoing room, its ceiling held aloft by tall tree-shaped pillars, most of its floor space taken up by an enormous swimming pool. The shallow end of the pool was empty, its green and blue mosaic glinting sadly in my coldfire light. There was still a bit of water in the deep end, sludgy black water smelling of yuck.

But despite the occasional glimpses of grandeur, there was mostly just mess.

Mess, and no stairs, no way out. Rangers never get lost. They always know where they have been, where they are going, and all the bits in between. Nini Mo navigated her way from Puento to Angeles, with both hands tied behind her back and a sack over her head, by sense of smell alone—that's fifteen hundred miles of burning desert! It was stupid, then, that I couldn't even find a doorway out or a staircase down. I knew Crackpot was big, but I'd never imagined it could be *this* big.

A tiny idea was forming in my brain that maybe Mamma had been right about the Elevator. I remembered Poppy and his shouting and the pinched look on Mamma's face as she waited for him to return. Only now did it occur to me that she had not gone looking for him herself—

Wah! A ranger would never think such things. A ranger must look with utmost logic at where she is and what she is doing, not succumb to dire fantasy. Nini Mo had not panicked when the Up-Drawn Bandana Society tied her to a log and threw her into the Dellenbaugh Gorge in *Nini Mo vs. the Cattle Coolers.* She had coolly sawed through the ropes with a spur and used her kilt as a parachute, then climbed back up the ravine and garroted every last ruffian. She had survived because she had been coolheaded and considering. I would be so, too, if only I could get my hand to stop quivering. The coldfire light was getting dimmer, and this time my Gramatica Invocation had no strengthening effect. I remembered that First Rule of Rangering, *Never let down your guard,* only too well now—now that it was too late.

The Second Rule of Rangering: *Take your bearings.* I had walked into a narrow closet, its walls tiered with drawers that went up over my head. I pulled one open, and a burst of dusty lavender boiled upward. Inside lay the legendary towels. Idden is pretty fastidious, and in her stories of Crackpot's glory, she always dwelled on those wonderfully fluffy towels. Now they didn't look so fresh and clean.

I went to the window and rubbed away the grime with my free hand. All I could see was my smudgy reflection. How could it be dark outside? Had I been lost so long that the day had gone by and night fallen, and now I wasn't only late for school, I had missed it entirely? I had to get out of here, and fast.

The Third Rule of Rangering: *Consider your options.* I did not want to climb out of the window into darkness. Goddess knew what hungry uglies were lurking down there, just waiting for a tasty little snack to plummet into their gaping maws. I had no option but to continue on. The dribble of panic I had been trying to swallow was turning into a torrent, and the coldfire light was almost gone. Though I tried to rekindle the Invocation, it would not spark again. A lone match would not be much aid against such very *dark* darkness.

So on I continued, down a short staircase, covered with well-torn carpet, and through a narrow corridor lined with empty chairs whose leather seats had rotted away. Then ahead— a thin slant of light.

I hastened toward it, passing through a room whose emptiness was indicated by the hollow echo of my footsteps. As I got closer, I could see that the light slanted from a slightly opened door.

But not just a regular door, regular-sized and everyday ordinary. This door was one of a pair, and these two doors were enormous, each as wide as a coach and twice as tall. They were smoothly silver, with no decoration of any kind, not even doorknobs or lock plates. The flat metal reflected the tiny spark of my coldfire light, getting dimmer by the second, and my own unflattering reflection, squat and wavery.

It was lucky for me that that door was slightly ajar; never would I have had the strength to push that mammoth weight open. My coldfire light winked out, but the brilliant summery shimmer coming through the crack kept the darkness at bay.

"There's no way out but through," I said, my voice thin and whispery. I had to suck my tum in and hold my breath, but I could just squeeze through.

THREE

Surprise. Denizens & Butlers. Many, Many Books.

*A*FTER SO LONG IN darkness, the bright light was blinding. For a second I saw nothing, then blurring gray spots swam across my eyes. After a few seconds the spots faded, and I found myself in a library.

And what a library! I had thought the Library Rotunda at Sanctuary was huge, but it was a tiny broom closet compared to this room, whose length seemed to go on forever, disappearing into a distant sunny haze. The width of the room was not so distantly long, but it was still plenty wide.

Like the doors I had squeezed through, all the surfaces of the room were sleek and silvery, the floor like polished steel, the bookcases angular and slick. To my left, the wall was one long sheet of glass, through which the hot sun spilled, making the dazzle that had so blinded me at first. The opposite wall was nothing but bookshelves, marching into the haze, climbing upward until they reached the round arch of a cloudy dragon-entwined ceiling far above.

But the books! Never had I seen so many books. Hundreds of sizes, colors, and shapes filled the bookshelves, and their brilliant bindings were the only contrast to the glittering silver monotone. More slick cases—these fronted with glass—stood freely about the room, and these contained more books, and there were still more piled on the floor in haphazard stacks. More books than I could read in a lifetime, even if I sat down in one of the stiff metal chairs that stood at intervals along the enormous windows and started reading right that very second.

I went over to the table that marched the length of the room. It was larger even than the Grand Council Table at the War Department—which means it was *big*—and it was covered in scattered papers, stacks of books, inky-pen wipers. Chewed pens lay haphazardly, as though they had been tossed down in disgust, and there was a lovely big glass inkwell shaped like a turtle, half empty.

The papers were covered with thick black writing in the style called Splendiferous. It's an old script, and very flourishing, with many long sweepy bits both above and below. Back in the day, it had been the official hand for writing official documents such as laws and proclamations. Now it's just old-fashioned and rarely used. It's an extremely hard script to read, and I couldn't make out any of the writing.

"Hey, don't touch that," a voice hissed in my ear.

My heart nigh to jerking right out of my chest, I snatched my hand back from the book I had been about to pick up, then turned around.

A boy stood behind me, glaring, his arms crossed. He was tall, his gangliness wrapped in a tattered black gown with trailing torn sleeves. Grayish hair straggled around a narrow, starving face; colorless eyes peered over a pointy snuffling nose.

"That book is older than this City and even more fragile," he said, "so keep your dirty paw to yourself." The boy shivered and huddled deeper into a thick black woolly shawl, which was liberally dusted with shreds of torn paper.

"Says who?" I demanded. "Who the heck are you? And what are you doing here?"

"This is *my* library," the boy said menacingly. He widened his flat white eyes and scowled. "I should ask what *you* are doing here!"

"Nayah," I answered. "This is *my* House, or rather my mamma's House, and therefore this library is hers. And so is the book."

The boy's scowl turned into a snarl. "Your mamma lives in this House by my leave."

"Ayah? Says who?"

The boy puffed up like an adder and bellowed, "I say so—I, Valefor, the Denizen of House Fyrdraaca—I say so and so it is!"

At least, I think he tried to bellow. Really he just kind of hooted in a loud reedy voice and ruined the effect by sputtering into a cough at the end. The windmill arms and the scraggly hair did not help his bombast, either.

Although I am ashamed to admit it, I laughed. He had tried to look so important and had only succeeded in looking silly. He coughed and coughed. I tried to swallow my laughter; he raised his head and gave me a look to cut glass.

"You are mean, Flora Fyrdraaca." The boy wheezed again, a terrible sound that made my own throat hurt in sympathy.

"And you are not our Butler," I said. "Mamma banished our Butler."

The boy stuck his pointy chin in the air. "Ha! I am an egregore of the fifth order—I can hardly be banished! Though Buck did try to get rid of me, this is as far as I can go, here to the Bibliotheca Mayor. If she banished me completely, the House would fall right down."

Could this actually be Valefor, our Butler? My excitement was tempered by skepticism. Praterhuman entities such as denizens, at least in my experience, tend toward the fantastic. At Sanctuary, Archangel Bob stands seven feet tall, and his crimson wings flutter behind him like two giant flags. Poor Furfur, at Saeta, even though he is run ragged by the hordes of lobbyists and sycophants always hanging around the Warlord, has a noble hound-dog head and is always perfectly dressed. Bilskinir House has been shut for years, but legend has it that the notorious Paimon is hugely and fabulously phosphorescent, and always hungry. This boy did not look fantastic at all, only scraggly. If he was our Butler, I guess he had fallen on hard times, like the rest of us at Crackpot Hall. But could it really be him?

"I know who you are, Flora Nemain Fyrdraaca ov Fyrdraaca the *Second*. Why do you not know me?" the boy said, scowling.

"Because I've never seen you before, and you sure don't look like a Butler."

He deflated a bit and wrung his bony hands melodramatically. "I know, I know. I'm really not in good shape. You should have seen me in my early days, before your dear mamma sucked me dry and cast me aside. Under Azucar Fyrdraaca, I had the mane of a lion and fingernails of gold. When Anacreon Fyrdraaca was Head of the House, I had six of the most perfect arms, and I was fifteen feet tall—"

"You must have banged your head a lot on the doorways then."

He stuck his lip out at me. "My hallways were taller then, too. You are a snippy one, Flora. I'm surprised at you, and disappointed, too. Surely you are the shortest Fyrdraaca that I can recall, and my memory is pretty good. And those little blue eyes—don't squint like that. It only makes you look mean. That hair—do you ever comb it? And that coat you are wearing! What a mess, those wide lapels and awful—"

Now I was not excited at all, just stung. It is true that I'm not pretty; my hair is rusty red and curly, with a tendency to frizz, and I am rather plump. But rangers don't want to be beautiful; they want to be anonymous. Nini Mo wasn't beautiful; she was strong and fast and clever, and those qualities are more important than looks. But it's irksome to have a complete stranger comment so personally on personal things.

"There is nothing wrong with my redingote," I said. "It's the latest style in coats."

"A slave to fashion, too! Fyrdraacas set the fashion; they don't follow it—"

"Well, you don't look so great yourself," I interrupted, to sting back.

"You should have seen me before. Then, I was the best House in the City—the brightest and most awesome. You could see my gleaming silver roofs all the way from the Alameda Hills, and at night, the glow of my lamps was visible even through the thickest fog. I was terrific. Until your mamma became Head of the House and cast me out of my rightful place, and struck me to this sorry state. Now look at me, this starveling, this! I am the House—"

"Prove it."

He stopped midspeech. "Prove it?"

"Ayah so. Prove you are our Butler. You say you are, but saying means nothing. You could be anyone."

"But I am Valefor Fyrdraaca!" he protested.

"So you say. Do something Butlery."

"But I can't. I am proscribed!"

"That's convenient," I said maliciously, as payback for his snarky comments regarding my clothes and cuteness. Of course he had to be Valefor—who else could he be?

He wrung his hands and said, agonized, "I *am* Valefor. How would I know you otherwise? My Will is Fyrdraaca Will—"

"Butlers have no Wills of their own. They are just servitors to their Houses."

He puffed. "Some servitors never gain power, and remain trapped forever within the Wills of those who made them, always stuck within their duty. But I, Valefor, have evolved so that I can act within my own Will, as it serves the good of the House."

"But if you have your own Will, how could you be banished?"

Another puff, almost a huff. "I am an egregore of the *fifth* order. I'm good, but I'm not perfect. I exist to serve the Head of the Fyrdraaca House, your dear lady mother, whose stubbornness knows no bounds. She banished me to this prison, but she did not dare abrogate me completely. I was not created to care for Fyrdraaca House—I *am* Fyrdraaca House, the very bricks, the marble, the mortar, the tile, the shingle, the nails, the crossbeams, the gold paint; to destroy me is to destroy your family—"

I should have been superexcited to have made such a fantastic discovery: our Butler, hidden away in our House. And at first, I was. But now that excitement was fading. Our Butler was not glorious and fantastic—he was weak and paltry and a whiner to boot. The disappointment was acute. It's like when Idden had such a crush on Relais Evengardia, the matinee idol, and spent hours mooning about the Cow Palace stage door, hoping for his autograph. But when she finally got to meet him, he was a complete and utter git, and her romantic love for him (and the stage) was squashed forever.

And with this surge of acute disappointment, I suddenly remembered that I was late-late-late, and now getting later.

I interrupted, "I am sorry, Valefor. Normally I would love to stay and chat, but I am very late, and I'm going to be in B-I-G trouble when I finally get to Sanctuary, because I don't have my library book, and this isn't helping any."

"Overdue library book, eh? And Naberius is a fiend on library books, too. I'd be surprised if he doesn't eat you."

"I will be surprised, too. So if you don't mind, I gotta get my book and get to school. I'm sorry I can't stay longer."

"What book?"

"*High Jinks in Low Places: The Autobiography of Nini Mo, Coyote Queen*, volume I."

Valefor sniffed. "That's awful tripe, you know. You should read something more educational. I have a lovely book on eschatological extensions and their role in immanentizing the—"

Ignoring Valefor's ramblings, I looked around the room, hoping for a way out other than the way I had come in, and there, set deeply within one of the massive bookcases, was a small silver doorway. It swung open at my touch, revealing a rickety flight of wooden stairs.

"You can't get down that way," Valefor said. "Those stairs lead to the Cellars of Excruciations. At least, I think they do. Thanks to your dear lady mamma, I don't know anything for sure anymore. But anyway, I wouldn't go down there unless I were feeling lucky. Are you feeling lucky, Flora Segunda?"

After my earlier encounter with the Elevator, I was definitely not feeling lucky. I stared into the dank tunnel leading downward and decided to try the windows instead. I am an extremely good climber.

The windows overlooked a sunlit yard, thick with snarled rosebushes and dusty green hedges. From the length of the Elevator ride, I would have thought we were at least five or six stories up, but it didn't look that far to the ground. Beyond, I could see the crenulated edge of another roof just beyond a cluster of eucalyptus trees. Judging from the angle of the sun, I was on the west side of the house, and that roof was probably the stables. When I took out my compass to check my guess, the needle spun like a broken top.

"It won't work here," Valefor said, breathing over my shoulder. "I am the lodestar of the House, and the needle will always point to me."

"It's spinning like a wheel."

"Well, then it's broken."

Huh, I thought. The compass was an award for Best Rope Climber at last year's Gymkhana Exhibition, and it was not broken. Anyway, I was pretty sure I recognized the stables, and outside was outside. I'd rather wander through the daylit garden than go back into the musty darkness. I climbed onto the broad expanse of the window seat and fumbled with the catch.

"What are you doing?" Valefor demanded.

"Getting ready to climb down that ivy vine," I said. "The one that is about to tear most of this wall away."

"Well, it's not my fault. Blame your dear mamma. If she let me do my job, then I would have this wall fixed, and all the other walls, too. And you wouldn't have to muck out the stables anymore."

"How do you know I muck out the stables?" I asked.

"Your boots have horse hoo all over them. Anyway, why are you leaving so soon? Didn't you just get here? Come and sit with me for a while and let's have a nice chat," Valefor said, suddenly all nicey-nice and beguiling.

"I have to go. I am late for school. I'm sorry, Valefor."

"When you take the dæmon on board, you must row him ashore." Valefor grabbed my sleeve with a hand that had about as much substance as a piece of paper. His flesh—if that is what it was—was faintly translucent, so I could see the wavering shade of my purple redingote through his thin fingers. I yanked but his grip was strong.

I was caught.

FOUR

Val's Strong Grip.
Explanations. A Kiss.

VALEFOR LOOKED LIKE a high wind could blow him away, but if a high wind came along, it would take me, too, because although I pulled hard, he would not let go. It was like being pinned by a shadow. I should have been able to just pull free of his diaphanous hand, and yet I could not.

"Let me go, Valefor—"

"I am so very, very hungry, Flora Segunda," he whined. "Can't you feed me?"

With my free hand, I fumbled in my dispatch case. You never know when you suddenly might feel a wee bit faint, so I make it a practice to keep a few little snackie things about me at all times. "Here, I have a chocolate bar. It's kinda squished, but you can have it. Take it and let me go." I pulled, but his grip did not slacken.

"Yuck—it's not nasty chewy food I want." The sunlight gleamed off Valefor's eyes and made them look as opaque as milk. I had never before wondered what Butlers ate, but suddenly the wonder was foremost in my mind—and not in a good way, either.

"If you hurt me, I will really tell Mamma," I said, more stoutly than I felt. I didn't like the way he was licking his lips.

"And then we'll both be in trouble, but whose trouble will hurt the most?"

Good point. *If force doesn't get you free,* said Nini Mo, *then fall back on surprise.*

"⟐⟊⟐ ⟐⟐⟊!" I shouted. The Invocation filled my mouth with a sour taste. And instead of sparking a small coldfire light, which I had hoped would startle Valefor enough to let loose his grip, a huge fuzzy ball of brilliant green coldfire flared, then dwindled into a tiny little green dot that vanished into itself with a brain-rattling, percussive *POP.*

My ears rang, my eyesight went black, and the world went fuzzy. When the blackness cleared and my sight came back into focus, I saw that Valefor had collapsed on the floor in a heap of dusty rags. I didn't feel so good myself; there was a heavy metallic taste in the back of my throat, like iron filings, and my teeth were buzzing.

"Where did you learn such an awful Word, Flora Segunda?" Valefor said, coughing out a huge cloud of dust. Now he looked even worse than before, as though he'd been left out in the rain and all his colors had run into a giant blur.

I clenched my teeth in an effort to get them to stop jittering around in my mouth. "It was supposed to just spark a little light."

"You shouldn't light a match in a powder magazine, Flora Segunda, then be surprised if the gunpowder explodes. Your Gramatica pronunciation is terrible. If you meant to Exhort an Ignition you should have used the Nominative case, not the Vocative. The Nominative lights, the Vocative implodes."

"It worked before just fine," I sputtered.

"You were lucky! Look what you have done to me—I was hardly here already, and now, thanks to your atrocious accent, I am almost gone! I haven't even the energy to rise!"

A tiny bad feeling was growing in me. Poor Valefor, trapped all alone in the library, and when he finally gets a visitor, she is mean to him and almost turns him into soup.

"What do you want me to do, Valefor?" I asked, relenting.

He perked up. "Just a wee little thing."

"What wee thing?"

"A tiny teeny thing that will be so small you won't even notice it."

"Such as?"

"Tiny teeny—"

"Plainly, Valefor, or I'm out of here!"

"Your Anima. If you gave me just a tiny teeny bit, it would go so far, and I would feel so much better, and you would be so nice."

"My Anima?"

"Ayah, your Anima—you know, your magickal essence, inside you, your spiritual energy—"

"I know what Anima is, Valefor, but how can I give you some?"

He sighed. "You have so little control over yourself, Flora Segunda, that every time you breathe out, you let a bit of your Anima blow away. Why waste it when you could give it to me? Please, I'll be your best friend, and it would taste so good."

Compassion is the vice of queens, Mamma always says, and she thinks I should toughen up. She says that I let the dogs take advantage of me and hog the bed, when they should sleep on the floor, and that I give too much of my pocket money to beggars, and that if I am to get along in this world, I need to harden my heart.

Well, I don't want my heart to be hard, and even if I end up like Poppy, trying to drink my heart to death, or like Mamma, trying to work my heart to death, at least I will know that I have a heart and I used it honestly. And maybe I owed Valefor something for making him worse. I couldn't really resist the poor Butler sitting there so forlorn and famished, too weak to even get up out of the heap that I had blown him into.

He said eagerly, "It's very easy—see, all you have to do is breathe out and I shall breathe in, thus I shall be fed. Easy as pie."

"All right." I knelt down beside him, and he reached for me with thin shivery hands. We bent our heads together. I closed my eyes, took a deep breath, and felt the featherweight touch of his lips against mine. Slowly I breathed out, then felt his shoulders shake under my hands.

"Ah, that is so happy," Valefor whispered. "One more time?"

I drew in another breath, and again exhaled. His lips grew warmer, and now I was shivering—not with cold, but with a skittery feeling deep inside, not entirely unpleasant. I opened my eyes. His pupils had dilated to enormous purple circles, bright as coldfire. Glittering. A faint tinge of color was creeping across his face.

"Just once more. The last, I promise."

I sucked a deep breath into my lungs, which suddenly felt deflated and small. Valefor's grip was much stronger this time. As I breathed out, a great darkness opened up before me, swirling with streaks of color. The skittery feeling inside turned warm, then hot, and suddenly I couldn't breathe at all. I yanked back, gasping.

Val said, distantly, "Thank you. You don't know how much better I feel."

I leaned against the window seat, sputtering. The room spun about me in fragments of light and color. I closed my eyes again, and the spinning slowed. I felt as though something had punched me in the gut. Something delicious.

"What a drama queen you are, Flora," Valefor said. "I didn't take that much."

I opened my eyes. The fragments slid back together with a click, and there was Valefor, looking an awful lot better. His face had rounded out, and his eyes were now iridescently purple. He shook out his gown and twirled it around. The fabric, now black and satiny, flared around his knees. "Isn't it nice?" he said.

It *was* rather nice, but I didn't want to admit it. The tight feeling of anxiety and gloom that I usually carry around in the pit of my stomach seemed less tight, less gloomy.

Still twirling, Val was giving off little sparks. He stopped suddenly, and his glittery eyes crinkled as he frowned. "You taste different, though. There's some unfamiliar spark about you. What can it be?"

"I don't know and I can't wait for you to figure it out," I said, standing up. A whirl of dizziness made me almost slide back down.

"Rebellion! That's it, Flora Segunda. You are full of irresponsible thoughts. So you want to be a ranger, join the Ranger Corps?"

"There is no more Ranger Corps. They were disbanded at the end of the War."

"Oh, that silly war, ayah, I remember. A ranger! Secret and sly, the rangers are. Other than Nini Mo, who knows a ranger? Who can tell where a ranger will be, *who* a ranger will be? I'm surprised at you, Flora, for harboring such deviant thoughts. Fyrdraacas go to the Barracks, you know."

I did not want to be reminded of this, particularly by a denizen who was making that remark with a superior little grin. "I gotta go. Ave, Valefor."

"Will you come back, Flora Segunda?" he asked anxiously.

"I don't know if I will be able to find you again."

"I'll mark the way," he promised. "And now that I feel better, I will make sure you land in exactly the right place!"

"I will try." I pushed the window open, swung down the uneven stone wall, lost my grip on the ivy, and fell, with a great puff of dust, into a pile of leaves.

Something thumped next to my head. When I got my wind back, I dug through the crackling leaves until I felt the spine of my overdue library book, which I had left on the settee in my bedroom. Just like Idden had said, Valefor and his magicking were helpful! Rolling to my feet, I looked up. The window was now closed, but I thought I could see a faint pale hand, waving at me frantically. I waved back and ran to catch the horsecar, feeling almost cheerful.

FIVE

Poppy Throws a Cake.
Barking Dogs. Broken Glass.
Temper Tantrum.

THAT EVENING, I SAT in the Below Kitchen, having a late dessert and thinking. Somehow, I had been lost for less time than I had thought. By running as fast as my short legs could carry me, I had made the 7:45 horsecar in time, and slid into the Round Rotunda just as the first bell was ringing. By the time the second bell tolled, I was safely in line, ready for Morning Assembly. At lunch, Librarian Naberius accepted my fifty-one-glory fine with a fishy grin, and handed over volume 2 of Nini Mo's autobiography.

No visit to Madama, no letter to Mamma. A narrow squeak, but a squeak all the same.

The rest of the day had been productive. In Dressmaking, I got the bodice of my Catorcena dress cut out. In Scriptive, I finished almost all the invitations, and in Literature, I got 100 percent on the pop vocab test. And all the while, my mind had spun around on the topic of Valefor, and it was spinning now still.

Poor Valefor, all alone and forlorn. I know a little something about feeling all alone and forlorn. Ayah so, he was pompous, that's true, but he was our Butler, and a part of our family. He was a magickal entity and must therefore know a lot about the Current, and therefore could probably be mighty helpful to me in my rangery aspirations. I wished that Udo, my best friend, were available to discuss, but—so annoying—he'd been under house arrest for two weeks and thus incommunicado for anything non-school-related. I wondered if the Elevator really would take me directly back to the Bibliotheca. I wouldn't mind talking to Valefor some more, but I didn't relish being lost again.

My thoughtful chewing was interrupted by thundering from above. When the dogs started to howl out a welcome, all the joy went right out of my chocolate hazelnut cake. Suddenly the luscious cake felt as heavy as a pair of shoes in my stomach. The dogs bolted out of the kitchen and up the Below Stairs, yelping joyously.

Once in a red moon, Poppy staggers down the Stairs of Exuberance and causes a lot of commotion. I always hope that he will save his acting out for when Mamma is home, because she puts up with nothing. The first sign of trouble from him and out comes her pearl-handled revolver and whack goes the barrel on the side of his head. Then she carries him back to the Eyrie, and we don't hear much from Poppy for a while.

I have a harder time handling him, because I don't believe in whacking people to make them behave, even though I admit that it seems to work for Mamma. She is a soldier and soldiers are prone to whacking, so it's understandable that she would feel comfortable with it. I have found that cajoling people and making nice is as effective as whacking, but it's hard to cajole someone who is drunk and half mad.

"Where's Buck?" Poppy demanded, materializing in the doorway like a dæmon from the Abyss. He pushed a dog down off his chest and nudged another one out of his way with a grimy bare foot.

"Mamma's on inspection," I said warily, from behind my fork. Like I said, I don't believe in whacking, but I was glad that I was closer to the knife board than he was. "Are you hungry, Poppy?"

Poppy doesn't eat much—crackers and cookies mostly, which I leave at the bottom of the Stairs of Exuberance or Mamma takes up to him. But sometimes he comes looking for something more substantial, and maybe that was all he wanted tonight.

"Where's Idden?" He sat down in the chair opposite me. His hands were steady and his eyes, sunken deep in the black stripe of the mourning band painted across his face, did not seem as bleary as usual. I had the sudden bubbling hope that he might be sober.

"She's gone back to Fort Jones," I said. "Her leave was over."

"Lucky her. You can taste the sky at Fort Jones," he said, reaching for my cake plate. "Get the hell down, Flynnie; you know that dogs can't have chocolate. It will kill you for sure." He paused the plate in midair and looked down at Flynn's begging face, considering.

"Here, Flynnie, here, pup," I said hastily, dangling a cinnamon cookie. You never can guess what Poppy will do next, and among all the dogs, Flynn is my favorite. Sometimes he sprays, and always he quivers, but he is my darling boy.

After Flynnie snatched the cookie, I tossed cookies to the other dogs, herded them all into the mudroom, locked the door, then put the key in my pocket. I wouldn't have minded sitting in the mudroom with them, myself, but it probably wasn't a good idea to leave Poppy alone.

"Where's Flora?" Poppy asked, shoveling the cake in. The last time he had come down from the Eyrie, I hadn't been home, so I hadn't seen him for about two weeks. He looked the same, though: like hell. His face was sharp as a blade, and his clothes were filthy.

"I'm right here, Poppy," I said, hoping he meant me, but pretty sure he did not.

"Not you. Flora. Where is she?"

He wasn't sober. My heart sighed, and I tried to distract him. "When was the last time you changed your clothes, Poppy?"

He paused midshovel. "What's wrong with my clothes?"

"Well, they are awfully grungy, Poppy. Wouldn't you feel better if you had some clean clothes? I'll get you some if you want."

"Where's Flora?" he demanded again.

"Do you want ice cream with your cake, Poppy?" I asked. "I got three kinds: chocolate, peach—"

"Where is Flora?" His voice was getting louder.

"She went with Mamma on inspection," I lied. I went to the icebox for the peach ice cream. He took the carton from me but, a moment later, abandoned the ice cream and sat silently, shoulders slumped, staring.

"What's wrong, Poppy?"

"I lost her, Flora," he said sadly. At least he recognized me again. "The Birdies took her from me."

"I know, Poppy, but it wasn't your fault." By Birdies I knew he meant the Huitzils. Huitzil means hummingbird and Birdie is the not-so-nice Califa nickname for our overlords.

"Your mother will never forgive me."

"She will, Poppy, but you must forgive yourself." Sometimes it is better to lie. Mamma never would forgive Poppy for losing the First Flora, but I privately felt that she deserved some of the blame herself. War is no place for a kid, yet Mamma had sent Flora to Poppy, and when he was captured, so was she. They were both taken to Anahautl City as prisoners. But although Poppy was ransomed, the First Flora was never seen again.

"Why didn't your mother leave me there? I deserved the darkness. I broke faith, Flora, I broke my word. I swore I'd never leave her and I did. I left her behind."

I didn't know what to say. I swallowed hard, blinking. The chocolate torte had become a huge wad in the back of my throat.

"Do you want some more ice cream, Poppy?" I asked lamely. Mamma would have known what to say, but Mamma wasn't there. At least, I thought dolefully, he wasn't throwing things. I kept an eye on the door, anyway. A good ranger knows how to make a swift exit.

He put his elbows on the table, and the sleeves of his tattered cardigan fell away, showing livid knife stripes along his inner arms, one so fresh it still oozed. "Do you think she will ever forget what I did?"

I wasn't sure which "she" he was referring to, but I said, "I am sure that she would understand."

"How can she understand in the dark? I never saw her after that, they kept us apart, but I could hear the screaming, maybe that was me, it was so far off that I couldn't quite make out the words, they gave me Moxley's heart on a soup plate, with barley broth and carrots, and I have always hated cooked carrots. They make me *sick!*"

He flung the plate against the wall, and the cake exploded into chocolate and hazelnut shrapnel. After that, he screamed and yelled and got the dogs all into a huge barking uproar, and then escaped the kitchen. Although I couldn't cajole him back up the Stairs of Exuberance to his Eyrie, I finally corralled him upstairs, in the Garterobe of Resolution, our only working potty, then locked the door.

I brushed back my messy hair and plopped down on the hall settle to catch my breath. In the dustup, I had knocked my elbow against a case full of ancient family artifacts, and now the bone throbbed in time to my newly pulsing headache. For a moment I thought I might throw up. Rangers do not cry, but my nose was running in a most unprofessional way.

"I had a ghost who was that noisy once, but you can bet that I got rid of him quickly." It was Valefor.

"I thought you couldn't leave the Bibliotheca." Despite the bad timing, I was a little pleased to see him. He was company, after all. I wiped my nose on the edge of my kilt. "Are you still banished?"

He smirked. "Ayah so, but I'm feeling a bit better. Not completely myself, but stronger."

Although his voice sounded less scratchy, the rest of him bordered on the transparent. I could see the wall behind him, through him. But the coldfire violet eyes still glittered.

"I can see through you," I said.

"Yes. I may be feeling better, but it's still a lot of effort for

me to get out. I could use another sip." He looked at me hopefully.

"*Flora!*" Poppy roared from the potty. "*Unlock this door right now!*"

"He needs a good thumping," Valefor said. "That would
shut him up."

"I don't believe in thumping people," I answered. "And besides, it's not Poppy's fault that he is this way. So thumping him
would hardly make him better. He's sick."

"Hotspur's drunk," Val said. "It's the curse of the Fyrdraacas. You'll probably go that way one day yourself."

I said hotly, "I don't drink."

"Not drunkenness, pinhead. I mean the madness. It's been
bred in the bone; you are all high-strung, like good hunting
dogs. The Fyrdraacas make magnificent soldiers and fantastic
lawyers, but it's the madness in them that makes them great."

"Mamma's not mad!"

"There is more than one way of being crazy, Flora," Valefor
said. "Some people are crazy for glory, some crazy for drink,
some crazy for duty. You'll see."

I doubted it. I had no intention of becoming a drinker like
Poppy, or a workaholic like Mamma, or a self-righteous git like
Idden. Being a great ranger requires many qualities, but mad-
ness and drunkenness aren't among them.

Valefor continued, "Ah, poor Hotspur. He was so glorious
once. The best of all the Fyrdraacas and the most beautiful, too.
Who would have thought this day would come? I remember,
when he was just a tot—"

"*Flora, damn you, let me out!*"

That crashing sound was probably Poppy throwing a chair
against the door. Mamma was going to be very angry if she
came home to find the Garterobe of Resolution trashed. We
only have access to one indoor loo, and I hate going outside to
the bog.

"You could threaten his life with a railway share," Valefor
offered. "I have a huge collection of them in the Bibliotheca
Mayor, and some of them are sharp as razors. Oh no, I forgot,

you are a *pacifist*. I would suggest charming him with smiles and soap, then. That would be a good nonviolent approach. Honestly, I can't see how you can be a Fyrdraaca and be a pacifist, too. It's an absolute contradiction in terms."

I was not happy to see Val anymore. He was a snippy snapperhead and he was not helping at all. I ignored his happy pontificating and went back to the potty door. Poppy's fits usually do blow over quickly. He screams and shouts for a while, and then he is done until the next time.

"Poppy?"

The hurtling noises abruptly stopped.

"Flora, please let me out." His voice sounded weak and far away.

"Are you done screaming and shouting?"

"Yes, Flora," he said meekly.

"Promise?"

"Flora—"

"Poppy, I have the key and I am not going to let you out until you promise to be good."

He turned threatening. "I'm going to tell your mother."

"Tell her what? That I locked you in the Garterobe of Resolution because you were screaming and shouting and that you threw my cake against the kitchen wall?"

There was a brief pause, and then his voice, less muffled, drifted through the keyhole. "I promise, Flora. Just please let me out. I need to get back to the Eyrie. I am feeling rather sick."

"I wouldn't," said Valefor, breathing down my neck. "Let him stew for a while."

"Get off." I pushed him away, my hand shredding through his arm like a knife through smoke. I gingerly opened the door and Poppy wobbled out. He sat patiently on the settle while I bandaged up the cuts on his hands. He had smashed the mirrors with his bare fists.

"My eyes are too green. I can't stand the way they stare in my face," Poppy said, as though that was an explanation.

"I shouldn't wonder," Valefor muttered. *"Look on my face, I have become death, murderer of calm."*

Poppy turned his head sharply, noticing Valefor for the first time. "What the hell are you doing down here?"

Val shrank behind me, wavering.

"If Buck catches you out, she'll cut you up and use you for a raincoat," Poppy warned.

"Hold still, Poppy," I ordered. He was shaking so hard that I kept smearing the Madama Twanky's Cut-Eze on his shirt instead of his arm.

"Ouch, careful with that stuff, it burns."

"Good on it," I said. "Serves you right. Who's going to clean up all that mess now, Poppy?"

"Make your little friend do it. After all, it is *his* House," Poppy said sarcastically.

Valefor snorted. "Hardly anymore. Your darling lady wife locked me up in the Bibliotheca Mayor, and this is the first time I've been out in I don't know how long."

"How *did* you get out?" Poppy asked.

"Poppy," I said, before Val could get me in trouble, "you should go back to your Eyrie and lie down for a while. I'm sure you'll feel better, then—"

"Watch him, Flora," Poppy interrupted. "He is bound to spit and that's going to burn. I warn you."

Whatever *that* meant. "Ayah so, Poppy, don't worry. I'll take care of everything."

Poppy shambled to his feet. "You'd better get back to the Bibliotheca before Buck gets back, Valefor."

Val sniffed. "I am not afraid of Buck."

Poppy looked at him somberly. "You are the only one. And you are a fool."

SIX

Cleaning Up. Val Makes an Offer. Wiggling Fingers. Another Kiss.

I COULD HELP YOU clean up," Val said, trailing behind me as I went downstairs to the kitchen to fetch a broom and let the dogs out.

The dogs slunk out of the mudroom dejectedly, then slunk off into the garden. Flynnie pressed up against my legs sadly and pushed his head into my hand to be petted. I hugged his solid meaty bulk, and he licked my face before squirming free to follow his sibs into the darkness.

"How can you do that? I thought you were diminished and without any ability." I got the broom and a garbage sack out of the mudroom, and Val followed me back up the Below Stairs.

"I am still weak, it's true, but you have lent me enough to allow me some freedom. So now we are friends and I stick by my friends."

The Garterobe of Resolution was a wreck. Shards of glass winked like fallen stars on the floor and in the bathtub. The sink was full of tooth powder and bath salts, and the walls and ceiling were stuck with soggy toilet paper. FOR THIS WE ARE SOLDIERS was scrawled in red lip rouge across one of the walls. Even if I got the mess cleaned up, I could not replace the mirrors before Mamma returned. Both Poppy and I were going to be in big trouble.

"My beautiful loo," Val moaned, peering over my shoulder.

"My beautiful loo. Do you have any idea how long it took me to make those mirrors? Weeks of utter concentration and focused desire. And the tiles—oh, the energy to make them the most perfect shade of bleachy blue, after which I was almost invisible with exhaustion—now all cracked, and filthy, too. Hotspur made a mess, but he didn't have far to go. Don't you ever wash the bathroom floor, Flora Segunda?"

"Well, can you do something about the mess?" I demanded, ignoring his crack. Valefor might not be afraid of Mamma, but I was. I did not want her to see this mess and say that I had not watched Poppy closely enough.

"Well, if I were to have more Anima—"

"How much?"

He grinned at me hopefully. "Not a lot, just more. What did you have for dinner tonight?"

"General Chow's tofu."

He wrinkled his long nose. "I'm not that fond of such spicy food myself, but all right. It's better than nothing."

"But be careful," I said. "You almost made me pass out last time."

"I'll be sweet as pie," he promised. His lips brushed mine and then parted to take my breath. A slow tingle started in my toes and wiggled its way upward, as though my blood had turned fizzy.

"That's enough," I said, breaking away. "You are making me dizzy."

Val grinned. "Ah, I feel so much better, you cannot be-lieve it!"

His hair, I realized, was not black. It was dark purple-blue, the color of a damson plum, and little threads of silver sparked in the thick curls now springing around his shoulders.

"Just clean this place up, Valefor. It's late and I have to go to bed. Tomorrow's a school day."

"You are a busy one, aren't you?" Valefor said. "Always rushing from here to there and there to here. You ought to just slow down and enjoy life. It's short enough as it is without you hurrying."

Ha! As though there was anything about life to enjoy. "Clean it up. Now!"

Valefor flourished a long finger. "ᴇ∧⤬𝄐ᴍᴵ"

When the sparkly purple Invocation faded, not only was the Garterobe of Resolution tidied up, but it was actually clean. The silver taps gleamed and the porcelain sparkled. The broken loo chain had been replaced, Mamma's cut-glass bottles were lined up neatly above the bath, and the towels were soft and fluffy. The mirror showed my astonished face and Valefor's smug smile.

"See how helpful I can be?" Valefor said happily. "The mirror is not exactly the same, of course. I don't have enough for that, but I don't think Buck's subtlety will extend to noticing the difference."

Valefor *was* helpful. While I let the dogs in, he whisked about the Below Kitchen, humming Gramatica under his breath and wiggling his fingers. When he was done, the kitchen was so clean that it almost sparkled. The copper pans hanging from the ceiling shone like stars, the stove glowed like a polished black pearl, and the floor looked clean enough to eat off.

"There we are! Let's have popcorn!" Valefor said when he was done.

"I thought you didn't eat food."

"Well, I don't eat to live, but sometimes it is fun to live to eat. Come on, Flora, tra-la-let's have a party! Oh please, let's!"

"I have to go to bed."

"Pah! Bed! There's time enough to sleep when you are dead, Flora."

"I am tired." Dealing with Poppy is exhausting and sick-at-heart-making, and now I wanted nothing more than to crawl into bed and stay there a week. It was a relief to have the mess cleaned up, and popcorn was tempting, but I still wanted my bed.

"You are a stick, Flora, that's what you are, an absolute stick," Valefor said.

I did not give in, but Valefor would not give up. Still begging, he followed me as I turned down the lights, banked the stove, and went upstairs. He leaned over me as I stopped by the Stairs of Exuberance, to listen for noise coming from Poppy's Eyrie. (Dead silence.)

"You are *bugging* me!" I shouted, after I had shut my bedroom door in his face and he had floated right through, anyway.

He looked hurt. "But I thought you liked me."

I threw my boots into the wardrobe and pulled my nightgown out from under my pillow. "I just need to go to bed and get some sleep. And I can't do that if you are following me everywhere. Can't you leave me alone?"

"I told you, Flora, we are connected now, and I can go where you go, at least around the House. I will be very quiet," he said, sitting down on the settee. But of course he wasn't. He chattered on about this and that, and that and this. Having someone around to clean things up was nice, but I could see now that it had its cost. *The meal's not free if you still have to leave a tip,* Nini Mo said.

". . . and a shame that a Fyrdraaca should be sleeping in a broom closet—"

"This was a broom closet?" I interrupted. My room is not fancy, but it's not tiny, either. It has a fireplace surmounted by a mantel carved with cunning little monkeys, two big windows that overlook the kitchen garden, a cushy settee, and a banged-up wardrobe big enough to play house in. Sure, it is messy, but that was nothing against the room, only against my interest in keeping it tidy.

"Well, not this room. This room was, I think, where I stored extra toilet brushes or something; I don't remember. Anyway, I mean there—" Valefor pointed to my bed. "That closet!"

At first glance around my room, you wouldn't see my bed at all, and you'd think maybe I slept on the settee. But then you would notice a set of doors on one wall, and when the doors slid open, there was my bed, tucked inside a little alcove, all snuggly and secret. I love my bed; when the doors are closed and you are pillowed down into your comforters with a dog at your feet, you are hidden and no one can get you. Had my bed been a broom closet?

"See how it is that the Fyrdraacas are constrained," Valefor said. "I am as wide as the sky when it comes to space, and here the Fyrdraacas are, crouching in utility rooms. Even your kitchen is just an extra kitchen I made in case some guest brought his own cook, and these rooms, all of them, spare servants' quarters for spare servants, and here you are living as servants in them. Or in your case, a slave, Flora Segunda."

Valefor was right. Why were we living in servants' rooms, like servants? Because we couldn't get to the rest of the House without the Butler. Whom Mamma had banished. Another thing to hold against her, I supposed. But not tonight. "I really have to go to bed, Valefor," I said. "Are you going to shut up or shall I kick you?"

"All right, all right!" He settled down on the settee and began to read one of my Nini Mo yellowback novels. I climbed into bed, pulled the door mostly closed, and put my nightgown on. The dogs had already settled in, and they shifted around to make room for me.

"Must you throw your clothes on the floor?" Valefor asked without looking up from his reading. He waved one hand and my stays and chemise drifted upward, then floated over to the wardrobe, tucking themselves inside. My kilt and pinafore wafted into the dirty-clothes bin, and my pullover flitted over to Valefor, who put down the yellowback to receive it.

"There's a giant hole in the elbow!" he said, accusingly. I'm terrible at darning. I can sew fine, but somehow when it comes to knitting, my stitches get muddled. Valefor smoothed the sweater between his palms, and when he held it up, smugly, the hole was gone. "You are welcome!"

"Thank you, Valefor."

"You *are* welcome."

"Well, then, if you are going to stay, at least turn the lights down."

The lights dimmed accordingly, and I slid the bed door shut and snuggled into the nest of dogs. Flynn squirmed his boniness between my feet, and Flash and Dash curled together against the wall. The sheets were doggy warm, but they could have smelled fresher.

I lay there and let the darkness overwhelm me. Sometimes it is very hard not to sink. Udo calls this feeling the little black ghost in my head, and while sometimes its wheedling is muted, I can never quite completely pull free of its influence. Sometimes it seems as though there will never be an end. Poppy will continue to be drunken, Mamma will continue to be gone, and I will march off to the Barracks and fulfill the Fyrdraaca family destiny, which is nothing but ruin and sorrow.

"Why are you crying?"

My heart jerked, and I lifted my head. The dogs hadn't moved, but Valefor's eyes, faint coldfire sparks, glimmered next to me.

"Pigface Psychopomp! I think I just lost ten years off my life."

"Fyrdraacas die young, anyway," Val said. "Where's your nightcap?"

I wiped my eyes on the pillowcase. "Go away and let me go to sleep."

"But you weren't sleeping," he pointed out. "You can't sleep and cry at the same time. And if you cry yourself to sleep, you'll only wake up with a headache tomorrow morning."

"I wish you would mind your own business."

"This *is* my business. I mean, I'm the House Fyrdraaca and you are a Fyrdraaca, so that makes it my business. Besides, you are getting my sheets wet. If anyone should be crying, it's me, over the decline of our family. Once so numerous and distinguished, oh, we had generals and lawyers, artists and statesmen, we were the beauty of the world, and now down to four Fyrdraa-cas, and none of you particularly distinguished compared to the Fyrdraacas of old."

He was a snapperhead, and for a savage sudden minute, I wished he'd stayed in his library and rotted. Cold feet squirmed against my ankles and I yanked away. Flynn growled and crawled to the other edge of the bed.

"Aw, finally, toasty. I get so very cold," Valefor said. "I remember when your great-great-great-grandmother Idden Fyrdraaca made this comforter. She cut up captured battle flags to make the quilt pieces, and when it was finished, she stuffed it with the hair of her enemies. Took her four years to get enough to fill the quilt. That's why it is so nice and warm."

Ugh! I had come across the quilt, brilliantly colored and crazily sewn together with bright swatches of silk, in one of the huge clothespresses in the laundry room. It had been on my bed ever since, and it was very warm, but I resolved now to burn it in the morning.

"Don't you have to get back to the Bibliotheca?" I asked hopefully.

"Oh no." Valefor laughed. "I feel so much better right now, I just can't believe it. Isn't this fun? It's just like one of those slumber parties I have read about. The girls lie in the dark and tell sad stories of the deaths of kings, and eat popcorn, and then they give each other green facials."

"You are not a girl."

"Oh. Well, yes, I suppose you are right, but now that I feel better, I could be a girl, if you wanted me to be—"

"No," I said hastily. He was confusing enough as he was. "Just stay the way that you are."

"Don't you want any popcorn?" the whiny dark asked.

I sat up, disrupting dogs and kicking aside cold feet. "Look, I am trying to go to sleep. I have had a long day and I have to get up early in the morning. All right? For Pigface Psycho-pomp's sake, can't you shut up?"

"Well, fine," said the darkness, snippily.

I flopped down, turned my back to the sulky silence, and pulled the covers over my ears. At least I didn't feel like crying anymore.

SEVEN

Sickness. Med-I-Cine.
Waffles. Val Proposes.

Valefor was gone when I awoke, and I did not feel so well. My head ached, my bones ached, and generally I felt punk. Rangers suck up pain and sickness; they don't let a little thing like weakness of the body get in the way of their obligations, so I dragged myself out of bed, did my morning chores, and got to Sanctuary just in time for first bell.

But the day was such a horrible loss; I should have stayed home. In my furry brain-haze, I left my Lit vocab list at home, so I got a zed on the hand-in, which meant that even though I got a plus-ten on the pop quiz, there went a fourth of my grade. In Scriptive, I knocked over the ink bottle and flooded out an entire stack of Catorcena invitations—twenty-five to do over. And after much finger-pricking, thread-snapping, and swearing in Dressmaking, I discovered that I had put the left sleeve of my Catorcena dress in upside down.

Every time I passed Archangel Bob in the hall, he would give me the eye, as though he had noticed I was not up to snuff and was wondering if he should send me to the Infirmary. With Mamma due home on Monday, I had too much to do to go to the Infirmary, and anyway, that was not where I wanted to spend my weekend, swallowing nasty medicine and eating nothing but oatmeal mush with spelt flakes. If you have to die in bed, it's better that that bed be your own. Nini Mo didn't say that, but I'll bet she would have agreed. Of course, she didn't die in bed, but it's the principle.

It seemed like the day would never be over, but finally it was, and before Archangel Bob could make up his mind and grab me, I schlepped home. I kicked the dogs into the garden, hung the laundry out, and mucked the horses. The dogs came back in, and I shut them in the parlor, leaving the terrace door open so they could let themselves out. I blearily climbed the zillion stairs up to my bedroom, where I flopped onto the settee and fell into a snuffling sleep.

Time became a sickly blur of waking, stumbling to the potty, stumbling back to the settee, and sleep. Waking, stumbling down to feed the dogs, back to the settee, and sleep. Sometimes it was daylight when I woke, sometimes it was night. Always I was shivery cold, shaky, and miserable.

Finally, I woke up feeling a little better, not nearly as shivery, but still terribly cold. And hungry, too. I didn't have the energy to get up, light a lamp, check on the dogs, find some chow. I didn't have the energy to do anything at all. I lay on the settee, staring miserably up into the darkness.

Then I remembered Valefor.

"Valefor," I croaked.

A thin wavery cloud coalesced at the end of the settee. I could barely make out Val's narrow face. The cloud crept down over me, and I shivered at the coolness. I put my palms up and he put misty hands against mine, and he immediately brightened into a more solid shape. He bent over and I breathed a deep breath into him, feeling him grow concrete, sucking the ache from me. For a few seconds, my insides felt airy, as though my skin were filled with nothing but a tingling purple light.

When Valefor stood upright, he looked the best yet, not at all a starveling. In fact, if it weren't for the purple eyes and his purple hair, he could have been a normal boy. He wasn't exactly pretty, but he sparkled.

Valefor grinned at me and waved his arms about. "Thank

you, Flora Segunda. I feel much better. You don't taste so good right now, but still, it's enough."

I flopped back on the pillows, feeling like I had inhaled little sparks of fire. I suddenly felt a lot more perky, albeit a tad breathless. "You are welcome."

With a gentle hiss, the radiators came on, even though I hadn't shoveled any coal in over a week. In the fireplace, the fire flared up, bright and friendly.

"This is much, much better," Val beamed, balancing on the settee arm. "Why didn't you call me earlier? You shouldn't be lying around like this, Flora. It's bad for your mental state. Once you lie down, you might not get up again for ages. Great-uncle Gussie once spent four years lying on the sofa in the Drawing Room of Depredations. You don't know how hard it was to dust around him."

"I've been sick."

"Ah . . ." Val fished around in his long hanging sleeves, then came up with a small green bottle. "I have just the trick."

"What is it?"

He proffered a spoonful of pinkish liquid. "Open up. It will make you all better."

I recoiled. I knew from experience that liquids that promise to make you all better usually make you wish you could die. "What does it taste—oof."

Valefor had shoved in the spoon. I started to choke and then the lovely buttery syrup flowed down my throat and seemed to settle into a warm fuzzy haze in my wheezing chest. Now I was really feeling pretty good.

"What was that?"

"Madama Twanky's Sel-Ray Psalt Med-I-Cine," Valefor replied. He'd replaced both bottle and spoon inside his flowing sleeve.

"It tasted like maple syrup." The Madama Twanky's Sel-Ray Psalt that Mamma forces me to take when I'm sick tastes like lamp oil.

"Well, I did improve a bit on the original, but it will fix what ails you."

"When is it?" I asked, pushing myself back up on the pillows. Ah, the lovely warmth puffing from the radiator. Ah, the lovely warmth in my bones.

"All times are alike to me, so monotonous and boring, but—" Valefor considered. "I think it's Sunday for you."

"Sunday!" Panic gurgled in my throat, in my voice. Sunday! The entire weekend gone. My dress, my invitations, my speech, the fifty tamales I had to make and distribute to the poor! Everything I was going to get done this weekend, just in the nick of Mamma coming home. And now she would be home tomorrow and I had done nothing. Even if I started immediately, I wouldn't have time to get it all done. "I've wasted the whole weekend. I'll never get all my chores done!" I slumped back down into gloom and felt babyish tears prickle at my eyes.

"Never you worry," said Valefor soothingly. "Valefor is here and he specializes in getting things done. But first, teatime!"

Out of Nowhere, Val produced a plate of waffles and a giant pot of orange tiger tea. While I gobbled the first solid food I'd had in forever, he started tidying. He twinkled his fingertips and suddenly my bedsheets were clean and the bed was made. (Pigface, I'd forgotten to get rid of that horrible comforter!) He waved a hand and my scattered Nini Mo yellowbacks hopped into a neat stack, and the painting of Mamma and Idden hanging over the fireplace straightened. He flapped my socks and they were hole-free. He fixed the upside-down sleeve of my Catorcena dress with a flip of one finger, and hemmed it with a wave of another. He tapped pen to paper and soon enough had a full stack of invitations completed, without a smudge or an ink blot. It was so wonderful to lie there, warm and full, and watch someone else do all the work. In just a few short minutes, my bedroom was cleaner than it had been in years and my Catorcena chores were nearly done. *Mamma, why are you so darn stubborn?*

"Well," Val said, finally, after I had drunk the last drop of tea and he had eaten the last waffle. He tossed the tea tray up in the air, and before I could shout, it was gone. "I have been thinking."

I yawned again. Between the medicine and all those waffles I was feeling awfully sleepy, but in a yummy tired way. "About what?"

He leaned over the back of the settee and grinned ingratiatingly at me. "I don't think the Elevator was being obdurate when it brought us together, Flora. That Elevator, that part of me, that is, knew what it was doing, even if you and I were slow to pick up on it."

"Hmm . . ." My eyelids weighed fifty pounds, and they kept dropping closed.

"Are you listening to me?" Val's breath smelled like nutmeg. I opened my eyes. His face was so close to mine that I could see the faint shimmer of golden freckles on his skin, which was as smooth as rubber.

"Do you have bones?" I murmured.

He said snippily, "Of course I have bones. Every stone in this house is part of my—"

"No, I mean, inside your skin, do you have bones? Do you have a liver?"

"What would I need a liver for—disgusting organ—of course not! But as I was saying. I could help you further, if you help me further, Flora."

"Ayah so?" I yawned again.

He continued, "You just don't know how boring and lonely it is to be so diminished, me who once had the world begging for favors. And it's not right, either, to close up such a House and let it molder away just because you are afraid—"

This woke me up some, indignantly. "Mamma is not afraid of anything." In her youth, my mamma killed a jaguar with a shovel. She's won the Warlord's Hammer twice. She's fought three duels, one bare-knuckled, and won them all. And, of course, she's been married to Poppy for twenty-eight years, which alone takes an awful lot of sand.

"Pah. You can be as brave as a lion on the outside, Flora Segunda," Val answered, "and fight bears with your fingernails and stare down monsters until they melt into little puddles of goo at your feet and still be a coward inside, in your heart, where it counts."

I rolled over and turned my back to Val. He was lucky I didn't believe in violence; otherwise, I would have punched his lights out for maligning Mamma so. The comfy feeling of chores done was receding into the more familiar feeling of gloom. Why did Valefor have to remind me of all this when I had been feeling so nice?

Val's nutmeg breath tickled my ear. "Don't sulk, Flora Segunda. It is not becoming to your lineage. I mean no disrespect to your dear lady mamma, but you have to face facts that this is not the way things should be."

"That's not my mamma's fault," I said into the cushion. "She does the best she can." *Which isn't good enough,* my brain whispered.

"No doubt she does, but that's not helping me, and it's not helping you, either. If we got together, we could help each other, and help your dear mamma, and even help darling Hotspur, too."

I rolled back over and stared up at Val's looming head. The coldfire burned purple in his eyes, like sparks of light deep in a black well. His lips were a faint shade of lavender, like very pale blueberries. He cocked his head and grinned at me, very sweet.

"What do you mean, help Mamma and Poppy?" I asked.

"You know," he said, "I remember the night the First Flora was born. It was strange weather. First came huge rain, then loud thunder, then an earthquake. An omen, don't you think? The First Flora was a stubborn little thing, and she was not going to come out. Such screaming and shouting and rushing to and fro, and, ah, the blood—I was never so strong, I think, as I was that night. Your mamma almost died. And you know why she didn't?"

I shook my head. Mamma never speaks of the First Flora.

Val looked smug. "Your father wasn't there, or I suppose he would have tried to help her, being a great one with the knife, Hotspur, always hoping to find something or someone to carve up. Your mamma was spewing blood and her eyes were growing dark. A doctor could not have helped her. But for me, for Valefor, what is a truculent baby and a dying mother? I just reached right in with one slender hand and I took a hold of that bad little girl's feet and she popped like a cork out of a bottle. Flora knew she'd met her match in me and there was no more insolence from her, I tell you."

"You are so full of hoo," I said. "Anyway, so what?"

"You ask your dear lady mamma," Val said, wounded. "And she will tell you I am saying nothing but the truth. I am the power of this House, Flora. The point is you all *need* me."

"Mamma is the power of this House. You are just the Butler."

"You decline without me. You dwindle. I told Buck, two wasn't enough, but did she listen to me? Of course not. See— she's already had to replace one!"

There were fewer Fyrdraacas in Califa than there had once been, but that didn't mean that we were in decline, did it? Fyrdraacas tend to die young, in all sorts of glamorous ways. It's not so good for the bloodline if people keep getting killed in duels (Great-aunt Arabelle), breaking their necks in cross-country horse races (Great-uncle Anacreon), drowned trying to swim across the Bay's Gate (Great-aunt Anacreona), or bit by a rattlesnake during a bar bet (Cousin Hippolyte), and not leaving any heirs behind. Pretty soon the family tree is pretty thin.

I answered, "Says you! There's still me and Idden. We aren't chopped mackerel."

"You are thin-blooded and miserable, that's what you are."

"We aren't." But my protest was halfhearted. I *was* a replacement, wasn't I?

"Suit yourself, then," he said, shrugging. "Whether you believe it or not does not affect whether it is the truth. It's not fair. I am oppressed, and nothing more than a slave to Buck's Will."

"You are just the Butler, a denizen—you *should* be subject to Mamma's Will. It was what you were made for, to serve her, as the Head of the Fyrdraaca family," I said meanly, for he had completely spoiled my happy mood.

Valefor glared at me. "Fyrdraacas come and go, but I alone of this House stand forever. Buck should understand that and treat me with the respect that I deserve. And anyway, it's not just me—we are *all* slaves to Buck's Will. Hotspur, Idden, you—"

"I have my own Will," I protested.

"Then why are you studying for the Benica Barracks entry exam?" Val asked slyly.

"I'm not." I wasn't, but I was supposed to be. I half hoped that if I failed the exam I wouldn't get in, although I'm sure that I would get in no matter if I passed or not. The Fyrdraaca estate may be worthless, but the Fyrdraaca name still has value.

"Why are you acting a slavey in your own home? Why do you have to get stuck dealing with Hotspur? Stuck with all the chores—the housework, the horses, the laundry?"

Each of Valefor's questions burned, for they were questions I had asked myself so many times but had never dared voice aloud. Underneath my gloom, there was the pinprick of anger. Why did Mamma have to be so unfair? Why couldn't she think of the rest of us for once?

He continued, "While I—whose Will it is to do those tasks—am locked away like a criminal."

"Anyway, we are both stuck, Valefor," I said, pulling the blanket up to my chin. "There's nothing we can do."

"Isn't there?" Val asked. He had perched on the settee arm, above my feet, and now he leaned forward, eyes gleaming.

"What do you mean?"

Valefor grinned at me hopefully. "I could be restored."

EIGHT

Discussion.
The Eschatanomicon.

SUDDENLY A TINY LICK of excitement was kindling against my gloominess. Could Valefor be restored? What if every day were like today, with working radiators and clean sheets? With delicious waffles and hole-free socks? The Elevator would always work, and there would be not a single dog hair anywhere. Could Valefor manage Poppy? I could live at Sanctuary and my nights would be blissfully scream-free. We would have our House back, in all its glory, and we'd be a normal family again, just like everyone else.

Then I remembered. "Mamma would never allow it."

"Why would Mamma have to know? I'd be very silent, just a little secret between you and me. I'd help you out, and Mamma would think you so clever, and no one but us would need to know." Val leaned in again, and again I saw the stars in his eyes. "Just think. Warm sheets, fresh waffles, no more stable duty, clean towels, you wouldn't have to clean the bathroom anymore, which I know you hate. No more dirty dishes or ancient leftover takeaway. Wouldn't that be heavenly?" The runnels of silver in Valefor's dark curls glittered. He wiggled a long finger enticingly at me. "And I can handle young Hotspur. I know where he lives. He'd be no trouble at all to me."

I closed my eyes to Val's enticements, which were mighty

enticing. Clean rooms and no chores. Fluffy towels and yummy snacks. And Poppy, handled.

Val's voice purred in my ear, deliciously. "In a little wink, I could have all those tamales made and your dress done. Your invitations sent and your speech written. Everything would be ready, and with no trouble to you. Everything in perfect order."

It *was* a delicious thought, and the more I thought about it, the more delicious it became. Oh, how blissful it would be to have order in the House and things working as they should. Valefor could do all the work, and I could get all the credit, and Mamma would never be the wiser. Maybe Val *was* the power of our family; after all, didn't everything start falling apart right when he was banished?

"But could you be restored, Valefor?"

"Of course. I am here, but weakened. Of course I could be made strong again."

"What would it take?"

"Ayah so? It would be easy, Flora, I know it would," Valefor said eagerly. "I mean, you want to be a ranger, right? I can taste it on your Anima. It's your heart's desire, your True Will, so what a place to start! Even Nini Mo would not have dared to jump in so quickly, but I know you can do it."

"I'm not an adept, though. Surely I would have to be."

"Well, Buck's not an adept and she was able to banish me," Valefor said. "Ayah, there's skill, it's true, but also the right Working."

"I don't know a Working that strong."

"Not yet, that is. See, Flora, I am so kind and generous. I have a giftie for you, and one I think you will like real well. Look here—"

He reached up and plucked Something from Nothing, then offered that Something to me: a red book, small as a deck of cards, with a glittery soft cover trimmed in golden emboss and studded with small pearls. A gilt hasp kept the book closed, but the hasp opened easily when I tugged on it. I flipped to the title page.

The Eschatanomicon,

OR,

Rangering for Everybody!

An Invaluable Collection of Eight Hundred
Practical Receipts, Sigils, and Instructs

FOR

Rangers, Adepts, Sorcerers, Mages, Bibliomantics,
Scouts, Hierophants, Gnostics, Chaoists, Priestesses, Sibyls,
Sages, Archons, Anthropagists, Avatars, Trackers,
and People Generally,
Containing a Rational Guide to
Evocation, Invocation, Augoeides, Smithing, Epiclesis,
Camping, Divination, Equipage, Retroactive Enchantment,
Mule Packing, Geas, Adoration, Cutting for Sign,
Bibliomancy, Transubstantiation, Hitches, Vortices,
Prophecy, Libel & Dreams, etc.

by

NYANA KEEGAN OV ADMOISH

"Free the oppressed!"

Valefor said, "It's a first edition. The later versions were expurgated, of course, which took all the fun out of them. But this one is intact, complete, and it's terribly rare. It's worth more than half the City, Flora. Don't read it in the bath. And look— it's signed."

The frontispiece showed a sketch of Nini Mo in a coyote-skin cape, rifle in one hand, pen in the other, and there on the fly-leaf was a thick black scrawl. Her calligraphy was very hard to read; each letter looked like a spiky thistle, and some had very long tails, but her signature was unmistakable.

Nyana Maudyn Keegan or Admiesh

"What does the inscription say?" I asked.

Val squinted, then read: "'To Little Tiny Doom and Fig. Dare, Win, or Disappear!'"

"Who is that? Little Tiny Doom? And Fig?"

"I have no idea; I don't remember exactly where I got the book. But see, Flora—*The Eschatanomicon* contains everything you need to know about rangering, or magick, or both, and I'm sure it has the perfect Working to fix me fine as I ever was before."

I stared at the book in my hand, stared at the thick slant of Nini Mo's handwriting. This book she had held in *her* hand; that black lettering had come from her pen. My head knew that Nini Mo—Nyana Keegan—was a real person, that she had once lived and breathed and died, as I lived and breathed and would one day die. I knew people who had known her, seen her, and talked to her. But yet, in my heart she was as fantastic as the stories that were told about her, and thus she seemed completely unreal.

But she had held this book in her hands, as I held it now. This selfsame book. Her flesh-and-blood hands. A small blot of ink followed her signature where her pen had slipped, as mine so often does. She had touched this book before, as I touched it now. These thoughts made my heart feel fluttery.

I flipped through *The Eschatanomicon*'s pages, which were as thin as lettuce leaves. The first few chapters were very rangery, indeed. "How to Make a Fire with Rocks." "Fording a River with a Rope." "Making a Mule Mind." "The Charm of Charm." "Sleeping in a Heavy Rain." "Tracking Backward." There were illustrations, too: tiny line-drawings of rangers fording rivers on rafts, rangers riding bucking horses, rangers hypnotizing rattlesnakes, rangers dancing the gavotte, and doing other rangery things.

But then, after chapter 11, the headings changed. "Retroactive Enchantments." "Sigils to Bind." "Sigils to Break." "The A–Z of Banishing." "Interior Evocations." "Exhalative Invocations." "Fun with Charms." The illustrations changed, too; now they showed rangers making Invoking Gestures, rangers wrestling with dæmons, rangers tossing lightning bolts, rangers turning into coyotes.

I flipped to the index, and there found what I was looking for:

"Restoration Sigils."

NINE

Waiting. Udo's Hat.
The Elevator Again.

I SAT ON THE EDGE of the Immaculata Piazza, leaning against one of the immense pillars that held up the main dome of Sanctuary, throwing scraps of bread to the doves. The Immaculata Piazza is protected from sun by the looming dome above, and sheltered from wind by large support pillars. It's a pleasant place to sit and wait for someone, which was good for me, because I had been waiting over half an hour for Udo, who was massively late.

Udo was finally out of the lockdown he'd earned by punching his horrible sister Gunn-Britt in the nose in a fight over the last tortilla. That sounds pretty bad, but Gunn-Britt is a pincher, and I had no doubt she gave as good as she got. There are seven kids in the Landaðon family, and they fight over everything. Seven kids, one mother, and three fathers. It's a terribly famous love story in Califa, and there was even a play written about it: how Udo's mamma was wooed by identical triplets and, having no way to decide among them, married all three. Udo's birth-father was in prison in Anahuatl City with Poppy and died there, but Udo still has two fathers left.

I've known Udo since we were tots. When I was too large to be easily portable on Mamma's trips but not large enough to stay home alone with Poppy, I would stay at Case Tigger (the Landaðon family home), which was fun and friendly, even with all those kids. Case Tigger is not a Great House, and it has no Butler, but it's homey and clean, and I love it there. But now that I have to Poppy-sit, Udo stays with me to keep me company. He would have done so this time, too, if he hadn't gotten popped for punching Gunn-Britt.

Although Udo is not destined for the Barracks like me, his parents are just as strong-willed about his future fate as Mamma is about mine, and he's just as annoyed at their planning as I am about Mamma's. The Landaðons are all lawyers; Madama Landaðon is on the Warlord's Bench, and Major Landaðon and Captain Landaðon are in the Judge Advocate General's office. As eldest, Udo should carry on the family tradition, but he'd rather go back to the original family profession: piracy.

His grandmother Gunn-Britt Landaðon had sailed with the Warlord, back in the days when the Warlord himself was a pirate and he hadn't yet scored his biggest prize: Califa. Now the Warlord is a warlord, not a pirate, and the Landaðons are lawyers, not pirates, and piracy in general is frowned upon, but that hasn't stopped Udo in his ambition.

If Nini Mo is my lodestar, then Udo's is the Dainty Pirate, whose exploits in the waters up and down the Califa coastline are notorious. The Dainty Pirate flouts the Warlord's Authority and refuses to sail with a Letter of Marque, which means if he ever gets caught, he'll be hanged. They call him the Dainty Pirate because his manners are exquisite, and so, too, his wardrobe. Udo thinks he's fabulous.

I had briefed Udo on Valefor during lunch, and he had demanded to see Val for himself, so we had agreed to meet after school and go back to Crackpot together. Which would have been fine, if he'd been on time, but Udo has a problem with punctuality that many detentions have not straightened out.

While I waited, I thought about *The Eschatanomicon*. I had stayed up most of the night reading it front to back. It really is a terrific book, full of all sorts of useful information and written in a friendly style, as though Nini Mo were sitting down next to you, talking to you as an equal. Magick books, in my experience, tend to be arcane and complicated, full of tortuous explanations and run-on sentences, and most adepts are superfond of superbig words. But Nini Mo eschewed the fancy words and spoke plainly. I didn't understand why the book was so rare, or why I'd never heard of it before. It was the best book on magick I'd ever read.

And after reading it, I was sure that I could restore Valefor, although a few details needed to be ironed out first, if only Udo would hurry up and arrive so we could go back to Crackpot and start ironing.

I was just about to give up and go to the Tuckshop for a mocha, and then let Udo arrive and wait for *me,* when at last there was a hollering *yahoo,* and here he came, resplendent in a black-and-white-striped frock coat over an emerald green kilt. Perched on his head was an emerald green hat the size of a wheel of cheese, well festooned with black and white ribbons and cruelly surmounted by an iridescent green-and-gold bird wing. Udo is the most conscientious dresser I know; half the time you need to put your sunshades on just to look at him. He is what the *Califa Police Gazette* would call a glass-gazing font of frivolity. If he weren't so disgustingly handsome, he'd look ridiculous. Instead, he looked glorious.

"Nice hat, Udo," I said. "I feel sorry for the bird that had to die so you could be stylish."

"Well, ave to you, too, Flora," he answered, reaching up as though to make sure the hat was still on his head, which it was, thanks to a hat pin longer than my arm. "I dug the bird out of Granny's old clothes-closet. It's been dead longer than we've been alive, and don't you think it's nice to make sure it didn't die in vain?"

"What took you so long?"

"Sorry. I got caught up in Arts Logic. Here, I brought you a mocha."

I took the cup he offered. Just what I needed, so lovely warm and chocolatey. "How much do I owe you?"

"Nayah, it's on me," he answered, airily.

I was shocked. Udo is notoriously cheap. Other than the

money he spends on his clothes, most of which he buys second-hand or makes himself, every glory he gets goes straight into his Letter of Marque fund. (Udo has no intention of paying for his piracy with his neck.)

"To what do I owe this honor?"

"Well, I missed you, Flora."

I had missed him, too, but I hate soppiness, so I said, all business-brisk: "So you should have."

Udo rolled his eyes and sat down on the bench next to me. "I can't stay out late tonight. Mam and the Daddies are going to the opera, and somehow I got stuck with squirt-wrangling. And I got six pages of cyclotomy to do for turn-in tomorrow. You'll be so lucky when you have Valefor doing your homework, Flora. Gunn-Britt was doing all my math, but she just raised her prices out of spite over the nose thing, and now I can't afford her. Do you think Valefor would do my homework, too? I guess you could just order him to—"

"I don't have a lot of time, either. I have to meet Mamma at the Presidio for dinner. She's finally back from Angeles."

"You are so lucky, Flora, that Buck is gone all the time. I wish *los padres* would go and take all those nasty kiddies with them. How bliss it would be to have no one to look after but blissful me."

"And Poppy, and the horses, and the dogs, and the chores—"

"The Warlord freed all the slaves but you, Flora."

"Don't I know it. Come on. We're burning daylight."

CRACKPOT WAS AS I had left it some hours earlier, with no sign of either Poppy or Valefor. A few stray smashing sounds drifted down from the Eyrie, but we pretended not to notice. Let Mamma deal with Poppy when she got home later; let him be *her* job, not mine. Or better yet, let him be Valefor's job.

The Elevator was waiting, grille ajar. I jumped in so quickly that it rocked back and forth slightly, squeaking at my weight. Udo followed and pulled the grille shut behind him.

"Take us to the Bibliotheca," I demanded, but the Elevator did not move. "Come on, chop-chop. Take me to Valefor in the Bibliotheca."

The Elevator remained stubbornly stationary, even when I stamped my foot.

"Maybe you should press a button?" Udo suggested.

"I never did before, but maybe so."

Together we peered at the buttons, which were less than helpful, listing:

THE POOL BOUDOIR
THE HAMMOCK LOUNGE
THE CELLAR OF SWEETNESS AND LIGHT
THEL'S RAPTUROUS SUNROOM
LIBROS

"This House is bigger than I thought," Udo said, and before I could stop him, he reached out and punched the LIBROS button.

The Elevator jolted a bit, dropping a few inches. I grabbed at Udo, and Udo grabbed at me, and we both fell against the wall.

"Udo! Who knows where we'll end up now!" I found my footing and stood up.

"It said *books* and a library has books, don't it?"

The Elevator recovered and began to slide downward.

"I thought you said the Bibliotheca was up," Udo said.

"It was, blast it all." I pushed all the buttons, some of them twice, but the Elevator just kept dropping, slowly picking up speed as it went. "But maybe this book place is entirely different."

"Hit the STOP button," Udo said helpfully.

"There is no STOP button." I pressed all the other buttons again, and then, for good measure, thumped on the panel.

"That red one—" Udo leaned in front of me. "There—"

"That doesn't say anything about stopping—don't—Udo—"

He pressed the button. The Elevator stopped abruptly, sending Udo careening into me and down to the floor, where his elbow crushed my liver painfully.

"Get off me—" I pushed him off and stood up, holding my hand against my side.

"See—I told you!" Udo looked pleased with himself.

"Ayah so, but now we are stuck between floors."

With a horrible groan that set my teeth to grinding, the Elevator bounced once, upward. Udo staggered against me again, almost pushing me off balance. The light went out. The Elevator shrieked like a baby.

And then it dropped like a stone.

Downward we plummeted, in pitch darkness. The roar of rushing air filled my ears to near bursting, or maybe that was just the pressure of our fall. Dimly, behind the rush, I could hear howling—maybe it was Udo, or maybe it was me. It was so dark that I couldn't tell if my mouth was open or not. I was pressed into the floor, feeling the Elevator shudder and leap beneath my hands and knees, my head swimming with nausea. I closed my eyes tightly against the darkness, and so dark was it that even the sparks of light you normally see when you squinch your eyes up were extinguished.

After a while, maybe it was forever even, it seemed like we were not moving at all, that we were suspended in a black void, and it was the Void itself that was moving, rushing by us in a howl. Perhaps this is what the Abyss is like, I thought, the impenetrable blackness, the scream of air; perhaps it was not the air screaming, but—

The Elevator hit hard and bounced upward, and so did I, catching my tongue painfully between my teeth. Something knobbed into my side, bright and hard. I jerked away and whacked my noggin into a stony object, which complained, "Owwww, that was my chin."

I opened my eyes. Gray light hazed in through the Elevator's open door. Udo sat on his heels, rubbing his chin with one hand and patting his hat with the other. The foot-long hat pin had kept it on his head, but now it was quite cockeyed. My head felt as though a hundred million goldfish were flapping their fins inside my skull. I tried to stand, but my knees wobbled me back down again. The grille stood open, so I did the easy thing and crawled out of the Elevator, into the huge expanse of the Bibliotheca.

TEN

Nausea. Discussion. Tea. Sigils.

THE FLOOR BOBBED and jumped with imaginary motion, and the mocha in my tum was threatening to abandon ship. Every time I raised my head, the Bibliotheca swirled into a blur of steel gray, and closing my eyes was worse: Then the darkness itself whirled and lurched. If I stared directly at one fixed point, my head started to slow down, but the second I moved my eyes, everything began to spin again.

Udo moaned, "Are you okay, Flora?"

I tried to look back to the Elevator without actually turning my head to look back at the Elevator, and I realized that Udo had crawled up next to me. I risked a glance and saw that his face was almost as green as his hat.

"I'm going to urp," Udo complained.

"Don't do it on me—"

"Floooooooooora!"

"Valefor?" I risked another turn of the head and saw that the Bibliotheca was shrouded in gloom. Today the light filtering through the windows was weak and gray, and rain skimmed the outside of the glass. It hadn't been raining earlier.

"Floooooooooooora!"

"Valefor—where are you?"

This time the only response was a wracking cough. I pushed up off the floor and stood, staggering over to the nearest table, to grab for balance. The floor tipped up and then down again, and for a moment my mocha was poised to spew. But then I got enough balance back to stand straighter and to see Valefor wavering, as thin and pale gray as newsprint. He looked terrible, much worse even than when I had first seen him. His hair stuck out like thistledown and his eyes gleamed wetly white.

"I am receding again, Flora," he moaned, and held his hands out to me. The floor swayed, but I lurched over to him, my own hands outstretched, and breathed so deeply that my chest grew tight with exertion. A cold misty feeling flowed over me, and Val's cold tenuous grip fastened upon me.

Val's lips were so faint that I could barely feel them press against mine. I breathed deeply out until my lungs felt sucked and empty, then inhaled again until they felt like balloons. It wasn't until my second exhalation that he began to solidify. First he felt wiry and thin like sinew, then tough and hard like bone, and then, finally, like solid flesh, warm beneath the grip of my hands.

I let go and pressed my hand on my chest, trying to hold my bouncy heart in, and gasped deeply. My insides felt as though my blood had been replaced with swirly giddy light, rushing golden through my veins. The dizziness was gone.

Valefor said happily, "Well, I feel much better! That was some good stuff, Flora. You are so full of lovely nice stuff: anger, guilt, sorrow. Yum!" He smacked his lavender lips and did a little dance.

"What was that with the Elevator, Valefor? It almost dropped us straight into the Abyss."

"That Elevator may go many places, Flora Segunda, but the Abyss is not one of them. I am sorry about the Elevator, but really you must take your complaints to darling Buck, for she is the one who has unstabilized me— Hey! Nice hat!"

This last was directed not at me, who was not wearing a hat, but at Udo, who was still sitting by the Elevator, looking slightly green. At the compliment, he grinned weakly and staggered to his feet, then made the courtesy that signifies Graciously Submitting before an Equal, which involved a bow so low that I was surprised his nose didn't touch the ground. Udo, like his hero the Dainty Pirate, is a fine one for manners.

"Thank you, sieur denizen."

"I love the bird wing, so beautifully cruel, and your kilt, what a divine shade of green. I do adore green, the color of jade and jaguar blood." To me: "He could teach you a few things about dressing, Flora Segunda. He's got style and flash."

Now Udo was grinning and I could practically hear the sound of his head inflating. "You do me a great honor with your compliments, sieur."

"Your manners are very nice, too," Valefor answered. "Much better than Flora's, here, who has forgotten to introduce us."

"You have not given me a chance, Val, for heaven's sake. Udo Moxley Landaðon ov Sorrel, Valefor, denizen—"

"Valefor Fyrdraaca ov Fyrdraaca," Valefor interrupted, returning Udo's courtesy with Deference to an Equal, an even deeper bow. "I have the right to the name as much as you do, Flora Segunda, maybe more. I am very pleased to meet someone with such exquisite taste, Sieur Landaðon, and glad to see that Flora has some friends with style. Surprised, but well-pleased. Tell me, sieur—where are hems these days? Are they ankle or knee—I am so out of touch, and Flora is useless."

"Knee for day, and calf for night," said Udo, "unless you are super-ultra-formal, when they—"

I interrupted. "Do you want to discuss fashion, Valefor, or your restoration? We don't have time to do both. Udo has to get to babysitting, and Mamma is coming home tonight."

"Restoration, then fashion," Valefor pronounced. "I shall have an entire new wardrobe, then, of shimmering samite! How bliss to get out of this rag!"

So we sat down in front of the fireplace to discuss. Valefor ignited a warming coldfire glow on the hearth and produced a lovely little snack with tiny sandwies, double bergamot tea, and lime meltaways.

"So, according to *The Eschata*, to create a servitor—," I said. I had read the chapter on denizens in *The Eschatanomicon* three times, but sometimes it is good to think out loud.

"I'm a denizen!" Val protested.

"A denizen is a kind of servitor, Valefor. You know that. A servitor is a magickal entity created for a general purpose. A denizen is a servitor attached to a particular place. A domicilic denizen is attached to a House."

Val said snobbily, "Still, a denizen is better than a plain old servitor—"

"That's true. A denizen can act completely independently as long as its actions are in accordance with the parameters laid down by the adept—"

"Who was?" Udo asked.

I was annoyed at being interrupted. "Who was what?"

"Who created you, Valefor? Was it Buck?"

Valefor answered, quite loftily, "Of course it wasn't Buck. She is only fifty-two years old. I out-age her by far. I was created by Azucar Fyrdraaca—"

"Which in Val's case," I said loudly, to get them back on track, "the parameters laid down by the adept were to take care of the House of Fyrdraaca. And these parameters were laid into the fetish that is Valefor's center. This fetish is the source of all Valefor's power, and now he's been disconnected from it, and that's why he is reduced and weakened."

"What's a fetish?" asked Udo. "Are you going to share those lime meltaways, Flora?"

I passed him the platter. "Every servitor has a physical item that binds it and links it to the physical world—"

"So it's kinda the physical representation of Val?" Udo interrupted.

"Ayah."

"Then shouldn't Valefor's fetish be Crackpot Hall?"

"No, the House is too big. No adept could charge something as large as an entire house. No one has that powerful a Will—"

"Azucar Fyrdraaca—," began Valefor, but Udo cut him off.

"So what's your fetish, Valefor?"

Valefor looked a bit embarrassed and mumbled something unintelligible.

I said, "What? I can't hear you."

"I have forgotten," Val admitted sheepishly.

Udo snorted. "You have forgotten? How can you forget something like that? That's pretty lame, Valefor. It's like forgetting your own name."

Valefor said plaintively, "I am insignificant and reduced, and I have been drained. There is so much about myself that I no longer know; why do you think it is taking me so long to write my memoirs? Buck has cut me off from much of myself, and, of course, my fetish, for with it, I should be whole and in command."

"So what do we do if we don't know what your fetish is?" Udo asked. "We can't reconnect you to it if we don't know what it is."

Val said eagerly, "You could kill Buck and let her heir take her place as the new Head of the House. Idden and I always got along quite well, I am sure *she* would restore me—oh ayah, it was just an idea. You don't have to get all stuffy about it, Flora. Remember, there will be Fyrdraacas in this House long after you are gone."

"I will not kill Mamma," I said, adding maliciously, as payback for such an awful suggestion, "I guess, then, you are out of luck."

Val turned the piteous all the way up to high and wrung his narrow hands together. "You don't know how it is, Flora. To be all alone in this empty room, to hear voices from so far away, lovely voices, and to know that they cannot hear you. To sit alone, with all these books telling the stories of other lives, not your own. And to feel yourself growing weaker and weaker every day, whilst your walls crumble and your family falls into ruin. And there is nothing you can do, alone, outcast, adrift, lost."

"There's got to be something that we can do, Flora," Udo said. "It sucks to be in lockdown; boy, don't I know it. I'm with

Valefor on this, all the way. Wasn't Nini Mo's motto 'Free the Oppressed'?"

"Thank you, Sieur Landaðon," Val sobbed. "You are so very kind."

"Quit crying, Val," I said. "We will find your fetish."

The sobbing stopped, and the tears on Valefor's pale cheeks were gone. "How?"

"We will use the Discernment Sigil."

ELEVEN

Discernment Sigil. Smoke.
Searching. A Tea Caddy.

Rangers, of course, are always looking for things—information, people, clues—and so *The Eschatanomicon* was full of sigils that find things. There was the Acquisition Sigil to find something you need but don't have; the Retrieval Sigil to find things you had but then lost. The Recovery Sigil, which seemed to be exactly like the Retrieval Sigil, only you had to have lost by your own fault the things you were looking for. The Discovery Sigil to find things that you didn't even know that you needed, and the Recollection Sigil to help you remember what you had forgotten. And the Revelation Sigil for things that were in front of your eyes but you were looking right through.

Some of these sigils were quite complicated. The Recollection Sigil was the obvious choice, but it called for several arcane ingredients (attar of crimson corn, starfish eyes, and a bowline knot), required that the adept prepare by drinking nothing but fizzy lemonade for three days before, and ended with the adept setting herself on fire. The Revelation Sigil would have also probably worked, but it called for six adepts and copious bloodletting. The Recovery Sigil required actions too disgusting to even contemplate.

But the Discernment Sigil, which helped you recognize what you were looking for when you saw it, seemed to fit the bill perfectly. It was short and sweet, required only two magickal Gestures, neither of which called for headstands or extra fingers, and it used only one very short and easy-to-pronounce Gramatica Word. No setting on fire and no blood-letting. It was not so much different from the Ignite Sigil, which I had done many times before. I was confident I could handle it.

"You will do it right, Flora Segunda, won't you?" Valefor said, worriedly. "If you do it wrong, your head could explode."

"If your head explodes, I am not cleaning it up," Udo said. He had grabbed *The Eschata* and was now flipping through it. "What about the Recovery Sigil; it looks like fun—"

"I've decided, Udo!"

"Who am I? Boy Hansgen?" Udo protested. "Who dropped and made you the boss?"

Boy Hansgen was Nini Mo's sidekick. When she died, he took over the Ranger Corps, and fought hard against the Bird-ies during the War. Afterward, when Rangers were outlawed and the Corps disbanded, he disappeared and hasn't been heard from since. He was a good ranger, but no Nini Mo.

"You are not nearly tall enough to be Boy Hansgen," I said. "Give me the book back, Udo. My head will not explode, I promise you. I know what I am doing."

Udo tossed the book to me, grinning at my awkward catch. "You are lucky I am so easy, Flora. If Valefor is the one who is supposed to be recognizing the fetish when he sees it, shouldn't he be the one who does the sigil?"

"He can't. His only purpose is to act in regards to the House. He can't act in any other capacity. So I will charge the Word, activate it, and then pass it on to him, so that he'll feel its ef-fects. Then he should know the fetish when he sees it. I would have rather done the Recollection Sigil, but this is the best we can manage."

"And once we have the fetish, then what?" Udo asked.

"We have to have the fetish first; then we'll be able to figure out how to restore Valefor. We won't know what Mamma did to disconnect them until we have the fetish."

"Well, let's fall to," Udo said. "I gotta be home by six, and I don't want to be late and risk another lockdown."

I didn't want to be late to meet Mamma, either; she frowns on tardiness as much as Sanctuary does, and after not seeing her in so long, I did not want to start out on the wrong foot.

So, Valefor cleared the table of its mess of papers, Udo took off his hat, and I reread the Sigil, to make sure of the steps. Read it another time, just in case. Udo arranged himself to one side of me, and Valefor across. Between us, I lay *The Eschata*, open to the Sigil, just in case.

My stomach was fluttering, in a very nonrangery way. I had never heard of anyone's head exploding from a wrongly done Working, but there is always a risk that problems will arise. *The secret to having confidence is acting confident,* Nini Mo said. I wiped my sweaty hands on my kilt and shifted so that my stays were not cutting so harshly into my back.

Strike hard, and with all your Will, Nini Mo said.

Closing my eyes, I rested my left hand on my knee and made the Invocative Gesture with my right. Pinching my left nostril closed with my thumb, I breathed in through my right nostril for four beats. Then I pinched my right nostril closed and exhaled through the left for four beats. Three times I did each side, and I started to feel the distant dizzy warmth that indicated the Current was building within me.

The fourth breath, I drew in through the right nostril, and then, pinching both nostrils closed, held the breath in. At first it was hard to focus; I kept hearing Valefor's cough, or the crunch of Udo's satin kilt as he fidgeted. Then my lungs began to grow tight and the urge to breathe started to build. I swallowed, feeling pressure in my ears, but ignored the sensation and focused my Will on the image of the Gramatica Word, focusing focusing focusing. The pressure grew, and the blobby darkness before my closed eyes bubbled and swam. Everything around me receded. The pressure burned; now there was nothing but it and the overwhelming urge to gasp.

Lungs scraping, I opened my eyes.

A thin light was spilling from the open pages of *The Eschata* lying before me. The light curled about itself, contracting into sparks, which in turn shifted and turned until they hung before me in the glowing sinuous letters of the Exhortation.

I opened my mouth and sucked in the glittering gnatlike letters. For a moment my mouth was filled with a sparkly crackling, and then, in shock and surprise, instead of expelling outward as I should have, I swallowed. The letters burned as they went down my throat, burning hot and burning cold. I gasped and started to choke, redness dotting my eyesight. My stomach convulsed in a horrible searing pain, and I doubled over, then the letters were boiling back up my throat in a scream: "ℒℬℐⅇℬℐℒ!"

The Word was as loud as thunder, as wide as the sky, as concentrated as a sword swing, as bright as a mortar flash. It flew as true as an arrow toward Valefor. He opened his mouth to receive it, and such was its force that he fell backward, disappearing under the table.

"Wow!" I dimly heard Udo say. My mocha had had enough; it no longer wished to be friends with me, and its desire to depart was extremely urgent. I leaned over and let it go. Afterward, my throat felt like it had swallowed a cat, a cat who had clawed all the way down.

"Valefor!" I croaked, wiping my mouth on my sleeve. My mouth tasted of fur; I spit, and spit again.

"I'm all right! I am fine!" Valefor popped up like a Springheel Jack-in-the-Box. "That was fantastic, Flora! Let's go, I feel great."

He danced his little happy dance, and I could see, clearly burning inside him, the glittery glow of the Sigil.

"That was something, Flora!" Udo said. "Did you hear that noise?"

"I didn't think it would be so big," I whispered. "Val, can I have some water?"

Valefor produced water and after about half a quart of guzzling down, and then a pint or so of spitting up, I started to feel better. My mouth still burned, and the rest of me felt as though

I had been beaten with a stick, but it was a good sort of pain, and it was mitigated by the happy sensation of success.

"Hurry! Hurry!" Val sang, "Let's go a-hunting! It's near, I can tell, almost on the tip of my tongue, let's go! I have eleven thousand rooms, so there's no time to waste!"

So we went, wasting no more time, Valefor leading the way. My trek through Crackpot before had been a bare little jaunt, but now we were on a full-fledged expedition. Up narrow staircases and down broad staircases we went. Through antechambers, bedchambers, closets, parlors, dining rooms, sitting rooms, furnace rooms, bathrooms, water closets, attics, cellars, receiving rooms, and on and on. All the while, Valefor kept up a running commentary, like a tour guide:

"... Slippery Stairs, where Anacreon Fyrdraaca broke his nose sliding down on a tea tray ... Beekeeping Room, don't bother them, Udo, and they won't bother you ... Formerly Secret Cubbyhole ... Because it can't be secret if you know where it is, that's why, Madama Smartie ... Luggage Mezzanine ... I wonder if that salesman is still in the linen basket, I should come back and check ... Eternal Atrium, look how large that tree has become, I must raise the roof in here or it's going to go right through the ceiling ... The Gun Room, what on earth did Buck do with my .50 caliber Gatling ... The Halfway Point—"

"Stop, Valefor, stop!" I said finally. I had a stitch in my side from trying to keep up.

"I gotta go, Flora," Udo said, halting as well. He's a championship fencer, but he also was looking a bit winded. Valefor, energized, was *fast*.

"I've got to go, too. *Valefor,* come back!"

Valefor slid back up the balustrade. "What? Why do you linger?"

"Haven't you seen your fetish anywhere, Val?" Udo asked. "We've been through half the House."

"Not even half. Remember, eleven thousand rooms?" Valefor said, "Come on—"

"Haven't you seen anything at all that could be your fetish?" I asked. "Nothing at all?"

Valefor hopped impatiently, "No. Come on!"

"I have to go, or Mam will ground me again," Udo complained.

I said, "And I have to go, too. We'll have to look more later."

"When?" Valefor cried. "Oh, when?"

"As soon as we can. It will be hard with Mamma around, but we'll think of something. Lead us back."

Valefor protested and whined and wrung his hands as he led us back through the maze of corridors, rooms, and galleries, Udo and I both urging him to hurry up, and he insisting we were going as hurriedly as possible. But then suddenly Valefor's whine changed to hoots of surprise.

"Flora! I can feel it! I can feel it! We are close, very close!" He took off at a dead run, and we followed him, barely able to keep up. A doorway loomed at the end of the hall, and Valefor effortlessly passed through it. The door was locked. Udo pounded and banged, and I shouted for Valefor to open it, and after a minute, he did.

Inside, the curtains were drawn. Valefor's thin purple glow and the liquidy luminescence of the Sigil cast tremulous light over the small room, stretching monstrous shadows. Valefor was flitting about maniacally, tossing things hither and thither: a fishing net, polo mallets, old boots, pillows, dead flowers.

"Valefor! Cool down!" I ordered, dodging the footstool coming toward me.

"I can tell—it's near—I can tell, Flora Segunda," he said excitedly, descending upon the narrow gilt bed that was pressed up against one wall and tearing the sheets and blankets asunder. Great clouds of dust rolled up, and I put my hand to my mouth to keep from choking.

"The window!" Udo gurgled, retreating back into the hallway.

I stumbled my way across the room and pulled at the curtains; the fabric tore in my grip, and with a clatter, the rod came down and almost beaned me on the skull. The cloud of dust that came from this plummet made the dust Valefor was roiling up seem like nothing, but once Udo helped me wedge the window up, we had fresh air and light.

Valefor was dismembering the bed, tossing the mattress over and dislodging a sheaf of yellowbacks. The walls were pinned with prints torn from old CPGs and polo flags, and a model sailboat perched upon the mantel. A yellowback whizzed by me and hit the wall, knocking a dartboard askew; I automatically bent down to pick the pamphlet up and grimaced. *Naughty Nan's Risque Review* was the title, and the illustrations were of scantily clad showgirls posing acrobatically.

"What room is this?" Udo asked, looking at a silver urn. Val had tossed it in his direction, and instead of dodging, Udo had caught it. "Hey, look, it's a trophy for best horseman at the Califa summer fair, and look who won it—Hotspur!"

"Bedchamber of Redoubtable Dreams." Valefor huffed, still chucking things. "Hotspur's bedroom, you know, when he was a kid. Can you believe all this junk? My fetish is buried in here somewhere under all this stuff. What a mess. I'll never find it."

"Poppy? This was Poppy's room?" I said, amazed. I looked around with new interest. Poppy had torn those prints out and stuck them on the wall? Those were Poppy's old cloaks hanging on the back of the door? Poppy's polo mallets in the corner and Poppy's hippo bank on the bookshelf? "Why would your fetish be in Poppy's old room?"

"I don't know—but it's here somewhere, I can tell, I can tell!" Valefor said. "I can feel it so close, it tingles, it tingles!"

"Is it this?" Udo asked, seizing a stuffed monkey that sat in the rocker by the fireplace.

"No!"

"This?"

Valefor said indignantly, "No! Not a blackjack, Udo, don't be a snapperhead!"

"Maybe, Val, if you quit throwing things around and stood

very quietly for a minute and focused, you'd be able to sense it better?" I suggested.

Valefor stopped his whirling and stood stock-still, clasping his hands under his chin as though he were praying, and closed his eyes. The Sigil burned inside him like a little sun, steady and bright, and its glow made his skin seem shimmery, like mother-of-pearl.

"Do you feel it?" Udo asked.

"Shut up, Udo—let me concentrate!" With his eyes still closed, Valefor extended one long arm in a point and began to spin. Once, twice, three times he twirled, his gown swirling around his legs and feet like water, his hair spinning out in a halo of purple. Then he stopped suddenly, his long finger pointing directly at the large trunk sitting in the fireplace alcove.

"There!"

"That dirty old trunk?" Udo said.

Valefor snorted. "No, my fetish is not the trunk, it's *inside* the trunk. Open it, Flora, open it!"

We dragged the trunk, which weighed enough to have a body in it, out of the alcove and toward the daylight spilling in through the windows. Its flat top was covered in about two inches of dust, but when I wiped the dirt away with the bed-sheet Udo handed me, purple paint was revealed. Spidery silver letters spelled out *Reverdy Anacreon Fyrdraaca ov Fyrdraaca*.

"It's Poppy's Catorcena chest," I said. It's the custom that on your Catorcena, your family gives you a special chest with your name on it. You store your Catorcena clothing in it, and later, your heirlooms, the things that are important to you and that you wish to keep always.

"It's pretty beat-up," Udo said, and so it was, the paint rubbed off in places, and the wood rough and split. It looked like maybe Poppy had actually used the trunk as luggage. Valefor was already unlatching the clasps on either side of the open lock-face.

"Hold on, Valefor," I said, grabbing at his arm. I could tell he was just going to start flinging. "It's Poppy's important stuff, and we need to be careful."

"I'm surprised at your sudden interest about any of Hotspur's stuff, Flora Segunda," Valefor said. "But ayah so—we shall be very careful."

Ayah so. The minute the lid was up, Valefor elbowed me out of the way and started tossing. My protests ignored, all I could do was try to catch what he threw before it got messed up or broken: a tiny pink baby dress and two little knitted booties, a leather tobacco pouch full of coins, a green velvet smoking cap, a leather-bound book, a hairy piece of leather—ugh, a scalp—this I also threw, rubbing my hands on my kilt to take away the yuck.

"Come on, Valefor," Udo said impatiently. He caught the cadet jacket Valefor lobbed, and then the forage cap that followed.

Valefor's response was muffled. He was leaning so far into the trunk that he was in danger of falling in completely. I grabbed the back of his gown and pulled him out, and he came, sputtering ecstatically: "I have it! I have it!"

"A shoe box?" Udo said.

"Not a shoe box—a tea caddy?" I said, disappointed. Somehow it had seemed to me that Valefor's fetish should be more exciting than a tea caddy. Or if a tea caddy, at least engraved silver or solid gold, but this one was only plain wood.

"This isn't my fetish! My fetish is inside," Valefor cried. "I know, I know, I am sure—can't you feel it? Open it! Let's open it!"

We pried the caddy out of Valefor's grip to examine it more closely, but it appeared to be nothing other than an ordinary tea chest, slightly battered, made of dark red wood. It was locked. I shook it gently and it rattled slightly—whispering, like sand shifting.

"Smash it open," suggested Udo.

"You can't do that," Valefor said, aghast. "You might break me, inside—"

"Can we pick the lock? Isn't there a chapter in *The Eschata* about lock-picking?" Udo said. "Gesilher has a set of lock-picking tools he sent away for, from an advertisement in the back of the CPG. I could go home and steal them from him."

There is an entire section in *The Eschata* about lock-picking, but the problem, as I pointed out, was there was no lock to pick. Or, rather, there was a lock, but it had no keyhole into which tools could be inserted. Instead, the lock plate was just flat and round.

"How do you unlock it if there's no keyhole?" Udo asked.

"It's a seal lock." I'd never seen one before; they are old and quite rare, but a strongbox with a seal lock was described in *Nini Mo vs. the Kickapoo Dollymop,* so that's how I knew about them. "The lock is keyed to a seal. To open it, you press the seal against the lock plate, and that turns the lock open."

"What seal?" Udo asked. "The Fyrdraaca seal?" He and Valefor were leaning over my shoulder, breathing heavily and tickling my concentration.

I tried to squint the seal pattern into focus; the pattern incised on the lock plate was very thin, almost invisible.

"It's not the Fyrdraaca seal. I can barely see it, but it's not anything I recognize. I think it might be a bear holding a staff. Here, you look."

Udo pronounced the seal to be a bear holding a parrot, but Valefor, after getting so close to the lock that his eyes crossed, pronounced it a falcon in flight. I looked at it again, and this time it seemed to me that maybe it was a hand holding a short whip with a tendrilly lash.

Distantly, a clock tolled, and its chime brought both me and Udo out of our inspection.

"Pigface! I gotta go," Udo said. "We'll have to finish this another time. I'm gonna get popped for sure, but it was worth it. Good job, Flora!"

"I was the one who found my fetish," Valefor protested.

"Ayah, but Flora was the one who did the Sigil that helped you do it."

"I have to go, too, Valefor, but we'll figure out what to do next later." I wasn't going to have time to change if I wanted to make the horsecar, and Mamma was probably going to be annoyed I was late, but in my warm glow of success, I didn't care. My Sigil had worked, and we had found the fetish. We would find the seal, too, and Valefor would be restored!

TWELVE

The Presidio. A Snack. Sneaking. Another Denizen.

WHEN FLYNN AND I got off the horsecar in front of the Officers' Club, scores of canvas-clad privates were industriously polishing cannons, cutting grass, and bagging eucalyptus leaves. Maybe there was an inspection coming up, or maybe they were just trying to stay one step ahead of Mamma. All I can say is that I am grateful that she saves the white-glove treatment for work. Without Valefor, Crackpot would never pass her official muster.

Normally I am happy when Mamma comes home; it means that things will be as back to normal as they can ever be, and that while my chores don't lessen any, at least Poppy is no longer my problem. She'd been in Angeles for two weeks, a long trip even for her. But this time part of me wished that she had not come back for a few more days, just enough time to deal with Valefor. Now that we had the fetish, all we needed was a way to get into the tea caddy. If we couldn't find the actual seal, there had to be another way to open the lock. *If you can't go in by the door,* says Nini Mo, *go in by the window.* The restoration was as good as done.

The Presidio is a pretty place, scattered with white buildings dappled by shade trees, surrounded to the south and east by sandy hills dusted with sea grass, and edged at the north and west by the glittering blue waters of the Bay of Califa. Despite being a place completely concerned with war, it always seems very peaceful.

Building Fifty-six, the headquarters of the Army of Califa, stands at the head of the parade ground, looking down its long slope toward the Bay. The parade ground is bigly huge, large enough to march ten regiments in unison, although the most I've ever seen is six, at the Fortieth Anniversary of the Warlord's Conquest, three years ago. In the middle of the parade ground four cannons guard the flagpole where the colors of Califa and the Warlord flap and snap in the perennial whippy wind.

Troops of soldiers were starting to assemble in front of the Adjutant General's office, preparing for the final afternoon Gun and Retreat. I hurried by, dragging the lollygagging Flynn behind me. If you are stuck outside within eyeshot of the Colors when Retreat starts, you have to stand at attention for the duration of the Color Guard marching out, saluting the Colors, lowering them, folding them, securing them, and removing them, while the Army band plays "Califa Forever" and the cannons sound the end of day. I've seen Retreat a hundred times, and I didn't need to see it again.

Guards always stand in front of Building Fifty-six, but they never stop me. They never salute me, either, but that I can live with. If something is brewing, or a bigwig is on the post making trouble of some kind, then the front porch is crammed with aides, guards, and strikers, and there will be a knot of horses out front, nipping at each other and kicking along the tie-up rail. Today the porch was empty, and so, too, was the waiting room, except for Lieutenant Botherton, who was standing behind the front desk, sorting mail.

He said, sharply, "Don't let that door bang— Oh, ave, Madama Fyrdraaca Segunda."

It was too late not to let the door bang, so I smiled sweetly and said, "Ave, Lieutenant Botherton."

Lieutenant Botherton gave Flynnie the evil eye. Dogs aren't allowed in official buildings, but I was willing to bet that the lieutenant was not going to point that out. Rank, or at least reflected rank, does have its perks.

"Has Mamma arrived yet?"

"The General's ferry docked safely earlier this afternoon, but the General has not returned from paying her compliments to the Warlord at Saeta House." Lieutenant Botherton swished his skirts away from Flynnie's friendly nose and sliced open another envelope. Yaller dogs, as everyone calls staff officers behind their backs, are notoriously stuck up. Their kilts are longer and their noses higher than anyone else's in the Army.

Daggit. Even after Valefor's tea, I was starving. And here I had rushed frantically, not bothering to change, sure I was late-late, and now no Mamma, no chow, zip. *Hurry up and wait,* says Mamma, *that's the way of the Army.* I think it's just plain rude.

"I'll be in her office, then." I scooted before he could say otherwise, dragging Flynnie away from the spittoon he was nosing. Building Fifty-six has been Army headquarters forever, so it's stuffed with all sorts of martial mementos and portraits of old soldiers. The hallways are lined with cases full of conquest booty and the walls hung with faded battle flags, and thankfully it is someone else's job to do the dusting.

Mamma's office is large and has enormous windows that overlook the parade ground. There's her desk, a few chairs, a stiff horsehair settee, and walls and walls of file shelves containing walls and walls of files. *An army may fight on its feet,* Mamma says, *but it marches on paper,* and here were the pages to prove it.

To solace myself for having to wait, I sat down behind Mamma's desk and began rifling. Two sealed redboxes sat on the blotter, waiting for Mamma's attention, but I didn't bother with them. Redboxes are usually full of the most boring papers imaginable: requests for mule shoes, counts of blankets, reports on irascible horses and uppity sergeants, all endorsed, in triplicate, and tri-folded. They are not worth the hot knife it takes to slide their seals off. The red tape dispenser was full, so I cut a few yards off and tucked it away in my pocket. Red tape makes particularly good bootlaces.

The left bottom drawer of Mamma's desk is always locked, but that's nothing to me—a little pin and a little pop and Mamma's secret stash is revealed: a solid block of black chocolate. I made myself a little choco sandwie and tossed a biscuit Flynnie's gaping way. The first sandwie was so yummy that a second naturally followed, after which I put the much smaller block back and returned the locks to right.

Outside, the evening gun boomed dully, drowning out the echo of the retreat bugle. The clock in the hallway chimed seven, and my tummy, despite the two choco sandwies, rumbled loudly. Where was Mamma? I peered out the window. The Retreat Guard had marched off and a detail was slowly making its way down the sidewalk, lighting the lamps. The Bay had faded to a dark blue velvet and more lights were pricking the windows of the offices, just as the stars were beginning to prick the sky above.

The choco left my mouth dark and sticky, and Mamma's sideboard held only faceted bottles of bugjuice, which burns rather than washes. Mamma doesn't drink, but I suppose that hospitality requires her to have libations available for those who do.

A long narrow hallway runs the length of Building Fifty-six, with a floor like polished silk. It's perfect for sliding down if you sit on a file folder, but if someone opens a door while you are flying, it's off to the Post Hospital and ten stitches in your grape. Believe me, I know whereof I speak.

The watercooler stands at the end of the hallway, next to the back door, which was open, in direct defiance of Mamma, who really hates drafts. Two figures sat on the back steps, haloed in cigarillo smoke, also in direct defiance of Mamma, who had made everyone else stop smoking when she did. I crept silently down the hallway, muting my footsteps by leaving my boots just inside her office. Stealth is made perfect only by practice, and besides, little ears can learn all sorts of interesting things when they maintain a low profile.

"... I read in the *Califa Police Gazette* ..." That was Crackers. He's chief clerk to the Chargé d'Affaires and can forge the signature of every officer over the grade of major. A very useful talent if it doesn't get you shot, and one which I had been cultivating myself, in my spare time.

"That rag! The CPG hasn't printed the truth in a hundred years." That was Sergeant Seth. She's a copyist, which has got to be the most boring job ever created by anyone anywhere. All documents that Mamma creates must go out in triplicate, and a copy has to be made and filed in the Commanding General's archives. That's what Seth does, sits at her desk and copies stuff all day long. I'd rather be eaten by bears.

"Maybe a rag, but they had witnesses. There's no doubt but that Paimon was up to something."

Today everyone had been discussing Bilskinir House and Paimon, its denizen—half the kids at school, the horsecar driver, and now the clerks. Supposedly, a group of Radical Chaoists, celebrating some obscure holiday on the beach nearby, had seen bright lights and heard distant roars coming from the House. Since the House had been closed for fourteen years, this was big news.

Sergeant Seth said, "Those Radical Chaoists were probably drunk, and that's where the lights came from—the bottom of a bottle."

"You can't deny that that group of kids disappeared last year, and there is naught explanation but that Paimon snacked them up. After being alone for so long, he must be very hungry. It stands to reason he'd grab a few edibles if he could get them."

Last year a school group from PS 94 had disappeared on a fishing trip, the wreckage of their boat later found on the rocks at Bilskinir's foundations. Mamma sent a squad to investigate, but they couldn't get near the House. A couple of weeks later, the school group started to wash up on the Pacifica Playa, in well-chewed bits. Sharks? Or a hungry denizen? No one was sure, but rumor seemed to favor the hungry-denizen explanation.

Seth said scornfully, "It's been fourteen years since Butcher Brakespeare died and Bilskinir House closed. A denizen couldn't survive that long alone. What would Paimon live on all that time?"

"Paimon was no ordinary denizen; he's an immaculate—self-contained. He must have still survived. Hadn't those bits been gnawed on?"

"That boat smashed against the Bilskinir rocks. Those kids drowned and were eaten by sharks."

"So you say, but show me the shark who'll cook his dinner before he eats it. Those bones were well charred—"

"Oh, there you are, Flora." Sergeant Carheña, carrying several redboxes, paused in the doorway of Mamma's office and totally blew my creepy cover. He said loudly, "Put those weeds out before the General sees you, or she'll smoke you herself."

Crackers and Seth scattered like buckshot. Evening had taken over Mamma's office, and my tummy was rumbling. Sergeant Carheña deposited the redboxes on Mamma's desk and lit the lamps, which cast a sunny glow in the dusk of the room. He's been chief clerk for as long as I remember and can make the most cunning hats out of linen paper and red tape.

"How are you, Flora?"

I sat back down in Mamma's chair and twirled once, just to see if it was still as fun as it had seemed when I was a kid. "Fine."

"How are your classes going?"

"Fine," I said. Twirling was not so fun. In fact, now I felt hungry *and* a bit sick.

"Are you looking forward to your Catorcena?"

"Oh yes, awfully."

"It will be a fine day, and you will be proud, I hope."

"Oh yes, awfully."

I looked out the window again. Two outriders on horseback reined up in front of Fifty-six; they were carrying Mamma's guidon and escorting a large black barouche.

Finally, Mamma.

THIRTEEN

Mamma. Wax Seals. Incredible News.

MAMMA NEVER JUST walks into a room. She strides into it and takes possession. Everyone stops what they are doing and looks to her, and now she's in charge. She says this attention is all about the rank, but I think it's more than that. The Warlord comes into a room and no one pays any mind at all, because despite the rank, he's just an old man with one leg. Mamma is so used to being the center of everything, she just *is* the center of everything.

So Mamma strode into the room, giving orders to Lieutenant Sabre, her aide-de-camp, who is almost always a foot behind her. When she saw me, she broke off and held her arms out: "Ave, Flora!"

"Ave, Mamma!"

She swept me into a giant squeezy hug and I squeezy hugged her back. She smelled of lemons, sea salt, and the Warlord's tobacco. Her gorget banged against my forehead and her golden aiguillettes scratched my chin, but I didn't care. Suddenly I was superglad that she was home. Flynnie bounced up and began to jump, yipping like a squeaky door, but, thankfully, he didn't spray.

"And I missed you, too, Flynnie." Mamma kissed Flynn, also, although I had already gotten the full force of the lip rouge, and thus he avoided being smeared. "Ah, now my chapeau is askew. Here, can you reach the hat pin?"

When she bent over, I could, just barely. Mamma was in dress uniform: tricorn hat, tight black frock coat, white wig, and red lip-rouge. I hate the dress uniform because in it Mamma doesn't look like Mamma at all, but like a bandbox soldier, cold and aloof.

Mamma unbuttoned her frock coat and sat down on the settee, hanging her gorget over Flynn's neck. He jumped up next to her and laid his head upon her knee. All the dogs adore Mamma.

"Finally, I can breathe again. Flora, would you get me a drink? Just a tiny. And put the Command Fan on my desk, would you, darling?"

I took the fan, the symbol of Mamma's authority, and laid it on her blotter, then went to the drinks cabinet. "Water, Mamma, or tea?"

"No, just a tiny drop of whiskey. Aglis, go tell Carheña to hurry up with those papers. I want them signed before I leave here today. And tell Botherton I want Captain Hankle's final report, ASAP."

"Whiskey?" I asked, surprised at her request, and a wee bit alarmed.

"As Nini Mo said, 'There is always an exception to every rule.'" Mamma actually knew Nini Mo, way back when, when Mamma was just a girl. Unfortunately, about all she remembers of the great ranger is that she was very short and smelled always of patchouli perfume.

I poured Mamma a tiny teeny drop of whiskey, and took it over to her. "What took you so long, Mamma? I've been waiting for hours." She took the glass and, in return, held her wig out for me to put on the wig stand on the sideboard.

"I'm sorry, darling. The meeting with the Warlord took longer than I thought it would. I have a splitting headache; that blasted wig weighs a tonne. Ah, that was just what I needed. Another wee drop?"

I refilled Mamma's glass with another wee, wee drop and sat down next to her, pushing the growling Flynnie off the settee to do so. He promptly tried to climb onto Mamma's lap; laughing, she pushed him down, scratching at his ears in consolation.

"How is Hotspur?"

"He's fine, Mamma."

"Orderly and well behaved?"

"Ayah." I had decided not to tell Mamma about Poppy's fit. That might lead to questions about damage, which would then lead to questions about cleanup. I was fairly certain that Poppy himself wouldn't mention it, either; he tends to forget such incidents almost as soon as they happen. I hoped he had forgotten all about Valefor, too.

"I'm glad to hear it." Mamma wiped off the rest of her lip rouge with her hankie and then looked like Mamma again. She is not beautiful, exactly, not like the Warlady or the Holy Headmistress, but she is better than beautiful, I think. Her nose is crooked because she's broken it twice, dueling and broncbusting, but the slant gives her face character. Her eyes are vivid green, and her short curls are the color of honey and they never frizz. Unfairly, I had gotten the Poppy end of the stick, the pointy chin and scowly mouth.

"How's your prep going?" Mamma continued. She kept looking beyond me, toward the door, as though she was in a hurry for something, or distracted.

A wee bolt of guilt stabbed me. "Fine, Mamma." Thankfully Valefor had mostly caught me up. He had even finished making my tamales, which was wonderful because I hate to cook.

"Did you get the invitations in the post?"

"Ayah, Mamma."

"I'm glad to hear that," she said. "Where is that Sabre? Listen, darling, do you want to run on to dinner and I shall meet you there? I have a few things to do here before I can leave, and they just can't wait."

The guilt was replaced with annoyance. I can't even say how

many times this happens: I meet Mamma for dinner, she sends
me on ahead, saying she'll be right there, and then I sit alone at
the O Club, moldering, until either she shows up just in time
for dessert or some junior aide shows up instead to *present the
General's compliments, and she is sorry she is delayed and instructs you to just
go on home.* "Mamma, so you always say, and you never come! I've
been already waiting for hours, and you've been gone forever."

As I complained, Lieutenant Sabre returned, with yet more
redboxes, and my heart sank deeper into irkedness. It would
take hours to go through them; I might as well just go home.
Only a little while earlier I would have been glad to go home, but
now, suddenly, I felt forlorn and disappointed.

Mamma sighed and rubbed the frowny line between her
eyes. "Aglis—"

"Sir?" Lieutenant Sabre kicked his heels together and practically saluted. Mamma runs through ADCs like water; she rides
them so hard that they usually break after a few weeks. Lieutenant Sabre had been with her for over a month now, and his
manners were so perfect and his posture so straight that he almost seemed praterhuman.

"I'll deal with those boxes after dinner. Are the papers ready
for me to sign? They should be ready by now."

"I will immediately ascertain, sir." This time Lieutenant
Sabre did salute, then turned hard on one heel and fairly
marched out the door. There's a saying in the Army: *He's so regular that he pisses at attention,* and if ever I had seen an officer who fit
that description, it was Lieutenant Sabre. I'll bet he wore his hat
even in the bath.

"Mamma," I pleaded, "can't it wait?"

Mamma sighed again. She looked terribly tired, as though
she hadn't slept well, which was also unusual, as she can sleep
even in the saddle. "Darling, here—as soon as I sign the papers,
then we'll go to dinner. After, you go on home and I'll come
back here to finish up. Ayah so?"

"Ayah so, Mamma," I said, slightly solaced. Maybe that was
better, anyway. Once Mamma got back to her office, she'd work

all night, which would give Valefor and me a chance to plan our next move.

"I just need to confirm a few Court-Martial sentences; it won't take me very long. You can seal my signature; I know you love to seal." Mamma rose from the settee and, after pouring herself another tot, sat at her desk and put her specs on.

I do love to seal, so I pulled a chair up next to her. There is something deeply satisfying about making a perfect wax impression; it takes more skill than you might think. Lieutenant Sabre, now returned, opened files and shuffled papers, and Mamma sharpened her pen. I lit the spirit lamp and set the wax crucible to the flame. Army sealing wax stinks of storax, bitter and pungent, but it smells good to me.

"All right, Aglis, let's go. We are burning daylight."

Sergeant Sabre read: "'Sergeant Micalah Tsui Sanford, Second Dandies. Charges: Insubordination. Specification One: On Flores 15, Sergeant Sanford, whilst drunk, did stand upon the squad room dining table, singing "Chicken on a Raft" to the dishonor and detriment of the service. Specification Two: When ordered by his superior officer, Lieutenant Felix Boyd, to remove himself from the table, Sergeant Sanford did call Lieutenant Boyd a square-headed—'"

"Just the verdict," Mamma said hastily.

"Mamma," I protested.

"Stay fresh and sweet as long as you can, my darling. Go on, Aglis, and skip the dirty details."

"I beg your pardon, General. 'Verdict: That Sergeant Sanford be sent down dishonorably from the service. Recommendation of the Judge Advocate General: Sentence upheld.'"

"I agree. Dictate addendum: *Sergeant Sanford shall be held for thirty days' hard labor, on bread and water, and then dishonorably discharged.* If there is one thing that I can't abide it's insubordination."

Lieutenant Sabre blotted the addendum and handed the paper to Mamma. Her pen dipped and flew. Mamma's signature is ornate and swirly. Try as I might I can never quite get my F to look so curly. When I have to turn in signed sheets for school, I always use Poppy's signature, which is a wiggly blur and very easy to copy.

Mamma handed the paper to me, and I rolled the blotter over her signature, carefully so that the ink did not smear. The wax was just about the right bubbly. There's an art to making sure that you don't splatter when you pour, but I've got years of practice, so it's no trouble to me. I can put 'em on or take 'em off, no big.

"I need your seal, Mamma."

She fumbled in her vest pocket. Mamma wears her seal on her watch fob, and when she tossed it to me, it was nice and warm from being tucked so close to her heart. I poured a perfect round dollop of hot wax, then pressed carefully. The seal of the Army of Califa is the same as the Warlord's seal, of course, five arrows bundled with a swirling ribbon. It looks quite nice impressed in wax, very balanced and round.

"You are piling up, darling," Mamma said, pushing another paper toward me.

"You are squiggling," I said. "That could be anyone's signature."

"But only one seal." Mamma skidded her pen across the paper, splotching ink. "Chop-chop."

I blotted and sealed. Sometimes, court-martials are quite interesting—murder or mayhem—but these were all stupid stuff: drunk on duty, uppity in the ranks, kicking the captain's cat. Nothing yummy at all. Soldiers can't hardly do anything that is fun, and if they disobey an order, no matter how dumb that order is, they are in for it. Here was a sergeant spending thirty days in the guardhouse for having dirty buttons (Mamma dropped him down to time served), here was a corporal spending four months in the guardhouse for snarking off to his commanding officer (Mamma gave him another month and a flogging). There was nothing interesting at all, and my tummy was really burning with emptiness now.

"Hang in there, Flora. We are almost done," Mamma said,

pushing her document over to me. "Where's Aglis with those papers?

Lieutenant Sabre had left the room, but now he returned with a folder. He handed it to Mamma, who flipped it open and dipped her pen.

"General, I beg your pardon but before you sign—"

"Ayah?"

Lieutenant Sabre was looking at me. Mamma paused.

"Flora," Mamma said, "my red-tape dispenser is low. Would you run out and get some more from Pecos? We are going to need it."

"Mamma—"

"Flora." She said my name in the Voice that makes colonels cry. I got up, a tiny part of me annoyed that she so obviously was dismissing me, but another part of me was suddenly apprehensively excited. Something was going on.

So I went, whistling cheerfully, as though going to fetch red tape was my favorite thing in the entire world.

"Close the door behind you, Flora," Mamma called.

I did, gently. Lieutenant Sabre has his own office, right next to Mamma's. They have an adjoining door, and this adjoining door, though closed, has a transom above it. The window was only slightly open, but slightly was enough.

". . . insists that you release the Dainty Pirate to his custody."

The Dainty Pirate? I stood on tiptoe, trying to get my ear closer to that open window. Not for the first time I wished I were taller.

"Not a chance in the Abyss. The Dainty Pirate is my boy. I got him, and I will spank him. You can tell Lord Axacaya's envoy to go home unsatisfied." Mamma's voice sounded hard, flat. "He's my prize and I shall keep him."

Mamma had captured the Dainty Pirate! Udo was going to absolutely die. The excited flutter in my tum became a full-fledged hurricane. But why was this incredible news a secret? For years, the Dainty Pirate had been the scourge of the coastline, robbing and plundering any vessel that crossed his path. Ayah sure, the Dainty Pirate had dainty manners and never actually killed anyone, but that didn't make him less of a thief. His capture would be a huge success for Mamma and increase her popularity even more.

Lieutenant Sabre coughed nervously. "I beg your pardon, sir, but Lord Axacaya's envoy made it clear that because of your previous association with Boy Hansgen, he doubts your ability to judge this case fairly. I beg your pardon."

Boy Hansgen? Nini Mo's right-hand man? No one had heard a jot from him since after the War, but he remained the most wanted man in Califa. What did Boy Hansgen have to do with the Dainty Pirate?

"Lord Axacaya is wrong in this matter. Many years ago, Boy Hansgen and I were friends, but I have no such friendship with the Dainty Pirate. This situation must be resolved quickly. If the word gets out that the Dainty Pirate is Boy Hansgen and he's in our custody, it's going to get ugly."

Boy Hansgen was the Dainty Pirate? I almost spit with excitement; if I hadn't been trying to be cool as a cloak-twitcher I'd have shrieked. The Dainty Pirate's true identity is unknown, and although the press is always speculating, no one had ever speculated that he was Boy Hansgen. Boy Hansgen alive? A real ranger—alive!

Mamma continued: "I want this warrant carried out immediately, Aglis, the sooner the better. Until then, I want him held in complete secrecy. It will be a disaster if the press catches wind of this. And I want him disposed of before Axacaya has time to get the news back to Anahuatl City. And Goddess knows, I don't want the EI to hear about this. Who knows what stunt those idiots might pull."

The EI—the Eschatalogical Immenation—is a revolutionary society devoted to the eviction of all Huitzil influence on Califa. They are completely against the law, but are often in the newspapers, although they never seem to do much besides paint slogans and post anonymous broadsides.

"Ayah, sir," Lieutenant Sabre answered. "There's a batch of prisoners scheduled to be removed from Presidio Guardhouse to the Zoo Battery prison tonight. I've arranged for Boy Hansgen to be moved with the rest, and I've instructed the Zoo Battery commander to prepare the gallows for tomorrow night."

The gallows? The gallows! Mamma was going to *hang* Boy Hansgen, the last ranger? Nini Mo's sidekick? The heat of my excitation went dead cold.

"Is he secure? I do not want him getting away, Aglis."

"He is secure, General. There is no way that he can escape."

"Good. Would you see what happened to Flora, Aglis—"

I abandoned my eavesdropping and rushed back to Mamma's office, pausing in the hallway for just a second, to try to compose myself. Lieutenant Sabre opened the door and gave me a severe look, which I ignored.

"There you are, Flora! I hope you weren't goldbricking," Mamma said.

"I wasn't fooling around, Mamma. Sergeant Carheña was gone and I had to go to supply for the red tape," I said sweetly, waving the wad of red tape that I had oh-so-luckily stuffed in my pocket earlier. My tone was sweet, but my tum felt sick.

"Here's the last one. And don't peek. It's sensitive."

She slid the document over to me. The top half of the page had been obscured with a blank piece of paper, leaving only Mamma's signature visible. But I knew what it was, and after I poured, I hesitated. My hand had trembled, and the wax had splotched most unprofessionally.

"Chop-chop, Flora. What are you waiting for?" Mamma said impatiently. "The wax is hardening."

I sealed the Dainty Pirate's death warrant.

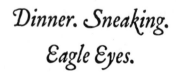

FOURTEEN

Dinner. Sneaking.
Eagle Eyes.

RANGERS HAVE TO learn to smile, and lie while they smile, and look content although they are grievous pained. But it's not easy to look carefree and blissful when your brain is churning like a flood. I could barely work my lips into a smile, and now I had an endless eternity of dinnertime to get through before I could make my escape.

Lucky for me, Lieutenant Sabre went to the O Club with us. Normally I would have kicked up a fuss over sharing Mamma after she had been gone for so long, but tonight I was glad to not be the full focus of her attention. Even Flynn, begging under the table, was a welcome distraction.

Dinner with Mamma at the Officers' Club is always a prolonged affair. As soon as you sit down, ancient officers start hobbling over to the table to compliment Mamma on this, or ask for her permission on that, or offer their opinion on another thing. Tonight was no different; in fact, it was probably worse because Mamma had been away for so long.

Between the endless interruptions, Mamma asked questions about the Catorcena, homework, Poppy, and the dogs. I answered, trying hard to squeeze my voice into some semblance of normal, but it was hard. Continuing lucky for me, though, Mamma remained somewhat distracted, and now that I knew the reason, her "wee tot" and the lengthy meeting with the War-lord made perfect sense. But so many other things did not.

How could she? How could Mamma send the last ranger to the gallows? Boy Hansgen—he'd been her friend—he was no less a hero than Mamma herself was. He'd never surrendered, never given up. If his capture was a secret, why didn't Mamma just let him go?

If I had been a better ranger, like Nini Mo, I could have teased information out of her without her even knowing I was teasing; I could have scryed the situation in the smear of gravy she left on her plate, or I could have burned my Will through Lieutenant Sabre's smooth forehead as he sat there at attention, chewing his steak, burned it right into his brain and known all his thoughts. But being only just me, all I could do was sit there, churning with questions, and try to look blissfully ignorant.

"Did you get your dress done, Flora?"

"Ayah, Mamma." Brief stab of guilt, but I *would* have it done next time she asked. In fact, Valefor might have finished it by now, for true.

"Are you all right, Flora? You seem a bit agitated."

Another sharp stab. "I think I am getting sick," I said, and then before Mamma could say anything more, the waiter whisked our plates away and asked if we wanted dessert. I did not, but alas, Mamma did, and of course Lieutenant Sabre followed her lead. I just wanted to get out of there before my facade completely cracked.

Mamma had finished quizzing me; now she turned her questions toward Lieutenant Sabre. Relieved to be off the hook, I sat there wishing dessert would hurry up—and then we had another interruption. A lieutenant in a red sash, which meant that he was Officer of the Day (the officer on duty when everyone else has gone home) and, thus, the interruption was official.

"I beg your pardon, sir," the lieutenant said, after saluting. "But I would not trouble you at dinner if it were not important."

"Ayah, so, Lieutenant Hulle?" Mamma asked impatiently.

The lieutenant leaned over and whispered into Mamma's ear. Her lips twisted and she put down the fork she had been fiddling with, then murmured something to Lieutenant Sabre, which I, darn it, could not quite catch.

Lieutenant Sabre whispered back. I tried not to appear attentive and twiddled my spoon, wishing I knew a sigil to enhance my hearing.

Murmur. Whisper. Murmur. Mamma. Hulle. Mamma. Sabre.

"Thank you, Lieutenant Hulle," Mamma said.

The lieutenant turned sharp on one heel and marched away, weaving his way through the tables that were now all staring at us.

Mamma sighed. "Will you excuse me, darling? I'll just be a moment, but I have something to attend to. Sit tight, Aglis, thank you." Lieutenant Sabre, half out of his seat, sat back down.

I could tell from Mamma's look that she was displeased. "What happened, Mamma?"

"Don't eat my cake, darling. I'll make it quick." She stood up, tossed her napkin on the table, and made her way toward the front of the Club.

"What is it?" I asked Lieutenant Sabre.

He was glaring at Mamma's back, the first real crack in his perfect yaller-dog facade I had ever seen. "Lord Axacaya. He wanted to speak with the General. He has the nerve to come here!"

Lord Axacaya is a powerful adept and Mamma's greatest enemy. He is not a true Califan; he came to the City many years earlier, fleeing from the Huitzil Empire. There he had been not just an adept, but divine. The Huitzils worship a hummingbird god, who feeds not on pollen and dew, but on blood and pain. The Flayed Priests of Huitzil take children from their real parents and raise them as the sacred offspring of this god. Then at a time ordained by the Flayed Priests' oracles, these divine sons and daughters are sacrificed to keep the Waking World in balance. (Thankfully, the Huitzils didn't make us take up that practice when we made peace with them.) Lord Axacaya was one of those divine children. When he was fifteen, he should have died under a sacrificial knife; instead, he fled and came to Califa, and with him he brought war. The Huitzils wanted him back, but the Warlord, after granting him sanctuary, wouldn't turn him over, and thus the conflict between our countries began.

And then later, when the War was not going so well for us, Lord Axacaya plotted with the Huitzils to turn Califa over to them if his life would be spared. If Mamma hadn't found out in time about his plotting, we probably would have lost the War completely. Instead, Mamma was able to force the Huitzil Empire to make peace, and though the terms were more to their benefit than ours, still we remain a free country, thanks to her. I think Mamma would have executed Lord Axacaya if she could have, but he's under Huitzil protection and, therefore, untouchable.

"It must be pretty important," I said, fishing. *And,* I thought, *it has to have something to do with Boy Hansgen.*

Lieutenant Sabre said viciously, "Pernicious traitor. The General should have ripped his lungs out while she had the chance. Now he lords over us all."

"If Lord Axacaya wants something, why does he have to ask Mamma for it? Why doesn't he just take what he wants? Mamma has no authority over him."

"It's not that simple. Under the Peace Accord, Califa maintains some independence and the right to conduct our internal affairs without interference—" Lieutenant Sabre stopped and looked at me suspiciously. "What makes you think that Lord Axacaya wants something from the General?"

Pigface Pogostick! I felt my face grow stiff and hard. I tried to arrange my mouth in an innocent smile. "Why else would he come here but to ask Mamma for something personally? I mean, he could have just sent a messenger if it wasn't important."

Lieutenant Sabre wasn't buying my feint. He looked at me so long that my face grew hot and my lips began to quiver.

Rangers do not quiver, nor do they show they are caught. "I think I'll take Flynnie out—" I said hastily, before my facade collapsed completely.

"Ah, the transom," Lieutenant Sabre said suddenly, and he smiled a bit. "I have found it useful myself at times."

"Transom? What transom?"

He looked at me appraisingly. "You will remember, Madama Fyrdraaca, that this is a matter of state, and you will be discreet?"

"You won't tell Mamma, will you?" I asked hopefully.

"Not if you swear on the goddess Califa to keep silent."

I glanced around to make sure no one was in whisper range, and then whispered: "Ayah, I swear, but I don't understand—the Navy's been chasing the Dainty Pirate for years. Why is Mamma keeping his capture a secret?"

"Shush—"

A plate of chocolate cake appeared before me, and then the waiter whisked around behind Lieutenant Sabre and plunked another plate in front of him, and then a plate in front of Mamma's empty place. A second waiter offered coffee, which I took, but Lieutenant Sabre declined for himself and for Mamma (which she wasn't going to be pleased about, I was sure).

As soon as the waiters were gone, Lieutenant Sabre said in a low voice, "When we sued for peace, what was the Birdies' first demand? The Ranger Corps be disbanded—the Birdies were afraid of the rangers' power and influence, and afraid of their magick. As Nini Mo's sidekick, Boy Hansgen was extremely popular. If word got out that the Dainty Pirate was captured, and that he was Boy Hansgen—think of the commotion. He'd be a hero and a rally for those who oppose the Huitzil overrule. At his execution, there would be a public outcry—maybe even riots. It's the General's job to keep the peace, as distasteful as sometimes that peace may be. And anyway, whatever Boy Hansgen may have once been, the Dainty Pirate is nothing but a common criminal."

"But why does Lord Axacaya want him?" I asked. "If Mamma's to execute him, isn't that what Lord Axacaya wants?"

"Ayah, but the General will execute him via Army regulations, and it will be short and sweet. Lord Axacaya would handle him according to Huitzil law, and that would be different."

"How?"

Lieutenant Sabre hesitated. "It would be messier. Also, Axacaya doesn't know that Boy Hansgen and the Dainty Pirate are one and the same, and the General thinks it best he remains ignorant."

"Have you ever seen him?" I asked. "Axacaya, I mean."

"Ayah."

"Does he really have an eye in the middle of his tongue?"

Lieutenant Sabre looked startled. "Gracious me, where did you read that, madama?"

"The *Califa Police Gazette.*"

"You should elevate your reading habits. The CPG is hardly the proper reading material for a young lady of good breeding—"

"Does he?"

"No," Lieutenant Sabre said, "but his eyes are black as pitch."

"Lots of people have black eyes."

"Not like this. I mean, his eyes are *all* black, even to the whites. He has trafficked so long in darkness that it has suffused his body, and now it stains the windows to his soul, reflecting his inner impurity."

I'd never heard of an adept whose eyes had turned to black, but then Lord Axacaya is a son of the Butterfly Goddess and he knows many dark and bloody arts.

It suddenly occurred to me that, though Lieutenant Sabre was being a surprisingly useful informant, I was missing out on an even more valuable opportunity to eavesdrop. Plus, maybe even get a glimpse of the boo-spooky Lord Axacaya myself.

"Excuse me, I have to go to the loo—I'll be right back." Before Lieutenant Sabre could comment, I bolted.

In the foyer, the Table Captain stood behind his stand, flipping through his reservation book nervously. The guards that normally stand outside the Club's front door were now standing inside, and they were holding their rifles at Port Arms, which is two positions away from Shoulder Arms, which is one position away from firing.

Earlier, the sliding doors to the Saloon had been open, though the Saloon itself had been empty and dark. Now those doors were closed, and two figures stood like sentries before them. They were heavily veiled, as formless as darkness, though their robes were a bright verdant green and fringed with brilliant feathers. The guards stared at these figures, and these figures—well, because of their veils, you could not see where they were looking.

"How are you, Madama Fyrdraaca Segunda?" the Table Captain said nervously. "Ready for your Catorcena? We certainly are." His eyes kept shifting from me to the veiled figures, then back again.

Normally, of course, people have their Catorcena parties at home, but in our case, that was out of the question, and so my party would be here at the Officers' Club. Ever since my sixth birthday, when Poppy ruined my party by standing on the roof of the garden shed and screaming at the goddess to strike him with lightning, I've had all my parties at the O Club.

"I am ready," I said, in a bright oh-I-am-just-a-harmless-silly-girl voice.

One of the figures swiveled in my direction, and somehow, just somehow, I knew it was looking at me. Suddenly I did not feel silly at all; I felt like someone was trying to rummage around in my head, picking through my thoughts, examining my teeth, poking my muscles, fiddling fingers in my brain. It was a horrible tickly feeling and made my insides feel all squirmy. I shook my head, but the feeling did not go away.

The veiling over the figure's head, I saw now, was sheer, but probably transparent enough to see through. The figure reached up a hand, long and graceful, bangled around the wrists with bracelets of jade and gold, and lifted the veil.

Two great eagle eyes stared at me, wide and unblinking, golden as an egg yolk. Above the eyes, iridescent feathers tufted upward into a quiff, and below, curved a sharp black beak.

A Quetzal! A Huitzil sacred guard. Never had I seen one, except as crude drawings in *Nini Mo vs. the Eagle Guards.* They say that Quetzals are born to women who lie with eagles, and they hatch out of huge green eggs, squirming babies with shrieking eagle heads. They say that the Quetzals tear out the hearts of sacrificial slaves, then eat them while they still beat. They say the Quetzals have no human feelings of mercy and love, only bloodlust and the killing instinct.

This Quetzal nerved my blood to shivering, with its unblinking golden eyes, the elegant narrow hand, the human form now evident beneath the robes. Valefor isn't human, but he seems human, he looks human, he acts human, and it's easy to forget that he's not. But this thing, despite its human attributes, had nothing in its eyes but a glittering hunger—the hunger of a predator. The Quetzal was unnatural, inhuman, and yet repellently beautiful, its sleek feathers shading from yellow amber into a deep yellow-red, the lethal beak as shiny black as wet ink. And those eyes, as round as two full moons, pitiless but also compelling.

I stood there, stock-still, caught in that gaze, unable to tear myself away. As mesmerized as a mouse who stands helplessly as death swoops down. Then the Quetzal let drop its veil and turned its great head away, dismissing me.

I turned and fled back to the safety of the dining room.

FIFTEEN

Case Tigger. Udo Upset.
A Plan.

MAMMA CAME BACK a few minutes later, looking grim, and she did not eat her chocolate cake. Neither did I; for the first time in my life, chocolate cake held no charms for me. Dinner was officially over. Mamma and Lieutenant Sabre went back to Building Fifty-six, and Flynnie and I were sent home in Mamma's barouche. Finally, I was alone, which was good because I could pretend normal no longer.

Back in the City, I got the driver, Sergeant Ziniea, to drop me at Hayes and Ash, near Case Tigger. It wasn't terribly late, only around nine o'clock, but already the light in Udo's room was out. The Landaðons are fiends on curfew, which is the one great negative whenever I stay with them.

Udo's room is on the second floor, facing the alley, but there's a handy dandy tree right outside his window. I have made the climb a zillion times, both up and down. I carefully opened the back-garden gate and stuffed Flynnie through, with stern instructions not to bark, and then swung myself upward. Udo's window was open; the Landaðons are fiends for fresh air, too.

The streetlight across the road was angled just right to throw a few shadows on the floor of Udo's room, and it showed the dim outline of a dresser and three beds. Poor Udo shares his bedroom with two younger brothers, but Gernot wets the bed and Gesilher kicks, so they all have their own beds.

"Udo," I hissed. I banged my shin against the dresser and stifled a curse.

The biggest bed groaned. Kicking off my boots, I climbed over the trundle bed where Gesilher lay wadded under a mound of blankets. Udo's bed is shaped like a sleigh and draped with curtains that hang from the ceiling. He always closes the curtains, as he bemoans his privacy. I brushed them aside. "Udo!"

Udo grunted and moved, half awake. "Go away, Ges—"

I poked him. "It's me."

"Flora?" he mumbled. Waking up Udo is like waking the dead. Actually, waking the dead is probably easier.

"Ayah, it's me—wake up." I poked again, then resorted to pinching. Udo jerked and rolled and then sat up, muffling curses. "Move over." I crawled under the curtains and into the bed, and Udo drowsily made room for me.

"What are you doing here?"

"Mamma caught the Dainty Pirate!"

That news immediately snapped Udo alert. "What?!"

"Keep your voice down or you'll wake the kids!"

"Buck got the Dainty Pirate? When? Where—"

"Is the house on fire?" Gesilher said from the darkness beyond Udo's bed. He's a worrier, always expecting to be poisoned, or burned, or smothered.

"Go back to sleep, kid," Udo said, unkindly. "The house is not on fire."

"Ayah." Gesilher was quiet again.

I said, "I just came from the Presidio—Mamma is back from Angeles, and she's captured the Dainty Pirate. He's been held in secret, and he's going to be hung tomorrow—" Here Udo groaned, but I continued, "He's Boy Hansgen! The Dainty Pirate is Boy Hansgen, Nini Mo's henchman—he's been incognito all this time!"

Udo gurgled at my news and bounced on the bed. "Boy

Hansgen! You've got to be joking me! Why was Boy Hansgen
disguising himself as the Dainty Pirate?"

"I don't know—but, Udo, they are going to hang him tomorrow night!"

"What about his trial? Doesn't he get a trial?"

"There isn't a trial, Udo. Mamma's already signed the warrant. She wants to make sure he's dead before anyone gets wind
of it."

Udo protested, "She can't sentence him without a trial—"

"She's done so, Udo, to keep him out of the hands of the
Birdies. She's keeping the peace—do you know what the public
might do if the news gets out that the Dainty Pirate is Boy
Hansgen? They could rally around him; it could cause riots—"

"You act as though you are defending Buck, that you think
she is right, and you say that you are going to be a ranger—"

"I am not defending Mamma, Udo, I'm explaining the politics to you."

"I don't care about politics. I care about the Dainty Pirate
being hung. What are we going to do—"

The door from the hall cracked open, slanting light into the
room. I burrowed down into the blankets, and Udo groaned
and made the fakest snore I'd ever heard. I lay as quiet as a tiny
crab and tried to hold my breath. For what seemed like the lon-
gest time, the light shone in silence. Udo snored again, and then
the door closed.

I burrowed upward. "You gotta keep it down, Udo! And I
gotta get home; I don't want Mamma to make it there first."

Udo bent his head toward mine, so that our foreheads were
almost touching, and whispered, "What are we going to do?"

"What *can* we do?"

"We have to rescue him . . ."

Rescue him! Was Udo *insane*? "We can't rescue him—"

"Are you kidding, Flora? You are always going on about
Nini Mo and what she would do. Do you think she'd let her
own henchman go to the gallows? Put up or shut up, Flora!"

Udo was right about that, that's for sure. Rangers are loyal to each other and stick hard to the rule *Leave no one behind.* When Nini Mo's accountant was killed in a raid, she dragged his body fifty-five miles on muleback to return him to his family for proper burial. She would never stand aside and let her sidekick be executed.

"...those guns in the gun room," Udo was saying, "and I have the pistol I got for my birthday last year; that's enough firepower to storm the guardhouse—"

I was only half listening to him. Why couldn't we rescue Boy Hansgen? All the way to Case Tigger, the knowledge that the last ranger would be executed tomorrow and I could do nothing about it had wormed and wiggled in my stomach like a bad egg sandwie. But Nini Mo says that what makes rangers stand apart from other people is that other people *don't* and rangers *do.* They act. Here was my chance to act like a ranger.

"No." I interrupted Udo's grandiose plan, which now involved two horse-drawn batteries and a squad of pikemen. "Nini Mo says you should only beard the bear in his den if you are coated in honey."

"Wouldn't that make the bear all the more likely to eat you?"

"She meant you should have the advantage before you face the enemy on his own turf. We don't have the advantage. We will need to be subtle, and we certainly don't want to get caught." I had decided to act, and with that decision, my tum felt much better.

A desolate howl rose from outside the window.

"What the heck was that?" Udo asked.

"Snapperhead Flynn—he thinks he's been abandoned—I have to get going—"

"We could wear masks—or Glamours! *The Eschata* was full of Glamours—Glamours that Confuse, Glamours that Befuddle, Glamours that Disguise."

"Ummm...," I said, considering. Udo was on to something. *The Eschata* did have an entire section devoted to Glamours, which only made sense, as rangers often require disguises, and the proper Glamour can disguise not only your face, but your whole body, too. "Lieutenant Sabre told Mamma that the Dainty Pirate would be transported to the Zoo Battery guardhouse tomorrow night, and thence to the gallows—"

"That's perfect!" said Udo, bouncing the bed again. "The road to Zoo Battery goes out along the Pacifica Playa, and that's beyond the City's border and there's nothing out there—no spectators, no witnesses. We could hijack the guard and steal the Dainty Pirate away!"

"He'll be pretty well-guarded, Udo. I don't think just the two of us, even in Glamours, could take an entire squad, maybe two. But if we had a release order . . ."

The order itself would be easy. I have a copious supply of official letterhead, which I have been nicking from offices for years, because you never know when official letterhead will come in handy. Udo's handwriting is as good as any clerk's, and I know all the official lingo. An Army special order is always achingly polite, full of *presents compliments, commends to your obedience, your humble servant.* I could very easily construct a special order demanding that the Dainty Pirate be handed to our custody.

"Can you forge Buck's signature?" Udo asked. Another howl raised up in sorrow—a good reminder that I needed to get home before Mamma did.

I said, "It's hard. I might be able to do something that would pass a casual glance, though probably not close scrutiny. But it's not the signature—it's the seal. We could never fake that."

"Pigface Psychopomp. Can you kip her seal, then, while she's sleeping or something?"

"I could, but I don't know that it would be wise, anyway. I mean, the guard is sure to think something is fishy—why would Mamma condemn a man to death and then suddenly turn around and release him? They are sure to question. We need a release order from someone no one would dare question, someone whose word would be law unchallenged. Who ranks Mamma?"

"Lord Axacaya?" Udo asked.

I thought of the grim-visaged birds and Lord Axacaya's demand, and a tiny thrill of revulsion rolled up my spine. "No. Who else?"

"The Warlord?"

I grinned in the darkness, and thought Nini Mo would approve mightily of my plan. "Ayah. The Warlord."

SIXTEEN

Home. Buck.
Differing Opinions.

I CAUGHT THE HORSECAR at Octavia. It was late enough that Flynn and I were the only riders, and the driver looked half asleep. Luckily, his horse knew the way. I sat at the very back, Flynn curled up on the seat behind me, and thought about our rescue plan. At the time of discussion, it had seemed the proper thing to do, but now it seemed like an awful chance. And yet, what kind of a ranger would I be if I did nothing to prevent Boy Hansgen from going to his death?

The horsecar left me at the Way Out Gate, Crackpot's back door (or delivery entrance, as Valefor had informed me). When I stopped by the stables to feed the horses, I saw that they had already been grained and mucked, and my heart sank. Mamma had beat me home. And I just couldn't face her right now.

Though I had defended Mamma to Udo, I couldn't defend Mamma to myself. I know she is sworn to uphold the Warlord, and that means she must uphold the Peace Accord, too, but how could she execute one of Califa's greatest heroes? A man who had once been her friend? She might have her reasons, but I did not understand them. Nor did I want to.

The dogs met me at the garden gate, caroling their pleasure at my arrival, and Flynnie flung himself forward to meet them. Any chance I had of sneaking in was lost in canine alarum. Still, maybe I could at least make it to my room. I very quietly opened the door, trying to slide in before the dogs could, but they leaped and pawed, and poured by me, almost knocking me down.

"Flora?" Mamma's voice drifted down the Below Stairs. "Is that you?"

"It sure ain't Nini Mo," I mumbled. The dogs scurried upstairs, which was well for them, because then I got a good look at the kitchen. When I had left to meet Mamma, the kitchen had been tidy and the dogs were locked up in the mudroom. Now the kitchen looked like the Flayed Riders of Huitzil had ridden through it once and then doubled back again, just for fun. The room was trashed. Someone, who could only be Poppy, had let the dogs out and unsupervised, and here was the result. Anger boiled up in me, so hot that it fair burned my throat. If I'd had a stick, I would have whacked something. Instead, I kicked the scuttle, which lay on the floor surrounded by spilled coal.

"Come to the parlor, Flora—I want to talk with you."

My heart, already low, disappeared into the depths of my boots. Mamma never actually talks *with* you; she talks *to* you. I trudged upstairs, a glassy sparkle of guilt glittering in my stomach. Had Lieutenant Sabre tattled after all? Or maybe Mamma had guessed? Or maybe she had found out about Valefor? I didn't know which was worse. No, I did. My knees felt rather weak. Nini Mo had faced the Flayed Priest Njal Sholto in a magickal duel, knowing that he was the greater adept, and thus she faced her own death. And yet she did not quiver. I would not quiver, either.

I would not quiver.

"Flora! Chop-chop!"

Mamma sat on the settee in the parlor, surrounded by a wash of papers. More were scattered over the low table before her, which also was stacked with the redboxes I had last seen on her desk at Fifty-six. The dogs had displayed themselves upon the hearth rug, like butter would not melt in their mouths. I could have kicked them all, a good boot right into the hinder.

Violence is not the answer, I know, but it's a hard impulse to strike.

"Where have you been, Flora? I thought you were going home." Mamma peered at me through her pince-nez. She'd changed out of her uniform into her purple silk wrapper, and her hair was standing up in spikes, as though she'd been running her hands through it.

"I'm sorry, Mamma. I stopped at the chemist's; I still don't feel so well." It was easy to sound forlorn and sick, partially because I really *did* feel forlorn and sick. My cold was still lingering.

"Why didn't you have the barouche wait for you?"

"There's no place to wait without blocking traffic."

"I don't like your riding the horsecar this late alone."

"I had Flynnie, Mamma."

"Ayah so, I am sure he would be good in a fight, poor coward. Flora, I went up to your room looking for you."

My stomach, which had started to warm, turned to ice again. *Do not quiver!*

"I thought you said you had finished your Catorcena dress. What did I find, not finished? Your Catorcena dress. I understand that sewing does not come easy to you, but that is no excuse for not being truthful."

"I'm sorry, Mamma," I said, and I was sorry—that I hadn't put the dress away. But then, I hadn't planned that Mamma might snoop; it's not her usual habit. And even more than sorry, I was relieved that Valefor did not appear to be anywhere evident. Although, blast him, he was supposed to finish the dress before I came home.

"I can accept your apology, but apologies are not going to cut it at the Barracks, Flora. They expect cadets to abide by their word and be truthful in all things. It is a hallmark of leadership to never dissemble."

Ha! Mamma could say that, and yet was she not dissembling in her dealings with Boy Hansgen? She did not practice what she preached. Rangers may lie, but at least they know that they lie. They are not hypocrites.

"I am sorry, Mamma."

"And the kitchen—you are supposed to make sure the dogs are in the mudroom before you leave, Flora."

Now, I would suck up the other stuff, but I was not going to take the blame for Poppy. "I did, Mamma, I did. Poppy must have let them out. They were in the mudroom when I left. It wasn't me."

"I stand corrected. In the future, then, perhaps you should put the dogs in the stable when you leave. Hotspur is not likely to go in there."

"Ayah, Mamma."

She sighed, and rubbed her forehead. She looked even more tired than she had at dinner. "I am sorry Hotspur is such trouble, Flora. You are good to look after him as you do. He has always needed looking after, poor boy."

In my mind, people stop being "poor boys" when they hit thirty, and Poppy was way past that mark, but I suppose Mamma has known him so long that it's hard for her think of him otherwise. Also, he does act very childish.

Mamma continued, "He has had a very rough time."

I didn't say anything because the only thing I had to say was rather mean. We must be nice to Poppy because he spent three years as a prisoner of war. But other people have rough times and they suck it up and move on. Sergeant Carheña lost his leg at the Battle of Calo Res, and he gets along just fine. There's a girl in my gymkhana class at Sanctuary whose little brother fell out of the back of an ice wagon and was crushed. She gets along just fine, too. Why does Poppy have to be special?

"Can I go upstairs now, Mamma? I have a lot of homework."

"I wish you would sit with me for a few minutes, Flora. It's been so long since we have been home together, and now I have to leave again. A messenger arrived from Moro; the Ambassador from Anahuatl City requires me to wait upon him, and I have to leave first thing in the morning. I'm sorry, darling."

Leaving again? Was this a stroke of luck! Mamma out of the

way, while Udo and I undertook our rescue plan. One worrisome detail easily taken care of.

"But I promise I will be back for your Catorcena. I promise. I'll be back in plenty of time. I promise."

"It doesn't matter, Mamma," I said. "Can I go? I need to get the kitchen clean before I go to bed."

"Leave the kitchen—I'll tell Aglis to send a squad over in the morning. And of course it matters. I promise I'll be back in time."

"It's fine. Good night." I turned around to go upstairs, and though Mamma called me back, I did not go. I didn't actually care about my Catorcena or whether Mamma was there or not. All I cared about at this particular moment was saving Boy Hansgen. Even Valefor had taken backseat to that; he could wait a little longer. Boy Hansgen could not. Mamma's departure made things much easier. Once Boy was safe, then I would restore Valefor, and if Mamma found out and didn't like it, to the Abyss with her.

When I got out of the bathroom, Mamma was waiting by my door; she never gives up, which is what makes her the Rock of Califa, I suppose. Persistence may be good for a general, but it is not such a happy quality in a mother.

"What do you mean 'it doesn't matter,' Flora? I thought you were looking forward to your Catorcena."

"I guess, Mamma."

"You have done an excellent job on your room, darling. I don't remember when I saw it this clean before, and the bathroom, too. I know you have a lot of responsibilities, and I am glad to see that you are, for the most part, handling them."

"Thank you, Mamma."

"I am sorry to have to leave again so soon, Flora, but I promise, before you go to the Barracks this summer, I shall take a nice long holiday and we shall do something fun, ayah?"

"Ayah, Mamma."

"I have to leave early, darling, so I won't wake you. Will you have cocoa with me before—"

A dog distantly barked, once, then twice, and then the entire herd erupted into a yodeling volley. There is only one reason the dogs howl this late at night.

Poppy.

Downstairs, glass crashed and the barking turned to howls. Mamma whipped around, then ran downstairs.

SEVENTEEN

Alone. Valefor. Next.

MAMMA LEFT AT oh-dark-thirty. She came into my room, but I pretended to be asleep and she didn't wake me—only brushed the top of my head with a kiss and slid the bed-door closed again. As soon as she was gone, leaving a faint whiff of sandalwood behind, I booted the dogs out of bed and ran to the window.

The outriders were already assembled; two of them were heaving Mamma's field desk into the back of a buckboard. Lieutenant Sabre stood by the back of the wagon, directing. The outriders finished levering up the field desk, then started on Mamma's trunk.

Usually I am sad when Mamma leaves, but not today. Today I was fearsome glad, and a part of me grimly wished she'd never return. This is very mean, I know, but sometimes my heart feels very very mean. Small *and* mean. Mamma could leave when she wanted to, but I'm stuck.

A striker held Jimmy's reins. The same wind snatching at the guidons was making Jimmy frisky, and he kept hopping a bit, so the striker had to also bounce, to keep him in place. The guidons dipped suddenly, and there was Mamma's bright head. She said something to Lieutenant Sabre, then took over Jimmy's reins, rubbing his nose soothingly. Mamma has a way with horses. No matter how wild they are, she can calm them.

I had not followed her all the way to the kitchen the night before. I had gone to the top of the stairs, and there I had stopped. Below, Poppy was shouting, the dogs were howling, and glass was smashing. Mamma's calm voice cutting through the clamor like thread cuts cake. Poppy's grating voice, rough with tears. *"The Human Dress is forged Iron!"*

"Shush, my darling, my sweet boy. Shush."

"The Human Form a Fiery Forge!"

"No, my darling, here, give the knife to me . . ."

That's when I ran back to my bedroom. I had slammed the door, crawled into my cold bed, and lay in bitter darkness the rest of the night, thinking bitter thoughts.

Now Mamma mounted, and Jimmy twirled a bit while she settled in the saddle, after rapping him on the withers with her crop. The last trunk was strapped down, and Lieutenant Sabre, who had been overseeing the stowing, mounted. Here was revealed Lieutenant Sabre's one military flaw: He had a terrible seat. His stirrups were way too high and his knees stuck out like wings.

The guidons went first, and then the buckboard. Mamma fell in next, then Lieutenant Sabre, and the entourage jogged down the drive. Because Crackpot's main gate is too heavy to be opened without Val's effort, the drive now cuts away and veers to the back of the House, toward the freight entrance. At the split, Mamma paused and looked back. I ducked behind the curtain, although I know she was too far to see me. I couldn't see her face, just the bobbing feathers on her tricorn hat. For a few seconds, she looked at the House, and then she turned and rode away.

I went back to my warm bed, and there found Valefor, usurping my place and seeming pleased with himself. He looked not quite the worst I had seen him, but not the best, either. Somewhere in between, faintly sparkling but faded to lavender.

"How happy that Buck should have to leave again, and now here is our chance. I can still feel that Sigil rumbling around inside me. I know this time we shall find it, I know we shall, Flora Segunda—let's start."

"I can't, Valefor." I found my wrapper and put it on, then looked for my slippers. Now that I was up, I might as well stay up. Udo and I had agreed that we would be cutting school today; his plan was to leave Case Tigger as usual, walk the kiddies to school, and then hit the horsecar. I had plenty of time to take a long hot bath before he came, if I went now. We had a long day before us, and it would be nice to be clean for it. Plus, I was too hungry to sleep. I needed a big breakfast and then to start preparing.

Valefor said, "Why not? We are burning daylight, and Buck is gone. When will she be back?"

"Tomorrow afternoon," I said. "Just in time for my Catorcena the next day."

"That should be plenty of time to—"

"No, Valefor," I said, then told him about Boy Hansgen. When I was done, Valefor's brow was furrowed in a pout deep enough to plant potatoes in.

"But what about me, Flora Segunda? Have you forgotten poor Valefor?" The tears were welling. Val was a regular fountain; it was a talent that I should cultivate. Crying on cue should surely be a handy ranger skill.

"No, I haven't, but we have to rescue Boy Hansgen first. He's on a deadline, and you are not, Valefor. He's going to be executed at midnight tonight, so we can't lollygag."

"But you care more about a stupid pirate than your own family?" Valefor sobbed.

"No, I don't. Don't be silly. But I have to prioritize—"

"Your own family!"

"Valefor, look at it this way. Boy Hansgen is a ranger. I know he'll be able to help us open the tea caddy. And he's an adept, too. He will know exactly how to restore you." I was making this up as I went along, but as I did, I realized that it actually made pretty good sense. If anyone would know how to open a seal lock without the seal, surely it was Boy Hansgen.

Val's sobbing turned into hiccups. "I might remember him, actually. Boy Hansgen, you said?"

"Ayah."

"Was he in a band? I think they played for Buck's twenty-first birthday—I do remember: The Infernal Engines of Desire, that was their name. It was a fancy dress party—come as your fear. I made the most wonderful cake in the shape of Horrors to Come and Delights to Pass, and real chocolate spouted—"

I cut him off. "So, see, Valefor, it's all part of the plan."

"Well, it could work," he said thoughtfully. "But you haven't forgotten about me, Flora? You will not forget. You promised you wouldn't."

I said soothingly, "I will not; I promise. But I can only do so much. Val, Poppy trashed the kitchen last night."

"I know. I heard him. Even in the Bibliotheca, I heard him. Oh, the noise. Well, I'll soon put a stop to that—it's first on my list."

"Could you fix the kitchen? And make me some coffee? Please. I'll give you more Anima."

So we bent our heads together, and this time I noticed that I could actually see my Anima. It was wispy and thin, a washed crimson that was almost pink, but I could see it. Again came the delicious feeling of sparkly well-being, and again I felt a whole lot better about the world—as though I had drunk two entire pots of coffee.

Valefor himself looked better than he ever had before; his form looked more solid and muscular, and his eyes were like chips of amethyst. For the first time, I noticed a family resemblance: Mamma's wide-set eyes and Idden's rounded chin. Poppy's bladed cheekbones and the Fyrdraaca nose, sharp as a tack. He really was quite good-looking in a matinee idol sort of way.

"You know, Flora Segunda," Val said, considering, "I think that perhaps I should make sure you don't forget me—and so I think that Valefor shall turn off the tap until you make good on your oath."

"'Turn off the tap'? What does that mean?"

"I mean, no more Valefor fixing everything nice and tidy. I mean, you are on your own until you come through, Flora."

"But you said you'd clean up the kitchen if I gave you more Anima!" I said indignantly.

"Well, now you know how it feels to be promised something and to receive it not. Turnabout is fair play."

"Valefor, I said I would do it, but all in good time."

"*Flora's* good time, and what time will that be? Well, Madama Fyrdraaca, you do as you please, and when you are ready, I shall be ready, too."

"I can clean the kitchen myself, Valefor," I said warningly. "I don't need you."

He was unperturbed. "Perhaps, but I think you've lost the taste for cleaning. And I think perhaps that you do need me. I am secure in myself. Say hello to Boy Hansgen for me."

He wiggled a little wave in my direction and dissolved into a froth of purple. Well, he could pout all he wanted; my plan did not hinge on him, anyway, though I had hoped to get him to help Udo and me with our disguises, and maybe whip us up a nice snack before we went to tackle the Warlord.

When it came down to it, I'd warrant he needed me more than I needed him. Although, he certainly was right that I had now *completely* lost my taste for chores.

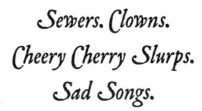

EIGHTEEN

Sewers. Clowns. Cheery Cherry Slurps. Sad Songs.

TRICKERY AND DISGUISE are the ranger's favorite tools. Easier to make a clean getaway if your target doesn't even realize it's been rooked. Easier to be given freely than to take by force. And the trick to getting what you want, Nini Mo said, is to make sure you phrase your request correctly.

The Warlord's favorite bar is a joint called Pete's Clown Diner, which is located in the most ruinous part of the City: South of the Slot. South of the Slot is famous for its hard-cases and blind tigers (or, to quote the *Califa Police Gazette,* "undistinguished personages and establishments of questionable clientele"), and not an area to be caught in at night unless you are suicidal or well-armed. Happy for Udo and me, who are neither, the Warlord's devotion to Pete's knows no schedule, and he's as likely to be found there at one in the afternoon as at one in the morning.

Early afternoon South of the Slot isn't pretty, but isn't life-threatening, either, as most of the dollies, mashers, twirlers, saltmen, and other lowlifes are still passed out in their beds or on the sidewalks. Or, rather, in the gutter, as South of the Slot has only a scattering of plank sidewalks.

We took the N horsecar, which traverses along the Slot that gives South of the Slot its name (there's a North of the Slot, too, but it's all banks—thieves of a more respectable kind, says the

CPG) and got off at Placer Street. Pete's Clown Diner is two blocks down, at Placer and Hazel, and within half a block, both Udo and I were wishing that we had worn shorter kilts and higher boots. Or better yet, ridden.

"Don't the garbage men come down here?" Udo asked. On the sidewalk the trash was ankle-deep; we would have walked in the street but that was knee-deep in mud, a rather unsavory looking mud that reminded me, both in looks and smell, of something I did not want to be reminded of.

"I guess not. Perhaps they are afraid to." I veered around the half-eaten chicken that lay forlorn on the sidewalk.

"Cowards. This is a disgrace." Udo hid his nose behind a white lace hankie. Since he was dressed as a drover, in leather pantaloons and overkilt and an orange-and-blue-plaid smock, it made him look rather conspicuously suspicious.

"Put the hankie away," I ordered.

"But the smell—"

"We are supposed to be in disguise. How many drovers do you think use white lace hankies?"

"Ones that don't like the smell—ayah, Flora, you win, as always." Udo replaced the hankie with a stogie; the look was more in keeping with his disguise, but the smell was only marginally better. Smoking is a horrible habit.

South of the Slot really *was* a disgrace; I agreed with Udo there. Farther down the street, a dead mule lay on its side, as green as a grape and so gassy that I'm surprised the corpse didn't float off into the sky. The sidewalk planking soon disappeared completely, and then the trash turned out to be a good thing because the only way to get through the mud without losing your boots was to hop from broken barrel to discarded box to abandoned fruit crate. When a wagon went by, its driver cursing a blue streak and snapping a whip over the struggling team, its wheels tossed up rotting garbage and sludge.

The buildings that lined the street were little more than shacks, hovels in near danger of collapsing. Rat-faced children peered through broken doors and empty windows, and occasionally a rat itself scampered by. Sometimes followed by a cat. Mostly not. Grubby men lurked in doorways, staring at us as we walked by, but no one stopped us. Perhaps Udo's smock had blinded them.

Pete's Clown Diner was made obvious by the clown dangling over its front door and the coach parked in front, with the Warlord's crest displayed in gold on its side. The dangly clown was, I realized thankfully, not a real clown, but just a dummy dressed so, and strung up. Still, it looked awfully lifelike hanging there, and the painted red smile looked more like a grimace. Garish red light flickered through the grimy window.

"Oh, Goddess bless us for what we do," Udo mumbled beside me.

"Remember the plan?" I whispered, fiddling with my veil. It was hard to see through, making everything dark and blurry and slightly spotted, but it was necessary for my mournful disguise. What grief-stricken sister, about to lose her favorite brother to cruel fate, would show her face in public?

"I remember," Udo said.

We clicked closed fists. "Ready."

Palm to palm. "Steady."

Knuckles to knuckles. "Go."

In Nini Mo's yellowbacks, the doors to a saloon always swing, but Pete's had no doors, just a row of beads that clicked as we pushed through them. In the yellowbacks, saloons are always loud and smoky, full of gallant gamblers and luscious bar-girls with hearts of gold. Pete's was dark, the air stale with smoke, and dim. No cow-band warbled on the stage, so the room was quiet, and I didn't see any gallant gamblers or luscious bar-girls, only a waitress with a face as seamed as an old shoe. Men and women sat at scattered tables, their heads drooping into their glasses.

To one side of the room stood a bar, slick and long. Behind the bar, a giant mirror tilted, reflecting the half-empty room, and the drover and the mourning woman standing in the doorway.

"My skin . . ." Udo groaned, coughing. I shushed him. Now was hardly the time to worry about his complexion. "Confidence is as confidence does," said Nini Mo, so I sailed forward to the bar and leaned on it, very cool-like.

The barkeep looked over his glasses at me. "What'll it be, madama?"

For a second my mind was completely blank. What do you order at a bar? A drink. What kind of drink? I couldn't think of any kind of drink, and then—

Udo said, "Beer."

The barkeep rolled backward and clutched at his chest as though Udo had punched him. "Beer? *Beer?* Young man, you insult me. Beer! This ain't no broom closet, no blind tiger, no gin joint. Pete's Clown Diner is a class establishment, with classy patrons, with classy palates. We make our own ice cream and our own whip. Not to mention toffee syrup. And me, Thomas Yin Terry, known throughout Califa as a mixologist extraordinary, who can make any confection you can dream of, and yet you ask for *beer?* I am shamed." He bent his head down, and a tiny silver tear dribbled down his cheek.

As he spoke, I read the menu written on the mirror behind him, and that's when I realized that Pete's was an ice-cream joint. The silver urn standing behind the bar, studded with levers, dispensed soda water, not beer. I was relieved that I was not going to have to choke down beer and pretend that I liked it. Ice cream is much better, and besides, I was hungry.

I said quickly, "I apologize for my brother, sieur. He's a drover, and they have no class—" Here Udo's foot stamped on mine, but I ignored the spike of pain. "I'll have a Cheery Cherry Slurp."

The barkeep brightened up. "Ah then, a Cheery Cherry Slurp. I've not had a call for that in many a day. A fine choice. And you, sieur drover?"

"A Broad Arrow Sling," Udo said.

"Another fine choice. Be seated, and Lotte shall bring."

We sat, at a table that was grubbier than Crackpot's kitchen floor. Only a look from me had kept Udo from dropping his hankie on the chair before sitting down, but it was hard to blame him. Despite my tummy's rumble, I was thinking that perhaps it would be a good idea to just *pretend* to eat the ice cream.

The Warlord sat in the back of the room, at a round table with three others, playing cards. I recognized him immediately, because, of course, his picture hangs next to Mamma's in every classroom and public building in the City. The Warlord wasn't exactly as his portrait showed: His hair was whiter, and his jowls heavier, but still, there was no mistaking him.

Once the Warlord was a fearsome pirate, who stole himself from the slave mills of Anahuatl City and then stole himself a small empire. Now he's pretty old and tired. I suppose final decay is unavoidable, unless you plan otherwise, which I do exactly—going out with a bang, like Nini Mo, long before my life descends into a whimper of old age.

Udo hissed: "There's the Warlord; what says your plan?"

"It says we should wait until we get our sodas!"

"We should move in—" Udo shut up while Lotte the Shoe-Faced Woman plunked the sodas in front of us, sloshing soda water and whip, and took my money. Now that the Warlord was sitting right there, just a few feet away, engrossed in his poker game, my nerve was sticking. The ice cream looked pretty clean, and I was starving; maybe I should eat it first and then—

"Do you want to buy some flowers?" Something tugged at my sleeve: a small child with a smudgy face.

"Git, sprout," said Udo rudely.

The child stuck her tongue out at him, and repeated to me: "Do you want to buy some flowers?"

"You haven't got any flowers," I said. The kid's dress had giant holes in it, and her little bare feet were blue with cold.

The child looked at me as though I were an idiot. "They are outside. If you come, I'll show you."

"I'm sorry, but I don't need any flowers. But here—" I fished in my purse and found a coin. The kid snatched the coin out of my hand and said, "Pinhead!" before flitting off.

Udo mumbled, "That was smart. Now every beggar kid South of the Slot is going to be pushing on us! Don't you know never to give out alms?"

"She didn't have any shoes."

"She probably did at home. I mean, who is going to give money to a beggar with shoes?"

"Maybe she really is poor, Udo."

A choked sob came from across the table. Udo was sniffling into his soda, tears running down his face, his mascara blurring. I was momentarily confused. A second ago he didn't care about the beggar, and now he was crying over her? Then I realized—blast Udo—he had started the plan without waiting for my signal.

"Ahhhh," Udo said, loudly, dramatically. "It's too much to bear, hermana. It's just too much to bear. Our poor Tenorio, so young, so young."

Under the table, I kicked Udo a good hard swift one in the knee, but he didn't let up. "Give us a song, Felicia, give us a song to remember Tenorio by. Here, I shall play the tune and you shall sing—"

We rose and went over to where a rickety pianoforte stood against the wall. When Udo flipped open the cover, dust puffed up, and when he put fingers to the keys the pianoforte wheezed just like a cat. The original plan had called for me to play and him to sing, but apparently Udo was in charge now, and my plan was nothing.

"Sing, hermana, sing for Tenorio." He banged out the first chords of "Who'll Tell His Mother." I had no choice but to sing, and so I opened my mouth and hoped that I remembered all the words:

"Somebody's darling so young and so brave
Wearing still on his sweet yet pale face
Soon to be hid in the dust of the grave
The lingering light of his boyhood's grace
Somebody's darling, somebody's pride
Who'll tell his mother how her boy died."

I'm not the best singer, but in this case, my wobbly notes were working for me, sounding like my voice was cracking with tears. The Warlord is notoriously susceptible to sob stories and sad songs—a susceptibility that our plan hinged upon.

The crowd, not fully appreciative, began to hoot and jeer, but Udo stubbornly played on, and I kept singing, even when someone threw a glass at my head. I ducked in time, and the glass slammed into the wall behind me, as explosive as a bomb.

NINETEEN

A Melee. The Warlord.
An Autograph.

THE GLASS-THROWING got the barkeep to shouting, which made Udo play louder. I reached for a high note and didn't make it, my voice breaking into a jarring yowl. Another glass was thrown, which this time hit a mark: the Shoe-Faced Woman, who went down like a buffalo. The shouting increased, and things other than glasses started to soar: a boot, a pineapple, a spittoon. Udo ducked down and I ducked behind him, but we kept on with our recital. Ice cream hit the wall above and showered down on top of us: Good-bye, Cheery Cherry Slurp.

"Hey now, hey now!" This roar bellowed over the hooting, the piano, my wailing. The hooting stopped, Udo quit banging, and I let my wail trail away. We had finally gotten the Warlord's attention, though not in the way we had planned.

The Warlord rose up from the poker table. "That's enough of that—that's enough, there! I'll be taking apart the next man to throw something, with my own hands, for interrupting the lady's pretty song like that. Let the lady sing." The Warlord might be old, but his voice was booming, and there was an expectation in it that his orders would be obeyed.

They were. Some of the crowd grumbled, but they sat back down. The barkeep and another man picked the Shoe-Faced Woman up and carried her away. A potboy came in with a broom and began to sweep glass.

"Go back to singing, madama," the Warlord said. "I like your song fine."

"I cannot, Your Grace," I sobbed, snuffling into the bottom of my veil. "I can no longer sing, oh, Your Grace, pardon me." I started to make the courtesy that signifies Abasement before a Superior So Superior That No Abasement Is Abased Enough, but since it requires going down on both hands and knees and the floor was so very dirty, I pretended to stumble on my way down.

The Warlord caught me. "Now there, now there. Rezaca, get the lady a chair and a drink of water. Come to me, my darling, and tell me what is wrong."

I sobbed and moaned and sat where bidden. At first it was hard not to laugh, but then the more I pretended to cry, the more I found I was actually crying, and pretty hard, too, as though something had twisted a tap inside me that I didn't even know was closed. Now that I was going, I could hardly stop, harsh gasping sobs that made my internal organs ache.

"Now, now, poor lady, why do you cry so?" The Warlord patted my knee with a very large hand.

"Our brother, Your Grace, our poor brother, he has so little time left in this world," said Udo brokenly. "And we weep for him, Your Grace. He is the favorite of our mamma, and how shall we tell her?"

Someone shoved a glass into my hand, and I lifted the veil just enough to gulp down the stale water, turning my sobs into hiccups. I swallowed another big gulp of water, swallowing the hiccups, too. "Oh, Your Grace, can you not help us? You are so kind and generous."

"Now then, tell me exactly, my darling, what you mean, and perhaps I can. Come, come here, take my hankie—" Out of the Warlord's green brocade vest came an enormous lace-trimmed red hankie, already well used. I took it, glad that the veil covered my grimace, and dabbed.

The poker buddy who had gotten me the chair said, "Your Grace, the game—"

"Shut up there, Rezaca. Go on, then, darling."

I said brokenly, "Your Grace, it is this: Our poor brother Tenorio enlisted in the Army, as our poor mother's sole support, her favorite child, too, and she with the goiters and the lumbago and the gout from a whole lifetime of washing clothes to feed us poor little children."

"An admirable son," said the Warlord. He motioned for my glass to be refilled. "Go on, dear madama."

"And so poor Tenorio fell in with a bad crowd, who enticed him to drink and gamble, and soon he had gambled away all his earnings and more besides and was deeply in debt. And then, when desperate to send his poor mamma the money she needed for her lumbago medicine, he borrowed from the company funds—" I paused to sniffle and let the drama sink in. "And then he was caught and sentenced to be hung, oh, Your Grace!"

Here I let loose with a wail and another round of wracking sobs, waiting, hoping, praying that our plan was working.

"Your Grace, the game!" said the poker buddy urgently.

The Warlord raised his hand without looking away from me. He said, his voice catching slightly, "Tell me how I can help you, little lady. I cannot bear to see such a sweet face so sad."

All the blood that I had not realized had left my head rushed back into it. "Oh, Your Grace," I said, and this time the wobble in my voice was from relief, "I know it was wrong, and so does Tenorio, but does he deserve to die for it? Our poor mother."

"Your Grace, I really think—," said the same annoying poker buddy, but the Warlord waved another *shut up,* then patted my knee again, although this time his pat was a bit more like a rub. I smiled sadly at him.

"If we were all to die for our mistakes, Your Grace, who then would still live? And how should we then learn?" Udo said earnestly.

The Warlord said, "Have you spoken to General Fyrdraaca about this?"

"She would not see me, Your Grace. She is strict with the law. But is there no room in the law for mercy? The Warlord's rule has always been just and kind."

"Ayah, so it has been. And so it should be—Rezaca, if you say another word, I shall fry you." Again with the rubbing hands. Then, before I could protest, the Warlord hoisted me up and perched me upon his massive knee. He might be old, but he was still pretty strong, even for a man with only one leg. "I shall speak to General Fyrdraaca on your behalf, my little parrot. How shall that be?"

"But Your Grace." I let the tears well in my eyes. "The execution is tonight, and by then it shall be too late."

Udo interjected. "And General Fyrdraaca has gone to Moro. By the time she gets back, our brother shall be gone, and our mother shall die of shame."

The Warlord encircled one squeezy arm around me, and this I did not like at all, but there wasn't much to do but try to look sweet. I could smell his breakfast on his breath: pickled herring. I sobbed, bending my head and jabbing my elbow into the Warlord's chest. He eased up on his grip.

"Your Grace, can you not show mercy? Can you not save poor Tenorio?" Udo sniveled.

"I can and I will!" the Warlord declared. "Get me paper, Rezaca. I cannot let this little lady be sorrowed, and for such a trivial thing. Have we not all had our bad gambling debts, a horror to pay?"

The annoying poker buddy protested. "Your Grace, it's hardly within our purview to interfere with the law—"

"Whose law is it? Mine! And I shall do as I see fit!" the Warlord roared. "Get me that paper!"

Rezaca was not moved. "Your Grace, General Fyrdraaca—"

The Warlord rose up, dumping me off his lap. Compared to this, his earlier roar had been but a whisper. "Am I not Warlord of this Republic? Is not my rule law? If you do not want yourself to be drummed down to the Playa with the Rogue's March, then you should be doing as I say!" Even though his ire was not directed at me, my stomach quivered. In his prime, the Warlord must have been a force. In anger, he was a force still. Now I saw a glimmer of how his earlier reputation had been founded.

"I have a piece of paper, Your Grace," said Udo helpfully. "And a pen and ink, too."

The paper was an ordinary sheet of paper, and so, too, the pen, but not the ink in the inkwell. It was an erasable ink, the idea being that when we got home, we could remove everything but the Warlord's signature and write in our own pardon. It was a clever trick that Nini Mo used in *Nini Mo vs. the Ring-tailed Alphabet Boy,* and she had helpfully included the receipt in *The Eschata.* It rather surprisingly was made using very common household ingredients that Crackpot had actually had on hand.

The Warlord sat back down, and I made sure I was out of his grabby range. He lay the paper down before him, sweeping the cards and piles of money out of the way. Udo uncapped the inkwell and handed him the pen. "Now, my spectacles, where are they?"

"Around your neck, Your Grace? On a chain?" Udo pointed out.

"Ah yes, my boy, you are a good one. Here then, give me a moment now." The Warlord put his spectacles on and rubbed his nose. He pushed the spectacles onto his forehead and rubbed his nose again. Dropped his spectacles down again and dipped the pen. Wiped it on his sleeve, and dipped it again. Sighed and tapped his gold front tooth with one fingernail, and then, just as I was about to scream with impatience, began to write.

He wrote several lines and signed his name with a flourish, and then, after dipping again, drew his seal from his weskit pocket. Udo continued his helpful theme by producing a stick of sealing wax and a trigger. Within a second, a nice round blob of wax had fallen on the paper and was pressed into the Warlord's personal seal: a hammer.

"There you have it, my dear. Mercy has a human heart, does it not? And let no one say that Florian Abenfarax de la Carcaza is not merciful. Blow."

I blew on the paper as directed, and then he rolled it up and handed it to me. "There shall be no more crying, eh?"

"Oh no, Your Grace, you are so kind, how can I ever repay you?"

The Warlord grinned and pinched my cheek. "Oh, we can discuss that later, my dear. Perhaps over an oyster supper?"

"Your Grace, we must hurry this to the Presidio," said Udo. "But after that, my sister would be most honored to share an oyster supper with you."

I would have kicked him, but he was too far away. I could only smile and say through gritted teeth, "Of course, Your Grace. I would be honored."

"I shall call for you. Where do you live, my dear?"

"Oh, I would be ashamed to have Your Grace call on me; it would hardly be proper. I shall come to Saeta House."

"No, no, my dear," the Warlord said quickly. "Meet me at the Empire Hotel on State Street, 10 P.M."

"Your Grace," I fluttered, and Udo fluttered, too, and then we fluttered our way out of there as quickly as possible.

We made it outside and were getting ready to make the return slog home, jubilant and crowned with victory, when a voice said, "You there!"

Our continued skedaddle was blocked by an enormous barge of a man wearing the Warlord's livery; our about-face was blocked by Rezaca, whom I suddenly recalled as the Warlord's Chief of Staff.

Were we caught? My tum sank into the toes of my boots and there quivered.

"You will hold up and listen to me well," Conde Rezaca said sternly. "You have received the Warlord's graciousness this time, but don't let this be a precedent. If you are wise, little woman, you shall not keep that appointment with the Warlord. In fact, I don't ever want to see you or your brother ever again, do you understand?"

My nerves twanged with relief. I had been afraid the Conde would demand the paper back, but this order was easy to agree to: Of course I had no intention of keeping the appointment. Udo nodded vigorously, and I said: "Yes, sieur, of course, thank you."

"Now get out of here before I decide to ensure your permanent absence from my sight. But wait—"

Our exit remained blocked by the Hulking Min-ion. Conde Rezaca stared at Udo, his lips pursed in consideration.

"Have I not seen you somewhere?" he said. "You do look familiar."

"I don't think so," Udo said falteringly.

"I am sure, sieur, that we are too low for your acquaintance," I said hastily. "Come, brother, and let us bother the august lord no more." I grabbed Udo's arm to hustle, but the Hulking Minion did not give way. As far as I knew, Conde Rezaca and Udo had never met before, but Udo does bear a striking resemblance to his two fathers, and Conde Rezaca probably knew them.

I pleaded, eager to get gone before Conde Rezaca's memory improved. "Please, sieur, let us pass and we shall trouble you no more."

Conde Rezaca nodded and the Hulking Minion stood aside. We put some speed into our skedaddle and were about half a block away, with the Slot well in sight, when another voice arrested us: "Hey!"

I turned and beheld the small beggar girl. Only this time she wasn't begging: She had a pistol and it was pointed straight at me.

TWENTY

Jacked. Mud. Tussling.

WHAT DO YOU WANT, sprout?" Udo demanded. "Put that toy away."

The Stealie Girl said stoutly, "It's not a toy, pinhead, and I want your purses."

"You are too little to be a criminal," Udo retorted. I elbowed him in the ribs, hard. If there is one thing I don't need Nini Mo to teach me, it's that you shouldn't be uppity to people with guns. Even if those people look about ten.

"Come on, Flora, let's go." Udo made a move to continue on, but I grabbed his sleeve. The Stealie Girl meant business; I could see it in her narrow eyes.

Though we were standing in full view, with wagons jolting along in the street and people passing along the boardwalk, no one seemed the slightest bit concerned by our situation. Probably two greenhorns getting jacked was a common sight South of the Slot.

The Stealie Girl demanded, "Gimme your purses."

"I'm not giving you a thin—"

I cut Udo off. "I have five divas; you can have that."

"Slowly," she ordered.

I reached slowly into my purse and removed the last of my savings. The girl took the bills, her pistol unwavering. Well, she could have our money; cash was the absolute least of my worries.

We had to get home and shift into the next part of the plan; already the sun was slanting low in the sky, signaling the end of afternoon, and I wanted to be on the Sandy Road to Zoo Battery before dark.

Also, I had just discovered that having a pistol pointed directly at you is very nerve-wracking. The mouth of the barrel seemed at least six feet wide, and at any minute it could spit a big huge nasty death right at me. My muscles were already clenching involuntarily, anticipating the pain.

I said, trying to sound soothing, "You can put the gun away, madama. We shall not argue with you."

"So you won't. Come on, Sieur Lug, give me your purse."

"I haven't got a purse," Udo said, which was true enough; he is so stingy that he keeps his money (when he's got it) tucked into one of his stockings. This makes it difficult for him to retrieve it, which makes it easier to get other people to pay.

"Well, then, I saw you all with the Warlord and I heard your drivel; it was sharp, to play on him that way, and I saw him give you that paper," the girl said. "Now you can give it to me."

"It's not worth a thing," I said, trying to keep the soothing smooth in my voice. "It's just a piece of paper. Here, you can have my veil. And Udo will give you his hat. They are worth something to a jobber. More than five divas, and more than a piece of paper."

"The Abyss I will," Udo retorted. "Listen, squirt, I'm one second away from blasting you. So turn around, march on, and leave us be. You got all our money, and that's all you need get."

"I want that paper," the girl said, stubbornly, "I saw the Warlord sign it, and his signature is worth a lot. I can get a fair amount for that. You can keep your ugly hat, but I want that paper."

"And I want a buffalo coat and a blue-tipped pointer—you've gotten all you are getting." Udo turned away, and the Stealie Girl cocked the pistol. The sound of the hammer snapping into place was awfully loud.

She said, "I will shoot you, and take the paper myself."

Udo froze, and then slowly reached inside his smock and pulled out the pardon. The Stealie Girl snatched the paper out of his grasp with one grubby hand.

My chest had gone tight with panic, but I tried to swallow the feeling away. *Be thoughtful, be quick, and overall be reasonable,* said Nini Mo. The Stealie Girl might have the gun, but I had my wits and could still be persuasive.

"Listen, madama," I said. "The paper is nothing; my friend here has ninety-three divas in cash at home. If you will accompany us there, it shall be—"

"You think me a ring-tailed baby, just been dipped in milk? I don't think so. What need do I have of ninety-three divas when I got this?"

Something elbowed me, almost pushing me off the sidewalk and into the Abyss of Trash that was the street: a masher on his way into the Azure Lagoon, the bar we were halted before.

"Heya, Ringie," the man said as he went inside.

"Heya, Cake," the Stealie Girl answered, and in her momentary distraction, Udo decided to act. He leaped. The Stealie Girl was small but she was sharp, and Udo was hampered by the tightness of his smock. They struggled, and the Stealie Girl dropped her pistol, which I managed to kick into the street.

Now all those people who had ignored us being jacked were interested in watching us fight, and a crowd quickly gathered, urging our melee on. Udo was shouting, and it looked like the Stealie Girl was biting. I tried to grab one of them, either of them, but only got an elbow in the chest for my troubles. All was confusion, with Udo and the Stealie Girl kicking and slapping at each other, screaming nasty, nasty things; the crowd hooting and hollering; and the paper—who had the paper? Where was the paper?

There—something white fluttered toward the ground. The Stealie Girl had dropped it. I grabbed and almost got kicked in the face; the Stealie Girl reached for it and was pushed aside by Udo. The paper flittered on the air and I lunged again, just as Udo did, our heads knocking together in a bright splurch of pain. Dizzily, I stretched and almost had it, but then a gust of wind snatched it out of my hand; the paper whizzed upward, and a man in a blue-and-green ditto suit made his own grab but missed.

Udo pushed me aside, frantically grabbing, and he almost had it. But then the Stealie Girl rose out of nowhere and pushed him hard. He overbalanced and fell over me—the paper fluttered beyond our grasp, off the boardwalk, and out to the messy, mucky ick of the street, where it was promptly run over by a buckboard full of cabbages.

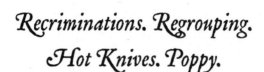

TWENTY-ONE

Recriminations. Regrouping.
Hot Knives. Poppy.

ALL THE WAY HOME on the horsecar, I blamed Udo and Udo blamed me, and no amount of blame changed the situation or made us feel any better, but it didn't make us feel any worse, either. To be so close, and yet to have defeat snatched from the jaws of victory was bitter, bitter indeed.

As soon as the buckboard had rumbled on its way, Udo and I had rushed out into the mucky street. All our frantic mucky excavations turned up were muddy scraps, and then *we* were almost run over by an ice wagon and had to confess defeat. The Stealie Girl had not waited around to see the result of our search, but had legged it immediately, with my five divas, of course, and Udo's hat, which had come off in the melee.

Though I don't normally believe in whacking people, I felt like making an exception for Udo and beating him with a stick. If only he hadn't bucked—I was sure that I could have talked our way out of the situation. Or let the girl have the paper and then jacked her back a few minutes later. Or something. But no, Udo had to jump in and act like an ass, and now we were completely and utterly screwed.

Udo said self-righteously, "I told you—if you hadn't given her that money, she wouldn't have thought we were easy marks."

"She thought we were easy marks, Udo, because we *were* easy marks. And you didn't have to be so fresh to her."

"She was just a kid—"

"Shush," I hissed. An old grammy was sitting directly in front of us, and there was an alert aura to her bonnet (garishly ornamented with a large orange velvet spider) that made me sure she was listening to every word.

"If you hadn't knocked into my arm, I could have grabbed it," Udo hissed back. "I had to do something—she was going to get away and you didn't seem poised to do any great deed."

This was so absurd that it wasn't even worth replying to, so I clamped my lips together, hard enough to hurt, and stared out the window. I was so angry, anyway, that if I spoke another word, that word would have burned my friendship with Udo to a crisp.

Not that I, for the moment, cared.

Rangers do not always meet with success, but they don't let failure stymie them. They regroup. Of course, rangers didn't let themselves be jacked like stupid idiotic greenhorns. *Don't dwell,* said Nini Mo.

A ranger always thinks again and regroups.

I thought and thought, but my thinking was not regrouping. My thinking was running around and around the idea that Nini Mo would have done some extremely clever daring deed and saved the day. Turned the Stealie Girl into a pretzel, or kicked her in the nose. Bedazzled her with another paper or charmed her with flattery. It's only after it's all over that you start thinking of all the clever ranger things you could have done. Only when it's too blasted late.

"I say that you yield to my plan now," Udo said. The grammy had gotten off at Tradis Street, and we were alone in the back of the horsecar. "We just saw how effective a demand backed by iron can be. Let us learn by that."

"Yield to your plan, Udo?" I said incredulously. "You must be mad! After what just happened, I wouldn't yield to your plan if it were the only plan left in the entire history of plans. In fact, I am thinking that maybe I should cut you loose completely. You are a liability."

"What were you going to do?" Udo protested. "You were standing there like a slug waiting to be salted. I didn't see you—"

"Shut up," I said savagely. "Shut up."

Udo retreated into wounded silence and stared out his own window. Well, let him sulk. I would think of something. I *had* to think of something. The horsecar trundled by Saeta House, and by the Arrow Clock tower, and I saw that it was almost three. What were we going to do?

"What about Valefor? Can he cough up a forgery?" Udo asked, without removing his stare from the window.

"I don't think so. His talents lie in housework and whining, and anyway, he's on strike because I put him on the back burner while we took care of you-know-who," I answered, without removing my stare from my own window.

The horsecar was now passing the Califa Lyceum, and I noticed that the marquee was advertising Relais Evengardia (he who Idden once adored) in *He Should Have Stopped While He Was Ahead,* his latest play. A line had formed in front of the box office. Relais Evengardia is the most popular actor in all of Califa, renowned for his portrayal of General Hardhands—

And then—huzza! Oh cleverness! Oh blissful day! A fully fledged idea leaped into my head, as though it had always been there and was just waiting for me to pay attention to it.

I turned back to Udo, who was still sulkily fixed on his window. "Hey! Remember when you competed in the Warlord's Annual Histrionic Extravaganza—"

Udo abandoned his sulk. "Ayah! I won Best Actor for my portrayal of General Hardhands in *A Cold Day in the Abyss.* I was really good; sometimes I think I should go on the stage instead of to sea."

"Remember, you got that citation from the Warlord? Signed and sealed?"

"Ayah, so what?"

"*Forgery* is so what. Listen." I dropped my voice to a whisper, and Udo bent in closely. "I can copy the Warlord's signature,

I'm sure. Particularly if I have a guide to go by. But it's the seal that's a problem—we can't forge that."

"Ayah so?" Udo whispered back.

"Remember how in *Nini Mo vs. the Mechanical Monkeys,* she forged the pass that got her into the Iron Mine of Arivaipa?"

"You know I don't read that trash, Flora."

"Ha! No trashier than *The Dainty Pirate Ahoy!,* I reckon, and a lot more useful right now, Udo. Look, she lifted the seal off the letter of invitation that Njal Sholto had sent to entrap her, and then put it on the forgery. It worked like a charm."

"Can you lift the seal off my citation?" Udo asked excitedly.

"I'll wager I can. Look, you go home and get the citation and meet me back at Crackpot. Go in the window, or something. Don't get caught, ayah so? And hurry about it. I think maybe we can salvage this yet."

Udo nodded vigorously. "I knew we'd think of something, Flora."

As far as I could tell, I had done all the thinking; no *we* involved at all. But now was not the time to get Udo's dudgeon back up again, not with the afternoon running out and night fast approaching.

"Here's your stop—go—" I yanked on the bell, and the horse-car jangled to a stop, and Udo jumped off.

Two hours later, after a brief stop for a snack (I was light-headedly starving), I was at my desk, the citation before me, heating the knife Udo had just finished sharpening. The art to lifting a seal lies in the heat of the knife and the patience of the forger. You have to get the seal warm enough to slide off the paper, but not so warm it melts away completely. Sealing wax is more pliable and elastic than candle wax, of course, and has a higher melting point, but you can go too far. I've practiced enough (Forgery 101) that if there is one thing I can do flawlessly, it's lift a seal.

But copying the Warlord's signature proved much less sweetie-pie. His letters are both quavery and legible, and these two qualities are very difficult to combine. All my efforts resulted in twiddles and squiggles, but nothing that would pass muster even in the dark. Udo tried, too, but he had no luck, either, no surprise.

"Let me have it back, and I'll try again," I demanded.

"I've almost got it, Flora. Quit leaning on me."

"We are running out of time—"

"That's because you are ragging on me," Udo said.

"Don't be a git—"

"What are you doing?" said someone else.

We lurched guiltily. There in the doorway stood Poppy. He wore a tattered dressing gown, and the short spikes of his hair poked every which way. The mourning band painted across his eyes was blurred, as though he'd been rubbing at it. He had a terrific black bruise on his right temple, as dark as a thundercloud.

"Do you need something, Poppy?" I asked.

He came into the room and sat down on the settee to waste our valuable time. "Only my life. But I don't think I left that here. What are you doing?"

"Nothing. I mean, just working on a paper," I said. "Homework, you know. Are you hungry, Poppy? There's soup. I can make you soup."

"Soup makes my teeth hurt, Flora. Anyway, I eat the air." He sat there, as comfortable as bedtime, and he didn't look like he was going to move anytime soon. Blast it! We didn't have time to waste dealing with Poppy, and he's so deceptive. He looked fine, albeit rumpled, but that didn't signify. Any moment he could break out in all sorts of horrificness; maybe last night was just a lead-up. The fireplace poker was out of reach. What would I do if he exploded?

But he didn't look as though he would explode. He scratched his chin, and said, "Forgery, eh? Didn't they used to boil people in oil for that once?"

"It's not forgery," Udo said. "It's an art project. I mean, it's a paper on—"

Poppy yawned and took a silver case out of his dressing-gown pocket. "I am no shavetail, Udo. I know forgery when I

see it. What are you making? Letter of recommendation? Fixing a bobtail? Commandeering a battery? Trumping a jump?"

A bobtail is when the bottom of a soldier's release paper is
clipped, removing the section where the recommendation should
go. I didn't know what trumping a jump is, and right now I
didn't care, either.

"A release, Hotspur, that's all; just a release," Udo said.
"Here, let me light that."

Ignoring my dirty look, Udo lit a trigger from the fire and
held the flame to Poppy's cigarillo. Udo is too casual around
Poppy; having been spared the worst of Poppy's scenes and having normal parents of his own, Udo doesn't understand how
bad Poppy can be.

"Someone in the calaboose?" Poppy asked.

I glared at Udo, trying to impart this glare with all the vigor
of *Do not tell him a single more thing at all, shut up* that I could, but I
could tell by the curve of his smile that he was not listening.

"Ayah so. Poor bugger," Udo said.

"He has my sympathy. Life is a prison if you cannot leave it
as you like. It don't look like you are having much success. You
got a mess of papers there."

"Well, it takes practice," Udo admitted.

The smoke wreathed Poppy's head like fog, and through it I
could see only the thin line of his lips. "I used to be a dab hand.
A handy talent for an ADC to have, you know, forgery. Sign the
papers yourself and save your boss the trouble. And if you're
skint, you can pay your bar tab off with your fakery. Here, let
me see if I still got the knack."

An idea was forming in my mind that perhaps, for the first
time ever, it might pay off to have a mad, irresponsible father. If
Poppy were as good at forgery as he said, then one of our problems was solved, and if he mentioned it to Mamma later, well,
who ever believes anything Poppy says?

Udo moved from the desk and gave Poppy fresh paper and a
pen. He examined the pen, announced the nib had lost its
sharpness, and demanded another. He sat straight as a ramrod

and squinted down at the empty sheet of whiteness. He dipped his pen and drew a thin line on his forearm to test the flow, and thus I realized that he was left-handed, just like me. Mamma and Idden are right-handed both, and now I saw where I had gotten the trait.

Poppy dipped the pen again, and then sloped it across the paper, smooth and even.

"'Juliet Buchanan Fyrdraaca ov Fyrdraaca.'" Udo read. "That's pretty good, Hotspur. It looks exactly right."

"Oh, Buck is easy. Now here's a huckleberry. Watch this."

Poppy wiped the pen off on his sleeve and dipped again. This time his pen skittered and hopped, swirled and twirled, slithered and jumped, and finally skittered into a long black slide. The result was elaborate and complex, twisty letters that arched up and plunged down, entwining each other like snakes. Even though I couldn't read the name, I could tell that whoever belonged to this signature was as big as boots, and firm in his or her authority.

"I wasn't sure I still had that one in me," Poppy said proudly. He blotted, then blew gently. "It's worth your life."

Udo said, "I can't even read it."

"'Banastre Micajah Haðraaða ov Brakespeare,'" Poppy said. "Old Hardhands himself. Ah, he'd have eaten my liver if he'd known I could copy him."

"Wow. What a signature." Udo was impressed, clearly thinking he needed to start working on a better signature of his own.

"He was a proper bastard, old Hardhands, but his warrant had class."

Now that Poppy's skill was established, there was only one signature I wanted, and I could wait no longer to get it. We had to be on the road within an hour if we wanted to make our interception.

"Can you do the Warlord?" I asked.

"I'm not sure. It's been a long time since I have seen it."

I pushed Udo's citation to Poppy, and he held it up, examining it carefully. "He has the handwriting of a five-year-old, our Warlord. It shall be easy as pie. Here, let me show you a trick."

He spun the citation around until it was upside-down. "It's easier to copy if you don't let the word get in the way. Think of it like a pattern you are drawing, like when your hair colors the sea."

I had no idea what he meant by that last comment. "Can you do it, Poppy?"

Poppy closed his eyes and ran his finger over the spindly letters. He made a few wiggly lines with the dry pen, incising an imprint upon the paper. After dipping the pen, he turned the edge of the nib so that the lines were thick going up and thin going down. He made a few little twirls, then drew a little pig with floppy ears and dancing slippers. He pushed his scribble paper away, lay a new sheet down, and dipped his pen freshly.

Then, swiftly, he began to write. The ink slid across the paper, as smooth as skates on ice, without hesitation, without pause. He raised his pen, pressed blotting paper down, and grinned. "There! I am charmed!"

I flipped the citation around, and we stared at the two signatures, side by side. They were perfectly alike, right down to the monogram that came after the name: *Florian Abenfarax de la Carcarza, ADLC.*

"You are a genius, Hotspur," Udo said.

Poppy grinned, and this grin rounded his bladelike cheeks and crinkled his eyes. For a moment he looked almost handsome. Then the smile drifted from his face, and he was the same sad Poppy again.

He dropped the pen and said, "But you know, I think I have forgotten how to sign my own name."

TWENTY-TWO

Strange Faces.
A Blue Light. Teeth.

NINI MO'S YELLOWBACKS always play up the excitement and adventure—they never mention the anxiety and alarm that comes before the excitement and adventure. The hour you spend riding toward your target, while your neck gets colder and your bottom goes numb. The knot of nervousness in your tum, which only gets knottier and more nervous as the place where you can still turn back gets farther and farther behind.

We left Crackpot just at dusk, slightly behind schedule but not by much. Broad-brimmed hats hid our faces, and underneath our concealing cloaks, we both wore stolen uniforms. Udo's was kipped from one of his fathers, and it fit him perfectly. Mine was borrowed from Idden's closet; it was the fatigue uniform she'd worn the summer she'd spent as Mamma's ADC, her third year at the Barracks. It was tight across the shoulders and long in the kilt, but otherwise would do.

Zoo Battery guards the southern end of the Pacifica Playa, far out at the end of Sandy Road in what are called the Outside Lands because they lie beyond the City's limits. No horsecar went out that far at night, and even if it had, we certainly couldn't take it without compromising our disguises. So we rode, me on Bonzo, and Udo on Mouse.

It's a longish ride, through Portal Pass, which marks the City's official limits, and across the Great Sand Bank, which stands between the Pass and the ocean's edge, and so I had plenty of time to think anxious thoughts. Nini Mo says that the time for thinking is before you make the decision, and once you've decided, it's time to act. That's easier said than done. Particularly when not everything has gone according to plan.

I looked at Udo, or, rather, at his back, since he was riding ahead of me. Mouse is a tail-biter, and it's always better to keep her teeth out of temptation's way. From the back, he looked like pretty much the same Udo. But when he turned to say something to me, he had the face of a stranger.

After Udo's close call with recognition at Pete's Clown Diner, we had agreed that stronger disguises were required, and for that we needed Glamours. This turned out to be easier decided than actually done. A Glamour should be easy baby ranger stuff, not too hard, and not too complicated. And the first Glamour, though tongue-burning and headache-making, had turned out just dandy.

Udo's own parents would not recognize him. I *knew* he was Udo and yet could hardly believe it. Now he looked ruggedly efficient; his chest was broad, his shoulders even broader, and his chin as squarely carved as a bar of soap. His face, perched above a bull neck, was leathery and wise, and his black eyes had a humorous squint to them. The biggest shock was the hair. Udo's fondness for his own blond locks has kept them long and flowing, but now his hair was so short that the scalp beneath was as tanned as his face.

In fact, Udo looked a little too much like Sergeant Shanks-worthy, the hero of the long-running yellowback series Sergeant Shanksworthy of the Steelheart Brigade. Though I wasn't a particular fan of Sergeant Shanksworthy, I guess the back of my brain had somehow decided that he was the perfect specimen of military manliness, and thus the Masking Glamour had so resolved.

"What are you goggling about?" asked Udo in a rumbling baritone that was as unlike his own boyish treble as the lion's roar is to the cat's meow.

"It's hard to get used to."

He pulled Mouse back so we were abreast, and the horses twisted their heads to snuffle at each other. "I know. It *feels* strange, too, as though my skin is too small. How do I look with a mustache?" He tugged one of the waxed spikes that stuck out at least two inches on either side of that stranger's mouth.

"I don't know what *you* look like with a mustache, but that face looks fine. Would that I looked so wonderfully different," I said, somewhat bitterly.

I was disguised not by a Masking Glamour, but by ten pounds of makeup that Udo had applied to my face with a trowel. This because the second Masking Glamour had failed utterly.

Magick is hard, I know that, and it takes long hours of practice to get things right. I thought I had been sticking to the easy stuff, the fail-safe stuff, but maybe I had just been lucky before. But what a time to fail! The Glamour had flickered briefly and then guttered, and all the Invoking, Evoking, and just plain Hysterical Entreaties to the Current had not gotten it to rekindle. I had tried other Glamours as well—a Concealment Glamour, a Dazzlement Glamour—but they only resulted in a pounding headache and the upchucking of my snack. Now, in addition to anxious, I felt rather dizzy and weak. I'd never realized magick involved so much urping.

"I swear I wouldn't recognize you in a hundred years, Flora. I swear that even Buck would not recognize you. You'll be fine," Udo said soothingly. "You'll be fine."

"I hope you're right, Udo. Get that horse over, she's squashing my leg. Do you remember the plan? You won't jump the gun like you did last time, will you?"

Udo edged Mouse sideways.

"I remember the plan perfectly, no fear, Flora. Don't worry. But remember, I will do all the talking. It will look odd if you keep piping up, when I outrank you."

The plan, of course, had been that I would lead and Udo

would follow. But now he had the mature, authoritative face, and I, though disguised, did not look old enough to be an officer, even a shavetail lieutenant. There was no way around Udo's having to take the lead, and my insides quivered at the thought.

"I'll be quiet as long as you don't say anything foolish, Udo. Do not deviate from the plan even a tiny little bit, I'm warning you."

"Never fear—oh, and it's Captain Gaisford to you, Corporal. I think we should get into character now. That's the secret to great acting—you get inside the skin of your part and never leave."

"Udo—"

"Captain Gaisford, Corporal, and don't forget it, or I shall write you up for insubordination. Ride on, we are burning daylight." He spurred Mouse into a trot. Sometimes the only way to win with Udo is to ignore him, so I merely urged Bonzo on and fell in after Mouse.

After a while, the smell of wood smoke began to seep through the fog, and then the shadow of a squat building suddenly reared from the gloom: the Bella Union Saloon, as notorious a deadfall bar as you would never want to see. The Bella Union sits right across the Califa city line, where the Sandy Road turns southward toward Zoo Battery, near the Presidio's back gate, and this central location has made it a favorite hangout joint for drunken off-duty soldiers. Mamma has declared it out of bounds to the military and twice sent patrols to burn it down. Twice it has sprung up anew, a blot upon the landscape that not even fire will erase. The *Califa Police Gazette* is always reporting dire doings at the Bella Union: ear-chewing, bar fights, tar-and-feathering.

A high-riding covered wagon stood in front of the Bella, THE HORSES OF INSTRUCTION inscribed upon the canvas in luminescent paint. Grunts carried musical equipment inside as a tall man stood by, watching and smoking, a hurdy-gurdy slung over his back. The Hurdy-Gurdy Man was clearly going for a deathly, gothick look: greenish black hair straggling out from under a moldering tricorn, sagging pink trunk hose. As I rode by, he looked up, his livid face wreathed in cigarette smoke, and flashed gold teeth at me, touching a salute to the front point of his hat.

The Bella Union behind us, darkness followed the fog's slow advance. My feet felt like blocks of ice, and my hands hardly gripped the reins. I wasn't sure if this feebleness was from the weather or all the Invoking I had done. Either way, I felt weak and tired.

Somewhere high above the fog, the moon must have risen, because the air was strangely light. I pulled up the collar of my sack coat; the wool rubbed the back of my neck, but moisture was dripping from my hat brim and I'd rather be raw than wet. Everything is always so much colder with a damp neck.

"Hey, Corporal—" Udo's blur made a vague gesture, and I turned around to follow his point. Just fog, thick and wet, but then, suddenly, there was a bright blue pulse of light, like a tiny fragment of sky cracking through the gray.

We reined in and watched as the light pulsed again. The horses shimmied, as though they could hear something we could not, and then distantly, we did hear something, a low rumbling that was as much vibration as noise. The horses shimmied again, squeezing together, and I kicked my foot out so Mouse wouldn't crush my leg.

"Cannon fire?" I guessed.

"Your ignorance astounds, Corporal Ashbury, but then what can you expect from a mere bouncer?" Udo answered. *Bouncer* is the Army nickname for cavalry, yet my hat brass proclaimed I was a webfoot, or infantryman. I started to correct him, but he cut me off. "Cannon fire does not spark blue. And besides which, that's north, and there ain't no guns to our north."

"Cannon fire can too spark blue if—"

Udo looked annoyed. "Your insubordination is grotesque. I do not know what the Army is coming to these days, with impertinence so common and respect so rarely valued. In my day, no mere corporal would ever dare contradict a ranking officer."

I almost answered Udo with something short and not so sweet. But I bit my tongue, because there was some truth to what he had said about staying in the skin of your disguise. Didn't Nini Mo once say that the best way to impersonate a rustler was to *be* a rustler?

"I beg your humble pardon, Captain Gaisford, sir. I did not mean to contradict you. Please enlighten me. If then, there are no guns to the north, what does lie in that direction that could create such a singular sight?" I asked.

"You are overdoing it, Corporal. Not so heavy on the sop, please. And the answer is Bilskinir House."

Bilskinir House, indeed. Another blue note pulsed, and this time the ground really did tremble underfoot for a moment. A shiver ran across the back of my neck.

"I guess the papers were right." Udo continued. "Maybe Paimon is awake after all. What do you think he's doing in there?"

"Making dinner, I wager. As long as I am not on the menu, then I bid him good eating. Come on."

"I give the orders, Corporal Ashbury," Udo said curtly. "Ride on."

So we rode on, leaving the blue bursts of light behind us. The cold was biting, and my hinder was going numb—surely we were almost there? What seemed like an eternity later, but was probably only about fifteen minutes, Zoo Battery loomed so suddenly out of the fog that Udo almost ran Mouse right into it. The wooden gates towered over us, at least twenty feet high and wide enough for four riders to enter abreast. Zoo Battery defends the southern end of the Playa and she houses sixty-five guns, so her red brick walls are high and thick. The gates were painted to look like teeth, giving the doors the appearance of a grinning, hungry mouth.

Udo dismounted, then advanced to bang heavily on the barred doors. His blows were tiny little puffs of sound, hardly louder than the distant crashing surf, but he had barely lifted his fist up from the third one when a cavity appeared in one of the lower teeth and an eye looked out.

"Who comes here?" the eye demanded.

"Friend, with the countersign." Udo sounded cool as lemonade.

"Answer, friend, with the countersign."

Here it was: No turning back. While Mamma had been attending to Poppy after his fit last night, I had spent a few minutes in the parlor, snooping through her correspondence book for passwords. I hoped that the Sign List I had copied hadn't been updated; I hoped that the passwords had not been changed. Here was the first test.

"Vilipend," said Udo, sounding rather bored.

The cavity closed.

Udo hitched his hat back on his head and scratched his nose. He tucked his reins under his arm, so as to adjust his sabre belt. He scratched behind Mouse's ear. The seconds clicked by. I thought I might scream. This was taking far too long; the guard should have recognized the countersign immediately, then opened the doors. They must have changed the password. My mind's eye saw through the Toothy Doors into the sally port beyond, where the guard was now assembled, rifles at the ready, to charge forward and blast the intruders: us.

"I will protest to Colonel Yangze," Udo said to me. "It's outrageous that we should be left lingering in the cold like this." Just as he raised his fist to hammer on the door again, before I could suggest we scarper, a crack appeared along the edge of one of the teeth. The crack widened and spread upward and down, and then became a door, which opened.

TWENTY-THREE

Inside. Orders. Swagger Stick.

Nini Mo said that caution makes you careful, but panic is a poison that will kill you. I had plenty of the first and no intention of indulging in the second. My heart was thumping so loudly in my chest that I thought it might pop right out, which would probably be good, because it would save me the pain of being shot.

"It's about time," said Udo. "This is outrageous! How dare you keep us waiting! I'll have you on charges for this."

A face appeared around the edge of the door, bespeckled and abashed.

"I am so sorry, so sorry, so sorry. It's just that we had mislaid the key, and then Danbury was asleep, and he's the only one who can pull the chain up to open the door. He was a pugilist before the Army, and he's ever so strong—oh, I'm sorry. Advance and Be Recognized."

"This command is a disgrace." Udo swept forward as though he actually were a stuck-up staff officer. He left Mouse's reins dangling, and I dismounted and grabbed them.

Udo said, "Lieutenant, I am on urgent business and I have no time to waste. Come, come, Corporal Ashbury, you are dawdling again." This last, over his shoulder to me.

It is true that Nini Mo said that acting as though you have every right is one of the tricks to getting away with a disguise, but it seemed to me that Udo was not acting as much as over-acting. Nonetheless, I hauled after him, towing Bonzo and Mouse behind me.

The portcullis door slammed shut behind Bonzo's tail with a rather alarming clang.

There's no way out but through.

Two guards with rifles stood behind the lieutenant, but their muzzles pointed down. In the fluttering lamplight, the lieutenant looked flustered and rumpled. His blouse was buttoned crooked and his hair was mussed. "I do beg your pardon for any perceived laxity, Captain, but also I must beg your pardon that you have not been recognized yet."

"Take my horse, and Corporal Ashbury's, too. I am Captain Seneca Gaisford, Judge Advocate General's Office. Escort me immediately to the Commanding Officer; I have a special order from the Warlord. Will you have me stand here all night?"

"No, of course not, sir. Lieutenant Wills Samson at your service. Do come in, please do." The lieutenant scraped and bowed and ordered one of the guards to hold the horses. I released the reins reluctantly. It had occurred to me that the horses were in as much danger as Udo and I, and I wished we had left them picketed outside.

We followed Lieutenant Samson through the dank, dark sally port, then into the parade yard beyond. Udo was haranguing the lieutenant for taking so long to let us in, and the lieutenant was parroting apologies. I myself would have told Udo to jump off a log, but that's the thing about the Army; when someone outranks you and gives you some, you have to take it. The parade yard was lit only by a few dim lamps, but I didn't need much light to see the ominous shadow of the gallows in the middle of the yard. The open casemates rising above the parade yard looked like black empty eyes.

Lieutenant Samson led us along the covered walkway and into the guardroom. After the outside chill, the guardroom felt warm and cheerful. Happy red and orange firelight spilled from the huge barracks stove. Although the holding cell was empty, two guards sat on a bench against the opposite wall, drinking from tin cups. The door to the Commanding Officer's ready room was closed.

The lieutenant offered us chairs. "Do please sit down, Captain. Might I get you some coffee? A little nip of something warmer? It's a long journey from the City; you must be almost frozen. What a night to be out in, what a night. Hendricks, get the Captain and his aide some coffee."

Coffee sounded wonderful, and I did feel almost frozen, but we couldn't linger. Udo said dismissively, "Never mind the coffee. As I said, we are in a hurry. I have important matters to attend to." He pulled our forged document from his dispatch case. "Take me to the Commanding Officer. I have a special order signed by the Warlord for the transfer of one of your prisoners to my custody. You will get him ready for transport. The Warlord wishes to speak to him immediately."

The lieutenant rubbed his hands together pleadingly. "Oh dear, oh dear. This is quite strange, oh dear."

"Are you saying that the Warlord's orders are strange?" Udo asked in a quiet, dangerous voice.

The lieutenant looked alarmed. "Oh no, oh no, of course not, sir. It's just that—"

"Just what?" Udo leaned in. His Glamour's black eyes squinted into angry slits. He looked like someone about ready to cut.

The lieutenant rubbed his hands and yanked on his sleeve buttons. "Let me just present your compliments to Captain Honeychurch, she's in charge here, and you can give your special order to her. Do please have a seat."

"I shall stand," Udo said imperiously.

The lieutenant took the special order from Udo and hurried into the office, closing the door behind him. Udo stood, one hand tucked into his buckler, looking completely unconcerned, and I only hoped that my expression was equally nonchalant.

"I will be filing a report." Udo said to no one in particular.

"A disgrace that a matter of such importance should be handled so carelessly."

Well, there he was certainly right. We had been left alone with two guards only, and the one sitting by the red-hot stove looked half asleep. In about three seconds, we could have disarmed them and taken control of the guardroom. Maybe two seconds. They weren't even armed. Their rifles rested in the rifle rack, which was locked. Of course, the guns Udo and I carried were not loaded; they didn't know that, and the threat might have been enough. But then we'd still have to find Boy Hansgen, and get the sally port unlocked. Better stick to the plan.

"You there—," Udo barked, pointing at the guard who was dozing by the fire. He strode across the room and grabbed the man by his collar, shaking him. "Are you asleep on duty? I'll have you shot!"

"I beg your pardon, sir, I beg your pardon!" The guard shook free of Udo's grasp and snapped to attention. Udo poked him in the chest with his swagger stick. I had tried hard to talk him out of the swagger stick—hardly any officers carry them anymore, since Mamma banned the impromptu smacking of enlisted soldiers—but Udo insisted it helped him stay in character.

"And your tie is untied and your blouse unbuttoned. I shall make a full report to the Warlord! Consider yourself under arrest as of this minute and report—" Udo raised the swagger stick like he was going to whack.

"Captain Gaisford, sir!" I said frantically, before Udo walloped the poor man and got himself arrested, and then me arrested, and then Boy Hansgen would hang, and that would be it for our plan. "Shall I see what is keeping Lieutenant Samson so long?"

The distraction worked. Udo turned back to me, and the guard sidled as far out of Udo's reach as he could, then stood at attention as though he were on review.

"I shall find out myself." Udo strode toward the office door, which luckily opened before he could kick it.

Lieutenant Samson beckoned to Udo. "Captain Honey-church will see you, sir."

"I applaud her good judgment," Udo said, then, as I advanced to follow, "Corporal Ashbury, you may wait."

Not on your life, I thought, and made move to follow. Udo poked me backward with the swagger stick, and I gave him a look that felt as though it should fuse glass but had no effect whatsoever on Udo's attitude.

"I told you to stay, Corporal Ashbury. I will have you on charges if you don't fall to."

I had no recourse but to stare desperately as the door closed behind Lieutenant Samson. Udo alone! We were doomed, doomed, doomed. What could I do? Nothing but hope for Udo's best, and somehow I could only imagine Udo's worst. My toes felt as cold as frozen grapes.

I sat on the bench, and the other guard, a small woman with gray-streaked hair, brought me coffee. "Those bosses. They are fresh. Here, this'll cheer you. I'm Hendricks, and that's Jam over there."

"Thank you," I said.

The coffee was hot, and as sweet as syrup, and it tasted like heaven. But the caffeine swelled up awful fantasies in my now-jittery brain. My eyes fixed upon the door, my imagination fired with dire possibilities: Udo threatening Captain Honeychurch with the swagger stick, poking or pointing, or perhaps even whacking. Udo can get carried away; that's exactly what led to Gun-Britt's broken nose, Udo not knowing when to stop. I should have held firm on that blasted swagger stick. Perhaps I should go interrupt them, with some excuse—

"A sloggy night to be out. And a sloggy night to die," Hendricks said. "Bad enough to end on the rope, but on a cold wet night as this, what's worse?"

"I can think of worse ways to go," Jam said. "There's always worse ways to go."

"You with the Dandies?" Hendricks asked me.

Mamma's regiment is the Enthusiastics, so why she had

Dandy hat-brass in her insignia-box was a mystery, but it worked out well for our plan. The Dandy Regiment is currently stationed on the Trinity Line, so there was no fear of running into any other Dandies.

"Ayah so." The door remained closed. Udo, oh Udo, don't be a prat or a fool or a twit. Oh please, Udo, please.

"I thought they were up north," Hendricks said.

"Ayah, I'm on detach. Medical leave, but now I'm better and was supposed to report to my regiment, but I got stuck on this detail—" I could hear the sound of Udo's voice, but not his words. Any minute that door was going to open to eject a furious officer and we would be All Done.

Jam said, "I pity you, that officer of yours is a right twit. He could use a good fragging. I'd like to punt that swagger stick right up—"

The office door opened and here came Udo, the lieutenant, and behind them, another officer dressed in sangyn: a Skinner! In my tum, my coffee began to burn. Of all the people for Udo to get uppity with! Only one regiment in the Army is allowed to wear crimson uniforms instead of the ordinary black and gold: the Alacrán Regiment. They are nicknamed the Skinners because of their habit of marking their kills with scalps. They are the Army's oldest and most decorated regiment, but they have a ferocious reputation for being arrogant and bloody-minded— and ruthless cold-blooded killers.

Poppy is a Skinner, and that, no doubt, is part of his problem.

A Skinner is not someone to be messed with, but Udo had not toned his high attitude down. If anything, he had nudged it up a touch.

"Well, now, I am glad to see that you understand your duty so clearly, sir," Udo was saying to Captain Honeychurch. "And attend to it so promptly."

Where the Skinner's left eye should have been was a blackened pit. Each cheek was marred by a slashing mark: the zigzag scars that all Skinners get when they swear their Regimental Oath. It's a mark of courage, supposedly, to stand firm while someone slashes at your face with a sabre. I think it's more a mark of foolishness.

"I follow the Warlord's orders," the Skinner said.

"As do we all, though some of us do so with more alacrity. I want you to know, Captain Honeychurch, that I'll be making a note of the condition of your guard to the Warlord—"

Captain Honeychurch interrupted him: "Lieutenant Samson, take the guards and retrieve the prisoner."

The relief that flooded through me was so huge that for a moment I thought I might slide boneless to the floor. Udo had not gotten us killed; we were almost home, we were going to pull it off, bless the Goddess now and forevermore.

"Attend, Corporal Ashbury!" Udo ordered, and I jumped to obey.

Lieutenant Samson nodded to the two guards, then unlocked the rifle rack so they could take their weapons. Private Hendricks picked up a lantern and lit it with a trigger. I followed them out of the warm guardroom into the icy cold night. Back along the covered walkway, across the sally port, and into a small dank room beyond, empty but for a clutter of open barrels and cracker boxes. Beyond that, yet another dank room, completely empty.

My pulse fluttered so strongly in my throat that I could hardly swallow.

"You must be careful with him," Lieutenant Samson was saying to me. I snapped to attention. "He's been put under a geas not to speak Gramatica, so his magick is greatly muted, but he's still dangerous."

"I will attend." I wondered who had put the geas on Boy Hansgen. A geas is a kind of magickal interdiction, superdangerous and very difficult. It can easily backfire on the adept, who then might find *herself* the one constrained, caught in a trap of her own making that she cannot escape. Who in the Army had such ability—and more importantly, why was *that* adept allowed to freely practice?

"I am surprised the Warlord sent such a small detail, but I

suppose it is not for me to question his orders," Lieutenant Samson continued.

"No, it's not," I said sternly. "We are all the Warlord's obedient servants."

Hendricks held the lantern high, while Jam bent to fiddle with a heavy iron ring embedded in the floor. A tug on the ring, and it pulled upward, levering a square of the floor open to display the dark mouth of an oubliette.

"Stand back," Lieutenant Samson said. "Drop the rope, Private."

Jam slacked the coil of rope and let it drop into the oubliette, and then leaned way in to shout, "Take the rope and I shall draw you aloft."

After a second, a distant answer came, unintelligible.

"He says he won't," said Jam.

Another unintelligible shout drifted upward.

"He says he's fine where he is, the damp is extremely good for his complexion."

Lieutenant Samson wrung his hands and looked flustered. "Oh dear. What shall I say?"

Hendricks offered, "Beg your pardon, sir, but tell him if he don't take the rope and allow himself to be drawn upward, we shall fill the oubliette with water, and close the lid. How will drowning be for his complexion?"

Jam leaned back over and shouted down the gist of Hendrick's suggestion, seasoning the recitation with some pretty spicy adverbs and adjectives, then relayed back to us. "He says that he wagers that he can hold his breath for a long time, and anyway, he'd rather be drowned than hung."

This time Hendricks leaned in and did the shouting. "You aren't to be hung yet, you fool—the Warlord wants to speak with you, and the execution has been suspended. Grab the rope and let us haul you upward!"

Pause, and another shout from below, and Hendricks said to Lieutenant Samson, "He wants a wash and a clean shirt, first, before he goes to the Warlord."

"Tell him yes, anything, just let us pull him up," Lieutenant Samson answered hurriedly. "The Warlord will be angry we've wasted his time."

It took all four of us to haul the rope up; Boy Hansgen weighed a ton. It would have been easier with a winch, but I guess that is the thing about oubliettes—once you put someone in, you don't normally aim to bring them up again. (Which made me wonder why they had stuck him down there to begin with—perhaps it was the most secure cell at the Battery?) We heaved and ho-ed, and the rope burned my hands even through my gloves, but finally, eventually, a dark shape emerged from the oubliette, dirty and damp.

TWENTY-FOUR

In the Jakes. Confession. An Awful Discovery.

THANK YOU, SIEURS," Boy Hansgen said, when he had achieved all the way out and stood up. He offered a sketchy courtesy—So Below Me I Hardly Bother—the manacles on his wrists and ankles clanking. "I hope that my poor starved weight didn't prove too heavy."

Boy Hansgen had a syrupy kind of voice, slightly accented, and musical. The lantern light was so dim that it was hard to make out many details; my overwhelming impression was of a white shirt and extreme grubbiness. And there was no way to get around his smell. The goddess Califa could probably nose him in heaven.

"I do hope you won't be complaining to the Warlord about your rations," Lieutenant Samson said plaintively from the position he had taken up behind Hendrick and her rifle. "You've had the same chow we've had."

"Ayah so, but perhaps your supper room is drier and your chow less sog. Or perhaps you are just used to hideous Army cooking. I will have that clean shirt now, and the wash." Boy Hansgen had the same easy tone of command in his voice as Mamma; even as a prisoner, he acted as though he expected to be obeyed.

"Do not try any tricky stuff." Lieutenant Samson was still

safely behind Hendricks. "We'll be happy to shoot you and give the Warlord our regrets."

"I care for nothing at the moment but clean," Boy Hansgen said, "and wouldn't dream of blowing my date with soap. Lead on, and I shall follow as gently as a hairless Huitzil lapdog." He twisted the last words into a tone that suggested *he* was nothing of the kind, but the others were exactly that.

Back we went across the sally port, Boy Hansgen stepping jauntily, as though he were on his way to a lovely dinner rather than a supposed interview with the Warlord, and then his death. He must really like to be clean; I do, too, so there we had something in common.

In the warm guardroom, Udo and the Skinner stood at Lieutenant Samson's desk, Udo signing papers and saying: ". . . recommend you to the Warlord for your assistance, Captain Honeychurch—"

"Here I be, the man of the hour, the boy of your dreams!" Boy Hansgen said, and clanked his manacles together again so they rattled loudly. Now, in better light, he was shorter than I expected, and older, too. But of course that followed—he'd been Nini Mo's sidekick, after all, and she'd been dead for over twenty-five years, so he would have to be pretty old. In the Nini Mo yellowbacks, he's always illustrated as a young man, with short spiky hair and a bass guitar tossed over his back. No bass now, and the blond hair was matted, silver under the dirt, but he still looked pretty pugnacious and tough.

He continued, "Captain Honeychurch, dear brave Captain Honeychurch, my heart is pattering with pain to have to leave your tender care so soon."

Captain Honeychurch glared and said, "Would that my care had been as tender as you deserved."

"You is kind to me," Boy Hansgen said snarkily, and the Skinner gave him a look that seemed to say, *You aren't even worth the effort of my knife.*

Udo finished signing and threw the pen down. He gave the

Dainty Pirate an arrogant once-over and said, "So this is the pirate who has caused the City so much ruin."

"I am that boy, and more besides. And perhaps just getting started!"

"I think you've come to the end, not the beginning."

"Hope springs, and who knows—maybe I will, too!"

Udo said, "The best you can hope for is a broken neck to save you the struggle of strangling."

Cut it with the snappy small talk, Udo, I thought, trying to telegraph that thought to him. *Let's get out of here.* But Udo was engrossed with his repartee and didn't glance in my direction.

Boy said, "You make such a dismal thought sound so cheerful, Captain What's Your Face. We have not been introduced."

"Captain Seneca Gaisford, JAG Office." As sign of his contempt, Udo made no courtesy bow at all.

"I am your obedient servant, Captain Gaisford." Boy Hansgen grinned and saluted with a closed fist to the chest. "But then, you knew that already. Lieutenant Samson here has promised me a cleanup before we go."

"I have no time for such things," Udo said. "We must leave at once. The Warlord is waiting."

"There's always time for soap. You don't want me to go stinky to the Warlord, do you?" Boy Hansgen smiled winningly at Udo. His teeth twinkled like ice cubes through the grime on his face. "We all know how delicate Florian is."

"Captain Gaisford," I said urgently, "we are late already." *Let us get going before we push our luck so hard that it breaks, Udo.*

"You do not need to remind me, Corporal," Udo told me. "I know my own schedule." He turned to the prisoner. "We have no time. I will see that you are given facilities when we reach Saeta. You have my word on it."

"At least let me piss. I promise I shall be quick. I'll be happy to do so in the fire if that's all the time—"

Captain Honeychurch ignored Udo's further protests and ordered us to take Boy Hansgen to the jakes. So Hendricks led him out, with Jam and me bringing up the rear, Jam's rifle at the ready. We crossed the cold, windy parade yard and into the shelter of a casemate. At the door of the jakes, Boy went on, but the guards halted.

"You go," Hendricks ordered Jam. "Keep an eye on him."

"Not me," protested Jam. "Not me alone. We should all go."

Hendricks shook her head. "We'll guard the door. If he overpowers you, at least we'll still be standing firm outside."

"I don't want to be overpowered," Jam said obstinately. "Let him overpower *you*. What if he changes me into a polecat?"

"He can't change anyone into anything, Jam. He's under a geas—he's powerless."

"Then, why don't you want to go—"

"I'll go," I said, both to move things along and because it was a chance to tell Boy we were here to rescue him. I didn't really care to share Boy's potty experience, but I could close my eyes, or stare at my boots, or something.

Hendricks said, "All right, then, Ash. Better unholster, and keep your gun on him. If he does get you, holler, and we'll make sure to bar the door so he can't get through us."

Which wouldn't help me any, I thought, *trapped inside,* but I wasn't really worried about Boy getting me—not once he heard what I had to say. Still, I drew my pistol and cocked it. "If he pulls anything funny, I'll shoot him."

Hendricks nodded approvingly. "That'll save the Warlord the price of rope. Go on, then."

The jakes was the kind that has five holes in a row, with nothing to screen them, and across, a row of stone trough sinks. The Army is *not* a good place for the potty shy. A small stove smoked in a corner, but it did little to melt the chilly rime off the stone walls. Boy Hansgen was already leaning over one of the troughs, scrubbing soap into his face.

"Um, excuse me," I said. What would Nini Mo say? Something exciting and dramatic, like *If you want to live come with me* or *Let us fly and be free.* But I felt silly just thinking those things. "Um—sieur."

The running water was loud, but I didn't want to run the risk of the guards outside hearing me, so I reholstered and stood by until he was done. Boy Hansgen scrubbed and scrubbed, and then straightened up, holding out his manacled hands. I gave him one of the ragged towels hanging over the troughs, and he dried his face, revealing a fantastically purple shiner around one blue eye.

He regarded me as he wiped his hands, and said, "You are in bad shape, girlie. You won't be able to hide it much longer—and if they catch you, they'll hang you, too."

I stared at him blankly.

"Do you have a cigarillo? I am dying for a smoke. You don't have to be coy with me. I don't care what boo-spooky stuff you are up to, but your superior officers will take a dimmer view of your traffic in the Current. You should have stayed out—"

"I'm not in the Army," I said. "I'm here to rescue you—"

Before I realized he had even moved, Boy Hansgen was looming, pushing me against the wall, which was cold against my back.

"Who sent you?" His breath stank, and his grip on my collar was choking. Before, he had been so humorous that he had seemed harmless, his reputation perhaps overblown. But now, the jovialness had dropped from his countenance and pure steel had taken its place. Suddenly, I was afraid.

"No one," I gurgled.

"No one?"

"I came myself, on my own, with my friend, Udo."

"The one calling himself Seneca Gaisford? The one Glamourized?"

"Ayah."

He eased his grip, incredulously. "Just the two of you? To pull my feet from the fire, just the two of you, and both of you kids?"

There was a hammering at the door, and Hendricks's voice: "Hurry up in there! You've had time for twenty pisses!"

"My bladder is full!" Boy Hansgen yelled back.

"Ash? Did he get you?"

Boy relaxed his grip so I could holler, slightly hoarsely, "I am fine—we'll be out in a minute."

"Hurry! That Captain Gaisford is crapping bricks over your delay."

"We come!" I shouted.

Boy Hansgen was still regarding me with a hard blue gaze that seemed to bore right into my brain. "Just the two of you, and no one else?"

It was impossible to lie to that look. "Ayah—we have an order from the Warlord for you to be released to our custody."

"Where'd you get the order?"

"We forged it."

He laughed and released me completely. "Well, budding rangers! Nini could have done no better. What is your name, girlie?"

I loosened my collar and rubbed my neck. "Flora Nemain Fyrdraaca ov Fyrdraaca." His praise had kindled a happy little glow in me that made the burn on my neck feel like nothing. *Nini Mo could have done no better!*

"*Fyrdraaca?*" Now he really did laugh, low in his throat. "Now, this is precious—one Fyrdraaca sends me to the gallows and another Fyrdraaca cuts the rope! But listen to me, girlie—you've got one of the worst cases of Anima Enervation I've ever seen."

"Anima what?"

"Have you been trafficking with a galvanic egregore—you know, a praterhuman entity, which gains its strength from human Will?"

A cold stream washed over me. I whispered, "Our denizen—Valefor—he's been banished and I was trying to help him."

"Banished? You mean abrogated? You've been letting an abrogated denizen siphon Will off you?" This time Boy's laugh was not amused. "Girlie, you are lucky I can see you at all—your denizen is sucking you of *all* your Will. Soon enough you'll be too far gone—"

The door thumped again, and then popped open. Hendricks,

her rifle pointed, said suspiciously, "That is long enough. Come on."

That cold stream had become a flood that was threatening to wash away the last bits of my composure. I gaped at Boy Hansgen, who gave me a steady look that seemed to say, *Don't panic,* before obeying Hendricks's command. But he was too late; I was already panicking. His awful assertion had driven everything but panic right out of my mind. What had Valefor done? What did Boy mean that I would soon be *"too far gone"*?

Jam prodded Boy Hansgen on, and, now smiling again, he went, stepping lightly.

"Hurry on, Ash," Private Hendricks said over her shoulder. "The captains are about to get into a duello. Are you all right?"

"Ayah so." In a haze, I followed Hendricks across the parade yard, this time barely feeling the cutting saltwater wind. As we approached the sally port, the sound of Udo, loud and indignant, pulled me out of my daze.

". . . an absolute outrage. You can rest assured that the Warlord will be told in detail of this insult, and you can rest assured that the repercussions will be quite serious."

"Here I am again, all clean and sweet," Boy Hansgen said happily, "and ready to meet my ex-liege lord—well, now!"

My line of sight was blocked by Hendricks. I peered around her, and every atom of my body turned into freezing ice when I saw who Udo was hotly protesting to, his swagger stick poking ominously.

Lord Axacaya's Quetzal guards.

TWENTY-FIVE

Panic. A Conflict.
Udo's Long Wind. Hat Brass.

ONCE IDDEN HAD TRIED to show me how Mamma killed that jaguar with a shovel, and in doing so, she punched me in the stomach. For a sickening second, I had wheezed and sucked, but my lungs would not inflate. That is exactly how I felt when I saw those Quetzals.

There were four of them, all unveiled, and their huge yellow eyes gleamed flat and iridescent in the flaring torchlight. Again I was struck by the awful combination of human and bird, the way the feathers shaded into skin. The unmistakable sharpness of those sword-edged beaks.

Udo and Captain Honeychurch had moved out to the sally port, and there we halted. Two Quetzals stood before the open gate, holding horses. Another stood with Udo and Captain Honeychurch, and it was with this one that Udo was arguing loudly. "My special order is signed by the Warlord and must be obeyed. I hope you remember, Captain Honeychurch, you owe no obedience to Lord Axacaya."

Boy Hansgen said, his voice slightly quavering, "Now I know just how the snake felt when he saw those shadow wings circling above. Not eagles, but *buzzards.*"

"We, all of us, are obedient servants to the Will of the Gracious Virreina, and Lord Axacaya is her dutiful son and his desires must be heard," said the Quetzal standing by Udo and Captain Honeychurch. Its voice was oddly sweet, and it sounded almost bored. "And he desires this man."

Cool, calm, and collected, said Nini Mo. *Panic poisons; levelheaded lives. She who holds out, holds all.* My chest felt light and airy, like I was breathing fog. I took a deeper breath, and then another. We hadn't lost yet.

"We are Califans first and foremost," said Udo. "And this is Califa still—"

A Quetzal interrupted. "Captain Honeychurch, you cannot deny a request by Lord Axacaya."

"Lord Axacaya has no jurisdiction here," Udo said hotly. "This is a military installation and under military rule. The Warlord is Commander in Chief." These last words were emphasized with sharp jabs of the swagger stick. I had a sudden vision of Udo torn into tiny shreds by those hooked beaks, but luckily for him, the Quetzal showed its respect for Udo's opinion by completely ignoring him and turning its attention to the Skinner.

"You shall not question Lord Axacaya's orders, Captain Honeychurch," the Quetzal said softly. "We will take the prisoner with us, and Lord Axacaya shall be pleased."

The other Quetzal had fixed its luminous gaze on Udo, and this gaze had apparently struck Udo dumb, for he did not now protest.

But Boy Hansgen did, a touch hysterically, "I beg you, Captain Honeychurch, as one soldier to another, do not send me to be torn apart by monsters. Let me hang, happy to die among my peers."

"You are no peer of mine," Captain Honeychurch said. "If it were up to me, I would have ordered you burned." The Skinner looked extremely unhappy, for which I could not blame her— either decision could end her career. Give over to Udo and let Lord Axacaya think his orders had been ignored, or give over to Lord Axacaya and risk the Warlord's wrath. Still, she was a Skinner and had taken the Warlord's oath—surely she knew where her duty lay?

"But does not mercy have a human face?" Boy Hansgen cried. "And look at them—there is no humanity there—no mercy. Please, Captain Honeychurch, can you not—"

"Captain Honeychurch, you have already ceded custody of this prisoner to me and, therefore, have not the power to grant Lord Axacaya's request." Udo had recovered, and his argument was actually a good one, though based somewhat on a technicality. "I am now in charge of this prisoner, and I say, you can go hang!"

"The Warlord owes obedience to the Virreina's representative," said the Quetzal.

"Ha! Lord Axacaya is hardly the Virreina's representative in Califa! What then is the Huitzil Ambassador?" Udo said doggedly. "And where's the order written? You cannot expect us to heed a verbal order—"

"I do not need a written order from Lord Axacaya," Captain Honeychurch said. "His servants are enough."

We were going to lose, I could smell it. Captain Honeychurch was going to give Boy Hansgen to the Quetzals, and part of me could not blame her. Which was worse, Quetzals now or the Warlord later? It's always best to procrastinate trouble.

If we were to come out triumphant, Something Had to be Done.

Who was going to Do It?

I looked toward Boy Hansgen, hoping he was poised to do something incredibly clever and flashy, to extract us all from the situation, but he did nothing. Standing between the terrified-looking Hendricks and Jam, he looked terrified, too. Maybe that was a ruse to throw us all off, so that any minute he could burst into some hideously clever escape attempt?

Any minute? Like right now? *Now?*

Boy Hansgen did not look like Someone Poised to Act. He looked like Someone Poised to Hyperventilate, or maybe Scream. His knees were practically knocking together, and only the firm grips of the guards kept him upright. He sure didn't have the nerve that the Coyote Queen had—I guess that is why he was just the sidekick.

Forget Boy Hansgen. What would Nini Mo do?

She would look for a Way Out. So, I looked.

The other two Quetzals—Minions, I suppose—stood before the gates, partially blocking that exit. Behind us, the sally port opened to the wide space of the parade yard, surrounded on all sides by three tiers of casemates, each alcove containing an extremely large gun whose barrel stuck out of an extremely small embrasure window. No exit there. If we somehow made it to the top of the parapet, there was nowhere to go but over the side, straight down into the pulverizing ocean surf. No exit there.

But Bonzo and Mouse had been brought up and now stood waiting behind me, a single groom at their reins. If we had a distraction and got by those Quetzals, perhaps we could just grab Boy Hansgen, leap onto the horses, and run?

The Quetzals' horses were Anahuatl Chargers, beautiful in a parade, useless in a fight, as nervous as chickens. Lord Axacaya sent Mamma an Anahuatl Charger one year for her birthday; I suppose he meant it as an honor, for they are very expensive. That horse was gorgeous, with a high narrow chest and the most beautiful bay color. But he was so high-strung that he jumped at the slightest whisper. He kicked at his stall so much that he blew out a tendon and had to be shot. Mamma had never even ridden him.

Bonzo and Mouse, on the other hand, are Bulrush Shermans, a breed known for being solid and unflappable. Mamma rode Bonzo in the War, and she used to joke that Bonzo should be the one called the Rock of Califa, because it was she who always held firm when Mamma herself wanted to scarper. I'd wager my life that those Anahuatl Chargers would curvet and stampede at the slightest upset, but that Bonzo and Mouse would remain steady, no matter what.

I'd wager not just my life, but Udo's and Boy Hansgen's, as well.

Sometimes being of no account is useful. The officers and the Quetzals were still arguing, and the enlisteds were terrified, so no one paid me the slightest bit of attention as I inched my way toward the gates. I pretended, just in case anyone did look, that I was scratching my forehead, and in doing so, managed to unhook my hat brass. The insignia is held onto the hat with pointy brass prongs; there's a stupid Army tradition that when you take the Warlord's oath and are given your insignia, you are repaid by having your hat brass driven into your chest by your comrades' congratulatory punches. Idden reported to me that being brass-blooded, as they call it, *hurts*. I'd wager those fancy horses would think so, too.

The Quetzal minions holding the reins were paying my sidling no attention, their gazes fixed on the argument. The groom holding Bonzo and Mouse was also staring agape at Udo, who was *still* in full-flood dudgeon. Captain Honeychurch was looking a wee bit more persuaded, but I wasn't going to risk it.

An Anahuatl horse flank was within poking distance. I was poised to punch, as soon as I was sure I would not be espied.

Then I heard: "Take him. And I bid Lord Axacaya joy with him."

Udo protested: "I will tell the Warlord!"

"You can tell the Warlord that I had to bow to the authority of our overlords," Captain Honeychurch said in a hard voice. "And if Califa is a client state and no longer has any Will of her own, it is no fault of mine, nor my regiment. You can tell the Warlord that!"

"I beg of you, Captain Honeychurch!" Boy Hansgen said desperately, but she turned away.

The guards shoved Boy Hansgen toward the Quetzals. He stumbled and almost fell, but they swooped in and grabbed him. They slung him over the back of one of those silly horses, and then they all rode away.

TWENTY-SIX

Ambushed.
Gramatica Exclamations.
A Coyote.

"WHO THE HELL ARE YOU?" a voice whispered in my ear. I gurgled and wiggled, but someone was lying on top of me, squashing my kicks and muffling my squawks. My face was pushed hard against oily scratchy cloth that smelled of sour milk and grease.

My brain felt mushy, confused. Where was I? What had happened? Udo—Boy Hansgen—in a sudden rush, the confusion cleared and I remembered.

Udo and I had been riding hell for leather, trying to catch up with the Quetzals. Our plan? We no longer had a plan, just the intention that maybe we could ambush the Quetzals and steal Boy Hansgen back. In military strategy, they call any maneuver with not much chance of success a Forlorn Hope, and that about summed it up. But after we had beat a hasty retreat from Zoo Battery, we had put our heads together and agreed that as Forlorn as the Hope might be, we still had to try.

So we'd put the spurs to the horses and set off in chase. The Quetzals were in a hurry, and those Anahuatl Chargers can really run. Already they had disappeared. But Bulrush Shermans can run, too, and steadily. I was sure we could catch up. Then, suddenly, dark shadows had sprung up on the road, shouting and flapping. In Bonzo's sudden curvet, I had lost my seat—flown upward. Then—*whompf*—darkness.

Now someone was pressing his arm against my face and hissing threats in my ear. Pain splotched my wrist, and I could barely breathe: My squasher weighed as much as a horse. Horse! Bonzo . . . Mouse . . . *Udo*—where were they? Were they all right?

The Squasher whispered in my ear, his breath meaty and warm, "I am dying to spit me some blackcoats, filthy bugger, but first I think we should have some fun. I need a set of ears to round out my collection." The cold edge of a knife wandered up the curve of my chin, and tweaked under my right ear, budding a spark of pain. My insides turned into slushy ice.

Then, thankfully, another voice hissed, "No ears—not yet."

"Aw, come on now, I been good," The Squasher whined. His weight eased up, and the arm across my face shifted, and I was able to turn my head slightly, uncovering my mouth.

"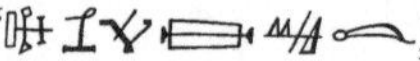," I whispered.

The Word exploded like a cork from a bottle, and for a second I thought I might explode, too. My brain went dark and tight, straining at my skull. My head throbbed, and I was engulfed in nothingness. Then my ears popped and I was myself again. The weight was gone.

I rolled over, forcing my stiff muscles to sit me up. My mouth tasted of iron sludge, and when I coughed, a giant wad of something nasty came up and out. A thin red glow suffused the air, and by this glow I could see the lee of a sand dune and trampled grass. Something lay upon the sand, moaning like a foghorn. A dark figure crouched over it, murmuring. There was no sign of Udo or the horses.

I started to crawl away, the sand cold against my hands. The dark figure looked up. In the thin red light, he was a blotch blacker than the night itself, which, now that the moon had risen and illuminated the fog silverly, wasn't so dark anymore.

"Where did you learn that word, little blackcoat?" the Dark Man hissed.

I had no idea. The Word had appeared in my mind like it had dropped there from the sky, and once it was there, it had to get out somehow or my head would have imploded.

The Dark Man continued, accusingly, "You turned Hubert's blood into oatmeal."

"He shouldn't have tried to cut my ear off," I croaked.

"Lucky for Hubert that I was here and able to turn his oatmeal back to blood. Else he would now be dead. It's strange to find a blackcoat with such a strong vocabulary. Who are you?"

Nini Mo says to never answer a question when you can ask one. "Who are *you*?" I asked, scrambling up and trying to keep one eye on the Dark Man while I looked around frantically for Udo and the horses.

"I'll trade you names, blackcoat."

"Keep your name, then, and get out of my way—I'm in a hurry."

The Dark Man stood. "Though I look more closely and see no blackcoat at all."

The slope behind me was steep, and sand is hard to climb. I could make a dash for it, but I'm not a very good runner, and in a chase, I wouldn't get far. Then I remembered the pistol at my hip. It wasn't loaded, but the Dark Man didn't know that. Nini Mo says sometimes the threat is enough.

I drew. The gun felt heavy in my hand, yet the weight was strangely comforting. That's the problem with guns: They pretend to be the solution to every problem.

"I have business elsewhere," I growled, "and so I bid you stand there while I go. If you seek to impede me, I'll shoot you."

The Dark Man answered, "I believe our business is the same. Are we not both hoping to get the candy and give the rush?"

"Give us the candy or we'll give you the rush" is the traditional shout heard on the holiday of the Pirates' Parade, but I guessed he was using it as a reference to the Dainty Pirate. Still, I played ignorant.

"I don't know what you mean. It's not Pirates' Parade."

"Perhaps not a parade, true enough, but I do believe there is a pirate. Allow me to introduce myself." The darkness fell away from the figure, as though he had cast it away like a cloak, and revealed the Hurdy-Gurdy Man I had seen outside the Bella Union Saloon. "Firemonkey, at your service. And we should quit playing games if we are to have the slightest chance of saving Boy Hansgen."

"The Quetzals took him," I blurted.

"So I know. Others from my organization—"

"You mean your band?"

"The band is just a cover, of course. No, the Eschatological Immenation. Who else?"

The EI! Mamma had been right to be worried about them. They did more than just paint slogans after all.

Firemonkey continued, "When we heard of Boy Hansgen's capture, we knew we must act. Some of my group have already gone ahead to intercept the Quetzals. Hubert and I came back because we thought you were the Warlord's pursuit." He paused. "Listen!"

I listened. Hubert had stopped whimpering, and all I heard now was the distant throb of the ocean, the rush of the night air, and my own breathing. "I don't hear anything, and I don't have time—"

"Listen, not with your ears! *Listen!*"

What can you listen with, if not your ears? I stood, trying to listen but to not listen. And, gradually, I realized that I did hear something, a deep vibration that was more of a feeling than a sound. There was a rhythm to the sensation, ebbing and flowing with my breathing, but like a tide coming in, it grew stronger and stronger.

"What is it?"

"It's the whirlwind sound of the world turning round," Firemonkey replied.

"What?"

"Someone is rending the Current—come on!"

He ran, quickly, and I followed, less so. The sand slid under my feet and my empty sabre sling kept entangling in my legs. Ahead of me, Firemonkey swept up the sand dune and paused at its peak to wave an encouraging arm toward me. Halfway up,

I skidded downward, feeling my thigh muscles squeal, my arm throb. Firemonkey jumped the crest and was gone. A shout arrested my slide; teetering, I turned and saw below me a waving figure and the bulk of two horses. Finally, Udo.

I half jumped, half ran back down the dune, and only Udo's sudden grab stopped me from ending up flat on my face.

"Where the hell did you go?" he demanded. "Are you all right?"

"I'm fine, and the horses, are they all right? Where did *you* go?" I pulled out of Udo's woolly embrace and squinted up. The jutting chin and heavy eyeliner were all too familiar: Udo's Glamour had worn off. It was good to see his face again.

"They're fine. Pigface, Flora, are you sure you are okay? Did you see those guys? Where'd they go?"

I answered. "I'm okay, but those guys, Udo, they're trying to rescue Boy, too. They are—"

"Pigface Psychopomp, Flora, *get down*." Udo gave me a hard shove, and I went sprawling. The horses jumped and scattered, and Udo himself hit the sand, half on top of me. A bitterly bright green light sped by us, barely missing our heads. It raced like a rocket, like hot shot, like a comet, and then got smaller and smaller until it winked out like a blink. The sand tilted up and tilted down, shifting like the deck of a ship. For a second, the whole world seemed to lift an inch and hover in the air. Then it jolted down again, with a tremendous thud. I felt as though every organ in my body had been pureed and poured back into my skin.

"What the hell was that?" Udo groaned.

"I'm not sure, but I know it was something Currenty. Come on."

"The horses—they've scarpered."

"Leave them; they know better than we do how to take care of themselves. Come on."

My feet turned in under themselves when I tried to stand, so I crawled my way up the sand dune instead, scraping my hands, tasting grit in my teeth, blinking away grit in my eyes. I started to slide back down, then felt Udo behind me, pushing. I paused at the top, bending to catch my breath, tasting iron on my tongue, my saliva too stringy to spit. The ocean ahead was a bright surge of silver, as fluid as mercury, and up the coast, Bilskinir House shone blue, like a malevolent morning star.

Distantly, a figure ran along the dark fringe of sand, pursued by Anahuatl horses. Udo, next to me, had pulled out his binoculars. "It's Boy; he's running hard, but they are gaining. Even if we got the horses, we'd never make it in time," he reported.

"Give me the binoculars," I demanded, yanking at the strap.

"Close your eyes," Firemonkey hissed in my ear. I started; I hadn't heard him crawl up next to me.

"Why?"

"Look beyond the Waking World."

I closed my eyes, and suddenly the steel-gray night was lit a glowing green, and the distant details of the chase snapped into clear focus. I saw then, not a man harried by a pack of horses, but a coyote, low and lean, running for his life along the shingle. And hot on his trail, four eagles.

Firemonkey said, anguish in his voice, "He hasn't got a chance."

"Can't we do anything?" Udo's free hand slid into mine, and I squeezed it tightly.

"No—they are too strong," Firemonkey answered. "They've already gotten my comrades. Damn those bloody birds to the Abyss!"

The Coyote ran, his spine stretched long and his muzzle pointed like an arrowhead, but the Eagles flying behind him were like bullets. He was not going to get away. One Eagle rose up, then skidded downward, snatching at the Coyote's back with outstretched claws. The Coyote stumbled, rolled in a tumble of legs, and writhed back to its feet, but another Eagle struck him down again. The others spun in a wide circle, darting and pecking, tearing with sharp beaks. The Coyote wove into the water, splashing, but the Eagles drove him back onto the sand, buffeting him with their huge wings. The Coyote lunged, his jaw snapping onto a wing, pulling the Eagle out of the air. The two dissolved into a blur of feathers and fur, the other Eagles swooping so low that their wings churned the sand up into a fine mist. Around and around the combatants they circled, and the mist became a whirlwind, so that I could see nothing but the spiral of sand.

My heart was beating so loudly in my chest that I couldn't even hear the thump of the surf. Udo was saying something, but I heard him dimly, all my attention focused on the now red-flecked sand devil, twisting and turning higher and higher. Udo's grip on my hand was crushing. The sandstorm flushed a deep crimson, then suddenly, as though an invisible hand whisked it away like a parlor trick, it was gone.

Now there was no Coyote, only a man on the bloody sand, so red he looked like he'd just been born. The Quetzals bent over him, their grotesque eagle-beaks tearing and pecking at his soft flesh. Then one stood, holding aloft something squishy and soft: Boy Hansgen's heart.

I opened my eyes.

TWENTY-SEVEN

Home. Stale Bread. Valefor.

FIREMONKEY AND what was left of the EI did not linger. As soon as they saw that it was all over, they scarpered, warning us to do the same before the Quetzals noticed us, or the militia came, or whoever/whatever else the magickal battle might have attracted turned up. So, Udo and I rode back to the City in a daze, silently. It was so late that even the streetlights were extinguished, so early that the only other traffic we passed were milk trucks, and the occasional cab, ferrying someone home from a big night out.

So much for *our* big night out.

At Crackpot, we silently took care of the horses and went on to the House. When we had left so many hours earlier, the dogs had been locked up in the mudroom, but now, when I opened the back door, no dogs, eager to pee, shot past us caroling joy at their release.

Even before I stepped into the kitchen, I knew what we would see. Although I had not completely cleaned up the last kitchen mess, I had tidied up some before we left. Now, once again, the dim overhead light showed a scene of gigantic disaster. The table was covered in spilled sugar and broken crockery. Chairs were overturned. The kettle had been knocked off the hob, and the ensuing flood had turned the hearth into a soggy waterlogged mess. The floor was covered with jammy paw prints, and the butter dish showed clear signs of licking.

"Oh Pigface. Not again," Udo moaned. "Those dogs, I could shoot them, each and every one. And then Hotspur next."

"Do you want a snack before you go to bed?" I asked. I stepped over a broken jam jar and kicked some onions aside to get to the sideboard.

"Shouldn't we clean up?"

"It can wait."

"Then I think I'll hit the rack. We have to get up in a few hours for school."

The dogs hadn't gotten to the bread box; the bread inside was stale, but I didn't care. I was so hungry I would have eaten it moldy. I took a knife off the knife rack and began to cut. Udo halted on the bottom stair, looking at me.

"We did everything we could," he said.

I chewed the bread; it made my jaw ache and tasted like nothing.

"Everything we could," he repeated.

I swallowed and tore another hunk off the slice.

"What more could we have done?" he asked.

"Nothing," I answered. "Nothing at all."

"You should go to bed, too, Flora. You look dead on your feet."

"I will, but I'm starving. I gotta eat something first."

Udo trudged up the stairs, and I righted a chair and sat down at the kitchen table, oblivious to the mess before me. Tea would have been nice, but I didn't feel like reviving the fire, and anyway, the teapot lay in pieces on the floor. I just sat there, staring into the shadowy darkness at nothing, chewing on stale bread.

Me and my happy splendid plan. My fabulous rangery skills, my magickal pride. I had thought I was so clever, and yet where had my cleverness gotten us? Nada, zip, *nunca mas,* nothing. I was an idiot, and a fool, and childish, and a failure. The long mirror over the sink reflected a sullen girl sitting in the middle of a huge horrible mess. Her eye makeup had smeared into pools of blackness, and her hair stood on end. Her lip rouge was blurred, making her mouth look almost bloody.

A nasty taste rose up in the back of my throat, bitter and burning, and I thought I might throw up. I leaned over, swallowing hard, and rubbed at my mouth with a gritty sleeve, scrubbing the rouge away. Now that girl in the mirror just looked washed out, a pale ghost. *She* would never be a ranger.

In a few hours it would be dawn.

In a few hours Mamma would be home.

Tomorrow was my Catorcena.

A little purple light shimmered, and became Valefor. He was looking pretty papery again, but I didn't care.

"Well," he said. "That was a fine time, Flora Segunda."

"Well-water," I answered. "Don't spoil with me, Valefor. I'm not in the mood."

"So much for heroic rescues. I am banished and even I could hear the screams. Such a magickal battle has not been seen since Hardhands—"

"Not now, Valefor!"

"Well, no matter. You did your best, which arguably wasn't really that good, Flora. But it's done."

"Go away, Valefor."

"Flora Segunda—you are far too serious. You give up so easily. Was it your fault that Boy Hansgen died? No, of course not. Your plan was perhaps not the best, and doomed to failure from the start, but it was kind of you to attempt it. He was going to die, anyway."

"Somehow you are not making me feel the slightest bit better, Valefor."

"Forget about Boy Hansgen. He's not the first magician to overreach, and he won't be the last. Let's move on to more important things."

"Yes, let's, Valefor. Let's, indeed," I said. "Are you familiar with the term Anima Enervation?"

Valefor shrank back a little, and his shape quavered. "Ayah so? What about it?"

"What is it, pray? Do tell me, Valefor. Enlighten me. You've always been quick to enlighten me before."

"I think, Flora Segunda, from your waspy tone, you know already."

"No, Valefor. I know that the Dainty Pirate thought I was fading, discorporeal, and he said that a galvanic egregore was sucking away all my Will, and I think he meant *you*, Valefor, and he said soon it would be *too late*. But perhaps you can explain it to me better, Valefor! Please do!"

Now Valefor wrung his hands, and his forehead wrinkled like a prune. "Is it my fault that your Will was so weak that it was so soon exhausted? And now we will both run back to the Current from whence we came."

"What do you mean, Valefor? Speak plainly and cut the mumbo."

"I was banished to the Bibliotheca and I had just enough stamina to keep myself strong from the wisps of Fyrdraaca Will that came my way. But then you came along and helped me out, Flora Segunda. It was so nice of you, and it enabled me to regain some of my former glory, though not a whole lot of it because, frankly, your Will was never really that punchy to begin with. But it was certainly better than nothing, though now your Will is running out, and so am I—I fear that I shall just dissipate back into the Abyss, and you shall go, too, for we are connected now—"

"Unconnect us, Valefor. Right now. Wherever you are going, you can go alone."

"Oh, but I can't, Flora Segunda. We are intertwined now; it's beyond my control, and there's nothing I can do."

"How could you let this happen?" I demanded.

"Me!? I am *weakened*, Flora—I could not help myself! You are the magician; I am just the denizen. It is your responsibility to take precautions!" The hands were still wringing, but his eyes narrowed into gleaming slits, and I saw that his hands weren't really wringing as much as they were snapping with an audible crackle.

I stared at him. I should have been angry, but somehow, suddenly, I didn't care.

"You are pernicious, Valefor. Now I see why Mamma banished you," I said dully.

"Pernicious! After all I've done for you, Flora Segunda, you are so ungrateful. All you wanted were your own little comforts, no true thoughts of Valefor, poor Valefor, you only pretended to be my friend. You never cared for my needs at all, so it seems to me that you only deserve what you are getting, faithless Flora!"

"Leave me alone, Valefor, just leave me alone." I lay my head down on the table, not caring if I got butter or broken glass in my hair, and closed my eyes. If I vanished, then none of this would matter anymore. No Catorcena, no Barracks, no Mamma, no failure.

"But, there is hope, Flora," Valefor said, eagerly. I felt him pat my hair hesitantly. "There is hope; we must not despair. You can save us still—"

"I don't care, Valefor," I said, without opening my eyes or lifting my head. "Just go away."

"But Flora, don't you want to redeem yourself? We haven't much time, but if I were restored, then I would be strong again and happy again, and so would you be, too, because we are connected. We are in this together, Flora!"

"I do not care," I repeated. "Go away, Valefor."

The little pats on my hair became little tugs, and I tossed my head against his grip. "Come on, Flora, just because you must be so morose doesn't mean that you should take me with you. Think of someone other than yourself for a change—"

I tugged away and stood up, knocking the chair down. Valefor hovered over me, his eyes white, his teeth white, his fingers long and pinchy.

"Leave me alone, Valefor, just go away and leave me alone!"

He tried to get in my way, but he was too insubstantial to make much of a roadblock. I pushed my way through him and ran outside.

Barbizon. The Pond. A Leap.

VALEFOR DID NOT—perhaps could not—follow me. The sky looked like milky tea and the moon was a swirly smudge just above the tree line. The gate to the back garden was open, and I went through it into the tangled wilderness beyond. Valefor had bragged quite a bit about the marvels of his gardens—how perfect his hedge animals, how tall his cypress trees—but as with the rest of Crackpot, there was nothing left of the glory but the brag itself. Without his care, the foliage had become a tangle of branches, and the grass high and hiding. A small footpath beat its way through the wilderness, and I could just make out its trace through the gloom, leading toward the Sunken Puddle, Crackpot's ornamental pond.

Just beyond the gate, at the edge of the Puddle, stands the grave of Barbizon, my great-grandfather Azucar Fyrdraaca's war horse. Her memorial is a statue so energetic that it seems as though Barbizon herself had turned to hard stone in the sudden act of curveting: She balances on muscular back legs, while an extended front hoof forever slices up at the sky, her teeth bared.

I sat down on a rock and stared up at Barbizon's shadowy bulk. The story goes that when my great-grandfather Azucar fell at the Battle of Creton's Harm, mortally wounded, Barbizon stood over him, keeping his enemies at bay with slashes of her sharp iron hooves, until at last my great-grandmother Idden fought her way through the rough din and helped Barbizon drag Azucar from the field. That, says Mamma, is true loyalty.

Something nosed against my leg, and I started, alarmed, before I realized it was Flynn. Dear darling Flynnie. I leaned over and squeezed him, and suddenly my emptiness was filled with a giant black sorrow, piercingly sharp. Now I was choking on tears that seemed to rip from my throat, leaving the taste of blood behind. Each breath I took cracked my heart a bit more, so that darkness spilled upward, outward, tearing my insides to shreds.

Flynnie's warm wet tongue lapped against my cheeks, slurped at my tears. He didn't care that I was a failure, an idiot, a baby. He loved me, anyway, no matter what. But who would feed him when I had entirely disappeared? Who would make sure Poppy didn't give him chocolate or leave the gate open so he could run into traffic and get squashed? Flynn squirmed, and I let him go, reluctantly. The sky had gone a thin pink—dawn at last—and Flynnie stood at point, quiveringly alert.

A gentle mist rose from the Sunken Puddle's surface, floating gently upward like cigarillo smoke. A small dark shape was moving fluidly across the water. Valefor, in his garden brag, had sworn three ancient turtles lived within the pond's deep, green waters, but if that was a turtle head, it was the biggest darn turtle head I had ever seen. And a big turtle could have a big head, but it would not stand up and clamber out of the water on hind legs, nor would it be tall and skinny. Or so white, either, like pale gleaming bone.

"Poppy! What are you doing?"

"Swimming," he answered, shaking himself like a dog. Flynn bounded up upon him, and he pushed the bounce down. "Could you hand me my towel? It's on that rock."

I tossed him his towel, then picked up the pack of cigarillos that fell out of its folds. He wrapped the towel over his shoulders, awkwardly, and sat down.

Mamma had warned Idden and me never to swim in the

Sunken Puddle, but that was one warning she didn't need to make. I had never had the slightest desire to go swimming in it. The water smelled like yuck and Goddess knew what icky things swarm within its sour, green depths.

"You shouldn't swim in the pond, Poppy." I sat next to him and snuffled my nose against my sleeve, but he didn't notice that, or the catch in my throat. Would he notice when I was gone? "You might get tangled in the weeds and drown."

"Not in this water. It's too buoyant. It's not really water, anyway. It's the Current, bubbling to the surface. If you dive down deeply enough, you can breathe the Current like air. It is marvelously refreshing, Flora—you should give it a try—you look like you need a little pick-me-up. It's delicious."

I ignored Poppy's crazy talk. I just wasn't in the mood for it. I should have gone back in the house, but I didn't have the energy to move.

Poppy put a cigarillo to his lips and muttered something under his breath. There was a small glitter of coldfire, followed by a long exhalation of smoke.

"Was that Gramatica, Poppy?"

"Ayah," he answered, sounding pleased. "Ayah, it was. I don't know much, but I know enough to light a few fires and to maybe make it rain, if I'm on a roll."

"It's forbidden for soldiers, Poppy, you know."

"So is forgery, darling, and that comes in handy sometimes, doesn't it? Anyway, Flora, you needn't sound so self-righteous. You got Gramatica words in you, too. I can see them floating around inside you—and not just little ones, but big fat bright ones, the kind that burn. Once Gramatica gets into your blood, you know, you can't ever get it out. It grows and changes you, if you don't take care."

A tiny shiver ran through me. I remembered the Oatmeal Word—it had sprung into my head and out of my mouth, yet I could have sworn that I had never heard or read it before.

The little winkie cigarillo butt flew through the darkness and plopped into the water. "You know that if ever the Fyrdraaca family is in true trouble, Barbizon is supposed to come to life and to our rescue, just as she did for Azucar."

"Ayah, Poppy, I've heard the story."

"Well, I often consider that I've sat here many times, and often felt in true trouble, and yet Barbizon has never leaped to my aid. So you know what that makes me think?"

"That's it's just a story?"

"No, no. That my trouble is never true trouble. And things, though I think them bad, are not really so." Poppy turned his gaze back from Barbizon to me. "You should have a swim, Flora. You look as dead as winter grass. Come on. We shall jump from the Folly roof, and it shall do you great good."

The Folly is a summerhouse that sits right at the pond's edge, like a cupcake on stilts. For generations, Fyrdraaca kids have used it as a clubhouse, but I hadn't been there for ages. Now, I glanced toward its shadow. "It's much too high, Poppy."

"Nayah, not at all; it's perfect. You have to run, of course, to clear the gutters and the patio deck below. But it's like flying—just wonderful. The arc of the air and the smack of the water. And then the pull of the Current."

"It sounds painful."

"Ayah, but deliciously so. Come on!"

He grabbed my hand and yanked, and I was so surprised that I didn't yank back but came right off the rock. During the War, Poppy was wounded, and during his captivity he was tortured, and so one of his arms doesn't work too well and he limps badly. But there was no weakness in his crazy, hard grip now, and I couldn't get free.

"Poppy!" I protested, bushes whipping at me as we ran down the path, Flynnie bounding behind, barking his approval, the rat dog. We bumped up the Folly's front steps and into the musty interior. At the stairs, I took advantage of a solid banister and grabbed, with a sudden strength that I hadn't had earlier when I was deep in my despondency.

"Come on, Flora, don't be a stick," Poppy said, pulling harder. I clung, and he tore, and because he had me with his good hand, he won. We thumped up two flights of stairs, and my protests did not weaken Poppy's grip at all. When Poppy threw open the attic door, the dust our feet had raised gleamed like fog in the pink dawn light that spilled in through the open casement window.

"Last one in is the Man in Pink Bloomers!" Poppy crowed.

I gave one last yank, breathless from our hurtle up the stairs, and got free.

"Poppy, please don't—"

He turned toward me, and by some weird trick of the pale light and the streaky shadows, his face looked like a skull, bleached and grinning a white bony grin. "You have to burn in order to shine, Flora." He pounced with a grip as hard as iron, yanking me into his run, and I had to follow or fall. The windowsill bruised my knees as Poppy pushed me over. I flailed about, grabbing empty air, and then I was jumping.

Immediately, my jump turned into a fall and then my fall turned into a plummet. The night blew by in a blur of shadowy trees, the sharp edge of the Folly roof, Poppy's loud shriek: *"Cierra Califa!"*

I hit with such a smack that all the air sucked right out of my stomach, and then I was twisting, turning, choking. Burning cold water weighed me down, pulling at me. In the darkness I could not tell which way was up toward air, which way was down toward death. My lungs swelled, my throat burned, and pressure roared in my ears. The compulsion to breathe forced my mouth open, and suddenly I was sucking in water.

A cloud of pinkness lit up the darkness, surrounding me in a nimbus of light. A thick syrupy warmth flooded my mouth, soothed my throat, a yummy goodness that tasted like apples and nutmeg, vanilla and ginger. I wasn't drowning anymore. I felt buoyant, almost frothy, as though my blood had been replaced with bubbly excelsior water. The water—the Current?—felt as warm as bathwater, curving over my body, caressing away all pain and tension. Other colors swirled in the pinkness—cerise, celadon, azure, umber, violet—and shapes, too, tremulous and serpentine. Below me, the light swelled into a brilliant glow of pinkness as bright as fire, and irresistible. I dove down toward this brightness, feeling the Current tingling and buzzing around me, but then my motion was arrested by a hard grip to the ankle.

I kicked the grip off, twisting and flailing, turning to see Poppy hanging in the Current beside me, as radiant as a star, his eyes glowing like green lamps. His movements were languid and graceful, with no sign of injury or crippling.

"Not yet." His lips shaped the words, and I could hear them as clearly as if we stood on dry land and he had whispered into my ear. "We must go back."

He grabbed my hand and began to pull me to the surface, which hung above us like a black ceiling, featureless and dark, and though I struggled and pulled, once again I couldn't shake free. The pink light was fading, and suddenly I was again choking on icy cold water, sputtering and panicking as my lungs began, again, to burn—and then my head broke the surface, and Poppy was pulling me to shore while I choked and coughed and splashed.

For a few seconds all I could do was lie on the sand, like a beached dolphin, spitting pond water and coughing, while a frantic Flynn licked my face and Poppy crouched next to me, laughing.

He crowed, "Did I not say? Oh, the Current is so sweet! I told you it was divine!"

"I almost drowned!" I pushed Flynn away and sat up, trying to spit the nasty taste from my mouth. "You could have killed me!"

"You can't drown in there, Flora. I told you, it's not real water; it's the Current. Do you not feel divine? Do you not feel better?"

Actually, now that my lungs were clear again, I did feel better. I felt drained and loose-boned, but better. Flynn pressed against me and I hugged his solid warmth. The air seemed less cold and the dark less dark, though perhaps that was just dawn coming on. The trees above me and the surface of the lake seemed edged in a pinkish glow, and my brain felt soothingly calm. For a few minutes I had forgotten about Valefor, forgotten about Boy Hansgen, forgotten about everything. Now I remembered, but somehow it didn't all seem quite as hopeless as it did before. My clothes felt heavy and wet, and yet that wasn't so bad, either.

"What was that light in the water, Poppy? Was it really the Current?"

"Oh, ayah. I told you, the wellspring of this lake is the Current. If you dive down to the very bottom, you can slip through the cracks into the core of the Abyss. All the Great Houses have their foundations in the Current, don't you know?"

But I didn't answer—he had stood up, and with that movement, the towel shrugged off his shoulders. In the thin dawn light I saw a large tattoo in the middle of his concave chest. A tattoo of a hand holding a whip. The same insignia as on the seal lock on Valefor's tea caddy.

"Poppy—that tattoo—what is it?"

He looked down his chin at his chest, grinning. "Like it, eh? It's my seal—the Flexing Whip."

"Your seal?" I choked. Suddenly I felt like an idiot. We had found Valefor's tea caddy in Poppy's trunk, so Poppy must have put it there. Why shouldn't the seal lock be his?

"Ayah, see." He tugged the cord around his neck up and over his head, and dangled it before me. "Take it. I don't need it anymore."

I took it, and there was the seal I needed to unlock the tea caddy that contained Valefor's fetish. As easy as that.

Poppy ran his hand over his cropped skull and frowned. "I'm sorry, Flora."

"Sorry about what, Poppy?" I asked, still staring at the seal.

"I thought the Current would help you, but it didn't. I can still see right through you."

TWENTY-NINE

Udo Shouts. Restoration. A Gramatica Word.

I FLEW FROM THE GARDEN into the kitchen, from the kitchen upstairs, so quickly that my feet barely touched the ground, set speedy on wings of panic and fear. Udo lay snoring on the settee in my room, still fully dressed, his big boots hanging over one end, his head almost hanging over the other. He hadn't drawn the blinds, and the room was already suffused with the slight glow of dawn.

I still clutched Poppy's seal in my hand; now I shoved it into my pocket and poked Udo, hard. "Udo, wake up!" He moaned and threw up an arm to ward me off.

"Uhhhh . . ."

"Can you see through me?" I hollered, yanking away the shawl draped over him and poking him hard again. "Can you see through me?"

Blearily he sat up. "What the hell is wrong with you—"

"Poppy said he could see through me! He said I was transparent! He said he could see right through me!"

Udo stood up, took me hard by the arms, and shook me. "Hotspur is crazy," he said calmly. "Calm down. And why are you all wet?"

I wrenched out of his grasp and flew to the mirror. I did look a bit blurry around the edges; my eyes were tiny blue marbles and my freckles looked rather gray. "I am blurry! I am fading! Valefor—"

Reflected in the mirror, standing behind me, Udo stared at me. He didn't look so good himself. His hair had disintegrated into a mass of matted elflocks, and his eyes were little slits of sleepiness. But he looked solid and firm, not insubstantial and flyaway.

I said hysterically, "Boy Hansgen said I had something— Anima Enervation—he said that Valefor was sucking all my Will. He said that Valefor would take it all and I would dwindle to nothing. He's done it, Udo! Valefor said we were connected, and as he goes now, so will I!"

Udo suddenly looked wide-awake. "Why didn't you tell me this before?" he roared. He grabbed me and shook me again, this time hard enough to clack my teeth together.

"I don't know. I just didn't. I forgot," I said weakly, knowing I sounded lame. "Anyway, never mind that. Valefor said there was no way to break the link between us, but that if we restored him, then he would be made strong again, and so would I."

"Do you believe him?" Udo asked. "You look all right to me, although maybe a bit wiggly about the edges. But perhaps I just need coffee."

"At this point he has nothing to gain by lying." I said. "And Poppy can see through me."

"Hotspur is crazy," Udo repeated. "What did you say the Dainty Pirate said you had?"

"Anima Enervation."

"Did you look it up in *The Eschata*?"

I shook my head. I had been too busy panicking to do anything that sensible.

Udo found an entire section on Anima Enervation—a section I could have sworn hadn't been there before or surely I would have noticed it and been warned. (Or maybe, Udo suggested, I had just not wanted to see it and had ignored everything that didn't suit my purpose? I doubted that, but didn't feel up to arguing with him.) The condition occurs when a galvanic egregore attaches itself to an energy source and then begins drawing so much Will that the source is completely drained and ends up with no Will at all.

Udo said, "Even if he sucked away your Will, that doesn't mean you would disappear, or be transparent—it only means you would lie around like a noodle, doing nothing."

"It is because I am abrogated," Valefor's voice said, from somewhere on high. We looked up from the book and didn't see Val himself, but his voice continued, "The abrogation is draining me, pulling me back into weakness, and now that Flora is connected to me, she'll be pulled, too, like me, from the Waking World to Elsewhere, and then to the Abyss of Nowhere."

"Break the link!" Udo commanded. "Leave Flora out of this!"

Valefor answered, still invisible, "I cannot; I haven't the strength to pull away, and neither does Flora. But if I were restored, we'd both be fine."

"Then we'll try the Restoration Sigil," Udo said. "If that's the only way."

"Finally, you all come to your senses!" Now Valefor's voice resolved into the rest of him. From the waist down, his figure had blurred into a purplish vapor, swirling and trailing like a train, and he looked airy and half transparent. "Finally, you do the right thing! Unlock my fetish, restore me, and I shall restore Flora!"

"You—" Udo made a lunge at him, but all for nothing, because Valefor whisked out of his reach, drifting up to float near the ceiling. "How could you do that to Flora?"

"Was it my fault she didn't know her own weakness? I'm just a poor redacted denizen, powerless and forlorn. I looked to you for succor, Flora—and look how I was taken in!"

"Taken in!" Udo shouted. He was balanced precariously on my desk chair and was trying to whack at Valefor, but Val was so wispy that Udo's snatches went right through him. "She was taken in by you, Valefor, by your promises—"

"I never promised nothing I didn't deliver! Didn't Valefor do your chores, Flora, and clean the house?"

"What price a clean house if Flora is gone?" Udo roared. "I don't want a clean house—I want Flora!"

"Stop it! Both of you. We don't have time for this!" I interjected. "Mamma will be home this afternoon, and my Catorcena is tomorrow!"

"Ayah so, but rest assured, Valefor, I'll be taking this topic up with you later," Udo said, climbing back down. "Where's that tea caddy? I'm going to get it open even if I have to smash it open. We've got to have Val's fetish."

"Smashing won't be necessary, Udo. I have the key." I fumbled in my pocket, withdrew the cord, and swung it before Udo's astonished gaze.

Udo grabbed at the cord and I let it fall into his grasp. "Pigface! Where did you get it, Flora? And why didn't you mention it earlier—"

"I got it from Poppy, just now. And, Valefor, how is it that you didn't recognize the insignia, when it was Poppy's seal all along?"

"Let me see that!" Valefor demanded, drifting down for a closer look. He snorted. "That's not Hotspur's seal! Hotspur's personal seal is Three Interlocked Rings Surmounted by a Star. I don't know whose seal that is, but—"

I cut him off. "Poppy said it was his seal, and anyway, it doesn't matter, because it's the same seal as on the tea caddy, and so it could be the dæmon Choronzon's for all I care, as long as it works."

"Flora," Udo said. He looked up from *The Eschata*. "I'm reading through the Restoration Sigil—and I think we have a problem."

"What problem?" I asked, feeling dismay start to prickle. Just when I had started to feel hopeful again.

"Well, to activate the Sigil, we need a Semiote Verb."

"A what?"

Valefor said helpfully, "A Semiote Verb is a Gramatica Word

that is so concentrated that it can only be in one place at one time. It's the most powerful type of Gramatica Word, very dangerous and not to be trifled with."

"In this case, we need the Semiote Verb *to Quicken,* in the Present Participle form," Udo said.

"And where is it?" I asked, dreading the answer.

"Bilskinir House."

THIRTY

Udo's Hot Words.
A Hot Bath. Muffins. Udo's Plan.

I SAT DOWN ON THE BED, my confidence dribbling away. Would this nightmare never end? Each time I thought we had a solution, another problem arose, and my energies were rapidly ebbing. Again I felt cold and empty, and as limp as a piece of string. "We can't do it, Udo. Paimon will eat us up! He'll gobble us down!"

"Oh, pooh!" said Valefor. "Paimon will do nothing of the kind."

"We can't give up, Flora. We can do it. We'll find a way," Udo entreated me. "We'll get the Word."

"I don't care if I disappear! Then I don't have to worry about going to the stupid Barracks, or stupid Poppy, or Mamma, or anything!"

Udo was horrified. "How can you say that?"

"It's the Fyrdraaca speaking," Valefor said. "It always comes out—"

I cut him off, shouting, "I don't care what happens to me! I just don't care! I'm a horrible failure and it's better this way. I thought I was so clever and rangery, and I wasn't anything at all but a *stupid heartless mindless snapperhead!*"

"Do you know who you exactly sound like, Flora?" Udo asked. He loomed over me with his arms crossed, looking lordly. "You exactly sound like Hotspur! Just exactly—'I don't care,'

'I'm so tormented,' 'If I die it'll be all the same to me,' 'Oh, leave me alone to my darkness!'"

Anger bit at me, snapping with sharp teeth, for of course he was right, and yet it made me bitterly mad to know that he was. I turned away, biting my lip hard and wanting to smack him. So much for my belief in peace—when it came down to it, I was a Fyrdraaca all the way.

"She is her father's child. What do you expect?" Valefor interjected. "But you should think, for once, of someone other than yourself, Flora."

"Shut *up*, Valefor!" Udo shouted, and then to me: "You are always complaining that he won't suck it up, that he whines like a baby, and now you are doing the same thing, Flora."

"Leave me alone, Udo!"

"You are always talking about Nini Mo and how she didn't give up. You're right—you'll never be a ranger, but not because you fail, because you *do* give up! Nini Mo failed plenty of times, and yet she kept trying. That's what made her great!"

"Leave me alone! *Get out, Udo!*" I shouted, and even to my own ears, I sounded shrewish and stupid, and that just made me angrier. His words cut me to the very bone, because even in my blackest state, I knew they were true.

"What is Buck gonna say if she comes home and finds you disappeared?" Udo demanded.

I said wildly, "Maybe she'll be glad—one less stupid Fyrdraaca for her to worry about." I pushed by Udo, past Valefor, blindingly, wanting only to get away from them, wanting only to hide. I ran down the hallway, Udo following me, and slammed the bathroom door in his face.

My chest hurt like I might cry, but no tears came. I turned the taps on the tub and, while the bath filled, looked at myself in the mirror. I did look slightly transparent; if I stared hard enough at my reflection, I could see through to the stained-glass window behind me. I shivered, but from cold or fear, I wasn't sure, then turned off the taps.

It was a relief to get out of my soggy clothes and slide into the hot water. I was so tired that when I yawned, it felt as though my jaw would crack. I leaned back and closed my eyes.

"Can I come in?" Udo's voice asked through the door. I sank down until the bubbles tickled my nose, then called my assent. The door opened, and the steam parted, and there was Udo, with a coffee cup in one hand and a muffin in the other.

"I brought you breakfast. Valefor's in such a cheerful mood that he broke his ban on helping, and cleaned the kitchen up." Udo set the cup and muffin on the edge of the tub and flipped the loo lid down to sit. "I'm sorry I yelled at you, Flora."

"I'm sorry, too," I said in a small voice. I reached a soapy arm for the cup. It was perfect: hot, sweet, and milky. Udo always remembers how I like my coffee.

Udo continued, "But you drive me mad when you talk like Hotspur, and there is no reason for it."

"But we just get in deeper and it just gets harder, Udo," I said. "And I feel so tired and slow. I can't go on."

"That's because Valefor is sucking your Will away, Flora. You gotta remember what you feel isn't real. It's just a symptom of the problem, not the problem itself. You know, you aren't the only one who feels pretty bad about last night, Flora—"

"Maybe, but—"

"Let me finish—but I can't afford to feel bad right now. I have a plan and I'm gonna do it, Flora, and if you don't wanna go, then that's fine, I'll do it myself. I'm going to Bilskinir and I'm going to get that Word, and then we'll restore Val and you'll be all right."

I felt tears burn and hoped that Udo would think it was just the steam. He was really too good to me. "How are you going to do that? Remember what the CPG said about the kids on the field trip getting eaten?"

"The CPG is just trying to sell papers; you can't believe anything you read there—remember last year when they ran that exposé claiming that the Warlord turns into a flamingo on the full moon? Valefor told me that Paimon was never that strong to begin with; he was really wrapped up with the Haðraaða family, and without them in the House to sustain him, he's probably withered away by now. I'm sure that he'll be no problem, and just in case, I'll be supersneaky. I reckon if I can get by Mam's curfew, I can get by some scrawny denizen."

"But what about that blue light we saw from the beach?"

"Valefor says there's a lighthouse. It's probably an automaton."

"But Bilskinir's a big House, even if there is no Paimon—how will you find the Word?"

Udo grinned and looked smug. "You should see how eager Valefor is now; he's practically rolling around like a hoop to be helpful. He found me this book." Udo displayed a small gilt-edged volume, *Califa in Sunshine and Shade: A Guide to the City and All Its Environs, Both Savory and Sweet.* "It has an entire chapter on Bilskinir, with a map, even. See"—Udo opened the book and began to read—"'. . . and most assuredly not to be missed is the Saloon of Embarrassment of Riches. Here is kept the Haðraaða family's greatest treasures, including Banastre Haðraaða's gilded baby shoes, the Bilskinir Dollhouse, the Orb of Great Golden Weight, the Plushy Pink Pig, and several Semiote Verbs.' It will be as easy as pie, Flora. I won't be gone more than a couple of hours, and we'll have plenty of time to restore Valefor before Buck gets home, and you'll be as good as new. What do you say?"

I closed my eyes. Udo, alone, risking for me; Udo's plan, which actually sounded like a pretty good one. I guess not all my Will was gone, because when I dug down deep inside to the depths of my heart, I found that I did not really want to vanish, leave Flynnie, leave Udo, leave Mamma. Would Nini Mo give up? She was my role model. Poppy was not.

A ranger is made, not born, Nini Mo said. *A ranger doesn't give in, or give out.*

I was born a Fyrdraaca, but I could make myself a ranger. I was tired and I wanted to sleep, but what fun is sleep if you do not dream—and do not wake?

I opened my eyes.

Udo, looking damp and wilted in the steam, said, "Well?"

"Hand me my robe and get out," I answered, and he grinned in relief.

THIRTY-ONE

Bilskinir.
The Causeway. Waves.

Rangers are masters at sneaking; it is their very rationale, their nature, their Will. Nini Mo snuck into the Virreina of Huitzil's seraglio and snuck the sixteen-year-old Infanta Eliade right out from under her mamma's nose before the Infanta could be sacrificed to the Huitzil goddess of rain. Then Nini Mo escorted the Infanta to Califa, where she married the Warlord and lived happily ever after.

If Nini Mo could sneak into the Virreina's seraglio and sneak the future Warlady out, then surely we could sneak into Bilskinir and steal a Semiote Verb. Of course we could, and then we would go home, restore Valefor, and live happily ever after, too.

Of course we could.

My heart remained optimistic, at least a little, but the rest of me was starting to feel pretty draggy. My head hurt, and my tummy growled with a hunger that even the maple-nut muffin couldn't satisfy.

We were going to miss another day of school, but that hardly seemed worth worrying about now. Even when Udo spends the night at Crackpot, he still has to walk the kiddies to school. So when he ran off to do that, I went down to the kitchen to try to plug the hole in my tum with a pound of bacon and two bowls of oatmeal.

An hour or so later, Udo returned, with egg-and-cheese on a roll and the extremely good news that a huge fog bank was moving through Ocean's Gate into the Bay and that Cow Hollow Harbor would be fogged in by noon. This meant that Mamma's ferry was sure to be delayed, buying us a little more time.

When we went to saddle the horses, we discovered that Mouse had thrown a shoe. There was no time to call the farrier; we'd have to double up on Bonzo, and this we did. Once again we rode out of the City, into the Outside Lands, via Portal Pass, only this time, when we reached the fork where Sandy Road goes south toward the Zoo Battery, we turned north onto Point Lobos Road.

The day, which started so sunshiny, had, as Udo predicted, turned cold and chilly. Even swaddled in Poppy's buffalo coat, I was cold, oh-so-cold, and glad that Udo rode behind me, for he radiated heat like a hot-water bottle. In front of me, Flynnie rode draped like a sock over my pommel. Twice we had tried to return him to Crackpot, and twice he had somehow caught up with us; finally, we had to let him come, but he hadn't been able to keep up. Luckily, Bonzo is pretty strong, and Flynn doesn't weigh much, and he was warm, too, although boney.

The easy rhythm of Bonzo's walk lulled me into a haze. I felt drifty and half asleep, or maybe I *was* asleep and this was all a dream—

"Look!" Udo pointed.

We had crested the Point Lobos Hill, and there, ahead, Bilskinir stood, silhouetted against a hovering fog bank. The House sits on a tall promontory, at the northern edge of the Pacifica Playa, and the rocks upon which it perches looked black as the best dark chocolate. They rose straight up from the water, so sheer that I'd wager not even a lizard could find foothold upon the glassy stone, and where the cliffs ended and the foundations of Bilskinir began was hard to say. I had never been this close to it before, and it struck me now that the House looked dark and ominous, almost brooding.

"What style do you think that is?" Udo asked. Flynnie wiggled and kicked, so I pushed him down off Bonzo. He skidded down the sand dune and rushed to the waterline, flushing a flock of seagulls off the sand.

"I don't know. Early Awful Baroque? It looks a bit like a wedding cake," I answered, yawning.

"An evil wedding cake."

"How can a wedding cake be evil?"

"It can be black, and ominous, and evil."

A roadway, rotten and broken, started at the beach and undulated up the side of the cliff, becoming lost from view around the northern edge. The smooth sandy beach gave way to rocks, scooped with shallow tidal pools, clotted with seaweed. Seagulls swooped and curled, their yelping cries echoed by the distant barking of sea lions.

I urged Bonzo down onto the beach, toward the roadway. Flynn scrabbled ahead of us, nosing seaweed and splashing through the water, barking at any bird that had the gall to come too close.

Soon we stood at the very root of the House, and its height above us seemed enormous and pressing. When I tilted my head back, the perspective swayed and wavered, and for a sickening second, I thought the entire House—turrets, spires, domes, buttresses, gingerbread, and all—was about to slide down upon our heads.

The tide was coming in, a green scrim of water surging up over the beach. Each wave came a little higher, and fell back a little less. The bottom of the roadway had flooded out, but I hoped not very deeply.

"How long do you think it takes for the tide to come in?" I asked Udo, pulling Bonzo to a halt, just above the water's edge.

"Not long," he said. "It's rising awful fast."

I didn't ask Udo how high he thought the tide would get. By the damp discoloration of the sand and the seaweed on the rocks, I could tell this part of the beach would be entirely flooded at high tide, and a good part of the roadway, as well.

"And then how long until the tide goes down?"

"Six hours, give or take."

"I hope Mamma is very delayed," I said dolefully.

"Or maybe Bilskinir has a back door," Udo suggested. "The guidebook didn't say anything about one, but there has to be a way out other than across the beach. Look: Snapperdog!"

Flynnie had abandoned his sniffing and was now splashing through the surf. He climbed onto a piece of the broken causeway and turned to look back at us, barking.

"Snapperdog says we are falling behind," Udo said.

"Flynn! Get back here!" I shouted, but Snapperdog is notorious for ignoring commands, and he ignored this one, too. He bounced down off the broken bit of causeway, disappeared into a smack of surf, and when the wave pulled back, reappeared higher up on the road, shaking off water.

I could not let Flynn go where I would not follow, so I put heel to Bonzo and nudged her on. The water splashed around us, first just lapping the edge of the road, wetting Bonzo's hooves. If that had been all, it would have been easy as pie, just as Udo had promised. But it seemed that as the road rose, curving up around the side of the cliff, so, too, did the waves rise higher and higher, keeping pace with the roadway's ascent.

I gave Bonzo her head, trusting that she knew better than I how firm her footing was, and she moved toward the shelter of the cliff side, as far from the edge as she could get. Ahead, through the spray, Flynn could be occasionally seen bouncing from rock to rock. The ocean was surging ever upward, and falling back less and less, so that soon Bonzo's fetlocks were wet. We drew our feet up as high as we could, to try to keep our boots dry.

"Good girl, good girl," I cooed. Bonzo's ears flickered and she continued onward, her head down, her muscles rolling under my thighs. Once she staggered, sliding, and for an awful second, I thought we were done for. I dropped the reins and grabbed at her mane, clamping on to her as hard as I could. Udo nearly cut off my breathing with his squeeze. Icy cold water surged, soaking us, but then Bonzo recovered her footing.

I twisted, craning my neck, and saw that the roadway behind us had vanished into the swirling gush of the incoming tide. *There's no way out but through.*

"This totally sucks!" Udo shouted, and I could not argue with him. I'm not afraid of the water, but these waves were strangely insistent, like grabby hands trying to snatch us, to drag us under. I twisted the reins tightly around my hands and was, finally, glad for Udo's viselike grip around my middle.

Bonzo, solidly, ignored the grabby water. Her head hanging low, she continued onward as surefooted as a mule. Now the sea was up above the stirrups, and I could not pull my feet any higher. Water slapped into my eyes; I blinked the sting away and wiped at my face with a wet sleeve. The coldness felt like acid eating at my flesh. My frozen fingers could hardly grasp the reins. Now the water was up to Bonzo's chest, swirling and sucking. The roar was thunderous.

Udo knocked me in the ribs, pointing, and I pushed my sodden hair out of my eyes. We had rounded a curve, and I could see ahead, at the top of a steep grade, the tall structure of a gate. A red figure posed in front: Flynn. If Snapperdog could make it, so could we.

Suddenly the waves fell back, and the water began to ebb. In a few seconds, the road was clear again, although still slick with seawater. The ocean had gone as flat as paper, the tide high, but not high enough to reach the road. And then a swell appeared on the water's smoothness, a swell that grew into a bulge and elongated upward into a wave.

With no urging from me, Bonzo broke into a jog, her hooves skittering on the wet rocks.

"Flora!" Udo moaned in my ear.

"I know—hold on. We'll be okay. Come on, Bonzo, come on, girl."

Higher and higher the wave grew, stretching like molten glass until it hung over us like a liquid ceiling, translucent blue and green, and still it did not surge downward. Even if Bonzo had been in the clear to canter, she would not be able to outrun the wave's break. But it did not break, only grew higher and higher. For a second, a minute, an hour, an eternity, the entire sea hung over our heads, heavy and smothering.

Then the wave collapsed. The noise was incredible, like the roar of a mob, or an avalanche, or a hundred cannons firing at once, or a thousand soldiers screaming together. My life did not flash before my eyes, like in books, but I thought of what Mamma would say when she found out that I had gotten Bonzo drowned, and that now she could not be mad about Valefor, and that I hoped I would see Udo on the other side, and I wished I'd been a bit nicer to Poppy, and—

Suddenly I realized the noise was receding and I was not drowned. I opened my eyes and saw that the water had been flung back by some invisible barrier. Bonzo had stopped and was looking about, bemused. Above us, around us, water thrashed and pounded, but not a drop touched us. Each time a wave rose, for a few seconds we were in a luminous tunnel of blue and green. Then the water would be repelled and the dreary daylight returned. The roadway was now smooth and dry.

"I think I just lost fifteen years off my life," Udo said. "And I almost pissed my drawers. Maybe I did piss my drawers. I'm so wet, I cannot tell."

A few more steps and we had reached the top of the road. Somehow I would have thought the gate to Bilskinir would be enormous and nasty, with spikes and bars and thorns and maybe gargoyles spitting boiling oil. But it wasn't. It was a plain white wooden gate, set in a plain white wooden fence, not so high as Bonzo's head. It was open.

Before this ordinary gate, Flynnie sat, licking his bottom while he waited for us. Beyond the threshold lay an immaculate sand driveway, as white and smooth as new snow. The sky ahead, framed through spreading trees, was as bright as blue paint, and the air was hushed and tranquil.

Looking over my shoulder, I saw that the waves had resumed their fury and were hitting the roadway hard. The crash of the surf shuttered us in, and I could no longer see the Playa

below. In contrast to the bright day before us, behind us the sky
was still gray.

Once again, Flynnie was point dog; while we hesitated, he
bolted onward. No giant Butler swooped down to snatch him
up as a tasty mouthful, and this emboldened us. But before I
could touch her sides with my heels, Bonzo took matters into
her own hooves and shot forward as though she had been spiked
from behind.

She flew through the gate and down the path, hooves kicking up all the nice white sand. I yanked hard on the reins and
not a whit did she slow down. We tore down the roadway, which
curved through a copse of tall shady trees, and rushed through
bright flower beds, blossoms kicking up around us.

"Whoa! Whoa!" I hollered.

Udo jounced behind me, his chin banging hard into the top
of my head, knees knocking into my sides. Bonzo shifted from
the jarring trot into an effortless canter. That made it easier to
stay on, but I could still not stop her.

"Hold on!" I could feel Udo starting to slip behind me, but
I couldn't do anything other than saw back and forth uselessly
on the reins. Ahead, the trees broke open to the blue sky and
the bulk of a gray stone building.

"I am holding!" Udo shouted.

"Whoa, whoa, whoa!" Something loomed up in our path—a
sundial, I think—and Bonzo bounded over it like a jackrabbit.
Then suddenly she skimmed into a halt, but Udo and I kept going and tumbled over her neck, toward the hard ground.

THIRTY-TWO

Kinda Creeping.
Not So Crawling. Caught.

WE WERE MUSSED, grass-stained, and breathless, but otherwise all right. My side burned from Udo's pointy elbow, and my back hurt from landing hard on the grass. The pain felt surprisingly good: It proved I was still solid. Flynnie stood over me, licking and drooling. I hadn't been dumped in years, and now twice in as many days; Nini Mo would not be proud.

"Get off!" I pushed at Flynnie, and heaved up to my feet. Bonzo had already recovered and was now tearing great gobs of grass out of the lawn, as though she had never done a snapperhorse thing in her entire life.

Udo clambered to his feet, grimacing at the grass stains on his jacket. "Now I'm wet *and* dirty." He wrung out the hem of his kilt and straightened his hat. "But at least I am alive."

"For the moment," I said sourly.

The way we had come was a wreckage of bent branches, torn turf, and crushed flowers. So much for our sneaking in. I hoped hoped hoped that Paimon was truly puny and weak, or we would be in serious trouble.

"You'll dry," I told Udo. "Come on. We should keep moving."

I retrieved Bonzo's reins and pulled her from her chomping. The weather had completely changed. No longer chill and foggy, the air felt warm and springlike, and the sky sparkled with gentle sunshine. I took my soggy buffalo coat off and shoved it into one of Bonzo's saddlebags. Bonzo's stampede had led us deep into the gardens, and now there was no sign of the House itself.

"Come on—we have to find the House. We don't have any time to waste."

"Flora," Udo said, very quietly and carefully. "Look."

Flynnie, who had been twisting around my feet, went taut and anxious. His tail sprang up, and his back drew out, his nose pointing. I followed his point, then froze.

Three red dogs stood in the middle of the sandy white drive, staring at us. Each of them was nearly as high as my waist, and they had squat toadlike heads with huge wide-set eyes and ears clipped into batlike triangles. Their massive jaws looked like they could snap up Flynnie with one crunch. They looked like they could snap up *Udo* in one crunch.

"Don't move," I hissed to Udo without taking my gaze from the dogs. They stared back impassively. Out of the corner of my eye, I saw Flynn's brushlike tail cautiously move from side to side. Carefully, slowly, maintaining my stare, I reached for Flynn's collar with my free hand and got it tight in my grip.

"Good doggies, nice sweet doggies!" said Udo brightly, friendly. The dogs ignored him; their silent contemplation was all about Flynn. Bonzo had taken advantage of my distraction to go back to grazing, and I didn't dare make a strong enough gesture to pull her head back up again. But the dogs ignored her, as well. I wished I had a weapon, a stick, a rock, anything, but I was afraid to move.

"Sweet darling puppies," Udo said encouragingly. "Precious sweet *babies*."

Then, Flynn yanked and jerked in my grip, trying to pull away. Though he's wiry, he's strong, and he easily tore out of my hold.

"Flynn!" I shouted. But of course Snapperdog paid me no never mind, just continued his headlong hurtle toward the Dogs of Doom.

They broke formation and flung themselves forward with a

sudden chorus of rumbly barking, which was answered by Flynn's hysterical yip. Flynn and the three strange dogs crashed together, and for one horrible sickening moment, I thought that was it. But instead of dissolving into a frenzy of snappy teeth and tearing jaws, they dissolved into a scrimmage of nose-licking and bottom-sniffing. Flynn began to spray with joy, turning around and around in ecstatic circles.

One dog bounced over to Udo and tried to lick his face, and another shoved his head under my hand to be petted: His thick silver-studded collar had an enamel badge on it that read BUMMER.

"You scared the stuffing out of me, Bummer," I said, rubbing his pointy ear. Bummer looked up at me, grinning a doggy grin, and licked my hand in a doggy apology. "Can you show us the way to the House?"

In answer, Bummer set off down the driveway at a trot, the other dogs falling in behind him. I tied Bonzo's reins to one of the lightposts that lined the drive, promised her we'd be back soon, and Udo and I followed.

Bummer diverged from the driveway onto a brick walkway. It curved around huge circular flower beds brilliant with ramrod-straight tulips, ambled through a copse of tall flame-tipped beech trees and droopy eucalyptus. The stillness was broken only by the purring of the fat doves preening on the close-cropped lawns and the papery rasp of the breeze-tossed leaves.

"The grounds look in awful good shape," Udo said, uneasily. "Don't you think if Paimon were really weak that they'd be a mess, like Crackpot?"

"Ayah." The same dismal idea had occurred to me. I thought about the invisible wall that kept the waves from washing us away, and I looked at the dogs cavorting with Flynnie, so sleek and well-groomed. These were not hungry dogs, and this was not an abandoned garden. Outside Bilskinir's grounds, the day had been cold and gray; here were gorgeous sunshine and clear skies. These were not the signs of a paltry starved denizen. A little tiny fear shivered in my blood. To keep everything so nice must require a great deal of power, and Bilskinir House had been empty of its family for over fifteen years.

Something was nourishing Paimon and keeping him strong.

I just hoped it wouldn't be us. Nini Mo said, *If you can't be secret, then you should be speedy.* "Let's hurry," I said, "and then get out of here."

"Ayah, let's," Udo agreed, and we picked up our pace.

The dogs trotted by a shrubbery clipped into the shape of a rearing gryphon, and by another, shaped like a manticore. We went down a slow slope of wide marble steps and by a flat reflecting pool. In the pool's center, the bronze figure of an archer stood tippy-toe, taut in the act of pulling back her bowstring. The water flickered with orange and white, and two bulbous eyes peered up at us: a fish the size of a large house cat.

"That's the biggest goldfish I've ever seen," Udo said. The fish flipped a fin against the surface of the water, splashing him, and he drew back in surprise. "I meant that nicely."

"Never mind the fish—come on."

But Udo lingered and the fish splashed at him again, this time smacking its tail and sending up a soaking sheet of water.

Then, behind us, a deep dark voice: "She wishes to be fed, but dinner is not yet ready. She must wait."

A chill started at the bottom of my feet and worked its way up, leaving my blood freezing cold in its wake. Udo stared at me, his eyes as round as marbles, his face a sudden sickly white. We were stock-still, and did not dare turn around. The back of my neck prickled coldly.

"Ave, Madama Fyrdraaca Segunda and Sieur Landaðon Uno." The voice was so rumbly I could feel the vibration in the back of my throat, and it reminded me, somehow, of chocolate, yet a silvery strand of lightness ran through it as well, like the gentle ring of a bell.

Udo and I turned around, and my hand groped for his. We squeezed, tight as death, and as damp.

Paimon loomed, taller than me, taller than Udo, taller than

Mamma. He wore a blindingly white flannel suit, and white patent leather shoes, long and pointy, like loaves of bread. A white straw skimmer hid most of his face, but not the tips of the tusks, or the long mustachio protruding beyond the brim of the hat. The tusks looked very sharp, and the mustachio was a lovely shade of velvety blue. I wasn't sure I wanted to know exactly what the brim of that hat was hiding. One enormous blue hand held a basket of violets, and another violet was tucked in his lapel.

"Welcome to Bilskinir House," he said, and again I felt the vibration of his deep voice in the back of my throat.

"Ave, sieur denizen, thank you, ave," I squeaked. I made a deep courtesy and, despite my quaking knees, managed to make it down and up again without falling over.

"Ave, sieur denizen," said Udo. His voice had dropped about four octaves. He gave Paimon a courtesy bow that was deep and flourishing and involved much inclining of head and waving of hat. Blast, I'd given Paimon the courtesy Respect to an Elder. Udo had given him the courtesy owed to a ruler, or overlord. Better idea.

The dogs gave Paimon no courtesy at all. They frisked joyously around his feet, bouncing and licking, pawing at his knees. He pushed them down gently with an enormous hand, whose fingernails, I couldn't help noticing, were as silver and sharp as pins.

"Well then, Flynn, I am pleased to see you again, as well," Paimon said. "Sit."

Flynn, who had never obeyed such a command in his life, promptly sat, looking up expectantly. Paimon's hand looked like it could squash his skull like a grape, but instead Paimon used those pinlike fingernails to scratch Flynn's ears. Flynnie closed his eyes and looked blissful.

"Thank you for receiving us, sieur," Udo said. "Your House is magnificent, and we are privileged to be granted this honor."

"I am honored by your visit," Paimon responded, and his courtesy was so low that his azure mustachio trailed on the ground.

Paimon looked as solid as bricks, as bright as noontime. He did not look the slightest bit forlorn or paltry—or hungry, for that matter, though this was no reassurance. To be that robust, he had to be well-fed, and what was he eating, then, if not tres-passers and those who strayed too close to his boundaries?

"We made a bit of a—I mean, there was a mess. Bonzo got too excited. I am very sorry, sieur denizen," I said, not particularly suavely. "Very very sorry."

Paimon gazed down at me and rumbled, "Think nothing of it. Bonzo was just in a hurry to get home."

"Home?" Udo asked.

"Ayah so. Did you not know that she was born in my stables? General Haðraaða Segunda rode her, and then, upon the General's death, she went to General Fyrdraaca. Who, I hope, is well?"

"Very well, sieur." I was amazed at Bonzo's secret history, but now her stampede made sense. After her ordeal in the water, she was eager to get back to a place she recognized.

"Come. You are wet and bedraggled, and I would not like to see you become ill. Will you do me the honor of coming this way?"

We had no choice but to follow, and so we did, not daring to protest. Now did not seem a good time to mention that we were there on a mission of thievery. Now did not seem like a good time to say anything at all. *Silence is bliss,* said Nini Mo.

So we followed Paimon past the fountain and through an arch in an enormous boxwood hedge, thick as a stone wall. Beyond the hedge lay a huge lawn, as lush as a velvet carpet, its gorgeous deep green studded with yellow and gold daisies. And there, at the far end of the lawn, was Bilskinir House itself.

No longer as dark and ominous as it had appeared from the beach, now the House glowed brilliant blue, a shade darker than the sky above. The deep blue, I realized, matched Paimon's own hue. Silver-tipped spires and turrets pointed loftily, and above all, a huge dome floated, looking like nothing so much as a giant scoop of blueberry ice cream. The roofs of Bilskinir glittered like silver fire, and the House shone like a sapphire, almost too beautiful to be real.

The dogs scattered across the lawn at a dead run, to menace the fluffy white sheep peacefully cropping the grass, but with one stern *no!* Paimon brought them back to heel. Although the lawn seemed to be as wide as a polo field, somehow we crossed it in only a few steps, and then went up a long swathe of light blue marble steps, whose risers were lined with slender trees with silver trunks and silvery blue leaves.

The stairs opened up onto a long portico, upon which sat a large round table surmounted by a cheerful blue and white umbrella. Next to the table was a tea trolley, and coming from it were the most scrumptious smells.

"Would you care for refreshments?" Paimon asked.

THIRTY-THREE

Tea. Sandwies. Explanations.

𝒲E WERE NOT ON the menu. The tea was gunpowder, my favorite, and the sandwies were egg and cress, pea-butter, and red raspberry jam. There were little heart-shaped cakes sprinkled with red sugar, dark brown gingerbread decorated with gold foil stars, and lemon meltaways. There was a cheese rarebit, and fat sweet-potato chips, and vegetable stir-fried rice. All of my favorite things to eat, oh-so-delicious and warming.

We had been prepared, if caught, for the worst. Yet here was just about the *best*: yummy food to fill the cavern that had become my belly, and Paimon so exquisitely nice, even if also somewhat overwhelmingly imposing. Nini Mo would have advised, *Be guarded,* and I was trying to be so, but the atmosphere was so ordinary, and Paimon so gracious, and the food so delicious, it was extremely hard not to be lulled. It was also hard not to gobble. With each bite, I felt a bit stronger, a bit more optimistic. Perhaps Paimon would just *give* us the Word if we asked nicely and remembered to say *please*. But the time didn't seem right yet; Nini Mo says that to be sure you get the answer you desire, you need to phrase the question nicely and to offer it at the best possible moment.

Beyond the stretch of green lawn, the patio overlooked a splendid ocean vista. The sea was only a slight shade lighter than the sky, and the color of both seemed faded compared to the House that twinkled behind us, as pretty as a spun-sugar treat. In the warm air, our clothes had already dried. The dogs had a table of their own, low to the ground, and each had a cushion to sit on and a silver plate off which to eat. Their manners were exquisite, too; they never barked or growled at each other, and even Flynnie seemed to be behaving.

While we ate, Paimon made polite conversation about the health of our families, various current events, and the latest polo scores. He was a big fan of the Monona Blowhots, who were already being called as the sure winners of this year's Pearly Mallet. Udo did most of the talking; my mouth was too busy chewing yummy delicious chow, and since Paimon was making sure that our plates never emptied, there was plenty of yummy delicious chow to chew. I felt much better.

Until I reached for my teacup, that is, and realized that I could see the vague pattern of the floral tablecloth right through my hand. I tried to pick up my knife, and it was soft in my fingers, gummy and hard to grasp.

"Ah," Paimon said, noticing my difficulty. He put the fish-shaped teapot down. "Please give me your hand, madama."

The hand he held out to me was as large as a dinner plate, blue as the twilight sky. His silver fingernails glittered. My own fingernails were purple, and Udo's were a garish cherry red, but Paimon's fingernails owed their shade to nature, not artifice, and, I noted again, they looked paper-cut sharp.

"Come now, it shall not hurt, madama," he chided.

His hand enveloped mine completely and the warmth of his grip, tight but not crushing, was reassuring. The wheeze in my chest loosened up, and some of the iciness melted from my bones. When he released my hand a few seconds later and I held it up to the light, my flesh had become blessedly solid again.

"How did you do that?" I asked.

"I gave you some of my Will, madama—but you needn't fear. You shall owe me no obligation for it. I have more self-control than young denizen Valefor does. And perhaps now is the time to discuss your problem and possible solutions to it. Please tell me all."

I let Udo tell the story, because I felt a bit foolish telling it myself. And also because my mouth was too busy chewing to talk. Somehow Udo managed to make me not sound like a complete and total idiot, and for that I was grateful to him.

"More tea, madama?" Paimon asked, when Udo had finished with a request that Paimon let us borrow the Semiote Verb, *for a while, a very short time, and we promise that we shall return it in perfect order very quickly, please, very pretty please?*

"No, thank you," I answered. I felt as full as a tick; I could not eat another bite.

"The tea was luscious," Udo said winningly. "We should hardly like to trouble you further, but the Semiote Verb is necessary to Flora's restoration. And we don't wish to sound hasty, but we are in a bit of a hurry. Flora has not much time."

"Please," I added, "please, sieur denizen, please?"

"I would be happy to give you the Verb," Paimon said. "But I cannot."

Suddenly I was hungry again. I reached for another egg sandwie, but this time it didn't taste nearly so good.

"Why not?" Udo asked.

"A Semiote Verb is extremely dangerous. Mispronounced, it could cause great harm, not only to the mouth that mangles it but also to the Waking World around it. I cannot allow it into untried hands. I beg your pardon for doubting your ability, but I must be careful."

I said piteously, "But it's my only hope. What else can I do? I shall disappear."

Paimon continued, "But besides the question of the Verb's potency, it would not affect Valefor's restoration, and therefore be of no help to Madama Fyrdraaca. Valefor has been abrogated by the Head of Fyrdraaca House—General Fyrdraaca. Only she has the power to restore him."

"Mamma," I whispered. "Mamma will kill me if she finds out what I have done."

"I doubt that very much. General Fyrdraaca has a temper, it is true, but she does not have a reputation for bloodlust. No doubt she will be angry, but hardly homicidal," Paimon answered.

"You don't know Buck," Udo said darkly.

"I think it is you who underestimate General Fyrdraaca, sieur," Paimon said. "But then I understand how it is when one wishes to avoid censure for one's actions. Anyway, I suspect that that option is moot, anyhow. General Fyrdraaca's ferry has been fogged in off Point Lobos, and the fog is not reckoned to lift until midnight. Flora doesn't have that much time; by then it shall be too late."

"I don't see any fog," Udo protested. "The sky has completely cleared."

"Within my vista, that is so. I do hate the chill and prefer the blue sky, and thus I arrange my view within my environs as such. But I assure you that outside Bilskinir's boundaries, the day is drear, and the fog thick."

Paimon could control even his weather! And Valefor said Paimon was the lesser of the Houses in the City. Why had I ever believed a word Valefor had said? What a fool—me.

"Then Flora is pegged," Udo said in anguish. "There's got to be something we can do."

"There may be," Paimon agreed. "It may be possible to destroy Valefor completely."

"But wouldn't that destroy Flora as well?" Udo asked.

"It would depend on the sigil used, and the skill of the adept."

"But I don't think I want to destroy Valefor completely," I said. "I mean, he can't really help himself, he is not supposed to be banished and he is so hungry—"

"Why are you sticking up for that pinhead, when he tried to do you in, Flora?" Udo demanded.

"He couldn't help it, maybe. It's hard to be so hungry—"

"Pah! I don't care about Valefor," Udo said hotly. "I only care about you."

"In any case, we must not act hastily," Paimon said. He stood up and began to collect our plates, then to stack them on the tea trolley. I grabbed the last cake before he whisked the plate away. Flynnie, done with his chow, came over and lay his heavy head on my lap.

"But we are running out of time," Udo protested. "You yourself said we didn't even have time to wait for Buck. We *have* to act hastily."

"I have some small influence over the passing of time within Bilskinir's boundaries," Paimon answered. "And thus I can offer you some latitude. Enough to give us time to consider alternatives. I have an idea, but I must seek advice before I offer it. Do not fear; my consultation shall not take long."

"Thank you, sieur denizen." I ignored Udo's protesting looks. "I could use a nap, and we do appreciate all your help. You have been so very, very kind."

"It is my pleasure. Come."

We followed Paimon through Bilskinir's humongous front doors, into a rotunda so lofty that the ceiling (if there was one) was lost in a sunny haze. I thought this must be the Hall of Expectant Expectations, where back in the day when the Pontifexa Georgiana Haðraaða ruled Califa, people would wait to be received by her. The hall was big enough to fit a crowd, but there was no place to sit. Here Paimon took our jackets and Udo's hat, and shooed the dogs back outside after giving them stern instructions to leave the sheep alone.

Califa in Sunshine and Shade had wasted few splendiferous adjectives in describing the House, but now I realized that no splendiferous adjective would ever do Bilskinir justice. The House was so splendiferous that I could not take all the splendor in; everywhere I looked, straining both neck and eyes, was such glory that it almost made me dizzy. We rode upstairs in an Elevator the size of a small boudoir, with walls lined in blue flocked velvet and mirrors that made it seem as though there were a dozen Udos and a dozen Floras. But there was only one denizen: Paimon had no reflection.

After escorting us down a hallway whose length was punctuated with portraits of dogs, Paimon halted in front of an enormous door. It opened, with no obvious action from Paimon, and he ushered us over the threshold. He clicked his heels together and bowed his enormous white-hatted head. "Rest. I shall return for you. Do not wander." The door closed behind him.

Udo reached out and tried the doorknob.

The door was locked.

THIRTY-FOUR

Sunk. A Water Elemental.
Footsteps.

"WE ARE TRAPPED!" Udo rushed to the window and rattled it, but that was locked, too. "We are trapped!"

The bedroom was decorated in an oceanic motif—if the ocean were bloodred. Crimson walls were traced with silver lines to represent the flow of water, over which swam sinuous eels, languid fish. Crimson carpets were scattered with woven shells, coral, seaweed. A polychrome mermaid perched on the huge chimneypiece, her carved crimson hair spilling over her round white shoulders and down her white bosom, to wrap around a muscular blue-green tail. A blue enamel stove crouched below the mermaid, in the fireplace cavity. A huge wardrobe, inlaid with mother-of-pearl, took up one whole wall. The bed was silver gilt, with a huge wooden tester and sangyn red curtains. Burnished blue gargoyles perched along the footboard; the tall headboard was painted with a scene of a stormy sea.

I hardly heard Udo. I climbed up on the bed, and sank into a feathery comforter that did not smell like moths, cedar, or dust. Oh, the bliss of a nap. I felt yummy-full and very tired, and reassured by Paimon's reassurances. Surely he, a great denizen, could come up with a solution to save me, and keep Mamma in the dark, and all would turn out happily after all. All I had to do now was rest.

Udo said, "The chimney is sealed. There's no way out. We are trapped. Are you just going to lie there?"

"I'm not just lying here," I said. "I'm thinking."

"Of what?"

"Of nothing."

"If you are thinking of nothing, then you are not really thinking. You should be thinking about how to get out of this trap." From the thuds and rattling, I gathered that Udo was trying the door again, and then the window.

"It's not a trap, Udo," I said, without opening my eyes. "Calm down."

"Ayah so? Flora, come on. You believed Paimon, what he said?"

"Why should I have not? He was so nice, Udo, and kind, and he said he'd help us."

"Ayah, right to the stew pot. Didn't you notice how the table was full of food, and yet he didn't eat anything? And how he kept urging food on us, as though he was fattening us up? And he never took his hat off, either, so we could hardly see his face. Don't you wonder why—what's he hiding? Slavering jaws? Fangs? And then he says he can't help us, and it is too late to get Buck to help us, so we are at his mercy, and then he locks us in here, to waste our time, until it is too late for you. How can he be so strong if he hasn't been eating someone, something? Look at Valefor—he's been alone barely fourteen years and he was hardly there, and yet Paimon looks as good as new."

I had not noticed that Paimon hadn't eaten, actually, being myself so busy eating. And Udo had a point about Paimon's obvious stability. And yet, he had been so nice, and kind, and *sincere*. Surely Udo was just being paranoid.

"Didn't Nini Mo say to expect poison from standing water?" Udo continued. The bed creaked as he sat down on it. "Flora— it's classic—you lure the prey into the trap, baited with honey, lull them, and then when they are relaxed and at their most tender, *snap* the trap shut."

"If Paimon were going to eat us," I said reasonably, "why

would he put us in the best bedroom in the House? I think from the design, this is the Bedchamber of Downward Dreaming. You should be excited, Udo. General Hardhands slept in this bed."

"And look where he is now," Udo said, which was stupid because even though Hardhands was dead, it had nothing to do with Paimon. The bed creaked as Udo stood, and then the window rattled again. "Look—Paimon said that he would slow time down, to give you more time, but the sun is going down. It'll be dark soon, Flora, and I don't want to be here after dark. Come on, Flora—focus. We have to get out of here—get that Word and get going—"

"Can I have a drink of water, Udo?"

"If I get you a drink of water, will you get up and help me figure out how to escape from here?"

"Ayah. I will, I promise," I said drowsily. Udo's footsteps stepped, then a glass clinked. "And with ice, if there is any—"

"Pigface Pogostick! Jumping Jethro-in-a-rattailed-kilt!" Udo yelped.

"You needn't swear just because I asked you for ice."

"*Hijo de mono y beso de naranja!*" I heard. "Who the hell are you, chupa?"

That wasn't Udo's voice. My eyes flew open. I crawled to the end of the bed and peered into the darkening room. Udo stood frozen, a pitcher in one hand and a glass of water in the other, and out of this glass something small and fishy was wiggling. It flipped up, and flapped a long tail as frilly and red as Udo's favorite crinoline, until it hovered in the air above the glass. It was only half fish; above where the waist would be if fish had waists was a humanish form dressed in a fancy black jacket covered with silver conchos, open to show a brilliant red weskit and a perfectly tied four-in-one cravat. Perched upon the cravat was an angry face surmounted by a top hat.

"Why did you disturb my siesta, idioto?"

"I beg your humble pardon, sieur," Udo said. "I didn't know you were in the pitcher."

The merman settled its top hat with a thump, then tugged on its weskit. "You never looked before you poured, did you, boy?"

"What *are* you?" Udo asked.

The merman scowled. "I am Alfonzo Guadaquevilla Ximenz Cimenes Perilla y Requesta, sieur." He made the tiniest of bows and tapped the brim of his hat. "I am not a *what*. I am a water elemental of the highest order, a direct descendant of Escarius of the Deep and of impeccable lineage. I need not ask what you are—that is obvious. You must be dinner. And about time, too. I am famished." The merman made a lip-smacking noise and slapped his tail on the air.

"Dinner!" said Udo. "Dinner!"

"Ayah, I can hear Paimon below, stoking the fire in the oven and mixing up marinade. And here you two are, so what else can this explain but dinner? You, sieur, look as though you might be a bit on the stringy side, but Madama"—and here Alfonzo flipped his tail and shot through the air toward me—"is quite nice and plump. A tasty little morsel, *muy dulce.* Though a bit waffly in the Will department, still tasty."

"I told you, Flora! I told you!" Udo shouted.

Alfonzo zipped around my head, flapping his tail as though he swam through water, not air, and poked at me with his cane. "You know, too, *dulcinea,* you look familiar to me. Have we met before? Elsewhere, perhaps? Madama Rose's Pirates' Parade party?"

I batted him away. "No, I don't think so. And Paimon isn't going to eat us. He said he'll help me! He was so nice."

The elemental answered, "He is a tender butcher, of course, and wishes to make your last moments happy."

"What did I say, Flora? I said so, didn't I?" Udo cried.

"I don't believe you," I told Alfonzo.

"Oh no? She who lives will see, eh? Or perhaps I should say, she who is eaten shall see. I think I shall go and I can lick the bowl. I hope there shall be sticky pudding for afters! *Mi favorito! Adiós, pequeños. Hasta la vista por cena!*"

The elemental flipped tail and hat and disappeared in a blue twinkle.

Udo looked triumphantly at me, and I looked woefully back. I didn't want to be eaten any more than I wanted to disappear to Nowhere. Would Paimon turn us on a spit like pigs? Boil us in a bag like pudding? The Huitzils sacrifice their enemies and make tamales with their ground-up bones, and mix their blood into hot chocolate and drink it. I thought of the Quetzals tearing at Boy Hansgen's bloody heart—

"I'll get the window if you get the sheets," Udo said. "We can tie them together and lower ourselves down, like the Dainty Pirate did when he was escaping from the Angeles calaboose."

My neck began to tingle.

"Udo—"

And then came the ominous sound of heavy footsteps in the hall.

THIRTY-FIVE

The Wardrobe.
A Ballroom. On the Run.

*P*AIMON!" UDO GURGLED. We clutched each other like a couple of shavetails, which didn't help a darn thing, but somehow Udo's grip was reassuring. If I would be eaten, at least I would not be eaten alone.

The door handle rattled. "Madama? Sieur Landaðon?"

"The wardrobe," Udo suggested in a strangled whisper.

Somehow we managed to stumble across the room to the wardrobe without making a huge amount of noise. Lucky for us it was so big. Despite its being stuffed full of clothing, we were both able to squeeze inside and pull the door shut behind us. We crawled as far back as we could, pulling the clothing over us, hoping for cover.

"I get points for being right," Udo hissed. "Next time maybe you'll listen to me—"

"Shush."

As the door creaked open, we froze, barely breathing in the lavender-scented mustiness. I surely hoped that Paimon could not see well in the dark, but I knew of course that he could. We huddled in agony, listening to the heavy tread enter the room.

"It is time for dinner," Paimon rumbled. Then, puzzled, "Madama? Sieur Landaðon?"

In my mind's eye, I could imagine it quite clearly: Paimon looking down in surprise at the messy bed, then lumbering about the room, lamp held high, examining each shadow for our cowering selves. He'd look under the bed, which of course would be innocent of us. He'd peer on top of the hard wooden canopy, for which he, naturally, would not need a ladder. He'd peek behind the billowing curtains; nope, we weren't there, either. We weren't crouched behind the fire screen; neither were we huddled inside the large clothespress at the foot of the bed, nor dangling by our sweaty hands from the windowsill. That left only one place where we could be, and I could picture that, too, with disturbing vividness: the wardrobe door flung wide, ruffling clothes, awful hungry roar, claws that catch, jaws that bite.

I crabbed through the clothing, pushing at the heavy folds in a panic, my wheeling arms colliding with something solid yet crunchy–Udo's nose, I was later to discover. Fighting the heavy fabric felt disturbingly like drowning, and what little air I could squeeze into my lungs was stale and flat. Then I ran into something woodenly hard: the back of the wardrobe. There was no place else to go. We were trapped.

"Madama?" Clothing rustled and moved on a current of cold fresh air. "Sieur, what are you—"

"ꝰ⊟✳⚖✕!"

Like before, the Gramatica Word popped into my brain and out of my mouth. It tasted like violets, and it whirled and gave off tiny purple sparks like fireflies. The bottom of the wardrobe fell away, and we were falling.

I landed with a hard thump, although something soft cushioned my fall. This softness was, of course, Udo, who swore at my weight and pushed me off him. I lay on my back, panting heavily. Above, a ceiling came into focus, painted with a riotous battle scene: screaming horses, spraying blood, clouds of smoke, and hacking swords.

"Pithfathe Psythopomp," Udo said, somewhat muffled. "I dink you broke by dose."

I sat up. There was just enough light to see that Udo's poor nose was a little spigot of blood, but it otherwise didn't seem too damaged. I shook out my slightly sticky hankie and tipped

Udo's head back. After a few seconds of pressure (me) and grumbling (him), the bleeding subsided and we were able to take stock of our surroundings.

The gray light showed us to be in a wide room, bereft of furniture or other décor. One long wall of windows from floor to ceiling looked out over a pale silvery sea. Waves crashed out of the darkness, hammering on the windows as though they wanted to be let in.

The opposite wall was one long mirror, reflecting both the pearly water and the rumpled forms of Udo and me. A huge fireplace—big enough to roast an entire regiment—filled the southern wall; the northern wall sank down into an orchestra pit.

"I think this must be the Ballroom of the Battle for the City of Califa," Udo said, "which is good, because it's not too far from the Saloon of Embarrassment of Riches. Though how we got here, I don't know. Where did you learn that Word, Flora?"

"It just popped into my head. Come on—we gotta keep moving. We have to get that Verb, and then get Bonzo and Flynn and get out of here."

"So now she listens and believes. Will we leave my hat behind? I loved that hat."

"Your hat is a casualty of war, Udo. We all have to make sacrifices, and that hat is yours."

"You are a hard woman, Flora Fyrdraaca," Udo said, and he grinned a little bravado grin to show me that he didn't really care about the hat, he was just trying to sound cool. "Come on. That door should lead to the Hallway of Indefinable Munificence, and then it's just a short way to the Riches place."

A door was cleverly recessed into one of the panels of mirror at the far end of the room. It gave easily under my hand and swung open to reveal an ornate hallway, plastered with clustering vines and drooping tree branches, now dusty and dull. The coast was clear; there was no sign of any hungry denizen.

Pausing midway down the hallway, Udo asked nervously, "Do you hear footsteps?"

I did hear footsteps, and not just that, but my neck was prickling again, as it had before. Somehow I knew that little prickle was Paimon, hot on our trail.

"Come on!"

We ran. Ahead of us the hallway ended in an arch and plunged down a tunnel-like flight of stairs. The risers were made of white marble swirled through with pale green streaks, and so, too, were the walls, which curved up to meet a low ceiling. Down down down we galloped, ten stairs, twenty stairs, fifty, a hundred. Down down, deeper into the green twilight that was emanating from the marble itself, a cold watery light like coldfire. The smell of the sea and the distant surge of water.

Nini Mo says that most courage comes from being too tired and hungry to be afraid anymore. If exhaustion and hunger were the hallmarks of courage, then I was the bravest person that ever lived. Yet, I didn't feel brave. I only felt sick and lost and like I had been hung out to dry in a rainstorm. Only Udo's painful grip was keeping me moving, that and the prickling on my neck that was growing more prickly by the minute. I put a hand out to touch the wall; it felt as warm as flesh, and it was vibrating slightly with the heaviness of Paimon's footsteps.

"I hope there's an elevator to take us back up," Udo said. "Going down ain't bad, but I don't relish climbing back."

"If Paimon catches us, I suppose he'll carry us back up," I said breathlessly. "I hope there's another way out."

"There's no way out but through," Udo said helpfully. "Hurry up, Flora, you are dragging."

"I'm coming, I'm coming," I puffed. Behind us the footsteps had grown louder and more rapid. Ahead of us, the stairs finally ended at an arched iron gate, its lintel twined with undulating luminescent letters that spelled out:

The Cloakroom of the Abyss

THIRTY-SIX

Dead Generals.
Dark Spaces. Caught.

ANOTHER ROTUNDA, whose diameter was much smaller than the Hall of Expectant Expectations and yet whose height seemed even more lofty. The sea smell was stronger here, thickly mingling with the pungent smell of Opanopex incense, wax, and a musty meaty odor I did not recognize. Through the still hush, I fancied I could hear the low sweeping sounds of the surf.

The center of the room was occupied by a small wooden boat beached upon a tall plinth draped in stiff red satin that obscured the boat's interior. A flickering lantern hung off the stern, and its bow took the form of a sinuous woman, her curved form and outstretched arms rising out of the wood, weed-green hair slick against her white sides. In the calm light, her eyes flickered with life and her red lips looked fresh and wet. She was, I realized, twin to the carved mermaid in the Bedchamber of Downward Dreaming.

The prickling on my neck was gone. "We lost him."

"How can you tell?" Udo asked.

"I just *know.* I don't know how but I do. I can feel him somehow when he is near, and I don't feel him now."

"Well, that's good, because I don't see any obvious way out other than the way we came, and if that way were blocked, we'd be pegged for sure."

"It's clear—he's gone—but I have to sit a minute, Udo, before

I can go up those stairs again. I'm starving, too." I sat down on the bottom step and rested my head on my knees. My tummy was burning and gurgling, and my head felt as dizzy as a dust devil.

"I'm surprised that you can think of food when you are so close to being chow yourself."

"Leave it alone, Udo."

"Flora, come and look at this."

I looked up to see that Udo had paused in front of one of the alcoves. "I can't."

"Flora—I'm serious. Come on."

I slogged myself to my feet. The alcove contained a bier, and sleeping on the bier was a sallow young girl holding a wizened baby, so shrunken its face looked like a skull. An inscription on the arch of the alcove said: SERENTHA FRYDONIA HAðRAAðA & FRYDONIE HAðRAAðA.

"Why would you sleep down here?" I asked.

"She's not asleep, I think," Udo answered. "She's dead. The Cloakroom of the Abyss is the Haðraaða family crypt."

Oh ugh and disgusting and yucky-yuck, but Udo was right. Each of the alcoves was occupied by someone who was sleeping a sleep from whence they would never awake. An old woman in a frothy blue dress, holding a perfect round orange in her hands: GEORGIANA HAðRAAðA I. A saucy little pug dog lying on a blue velvet pillow, its pink tongue poking from a slightly open black muzzle: HER GLORY'S FANCIFUL SHADOW. A man in full armor, his face hidden by a pig-snouted helmet, a sharp sword balanced on the length of his body: ALBANY BANASTRE BILSKI-NIR OV HAðRAAðA.

The bodies looked so alive, so perfectly asleep. It was hard to believe that our whispers would not wake them up. But they made me shiver. No matter how lifelike they appeared, it didn't change the fact that these pristine figures, so painted and curled and gussied up, were dead. They were cheats, facsimiles, and somehow it seemed indecent to allow them to lie there so exposed.

"I hope my hair looks that good when I have been dead three hundred years," Udo remarked, looking at an elegant old man in a flowery kimono and stiff elaborate upswept curls. EOS SABRE, according to the inscription.

The next alcove had no body, only an ivory-handled hunting whip, its slender snaky hunting lash twined around a copper-red braid, lying like a substitute effigy on the sangyn marble slab. The arch above had no inscription.

"I'll bet that one was for the Butcher Brakespeare—General Haðraaða Segunda. It's 'cause she didn't have any kids that Paimon got left all alone, I suppose," Udo said. "Wasn't her nickname Azote, and doesn't that mean 'whip'? I suppose there was nothing left of her to bury after the Huitzils ate her." He turned back toward the boat in the center of the room. "And that leaves . . . who do you think, behind those curtains?"

"I don't know and I don't care, Udo," I said. "I'm ready. Let's get going. I am so tired now, I just want it over with. Fading, or restoration, I don't care, I just want to be done."

"Come on, Flora. This may be our only time ever to be here. Aren't you the least bit curious?"

"No, Udo. I'm not. I'm just hungry and tired. We still don't have that Verb yet. Come on."

"You are no fun," Udo said, and then craftily: "Or are you scared?"

"Udo." I moaned. "We don't have time for this."

"I think Flora is scared. Flora is scared!" Udo sang gleefully. "I dare you to climb up there and look."

"I don't have to take your stupid dare, Udo, or play your stupid games. Come on, if you are so hot on it, then I dare *you* to look."

"You can't block a dare with a dare, Flora. Come on, I triple-dog dare you!"

There's no block for a triple-dog dare, and no backing out, either. And no point in further hesitation. When you must strike, strike hard, Nini Mo said, and strike them to the Abyss. I walked over to the boat—which, closer up, I realized was actually a fancy

catafalque, not a boat at all—then climbed up the little flight of
stairs and pulled aside the long billowing drape.

A prone figure lay under the slick shroud of a flag, not Califa's national flag, but a banner of sangyn silk that had no ensign.
With one tentative hand, I gingerly picked up the edge of the
fabric, drew it back, revealing a white face, a wide chest, and two
folded hands.

I didn't need an inscription to know who this was. His portrait hangs in every civic office and schoolroom in the City, and
though now that famous face was white and still, it was unmistakable. A tiny little shiver ran up my spine and into my tummy,
which began to quiver.

Banastre Haðraaða, the Warlord's Fist.

"Hardhands," Udo breathed, now leaning behind me. "Look
at him. He's a real stunner."

Hardhands was beautiful, it was true, but it was an icy-cold
beauty, glassy, and I don't think that was just because he was
dead. His hair, pulled back into a long braid tucked under his
dark red officer's sash, was as white as snow. His taut lips were the
palest pink, and his eyelashes lay like black feathers against his
paper-pale skin. Long white hands with sangyn-colored nails
were folded on his chest, as though they had once clutched something—a sword, perhaps, or maybe a pistol—but now they lay
empty, slightly cupped. He wore the sangyn-red Skinner uniform, its long sleeves trailing off the edge of the plinth, spilling to
the floor like blood, but his cheeks were not marred by the Skinner scars.

"He looks pretty good for a guy whose wife shot him in the
throat with an arrow," Udo said.

"No one ever proved that Butcher Brakespeare really shot
him in the throat—" I stopped, caught suddenly by a glance at
my hand, which still held back the curtain.

"Udo," I quavered.

The knobby lines of my bones shone through my flesh, like
rocks at the bottom of a clear mountain stream.

"Pigface Pogocrud," Udo said. "Don't panic, Flora—we still have time, I swear. It will be okay. Come on."

He pulled the flag up over that cold beautiful face, and I was glad to see it disappear. It was exactly the kind of face that could haunt you in your dreams. And my dreams were crowded enough as it was.

As we clambered down the tiny stairs and struggled to put the drapes back as they were before, there came the faint sound of footsteps. A voice drifted down the stairwell, our only way out.

The iron gate at the top of the stairwell squeaked as unseen hands pushed it open. We wasted no time frozen in fear, but scrambled about, trying to find a safe spot. The funeral urns by the doorway were far too big; the little alcoves were not big enough, and I didn't fancy getting too friendly with any of the pallid dead.

"Hey," Udo hissed. For a second, I couldn't find him, then saw a frantically waving hand and part of Udo's head, poking out from underneath the drapes that hid the bottom of Hardhands's catafalque. "There's plenty of room—hurry!"

The footsteps were closer now, ringing like bells, and I thought that I could hear the ominous scrape of claws on the marble. I skidded across the floor, almost banging myself right into the edge of the catafalque. It was a tight squeeze, sliding underneath, but I made it, sucking in a lungful of dry dusty air. Udo dropped the drape, and again we were in pitch-blackness.

The space was cramped and the stale air tasted of sickly-sweet decay. The thought dropped into my brain that perhaps the figure above was merely an effigy, and down here, bony and sharp, was the real thing, twisted sinews and gritty bones, and perhaps it did not want to share its space. I buried my face in the back of Udo's jacket, trying to choke that thought down.

The footsteps tapped, tapped, tapped, stopped.

Tapped, tapped, stopped, tapped, stopped.

"Ave?" The voice, echoing off the marble, sounded as though

it came from behind me, and I almost jumped out of my skin. I clutched at Udo, trying not to make a move, a sound, a rustle, a breath. We lay there in terrified silence, and only the mouthful of cloth I was biting kept me from screaming.

"Ave? Who's there?"

It was not Paimon's bell-like voice that spoke these words. But if not Paimon, who? The voice sounded distantly familiar. The footsteps came closer and I felt a swish of air as the drapes twitched.

"How about you, you old bastard?" the voice asked, and stairs squeaked. "Have you been gibbering around again? Snapperhead son of a bitch, it does my heart glad to see you lying there like a cold stiff log. I only rue that I was not the one who stretched you there, tinpot Pigface—"

The swearing stopped, and it was my fault. Udo's hair was tickling my nose, and though I tried to hold back the sneeze, I could not. It was a small sneeze, as muffled in Udo's back as I could make it. I held my breath and Udo pinched me, as though I needed any reminder to be quiet.

"Well now," the voice said. "I never heard of a ghost with a cold."

I stifled another sneeze, and then suddenly a hard hand was on my foot, yanking. I couldn't help it, my sneeze turned into a scream, and though I kicked and grabbed and Udo grabbed on to me, the grip was like iron and would not let me go. I slithered along the floor, underneath the drape, and then I was squirming and shrieking and kicking in the open air.

THIRTY-SEVEN

Caught Again. Where? Paimon's Hat.

WHAT HAVE WE HERE, then? A little ghost? Or a little spy?" The man with the grip inspected me at arm's length. It was a hard grip and a long arm, and the man's face was not friendly, though there was something familiar about it. In his free hand, he carried a lantern, and this he held up so its light shone on my face.

"Let her go," Udo said heroically, taking the wrong cue to exit his refuge.

"Two little spies! A matched set." The man laughed, and by this laugh, I knew him. It wasn't as hysterical as the last time I'd heard it, but it was otherwise the same.

"Poppy!" I squeaked, for it *was* Poppy. A Poppy strangely different, but Poppy all the same. No mourning band was painted across his eyes, and without its smudging, he looked younger, his face fuller, less skeletal. The Skinner scars on his cheeks looked vivid, fresh. His eyes were clear and steady, and the arm that held up the lantern showed no sign of injury or constraint.

And his hair! A copper-red braid the exact shade of a brand-new glory hung over his left shoulder and trailed down to tuck into the sash of his dressing gown. As long as I could remember, Poppy's silver hair had been cut razor short, almost to his skull. Mamma and Idden are both blonde, but my hair is red, and now I knew why.

"Poppy! It's me, Flora!" I cried.

"What are you doing here, Hotspur?" Udo asked.

Poppy squinted. "You know me?"

"Of course we do. You are Reverdy Anacreon Fyrdraaca, called Hotspur," Udo answered.

"Ayah so, but who are you?"

"But it's me, Flora—me. Your daughter, Flora, and Udo, too. See, it's Udo. Don't you know us?"

Poppy said grimly, "It is true that I have a daughter named Flora, but she is only six years old, and home, tucked safely into bed, I hope. And I don't know any Udo." Poppy let me go. "I think Paimon should explain what is going on here—"

"No!" Udo and I shouted, almost together. "Not Paimon."

"Look, Poppy," I said, desperately. "Look!" I yanked at my collar, and pulled out my identification badge. Mamma insists that Idden and I (and the dogs, too) wear our badges all the time. One side has my name; the other, the Crackpot seal. It is to identify us in case we are ever lost. I guess I was pretty lost now.

Poppy took the badge and held it in the lantern light. "'Flora Nemain Fyrdraaca ov Fyrdraaca,'" he read, and then looked at me, wonderingly. "I recognize that badge; I had it made when you were born. Flora! Why are you so old? What happened?"

"I don't know, Poppy. We got lost in the House, running from Paimon, Udo and me, and somehow now we are here, and you are, too—"

Udo interrupted, "I think that time is out of whack here. Paimon said he'd slow it down, but maybe he's turned it too far back or moved it forward or something."

"How old are you, Flora?" Poppy asked.

"Thirteen—I mean, fourteen. Tomorrow," I answered.

"Look at you, Flora! Your hair was so fair, and now it's so red, and what on earth are you wearing? Is fashion so bad in the future? Come and kiss me, baby."

Normally I don't like to hug Poppy, but this time I went to his embrace willingly. Poppy's arms were strong and warm, and he smelled of pipe weed and bay rum. I kissed him, his cheek scratchy beneath my lips, and hugged him so tightly that he gurgled in mock alarm. He said, over my head, "And who, darling boy, are you?"

"He's my best friend, Poppy. Udo Moxley Landaðon ov Sorrel," I said into Poppy's soft woolen chest.

"Sorrel? Moxley has a son—wait until I tell him! He'll be so tickled!"

Udo said in a strangled voice, "My father! You know my father?" Udo's birth father was killed before Udo was born, and though he still has two fathers, I think it bothers him that he never got a chance to meet the one who engendered him.

"Of course. Damn, if only Moxley weren't at the War Department with the General, we could march straight up and say hello. I'm sure he'd be thrilled to meet you."

"My father was Buck's adjutant?" Udo said, bewildered.

"Buck—a general!" Poppy laughed. "I told her she'd never escape family fate! General Fyrdraaca—that's hilarious. No, not Buck, but General Haðraaða Segunda. Your father and I are her aides, which is why we live here at Bilskinir. And let me tell you, I've had some pretty strange things happen to me in this House. Once, I was on the way to the loo in the middle of the night, and a set of tiger fire irons chased me—and they would have gotten me, too, if I hadn't managed to beat them down with a hat stand. But never this strange as to meet my own grown daughter. Tell me, why on earth were you hiding under Hardhands's bier?"

"We were running from Paimon—he is going to eat us!" Udo answered. "He's still going to eat us if he catches us. You've got to help us, Hotspur!"

"Don't worry about Paimon, I can handle him," Poppy answered. "Now, darling, don't cry."

I couldn't help it. It was all too much. To be so hungry and then so full and then so hungry again. Being chased, hiding, and now this Poppy, tall and true and beautiful, and talking very fast but not the least bit crazy. Poppy as he once was, as I had never known him. Sane. Beautiful. Normal.

"Poppy," I gasped. "I'm in terrible trouble—"

"Ha! I doubt that any trouble you are in is any worse than any trouble I have been in. I am the troublemaker in this family, I'll have you know!"

Udo said, "Well, it is pretty bad, Hotspur."

Poppy squeezed me tightly. "I'll be the judge of that. Did you accidentally burn down the Redlegs' hay shack?"

"No—"

"Did you get caught stealing the Warlord's best hat for a dare?"

"No—"

"Did you lose twenty-five thousand divas at whist?"

"No—"

"Well, then, my title remains secure," Poppy said triumphantly.

I moaned. "It's worse than all that. Mamma shall kill me if she finds out—"

Udo interrupted, "Look—Flora's disappearing. We don't really have time to explain. We came to Bilskinir to get one of the Semiote Verbs—it's the only thing that will fix her, but Paimon won't help us."

"We'll see about that," Poppy said grimly. "If Flora is in trouble, Paimon will be helpful, or he'll be sorry. *Paimon!*"

"No!" Udo and I yelled together. "He'll eat us—"

"Ha! I'd like to see him try to eat my child! *Paimon!*" Poppy hollered.

My neck began to prickle. With an audible pop, the air before us whirled into a Vortex, whose diameter grew wider and wider, until Paimon stepped out of the nimbus of blue coldfire.

Udo gave a little shriek, a squeaky little mouselike sound that didn't sound heroic at all. My own scream didn't sound particularly heroic, either. But I couldn't help it.

Paimon had taken off his hat.

THIRTY-EIGHT

Paimon's Suggestion.

*P*AIMON'S HAT HAD only hinted at what lay beneath its shadowy brim: a peek of blue mustachio, a twinkle of tusks. But without the hat, the full monstrousness of Paimon was revealed in all its monstrousness. Two great curling horns, as thick as my neck, sprang from a broad blue forehead. Eyebrows as tufty as mice shadowed round blue eyes, whose pupils were narrow and slitty, like a goat's. Silver spectacles balanced on a leathery black oxlike nose. His jaw, big enough to chomp me up in one bite, supported the enormous tusks that sprang from either side of his enormous mouth, filled with equally enormous white teeth, as large as domino tiles. Long fringy ears, somewhat like a cocker spaniel's, framed this grotesque face, their prettiness making the rest of Paimon's face seem all the more horrible in comparison.

When he saw us and Poppy, Paimon's eyebrows lowered and his mouth opened, roaringly: "Major Fyrdraaca, what are *you* doing here? Flora, Udo, I have been looking everywhere for you."

"Poppy! Don't let him eat us!" I cried. Udo and I had scurried behind Poppy at the first sight of Paimon, and now I peered around his back, not able to take my eyes off the denizen. I had never seen anyone so big or so blue. The Quetzals were the marriage of bird and human, and each taken alone would be

fine. It was this unnatural combination that caused their gro-
tesqueness. But Paimon was like nothing else I had seen before,
the monster from a nightmare, the horror under your bed, the
thing that gets you on the way to the loo in the middle of the
night.

"Eat you!" Paimon said in dismay. "Eat you! Where did you
get the idea I would eat you?"

Udo answered, "That water elemental—Alfonzo—*said* you
were going to eat us."

Paimon rolled his golf-ball-sized eyes and looked a little
hurt. "Alfonzo is extremely untrustworthy. You should not
listen to him. I have no intention of eating anyone."

"Never mind the eating, Paimon," Poppy said. "What the
hell is going on here? Why is Flora here, strangely aged, and why
is she disappearing? And why won't you help her?"

Paimon sighed, a sigh that was almost a roar. "There has
been some terrible misunderstanding. I knew I was thrown off
balance, but I didn't think it was that bad. Madama Fyrdraaca's
current instability is disruptive, and this disruption has made
your times overlap. I apologize for the confusion; this is really
not good. You should not have met. It's bad precedent. You
must go back, Major Fyrdraaca."

"No matter, that. It's only eight years," Poppy said impatiently. "We have met, and now I want you to help Flora. Give
her what she needs."

Eight years? This could not be Poppy eight years ago. I remembered that Poppy well. That Poppy had ruined the slumber
party I had for my sixth birthday by climbing onto the roof of
the stables and howling like a coyote all night long. This was not
that Poppy. With horror, I realized he thought I was the other
Flora. He was trying to save the First Flora. He didn't know me
at all.

"Poppy, I'm—," I started to say, but Paimon interrupted.

"What she asks for is useless. The solution she has suggested
will not solve her problem." Paimon's words were directed at
Poppy, but he aimed a glinty blue twinkle at me that clearly

meant *Not another word,* and so glinty was that twinkle that I had
to obey.

"And what exactly is this problem?" Poppy asked.

I will do the explaining, said that glinty blue twinkle, and explain Paimon did—an explanation that was basically the truth,
with one big exception: He didn't mention that Valefor was
banished, only that he and I had become intertwined and I was
attempting now to extricate myself, before I disappeared. And
he did not explain that I was the *Second* Flora.

If only that blue glint would glint elsewhere, I would protest,
but then it occurred to me that Paimon did not want Poppy to
know the details of the future, and I saw that was probably right.
Would I want to know that my future was lost, that my sanity
hung by a thread, that only failure and pain lay ahead? Probably
not. But still, I wished that Poppy would know it was *me.*

When the story—still woeful for all that it was now shorter—
was over, Poppy shook his head. "That Valefor is a tricky one.
Watch him like a hawk. He's sweet, mostly, but boy, can he be
trouble when he wants to be. Buck has to keep close tabs on
him. Well, obviously, we need to call Buck. She'd get Val back in
line pronto."

Udo said, "Buck's away, and she won't be back in time to
save Flora. By the time she returns, it will be too late."

"Now, I could send Buck a letter. She'd get it and be fore-
warned about the future," Poppy said.

"Ayah, but you didn't, because if you had, then she'd know
already," Udo pointed out. "And she wouldn't have gone anywhere."

"Ayah, that is true enough," Poppy admitted. "Paimon, can
you slow Flora's evaporation down? Keep her from disappearing until Buck returns? Don't worry, honey. Hold on."

Poppy reached out to me, to pull me back into his embrace,
but his arms went through me as though I were made of smoke,
diaphanous and gauzy.

"Poppy!" I gurgled. I tried to clutch him, but my reach was
just as tenuous.

"I can see through her now!" Udo yelped.

A geyser of hysteria was building inside me and about to blow, and then two large white flannel arms pulled and held me tightly to a hard silk chest. For a second, I could barely breathe, in that barrel-chested embrace, then I realized that I didn't have to breathe at all.

"I don't understand," Poppy said. "How can you touch her and I can't, Paimon?"

Paimon answered, "I can manifest in the Waking World, but I am actually of Elsewhere. I am manifested in both the here and the now—her now and your here. Thus she is clear to me."

"But I want to be in Udo's here, or Poppy's here," I gasped.

"Paimon, you are the oldest House in the City—you have to be able to do something," Poppy demanded.

"I have done all that I can do," Paimon said, "though I have a suggestion to make. But I do not think it will meet with your favor."

Poppy said, "I don't know that this is the time to be squeamish. We shall do what we shall have to do. Let loose the advice, Paimon."

"There is only one person in Califa who can help Flora."

Poppy said impatiently, "Who is that? Don't be all spooky about it."

"Lord Axacaya," Paimon answered.

THIRTY-NINE

Desperation. Decision. Departure.

Of all the suggestions Paimon could have made, this was the worst. My hope, which had sprung up when Poppy had proved to be so calm, so logical, so sure that we could figure something out, deflated like a punctured balloon. *Oblivion is only one step away,* Nini Mo said, and bitterly now did I understand what she meant. Perhaps there truly was no hope, and I should just give up. But I looked at Poppy, so straight and tall, and Udo, so faithful and true, and I did not want to give up, for them. I did not want to lose them.

"Axacaya!" Poppy echoed. "That tin-potted backdoor horn-swoggling drummer? That jabber-jawed mincing malicho? He wouldn't help his own mother stay afloat in a stormy sea."

"He is the greatest adept in the City," Paimon said. "He himself straddles the Line, with one foot on either side of the divide between the Waking World and Elsewhere. He is the only adept alive who has crossed the Abyss and returned again. If there is a way to save Flora, he shall know it."

I looked at Udo and Udo looked back at me, his jaw clenching. I knew he was remembering what I was remembering: Boy Hansgen's death. And wondering whether or not Lord Axacaya knew of our involvement in his failed rescue. How could we ask Lord Axacaya's help after that?

"But Lord Axacaya is Mamma's greatest enemy," I said weakly. "Why would he help me?"

"You do not know until you ask," Paimon said. "And do not think that your situation only affects yourself. You and Valefor are being pulled back into the Abyss—the denizen of one of the great Houses of the City is disintegrating. This affects all the Houses, and not happily, either."

"Sod Valefor—what about Flora?" Udo said rudely. "He can go if he wants. It is her we have to save."

"They are the same now," Paimon said. "As one goes, so, too, the other, unless they can be disconnected."

"And I hate like hell to ask Axacaya for anything," Poppy said doubtfully. "I doubt if either Buck or the General would like me to have that kind of a debt."

"For Pigface sake, Hotspur," Udo burst out. "Do you think that Buck is gonna like it if Flora evaporates? What's she gonna say to that and if we could have done something to stop it and didn't? I'll go to Axacaya myself if I have to, and I'll *make* him help, Flora. You can count on it."

I blinked. When I looked straight at Udo, he was the same old Udo, but then when I blinked, it seemed that in his place stood a tall broad man, tanned from the sun, with fierce blue eyes, his waist girded with a heavy gun belt. Then I blinked again, and there was just scrawny Udo standing there. When I looked long at Poppy, I saw a skinny boy, pale face free of scars, ropes of blazing red braids looped about his neck and shoulders. Another blink, and there was Poppy, looking unhappy and lighting a cigarillo again. I couldn't believe how beautiful he was.

"We have no choice," the man who was Udo said, glowering.

The boy who was Poppy rubbed his face and blew a tendril of smoke. "Ayah, you are right, of course, Paimon."

Paimon, no matter how many times I blinked, looked the same as ever, towering and monumental, and now damp with my tears. I looked down at my hands; they were like glass, and all trembly. Never to touch Udo again, never to pet Flynnie.

Poppy had smelled so deliciously of bay rum and pipe weed; Udo of cinnamon soap and muffins. Now I could smell nothing. I would never smell anything again, not wet-dog Flynnie, or Mamma's flowery hair pomade, or oranges. Never taste coffee, or maple-nut muffins, or chocolate. Paimon's coat was soft beneath my face, but he had no heartbeat. I could distantly hear Udo and Poppy arguing, but already their voices were becoming dim, and soon I would hear nothing at all. I would float through Elsewhere, like a ghost, and gradually even Elsewhere would fade and I would grow dimmer and dimmer and then be gone.

What could Lord Axacaya do to me compared with that? He could refuse to help me. Would I be worse than I was now? Nini Mo said that you must *dare, win, or disappear.*

"I will go see Lord Axacaya," I said in a small voice. And then, when no one paid any attention, I summoned up all the loudness I had left in me and said, in what turned out to be a shout, "I will go see Lord Axacaya!"

"An' you will," Poppy said firmly. "But not alone. I shall go with you—I wager I can influence Axacaya to assistance."

"And me, too," Udo said.

Paimon shook his massive head, his ruff flying. "I am sorry, but you cannot, either of you. Flora is almost gone into Elsewhere, and there you cannot follow her, neither of you being adepts. I will escort her, but you both must return to your proper places."

"I will go," I said. "Udo, you should go home, take Flynnie and Bonzo. Maybe you can stall Mamma, if you have to."

Udo protested, but what else could he do? Soon he would not be able to see me at all, and he could not follow me Elsewhere. So he agreed.

"But I do not want to have to explain to Buck what has happened," he warned. "Do not leave me holding the bag, ayah, Flora? It would be pretty mean to float off into the Abyss and leave poor me to get walloped. Ayah so?"

"Ayah so," I promised Udo, and hoped very much that I

could hold to this promise. "And don't forget to feed the dogs and to let them out. They are probably explosive by now."

"As long as you are still bossy, Flora," Udo said, "there is hope. How do I get out of here, Paimon? Also, can I have my hat back?"

"Go back up the stairs and I shall meet you and escort you to my gates," Paimon answered.

At the bottom of the steps, Udo paused and looked back at Poppy. "Hotspur? My father—could you tell him . . ."

"Tell him what?" Poppy asked, when Udo didn't continue.

"Tell him I said hello," Udo said quickly and, turning about, disappeared up the stairs and into the darkness.

And so Udo was gone, and I hoped with all my heart that I would see him again, that this was not the last time for us. And I resolved, if I did return, to be a bit less snarky about his foibles, and also to give him the fuchsia umbrella I had gotten for my birthday the year previous and which he had been coveting. It is funny the trivial things you can think about, even when the situation is dire.

"Give us a minute, Paimon," Poppy ordered. "And then I will let Flora go."

"A minute only, Major," Paimon said. "We have a long way to go."

Poppy crouched down so that we were more of the same height. I had never realized how toweringly tall Poppy really was; my Poppy's permanent list made him seem shorter.

He said, "It is funny, young Flora, you seem too serious to be my child. Even transparent, I can tell that you are not a sunshiny girl. And you were so happy as a child, always laughing and singing. Flora . . . why did you not tell me what was wrong? I know you did not, or you should not be here now. For had I known, I would not have let it get this far. And yet—I know now, and still I did not help you when you needed me."

"Poppy . . ."

He looked at me gravely. "I wasn't born in a barn yesterday. I can tell that Paimon has withheld information from me. No doubt he doesn't want me to know the future, and if he doesn't want that, then I can only guess it isn't good. And yet, it cannot be all so bad, Flora, for you are grown so beautiful and strong. But I think there can only be one reason why I would not help you—but you needn't fear telling me. I do not fear dying, Flora. I expect it. Fyrdraacas don't die in their beds. I only hope that I make a good death. And I'm sorry that it means I will not be there for you. Will not see you grow up."

"Poppy . . . it's not that—" I choked.

"And even now I cannot be much help to you. And for that I am sorry, too. But you may trust Paimon, and, Flora, you must trust your mother, too. She loves you and Idden more than anything, and she will never let you down. I remember when you were born—you insisted on entering the world feet first, with the cord wrapped around your neck. You should have died, most babies would have, but you were too tough then, and you are too tough now—a true Fyrdraaca."

"Poppy, you don't understand—" I sobbed, "Poppy—"

Paimon chimed closer and cut me off before I could say more. "We must go, Major Fyrdraaca. I'm sorry."

"All right, Paimon. Now listen to me, Flora. Everything is going to be all right. Axacaya is spooky, but he is just a man. Remember that. He is just a man. But you are a Fyrdraaca. Remember Barbizon?"

"Ayah." I sniveled.

"Had she climbed off her pedestal when you left Crackpot?"

"No."

"Well, then, see, the trouble ain't so bad. Come on, girlie, don't cry—it only spoils your aim."

"We must go," Paimon said urgently. "Come."

Poppy kissed the air above my forehead, and I kissed it back. "Cierra Fyrdraaca, Flora."

"Cierra Fyrdraaca, Poppy." Paimon yanked me by the arm and sailed through the doorway. I turned back and caught a quick glimpse of Poppy, framed tall and straight, his hair glowing in the lamplight, and then he was gone.

FORTY

A Balloon. Bath Time. Looking Good.

I STUMBLED AFTER Paimon, with only his grip keeping me going. He dragged me onward, through endless hallways, up endless stairs, around endless corners, through endless galleries. I could barely keep up, huffing and puffing like a whirligig, then I stumbled over a riser, flew up in the air, and drifted like a kite, controlled by the firm grip of Paimon's hand. Now I really was bobbing along like a balloon, and it was actually kind of fun. Like swimming without worrying about getting water up your nose or some snapperdog cannonballing onto your back and almost drowning you. I bounced and flew, feet trailing behind, hair whipping, and the wind was such a blur in my face that I could not see a thing.

Finally, we stopped, and when Paimon let go of my hand, I floated to the ground with a gentle thump, and there I lay happily. The carpet was as soft as grass. I blinked and saw that it *was* grass, sweet and warm, dappled with white daisies and egg-yolk-colored buttercups. I flopped over on my back and looked up at the periwinkle sky, spangled with little green butterflies. A fresh breeze ruffled my hair.

"That was cool," I said. "Can we do that some more?"

"No," Paimon intoned. "You must get ready to visit Lord Axacaya. You cannot go to him dressed like that."

"I am afraid, Paimon," I said smally.

"Why is that?"

"Lord Axacaya hates Mamma, and his Quetzals tore out the heart of Boy Hansgen. What if his Quetzals want to do that to me?"

"They will not. Come, Flora."

I sat up reluctantly. "Why are things shifting back and forth?"

"You are Elsewhere now," Paimon said. He rustled around in a tree trunk—no, a wardrobe—no, a tree trunk. It was awfully confusing. "Where things can be more than they appear."

"So that was Udo as a man that I saw?"

Paimon turned, clutching a mass of red froth to his chest. "Ayah."

"If that was Udo as a man, then that was Poppy as a boy? Why did I see Udo forward and Poppy back, instead of both back or both forward? That doesn't make sense." Nothing in this House made any sense. It was enough to make you sick. "I am confused, Paimon."

"Udo has no past and Major Fyrdraaca has no future."

I followed Paimon by a leafy bower, invitingly plump with pink pillows and a trailing canopy of roses and grapevines. The bower looked so cool and delicious that I wanted nothing more than to fling myself into its depths, lie among the poppies and rose petals, and dream of long languid rivers, of floating aimlessly in a narrow lulling punt, trailing my hand in the cool water, and drinking gin fizzies. Then I blinked again and saw the bower to be a large overstuffed bed, heaped with pink pillows and covered by a carved wooden lattice.

Paimon heaped the dress on a rock and held out a hand to me. "In you go. The water is perfect." I blinked, and a pool became a steamy bathtub filled with glimmering bubbles.

"Can you make things be one or the other?" I asked. "I am getting rather dizzy."

"You must focus, madama. In you go."

I decided that I liked the glade better, and with that decision, there was no more bouncing back and forth. I threw my clothes at Paimon, and the splash I made jumping in was so big that he got drippy and wet. I floated and spun in the soothing water, staring at the serene blue sky, until Paimon started scrubbing. No matter how hard I wiggled and complained, or even bit, his right hand was like iron and his left hand was like sandpaper, and by the time he was done I felt like a shrimp that had just been boiled and peeled. But, Pigface, was I clean!

"I thought I was discorporeal now. Why do I have to have a bath and change clothes if I have no real body?" I asked. "What's the point?"

"You are seeing things as you are used to seeing them, in corporeal form, so that they make sense to you. But what you are seeing are symbols. It is not your body that you are cleaning, but your true self. You cannot go to see Lord Axacaya with a grubby soul, can you?"

"No," I admitted. "I guess not."

"You must go to Lord Axacaya as a supplicant, but yet you wish him to understand that your request is an important and serious request, made respectfully. Therefore you must look serious and respectful."

Nini Mo says that to get something you must look as though you don't actually need it. If you look hopeless, even if you *are* hopeless, why would anyone help you out?

Paimon plucked me from the pool like I was a sodden tea bag, then wrapped me in a fluffy towel the size of the City before bearing me back to the bower. There I was slithered into a chemise, stuffed like a sausage into stays, and laced tighter than a drum.

"I can't breathe!" I puffed, as Paimon cinched the laces tighter. He almost yanked me off my feet, and I grabbed at a tree trunk for support.

"Do not hold your breath," he ordered. "You do not need to breathe here."

Paimon the Merciless continued to tug until I thought I would break in two, and before I could protest, he tossed a froth of vivid red over my head. I emerged from the rosy foam coughing and gasping, and when I was done choking and Paimon was done lacing and tucking, my cheeks were almost as red as the dress.

"I look like a bloody nightmare," I protested when I saw my filmy reflection in the mirror. "I cannot wear this to meet Lord Axacaya. I don't look serious or important at all."

The skirt was huge and fluffy, like a giant blown rose or a waft of cotton candy. Sleeves puffed like balloons from my elbows, but my shoulders and neck were chilly and bare, and the neckline was cut awfully low.

"You look very fine," Paimon said, slightly hurt. "I designed this dress myself, madama, and it suits you perfectly."

"But I look all fluffy!"

"You look grown-up." Paimon descended upon me, with a brush in one long hand and a sheaf of combs in the other. He twiddled and twirled and brushed and bouffanted. When he was done, my hair, normally so frizzy, was a sleek mass of curls hanging in perfect spirals down my back, caught by each ear with a spangled diamond clip. The hairbrush was replaced by maquillage brushes, which fluttered over my face like little butterflies, dipping and swirling color on my eyelids, cheeks, and lips. Last, Paimon handed me crimson gloves, soft as butter, and then a fan case.

Two thin chains unwound into my hand, dangling from a heavy silver clip. The fan withdrew from the sheath easily and when I flipped my wrist, it unfurled with a snap. Paimon clipped the fan frog onto my sash so that it hung on my hip like a sabre or a holster.

"There, madama," Paimon said, proudly. "It has been a while since I have acted as a dresser. General Haðraaða was quite particular about his attire, but General Haðraaða Segunda was very careless with hers. I am pleased to see that I still have the touch. You look fine."

He flipped a full-length mirror out of Nowhere, and there I was, reflected in its silvery shimmer, and I did look fine. I wouldn't say I was beautiful, but I wasn't bad. Udo is right—it's amazing what a little maquillage can do for you, particularly if you don't lay it on with a trowel.

And Paimon was right, too—I felt a whole lot more confident about facing Lord Axacaya.

"I hope I am irresistible," I said.

"You will do," Paimon said, with satisfaction. "Come."

FORTY-ONE

Many Rooms. Many Times. Advice.

NOW I DISCOVERED that if I gave a little skip and swished my buoyant skirt in bell-like fashion, I could glide for several feet, at least, before I needed another little push to send me aloft and forward again. It was like flying, only instead of wings I had the huge poofiness of my skirts to keep me moving.

Paimon wafted down an enormous stairway, wide enough to march an entire squad abreast, his shoes making a delicate tapping sound on the porphyry steps, and I floated down after him effortlessly. A little snake's head at the end of the banister winked at me as I sailed by.

"Don't dawdle," Paimon said over his shoulder. "We have a long way to go."

"How are we going to get there?" I whisked my skirts faster to catch up with him.

"You shall see. Come!"

A narrow greyhound slid up to me, rubbing his head on my skirts, and when I bent down to pet his soft head, another cold nose shoved its way into my hand—a slender red dog who was not Flynnie. The greyhound growled, and I thumped him once between the eyes with my finger. "I have two hands. I can pet you both."

Paimon turned, wafting disapproval. "Get down, Kria, and

you get down as well, Parzival. You are going to get dog hair all over madama's dress. Madama, please do not encourage them."

"How come I can pet these dogs and I couldn't pet Flynnie and the others?"

"Because these dogs are dead," Paimon answered.

"You mean they are ghosts?" They looked pretty solid to me, and they felt pretty solid as well, although Parzival seemed a little bony.

"That's a colloquial term. But yes, ghosts, if you will."

"Poor things. I'll bet they get lonely being ghosts all the time."

Paimon gently took my arm and drew me away from the disappointed doggies, who fell into a trot behind us. "We must hurry, madama, we are late as it is."

"I'm sorry, Paimon," I said. "It is hard to concentrate. I feel all drifty and dreamy—like none of this is real."

"In the strictest sense of the Waking World, madama, none of this *is* real. Although in the strictest sense of Elsewhere, none of the Waking World is real. Elsewhere is a place of shifting and constant movement, and it takes a great deal of concentration to hold yourself together in it. However, you must try, or else you will drift so far into Elsewhere that even Lord Axacaya will not be able to help you back, for there will no longer be any you to return. That which was Flora will have splintered into a thousand tiny bits and scattered into the Abyss, and you will be gone forever."

Forever. The word shivered through me, spreading coldness. I focused on the hard heat of the dog's head beneath my hand, and Paimon nodded approvingly. "That's better. Come. We must go through some of the most distant reaches of the House. You must stick close to me, madama. Should we lose each other, it may take me some time to find you again."

I nodded. Now that I was used to his face, Paimon didn't seem monstrous at all. His ears were so silky and soft-looking, and his eyes were filled with kindness. And he was such a pretty shade of blue, damson twilight, blueberry dawn. I clutched his hand tightly, and on we went, the two doggies close behind us.

Through a solarium, weaving in and around elegantly dressed people clutching wineglasses and eating little snacky things, their chattering voices far and distant like a melody on the wind.

Through the Ballroom of the Battle of Califa, now filled with rows of narrow beds, white catafalques for silently suffering soldiers, pristine bandages dabbled with blood, the silence broken only by the occasional stifled sob.

Through a dining room, the clink of glasses and dull murmur of conversation in pale candlelight. I caught sight of a bobbing gold feather—Mamma, with a huge pregnant tummy that kept her from pulling in close to the table.

"That's Mamma," I said, trying to pull away from Paimon. But he refused to drop his grip.

"No, it's just a memory of your mother and a meal here she had many years ago," Paimon said, drawing me onward past the head of the table where a Skinner sat, looking as though she could chew glass.

Down a darkened hallway, past a small child in a white nightgown, sleepily clutching a plushy pink pig, rubbing her eyes and crying distantly, "Bwannie . . . Bwannie."

Through the Ballroom again, this time thronged with dancers, the officers in unfamiliar green and gold uniforms, their golden gorgets gleaming in the lamplight. The civilians had towering hair, sculptured into swirls and crests, and inset with little trinkets—a ship, a castle, chirping red birds. Outside, the sea thrashed at the windows, and the sky was filled with falling red stars. Not stars, but hot shot—cannonballs.

Then before us curled a familiar iron gate, familiar green jade steps sinking downward into limpid darkness: the Cloakroom of the Abyss.

The flaring light and the dusty clothes were the same, only now the marks of death were all too clear on the still faces. Georgiana Haðraaða was flushed purple with poison, and the orange she held was shriveled. Serentha Haðraaða's lips were locked in the rictus of travail, her skirts crusted with dried blood, and the malnourished baby was also malformed, with a crooked little back and flipper hands. The little pug dog Fancy's muzzle was flecked with foam, stubby paws and legs rigid and stiff.

I was awfully glad that the drapes to Hardhands's cata-falque were closed. I did not want to see what was behind those sangyn curtains, which, as we passed them, seemed to move as though perhaps the thing they concealed had stirred.

We circled the room and then ascended the same steps we had just come down.

"Why are we going back the way we came?" I asked.

"You can never go the same way twice, madama," Paimon said. "The way may appear the same, but it is different and so are you."

He was right. Now at the top of the steps was a small door, narrow and not tall enough for Paimon to go through. It was closed.

"I can go no further," Paimon said. "You must go alone from here."

"Can't you go with me?" I asked hopefully.

"I cannot. This is the limit of my authority."

"Lord Axacaya is Mamma's great enemy."

"Does she say so, or does he?"

"She does. She hates him for what he has done to the City, and to the Republic. Do you think he'll really help me, knowing how Mamma feels?"

Paimon put an enormous hand on my head. His touch was as light as swan's down. "Sometimes we believe things to be true that are based not in truth but our own fears and desires. Some-times things and people are not what they seem to be. Sometimes people have the same goals but different ideas about how to reach them, Flora."

"And Poppy—"

Paimon's touch became heavier. "The time for thought is

past, Flora. You must not think. You have made your decision. You must act."

He held out a little red leather box, snapped shut with a gold clasp. "It is rude to visit someone and not take them a gift. Give this to Lord Axacaya as a token of your appreciation. And when he asks you to tell him your situation, do so clearly and truthfully. Be respectful and humble but not servile. Be polite, but do not grovel."

I took the box, and gratefully. "Thank you, Paimon, for everything. I am sorry that we ran from you. You have been so nice. Thank you very much."

"It is my pleasure to serve you. I hope perhaps you will visit me again sometime. Remember, Flora: *Dare, win or disappear.* Now go forth."

Paimon's tusks brushed my forehead, smooth and cooling, and when I kissed his cheek, it felt petal soft under my lips.

I pushed the door open and stepped forward.

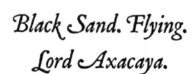

FORTY-TWO

Black Sand. Flying. Lord Axacaya.

SAND CRUNCHED UNDER my feet, and ahead of me stretched a long beach: the Pacifica Playa. But not the Pacifica Playa as I had ever seen it before. The sky and surging sea were the same quicksilver gray, but the water pounded on sand that glittered black as soot. It was as though someone had reversed night, turned the light to dark and dark to light. The air was strangely still. The surf rolled silently up onto the sand, then silently surged back. If the sky above had stars, they were invisible against the silver.

I turned to look the way I had come and saw Bilskinir shining blue on the cliff above me. It was a cheerful gleam of color in an otherwise colorless world, which despite the silvery glitter seemed drab for the lack of any contrasting shade.

There was movement in the sheen of the silver sky: an eagle. The bird circled me, at first so high I could barely make out the sweep of its wings, but then swooping lazily lower to drift menacingly around me. Though a sizzle of fear shot up my spine, I did not give ground, even when the eagle wheeled up, then dropped into a screaming dive, claws outstretched, directly toward me.

At the very last minute, the eagle pulled up slightly. Then eagle legs stretched down into human legs, and the eagle body transformed into a lithe human form, and as elegantly as a dancer, it landed on the sand before me. The eagle feathers had translated into a knee-length feathery kilt and a feather cape, but the sleek eagle head, all enormous green eyes and hooked beak, had not changed.

"Ave, Flora Fyrdraaca," the Quetzal said in a soft fluid voice, then sank into the deep fluttering courtesy that signified Meeting as Equals, but Me Slightly Above. "I, Axila Aguila, give you greetings."

I responded with a courtesy of my own, a courtesy that said Before You and Better. "I, Flora Fyrdraaca, return those greetings with great pleasure. I am happy to make your acquaintance."

"We have met before," the Quetzal said, "at the Zoo Battery, when you tried to steal the traitor from us."

The Quetzal recognized me! Again I felt that wave of terror skitter up my spine, but I ignored it and said firmly, "You were stealing him yourself."

"Perhaps so," said the Quetzal, and it seemed like there was a hint of humor in its voice. *"Cree el ladron que todos son de su condición.* A thief believes everyone else is a thief, too. Axacaya has sent me to act as your escort."

"How did he know I was coming?" I asked, wondering what exactly it had meant by the thief remark. That I was not the only thief, or that I was paranoid?

"He swims in the Current, and nothing there is hidden from him. He has been waiting for you. Will you come?"

There is no way out but through.

"I will."

"We shall go, then." The Quetzal spread wide its arms. The feathered cape fell away from its torso, and by the clingy drape of its thin white chemise, I saw, with a jolt, that the Quetzal was female.

"Come," she said impatiently.

I realized that she wanted me to step into her embrace, and I hesitated. The idea of touching the Quetzal made my insides quiver. I did not want to get close to that razory beak, those claws. Somewhere, once, I had read that eagles are so strong that they can crush bones with their talons. True, the Quetzal's talons curled at the end of human fingers, but surely they had the same strength.

The Quetzal turned her head in a smooth swivel left, then right, and her eyes flashed luminous green, like a cat's eye caught in a light. "Will you have Axacaya wait?"

. . . but through.

I no longer had any bones to crush, no flesh to tear, and what could she do to me that was worse than I had done to myself? Squeezing my shoulders together in a bit of a huddle, and twisting my hands together at my throat, I stepped forward into the Quetzal's embrace and closed my eyes. She folded wiry arms around me, clutching me to her chest, which, save for her soft breasts, was hard with muscle. She smelled faintly metallic, the odor of old dried blood, and also of acrid vanilla. The bare skin of her neck against my cheek felt downy.

With a sound like ripping silk, her wings tore at the sky. I felt the spring of her leap, and we were aloft. Air roared by, as loud as a train, and the darkness pressing against my eyes spun and whirled. The beat of her flight filled my ears with a rhythmic pulse that matched the throbbing heartbeat beneath my head.

Onward, onward, we soared, and time seemed to vanish into the tidal flow of our journey, the steady pull of movement flowing around me, over me, inside me. The sensation of speed filled me with a huge excitement that made me want to shout with joy.

Then, we spiraled into a descent, and lightly, I felt the bump of landing. I opened my eyes and saw that I stood in a large courtyard. Luminarias blazed in the dusk like stars fallen to Earth, and by their light, I saw glittering red and gold mosaic under my feet, a tall fountain, and flowering plants everywhere, climbing up the white mud walls, spilling over wrought-iron balconies: fuchsia and white bougainvilleas, yellow marigolds, blue chrysanthemums, lavender orchids, fragrant orange trees, and a dozen flowers I didn't recognize.

"Xochiquetzal. You say Mariposa. Lord Axacaya's House," the Quetzal said. She released me from her embrace and led me across the courtyard, through a carved wood archway, and into a narrow gallery. Butterfly lamps hung from the vigas overhead, and more luminarias lined the walls, illuminating a fantastic mural: a ceremony in which red played a prominent role, a jade-masked priest holding a knife aloft, four eagle-headed priests stretching a screaming figure over a plinth—a Birdie sacred sacrifice.

"I have brought her to you, Axacaya," the Quetzal said. I turned my attention from the lurid wall-painting toward the dais at the far end of the gallery, where a figure had stepped out of the darkness.

Lord Axacaya.

The Quetzal's wings fluttered and her head inclined: I Serve You at My Own Discretion. "I am done."

"Thank you, Axila," Lord Axacaya said, his words slightly slurred with a low musical accent. "I shall call you back when I am ready."

His hand flashed in a throw, and something soared through the air. The Quetzal caught the toss, glanced at her catch, and then continued the movement from her hand to her beak. When she turned back to me, I saw that both hand and beak were stained red with blood.

The Quetzal paused in her exit and stared at me with that fixed green gaze. "Go with the goddess, Flora Fyrdraaca." And then with a flutter of feathers, she was gone. Lord Axacaya and I were alone.

Courtesy. Gifts.
Chocolate. Please.

AGLIS SABRE, Mamma's ADC, had told me that Lord Axacaya did not have an eye in the middle of his tongue, but the
Califa Police Gazette often represents him as a hideous old man
who has a skull face and snakes for hair and who drinks the
blood of his enemies from a jade cup. And yet the man who
stood before me was in all ways just a man, as Poppy had said,
not old or hideous or skull-like.

Lord Axacaya was tall, with spiraling yellow curls cascading
past his shoulders. Like the Quetzal, he wore a feathered kilt, but
the feathers were iridescent green and blue, silver and gold, glittering and catching the light like jewels. A jaguar skin was tossed
over his shoulders; the jaguar's head hung down over his chest, its
glazed eyes gazing out at the world mournfully. A jade labret
shaped like a butterfly pierced his lower lip. He held in his left
hand a jade mask, the kind that Huitzils wear on formal occasions, and, in his right hand, a feathery fan, whose golden quills
were fully three feet long.

Aglis Sabre had been wrong about Lord Axacaya's eyes.
They were not black voids but the galvanic blue of the hot summer sky, like the glowing heart of a coldfire spark. He looked
young, in his twenties perhaps, but I knew him to be older than
Mamma, and she is fifty-one.

"Welcome to my House, Flora Fyrdraaca," Lord Axacaya

said. The words were clear and loud, but his lips had not moved. He bowed his head slightly and fluttered the fan sign that meant Honor without Reservations.

"Thank you for receiving me," I said, glad that I had gotten an all-perfect mark in the Fan Language section of Politeness and Charm class last term. I unholstered my own fan and ripped it open with one sharp twist of my wrist. I curtseyed Respect to an Elder and fluttered Gratitude from One Equal to Another.

Poppy had said to remember I was a Fyrdraaca, and I was going to remember it and hope that memory kept the trembles at bay, but it was hard not to tremble. Lord Axacaya looked human, but he also looked disdainful and arrogant, and there was no spark of kindness or compassion in his glittering blue eyes. They were as cold and calculating as the predator eyes of his Quetzal guard.

I held out the little box Paimon had given me and was glad to see that my hand did not shake. Neither, somehow, did my voice. "Please accept this token as a sign of my appreciation for your reception."

Lord Axacaya advanced toward me and took the box, his hand brushing against mine. Even through my glove, I could feel the heat of his skin. He radiated warmth like a stove, warmth and the thick rich smell of chocolate and cinnamon. It was a heady smell, dark and musky. His wrist was encircled by an intricate blue tattoo of a curling snake whose head came down over the back of his hand, its tongue extending the length of his index finger.

"How thoughtful of you," he said, and this time his lips did move, mouthing the words but turning slightly up in what might have been a tight smile.

When Lord Axacaya opened the box, a ladybug crawled out. It perched on one edge of the box, wiggling its antennae curiously, and then crawled down onto Lord Axacaya's hand. The insect was larger than a regular ladybug, about the size of a glory, and it had only two black splotches on its crimson back, shiny as enamel. Surely it wasn't really a ladybug, but what, then, was it?

The bug fanned its outer shell, and a blur of brilliant coldfire light spilled out from under the red and black carapace.

"The Semiote Verb *To Will,* Indicative Past Plural," Lord Axacaya said. "Isn't it lovely?"

A Semiote Verb! Not the one we had been wanting but equally as valuable. Hardly a gift. More like a bribe. I felt a wiggle of guilt that Paimon had given away something so costly on my account, and vowed then, if I got home—*when* I got home—I would be sure to write him a thank-you note.

"This is an extremely generous present, Madama Fyrdraaca." This time Lord Axacaya's smile was slightly more genuine, though it also, unfortunately, showed me that his teeth had been filed into points. I shivered involuntarily, but if he noticed, he didn't show it. Gently, he jiggled his hand, and the ladybug dropped back into the box, which he closed.

He said, "Come, I shall offer you refreshments, and then we shall discuss your situation."

I followed Lord Axacaya's gesture to a brazier stove shaped like a squatting monkey, which sat to one side of the room. Arranged before the brazier were two stone stools, one carved to represent a rabbit, the other a jaguar. The carvings were the Birdie style, angular and square, and vaguely I remembered that each animal was sacred to the Birdies. I sat where Lord Axacaya indicated, upon the jaguar, my skirt poofing like a marshmallow around me, and watched as he stirred the pot on the stove, frothing its contents with a whisk he held between his palms. He poured the liquid into a cup shaped like a skull and offered it to me.

Oh dear, the cup *was* a skull, its top removed and its brainpan lined with gold. *Don't let them see you flinch,* said Nini Mo, so I took the skull with no comment and no grimace. But this time, alas, my hand did shake.

"Love is all we Desire," Lord Axacaya said. It's a traditional blessing, which we never say at home because Mamma disbelieves in piety. But it precedes all meals at Sanctuary, so I knew the correct response.

"Will is all that we must Do."

The chocolate, I hoped, was not mixed with blood. It was thick as mud, hot, and spicy, and it tasted delicious. I drank, then licked my lips, hoping that I did not now have a chocolate mustachio.

Lord Axacaya drained his own skull cup and set it aside. He looked at me coolly and distantly, as though I were a specimen, interesting but maybe not *that* interesting. "Now, madama. Perhaps you will tell me why you have come to me."

Paimon had said to be clear and truthful. But where to start?

"At the beginning, perhaps?" he suggested. "That is where most stories begin."

"Can you read my mind?" I asked, startled. If he could hear the things I was thinking, he'd be even less likely to help me. "That's not very polite." Then I could have kicked myself. This was not the time for snark.

Now it was his turn to look startled, as though he were not used to people correcting him, which I suppose he wasn't, being almost a god and all. For a minute I thought I had blown it completely, but then he said, "I beg your pardon, madama, you are correct, of course. In my defense I say that I was not so much reading your mind as your face. Elsewhere thoughts are as good as actions, in some respects, and your face is quite expressive."

Then I am sunk, I thought, trying to arrange my face into an attitude of blankness.

"Go on, I did not mean to interrupt you."

I plunged in. "Valefor, our denizen, is abrogated, you know, and I found him and tried to help him get a little energy, but then somehow we became intertwined and he infected me with his dissolution. Now he is fading back into the Abyss, and I am, too, that's why I am Elsewhere now. I thought maybe if I restored him, then that would stop my evaporation, but Paimon says that only Mamma can restore him, because she's the Head of our House. And he said that the only thing that would help me would be for the link between Valefor and me to be broken, and then I would not fade," I said. And because Nini Mo said that flattery was a useful grease, I added, "Paimon said you were the greatest adept in the City and that perhaps you could break this link."

Lord Axacaya listened to all this without comment, looking almost bored, and when I was done, he stood up and poured me more chocolate. Turning back to me, he said, "I am surprised at your magickal doings. It is no secret that General Fyrdraaca does not approve of the magickal arts."

"Mamma says magick is a trick that the goddess plays upon us."

Lord Axacaya answered by whispering a soft Gramatica Word. The Word danced in the air in front of me and twisted into a note of fire, then became a brilliant dragonfly that flitted away. "Magick is a trick we play upon ourselves. The only true power lies in our Will. All else is vanity and games."

I said impatiently, "It's a trick that Val has played upon me, and I don't like it one bit."

Lord Axacaya twitched his shoulders, and his movement made the jaguar's eyes flash with life. He said coldly, "A trick? Whose trick? And whose vanity? There is much of both in your story, madama, in the details that you left out in your telling."

He continued, "You say Valefor tricked you, yet your desire to help him was rooted in your own selfishness. You sought to spring Valefor from his prison only to relieve yourself of your chores—a mighty poor excuse to go against your mother's dominion. You dragged your best friend, your dog, and your horse into a dangerous situation, and took little regard for their safety, and they easily could have been killed.

"But that is not all, is it? Let us see . . . Oh yes, you attempted a major magickal Working, with no preparation or guidance. There, not only could you have permanently damaged yourself and your friend, but you could have torn the Current, you could have thrown the Waking World off balance. What you set in motion could have destroyed us all.

"And that stunt with the Dainty Pirate? What right had you to decide if he lived or died? What do you know of the facts of his case, the damage he has caused to Califa, to the Republic? The danger he posed to our future? Did you think you could hide your involvement? What will the Warlord say when he hears about that?"

Tears burned my eyes like acid, even as I bit my lip and tried not to blink, tried to hold them back.

"What else? Forgery, theft, and falsehood. Deception, shirking, and treason. You certainly have missed no vice, have you, madama? You have been nothing but thorough in your depravity. Why should I reward such behavior? Why should I help you?"

"Paimon said that Valefor's disintegration affected all the Houses, that it could pull the Current off balance," I said, very small.

"Bilskinir, perhaps, and the other Great Houses, old and decadent, but your foolishness cannot affect me. My House was built by my Will and is strong enough to withstand your games. So why, then, should I help you?"

"I don't know," I whispered. *Don't reward failure,* said Nini Mo. Everything he said was true, and if true, surely I deserved everything I got. I bowed my head, feeling the tears dribble and feeling myself shiver and shrink. How could I have been so stupid? Why should I be saved?

He continued, "Your story fits well with what I have thought for years. The Fyrdraacas, as a family, have always lacked verve. Your entire bloodline is sour; there's no hope for it anymore. Any spark that your family might have once boasted of has long since guttered out. No wonder it dwindles and dies out. Look to your mother, buried in her work, a slave to her enemies, ignoring her child, allowing her to run wild, no discipline, no guidance, no respect."

"Hey—" My protest was a squeak.

He said scornfully, "And then there is Hotspur, reckless and indifferent to the safety of others, now boiling in his own misery. When faced with adversity, he broke, his Will as thin as a thread but not half as strong. Incurably romantic with his falsely placed love toward the greatest criminal Califa has ever known—"

"Mamma is not a criminal!" I yelped, unable to keep silent any longer.

"Not General Fyrdraaca, you little fool. Butcher Brakespeare. Cyrenacia Sidonia Brakespeare ov Haðraaða. General Haðraaða Segunda. Didn't you know that he was her lover? All Califa knew and not you? Did he not snap after her death? Descend into madness because he could not live without her? Even the loss of his own child was nothing compared to the loss of his mistress."

"That's not true!" Even as I protested, doubt wormed at me. Like a flash came the memory of that empty slab in the Cloakroom of the Abyss—the whip twined with a braid of brilliant red hair. Poppy's hair, I realized. I thought he had clipped his hair short in mourning for the First Flora, but had he? Did he wear the black mourning band for her, or for someone else?

Lord Axacaya continued on: "Look at you now—you are no better than your father. The slightest bit of pressure and you snap like a twig. You cry and you wring your hands, and you disappear. And you thought to be a ranger. *Dare, win, or disappear!* You have made your choice, Flora Fyrdraaca, to disappear!"

These words stung me like poisoned darts. Was I no better than Poppy? I had scorned him because he gave up. He gave in. *A ranger,* Nini Mo said, *will never willingly dance with death.*

Dare, win, or disappear.

A red spark flared in my darkness. Anger at myself for giving in. Anger at myself for sitting helplessly while Lord Axacaya slandered my family. That spark was hot, and against the dampness of my despair, it felt good. It felt great. It felt *real.*

"No, you are wrong!" I cried. "I will not go. I will not disappear. And you are wrong about Mamma—wrong about Poppy!"

"Am I?"

Ah, that sharky grin, how I'd like to smack it off his face.

With each second my anger grew, and so, too, my determination to prove Lord Axacaya wrong—wrong about me, wrong about the Fyrdraacas.

"Mamma and Poppy were loyal to Califa; they fought for her honor. What did you do? You betrayed the country that took you in, and you sold out Poppy, and you would have sold out Mamma, too, if you could have! You work for Califa's enemies—it is you who are the traitor!"

Lord Axacaya's eyes blazed like cold fire. "You talk treason, to speak to me that way, girl. And yet, I know you are not responsible for yourself. You are a foolish child. And it is the parent who must take the blame for the foolish child. I can send my Quetzals to Crackpot and arrest Colonel Fyrdraaca. Is he not responsible for you in your mother's absence? I can have him killed, and no one shall resist my authority. He'll be dead by morning."

"You will not touch Poppy!" I cried. "I will not allow it!"

"How will you stop me, madama? Are you not diminishing and fading? Are you not weak-willed?" Lord Axacaya said scornfully. "Should I be afraid of you?"

"You pernicious pinheaded mincing malicho TRAITOR! I will see you in the Abyss before I allow you to bring the Fyrdraaca family down!" I screamed. Every drop of blood had turned to fire, and this fire was eating through my flesh, eating through my skin. My throat translated my anger into a shriek of rage that hung on the air like greasy smoke.

I was *furious*. And it felt good. It felt wonderful. It felt *fabulous*. Scalding heat flowed up my toes, into my legs, burned through my stomach, and into my mouth. Thick guttural Gramatica Words sparked and snapped in the swirling air, which now smelled thickly of my ire. Anger consumed me like a fire consumes wood, and there was no room for us both inside me.

I opened my red mouth and let out an almighty screech of fury, a screech that tore my throat and burned my ears, and seemed to last forever, a horrible sound that rent the air in front of me. My scream rose higher and higher, the noise translating from Wordlessness into the Oatmeal Word, magnified a hundred thousand times from whence I had last spoken it.

"⸙⸕⸘⸙⸕ ⸙⸘⸕⸘⸙!" The gash became a magickal Vortex, a roiling daisy wheel of fuliginous darkness that rolled forward to envelop Lord Axacaya.

FORTY-FOUR

Will. More Chocolate.
A Revelation.

THE VORTEX WHISTLED as it blurred and gave off a spiky blue and green coldfire light, like gashes of lightning, acrid and hot. Then, with a sound so loud I could not hear it, but could only feel the tremendous buzz of its vibration, the Vortex flared into a blinding burst of coldfire and was gone.

My skull rang with a noise that made my spine vibrate, my ears buzz. My vision dissolved into sparkly whiteness. It felt as though I was turning into oatmeal, melting into a puddle of starchy goo—a horrible sensation, quivering and shivery, that seemed to be getting stronger and stronger. And then suddenly the world snapped back into focus again. The awful sensation of oatmealness vanished. Now I felt heavy, not with the weight of desolation and despair, but with actual weight, the feeling of flesh and bone. I held up one hand to the light; it was plump and white, and I could not see through it. I pressed my other hand against my chest, and felt the slight bump of my heartbeat. I felt alive.

I felt *real*.

Lord Axacaya stood where the Vortex had been. He stepped toward me, his now obsidian eyes blazing. He brought his hands together in a thunderous clap that seemed to shift the ground beneath me, and I scrambled backward, skittering away from him.

What had I done? I had thrown the Oatmeal Word at Lord Axacaya, and he had stood through it, and now he was going to smite me. A tiny voice said, *At least you don't go willingly.* But that tiny voice was an awful little consolation—all my troubles for nothing. I only hoped it would not hurt too much. At least he was not setting those Quetzals on me—

Then Lord Axacaya clapped again and again, and he spoke in a voice not furious but friendly: "Welcome back to the Waking World, Flora." He smiled, a genuine smile that wiped all disdain and arrogance from his face, which now looked much older. Thin lines radiated from his eyes and lips, and his butter-colored hair was threaded with shimmering silver. And his eyes were so very black now, yet there seemed to be shimmering movements within their depths. Lieutenant Sabre had been right after all.

"What happened?" I croaked, bewildered. I was solid again, but how was I real?

"You are yourself again. You have regained your Will."

"How?" Each word felt like a razor blade, and my lips were sore, too.

"You asserted yourself. You stood up for your Will. Come sit down, and we shall have more chocolate. You look like you need it." He gestured toward the stools. Daylight now stippled the floor, filtering down from the *latillas* above, and hung in the still air like little clouds of sunlight. The luminarias were doused.

"By getting mad? By using the Oatmeal Word?" I sat down heavily on the jaguar.

"Oatmeal Word?" He sounded puzzled.

"What I said. That Gramatica Word." This time, I was relieved to see, the cup Lord Axacaya handed me was made of carved jade, shaped like a flower. But the chocolate tasted as rich and sweet as it had Elsewhere, and it smoothed away the pain in my mouth and throat. My tummy rumbled, but now my hunger was just plain old hunger, not ravenousness.

"Ah, you mean the Gramatica Adverbial form of *Convulsion?* No—that was just a symptom of your rage. You spoke it well, though; I was hard-pressed to withstand it. No, the solution to your problem, Flora, was Focus and Will. Nothing is stronger than your Will. Not even your little friend Valefor. He tried to pander your Will to his, but he could only do so because you let him. No one can take you from yourself, Flora, unless you allow them to. But you needed to be jolted to that realization, and so I provided you with a spur. I am sorry to have sounded so harsh, but you were pretty far gone. I wasn't sure that you could come back."

"Am I still linked to Valefor?"

"You will always be linked to Valefor. He is a Fyrdraaca, too, and the bond between you cannot be broken. But I would advise not allowing him to siphon your Will in the future. He is hungry—he cannot control himself. But he should not be encouraged, and as you have learned, it takes a great deal of strength to keep a hungry denizen at bay. Best not to take chances."

"But will he keep fading away?"

"As long as Fyrdraaca House stands, he will remain."

I sat there, trying to wrap my jellied mind around what Lord Axacaya had said. It was my Will that brought me back, and that Will had been activated by my anger. That much I understood. But why had he helped me? He was Mamma's enemy, wasn't he? I had worked against him, as far as the Dainty Pirate went, and he knew it—didn't that make me his enemy, as well?

I said, "I don't understand, Your Grace. You said you would not help me. You said I was irresponsible and foolish."

"So you were," he answered. "But courageous all the same. It was foolish to go against your mother and try to assist denizen Valefor. But it was a brave thing, and it was the right thing, to try to free Valefor from his bondage. He may be a servitor, but he is a sentient being. Should he not have the right to his own Will?"

"You said my family was a failure, but the failure is all mine. Please don't blame Mamma and Poppy for my actions. I will take my punishment if I must, but don't hold them responsible. What I have done is not their fault."

"I hold you responsible for your actions; you and no other," Lord Axacaya said. "What I said before about the Fyrdraaca family—I stand by those statements. I am no friend of your mother's, nor is she a friend of mine. But there is a saying: The enemy of my enemy is my friend. We share a mutual antipathy toward our Huitzil overlords; I have no more cause to like them than she."

"But," I said, bewildered, "I thought you were allies with them. You act like you are their friend; you do their bidding."

"Can I not smile and lie while I smile?" Lord Axacaya said. "Sometimes, Flora, you must grit your teeth and bear it until such time comes when you can bite."

"If you are against the Birdies, then why did you want the Dainty Pirate? Why did you have him killed? Mamma had no choice—she had to uphold the Peace Accord or risk herself—but you? He was their bane. He made no secret of working against them!" I burst out. Even as I did so, I thought, *Oh Flora, you should probably keep your mouth shut and stay ahead while you can,* but my mouth would just not stay shut—I had to know. "Why did you have him killed, then?"

"Did I have him killed?" Lord Axacaya asked with a smile.

"I saw it! I saw your eagles rip him apart! Udo was there—he saw it, too!"

"Did you? Things—and people—are not always as they seem. If you have learned nothing from your studies of Nini Mo, you should know that. Was she *ever* what she seemed? It is not enough to *see* something; you must know what it is that you have seen."

Now I was annoyed, and exasperated. Why couldn't he just say what he meant instead of having to be all mysterious and boo-spooky? Is there something about adepts that they just cannot speak plainly, that they have been too muddled by power and mystery?

Lord Axacaya laughed. "Well, then, I will say— unmysteriously and un-boo-spooky—Boy Hansgen is not dead."

FORTY-FIVE

Udo. Pie. Surprise.

I HAD THOUGHT I'D had all the surprises I could ever have, that nothing could ever surprise me again. But I was wrong. If Lord Axacaya had suddenly turned a cartwheel and set his own hair on fire, I could not have been more thunderstruck.

"He's not dead?" I repeated. "He's not dead? Why isn't he dead? I saw him die! I saw the Quetzals tear him to shreds and rip his heart out!"

"I'm afraid you and Udo stumbled into a little bit of sleight of hand designed to make it appear that Boy Hansgen had met his reward. You did complicate matters tremendously, and I have to admit that initially I was quite annoyed by your intervention. But then Boy persuaded me that you and Udo had done no harm and, indeed, had shown quite a bit of courage and initiative—qualities in rather short supply these days."

"But I don't understand. Why did you want us to think that Boy Hansgen was dead?"

"Not you, my dear, but others who were watching and taking an interest in his fate."

"You mean Mamma?" I was still confused.

"General Fyrdraaca—and the Birdie overlords—and others, perhaps, too. I'm sorry, Flora, but I can be no more specific than that. You understand that this is a deep, deep secret? I must swear you to silence. If it should get out that he yet lives, then it would be a great danger to him—and to our plans. Will you swear?"

"I swear," I said, thinking, *Well, I won't tell anyone but Udo, that is.* And also thinking, *I still am pretty super-darn confused, but what a relief to know that Boy Hansgen hasn't been ripped to shreds after all.*

Lord Axacaya stood and snapped his fingers. A spot of sunshine coalesced into a servitor with a sad camel-head and sad camel-eyes, who answered, "Your Grace?"

"Sitri, Madama Fyrdraaca is leaving now. She is in a hurry. Please have the closed coach brought around. She wishes to be both swift and discreet."

The next thing I knew, Lord Axacaya had kissed my hand and Sitri was practically frog-marching me down the gallery, through the courtyard now flooded with sunshine, and into a carriage. Thus an end to that ordeal, and I had, in fact, made it through.

The ride home, my brain boiling like a teakettle at high noon in the Arivaipa desert: Lord Axacaya—Mamma— The enemy of my enemy is my friend— Boy Hansgen alive— The Quetzals— Poppy's dead general—

Poppy.

Though all these thoughts roiled within my brain, it was Poppy who kept boiling back to the top. Poppy as I knew him today and Poppy as I had seen him at Bilskinir. A crazy, shifty-eyed old man, bending and halting. A bright-eyed, bright-haired young man, tall and straight. Poppy with his shaking hands and his hollow eyes. Poppy laughing at the thought of burning down the Redlegs' hay shack. Poppy screaming and clawing at his face with his own hands. Poppy kneeling before me, trying to hold on to me. Poppy now. Poppy then.

And Poppy and Butcher Brakespeare, his dead general. Had he loved her? He'd been her aide and had been captured with her by the Huitzils and gone to prison with her. But that had nothing to do with loving her. What about Mamma? Had he never loved her?

When I came through Crackpot's back gate, Flynn was

waiting. He yipped and curled with excitement, and tried to jump up on my poofy skirts. I pushed him down and kissed his nose, happy that I was solid enough for him to jump up on, never mind if he got paw prints on my dress.

The stables were empty of Mamma's horse, which meant, to my extreme relief, that somehow I had beat her home. Bonzo nickered, and pawed at the bars of her stall, in expectation of carrots and sweet feed. I fed her and Mouse, and made sure they had water. Never had horse chores seemed so satisfying, and never again would I complain about mucking out the stables.

I came in quietly through the mudroom and found Udo sitting at the kitchen table, eating pie. A pistol lay to one side of his plate, and a stack of papers and an empty inkwell were on the other. Although he was shoveling the fork in as fast as it would go, he didn't look like he was enjoying his food very much. A ring of dogs stood around him expectantly, and when they heard my step on the stairs, they broke into a belling bay and rushed me.

Udo looked up and choked, spitting crumbs. "Flora! Are you real?"

I waded through the dog pack, petting and kissing as I went. "Real enough to be pissed at you! I am off facing my doom while you sit on your hinder eating pie?"

Udo abandoned the pie and vaulted the kitchen settle to squeeze me tightly, swinging me up in the air. "Oh Flora, you are a sight for sore eyes—I thought you were gone for good!"

"Put me down," I said, pummeling his shoulders. "I can't breathe!"

This demand only caused him to squeeze me tighter, and then I found that I was squeezing him back. He felt hard and real, and my eyes began to water in a most babyish manner. I no longer minded that he could toss me around, but I didn't want to encourage him further, so I said, "Put me down, Udo! You are mussing my hair. Paimon worked hard on it."

Hair mussing is a mortal sin in Udo's eyes; he sat me down gently on the edge of the kitchen table, then stood there, grinning like a fool.

"Flora! I'd given up hope! You look fabulous—where'd you get that dress? And your hair—you actually look like a human being! I thought you were gone for good, oh Flora! Flora—Flora! Guess what! The Dainty Pirate is alive!"

"I know, but how do you?" I got off the kitchen table and shook out my skirts.

"I saw him! He came here—"

"What?!"

"Ayah, see, I got back to Crackpot, and I sat here all night trying to think of what to do, but I kept thinking, *Wait, just wait another minute and she'll walk in the door.* Then, finally, this morning, I gave up, and I thought to myself, Udo, you can't stand this another minute. You have to go to Mariposa yourself and find out what has happened and, if you have to, gut Axacaya like a deer, if Flora needs revenge. So I thought I'd better fortify myself with pie before I went, and then once I finished that pie, I was going to march right over there, and Lord Axacaya and I were going to have strong words!" Udo said, in a tone I had never heard before. It was cold as ice and so, too, were his eyes. I was reminded of the vision I had of Udo as a man, the future Udo, and suddenly that Udo did not seem so far off.

"But what does this have do with the Dainty Pirate?"

"I'm saying, Flora—let me finish—so I was almost finished with my pie. There's a knock at the back door, and I go to answer it, and it's this guy, with a big pile of gifties, and he says, 'I have a delivery for Flora Fyrdraaca,' and I say, 'She's not here,' and he says, 'Well, you can sign for them,' and brings them in—and then suddenly I realize that he's familiar to me. And then I realize that it's the Dainty Pirate!"

"What did he say? Did he explain what happened? How did he get away?" I asked eagerly. The Dainty Pirate *here*! And I had missed him, blasted bloody blast.

"He didn't say, Flora—he just delivered the packages, then left."

My excitement deflated. "But how did you know that he was

the Dainty Pirate, then? He could have just been some delivery guy."

"But I recognized him, Flora; I swear to you it was the Dainty Pirate. I mean, I couldn't just say, 'Hey, are you the Dainty Pirate?' because he's a wanted man, and supposed to be dead, and he'd deny it, anyway. But it was him, I swear, I know it. He winked at me on the way out—he knew that I knew, and I knew that he knew that I knew—we both knew."

"Did you open the packages that he brought?" I asked. "Where are they?"

"I put them in the parlor. I waited for you. Wasn't I nice?"

We stampeded upstairs and into the parlor, which was full of presents piled on the chairs, the sideboards, the tables. I had no idea I had so many friends, well, not really me, I guessed. People who wanted to keep on Mamma's good side. Still, it is cheering to get stuff, even from people you don't know. Udo threw packages around until he found the right ones: a big one and a small one, both wrapped in bright polka-dotted paper, green and gold—the Dainty Pirate's colors!

"See, this one is addressed to you, Udo," I said, pushing the large box to him.

Udo ripped paper and, delving deep into the box, withdrew a hat. Not just any hat, but the most marvelous bicorn hat, its brim pinned by a green and gold cockade, and its crown surmounted by a bright red feather—just the sort of hat a pirate would wear. In fact, it was the exact hat that the *Califa Police Gazette* always shows the Dainty Pirate wearing, right down to the garish plume.

"I told you! Open yours," Udo said triumphantly. "Pigface, what a gorgeous hat!" He put the hat on, points front to back, and I had to admit that he did look quite handsome, very piratical, even.

My box was smaller, and inside was the most beautiful compass I had ever seen, with a rosewood case and golden pointers and mother-of-pearl inlay. I held it in my hand, and the arrow jiggled and spun a bit, and then, head-steady, pointed north.

Udo said, tossing through the packing paper, "There's a note, but it's blank."

"Give it here." The paper did appear to be blank, but surely it could not really be. Why would Boy Hansgen have included a note and not written anything on it? "Wait a minute. Get a trigger."

I carried the paper to the parlor table lamp and removed the glass chimney. Udo lit the wick and I held the paper to the bare flame, close enough to heat but not enough to burn. Letters began to appear, pale yellow, darkening to brown.

"Well, now. Clever," Udo said admiringly.

"It's an old ranger trick. Lemon juice. Invisible until it reacts to heat. Here." I handed the paper to Udo, and he read aloud:

Dear Flora and Udo:
Please accept my most sincere gratitude for your attempts to salvage me from an unsavory fate. As you see, although appearances may have lent themselves to indicating otherwise, I was able to make my escape. Someday I hope to explain further. Until such time, please allow these small remembrances to represent my deepest thanks.
The Dainty Pirate

"Wow! Flora! See—we weren't in vain after all! See? It all worked out," Udo said, admiring himself in the mirror. "The Dainty Pirate is alive, and so are you—and ain't life grand? You have to tell me all about what happened at Mariposa. What was Lord Axacaya wearing—"

The hall clock chimed, and suddenly I forgot all about the Dainty Pirate— *Noon!* It was noon! My Catorcena ceremony was to start at two thirty. Noon! My stomach went cold, a chill that spread its way down my legs and into my feet, up my body, into my head. For a moment, the kitchen went black, and I actually thought I might faint like one of those silly greenhorns in a Nini Mo yellowback.

"Udo, it's already noon! What happened to Mamma?" I said, a touch hysterically. "Mamma didn't come home, did she, already?"

"Oh, ayah, we are lucky, so darn lucky, Flora. That fog bank that Paimon mentioned yesterday? It never lifted; it's sitting there still. No ships can get through the Gate. Maybe we might even have to postpone the ceremony, if she can't get through."

I resolved to send Paimon more than just a plain thank-you note. Maybe candy, or perhaps a smoking cap.

Udo turned away from his preening. "Pigface, am I glad to see you. Now you gotta tell me everything that happened with Axacaya—I hope you didn't sign anything. He didn't make you sign anything in blood, did he? What was he wearing? And what about Valefor? Is he gone for good? But the House didn't fall down."

"Valefor should be all right, but he won't be making any more waffles. He's trapped in the Bibliotheca again," I answered. I knew that I was going to have to go find out how it was with Valefor, but I wasn't entirely looking forward to seeing him again so soon.

"Well, he deserves to stay there after all that, the little snapperhead. Why do you look so downcast, Flora? You are saved. The Dainty Pirate is saved. Everything is working out just dandy."

I said gloomily, "Ayah so, maybe, but there's still my Catorcena, and I haven't finished my dress, or my speech, and now there is no time."

Udo evicted a dog from the settee and sat down. "Don't be a snapperhead, Flora. Look at what you are wearing. It's the most magnificent Catorcena dress I've ever seen. It will do just as well as that other old rag, which wasn't half as nice. You even got cleavage. And the House, it's clean enough, I doubt Buck will notice if it's any cleaner—she won't be home long enough. The kitchen was the big thing, and I got that mostly done. And as for the speech—here—" Udo thrust a stack of papers at me. "Last night I was just sitting here, going crazy, and so I thought

I had to do something, waiting for you to come back, so I wrote your speech for you."

"Really?" I read the top sheet: *First and Most Fabulous of all the Fyrdraacas, Azucar Fyrdraaca was known for his fashion sense and exquisite taste* . . .

"Well, I guess you'd have to say I didn't really write it, exactly, Flora. I mean, you'd already written a lot. I just fixed what was there. I lost the lines about being a slave, and how Crackpot only has one potty. Actually, I guess I had to redo most of it. You are lucky I'm a fast writer, and pretty good at the flattery, too."

"Thank you, Udo," I said. "It's kinda cheating, though, isn't it?"

"Well, it's really a collaboration. I never heard any rule about a collaboration, and besides, beggars can't be choosers, Flora. You speak it from the heart, like you mean it, and that's what counts, I think."

The rumble of cannon fire shuddered through the House, and the dogs jumped up, alarmed, and flung themselves out into the back garden, yelping.

The ferry-arrival gun.

Mamma would be home within the hour.

FORTY-SIX

The Bibliotheca Again.
An Understanding.

SO UDO WENT HOME to change, for he couldn't go to my Catorcena, he explained, with me looking better than him. And I had two things to do before Mamma came home, both of which I dreaded but felt I should do. Had to do. *Must* do.

I was determined that the Elevator should give me no trouble, and after I told it so in no uncertain terms, it got the message, for it whirled me upward as though its cables were greased with butter.

The thin light streaming in through the windows of the Bibliotheca threw shadows, wavering and gray, but there was no sign of Valefor, or even sign that there ever had been a Valefor. The room looked anciently abandoned, dusty and derelict.

"[illegible]," I said, and a Gramatica flame kindled before me. A tall candelabra sat upon the library table, and I used the coldfire spark to light it. The candlelight projected cheerful warm light a few feet into the darkness, and that was all. The pages covered with Splendiferous script that I had seen on my first visit to the Bibliotheca were scattered on the table; I held one to the light and squinted until I could make out the title: *I, Valefor Fyrdraaca ov Fyrdraaca, This is My Story.* Val's autobiography.

"You should have learned by now to mind your own business," Valefor wheezed from high above me somewhere.

I let the paper waft down to the surface of the table and peered up into the dimness, trying to find a form to match the face, but he was hidden in the gloam.

"Come on down, Valefor, where I can see you."

He ignored the request. "What gloomy thoughts to match a gloomy face. I would have thought that you would have returned triumphant, the woman girt with the sword before her, and instead, here you are, as dumpy as an apple cake but not nearly so sweet."

"Lucky for you, Valefor, that I still don't believe in violence," I answered. "Otherwise, perhaps, I should rip you up into tiny little bits and throw you to the four corners of the earth. Come out where I can see you."

"And every corner girded with fire and ice," Val said, unimpressed. He drifted out of the murk, coughing. "I guess your pacifist nature works to my advantage, for once."

"I see, denizen Valefor, that you are not looking so perky now."

Indeed, gray and tattered, he looked more than ever like a ratty dust rag. His hair straggled gray, his gown straggled gray, and his eyes were the same color as his skin: gray. Having been so recently flyaway myself, it was hard not to feel a spark of pity for him, but I didn't let this show.

"It's true," he said dolefully. "You are saved, and brilliant, but I am the same as I was before, forlorn."

He looked woeful, and within me, the pity warred with irritation. I remembered how desperate I felt when I thought I would blow away in the wind and never see Mamma and Poppy and Idden and Udo and Flynn again. Such desperation I would not wish even upon my enemy, and Valefor was not my enemy. He was, for better or worse, a member of my own family.

"However," I said, "that's no excuse for taking advantage of me."

"Maybe not," he agreed. "Does not your revenge feel good? You, free and clear, and me, still locked up, alone, quickly diminishing."

"Pooh," I said. "Revenge is not my motive. Despite your insidious little tricks, I would not see you diminish any further."

"You are not your mother's child, then, for sure," Val said. "But whether you wish revenge or not, revenge is surely what you will get, because without my restoration, I am lost. You may not be fading, but I still am." Here he sobbed and wrung his wasted hands together in a very melodramatic fashion.

"I couldn't restore you, anyway. Didn't you know that? Only Mamma can release you, just as only Mamma could lock you up. You, the Fyrdraaca House, and she, the Head of that House."

"I wasn't sure," Valefor admitted. "But it seemed worth a try. Well, Flora, you did your best; do not think of me when I am gone, though I suppose that you will perhaps miss my slaving, no?"

"Perhaps. Perhaps not. I cannot free you, Valefor, and I guess I ought not to have tried. But you are not diminishing further, Lord Axacaya said. You shall no longer grow strong, but you shall not further fade, either."

"Small consolation to be stuck like this."

"Maybe, Valefor. But it's better than disappearing completely, eh? And Lord Axacaya said that we are still linked, we shall always be linked, for we are both Fyrdraacas. If you focus strongly, you should be able to take some small solace in that, and perhaps it will strengthen you a bit." Lord Axacaya had not actually said focus would give Valefor strength, but it seemed to me that it couldn't hurt to give him a little hope, could it?

At this, Valefor perked up a little bit. "Are you still my friend, Flora Segunda?"

"If you behave, and no tricks."

"What about my fetish?"

"I will keep it safe, Valefor. And maybe one day I can get Mamma to restore you. But you must behave."

"I will try, Flora Segunda, I really will, but it is hard. My gift is rhetoric and confabulation, and it's so hard not to practice what I have no choice but to preach. You should understand something of exaggeration, being so prone yourself."

"We are not talking about me, Valefor, we are talking about you. Will you promise not to trick me again?"

"Trick you once, shame on you; trick you twice, shame on me," Valefor said, which I took to be as much of a promise as I could expect from him. "If we are still friends, will you bring me newspapers, and maybe a muffin or two? Even a little kitten or a mouse, if I am good? A tiny spark of Will to keep me perky?"

"We'll see, Valefor. We'll see."

And so Valefor.

And now Poppy.

FORTY-SEVEN

Poppy.

I DDEN AND I HAVE never been expressly forbidden to go up to Poppy's Eyrie, we just never have any inclination to do so. Better to leave him alone. Today I was not going to leave Poppy alone. Today I *could* not leave him alone.

I can't imagine why the stairs were named the Stairs of Exuberance when there was nothing particularly exuberant about them. They were narrow and gloomy and lit only by slender slits in the heavy brick walls. Round and round they circled; wide on the outer edge, narrow on the inner. By the time I got to the top, I was dizzy from the spirals and, thanks to Paimon's tight lacing, breathless from the climb. I paused on the threshold of the half-open door (imagination would have it barred and bolted from without, like in a lurid mystery novel) and rested my burning leg muscles. They didn't call the top of the tower the Eyrie for nothing.

"Poppy?" I peered around the doorjamb. When I got no answer, I sidled in, careful to keep the door to my back. A good ranger always knows what is behind her.

Four windows, one in each wall, stared at me like four wide eyes. There was a narrow iron cot, no wider than a grave but not nearly so deep. Since Poppy always looks like a corpse, I would have thought that the Eyrie would be an equal mess, all dank and crumpled, messy with blood and bottles, and Goddess knows what else.

But it wasn't. The cot was neatly made; the wooden floor was neatly bare. A small altar sat in the northwest corner, which is, of course, the direction from which Death comes.

Poppy knelt in front of the altar, his head bent, his shoulders hunched. The doors to the altar were closed, which is tremendously sacrilegious, even I knew that. The Goddess must be free to come and go as she Wills and it is an insult to her to shut her doors against her.

"Poppy," I said, quietly. My hands were shaking, and I scrunched them into the fluff of my skirt, clutching fistfuls of fabric. "Poppy."

"I'm sorry," he said, without looking up. "I'm sorry."

He turned his head then, though he did not raise his eyes, and I saw his face. It was masklike, his eyes sunken in the painted black band that bisected them. His eyes were dull and muddy. The contrast between that weary sad face and the handsome face, the bright green eyes, of the Poppy I had met at Bilskinir twisted painfully in my stomach.

"Sorry for what, Poppy?" I asked.

"Sorry that I failed you. Sorry that I could not save you. Sorry that I let you go—let you go on into the darkness, alone."

"I didn't go anywhere, Poppy. I am still here." I reached my hand out and tentatively, lightly, touched his shoulder, which felt fragile and bony beneath my fingers. "You didn't fail me."

Now, finally, Poppy lifted his eyes, and he looked at me, and with that look, his gaze sharpened like a knife, with sudden avid confusion and a strange sort of hunger.

"Flora? Is that you?" he asked wonderingly. "You are real? You are not a ghost?"

"I am not a ghost," I said firmly. "I am real."

Poppy stumbled to his feet and reached out to clutch me. I hugged him back, feeling the ridge of his ribs underneath his sweater, smelling the acrid odor of his sweat. Underneath that smell was another, one I remembered from the embrace of the other Poppy: pipe weed and bay rum.

He said, in a rush of words, "Flora, I tried, I told Valefor to leave you alone. I fed him to keep him off of you, and I took the fetish from Buck to give it to you, but then I forgot where I put it, and I couldn't find it in time. I thought you were the other Flora before, and when you were lost, I thought you were safe, but then I realized later you were not her, you were yourself, and I thought maybe if you swam in the Current it would fix you, but it didn't do any good. I'm sorry, Flora, I'm so sorry."

Suddenly it all made sense, although in a muddled Poppy way. He had remembered and tried to help, but so confused had he been that I hadn't even recognized his help *as* help. Poppy's warning to me about Valefor. Valefor's fetish in Poppy's Catorcena chest, locked with Poppy's seal. Poppy, dragging me off the Folly into the Current, hoping it would fix me—though it hadn't, it *had* given me enough jolt to go on a little longer. Poppy, even in his crazy confusion, had tried. He had done the best he could.

My throat closed in on itself, choking down the words, letting out only the most horrific gasping noises. Each wrack seemed to shake me to the core, dislocate my shoulders, wrench my ribs, but I could not stop. I closed my eyes, burning and blurring with running eyeliner, and Poppy's arms smothered me into the roughness of his sweater, holding me too tight to shudder anymore, and then, at last, I could stop.

"I want . . . ," I said into his chest, when I could talk again. "Poppy, will you come to my Catorcena?"

He didn't answer, only slackened his hug and let his arms fall. He sat down on the edge of the cot and bent his head again. Little lines of blackness ran down his cheeks. "I can't, Flora."

"Please, Poppy. Please."

"I can't, Flora, I can't bear the light. I can't see their faces. I can't."

I said, with more firmness in my voice than I felt in my knees, so tired and wobbly: "You can't mope forever, Poppy. *Dare, win, or disappear!*"

"I'm sorry, Flora."

"I don't want your apologies, Poppy."

"But I don't have anything else. They took it all. I have nothing left," he said sadly.

"That's not true," I said, stung to hotness. "You have Mamma, and Idden, and me. And Flynn, and Flash, and Dash, and Lash, and Screamie. Even Valefor. Aren't we something? Don't we matter? We must matter; you must care, or you wouldn't have tried to save me. Poppy, don't you remember, when we were at Bilskinir and we said good-bye, and you said that you don't fear dying but you were sorry for not being there for me and for not seeing me grow up. Poppy! You are not dead! Remember you said that Fyrdraacas are tough? Fyrdraacas don't give up! You are Reverdy Anacreon Fyrdraaca. Poppy, *please.* Please don't give up. Please try."

He just sat there with his head bowed, and I wanted to whack him, which I knew was a totally useless want, not helpful at all, but it made me so angry to see him so forlorn. For a minute, in his arms, I had thought, foolishly, that somehow things might be different now. But no, that *was* a foolish thought. Poppy was just the same as always. Weak-willed and broken.

"You love your dead general, Poppy, more than you love Mamma, or Idden, or me," I said in a mean little voice. "Is that who you are mourning? Is that who you think about all the time? Not me, not Mamma, not Idden, not the other Flora. *Her!*"

He looked up at me, his face agonized, and I knew then it was true, what Lord Axacaya had said. He answered, "You don't understand, Flora—"

"Fine, Poppy. Have it your own way. I don't care. Sit in your tower and think of her. *I don't care!*"

Outside, a bugle sounded Boots and Saddles. I ran to the window. Below, looking like little toy soldiers, were Mamma and her escort, flags flying. The bugle sounded again, and abandoning Poppy, I tore down the stairs to answer its call.

FORTY-EIGHT

Mamma. Orders. The Barracks.

I MET MAMMA JUST AS she swept into the parlor in a tide of yapping dogs, singing, "*With your rifle come and stand, with your rifle come and stand, gather round and assemble, gather round!*" to the tune of the Assembly bugle call. "Where's the birthday girl? Where is she!"

"Mamma!" I waded through the sea of dogs to meet her, and she enfolded me in salt-smelling buckskin arms and kissed my forehead with cold lips. I hugged her back, glad that I was real enough to do so, and also glad—oh, so glad—that she didn't know how close I had come to never being able to hug her again. "Mamma, I'm so glad you are home!"

"I'm sorry I am so late," Mamma said. "I thought I would miss the entire ceremony. That blasted fog, I was cursing the weather and the Goddess; the pilot said that he'd never seen such a fog bank before, so thick and squat; we thought maybe it would never lift. But it did lift and here we are, like the cavalry in the nick of time. Get down, wretched dogs, get *down!* Will you forgive me, darling?"

I hugged her tightly. "It's all right, Mamma. You are here now, that's all that matters. But Mamma..." Guilt twinged at me, and for one mad moment, I almost blurted out everything.

Mamma saucered her forage cap toward the bust of Azucar

Fyrdraaca, but it missed its mark and was immediately seized by a chasing dog. "Dash—drop that hat—what is it, darling?"

"I skipped school!" If I had to confess something, that seemed the safest sin to admit to.

"Oh pooh! A little fault, I think, on this big day. Look at this room, it's so full of gifties there is almost no room for us! Are you ready, darling? I'm sorry to cut it so close—you look lovely, how well your dress turned out—but we need to redo your maquillage, darling. I sent Aglis on ahead, to make sure that everything was ready at the O Club."

With a flurry of commands, Mamma took charge. She ordered her outriders to load my gifties and the dogs into the barouche. She ordered me upstairs to get my cloak and hat, and not to forget my speech. She ordered herself upstairs to get her dress uniform, and then ordered me to help her find her silver aiguillettes, which we didn't find because, she suddenly remembered, they were in the luggage she had taken to Moro. Back downstairs, she ordered her outriders to get Flynn back into that barouche and keep him there. Twenty minutes and twenty more orders and we were ready to go.

"And now, do we have everything and are ready to go, darling?" Mamma asked, surveying the parlor one last time. "Your speech?"

"I have it. Mamma—" I had something to say and now seemed like as good a time as any to say it.

Mamma didn't hear me. She said, "I lost my Catorcena speech, what a disaster! My lady mother almost had apoplexy. I had left it on my desk and then that blasted denizen came and tidied it up, and couldn't remem—" Mamma stopped midword. She was looking beyond me, at the doorway, her face suddenly rigid and set.

There stood Poppy, his face white as paper but scrubbed completely clean. His eyes were muddy green, but they were clear. The Skinner scars on his cheeks were faint, barely visible. He had changed out of his ragged clothes into a green and gold brocade frock coat, black kilt, and polished black boots. His stock was untied. His hat, a gorgeous beaver bicorn, with black fur trim and a bright silver cockade, was on crooked. Poppy smiled at us, a small shy smile that lit like a lamp, and suddenly that beautiful young man I had seen at Bilskinir stood before me—bent, twisted, older, but still recognizable.

"Happy birthday, Flora," he said. "Ave, Buck."

"Ave, Hotspur," Mamma said. "What you are doing down-stairs?"

"It's Flora's birthday."

"So I know," answered Mamma. They looked at each other and something passed between them, something I couldn't quite read. But one thing was clear: Though Poppy may have loved his dead general, he loved Mamma, too. And Mamma loved him back.

"Can you tie my tie, Buck?" Poppy said. "My arm don't reach that high." He came forward and stood in front of Mamma expectantly. She quickly knotted his tie and tucked the ends into his weskit, then reached up to straighten his hat.

"Do I pass inspection, General?" Poppy asked, with the shadow of a smile.

"You will do, Colonel. There! We are all ready. You both look very nice," Mamma said brightly. "I hope I can get cleaned up well enough to match, or I shall be the disgrace of the family. Shall we go?"

Now or never. After I had faced Axacaya, after I had faced Poppy, what could Mamma say? It was my birthday. And Poppy had washed his mourning off and come out of the Eyrie to face life. Maybe things—people—could change after all. Or at least *try* to change.

"Mamma— Poppy— I want to say something."

"Ayah, darling? What is it?" Mamma said impatiently. "We don't have much time. Can it wait until later?"

"No, Mamma. It can't."

"They won't hardly start without Flora, Buck," Poppy said. "Let us sit down for a minute and listen."

"All right, but quickly." Mamma sat on the settee, and Poppy sat down next to her, taking her hand in his and holding on to it tightly.

I moved in front of the fireplace and took a deep breath. Somehow Flynnie had again escaped the barouche, and now he ingratiated himself between Poppy's legs. Poppy rubbed his silky ears absentmindedly and stared at me. Mamma was looking at me quizzically.

Dare, win, or disappear.

"Mamma. Poppy. I don't want to go to the Barracks," I said in a big rush, the words almost blurring together. "It's not for me, I know it's not. I know that's probably disappointing to you, but I really don't want to go. I know all the other Fyrdraacas went, but please, not me. My Will lies elsewhere."

Mamma didn't answer. She looked at me, but at least it wasn't that cold *I'm in Charge and You'd Better Not Gainsay Me* look. It was more of a *Where Did This Come From; I Can't Believe I'm Hearing This* look.

Then she said slowly, "All Fyrdraacas go to the Barracks. It's our family tradition."

Poppy said softly, "Perhaps, Juliet, it's time to start a new family tradition."

Mamma turned her Look upon Poppy, but he only gazed steadily back.

"You never mentioned this before," Mamma said to me.

"You never gave me a chance, Mamma. You never acted like you cared what I thought."

"You have your duty, Flora."

"Ayah, I know, but there is more than one way to be loyal, Mamma."

"We don't have time to discuss this now. It's a serious thing you have said, Flora."

"I know, Mamma. I know that we don't have time now, and it's all right, but I just had to say."

"All right, Flora. Your objections have been so noted and will be discussed further at a later time."

"Thank you, Mamma," I said, relieved. "That's all I ask. I know it's a serious thing and must be discussed seriously, but that's all I want—to discuss it."

Nini Mo said talk was cheap and it is action that counts. She was right, but I now realized it takes a certain amount of words to get things done. I guess I wasn't a ranger yet, nor had I yet escaped the Barracks, but I had escaped something much worse—Nothingness. I was still me, and right this moment it felt pretty good, actually, to be me, Flora Nemain Fyrdraaca ov Fyrdraaca.

Behind Mamma and Poppy's heads, above the bust of Azucar Fyrdraaca, a purple spark glimmered briefly and then was gone.

AFTER

*L*ATER, AFTER WE HAD ridden in the barouche to the O Club—Mamma, Poppy, me, and the dogs, like we were a real family, with Mamma looking at Poppy as though she couldn't quite believe it, and the escort following behind, loaded with my gifties—

Later, after I had made my speech and sworn my oath, and curtseyed to the Warlord (who, thankfully, did not remember we had ever before met), and received the Warlord's beery kiss upon my cheek—

Later, after Mamma welcomed me to adulthood and presented me with my Catorcena chest, and the gifties were opened, most of them pretty good, except that someone had sent me a plushy pink pig, as though I had just turned four, instead of fourteen—

Later, after my Catorcena cake was cut, and slices handed around, and toasts made, and congratulations offered, and Dash and Flash stole a turkey off the buffet and were chased from the room by a posse of infuriated waiters—

Later, after I had danced with the Warlord, who trod heavily upon my toes, and then with Mamma, who was as light as a feather, and then with Poppy, who was surprisingly spry, and who had not gone near the punch bowl all evening—

Later, after all that, I was in the loo, trying to figure out how to wad my giant poof of skirts into such a small stall, when I remembered the small box Poppy had pressed into my hand at the end of our dance. Before I had been able to open it, Udo had descended on me and I had shoved it into my pocket as he whisked me away for a mazurka. And after Udo, Lieutenant Sabre and a waltz, and then Udo again, and so I had forgotten all about the little box.

Now I pulled it from my pocket. The box was small, made of worn red leather, and held closed with a small gold clasp. Inside, a tarnished silver badge lay on a crumple of velvet. Not a civilian identification badge, like the one Mamma makes me and Idden wear, but an actual Army-issue badge, enameled in smoke gray and dusky purple, the kind you wear around your neck so they know who to ship you to when you are killed.

On one side was the logo of the Ranger Corps: the Unblinking Eye.

And on the other side, the name of the badge's owner:

REVERDY ANACREON FYRDRAACA OV FYRDRAACA.

Poppy.

FLORA'S DARE

How a Girl of Spirit
Gambles All to Expand Her
Vocabulary, Confront a Bouncing Boy Terror,
and Try to Save Califa
from a Shaky Doom
(Despite Being Confined to Her Room)

Tierra Califa

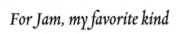

For Jam, my favorite kind

In what distant deeps or skies
Burnt the fire of thine eyes?
On what wings dare he aspire?
What the hand dare seize the fire?

—WILLIAM BLAKE

What I Learned Last Term

An Essay by
Flora Nemain Fyrdraaca ov Fyrdraaca
Senior Class
Sanctuary School
City of Califa
Republic of Califa

1. Do not trust banished Butlers who promise they will do your chores but are actually tricking you into giving them all your Will so that you start fading into Nothing.
2. Accidentally inhaling a Gramatica Invocation really hurts and can result in very sparkly upchucking.
3. The trick to forging a signature is turning the original upside down before you try to copy it.
4. After a week in the bottom of an oubliette, even great heroes smell pretty bad.
5. Eight-foot-tall blue praterhuman entities with razor-sharp fangs, needle-sharp mustachios, and shiny sharp tusks can actually be quite nice.
6. It is easier to face your greatest enemy when you look fantastic.
7. Nothing is stronger than your own Will.

OF COURSE, these things are not what I was *supposed* to learn last term.

When Archangel Bob gave out this assignment (and I'd like to point out it's entirely unfair to have to do homework over the holiday break), I know he expected me to list the things I'd learned last term at Sanctuary School. And I was supposed to learn a lot. For example, in Charm and Deportment I was supposed to learn how to say no without giving offense. In Scriptive I was supposed to learn how to write beautifully in Splendiferous Script. In Dressmaking I was supposed to learn how to inset sleeves and make cartridge pleats. In Math I was supposed to learn how to calculate square roots.

Ayah, so I did learn how to read Splendiferous Script (though I never quite managed to learn how to write it—at least not legibly), but who uses Splendiferous Script anymore? Only government clerks and really old people—neither of which I am. I didn't quite manage the rest of the lessons, but so what? If people get offended when you say no, isn't that their problem, not yours? I don't like cartridge pleats; they make your waist look too big, and my waist looks big enough as it is. And who needs to know how to calculate a square root? Only engineers, accountants, and gunners, none of which I plan to be.

I am going to be a ranger. And rangers do not waste their time sitting in a classroom. The greatest ranger of them all—Nyana Keegan, better known as Nini Mo—chronicled her adventures in a series of yellowback novels called Nini Mo: Coyote Queen. (*Coyote* being the slangy term for ranger, of course.) There is no yellowback called *Nini Mo Sits in Math Class,* or *Nini Mo and the Curse of the Overdue Library Book,* or *Nini Mo vs. the Term Paper on the Orthogonal Uses of Liminal Spaces in the Novels of Lucretia McWordypants.*

Rangers are not bound by rules and regulations. Rangers move silently through the world, unnoticed and unknown, and yet they see everything. They are clever, cunning, and shrewd. Rangers are adept at working the magickal Current. They can cross from the Waking World to Elsewhere as easily as moving from one room to another. They follow their own Wills, not the Wills of others. They are to their own selves true. They seek out secret truths, and find that which has been hidden.

Nini Mo did not let school interfere with her education, and neither do I. To be fair, I will admit that sometimes the stuff they try to stuff down you is helpful: For example, when you are running from a hungry domicilic denizen you are pretty glad that you didn't skip gym class. And when you have to go to your family's worst enemy and beg for his help, it is useful to have practiced your manners in Charm and Deportment until they are perfect.

But overall, after ten years of school, I can state with authority that formal education is all about sitting and listening and repeating and reading, and doing busy work. Calculate, *If Udo has four cupcakes and you have six cupcakes, which cupcake is blue?* And, *Define the word* defenestration *and use it in a sentence. (Before you defenestrate your math book, you should open the window first.)* Write out, *I will not return my library books two weeks late ever again,* one hundred and fifty times. Maybe these things are useful in school, but they are not very helpful in Real Life.

And this I learned the hard way—in Real Life.

My Real Life education started in the middle of last term, when I accidentally found Valefor, our family's long banished Butler, locked in the Bibliotheca Mayor. Val was pretty sad about being locked in the library, powerless to keep up our House; I was pretty sad about the decrepit state of Crackpot Hall. We struck a deal: In return for help with my chores (I know—it does sound stupid now, doesn't it?—but I had *a lot* of chores), I would share my Anima with him—my Will, my spirit—and try to restore him. (This turned out to be Lesson One.)

To restore Val, Udo (my best friend, who also does not allow school to interfere with his education—or his fashion sense) and I had to find Valefor's fetish, which we almost did, thanks to a handy-dandy Discernment Sigil we found in the handy-dandy magickal handbook *The Eschatanomicon.* (Here's Lesson Two.) But before we could restore Val to full power, I discovered that Mamma, who is the Commanding General of the Army of Califa, had captured the infamous Dainty Pirate and was going to hang him. The infamous Dainty Pirate turned out to be Boy Hansgen, the last true ranger, in disguise. Udo and I couldn't let the last true ranger die, so we tried to rescue him. This involved a forged order of release and a deep-cover infiltration of Zoo Battery, where he was being held. (Lessons Three and Four.) We almost succeeded, but at the last minute, Boy Hansgen was snatched away from us, and killed.

This failure was crushing, horrific, excruciating, awful. But the worst was to come: I then discovered that Valefor had infected me with Anima Enervation—a dreadful magickal wasting disease of the Will. If we did not restore Valefor immediately, he would dwindle and disappear into the Abyss of Nowhere— and take me with him.

But the Restoration Sigil required a Semiote Verb—a Gramatica Word so concentrated that it could be in only one place at a time—and that Semiote Verb was kept at Bilskinir House. Ayah, Bilskinir House, the House of the Haðraaða Family, closed ever since the last Haðraaða died years ago. Closed and guarded by a fearsome Butler called Paimon, a denizen whose sharp appetite and sharper teeth were legendary for their ferocity.

We had no choice. If I was to be saved—if Valefor was to be saved—Udo and I had to get into Bilskinir House, and hope to sneak by Paimon, steal the Word, and scarper without running into any sharpness—teeth, tusks, or otherwise. Lucky for us, Bilskinir was not nearly as boo-spooky as we'd heard, and Paimon, although fearsome, was welcoming. And an excellent cook, too, which I suppose makes sense, as by their very nature domicilic denizens are domestic. (Lesson Five.) But instead of giving us the Semiote Verb, Paimon gave us really awful news. Only Mamma, the Head of the Fyrdraaca House, could restore Valefor. And Mamma was out of town. By the time she came home, it would be too late; Val and I would have vanished into the Abyss of Nowhere.

After a slight misunderstanding and an accidental side trip into Bilskinir's past, where we met Poppy, much younger and far less crazy than he is now, Udo and I came up with a new plan. I had only one hope: Go to Lord Axacaya, the City's greatest magickal adept—and Mamma's greatest enemy—and beg him for help. I quivered at the thought. But, *Desperation makes you desperate,* said Nini Mo. I had no choice. (Lesson Six.)

Well, Lord Axacaya wasn't so very helpful. In fact, he was downright mean. He pointed out the flaws in my recent behavior: that I had gone behind Mamma's back to help Valefor in the first place, that I had no business meddling in the City's politics by trying to rescue Boy Hansgen, and that I had lied, cheated, stolen, and forged. True, in retrospect, I *had* been quite a snapperhead, but that was no reason for Lord Axacaya to threaten my family, which he did, saying that it was Mamma and Poppy's fault that I was so badly brought up, that it was Poppy's fault I was gallivanting around causing trouble. The meaner Lord Axacaya was, the angrier I got. If I'd been a snapperhead, that was *my* problem—Mamma and Poppy weren't to blame.

I exploded in rage—and my fury saved me. My anger strengthened my Will and broke the link between me and Valefor. I refused to be pushed around anymore by anyone, and that turned out to be the thing that saved me. (Lesson Seven.) And Lord Axacaya had only been baiting me, to get me to stand up for myself; once I was myself again, he was really quite gracious. I'm not sure why Mamma hates him so.

(Oh, and Lesson Eight: Don't always believe your eyes. Udo and I had thought we had seen Lord Axacaya's guards kill Boy Hansgen, but they had only made it look like they did. Actually, they had allowed Boy Hansgen to escape.)

So that's a short summation of what I learned, and how—and why. *A ranger learns from her mistakes*, Nini Mo said. I made plenty of mistakes, and I think I've done a pretty good job of learning from them.

Now, I'm supposed to finish up this essay (which, of course, I'll never turn in—*not everyone needs to know everything*, said Nini Mo) by discussing what I want to learn next term, my last term at Sanctuary School.

Well, I would like to learn how to start a fire with a piece of ice. How to load one hundred pounds on a mule. How to hold my breath for ten minutes. And most important: I want to learn Gramatica, the language of magick.

True Invocations and Sigils require Gramatica, and Gramatica is fiendishly complicated. The words are sounds, but they are also gestures, and colors, and lights. Gramatica is also horribly dangerous. If you mispronounce a Word, awful things can happen. You could try to open a lock and instead turn your head backward. You could try to light a match and instead set your hair on fire. All because you had inflected up when you should have inflected down, or *klick*ed where you should have *klack*ed, or stood on one foot instead of three. One mispronounced Gramatica Word and you could evaporate all the water in the Bay, or summon up an ice-storm elemental, or turn time back.

I know a few words of Gramatica, but they are tiny small words that do tiny small things: ignite coldfire sparks, charge small sigils—nothing big, nothing interesting. If I'm going to be a ranger, I'm going to have to learn a whole lot more.

And Sanctuary definitely does not teach Gramatica.

ONE

Dirty Dishes.
A Brief Recap. Woe.

Finally, the term was over and two weeks of freedom loomed. Two weeks of freedom from Sanctuary School, that is. There was no escape from Poppy.

"I think," I said, sorrowfully, "that I liked Poppy better when he was drunk." My back hurt from leaning over the sink, and the dishwater was now cold and greasy. Happily, I was on the last pan. It was crusty and black, but it was the last. The last pan, the last chore, and then, I would be free for the first night of term break.

"There is no pleasing some people," Valefor replied from his vaporous perch high on top of the kitchen dresser. Valefor was the one who should have been doing the dishes, and everything else as well. Thanks to his banishment, he was a mere wisp, and his helpfulness was limited to criticism, which I did not find helpful in the slightest. And he had to lay low, too. If Mamma discovered him flitting about, he would be in a World of Hurt.

Valefor continued. "You complained when Hotspur was drunk and wallowing all the time; now he's straight as straight, and you complain about that, too, Flora Segunda."

I put the last pan in the dish drainer, then straightened up, feeling a hundred years old, and as though I'd been washing up for ninety of those years. It was only Mamma, Poppy, and me at home, yet somehow we were generating enough dirty dishes for an entire regiment. Poppy's fault, really; he was cooking meals big enough for an entire regiment, even though Mamma ate only breakfast at home, I ate dinner at Sanctuary School, and it was usually just Poppy and me for supper.

"I never thought he'd turn out to be such a tyrant," I said. "He's a hundred times worse than Mamma. At least Mamma isn't around enough to crawl down your throat. Poppy never leaves the house. He's always here. There's no escaping. Flynnie, get out of there."

At my gentle kick, Flynn slunk away from the garbage can, looking dejected, as though he'd never been fed before in his life. Which was, of course, false, as he'd not only already had dinner, but had licked the plates before I washed them—saves on the scrubbing, you know.

"Hotspur is overcompensating," Valefor explained. "He always goes too far. When he was brave, he was the bravest ever. When he was in love, you'd have thought no one had ever loved so much. When he was crazy, no lunatic ever howled so loud. And now that he's sober, he's so straight you could rule your paper with him."

"Can't he just be somewhere in the comfy middle?" I pulled the plug and let the nasty water glug out of the sink. There, that was it. Punto finale for Flora and the dishes. Punto finale for my last chore of the day. And not a moment too soon. The kitchen clock was about to chime eight. If I didn't get a move on it, I was going to be late meeting Udo, and I hate being late. *The only thing that it's good to be late for,* said Nini Mo, *is your own funeral.*

"No Fyrdraaca ever sat in the comfy middle," Val pronounced. "We are all about the razor-thin edge of extreme. It's our family hallmark."

"Ha," I said, sourly, for he was certainly right there.

"Anyway, you wanted things to change, and they did. So stop complaining."

"Ha." Even more sourly, for he was right there, as well.

My Catorcena—my fourteenth birthday whereon I became officially an adult—was three months past, and things *had* changed, and yet nothing at all changed, really. Of course, I hadn't expected miracles—I wasn't *that* childish, even at my most optimistic—but immediately after my birthday celebration, things had looked mighty promising.

Take Poppy, for example. During the Huitzil War, Poppy had been a prisoner, and almost executed for war crimes. At the end of the War, Mamma ransomed him, but Poppy came home sick, crazy, and a drunk. And so he had remained until finally he had promised to try to forget the woes of the past and stay sober.

He had kept his promise. But Poppy sober was almost as bad as Poppy drunk, only in an entirely different way. Drunk Poppy was a lunatic. Sober Poppy was a tyrant. A martinet. What in the Army they call a whip. What I call a giant huge pain in my hinder.

Sober Poppy had turned Crackpot Hall into an Army camp. There was Reveille (Get Up), Mess Call (Get to Breakfast), Assembly (Inspection before Leaving the House), Drill Call (Do Your Homework), Guard Mount (Take the Dogs Out), Inspection (Is Your Room Clean?), Reinspection (What Did I Tell You about Dusting?), Tattoo (Time for Bed), and Retreat (Lights Out). I was surprised that Poppy didn't actually get a bugle and stand on the stairs sounding the calls. Maybe he just hadn't thought of that yet.

Poppy had become a despot who skulked around the house, his face like a block of carved ice. I don't think Poppy actually slept; he just stayed up all night polishing and dusting, scrubbing or sweeping. Crackpot was still decrepit, but now at least it was clean.

And cooking. When Poppy was a souse, I would not have pegged him to have much interest in cooking, but now, next to cleaning, cooking was all he did. He made bread and cakes, pies and cookies. Stews and soups, gelées and galantines, roasts and chops, tortillas and tortas. The pantry was full of food, the icebox was full of food, Mamma was full of food, I was full of food, Udo was full of food, even the dogs were full of food.

Only Poppy was not full of food; I never saw him eat a single thing.

All I had wanted was order. Instead, I got tyranny.

Mamma, of course, was exempt from Poppy's discipline, as she outranked him, but I had no choice but to hop to. My only relief was school; never before had I been so happy to escape to Sanctuary each morning, and I loitered there in the afternoon as long as possible. But eventually I had to go home.

The only bright side to Poppy's behavior was that it was doing a great job of reminding me that I did not want to follow the Fyrdraaca family tradition. Fyrdraacas attend Benica Barracks Military Academy and then go into the Army. As far back as anyone can remember, this is so: Mamma went, Poppy went, my sister Idden went—even the Fyrdraaca dogs have gone. Fyrdraacas are soldiers. It's our family rule.

What has soldierly duty gotten this family? Mamma is Commanding General of the Army of Califa and everyone thinks she's a great hero for saving Califa from the Birdies, as we call the Huitzils. Thanks to Mamma's peace accord, we are a client state instead of a conquered one. But she's a slave to duty; she's hardly ever home, spends all her time pushing paperwork, handling the Warlord, bowing to the Birdie Ambassador, trying to keep the Republic together.

Poppy was aide-de-camp to the Butcher Brakespeare, the commanding general before Mamma, and narrowly escaped being executed with her. Instead he spent three years in a Birdie prison, where he was abused and tortured. He came home a broken drunken wreck. That's how soldierly duty worked out for him.

My older sister, Idden, is what they call a paper-collar soldier—in other words, perfect. She graduated first in her class at Benica Barracks, she's made captain after only six years out of the Barracks, and may well be commanding general herself one of these days. But now she's posted to Fort Jones in Trinity Territory, where you could die of boredom and it would take the news two weeks to reach civilization. Now that Califa is a client state, the Army just sits and does nothing.

And my other sister, the First Flora. Flora Primera wasn't a soldier, just a six-year-old girl when she was captured with the Butcher and Poppy. When the Butcher was executed and Poppy imprisoned, the Birdies took Flora Primera—and Mamma could never find out what had happened to her. Perhaps the Birdies sacrificed her to one of their bloodthirsty gods. Maybe they ate her, like they ate the Butcher Brakespeare. Maybe they fostered her to a Birdie family and now she's forgotten all about Califa. Flora Primera wasn't even a soldier, but she was sacrificed for Fyrdraaca soldierly duty.

That leaves me, Flora Segunda. I have no intention of wasting my life on soldierly duty.

I had finally gotten my nerve up to tell Mamma that I did not want to go to Benica Barracks, and that was some nerve, let me tell you, because Mamma is used to being obeyed. To my surprise, Mamma had not exploded at my impudence. Instead, she had promised that she would consider my desire and we would discuss it further.

Except Mamma never took the time to consider or discuss. Immediately after my Catorcena she'd gone off to Arivaipa Territory on a three-month inspection; she'd only just returned and already the redboxes were piling up in the office, full of paperwork she had missed while she was gone. I had hardly had a minute alone with her since she'd gotten back. When she wasn't at Headquarters, she was with the Warlord, and when she wasn't with the Warlord, she was in her study, surrounded by redboxes and her aide-de-camp, Lieutenant Sabre, while various other staff officers tramped in and out, making personal conversation with Mamma impossible.

I hadn't yet mentioned to Mamma my specific ranger ambitions; I thought I would take things one at a time. Did Nini Mo wait for her mother's permission before following her Will? She did not. Nini Mo's mamma, a wer-coyotl of great power, encouraged her in all ways, but even if she hadn't, that wouldn't have stopped Nini Mo. She followed her own Will and let no one stand against her.

I wiped down the table again and took a last look around the kitchen. I didn't want to give Poppy any excuse to confine me to my room. So far, I'd been confined for not polishing my boots, for coming to breakfast with my jacket unbuttoned, for giving Poppy an insolent look when he suggested that I run up and down Fyrdraaca Hill several times for exercise, and for not standing up when he entered the kitchen. (Was he my commanding officer? *No, but I'm your elder deserving of respect,* he had said. Respect!) I didn't have time to be confined tonight.

Tonight I had plans.

TWO

An Earthquake. A Curfew.
Lying about Puppets.

LEAVING BEHIND a spotless kitchen, I went to report to Poppy, the woefully hungry Flynnie nudging at my heels. I love Flynn, the runt of the Fyrdraaca red-dog pack, but sometimes he can be a real pest. I found Poppy darning my socks in the parlor, surrounded by Flynnie's older and more handsome siblings, Crash, Dash, and Flash. Poppy sat on the settee stiffly, as though he were at attention in front of some invisible review. Once, he had been considered handsome, but you wouldn't know that now. He was gaunt and bony, his cheeks sunken. For years he'd kept his hair cropped close to his skull, as a sign of mourning. He was letting it grow again, and it was now a shade of silvery red that softened the angles of his face. Poppy's knitting needles clicked like cicadas as he stared fixedly into the fire, his eyes blank and unblinking. He was obviously thinking about something, but what—Idden? Flora Primera? The Butcher Brakespeare, whom he had loved so well? Tomorrow's menu?

I knew what *I* thought about every time I saw Poppy: the ranger badge he had given me at my Catorcena. The ranger badge with his name on it. I now wore it on a chain around my neck. I longed to ask him what his giftie meant, but I dared not presume. His face made it clear he invited no questions. It was hard for me to believe that he had ever been a ranger, truly, for surely no ranger would ever have broken as he did. No ranger would have gone mad or drowned his sorrows in bugjuice. Before Poppy retired, he was a member of the Alacrán Regiment, the most fearsome regiment in the Army of Califa, but that didn't really signify, as the rangers had all been undercover. He could have been both an Alacrán and a ranger, and I longed to ask if that was so—and yet I dared not.

On the coffee table, a cigarillo burned in a little nest of cigarillo butts. Instead of eating, Poppy smoked. I guess you can only give up one horrible habit at a time, but the smoke was making my lungs itch and my nose run, and it smelled foul. Even the dogs were snuffling. But I didn't dare complain about that, either. Next to the ashtray lay a letter: I recognized Idden's perfect handwriting. She writes to Poppy every week. The rest of us are lucky if we hear from her every six months.

"Poppy?"

"Ayah?" He looked away from the fire, toward me, as the needles continued to clack.

"I'm done with the kitchen. Can I be dismissed?"

"Are the dishes put away?"

"Ayah, sir."

"The table is wiped?"

"Ayah, sir."

"Floor swept?"

"Ayah, sir."

"Stove banked?"

"Ayah, sir."

"Sink trap cleaned out?"

"Ayah, sir."

"Where are you going?"

"The Blue Duck."

"Be back by eleven. Dismissed." He turned his stare back to the fire.

Eleven! This was outrageous! During the school year, my curfew was at eleven. Now that I was on vacation, surely I should have a later evening. I wailed, "Poppy! It's almost eight now. Weatherhead, the opening act, doesn't even go on until nine. Udo and I won't get to see the main act if I have to be back by eleven."

The needles continued to click. Poppy didn't answer. I longed for the days when I could do anything I wanted. So what of a clean house and yummy chow if I had to live like a prisoner? *Sometimes by the time you get it, you don't want it anymore*, said Nini Mo. Pigface, was she right!

I tried to sound calm and adultlike. "Poppy, it's not fair. It's the holidays—there's no school tomorrow—I don't have to get up."

The floor wiggled under my feet. For a second, I thought, *Too much cake at dinner!* But then the dogs jerked up in alarm, and Flynnie let out a sharp yelp. The shaking was not just me.

The room filled with rattling: pictures clacking against the wall, glasses jingling against each other. The floor vibrated as though somewhere a giant was energetically dancing the mazurka. I lurched toward the doorway, the dogs dove under the coffee table, and Flynnie launched onto Poppy's lap. A loud grinding rumble drowned out the rattling.

An earthquake! And the second one of the week. The City has always been susceptible to shaking, but recently these tremors had become more frequent. I clutched the doorjamb, watching a spider-crack appear in the ceiling. Doorways are supposed to be the safest place in an earthquake, but Crackpot was so rickety that safety was probably relative. Poppy clutched Flynnie and continued to stare at the fire, whose flames were dancing as though blown by wind. Then, suddenly, the trembler stopped. It had seemed forever, but probably was only a few seconds. Other than the thin crack in the ceiling plaster, everything was all right.

Poppy hadn't moved from the settee. Now, as though nothing had happened, he said, "All right, Flora. It is true you are on vacation. Be home by midnight. But not a minute later, do you understand? We have an early day tomorrow. I want to go over *Hardel's Tactics* before lunch."

"Ayah, Poppy." I sighed. If he could be nonchalant about the fact that Crackpot had just about fallen down upon us, well then, so could I.

"Did you feel that?" Mamma demanded from the doorway. "I was almost squashed by a stack of redboxes. Everyone all right?"

"Ayah, Buck, we are fine," Poppy answered.

"These earthquakes, they are beginning to be worrisome. That one last week really rattled the Baker Cliffs. We are going to lose Baker Battery if this keeps up."

"That would be terrible, Buck," Poppy murmured.

Mamma shot him a Look. "Baker Battery is one of the City's first lines of defense, Hotspur."

I did not care about Baker Battery. I cared about my curfew, so I jumped in. "Mamma, it's the first night of term break—"

"Is it? Lucky girl to get a holiday. I wish I had a holiday." Mamma perched on the fire-fender and looked longingly at Poppy's ashtray. She quit smoking some years ago, but I know she still misses it. (I also know she packs in the snus when she thinks no one is looking.) "I hope you have fun plans. I've been wrestling all evening with the seating chart for the Warlord's Birthday Ball and I can't think of anything that is less fun than that."

"I'm going to a show with Udo, but Poppy says I have to be back by midnight, and it's already eight—"

Mamma frowned. "I hope you are not trying to circumvent Hotspur's authority, Flora."

"But it's not fair, Mamma," I complained.

"Your father is in charge of household matters, Flora, and I will not second-guess him. Don't try to jump the chain of command."

Chain of command—was Mamma joking? Judging from her face, she was not. In fact, she looked very grumpy. Recently Mamma had been a real bear; she really did need a holiday.

"Every minute you waste arguing, Flora, is a minute you lose from your show," Poppy said. "If I were you, I'd quit malingering and get going."

"Is there any dessert left, Hotspur?" Mamma asked, and thus I knew the topic was closed.

Age of majority hoohah, I thought sourly, as I ran upstairs to change. I might be an adult but I was still a slave.

"Did you feel that?" Valefor met me at the door of my bedroom, wringing his papery-thin hands, his wispy white hair standing on end. "My foundations were shaking. I thought my roof might go. They are getting more frequent, these shakings. I can't take much more. I'm going to fall in."

"Sorry, but there's nothing I can do about it. Poppy said I had to be back in by midnight. Can you believe it?"

"A curfew! Oh, it's awful to be you, Flora Segunda."

"Don't I know it."

Udo and I were not in fact going to the Blue Duck as I had so blithely lied to Poppy. The Blue Duck is a fine club, a dandy club, a trendy club—if you are twelve years old and like puppets. In fact, that is exactly what was playing there tonight: Sylvestris Jaciodes's Stilskin Puppet Show. I am far too old for puppets. Instead, Udo and I were going to the swanky cool Poodle Dog club for reasons I shall soon explain.

I had not totally wasted the three months since my Catorcena with schoolwork, Poppy work, and chores. I had spent every spare moment studying *The Eschatanomicon, or, Rangering for Everyone!,* Nini Mo's famous handbook. Valefor had found a signed first edition in the Bibliotheca and given it to me—the most useful thing he ever did for me, I think.

The Eschata tells you everything you might ever need to know about being a ranger—magick stuff and nonmagick stuff. I'd been working my way through the book carefully since my birthday, concentrating on the rangery stuff: tracking and fire-starting; how to ford a river, find your way through a maze, or follow a man down an empty street in broad daylight. I read all those chapters over and over again, memorized them, took notes, made diagrams. I practiced tying knots, and I worked on secret codes. I learned how to start a fire with a piece of glass and some tinder. I memorized the heliograph gestures and practiced dowsing for water.

The Eschata has a short appendix on Gramatica vocabulary, and I had memorized and practiced most of the Words contained therein, but they were small Words that empowered very small sigils. I could create a small coldfire light. I could banish small malicious entities. I could create a small disguising Glamour. But I couldn't say anything important. To do truly large workings or very powerful sigils, you need not only a great Gramatica vocabulary, but you have to speak entire Gramatica sentences. Conjugate verbs. Modify nouns. Diagram sentences. Speak fluently and without hesitation or mispronunciation. Unless I learned Gramatica, I would never be a true ranger—a true magician.

So I needed to find someone to teach me. But who? Most of the people I know are soldiers, and soldiers are forbidden to meddle in the Current (there's no honor there, you know, achieving through Will what you could achieve through Blood). Mamma hates magick, calling it a cheat, and so as a family, we do not associate much with magicians.

However, I am not without my own resources, and I had three options in mind. Nini Mo counseled that rangers should consider all the facts and factors before they decide upon a course of action, so I had carefully considered each of my three possibilities.

First was Boy Hansgen, the Dainty Pirate, the only member of the Ranger Corps left. He did owe me one, for trying to rescue him from certain death, but after delivering a thank you note and giftie, he had completely vanished. Both the Alta Califa and the Califa Police Gazette had run editorials commenting on his sudden disappearance from Califa's waters, but they had no good explanations for his abrupt cessation of piracy. The Alta Califa suggested he'd finally seen the error of his ways and reformed. The CPG guessed maybe his ships had been sunk in a storm. No matter: He was gone and I didn't know how to find him, so that way was closed.

Next: Lord Axacaya. He's the greatest adept in the City, probably the greatest adept in the entire Republic. Mamma hates Lord Axacaya not only because he is an adept. She hates that he's Huitzil by birth: born a Birdie, brought up by the Flayed Priests as a divine child, and fated to be sacrificed to the Hummingbird god, who feeds not on nectar, but blood. Lord Axacaya escaped this destiny, came to Califa as a refugee, married the Warlord's daughter, and has been here ever since. Mamma believes Lord Axacaya is a Birdie pawn, but I'm not so sure.

However, there were two problems with approaching Lord Axacaya. The first was exactly that: How to approach him? I didn't dare just ride up to Casa Mariposa and ask to see him, and we don't exactly move in the same social circles. My one hope was the Warlord's Birthday Ball. The Ball is Califa's biggest social event of the year; everyone who is anyone in Califa attends. Including Lord Axacaya. I had lobbied Mamma hard to let me go, too; now that I was an adult, should I not be included in all Fyrdraaca family activities? After all, Poppy was going, and there was no doubt that I could behave better than Poppy.

But Mamma had flat-out refused me permission, saying that the Warlord's Birthday Ball was a political and moral snake-pit and she didn't want me exposed to such danger. Of course, I also didn't dare tell Mamma that I had been exposed to things far more dangerous than a silly birthday ball, but my other arguments were futile. Mamma remained firm. They don't call her the Rock of Califa for nothing.

The second problem, frankly, was that I didn't relish the idea of going to Lord Axacaya with my hat in my hand. I had done that once before, out of dire necessity, but asking for two favors seemed like pushing it. I do have my pride. He'd helped me before but made no suggestion he'd do it again.

So my quest to learn Gramatica hinged on Firemonkey, the

leader of the Eschatological Immenation, Califa's rebel faction, which is devoted to the expulsion of Birdie influence from Califa. No one really takes the EI seriously; they paint slogans and distribute seditious pamphlets, the extent of their revolutionary tactics. But Firemonkey is also a magician; this I discovered when I first ran into him, when he and I both tried to rescue the Dainty Pirate from being executed by Lord Axacaya. We had both failed—or so I thought until I found out that the Dainty Pirate had been working for Lord Axacaya all along as a double agent, and that the murder was only a ruse.

Nothing is worth more than information, said Nini Mo, and I hoped that Firemonkey would be interested to learn about Lord Axacaya's ruse, interested enough to trade education for it. I had no interest in Firemonkey's revolutionary politics, which I would have to make clear to him. It's not that I think Califa is fine under Huitzil rule; of course I would like Califa to be a free republic again. The EI, however, wanted to get rid of not just Huitzil law, but Califa law, too. They believe everyone should be free to do whatever they want—the Law of Will, they call it. A recipe for disaster, I call it. There has to be some law or people would just throw their trash in the street, and take advantage of old grannies. *People will do*, said Nini Mo, *exactly what they think they can get away with.*

Firemonkey, wonky politics aside, was my best bet because he, unlike the Dainty Pirate and Lord Axacaya, was approachable. Firemonkey's cover for being a revolutionary was as the lead singer for the band the Horses of Instruction. Who just happened to be playing at the Poodle Dog tonight.

The ranger who helps herself is helped by the best, said Nini Mo.

THREE

Udo's Bank Account.
Sold Out. Udo Drools.

Mamma had to return to the Presidio for an evening inspection, so she dropped me off at Case Tigger on her way. This ride lessened my lateness a bit and saved me the horsecar fare. At Case Tigger I ran the gauntlet of parents (one mamma, two daddies), siblings (six—all absolute horrors), and various pets before finding Udo in the loo, primping.

Udo is sickeningly good-looking: his jaw perfectly square, his hair perfectly gold, and his eyes perfectly blue. He is also sickeningly vain and spends much of his time trying to improve upon perfection. I pried him away from his mirror, where he was taking forever to decide between red lip rouge or blue, and if his hair looked better on the top of his head in the shape of a rolled doughnut, or braided into five plaits and dangling free. After I told him that the red lip rouge made his face look too thin and the doughnut hairstyle made his face look fat, he quickly decided on braids and blue and we were able to make our exit.

We caught the N horsecar just as it was pulling up, and managed to get the last two seats. Udo fished a silver case out of his greatcoat and lit up a foul clove cigarillo.

"Don't you think you have enough nasty habits, Udo?" I waved my hand ineffectually through the blue smoke. "You'll ruin your lungs."

"Ha," he said. "Ayah, but I can blow a smoke ring."

"That'll be some consolation when you die of black lung," I said. "We'll put that on your memorial stone: Ayah, but he could blow a smoke ring."

"You are an old crab, Flora." Udo added insult to injury with a nip from his flask—another bad habit I did not intend to acquire. "And you get precious little fun out of life."

"I'd get even less if Poppy had his way. I have to be back by midnight," I said morosely. "Can you believe it? On the first night of vacation."

Udo hooted. "Midnight! That's outrageous. The Horses of Instruction won't even have gone on by then, probably. You're going to miss the show."

"*We're* going to miss the show."

"*I* don't have a curfew."

"If you plan on coming back to Crackpot with me, then you're on the same curfew I am."

"The whole point of going home with you, Flora, is, that way, the Daddies don't know what time I get home. If you've got a curfew, then that defeats the whole purpose."

"Sorry," I said, not in the least bit sorry. Before I could tell Udo about my plan to approach Firemonkey, he started up on his favorite topic.

"Look, Flora, I've been thinking about the Letter of Marque."

Oh no! Here we went again. Udo's pirate ambitions had not abated, not even after the Dainty Pirate incident. If anything, they'd grown even stronger, and now he was even more obsessed about obtaining a Letter of Marque. A Letter of Marque is a document issued by the Warlord authorizing the bearer to seize and confiscate property. It makes piracy legal, as long as you are willing to give the Warlord a cut of your prize.

If the Dainty Pirate had had a Letter of Marque, Mamma would not have been able to sentence him to hang. And of course since Udo didn't want to end up dangling from a rope, he was determined to get a Letter of Marque, but they cost a lot of money. Udo is cheap and pinches every diva until it squeaks, but he was still a long way away from the purchase price. And all his money-making ideas were harebrained and ignored the most obvious solution: Get a job. I was sick of the subject, and anyway, I had other things to worry about, like Firemonkey.

"Can't you leave it alone for one night, Udo?"

"Ha! The Fyrdraacas are one of the most wealthy families in the City. Easy for you to say to forget all about money."

"Maybe so, but I'm not the Heir to my House, so I get zippo, zilch, nada, nothing. Idden gets all the swag and the House, and I'm a pauper."

Udo waved dismissively. "You've got your allowance from Buck, but I must make my way through life on my wits, and ships don't grow on trees. Neither do Letters of Marque. Do you have any idea how much one costs?"

The exact amount was seared on my brain by Udo's constant whining. "A hundred and fifty thousand divas. But the Warlord doesn't issue Letters of Marque anymore. The Dainty Pirate didn't have one."

"Only because he refused to recognize the Warlord's authority, not because the Warlord wouldn't give him one. If Florian sees enough of my gold, he'll write me one up, I promise. That's why I need cash!"

"You could get a job, Udo."

Udo rolled his eyes dismissively. "I have a better idea." He took off his hat and fished a crumpled piece of paper out of its crown. I knew what was coming: another crazy scheme. Earlier crazy schemes: chicken-farming in Case Tigger's backyard (nixed by city zoning), organizing the siblings into a street-sweeping brigade (nixed by the Daddies), renting his little brother Gesilher out for medical experiments (nixed by Gesilher's demand for 20 percent). Now what?

Udo continued. "Look, I have a cunning idea of how to get

some cash, and it'll be easy, too. I happened to be walking by the post office on the way home this afternoon, and look what I noticed on the wall!"

I smoothed the crumples out of the paper and angled it toward the overhead light. "'Dead or alive,'" I read. "'Ringtail Peg, the Masher Queen. Wanted for grand larceny, gambling, fixing, mashing, arson, and murder. Five thousand divas in gold payable upon delivery of prisoner or corpse. By command of the Attorney General of Califa, under the Warlord's Sigil and Sign.'"

"See?" Udo waved more papers. "There are tons of them. Droolie Bee, wanted for larceny, fifteen hundred divas in gold. Firefly Andrews, tax evasion, two thousand divas in gold. Springheel Jack, fifty thousand divas in gold. It would be easy money! Just like taking candy from a baby. We'd be rich and we'd be doing the City a favor. What? Why are you giving me that evil eye?"

"You want to take up bounty hunting?" I said. "You have got to be kidding me!"

"Think on it! Five thousand divas in gold. And keep your voice down—I don't want anyone to steal my idea."

"Udo, you don't like to get your hands dirty and now you are suggesting that we go out and track down criminals and bring them in? How are we going to do that?"

"Well, I figure we'd need some capital, but I'm willing to put out a little to get a little back. We go South of the Slot and—"

"And get ourselves robbed. Remember what happened last time we went South of the Slot? We were jacked by a ten-year-old kid!"

Udo ignored my cold hard truth. "And check out some of those dives."

"Remember the last dive we checked out? Pete's Clown Diner? We got caught in a riot!"

Again, with the ignoring: "Grease a few palms—"

"We'll be killed, or worse."

Udo said huffily, "Would you let me finish! Grease a few palms and then track them down, tie them up, and bring them in. It will be easy. I mean, they don't even have to be alive, so if they give us any trouble, we just peg 'em and we still get the cash. And even though it was my idea, Flora, I'll be happy to cut you in for 10 percent."

"Oh how kind," I said sarcastically. "Ten percent of being robbed, killed, or worse. You are so generous."

"It's a good idea, Flora. Didn't Nini Mo go into bounty hunting for a while?"

"Ayah, but she was Nini Mo, the Coyote Queen. She had her reputation behind her. They just took one look at her and folded. I don't think the people you have mentioned are going to let you walk right up, introduce yourself, and say, 'Oh by the way, I'm taking you in, dead or alive; would you please come with me.'"

Udo said, exasperated, "Well, of course they will not. I'm not an idiot, Flora. I thought of that, too. See?" This time he fished in the inner pocket of his greatcoat, then displayed a small red enamel case. "This is going to make all the difference in the world."

"It's a compact. Are you going to powder their noses if they refuse to come with you?"

"Well, in a manner of speaking, yes, I am. This is no ordinary powder—no, don't open it! If you spill it, we'll be in super-big trouble. It's Sonoran Zombie Powder. One whiff of this stuff and you are no more willful than a piece of cheese. They use it in Huitzil to control sacrifices and wanton wives. Makes the most obnoxious hellion as smooth and easy as glass."

"Where'd you get it?" I took the compact from him and inspected it more closely. The red enamel top was embossed with a sigil shaped like a spiky wheel, and the clasp was cunningly fashioned like two hands holding each other at the wrist. The label pasted on the bottom read: MADAMA TWANKY'S SONO-RON ZOMBIE POWDER.

"Oh, I have my sources," Udo said mysteriously.

"You got it from an advertisement in the back of the *Califa Police Gazette,* didn't you? Those adverts are all cheats, Udo. Remember when you ordered that lotion that was supposed to turn your skin the color of bronze, and it turned you green instead? You've wasted your money."

"Ha! Fool me once, shame on you; fool me twice, shame on you. Do you think I'm a baby, new-dipped in milk? Of course, I tested it out already, and it worked perfectly. On the way home from Sanctuary, I stopped at the Park and zombified a duck. It followed me right home and we ate it for dinner."

"Udo!" That poor duck. Before I could ask him how he could be so mean, the horsecar jolted to a halt.

"Back door! Back door!" Udo pounded on the handrail. The door popped open and we scrambled out into the drizzly night.

The street in front of the Poodle Dog was packed with people; I'd had no idea that the Horses of Instruction were so popular. It looked like every wolfgirl, b-boy, gawker, masher, glitterette, and gothick in Califa were loitering outside the Poodle Dog, hoping to throw themselves at the band's feet. A knot of City militia stood to one side, watching the crowd suspiciously.

I grabbed at Udo's sleeve, trying to keep up with his push through the crowd. "Did you get tickets already?"

"We'll get them at the door!"

"I thought you said you were going to get tickets!" My heart sank. If we didn't have tickets already, we were out of luck.

"There's a line!" a b-boy protested as Udo tried to push his way past. "And the end of it is back there."

A chorus of angry voices joined the b-boy's protests, and in the face of clear-cut menace, we fell back to find the end of the line. When we finally found it, my heart sank further. It was two blocks away from the club and there was no way we were going to get in.

"Pigface Psychopomp," Udo swore. "I never thought the show would be this packed."

"What are we going to do now?" I demanded. "My whole evening is blown, Udo."

"We'll go around back and see if we can get in that way. After all, we know Firemonkey. We ought to be able to get through the Bruisers that way."

Udo's suggestion seemed like a long shot, but it was our only shot, and it would get me closer to Firemonkey, anyway. We tried to make our way to the alley that led to the backstage entrance; the throng was thick. We were pushy, but it was still hard going, and at the rate of our progress, we weren't going to get around back before my curfew was up. Blast Udo!

Then, before us, a Chickie materialized out of the crowd like cold air bursts out of an icebox. The crowd fell back for her and she pointed a gloved finger at Udo. "Come with me."

In the fluttering streetlights, the Chickie looked like congealed darkness: hair black as coal, eyes black as coal, lips black as coal. Her skin was corpse white, and just in case the moonlight was too strong for her fragile coloring, she was sheltering under a large black parasol. A gloom of Boy Toys stood behind her, each dressed somberly in black sack-suits, black ties, black shirts, and each with some variation of a bored snarl on his face.

"Me?" Udo croaked.

"Ayah, you," the Chickie said impatiently. "Come on. The show's about to start."

Udo stood mesmerized, staring slack-jawed at the Chickie, though whether he was drooling over the Chickie herself or her fabulous leather trenchcoat with the huge ruffy black wolf fur collar was unclear. She turned and the crowd continued to melt out of her way, as ice melts before salt, and Udo, hypnotized, followed. Well, I wasn't going to wait outside—alone— nor was I going to let Udo go forward—alone—so I, too, sailed, falling in behind the Boy Toys, who didn't even give me a glance.

Past the rest of the line we went, and not a quibble came from the queue. The Chickie's powers to strike dumb were not confined to Udo. The doorman said not a word as we approached, just unclipped the red velvet rope and waved us in.

FOUR

The Poodle Dog. A Bruiser. A Disgusting Potty.

INSIDE, THE POODLE DOG was a mob scene: wall-to-wall, floor-to-ceiling hipsters, packed tighter than pickles in a jar. The air was heavy with the smell of Madama Twanky's Bear Oil hair pomade and a gauzy haze of cigarillo smoke. Outside, the night had been chilly; inside, it was so hot that I immediately regretted wearing my redingote. Not two steps and I was bathed in sweat.

The Inside Mob parted for the Chickie, just as the Outside Mob had, with Udo, the Boy Toys, and me coasting along in her wake. Up the stone staircase we marched, to where it widened into a landing and split into two sweeping curves. Then around the right-hand curve and out onto the dance floor.

The Poodle Dog's grand hall is designed to look like the courtyard of a small village. Fake stucco covers the walls, creating a facade of small stone houses, each with doors that don't open and windows that look into darkness. High above, fake rooftops support the balcony. Higher above, the rounded ceiling is painted a vivid nighttime blue, pricked with ignis stars, and swirling with lights that simulate clouds. A huge red velvet tent takes up the far end of the hall; when the show starts, the front of the tent rises, revealing the stage behind.

Ahead, the Chickie, Udo, and the Boy Toys were swallowed whole by the crowd, and I was abandoned. I had meant to enlist

Udo's help in getting to Firemonkey, but clearly he now had no time for me. Well, let them go. I would have more success without Udo hanging on my neck, anyway.

One of the many annoyances of shortness is that you are invariably crushed in a crowd. And you can't see anything. And people spill their drinks on you and ash their cigarettes in your hair. It seemed as though everyone at the club was taller than me. Thus, my view was mostly of people's chests, even when I hopped. But even if I had been in the front row, once the show started I still would not have been able to see the stage because Weatherhead, the opening act, is notorious for their pyrotechnics. Their music is great, but best not to stand too close or you might find yourself on fire.

In anticipation of a crowd, I had left my spurs on; it's amazing how a few good jabs will get people out of your way. By this action, I was able to make my way through the throng. One small benefit of being short is that you can slide out of the way before people realize it was you who just put a rent in their red velvet knickers. *Hurry, before they notice,* said Nini Mo.

In front of the stage, a mosh pit had already formed. Bullyboys in lacy black kilts and wolfgirls with electric-blue hair were kicking and shoving and flinging themselves against each other, smacking heads and fists—this despite the only music being the dull roar of anticipatory chatter. In the flickering footlights, the red gape of the still-curtained proscenium arch looked very much like a hungrily gaping mouth.

I skirted the mosh pit and kicked my way toward a small wooden door set in one of the towers that flanked the stage. Halfway there, I saw a flash of moldering green and, by bouncing up on my tippy-toes and craning my neck, spotted the back of a familiar tricorn hat: Firemonkey. Behind him filed a chubby man in a gauzy white robe, carrying two drumsticks, and a tall figure in a wide-brimmed hat, pulled low, and a black leather duster, with a banjo slung over one shoulder.

I put some muscle into my push, adding elbow to spurs, but the crowd had thickened and I couldn't seem to catch up to him—Firemonkey was always just out of reach. And then suddenly my way was barred by a wide expanse of purple-and-yellow-checked weskit, a noxious color combination that no doubt would have had Udo salivating.

"Where are you going, girlie?" A huge round face floated above the floppy black tie that emerged from the weskit: a Bruiser set to guard backstage access. I pretended I didn't hear and tried to dodge around him, but I was blocked on one side by a sweaty bully-boy and on the other by a rum-bubbler, so the only way in was through the Bruiser, who was as solid as a brick wall.

"You got a backstage pass?" the Bruiser growled, and though he didn't raise his voice, I could hear him easily. There was something strange about his face. It seemed oddly flat and one-dimensional, as though it was a flesh-colored mask. His lips moved stiffly, and his eyes were two points of emptiness sunk into hollow sockets.

"A what?" I pretended ignorance. The longer I stared up at the Bruiser, the more papery flat his face seemed, and I realized why: He wore a Glamour. I blinked, and for a brief flashy second saw what was behind the Glamour. Small tusks punctuated a large flappy mouth, and tiny pink eyes glared under tufty mouselike eyebrows. I recognized him from the Entity Spotter appendix in the back of *The Eschata:* an obstructionist dæmon; extremely bad juice and almost impossible to get through. If Firemonkey had brought him in for muscle, he really did not want to be disturbed.

The Bruiser growled, "Backstage. You ain't allowed backstage if you ain't got a backstage pass. You got no pass, you skedaddle."

"Look, I have to speak to Firemonkey. It's important. You are impeding my way." I tried bluster and made to push by, but he was as solid as a rock. "Let me pass."

"Firemonkey don't talk to no one before the show. They all wanna talk to him. He gotta have quiet to banish and invoke. He don't talk to no one."

If blustering fails, said Nini Mo, *try flustering*. I remembered also from the Entity Spotter that flattery was an obstructionist dæmon's weakness.

I looked up at the Bruiser through fluttering eyelashes. "Oh sieur, I do so adore your weskit. It's supercool. Where did you get it?"

The Bruiser looked down at himself, and a tiny smile floated over his pudgy lips. He tucked bananalike thumbs into the edges of the weskit and preened. "I designed it myself. And made it, too." He was puffing up, literally. If I slitted my eyes, I could see through the Glamour, see his head actually inflating like a balloon. His forehead distended upward, and his eyes began to bug out like little red marbles. Yuck.

"You are so clever," I wheedled, thinking, *I can't believe I sound so soppy*. But it was working. "Do you design professionally?"

"I gotta shop down in LoHa; make suits, too. Fine tailoring, no fusing for me, all hand-stitched. I give you me card, you come down, lolly, and I make you over, better than that slop jacket you got on." The Bruiser fished in the pocket of the awful weskit and pulled out a damp piece of cardboard, which I had no choice but to take. "I make you pretty."

"Thank you, sieur, but please . . ." I grinned sweetly at him and turned the flutter up to hurricane level.

The Bruiser hesitated. I almost had him; I could feel it. He was going to let me through. Then, just as he was about, I was sure, to give into my sweet flattery, there was a roaring cheer, and the club plunged into darkness. Red and white sparks arced into the air, and a drum pounded like thunder. In the spitting, sparking light, I saw that the Bruiser was gone, and the stage-access door firmly closed.

Pigface Psychopomp, I had been so close!

Well, there was still the outside backstage door. Firemonkey had to leave the club somehow, at some time, right? And maybe I would have better luck with the Bruiser stationed there, or maybe the door was left unguarded and was merely locked. Without an audience, I was confident that I could pop the lock pretty quickly. Lock-picking is an elementary skill I mastered when I was just a tot.

I pushed through the crowd, which was now bouncing up and down to the heartbeat rhythm of Weatherhead's music. The drone was so loud, it made my ears ring, vibrated my legs, and made the back of my throat hum and buzz. Spicy black fog rolled down off the stage, parting long enough to give a quick glance at a yellow mackintosh spastically jerking across the stage. Something wet and spongy hit my head, bounced off my shoulder; my hand came away wet and red, smelling of liver. Weatherhead were throwing organ meat.

I had just washed my hair that morning; time to take cover. And I had to potty. Better get that done before I started on lock-picking. I kicked my way down the stairs toward the pisser, looking out hopefully for Udo, but not seeing him anywhere.

The pisser was full of jostling girls trying to adjust cleavage and maquillage in front of a cracked wall mirror. After the darkness of the club, the bright gaslights made my eyes water. In the mirror, my reflection was raccoon-eyed with smudged black eyeliner. My hair looked like I had been hit by a bolt of lightning; it stuck straight out from my head in a frizzy red halo. I wetted my hands and tried to smooth it back down, though I knew that would only make the frizz worse.

A wolfgirl exited a stall and I nipped in before the door slammed shut behind her. The walls of the stall were scrawled with graffiti, and what wasn't illegible was obscene enough that I wished it *were* illegible. The floor was slick—I hoped it was water, but maybe it wasn't. Greenish water gurgled in the toilet, which was missing its seat. Even before Poppy started cleaning, the potty at Crackpot had never been half this bad. Our outside bog, which we have to resort to if the inside pipes get plugged, is dark and spidery and the seat has splinters, but it is never this horrible. But I really had to go. *Don't stand on ceremony when you gotta squat,* said Nini Mo.

I tucked my kilts up as high as I could and was glad that I had remembered my hankie; of course there was no potty paper.

I was about to cautiously squat, when there was a loud gurgle behind me and a splash of cold wetness on my hinder. I jerked up and around. The water in the toilet was bubbling, and these bubbles were popping into an awful smell. I buried my nose in the crook of my arm, trying to drown out the stench with the smell of lavender laundry soap.

"Hey!" The stall door behind me thumped. "I gotta go! Hurry up!"

Nasty water began to rise up and over the toilet's rim, and I danced back. Something was starting to slither up out of the water. This something was shaped like a long wiggly parsnip: a pallid white tentacle. Long and pointy, its tip was covered with suckers, just like the little squiddies that Mamma loves so much, marinated in soy sauce and grilled. Only this tentacle was much, much bigger. Bigger around than my arm, in fact, with suckers as large as tea cakes.

"I GOTTA GO!" The door banged again. The tentacle wiggled in the air, bending this way and that, as though it was searching for something. I stood like a rock, motionless, hoping that the tentacle wouldn't notice me. I couldn't open the stall door without moving toward the tentacle, and this seemed like a very bad idea. It paused for a second; I held my breath. The tip pulsated bright red, and the rest of it blushed a deep pink; and then, with a lashlike motion, the tentacle snapped toward me.

I jerked back, banging against the stall door—not far enough. The tentacle had grabbed a wad of my kilt. I twisted and turned, trying to get free without ripping my kilt too badly, but the tentacle had a hard grip.

I grabbed my kilt hem and yanked. The fabric tore and I was free. I pressed against the door and tried to flatten myself down as though I were a piece of paper. The tentacle jabbed in my direction, but it seemed to be at the end of its reach, and I was now out of range. Out of range, but trapped.

Carry the important stuff on you, Nini Mo said, and there are few things more important than fire. I fumbled in the inside pocket of my redingote and found the trigger case I had *borrowed* from

Poppy (who didn't need his smoking encouraged with easy access to matches). The tentacle was straining and stretching; it knew I was just out of reach, and was trying to close the gap. With fumbly fingers I managed to open the silver case, withdraw a match, and strike it against the wall. The triggers were supposed to strike anywhere. The match head sputtered and did not light.

"Pigface!" I swore, and shook out another trigger. My hands were shaking in a most unrangery way. I didn't look in the direction of the tentacle, but I knew by the sloshing sound that it was still there. I flicked the second match head with my finger; the trigger snapped and blossomed into a happy orange flame, small but hot.

I flicked this match onto the tentacle, which writhed and withdrew, but then shot forward like a striking rattlesnake and grabbed my waist, almost yanking me off my feet. I dug my heels in and grabbed onto the purse-ledge, but the metal shelf was slick and my hands slid right off it. The tentacle squeezed tightly; my lungs sucked together and for a moment the world went spotty black. Only the steel bones of my stays were keeping me from being snapped in two; putrid water sloshed over my toes. My knife was in my boot; I couldn't reach it.

Then I remembered the fan hanging at my waist, tucked into one of Mamma's old sabre slings. Paimon had given it to me as part of my Catorcena outfit, and though it looked fragile and delicate, the tips of its ribs were razor sharp. Now I fumbled for it, wincing at the slimy slick warmth of the tentacle—luckily the fan case itself was hidden in the folds of my kilt. Gasping for breath, I managed to hook a finger into the ring at the end of the fan and pull hard. The fan flew up in the air, and I caught it, ripped it open with a flick of my wrist, and slashed it downward.

The razor barbs of the fan sliced the tentacle like it was butter. Spurting slime, the tentacle let go of my waist, wiggling and writhing. I slashed again. The tentacle slithered back toward the potty, and I pursued it, hacking at it. With a giant slurp it sucked back into the water and was gone.

The stall tilted up—I fell against the door heavily, banging hard against the purse-ledge. Plaster showered down, and outside the stall door, people began to squeal. The trembler stopped abruptly. I yanked the door and stumbled out, running into a pissy-looking dollymop.

"Took enough time! Pigface, what the hell were you doing in there? Contemplating infinity?" She started to push by me. "I almost peed my drawers."

"You'd better be careful," I said breathlessly. "Something grabbed me."

"What?" The girl paused.

"Something crawled out of the toilet and tried to grab me."

The girl peered into the stall, then said scornfully, "There's nothing in there, snapperhead. You've had too much jake."

I peered around her, and indeed there was no tentacle, no bubbly water, no slime. The toilet stood serenely in the middle of the stall. The floor wasn't even wet. The trigger case lay where I had dropped it, and I leaned over to scoop it up.

Had I imagined the whole thing? I held up the fan; glowing green slime dripped off the barbs.

I had not.

FIVE

Firemonkey Incites.
A Mob Scene. Crushed.

I STAGGERED OUT of the pisser into a roar that practically propelled me backward. Most of this roar was music: the high-pitched, whiny grind of a hurdy-gurdy; the dull, headachy throb of a bass propelled by staccato drumming. But some of it was shouting, a persistent chant I couldn't understand. I recognized the tune, though: "Nonny O!," the Horses of Instruction's most popular song.

The tentacle had really unnerved me, and my desire to get far, far away from that toilet was really strong. All I wanted now was to go home. *Rangers don't retreat*, said Nini Mo, *but they know when to regroup.* The Horses of Instruction might just be starting, but I was done.

I fought my way through the noise, which was like trying to stand against a high wind, elbowing through the crowd, trying to find Udo, so together we could make our escape. The hall was dark, lit only by intermittent flashes, and when these split the gloom like bolts of lightning, I saw a hazy, gyrating mass of people, thickly packed. The figures were indistinct, shadowy, and none of them seemed to be Udo. Where had he gone, the snapperhead, just when I needed him most? I slid between a woman in a heavy leather jacket, well festooned with chains, and a bald man coated in silvery paint, and found myself at the stage.

Above my head, the stage lights flickered with a garish blue glow, illuminating Firemonkey, blackish-green hair straggling out from under a soggy tricorn, pumping at the handle of a hurdy-gurdy as though he were possessed. To his left, a cadaver flogged an upright bass; on his right, the duster twanged on a banjo that hung down around black leather knees. This close to the band, the noise made my ears ring and my stomach heave; Firemonkey must have invoked the biggest amplification dæmon ever to get such loudness. Forget Udo, I had to get out of the Poodle Dog before I puked. He'd have to make it home on his own. But before I could turn around and try to push my way to open air, the music stopped. The audience continued to chant. Suddenly I understood what they were shouting.

"*Azota! Azota! Azota!*"

The Butcher Brakespeare's nickname.

Firemonkey raised up his hand and, when the crowd quieted, cried, "She died so that we might live!"

At first I thought he meant the Goddess Califa, but when the crowd resumed its chanting, I realized he was referring to the Butcher. Firemonkey raised his hand again, and again waited a few seconds for the chanting to die down.

"But despite her sacrifice, we live like slaves! Should Florian not die so that we may live free? So that Azota shall not have sacrificed in vain?"

The crowd howled its agreement.

The queasy feeling in my stomach suddenly had nothing whatsoever to do with the music and everything to do with the fact that Firemonkey was preaching treason. I remembered the militia outside; nothing riles them faster than someone stirring up a crowd to sedition. I had no desire to end the night in the City Gaol; I would miss my curfew for sure, then. My urge to get out of the Poodle Dog became overwhelming. But despite my kicking and prodding, I was stuck. The people around me were staring raptly upward, immobile.

"*Cierra Califa!*" Firemonkey cried, and threw his arms wide. A huge curl of coldfire roiled out of his greatcoat. The coldfire flowed upward, twisting and turning until it formed an insignia that glowed in the darkness like a rope of fire: the sinuous twist of an azota, a riding whip, the source of the Butcher's nickname.

"*Azota and Cierra Califa!*" Firemonkey roared, and the crowd roared back while the band launched into "Calífa Strong and Mighty." The crowd began to gyrate and bounce again in time to the music, their chanting frenzied. But then abruptly the overhead lights flipped on, and the coldfire insignia was suddenly invisible in the bright glare. The roars of excitement were pinpricked with screams.

"In the name of the Warlord, you are all under arrest!" someone shouted from the back of the hall. The crowd erupted into screaming and pushing. *The best place to be in a stampede*, said Nini Mo, *is not in a stampede*. But I was still stuck, pressed hard up against the stage. The crush was suffocating; I could barely breathe, and what air I was able to gasp was tainted with smoke and perfume. If I went down, I'd be trampled underfoot in no time, and there'd be nothing left of Flora but goo on the soles of a lot of supertrendy shoes.

Then an iron grip grabbed my shoulders and hauled me up over the edge of the stage. I stumbled upright, wheezing. The Horses of Instruction's banjo player had me by the arm and was now dragging me across the stage. Firemonkey and the cadaver had disappeared; the chubby drummer was still drumming, his head flinging back and forth like a pendulum, heedless of the pandemonium. The banjo player and I ran into the wings, past the amplification dæmon still caught in his protection circle. He snapped his crocodile-long jaws at us as we passed, but the charged circle held and his gnashing teeth snapped empty air.

Backstage was a melee of frantic roadies and screaming groupies. The banjo player was taller than me and used that height and bulk to clear a path. Shoving people out of our way, we ran down a corridor, and then flung ourselves through a doorway. I fell against a row of costumes, coughing and wheezing, my lungs burning. A bright girdle of pain now encircled my waist where the tentacle had squeezed me. I coughed until it felt as though my lungs had been torn into fragments, but when I was done, despite the pain, I felt better. At least I could breathe again. The banjo player had slammed the door shut behind us and now leaned against it, regarding me.

"You all right?"

"Ayah. Thanks for grabbing me."

"My pleasure, Tinks."

The banjo player pulled off the wide-brimmed hat. And there was my sister Idden, grinning at me, looking exactly the same as the last time I had seen her. Except that now she was as bald as an egg.

SIX

Surprise! Revolutionary Fervor. A Hasty Exit.

I GAPED AT IDDEN like a greenhorn at her first sight of snow. Of all the questions that ran through my head—*What are you doing here? How did you get here? When did you learn to play the banjo?*—what came out of my mouth was, "What happened to your hair?" Idden has always looked a lot like Mamma: same blue eyes, same high cheekbones, same yellow hair. Even without hair, the resemblance was still strong.

Idden laughed, her gold lip-plug (also new) winking in the sputtering light. "I got tired of washing it. Cool, eh? Give me a hug, tiny sis."

We squeezed each other so tightly that the buttons of Idden's duster ground into me painfully. She smelled like cigarillo smoke and lemon verbena, and she felt thin and bony.

I asked, "What are you doing here? I thought you were at Fort Jones."

"I was, baby, but obviously I'm not anymore."

"Are you on leave?"

Idden laughed. "You could say that. Toothache-leave."

Toothache-leave—that's Army slang for deserting. I yanked out of Idden's embrace and stared at her. Idden had deserted? Never in the history of the Fyrdraaca family had anyone ever deserted! I could not imagine it. Deserted! And though enlisted soldiers desert sometimes, officers hardly ever. Enlisted soldiers have to serve out their term, but officers can resign at will and therefore have no reason to scarper. I had never heard of an officer deserting.

Idden grinned. "Got nothing to say to that, Tinks?"

"Mamma is going to kill you!" I said, ignoring the provocative use of my despised kiddie nickname.

"She'll have to catch me first," Idden said, "and I'm guessing from your reaction that she doesn't even know."

"We all thought you were at Fort Jones. Poppy just got a letter from you. But, Idden, how could you desert? What were you thinking? They'll shoot you if they catch you."

"Let them try," Idden answered. "You don't look any taller, Tinks. I think you've stunted."

Again, I ignored the slur. That's one of Idden's tricks, to deflect you from topics she doesn't want to discuss—try to rile you with unflattering personal observations and stupid nicknames. I refused to be deflected.

"You never answered me."

Idden gave me a superior little smile that I knew only too well. "Because I'd had it, Flora. I've been pushed around long enough. I'm sick of Buck, sick of the Army."

"Why didn't you just resign? That would be better than running away."

She snorted. "Ha! Do you think for one minute that Mamma would let me resign? She'd never accept my resignation—I had to get out without her knowing. And anyway, I don't recognize the Warlord's authority anymore, so I consider my oath to him null. He's a Birdie puppet, Flora. Obeying him is like obeying the Virreina of Huitzil. He has got to go, and all his lackeys, too. Collaborators all, even Buck."

"Mamma is not a collaborator! She's just trying to keep Califa safe."

Idden looked scornful. "Safe for what? Safe for whom? Safe for the rich and the powerful? What about everyone else? Slaves— one and all. First slaves to the Warlord, who sold them to the

Birdies, now slaves to them, too. Safety in slavery isn't worth having."

I'd never heard Idden this worked up about anything before. She'd always been mild as milk toast and done exactly as Mamma had said. Not only done it, but acted as though Mamma's Will was hers as well, that their desires were exactly the same. Maybe Idden had gone mad. Maybe she had Army Green Sickness—it happens to people who spend too much time in too isolated a post. They start imagining things, and become paranoid, and then nostalgic, and eventually have to be taken away to the Califa Asylum for the Unfortunate and Lost. Mamma could hardly be mad at Idden for being insane, could she?

Idden continued, "My duty to Califa is higher than my duty to the Birdies' puppet. I am loyal to Califa and those who died for her—like Azota Brakespeare!"

"But she was a murderer and a war criminal," I protested. "And she almost got Poppy killed."

Something flared in Idden's eyes and she pinched me hard. "Birdie lies! They made her out to be a criminal so they could get rid of her. I knew her, Flora, and she was nothing as they say. She loved Califa, and she died trying to keep Califa free. Mark me, Flora. Change is coming. The tree of liberty must be watered with the blood of tyrants."

"What does that mean?" I asked, almost afraid of the answer.

"It means, Flora, that there comes a time when we have to decide either to risk death for freedom, or to live as slaves. I have made my decision; that's why I joined Firemonkey's band. Califa must be free."

"But, Idden—"

The shouting and screaming outside had gotten louder, and now people were pounding on the door, demanding to be let in. It did not seem a good idea to open the door, but the only other exit was a small window high on the back wall.

Idden cut me off. "Look, I don't have time to argue with you now. We have got to get out of here. The militia will be here any minute, and neither of us wants to end up in gaol. Come on."

"But we're trapped!"

"You'll see—come on." Idden unbuttoned her duster and drew her service revolver. "Fire in the hole, Tinks."

I covered my ears just in time; she fired twice, the shots echoing explosively. I ducked my head, barely avoiding a face full of flying debris, and when I looked back up, the small window gaped open, and my ears rang. The acrid smell of black powder was choking.

"Ayah, Tinks, this is where you get off. But first, Flora, swear you will not tell Buck that you saw me."

I saw the grab coming and tried to dodge, but Idden was quick, and she's much taller than me. Despite my kicks, Idden got me into a headlock from which I could do nothing but spit ineffectually.

"Swear it, Flora!"

Nini Mo says an oath sworn under duress is not binding. I couldn't cross my toes in my boots, and Idden had my hands pinned, so I crossed my eyes and said, "Ayah, so, I promise."

"I think only of your best interests, Flora," Idden said, releasing me. "You don't want to be there when Buck finds out I'm gone. And you sure don't want to be the messenger."

I glared at her. "Ayah, so you say, but you know what—you sound just like Mamma when you say that!"

"You can't rile me, Flora, so don't even try. Come on, boost up."

Idden crouched by the window, linking her hands together into a cradle. I stepped and she boosted me up to the window, grunting. "Pigface, you've grown."

"Thanks to Poppy's food." I puffed, grabbing at the window frame. The edge of the sill was ragged and some glass remained, but Idden's propulsion gave me no choice but to go through. The window opened into an alley; below me was a six-foot drop, but, lucky for me, about half of that drop was taken up by a giant trash bin. Before I could protest, Idden heaved me the rest of the way through the window. I hit the closed top of the bin with a painful thump, scrabbling for a handhold, and just barely managed to keep myself from rolling off the side. A horde of hipsters were roaring down the alley, pushing, shouting, and screaming, and it would have been bad news for me if I had landed in their path.

Idden's head poked through the window. "I'm sorry I missed your Catorcena. If I could have gotten leave, I would have."

I glared at her. "You talk pretty big, Idden. But you are going to get yourself killed. You aren't being fair to Mamma, or Poppy, either. Think of all they have gone through."

"My country comes first."

"Now you sound just like Mamma," I jeered.

Idden glared back at me. "You'd better get going. Toss me a kiss, Tinks."

"Aren't you coming?"

"I got another way to go—better get yourself out of this alley before you are blocked in. Fine, keep your kiss. If I'm dead next time you see me, you'll be sorry you were such a stick, Flora."

And then Idden pulled her head back inside and was gone.

I jumped off the trash bin and squeezed between its side and the wall: A tiny bit of shelter but better than nothing. That window hadn't been such a good exit after all; at the far end of the alley, the militia had already thrown up a barricade. At the other end, the rioters had pulled another bin in front of the club's fire door, and from behind this barricade they were shouting and screaming at the militia. Me, the monkey in the middle.

How was I going to get out of here? *If you get in*, said Nini Mo, *you can get back out again.*

Something much larger than a brick hit the wall above me, which sent a roar of noise through my ears and practically knocked me down. Now everything sounded distant; my ears were ringing. Cautiously, I again peered around the edge of the trash bin. The militia were firmly entrenched at the far end of the alley; behind their stacked riot shields, cavalry had formed

up. The riot line broke open to allow a caisson to pull forward.
Behind it came another carriage, upon which sat a gleaming
fieldpiece: a gas gun.

Gas guns shoot canisters containing a burning acid smoke.
One breath of that and you are coughing up the bloody shreds
of your lungs. Get the stinging smoke in your eyes and you will
be lucky if you ever see anything again. Despite my best efforts,
panic began to bubble up my throat. I was no longer the monkey in the middle. Now I was a sitting duck.

If you need a light, said Nini Mo, *look up for the stars.*

Above my head, a fire ladder dangled, its bottom rung just
about out of reach. Jumping didn't close the gap, and if I tried
to heave the trash bin into range, I'd expose myself to the firing.
The cannoneers had unlimbered the gun and swiveled it around
until its barrel pointed down the alley. The barricaded hipsters
began to jeer loudly. The battery ignored their cries, and the
gunner began to sight the gas gun.

Not for the first time did I bemoan getting the short end of
the Fyrdraaca stick, height-wise. Even with my highest hop, I
could not reach the bottom rung of the ladder. I pulled off my
sash and began to scrabble in my dispatch bag for something
weighty to tie onto the end, with the intent of making a grapple
that I could use to pull the ladder down. A brick hit the wall
above me and shattered into dust.

"Pigface Psychopomp!" Nini Mo says you should always remain graceful under pressure, but it was hard to be graceful
with death whizzing over my head. My long wooden pencil case
was pretty heavy; maybe that would work. I was tying the sash
around it when the lid of the trash bin swung open and a tou-
sled head grinned down at me.

"Hey, Flora, talking to yourself?"

"It's about time you showed up, Udo." The sudden relief at
seeing him almost made me feel faint. "Get out here and pull
that ladder down before we are snorting our lungs out our
noses."

Udo jumped out of the trash bin and reached a hand back to

haul the Chickie out after him. She was wearing his greatcoat and both of them had mussed hair and smeared lip rouge. Udo didn't need to climb on top of the trash bin to snag the ladder down; he just reached up one long arm and pulled.

A gas canister whizzed by us, trailing sparks and smoke. This put a hustle into our scramble; it's amazing how fast you can move when the threat of scorched lungs is literally hot on your heels. The Chickie went up the ladder first, in a flurry of black skirts; I was next. At the top, the Chickie paused, blocking my way.

I started to give her a good shove, and then saw, beyond her, flickering red light.

The roof of the Poodle Dog was on fire.

SEVEN

Fire. To the Horsecar.
A Shoot-out.

THE FIRE HAD NOT YET fully engulfed the roof, so we were able to weave a path around the little licks of hot flame. But the thought of all the flammable alcohol and hair products that might still be in the club below, coupled with the wafting gas behind us, made me very eager to get off the roof as fast as possible.

We were not the only ones who had thought of this escape route; on the far side of the roof, other clever shadows were creeping out of the stairwell and dashing past the flames to leap the gap between the Poodle Dog and the warehouse next door. We rushed to follow their example. The buildings were packed so tightly together that the distance was not too great; but still, it wasn't a short jump. Udo went first, his half-undone braids flapping, then turned to offer a hand to the Chickie, who ignored the gallant gesture. She made a graceful ballet leap and a graceful ballet landing on the other side.

At the edge, I hesitated. The gap was large and my legs are short. But the heat behind me was hot, and Udo was shouting, and Nini Mo once leaped fifteen feet over a chasm sixty feet deep—without a running start. But surely her legs were longer than mine, and stronger, too. And she wasn't wearing pinchy stays that kept her from sucking in a good deep breath.

"Come on, Flora!" Udo shouted. The Chickie was tugging

on his arm impatiently. That gesture steeled my resolve; I was not going to let her leave me behind.

Dare, win, or disappear, I thought grimly. For luck, I clutched at Poppy's ranger badge hanging from my neck, and as a whiff of smoke wafted over me, I ran forward and hurtled myself across the gap, gasping like a teakettle. There was a dizzy roar in my ears, swooping blackness, and then I was in Udo's arms, and Udo was staggering backward, moaning theatrically.

"You weigh a ton, Flora."

"Come on," said the Chickie impatiently. "I'm getting smoke in my hair."

I jerked away from Udo, annoyed. We tore across the roof, weaving past chimney pots, around piles of broken beer bottles and soiled mattresses, and then slid down the fire ladder onto Kautz Street, which was thick with people. Some of these people, like us, were trying to scarper. Others were running toward the ruckus, confusing those of us trying to advance in the opposite direction, as Nini Mo once defined *retreat*. Cries of "*Azota and Cierra Califa!*" mixed with the sound of sirens, the rhythmic rat-a-tat of the gas gun, the howls of pain. Something very fast whizzed by my head, so close that I could almost feel it parting my hair.

We pelted around the corner onto Geary where, up ahead, the welcoming lights of the J horsecar were gliding out of the darkness toward us. Waving our arms frantically, we got to the stop just as the car pulled up.

Udo, the Chickie, and I flashed our car passes at the driver and headed for the back. We plopped down in the last row; I peered out of the window. The sirens were getting louder and the streams of people thicker; in a minute the J horsecar was going to be stuck in the crowd. But the car didn't leave the stop.

"Come on!" Udo shouted. "Get going!"

The driver was yelling at a man who was standing in the car doorway. "You gotta pay the fare!"

The man didn't answer, just tried to move past the driver, who threw out a barricading arm.

"Fare!" the driver said again. He had closed the door, but through the glass, I could see several angry-looking people with large guns converging on the trolley. The stranger did not answer. "I ain't going anywhere without your fare, bud."

"Pigface!" Udo was searching his pockets. "I don't have any change. Do you have some change, Zu?"

The Chickie ignored the request. I dug in my pocket, rushed back down the aisle, and threw a lisby in the fare basket. The driver, satisfied, dropped his arm, and the man went past me without a word of gratitude. The car clanged forward, just as large sweaty hands pounded against the door.

"Thanks, Flora!" Udo said when I lurched back to my seat. He and the Chickie were now snuggling. Most of Udo's lip rouge had transferred to the Chickie's lips, which now gleamed blackly blue. The stranger plopped himself down in the second to last seat, next to me.

I peered out the back window to see if we were still being pursued. We had already passed the last streetlight at Fluery and the Slot, and the darkness behind appeared empty of angry running guns. I breathed as much a sigh of relief as my pinchy stays would allow.

"What the hell happened back there?" Udo asked. "The Zu-Zu and I went outside for a few minutes and the next thing we knew we were in the middle of mayhem. We had to take cover in that trash bin." It was a testament to his bedazzlement that he didn't complain about crawling into a trash bin; normally, Udo would rather be shot than get dirty. He gave the Zu-Zu—what a stupid name—a moony look.

Udo was hardly even breathing hard. Neither was the Zu-Zu; other than the smeared lip rouge, she looked as composed as though she had just been for a stroll in the park. She snapped open a black beaded purse, removed a small black compact, and began to repair. I, on the other hand, thanks to my too tight stays, was wheezing like a hurdy-gurdy, and a bright spike of pain was trying to cleave my brain in two.

I glared at Udo. "If you'd been in the club, where I was look-ing for you, you'd have known what happened. You missed the big rally," I said, when I could do so without too much wheeze.

Udo grinned at me, and I felt like smacking him. "I was busy."

"Well, then, I guess you didn't miss much."

"Weatherhead's drummer exploded," the Zu-Zu said. I'll bet she had spent hours practicing her husky voice, so perfectly bored-yet-cool. "It's the fourth drummer they've lost this year. They shouldn't use percussive dæmons. They are too unstable."

"The Zu-Zu is in a band," he said admiringly.

"Huzzah," I answered. "Anyway, that's not what happened. Firemonkey got up onstage and incited the crowd into a mob." I decided to wait until Udo and I were alone before telling him I had seen Idden; Fyrdraaca family business was none of the Zu-Zu's affair. Nor was the tentacle attack, which I recalled with a shiver.

The Zu-Zu pursed her blackened lips in a pout at my cor-rection, then tossed back a lank black lock of hair from her paper-white forehead. Udo gave me a dirty look.

"What time is it?" I asked him.

He hauled his watch out of his pocket. "Eleven forty-two."

"Pigface, I'm going to get canned if I'm not back by mid-night."

"Flora," Udo told the Zu-Zu, "has a curfew."

"Pity." The Zu-Zu looked unsympathetically at me. She smiled slightly. I had the sudden urge to smack her.

Instead I said maliciously, "You have a curfew too, Udo."

"Oh no—I just have to make sure Flora gets home safely, and then I'm free." Udo smiled at the Zu-Zu. "I haven't had a curfew since I was a sprout."

Now, this was a big fat lie. Udo *always* had a curfew, even back in the days when I did not. The Daddies are pretty strict—with the six kids, they have to be. Otherwise the nuts would take over the nuthouse.

Before I could point this out to him, something hit the back window, not hard enough to break it, but hard enough to make me jump. I looked back.

"There are people with guns chasing the horsecar, Udo," I said. "And I don't think they are militia."

Udo and the Zu-Zu turned around and peered out the back window.

"I was afraid this might happen," Udo said. "Though I was hoping we could lose them in the mob scene."

"Lose who? What are you talking about?" I asked. "Why would men be chasing us?"

"Oh, probably because of him." Udo pointed toward the man whose fare I had paid. He had been sitting so quietly that I had forgotten all about him. The man was staring straight ahead, his hands neatly folded on his lap, his face slack and stupid. He looked asleep, almost, but his eyes were open. A thin string of drool dangled from his lips.

Udo chortled, and my stomach twisted up. He was grinning too much like a fool not to actually have done something incredibly foolish. "Don't you recognize him, Flora?"

"It's too late to play games, Udo. Just tell me."

Udo scrunched his face in disappointment. "It's Springheel Jack, of course! Pigface, Flora, he's just been all over the CPG for the last two weeks and you don't even recognize him?"

Springheel Jack! The cutthroat bunco artist and cat burglar! The leader of the infamous Red Heels gang, which practically controlled the South of the Slot. Only last week the CPG's front page had trumpeted Springheel Jack's latest exploit: He'd gotten into a bar fight with the equally infamous Gallus-Meg and gnawed off her ear. Later, when sober, he had returned it to her in a silver locket, accompanied by a gallant note saying that it was not normally his habit to gnaw upon ladies and she must blame his ill manners on too many Pisco Punches. The press had swooned over his gentility, but it didn't seem to me that a note of apology was much return for having your ear chewed off.

At the moment, however, Springheel Jack didn't look particularly aggressive. In fact, he was dribbling like a fountain.

"Why is he following us?" I asked. "And why is he drooling?"

"It's a pretty story; see, the Zu-Zu and I had nipped outside to get some air, you know," Udo said, "and who should we see but Springheel Jack pissing against the wall. Even though it was dark, I recognized him by his boots instantly."

I peered at the floor. Springheel Jack's footwear was indeed somewhat noticeable—great big sparkly red boots with five-inch heels. Little snake heads sprouted from the toes, but they, too, were droopy and half asleep. In the thin light of the horsecar, the boots glittered like rubies.

Udo continued, "I played it cool. I just sidled up to him and asked him for a light, and when he leaned over to light my cigarette, *aquí*!" He brandished the red enamel compact. My heart sunk so low that I swear it fell through the bottom of the car and right onto the road below.

"You snapperhead!" I added a few choice adjectives to the noun. "What were you thinking?"

Udo glared at me, puffing. "I was thinking about the bounty on his head, fifty thousand divas, that's what I was thinking."

"Udo told me his plan," the Zu-Zu interjected. "I thought it an excellent idea and it showed a lot of initiative."

I ignored her, because obviously she was a snapperhead, too, and, anyway, who cared what she thought? I said to Udo, "Plan? There was no plan! We discussed the bounty hunting and decided it was a stupid idea—"

"No, *you* decided it was a stupid idea," Udo said hotly. "I thought it was a brilliant idea. And I was right! Look at him, fifty thousand divas on his head, and as easy as pie. If we hadn't had to run, we wouldn't even have broken a sweat!"

"I think it was a brilliant idea, Udo," the Zu-Zu said. "Never mind her."

"With his gang after us, trying to kill us, or worse!" I said, still ignoring her. "What are we going to do now, Sieur Brilliant Plan?"

Behind Udo, through the glass, I saw the dim shadow of a

man, waving something that was much too long and shiny to be his hand. Good rangers know when to act on instinct. I rolled to the floor, flailing at Udo to do the same, just as the window next to me exploded into a slivery halo of glass.

EIGHT

Angry Outlaws.
An Ominous Appearance.
Udo Makes a Choice.

I CROUCHED ON THE FLOOR and felt the glass pelt down upon me like little nuggets of razor-sharp rain. The window on the other side of the car cracked, thus leading me to the brilliant conclusion that we were flanked on both sides. That was bad, superbad, but surely it couldn't get any worse—until I realized that the *pop-pop-pop* coming from above my head was Udo firing back with the little revolver that he had gotten for his Catorcena, and which I hadn't realized he was carrying. *It can always be worse,* said Nini Mo, *and usually will be if you wait long enough.*

"Udo!" I yelled, crawling under the seat and grabbing at his twitching feet. The floor of the horsecar was disgusting, sticky with spilled liquids and awash in torn paper. Why couldn't people take their trash with them?

"I got one! I think I got one!" Udo dropped back down and broke open the frame of the revolver, spraying empty shells in the air. "Zu—reach in my left breast pocket and hand me some more cartridges."

The Zu-Zu had dropped down onto the seat when the shooting started, thus keeping her pristine self above the trash. Now she rolled onto her side, fumbling in the pocket of Udo's greatcoat, as unperturbed as though she got caught in a firefight every day.

"What the hell are you doing, Udo?" I hissed.

"What the hell does it look like? Defending our lives!" He dropped the last cartridge into the cylinder and snapped it closed. Before I could stop him, he bobbed back to his feet, firing wildly. Udo's desire to impress the Zu-Zu was going to get us killed.

The horsecar, which somehow had kept moving during all the implosions and explosions, suddenly jolted to a halt. The driver's yelling was punctuated with another shot, then ominous silence.

I gingerly poked my head up next to Udo's, expecting any minute to feel the horrible bite of a bullet blowing my head off, but the firing didn't start up again. Two men in long white trench coats were hauling something thumpy down the front steps: the poor driver. The windshield was liberally sprayed with blood.

It was time, yet again, to advance in the opposite direction. In other words, to retreat. I looked wildly around to see how to accomplish that action and noticed the emergency door. Reaching up, I twisted the door handle, trying very quietly to jiggle it open. Someone from the front of the car hollered: "Hey! You, in the back! Let Jack go and no one will get hurt."

Udo fired again, but this time my whacking arm ruined his aim and the shot disappeared through the roof.

"FLORA!" Udo shouted, pushing me away and dropping back down. I fell against the emergency door, adding a bruising pain on my side. The Zu-Zu smiled at me. I did not smile back.

"Come on, kiddies, the game is up!" the outlaw yelled.

"My game has just started!" Udo shouted back, the snapperhead. I gave up being stealthy and pushed the emergency door hard. It popped open, and the Zu-Zu peered around outside, then nodded encouragingly to me. I motioned with my chin, and she rolled off the seat and slid down into the darkness.

"Come on, Udo! Hurry!" I hissed.

Udo gestured toward Springheel Jack, who sat stock-still, oblivious to the ruckus. "I'm not going without him."

Something had to be done to give us enough cover to grab Springheel Jack and run. We needed a diversion. Maybe if I could lob a ball of coldfire at the outlaws, that would distract them enough to let us escape. A coldfire ball is easy—I've done it many times and never gotten it wrong.

"⟨sigils⟩" I whispered, holding out my palm. A bead of coldfire bloomed above my open hand, smaller than I would have liked.

"⟨sigils⟩!" The coldfire light increased in size until it was about the size of a grapefruit. Cradling it in my hands, I popped up and threw the ball as hard as I could toward the outlaw—who neatly caught it and said, with an evil laugh, "I'll return this to you, missy." And then he suggested something that didn't sound very pleasant.

Clearly I needed something bigger. Much bigger. But I didn't know any bigger sigils—well, I knew some bigger sigils in principle, but not in action. What would Nini Mo do? She'd dazzle them with a Scintilla Sigil, or confuse them with an Ambiguity Sigil, or turn them into goats with a Transubstantiation Sigil. But while I knew *of* these sigils, I did not know their Gramatica.

The outlaw was advancing down the aisle. My mind had gone blank with terror—surely not a problem Nini Mo ever faced—and a funny taste was growing in the back of my throat, a rotten meaty taste. I swallowed hard, but that just made me gag, and when I opened my mouth to spit, a low ominous noise came out instead, a noise that vibrated my teeth and made the hair on the back of my neck tingle. A pale sickly glow began to seep through the car, the kind of light that makes the living look dead and the dead look decomposed. With detached horror, I realized that the glow was coming from me. I stood up and stepped out into the aisle, coldfire writhing like galvanic green ribbons from my outstretched fingertips. The outlaw dropped his gun and screeched.

"Flora—what are you doing?" Udo asked from somewhere behind me, his voice breaking.

"꜀꜀꜀!" The Word exploded from my mouth, its glittering coldfire letters whirling in a haze of furious fuliginous blackness, its edges as sharp and black as a Birdie obsidian sacrificial knife. The Word flung down the aisle, making *whomp-whomp* noises, and caught the outlaw square in the kisser. He screamed, a horrible sound that plunged into my brain like an ice pick in the ear. For a moment his head was separated from his body by a thick line of blackness, and then his head flew upward, buoyant on a spray of blood. He was still screaming, or maybe that was air howling as it escaped from his neck. Whatever the noise, it was horrific.

A sharp poke pushed me out of my daze. Udo was shoving me toward the emergency door. I crawled over to the door and rolled out, catching myself just before I hit the pavement, where the Zu-Zu waited. Udo prodded at Jack, who staggered out after me. We broke into a tearing run, eager to leave the howling shrieks and screams and the pallid glow of the horsecar as far behind as possible. No one followed.

Somehow, somewhere, we stopped running. Or rather, Udo and the Zu-Zu stopped, and then I couldn't run anymore and had to stop, too. In fact, not just stop, but sit down, not just sit down, but collapse, which I did. The curb was dirty and wet, but I didn't care. I had to get new stays; I was squeezed so tightly into the old ones that my lungs were sucking against each other, and all the blood was bouncing around inside my skull, so that I felt as though I was going to upchuck.

Udo leaned over, folding his arms around his stomach, gasping. "What ... hell ... Flora ... hell? Your hair ... on fire ..." His braids flopped over his bright red face.

"An Ominous Apparition, followed by an Active Protective Sigil," the Zu-Zu said. She was barely winded, but her hair, I noticed happily, had become even more disarranged. "Where did you learn all that, Flora?"

"I didn't," I gurgled. "I dunno—"

"Whatever. I want a coffee," the Zu-Zu said. "Let's go to el Mono Real, Udo, and you can get me a coffee."

I straightened up and tried to look refreshed and relaxed, as though I invoked Ominous Apparitions, flung forth Active Protective Sigils, and ran pell-mell from killers all the time, no big. What I really wanted to do was expel the contents of my tum and then collapse on the ground in a little pile of goo. "What about Springheel Jack?"

The outlaw had kept pace with our flight and had stopped with our stop; he didn't look winded at all, or concerned, or worried. Just blank and drooly.

"Oh, he can have coffee, too, if he wants," the Zu-Zu answered. "Come on, Udo. We're only a block from el Mono Real. I'm perishing."

"Ayah, so," Udo agreed, as though he was actually going to go with the Zu-Zu for coffee, thus leaving me to wait and see if the outlaws caught up with us.

"Hey! What about Jack's gang?" I demanded.

"Are you kidding, Flora? I think at this point they probably know better than to mess with us," Udo said. "Come on, let's get coffee."

"And what are you going to do about Jack?"

The Zu-Zu was already drifting down the street, a blot of imperious spookiness who didn't seem to care if we followed her or not. Udo glanced at her and then back at me, and took two steps in her direction. "Turn him in tomorrow, Flora. Come on."

"I have to get home, Udo. I've got a curfew, remember, and so do you."

'Don't be a stick—"

The Zu-Zu had stopped and turned. "Udo!"

"Come on, Flora," Udo said, half-pleadingly.

"I have to go home, Udo. You can go get coffee, if you want—with your pallid girl and your zombie pard. But I have to go home."

Udo stood up straight and said loftily, "Then go. No one is stopping you."

And with that, Udo trotted after the Zu-Zu, Springheel Jack close on his heels, leaving me standing alone in the middle of the empty street.

NINE

Just in Time.
A Handy Map. Bilskinir Baths.

By RUNNING—actually more like loping, or maybe even staggering—and then taking a shortcut up Crackpot Hill (via the Straight-up Stairs, which are indeed straight up), I managed to slither in through the mudroom door just as the kitchen clock began to chirp twelve times.

I was winded, sore, sweaty, and starving, but I was on time.

The kitchen fire was banked and the lamps doused; the room was dim and dogless, but filled with a delicious smell. In the low glow of the night-light, I saw a row of hand-pies sitting on the sideboard—more of Poppy's industry, I guessed. In addition to being thrashed, I was ravenous, so I snatched up three pies and stuffed them into my dispatch case before heading up the Below Stairs, making sure to skip the fourth step, which squeaks.

The parlor was also dim and dogless, but I could see that the bust of St. Stostikaos was empty of Mamma's hat, indicating she hadn't returned from Headquarters. Sometimes Mamma is at the Presidio all night. Often this is annoying, but tonight it meant one less parent to sneak by, so I was grateful for her absence.

Since he'd sobered up and come down out of the Eyrie, Poppy had been sleeping in Mamma's room, and as I crept by their door, I saw it was closed. He must have gone to bed early and taken the dogs with him—lucky, lucky for me. I crept the rest of the way down the hallway, trying to muffle my wheezing, to my bedroom, where I found Valefor lounging in my bed, reading a yellowback, and eating toffee.

"You are nearly late," he said, crunching loudly. I closed my bedroom door and locked it. "And you have liver in your hair." *Crunch, crunch.*

"I know, Sieur Bossy Boiler."

I felt as though I had just crawled across the entire Arivaipa desert. The thought of collapsing upon the settee and never moving again was blissful, but I had to get clean first. If Poppy smelled the smoke on me, saw the liver or the broken glass in my hair, he'd be mighty suspicious. The Stilskin Puppet Show does not involve pyrotechnics or organ meat.

I pitched my stays and pinafore on the floor and got my dressing gown out of my wardrobe. "Is Poppy in bed?"

Crunch, crunch. "Oh, no, he's gone."

"Gone?! Where did he go?" Poppy hadn't left Crackpot in years. "Did he take the dogs?"

Crunch, crunch. "He locked them in the stables when he left. I don't know where he went. You are lucky he's gone. You stink of smoke, magick . . . and failure, so I'm guessing it didn't go so well."

"Go kiss a horse, Valefor," I said rudely, and went to take a bath.

In the loo I saw that Valefor was right: I was a mess. My hair was matted with liver, sparkly with glass shards. The smell of smoke hung about me like a pall, and my eyes looked like soft-boiled eggs. My teeth were zinging with a galvanic buzz—an aftershock of the Ominous Apparition, I supposed. The hem of my kilt was shredded, and when I pulled off my grimy chemise, I saw I had a livid welt mark around my waist, along with red lines from where my stay-bones had been squeezed into my flesh. All the little pains had merged into one giant throb.

Lots of rose-smelling soap washed off the liver and smoke. But nothing could erase the smell of failure. Clearly, Firemonkey was a dead end. The Horses of Instruction would have to leave the City if they wished to stay ahead of the militia, and how could a man on the run teach me Gramatica?

And then there was Idden. Blast her! Couldn't she have run off to be a gambler or a farmer? Something harmless? Well, she had made her bed, and I hoped she enjoyed lying in it; when Mamma found out what Idden had done, she was going to explode—and who knows what that would mean for the rest of us. The more I thought about Idden, the more I felt like kicking her, which reminded me of someone else I would like to kick: Udo.

After all we'd been through, how could he leave me in the lurch for that stick girl? She'd just given him a Look and away he went, with not a thought of me, his best friend—me who had just kept him from ending up as some outlaw's bull's-eye. Well, fine. If Udo wanted to play it that way, I didn't need him. I had more important things to think about than Udo, his stupid Chickie, and his zombie outlaw.

Like the tentacle that had tried to kill me. I had never heard of a tentacle erupting out of a toilet before. Mamma loves to tell the story about how when she was a shavetail lieutenant in Arivaipa Territory, her commanding officer was attacked by fire ants while he was sitting on the pot in the Officers' Sinks. And last year the CPG had reported on a guy who'd had his hinder bit when a rat popped out of his potty. But that's completely different than a tentacle. After all, you expect fire ants in the desert. And it's not unusual to find rats in a sewer, though you hope they will stay there and not pop up in your pot when you are sitting upon it.

How could a tentacle even get into a potty pipe to begin with? I don't know much about Califa's water pipe system, but if it was full of tentacles, surely you'd read about it in the CPG. People would be constantly complaining. There would be editorials published, and questions asked in the Warlord's Grand Council. That's what happened after the rat-bite incident—the whole City talked of nothing else. After a lot of hullabaloo, Lord Axacaya promised to take care of the problem, and he did, with an Anti-Rat Sigil or something, and since then the City has been remarkably rat-free.

I peered over the rim of the tub at the potty. It sits up on a little wooden platform, thronelike. The lid was down, and surely it was only my imagination that, for an instant, it looked as though it was quivering—as though something inside wanted to get out. *Was* it my imagination? The longer I stared at it, the more the porcelain lid seemed to wiggle.

I stood up with a splash and grabbed my towel. The potty lid was firmly down—the quivering had been all due to my anxiety and the only ripples in the tub were those made by my hasty exit. Still, I toweled off hastily, and as I left the bathroom, I pulled the door firmly shut, just in case.

"You've gotten rid of the smell of liver and smoke," Valefor allowed, still lounging on my bed, "but the failure is still strong. I can't stand that smell. Maybe you should sleep on the settee?"

"It's my bed. *You* can sleep somewhere else."

"Don't be mean, Flora," Val said, not moving.

I hung my towel on the fire-fender and, after fishing *The Eschata* and the apple pies out of my bag, climbed into bed and slid the door shut, so that Valefor and I were snug and hidden away. Even if a tentacle *did* come out of the drains, and *did* find its way down the hallway and through my bedroom door, it wouldn't find me, for my cupboard bed vanishes behind a paneled wall when the door is closed.

"Do you know anything about tentacles, Valefor?" I asked. Valefor's glow was thin and wavering but it was enough to read by. I opened *The Eschata* to the Entity Spotter Appendix, and began to page through to the Ts. The pies were delicious; Poppy really knows how to make a proper piecrust—flaky and crisp. My piecrusts always turn out soggy.

"Tentacles?" Valefor said, yawning. He had taken all the pillows and piled them up behind him, and I noticed he was clutching the pink plushy pig that someone, apparently under the impression that I was turning four instead of fourteen, had given me for my Catorcena. "Wiggly things. Sometimes they have suckers. Sometimes they glow. Don't bogart all the pies, Flora. I'm hungry."

"After all that toffee?" I said, but I passed him a pie. *The Eschata*'s entry for *tentacle* said: *A long flexible fleshy appendage used as a sensory organ or appendage. Can be tipped with suckers, barbs, hooks, or luminescent pads. Can be found singularly, or in multiples. In small doses, a delicious snack. Larger—very bad news.*

"What entities have tentacles, Val?"

Valefor said, spraying crumbs, "Well, that last time I saw him, Virguex, Sucker of Souls, had tentacles."

I flipped to *Virguex*, who turned out to be a tenth-level apoplectic entity, who, as his name suggested, liked to suck people's souls away via a long hollow tongue with a barb on the end. First he pierced your neck with this tongue, and then he slurped. Yuck. Virguex did not sound like the kind of entity you would want to meet in a dark alley at deepest midnight unless you were armed with the Semiote Verb *To Smite*.

Fortunately, Virguex was not my guy, as the Entity Spotter soon made clear. When I finished reading Virguex's entry, the black letters on the page began to jiggle and wiggle, unraveling to become one long black thread that reworked itself into an image: a mug shot of an ugly dude with jagged fangs, a domelike head covered with short wormy tentacles, and a lolling tongue that was so long he could have tied a knot in it and worn it as a cravat.

"Not him," I said.

"Hmmm," Valefor said. "If I were more myself—a little less hungry—my memory might be a little better, Flora Segunda. That pie was good, but it wasn't filling."

"I'm not giving you any of my Anima, Valefor. How dumb do you think I am after last time?"

"Not dumb as I would like." Valefor sighed. "Why can't you be more like your great-uncle August? He was dumb as a sack of hair. So dumb he set his own drawers on fire trying to light—"

"The tentacle, Val."

"There are lots of different kinds of tentacles. Aren't rangers supposed to be observant and specific? Can't you be more descriptive?"

"You know, like the little squiddies that Mamma likes to eat fried. That kind of tentacle. Only much, much bigger. As thick around as my arm, and with burning suckers at its tip."

"A squid tentacle?" Valefor yawned into the pink pig. The pig had no mouth, just a plushy pink snout and beady black knotted eyes, but it somehow managed to have a slightly smug expression. "*Squids* have squid tentacles."

"Squids aren't that big."

"The Loliga is. If there aren't any more pies, I think I shall go to bed, I'm so dreadful tired."

"Loliga? What's the Loliga?"

"You are so ignorant, Flora Segunda. Don't they teach you anything at Sanctuary—*oooof!*"

I had kicked Valefor hard, and now he shot upright, protesting. "Don't be angry at me, Flora Segunda. It's not my fault that your education is deficient."

"Your entire existence is going to be deficient if you don't quit jacking me around, Valefor. What is the Loliga?"

Valefor rolled his eyes, huffed and puffed, then said, "Long ago, before you were born, little girl, the great adept Georgiana Haðraaða coerced an egregore of the ninth power into the body of a giant squid. She hid the Loliga under the City and then used it to blackmail Califa's citizens into making her Pontifexa. That's how the Haðraaða dynasty came to power, before your puffy little Warlord overthrew it. Georgiana threatened to loose the Loliga upon the City if they didn't bow to her. Which they did, of course, the cowards. Now, if it had been up to me, I should never have given in."

"Why didn't you ever mention this before, Valefor?" I demanded. I couldn't believe that there was a giant magickal squid hidden somewhere under the City and I had never known it until now. All my exhaustion and throbbing was suddenly subsumed in a wave of excitement.

"Well, it never came up before. How was I supposed to know it was important? You never mentioned you were being attacked by a giant squid before."

"But I never was before tonight."

"Then, you didn't need to know until tonight," Val said smugly. "And anyway, how was I supposed to know that the Loliga was still there? I'm cut off from the Current—I have no idea what is going on out in the world, except what I read in the newspapers. Now that there are no Haðraaðas left alive, I would have figured that the Loliga had long since been freed."

"Well, obviously not, if it's attacking people. But why me?"

Valefor shrugged. "I'm sure she wasn't after you personally, Flora Segunda. Don't be so conceited. Probably, she was just looking for a snack and you happened to be there, fat, dumb, and happy. I hope the Loliga keeps out of my drains. That's the last thing I need, on top of all those silly earth—" Valefor broke off and looked at me, horrified.

I stared back, and I knew we had just been struck by the same horrible idea.

"The earthquakes, Valefor! Could they be caused by the Loliga?"

"That was Georgiana's threat, Flora Segunda! Earthquakes. Oh, why didn't I think of this before? It's a pity to be so proscribed. If I were myself and powerful again, I would have considered this earlier."

"But Georgiana is dead, and so are the rest of the Haðraaðas. There is no blackmail anymore."

"But they must have died out without freeing the Loliga."

"And a sigil is only as strong as the magician who creates it." No sigil will last forever, no matter how strong the magician's

Will may be. Georgiana Haðraaða was long dead, and the last Haðraaða—the Butcher Brakespeare—had died years ago. Whatever sigil Georgiana had used to proscribe the Loliga must be weakening and allowing the Loliga to struggle—and endanger the City.

Valefor wailed, "This is terrible, Flora Segunda. The Loliga is an egregore of the ninth degree—one of the most powerful entities ever to manifest in the Waking World. After all this time a prisoner, she's probably very angry. If she got free, who knows what she could do! I don't want to be destroyed! I'm already fragile."

"None of us wants to be destroyed, Valefor," I answered. "We've got to do something."

"Like what? We can't do anything against an egregore of the ninth degree. Oh, when I was not banished, I would have been more than her match, but not now, forlorn and almost empty—and you are just a girl."

"What would Nini Mo do?"

"You are not Nini Mo." In his panic Valefor had grown even more wispy; now he was merely a face floating in vapor. I had never seen him this discombobulated before.

A threat to the City should be Mamma's affair, but what could she do against a magickal entity? Not only was she not a magician, she hated magick. She'd probably try to handle the problem with military force and that would only compound it. The Warlord—he's a joke, and he'd only refer back to Mamma.

What would Nini Mo do if she couldn't handle the problem herself? *Leave ditch digging to the ditchdiggers*, she'd say. Leave it to the experts. And as far as experts in magick, there was only one person in Califa who might know what to do about an egregore of the ninth degree.

"I've got to tell Lord Axacaya about this," I said. "Maybe he knows already. But if he doesn't, he needs to. He's a powerful adept. Surely he'll know what to do."

Valefor was doubtful. "I don't know, Flora. I mean, I know

he helped you before, but you can't trust him. He was born a Birdie. He might think it was fine for the City to be destroyed."

"I don't think so. He's lived in the City for years, and even when he could have betrayed her to the Birdies, he didn't."

"Flora?"

At the knock on my bed door, Valefor blinked out. I hastily shoved *The Eschata* under my pillow before sliding the door open.

I yawned and stretched as though I had been asleep. "Ayah, Poppy?"

Poppy had a lamp in his hand, held low so that I couldn't see his face. Flynn wiggled through the opening and squirmed in between me and the wall. "I was just checking to make sure you were here."

"I was asleep, Poppy."

"Is Udo here?"

"He decided to go home."

"Who were you talking to?"

A quiver of quicksilver fear ran through me. "No one, Poppy. I was asleep."

"You must have been talking in your sleep, then."

I snuggled down and closed my eyes, as though I couldn't keep them open another minute. After a few seconds, the reddish light waving on my eyelids went away and the door slid shut. I was exhausted, yet I could not sleep. A giant squid under the City—earthquakes—Udo—Lord Axacaya—tentacles—the Zu-Zu—falling buildings—Udo—Crackpot Hall in ruins—Mamma and Poppy squashed—Udo.

Forget Udo. I had to focus. Maybe Lord Axacaya already knew all about the Loliga, but I had to tell him just in case. Tomorrow was the Warlord's Birthday Ball. Mamma had said I couldn't go with her, but that didn't mean I couldn't go at all. There had to be a way to sneak in. I could use a Glamour as a disguise and get to Lord Axacaya that way. And surely bringing this situation to Lord Axacaya's attention would speak well of my initiative and experience. Surely it would impress him.

Surely it would show him that I was mature and levelheaded and had learned from my previous impetuous behavior. Surely it would show him that I was worthy of his teaching. Worthy of being taught Gramatica.

The ranger who saves the world, said Nini Mo, *also saves herself.*

TEN

Waffles. Headlines.
Seating Charts.

I GOT UP AT DAWN to research Georgiana Haðraaða in the history book we use at Sanctuary, *The Grand History of the Republic of Califa and Its Glories and Golden Ages.* Unfortunately, it has a lot to say about the wonders of the Warlord and how fabulous it was when he conquered the City and liberated it from the tyranny of the Haðraaða Pontifexas, but very little about the Haðraaðas themselves. There had been three Georgianas; the one I was interested in was the second. She was described as a cunning adept and a ruthless leader, but there was no mention of a Loliga. If I had been able to get to Valefor's Bibliotheca, I might have found more useful books, but I didn't dare use the Elevator with Poppy around, and there's no way to get to the Bibliotheca without the Elevator. Even then you take a chance of ending up not in the Bibliotheca but lost somewhere in the banished depths of Crackpot Hall—perhaps never to find your way home.

But then, a stroke of luck. I was flipping through *The Eschata* again, hoping to find something useful that I had missed, when I noticed a small piece of folded paper stuck between two pages.

The paper was a map entitled "The City of Califa's Fundaments, including Underground Tunnels, Rivers, Sewers, Galvanic Currents, Reservoirs, Streams, Cache-basins, Back Doors, Beaver Lodges, and Other Subterranean Landmarks." Nowhere was there a giant X marking the Loliga, but as I studied the map, I noticed that all the lines of Current eventually crossed at the exact same point: a Vertex of great power. If I were a great adept hiding a giant magickal squid under the City, I would lure her to this Vertex and use these lines of Current to trap her. In the Waking World, this Vertex corresponded to the location of the ruined Bilskinir Baths.

The Bilskinir Baths were a natatorium complex built by Albany Bilskinir, the husband of Georgiana Haðraaða Primera. Like Bilskinir House, the Baths were located on a cliff overlooking the Pacifica Ocean, though the House and Baths were some distance apart. During their heyday, the Baths were one of the wonders of the City, particularly the great Salt Pool, which was refilled with fresh ocean water every day. During the reign of Georgiana Segunda, the Baths had been almost totally destroyed when a ship full of dynamite had run aground against the Salt Pool's retaining wall and exploded. Now I wondered: Had the Baths really been destroyed by dynamite, or had the Loliga put up quite a fight?

The Warlord's Birthday Ball was to start around seven in the evening. After breakfast, I would need to spend the rest of the day planning. I had to make sure that I had a good strong Glamour; the last thing I wanted was to be recognized. And I had to find something to wear—not so splendid that I was memorable, but something that made me look as though I belonged. *Clothes make the ranger's disguise,* said Nini Mo. My wardrobe is pretty deficient. I did have my red Catorcena dress, but it was awfully fluffy and I did not want to look fluffy. I wanted to look sleek and cool. Maybe Udo could help.

Udo. In my excitement about the Loliga and the map, I had forgotten about Udo. Now I remembered and went downstairs to breakfast in a very grumpy mood.

"How are you this morning, Flora?" Poppy bustled about the kitchen; buttering waffles, pouring coffee and orange juice, frying bacon. The bacon smelled so delicious—porky and fat— that I took three slices.

"Fine." Maybe I could sneak something from Mamma's closet. Though she hardly ever wears civilian dress, she has a lot of clothes.

Poppy glanced at me, but didn't say anything else, just refilled my coffee cup and sat down across from me while I ate my waffles, ignoring the dogs hovering vulturelike around his chair.

"You all right? You seem rather stiff this morning," Poppy said.

"I'm fine," I lied, though I felt about a hundred years old. "Where's Mamma?"

"She's not up yet," Poppy answered. "She was at HQ late. Did you see today's *Alta Califa*?"

He pushed the paper over to me, and when I flipped it over, all the blood rushed out of my head and plummeted to my feet.

POODLE DOG GOES POOF!
FIREMONKEY SINGS SEDITION!
Drummer Implodes. See back page for details.

"It's a good thing your show wasn't at the Poodle Dog; the place burned to the ground last night," Poppy said. "There was a riot and the militia had to get out the gas gun to clear the streets. I believe in freedom of speech, but this Firemonkey goes too far."

"Ayah. I'm thankful we missed it." I peeked over the top of the paper to try to gauge Poppy's mood. He was sipping his coffee almost meditatively. But guilt made me paranoid, and his very calmness was worrisome. Did he realize I had come in late? The Army is all about honor; if you know you've done something wrong, even if no one else does, you are supposed to turn yourself in. I had no intention of turning myself in.

Poppy continued, "Califa is in a precarious position. The Birdies will stomp us if we step even an inch out of line. We must do nothing to antagonize them."

I swallowed my last bite of waffle and said, "These waffles

are fabulous, Poppy. The batter is so light and fluffy. Can I have another?"

Poppy got up and reloaded the waffle iron with batter, but he wasn't deterred from his topic. "Treason and sedition can't be tolerated. Firemonkey says he speaks for Califa's own good, but if he had his way, he'd pull her to her ruin. I hope the militia catches up with Firemonkey and his moronic cohorts—the sooner the better. Blood-eagle the lot of them."

His words surprised me. Surely Poppy had no love for the Birdies, not after what they had done to our family, to the First Flora. Like the rest of us, he had to suck it up—outwardly, at least. But I would have thought that privately he'd approve of anyone causing the Birdies woe. And also, that he would support any movement designed to rehabilitate the Butcher Brakespeare, his long-dead love.

"I'm sure the militia will catch up with Firemonkey, Poppy." I hoped, of course, that they would not.

"I hope so. Thank heavens no Fyrdraaca has any concern with Firemonkey or his idiotic propaganda. It would be devastating for this family if any of us were found to harbor such sympathies. We, above all other Califians, must be seen to be true to our oath of fealty to the Virreina of Huitzil. The slightest hint of treachery could mean our destruction."

My breakfast began to bubble in my stomach. I had not thought so particularly about what it might mean if a *Fyrdraaca* were involved with the EI and its stupid plotting. Would Idden reflect upon us all? Surely the Birdies would understand she had acted on her own . . . wouldn't they? I remembered the Butcher Brakespeare—a Flayed Priest had cut her heart out and eaten it. I didn't want anyone to eat my heart. Or Mamma's. Or Poppy's, for that matter. Or even stupid Idden's.

Poppy dropped another waffle on my plate, and I stared at it.

"What's wrong? You look ill."

"Too much bacon, I think, Poppy," I said, trying to twist my stiff face into a smile.

"I used to love bacon," Poppy said, "but now the smell makes me rather sick. It smells too much like—well, never mind. Here, I'll give your waffle to the dogs." He whisked my plate away, and I was glad to see it go. "Or, better yet, to your mother."

"Good morning!" Mamma sang out, as she came down the Below Stairs. She was in her red silk bathrobe, and her hair stood straight up. She sat down at the kitchen table and Poppy put my plate in front of her. "Waffles, oh how I love waffles, and Hotspur makes the best waffles ever. You look bleary, Flora. How was the show?"

"I missed most of it," I said, "so I don't know. I had to be home, you know."

"Poor punkie," Mamma said. "Even your gloomy face can't bring me down today. I'm in a happy, happy mood because I finally got the stupid seating chart for the Warlord's Birthday Ball worked out. I am a true genius, let me tell you. It's no picnic trying to make sure that no one ends up next to their worst enemy and yet hierarchy is followed. Protocol is a real bitch. Pass that bacon over here, I'm starved."

I passed the bacon but Mamma had put her fork down and picked the paper up, and the sharp line between her eyes turned into a knife slash. "Pigface Psychopomp!" Then she said something else, much worse.

"Buck!" Poppy said sharply. "Language."

Mamma waved the paper angrily. "This is just dandy. Florian's going to squee, for Califa's sake. Those idiot militia morons. They shouldn't be allowed out of bed in the morning—turning a gas gun on civilians!"

"At least it's not your fault, Buck," Poppy said. "No one can blame you."

"It's not a matter of blame," Mamma complained. "I was almost to the point of getting the Birdies to withdraw their detachments from Califa—I had them believing we no longer needed such oversight, and now this. I'm going to kick Colonel Oset from one end of the City to the other. And why didn't anyone inform me of this earlier? Where was the Officer of the Day? I'm going to kick him, too!"

Mamma threw the paper, and swore again. I would have felt sorrier for Colonel Oset if I hadn't seen the gas gun in action. Instead, I felt like being kicked by Mamma wasn't nearly enough punishment. But Mamma's ire seemed more about the militia's reaction than the Horses of Instruction's instigation, which was good. Good for Firemonkey, and for Idden, too.

"I've got to get back to the Presidio," Mamma said. "Wrap me up some bacon, will you, Flora?"

Poppy plunked a coffee cup down in front of Mamma. "Buck, it's over now—rushing won't do you any good. They know you are coming and bringing hell to pay. Let them stew."

"True enough—" Mamma was interrupted by a barking chorus. The dogs had left off their begging to hurtle themselves toward the back door, woofing a welcome to Lieutenant Sabre, Mamma's aide-de-camp, who had appeared in the doorway, his hat in his hand.

"Did you see the paper, Aglis?" Mamma said, when the dogs had subsided enough to allow Lieutenant Sabre to come into the kitchen. Alas, he did not emerge completely unscathed; his skirts were now covered in paw prints and dog hair, ruining his usual perfection.

"I did, General," he said. "Ave, Colonel Fyrdraaca, Madama Fyrdraaca Segunda."

Mamma said, "I want to give a statement to the press immed—"

"I'm sorry to interrupt, General," Lieutenant Sabre said. "May I speak with you privately? It's important. Very important."

Lieutenant Sabre, I noticed, looked rather pale, and his lips were pinched together so tightly that they were almost white. But, like a good yaller dog, the golden buttons on his frock coat gleamed, his collar was perky, and his tie perfectly tied. I used to think that Lieutenant Sabre was terribly stuck-up. But he's the only aide Mamma's ever had that lasted more than a few weeks, so he clearly has sand.

"I already know all about the idiot militia, Aglis."

"It's not that, General," he said, and suddenly I knew exactly what it was. My stomach sank into my slippers.

"All right, then. Come upstairs to my study." Mamma took her coffee cup, and Lieutenant Sabre followed her upstairs. I watched them go, the sour feeling in my tum growing. Mamma was already in a bad mood; it was only going to get worse. Blast Idden—she wasn't even here, and she was causing trouble.

"He looks like a man going to his execution," Poppy remarked, and he would know what a man going to his own execution would look like, I supposed. "Poor bugger."

He went back to frying bacon and I fiddled with my coffee cup, tense and waiting. After a few minutes, noises began to echo down the Below Stairs. At the stove, Poppy froze, bacon dangling from his tongs. The dogs swiveled their ears, though their eyes never left the bacon. I froze, cup in hand.

Mamma was shouting. Shouting! Mamma never shouts. The angrier she is the quieter she gets; you have to lean in to hear what she's saying, and each word hurts all the more for having to strain to hear it. Mamma shouting: This was worse than I had expected.

"Finish your breakfast, Flora," Poppy ordered, abandoning the bacon and running upstairs, dogs falling in behind him.

Of course, I didn't just sit there. By the time I got upstairs, Poppy had vanished into Mamma's study; the door was closed, but that didn't mute the shouting. I hardly even had to lean against the door to hear what she was saying.

"—the hell did it take this long for him to inform me?"

Mumble, mumble. Poor Lieutenant Sabre, the bearer of bad news through no fault of his own.

"Calm down, Buck." Poppy.

"Three weeks—she's been missing three whole weeks and I only find out now!" Mamma shouted. Warm fur pushed against me; I looked down to see the dogs huddling around my legs. Their ears were flat on their heads. Somehow dogs always know when something bad has happened. I petted them reassuringly, though I did not feel reassured at all.

For the next few minutes, Mamma shouted, Poppy and Lieutenant Sabre tried to be soothing, and I huddled against the door, my ears burning. Most of Mamma's anger was focused on the fact that Idden's commanding officer hadn't sent a courier as soon as Idden had disappeared from Fort Jones. He had waited a full week before marking her absent on the post returns, and another week before changing her to absent without leave. Only then did he send a courier to the City with his report, and due to heavy rains, the journey from Fort Jones to the City took an extra three days. That's why Idden had been gone for three weeks, but the report had only arrived now. I felt sorry for Idden's commanding officer, caught between a rock and a hard place—Idden's desertion and Mamma's fury. He had probably hoped Idden would come back before he had to report her.

The door flung open. I jerked out of the way, just in time, and Lieutenant Sabre came barreling out. He shut the door behind him and stared at me, wild-eyed. He was practically quivering.

"Are you all right?" I asked.

"I'd rather face all the Flayed Riders of Huitzil," he said, "than the General when she's angry."

"You and me both."

Lieutenant Sabre unbuttoned his tunic and breathed heavily for a minute, then took a case out of his sleeve and wedged a little packet of snus into his lip. He wiped his forehead with his hankie and then rebuttoned his tunic.

"The General is threatening to go to Fort Jones to investigate," Lieutenant Sabre said. "She doesn't believe that Captain Fyrdraaca deserted. The General thinks that Captain Fyrdraaca may have met with some misadventure, perhaps while hunting. That she might have fallen in a ravine or been attacked by a wild animal."

Huh, I thought. *If only Mamma knew, she might wish Idden had been eaten by a bear.*

"What do you think?" I asked.

Lieutenant Sabre snorted. "Captain Fyrdraaca was acting

quartermaster at the time of her departure from Fort Jones. She is missing and so is the entire quartermaster treasury. That seems pretty definitive to me."

Pigface! Idden had forgotten to mention that to me. So if they caught her, they could court-martial her for desertion *and* theft. Fabulous, Idden, just dandy.

"Can Mamma go to Fort Jones?" I asked.

"She'll have to get permission from the Warlord, but, of course, that's just a formality. He'll hardly tell her no. But it's a bad time for the General to be absent from the City. The EI causing all that commotion, the Warlord's Birthday. We need the General here. She's a stable influence, and it would look bad to have her gone right now."

And Idden long gone from Fort Jones, too, I thought, *so an entirely wasted trip.*

"Maybe the Warlord won't let her go," I said, hopefully.

"Lay off, Reverdy!" Mamma's voice rose again. "I need your support here!"

Lieutenant Sabre and I leaned back against the door and heard Poppy say, "Be reasonable, Buck. Rushing off to Fort Jones isn't going to solve anything. If Idden has deserted, she's long gone."

"I refuse to believe that Idden would ever desert," Mamma said. "She is probably lying at the bottom of a ravine somewhere."

"For three weeks, Buck?" Poppy said quietly. "Then there really is no point, is there? Hardy's letter said they searched for her and found nothing—no horse, no dogs, no Idden. And taking the QM funds is a sure sign that she scarpered. She's gone, Juliet. She's gone."

For a moment there was silence, and then Mamma said, "I can't go through this again, Reverdy. I just can't. I can't lose another child. I have to find her."

"And if you find her? What then? Are you going to court-martial her and shoot her?"

"Of course not."

"How are you going to have any choice? Will you be so openly partisan?"

Another silence, and Lieutenant Sabre and I looked at each other. Mamma would never have her own daughter shot, would she? Would she? The look on Lieutenant Sabre's face said he certainly thought she would. *Oh Idden, you snapperhead.* I really hoped she had covered her tracks well. I hoped, hoped that she and the other Horses of Instruction were far, far from the City now. Long gone.

We heard the footsteps just in time and retreated halfway down the Below Stairs, so it wouldn't be obvious we'd been listening. Without giving a look our way, Mamma flung herself upstairs, her face as hard as stone, her dressing gown flapping.

Poppy stood at the top of the Below Stairs, looking down at us. "She's going to Fort Jones," he said. "I tried to persuade her otherwise, but when has Buck ever listened to me? You'd better get packing, Aglis. You have a long trip ahead of you."

"My condolences, sir." Lieutenant Sabre saluted and skedaddled, no doubt wishing he could flee somewhere no one had ever heard of the Fyrdraaca family. I knew how he felt.

"I'm sure she's all right, Poppy, wherever she is," I said, after a moment.

"I hope you are right," Poppy answered. "If you heard from Idden you would tell me, wouldn't you, Flora?"

One of the annoying aspects of Poppy being sober is that he now is much harder to deflect. He was looking down at me with a green gaze that pierced me to my very soul and made me want to start to blather. Mamma can do this easily, but I had not known Poppy had the same talent. Guilt stabbed at me.

He continued, "I don't care if she deserts from the Army a thousand times over. I just want to know she is all right."

Mamma had said: *I can't lose another child.* The first Flora gone, and now Idden. I was the only Fyrdraaca child left. My waffles churned into a painful throb and for a moment I thought about spilling my guts—not my breakfast, but my guilt. Why should I cover for Idden? I didn't know where she was. And I *had* crossed on the promise not to give her up, which meant it wasn't bind-ing. But what if I did tell Poppy I'd seen her? How could he help her? He could barely help himself. And if he told Mamma, then she would have no choice but to court-martial Idden and maybe even shoot her.

When in doubt, keep your yip shut, said Nini Mo.

So I said, "Idden can take care of herself, Poppy. I'm sure she's fine."

"No doubt you are right, but I wish I knew for sure. The Fyrdraacas dwindle," Poppy said sadly. "I think we can fall no further, and yet there's always more down."

ELEVEN

Mamma Departs.
Tactics. Getting Dressed.

BY LUNCHTIME Mamma and Lieutenant Sabre were on the steamer for Aurora, the first leg of the journey to Fort Jones. I felt terrible that she was making such a long trip for nothing, but what could I do? I couldn't think of any way to tell her the trip was pointless without giving away Idden. And I still had to worry about the Warlord's Birthday Ball.

In all the hullabaloo, I hadn't had time to work on my Glamour or try to rescue my wardrobe. But then, unexpectedly, Idden did me a favor. On the ride to the docks, Mamma was full of instructions—one of which was that Poppy should send his regrets to the Warlord. She did not want him going to the Ball alone.

I saw my chance and leaped, offering to go with Poppy. I pointed out that the Warlord might be insulted if our family made no showing at all. Poppy, surprisingly, sided with me, saying that at such a volatile time it was important for our family to show the Warlord support.

Reluctantly, Mamma agreed. At the docks, she hugged Poppy good-bye and kissed each dog on the nose. Then she hugged me and whispered in my ear, "Keep an eye on your father, Flora." I whispered back that I would, and then the steamer was chugging out onto the deep blue bay, Mamma a dark blur, getting smaller and smaller until we could not see her at all. But her flag stayed visible until the steamer rounded Black Point and was gone.

Once again it was just Poppy, me, and the dogs.

Of course, in the Fyrdraaca family there's always a catch, and in this case, the catch was that Poppy did not think that I should get the day off just because we were going to the biggest social event of the season. Despite my protests that I needed to prepare for the Ball, Poppy insisted on study time.

By the time he finally released me, I was so sick to death of tactics that if I had been called upon right that moment to lead a Flying Wedge, or Oblique Left Double-Time, or enfilade the enemy using Honeychurch's Backward Line-Breaker, I would have just lain down on the ground and let my troops ride right over me.

Not all battles are fought on a battlefield and not all weapons draw blood, Nini Mo said. Released from Poppy bondage, I could turn my thoughts completely toward the tactics to use at the Ball. I couldn't just walk up to Lord Axacaya in front of everyone. I had to be subtle and discreet. I had to be calm and deliberate. I needed to give the impression of being a reasonable adult who should be taken seriously.

Nini Mo says you should dress to fit the occasion, but that was easy for her to say. I'm sure she had a huge wardrobe of fabulous clothes, and if not, at least she had her own money to buy as many clothes as she could want. Nearly all my clothes were hand-me-downs from Idden. I remembered painfully that the Zu-Zu's fashionable clothes were surely not castoffs. Which reminded me painfully of Udo's treachery. He went off with *her* and left *me* in the lurch, the dolt. How could he? I would never desert him, no matter what. He was faithless. I should have known it would come to this. Udo is pretty but he has no staying power. Well, I hoped he enjoyed his new scrawny little friend. She was welcome to him, and he to her. *Have fun, Udo.*

"Your kilts are too short, and your sleeves not long enough." Valefor had perched on top of my wardrobe. He'd recovered a bit from his fright the night before, but not much. Now he was so wispy that if he didn't hold on tightly to something, he bobbed up toward the ceiling, so he split the difference by holding on to something up high. "No one wears lacy collars now, nor pinafores unless they are doing yard work, Flora Segunda, and you are going to the Warlord's Birthday Ball. The press will be there, and they will write that the Fyrdraacas have lost all their fashion sense. I shall die of shame."

I surveyed the mess strewn on the settee, on my bed, on my desk, heaped on the floor: every piece of clothing I owned, including the fluffy Catorcena dress, everything Idden had left behind, and some things pillaged from Mamma's closet, which were just as old and out-of-date. "I think it shall take more than shame to kill you, Valefor. What am I going to do? I haven't time to go buy anything. And how do you know so much about what is in style?"

Valefor said primly, "I may be stuck in this house, but I can read. Udo's been giving me his old *Warlord's Wear Weekly*s. I like to keep up. Clothes really do make the woman, Flora."

It was stupid, but I rather felt like wailing. Never before had I been vain, for what cares a ranger about appearances? It's getting the job done that counts. But what if the job requires you to look, if not fabulous, at least presentable? Maybe even alluring? I was not in the least bit alluring. Maybe I was the ugly ducking who would, one day, spawn into a swan. But somehow I didn't think so. Life is rarely like the stories. If it were, my clothing problem would be quickly settled.

In the sentimental yellowbacks, there's always a point where the hero is stuck—has nothing to wear, can't get her homework done, has to make dinner for ten but doesn't know how to cook—and just as she is about to howl, there's a mighty flash and her magickal auntie appears and makes it all right. Conjures up a fabulous outfit, or finishes the stupid word problem, or whips up a delicious eight-course menu. A magickal auntie would sure come in handy right now. Instead I had a red dog snoring in my bed and a useless denizen lurking on top of my closet.

"If only you were more useful," I said to Valefor. "If only you could conjure me some new clothes."

"Whose fault is it I'm not useful? You cannot put that against me, Flora Segunda. I tell you, I was a real style-setter before. The outfit I made for Hotspur's Catorcena was a real stunner—two days later everyone in the City was wearing its knockoff. *À la Fyrdraaca* they called it. The frock coat had a double tier of puffs on the sleeves, and the skirts were pinned back into a huge train . . ."

I tried to ignore him. He was chock full of reminiscences of his past glories, and listening to them only made me more depressed. Well, it would have to be the Catorcena dress that Paimon had made for me. It was the only dress that fit and looked appropriately splendid, even if it was fluffy. I wished it wasn't quite such an awful shade of red and that perhaps the skirts were not quite as ruffly, but they were impressively wide, which somewhat canceled out the ruffles. And the neckline *was* plungy. I certainly outshone the Zu-Zu there, no problem. She had as much cleavage as a washboard. I would wear Mamma's pearls (pillaged from her jewelry box) and carry my birthday fan, and if Valefor could help me with my hair, I wouldn't look too bad.

But first I had to get into those damn stays, which I dreaded. I'd let the back laces out as far as they would go, and it was still a struggle to get the busk closed. One of the steel bones was rubbing a raw spot under my arm, right through my chemise. As soon as Mamma got home, I was going to demand that we go to the Army-Navy store and get new underpinnings.

I was hopping and swearing and Valefor was urging me to suck it in, though it was sucked in as far as it would go, when a rap on the window made me jump. Blast it, I had almost gotten the bottom snap of the stays hooked. Now I would have to start over.

"It's Udo," Valefor said helpfully. Who else would it be? Udo's the only person besides me who knows the trick of climbing through my window.

Udo swung in over the sill after I opened the window. "Why'd you latch your window?"

"To keep undesirables out," I said. "Where's your Chickie, Poo-Poo, or whatever her name is?"

"Did a hurricane come through here? Pigface, what a mess." Udo tossed aside the clothes draped on the settee, then threw himself down. Flynnie got up from his snooze on the bed and ambled over to sniff his hand. "Her name is the Zu-Zu, as you well know. We had our coffee, and a few other things besides . . ." And here he smiled in a most sick-making way. "Then she had to go to band practice; Califa's Lip Rouge, that's the name of her band, did I mention? She's the lead singer. I couldn't very well take Springheel Jack back home to Case Tigger, right? Anyway, I'm supposed to be staying here with you. So here I am."

"*Last night* you were supposed to be staying here, Udo. It is not last night anymore."

"The weekend," he said airily.

I looked out the window but saw no zombified outlaw below. The gate to the kitchen garden was open, and Dash and Flash were nibbling their way through the tomato plants, while Crash was digging a hole in the asparagus bed. Blasted dogs. I leaned out the window and hollered. They looked up, heads cocked as if to say *What on earth can be wrong with Flora?* And then went back to their munching and digging.

"You left the garden gate open, Udo," I said, slamming the window shut. "The dogs are in there making a mess."

"Sorry. Look, Flora, I put Springheel Jack in the stables—"

Valefor shrieked like a teakettle. "You put a zombie in my nice clean stables?!" I had told Valefor about Udo's little scheme earlier, and he had been even less impressed with the plan than I had. And if *Valefor,* the Very King of Bad Ideas, thought the idea was bad, then it must be bad indeed.

I didn't care about the clean stables at all. "How long does that powder last, Udo? What if he comes back to himself suddenly in our stables? Did you think of that?"

"I did, actually, Flora. But it ain't going to be a problem."

"Why is that? And get your boots off my settee." I pushed Flynn away from whatever he was licking up off the floor. Only two days earlier I had spent several hours polishing it, and I didn't want to have to redo so quickly.

"My stables! What if he scares my pretty horses?" Valefor moaned.

"He ain't gonna bother your horses, Val. Now don't be mad, Flora, but Springheel Jack is dead."

"What do you mean, dead? Flynn—get away. What do you mean he's dead?" I demanded.

"Well, I guess he was hit during the gunfight, Flora, and the zombie powder kept him moving. I didn't notice it until I got to the stables, and, well, the back of his head is gone." Udo looked rather chagrined.

Valefor shrieked again. "Is he dripping? He'd better not be dripping, Udo. Oh, to be so helpless, while I am ruined. He's not dripping, is he?"

"Udo." I moaned. Why was I cursed with relatives and friends and dogs? Why couldn't I be an orphan? And a hermit, too? A hermit orphan who was allergic to dogs. The blasted dog wouldn't leave the licking. I put a foot in his ribs and gave him a soft boot, to no effect. "Oh, Udo . . ."

"Don't get yourself all twisted, Val. He's not dripping; I wrapped his head in a feed sack. So he's fine. But anyway, Flora—it's not just that—"

"I smell blood," Valefor said suddenly. He began to crawl down the front of the wardrobe, spiderlike, snuffling. "Full of delicious Anima."

"Ayah, that's what I'm trying to say," Udo said triumphantly. "I've been shot!"

TWELVE

First Aid. Apple Gin. Udo's Pockets.

UDO *HAD* BEEN SHOT, the wretch. His shoulder was a sticky bloody mess, and more blood was dribbling down his arm, and trailing on my nice clean floor, delicious to dogs. I felt faint, but a ranger cannot flinch. Nini Mo didn't flinch when she had to amputate her scout's arm with a sewing awl after he got mauled in *Nini Mo vs. the Chupacabras*. She just gritted her teeth, shoved a stick in Frank's mouth, and started sawing.

Pushing the lip-licking Valefor out of the way, I helped Udo pull off his coat. The cloth was stuck to the wound, and he whined and swore as I eased the fabric away.

"It stopped bleeding earlier and so I thought it was nothing, but now it's started again. I must have strained it climbing up the side of the house. Be careful of that—it's one of my favorite shirts," Udo complained as I tried to unstick the linen using water from my teakettle and a hanky. "Owww."

Valefor drifted over us, making disgusting little noises and begging for a taste.

"The shirt is ruined, Udo, and, Val, get away—you're a Butler, not a vampire!"

"But the lovely Anima," Val whined. "It's just going to waste, and I'm so famished."

I drew Udo's shirt over his head and off, thus revealing a clotted red mess on his left shoulder. My tum twisted and my breakfast rose upward. I swallowed hard; I was not going to give Udo the satisfaction of urping. Valefor grabbed the bloody shirt and whisked back to the top of my wardrobe, where he began to make slurpy sounds.

"How could you go this long without doing something?" I said. "Doesn't it hurt?"

"I didn't even feel it," Udo twisted his head so he could inspect himself. "I can hardly feel it now. Anyway, I was busy with other things."

The Zu-Zu, I warranted, and suddenly I felt very mean and rather hoped that the wound hurt quite a bit.

"Wait until the excitement wears off." Valefor had stopped smacking. "And then you'll be howling like a monkey. I remember when the Butcher Brakespeare shot Hotspur, it was the night of Pirates Parade and he—"

"Val—*shut up*. You are distracting me," I said. Pouting, he obeyed. I poured more water and dabbed at the wound, while Udo squirmed and ground his teeth. Eventually was revealed a long red furrow running the length of his bicep, skimming the top of his shoulder.

"Oh, it's nothing," Udo said, disappointed. "It's just a little scratch. The bullet must have been spent when it hit. And I never even felt it. Ain't that weird—you should know when you get shot, but I didn't even notice."

"You need to see a doctor," I said. "Maybe it's worse than it looks. It could get infected."

"No way!" Udo answered in alarm. "If I go to a doctor, they'll want to know what happened, and it'll get back to Mam and the Daddies, and then I'll be in a world of hurt for sure. It's just a scratch."

"Udo, you've been shot, for Califa's sake! You have to see a doctor. I told you that stuff with Springheel Jack wasn't a game—someone was going to get hurt."

Apparently Valefor was done with the shirt, for now he drifted down from the wardrobe. "Pah, you are an old nurse, Flora. It's nothing. Just wipe it out with some bugjuice, bind it up, and he'll be fine. But we have to do something about that drippy outlaw."

Springheel Jack! We had to get Jack out of the stables before Poppy found him. And I had forgotten I was supposed to be getting ready for the Warlord's Birthday Ball. It was almost time to leave. But how was I going to explain to Poppy that I had to take Udo to the surgeon? No lie I could possibly think of was going to be good enough to satisfy Poppy *and* keep us out of trouble. And if I missed the Ball, who knew when I would have a chance to get close to Lord Axacaya again. Blast Udo!

The Eschata has a whole section on first aid, for rangers often operate far beyond the reach of doctors, or have medical needs that they do not wish to disclose. Luckily for Udo, I'd read that section three times already and even done some practice by bandaging up Flynn. The wound didn't look that bad. It had already waited and Udo hadn't yet died. Surely it could wait longer.

But suddenly Udo was not quite so perky. He lay back on the settee, his face pale, his eyes closed, while I tore up one of my outgrown chemises. He wiggled only a little as I carefully cleaned the scratch with the bottle of apple gin I had long ago confiscated from Poppy and kept around just in case. I folded a piece of the cloth into a nice little pad, soaked it with the bugjuice, and then secured it over the wound with a goodly quantity of brown paper tape. Nini Mo advises that you can pack a wound with cobwebs, but I didn't have any, so the apple gin would have to do.

I said, "There, you are done. If your arm turns green and falls off, Udo, it won't be my fault."

"Pooh," said Udo, drowsily. "You aren't a very nice surgeon."

"You are lucky I didn't just whack your whole arm off as a precaution."

"Ha-ha," Udo said weakly, and I poked him in the chest.

"Hey. You can't pass out now, Udo. We have to figure out what to do with Springheel Jack."

"You'd better give him another jolt of that apple gin," Valefor suggested, and for once his idea was a good one.

Udo took the glass of gin. "Turn Jack in is what we are going to do," he said. His hands were now shaking so hard he could barely get the glass to his mouth. I took it from him and held it against his lips. He drank, sputtering, but I didn't take the glass away until the entire jolt was gone.

The kitty-clock on the mantel said it was five o'clock. I had to leave in forty-five minutes. The gin had turned Udo's cheeks bright red, and now his eyes looked glassy, though that might have been the shock of the gunshot catching up with him. He wasn't going to be good for anything. Once again, it was all up to me.

I said, "Look, Valefor, can you get to the stables and guard Springheel Jack? Make sure that Poppy doesn't go out there. If he looks like he's heading that direction, then come back and tell me quick and I'll try to distract him. We're going by cab, but Poppy might decide to check on the horses or something. I've got to finish getting dressed and then I'll be down to move Jack to a more secure location."

"He's going to spoil," Udo mumbled. "We gotta turn him in." He was snuggling up with the pink pig, his face buried in the pig's fat neck. The pig stared at me with beady little eyes; now his expression seemed rather amused.

I said, "We can't do anything right now, and I have an idea where to stow him. Go on, Valefor. We haven't got any time to waste. Can you get there? You should have gotten *something* out of Udo's shirt."

Valefor stuck his nose in the air. "You are bossy, Flora Segunda."

"Go!"

With a wiggle, Valefor disintegrated. Now that I had purpose, I was able to snap my busk with minimal fuss. I yanked my laces as tightly as they would go, tied them off with a bow, then slithered into the red dress. Caught my hair back with my red Sanctuary ribbon and hung my fan case on my sash. In the beauty section of *The Eschata,* Nini advises that even if you wear no other maquillage, you should always wear lip rouge. I didn't have any lip rouge, but Udo would. He was asleep, so he would hardly squawk if I borrowed it. Snatching up his jacket from where I had tossed it, I went through his pockets, finding a crushed box of Madama Twanky's Coffin Nails, a silver lighter engraved with the initials O. A., his bankbook (in which the balance clearly showed that Udo was in no danger of being broke), a lip rouge in the shade of Death in Bloom—and a package of Madama Twanky's Netherglove sheaths, size extra large.

Quivering, I dropped the coat and stared at Udo. Could he and the Zu-Zu possibly . . . ? But they had just met—just yesterday! Surely Udo wasn't that rash? How could he, with such a skanky slag?

I opened the tin and saw that the sheaths were all there. Well, why should I care if one *was* missing? If Udo wanted to fondle that stick girl, then all the more welcome he was to her. They were equal to each other in vanity and idiocy. I had bigger things to worry about than Udo's bad taste in women: the Birthday Ball, Springheel Jack, Idden. Udo's love life was low on my list. Actually, Udo's love life wasn't on my list at all. Not even at the very bottom.

"You look nice, Flora." Udo opened his eyes as I leaned over him to tuck the blanket up over his shoulders.

"Thanks."

He said, sleepily, "But you need some lip rouge; Zu says you should always have a good lip rouge."

"Huh," I answered, the little glow of his compliment now extinguished.

"Zu is a stunner, don't you think?"

"If you like them with one foot in the grave," I said sourly, but Udo didn't answer. He'd passed out.

THIRTEEN

Wheelbarrows. The Icehouse. An Ant.

I GALLOPED DOWN the Below Stairs and, at the bottom, skidded to a breathless halt, startled. A bright red stranger stood at the stove, his back to me. This stranger wore the Alacrán regimental dress uniform; his frock coat, a deep bluish crimson called sangyn, had gilt-encrusted bat sleeves, and the hem of his sangyn kilt just brushed the top of his polished black boots. His sangyn wig was in the style called the Flail, because the long braids are gathered together so they look like the lash end of a whip. His sabre sling was empty, showing he was prepared to dance, not fight. But the gun on his hip showed he was prepared to dance *and* fight.

The sangyn stranger turned around, and was, of course, Poppy.

His face was painted as white as bone, the scars on his cheeks, one slash to each side of his nose, striped with red. His lips were red, too, bright and shiny, as though touched with blood. Two lines of small sangyn marks dotted his forehead. I didn't have to count to know there were sixteen of them: the number of scalps that Poppy has taken. The Alacráns are the only regiment in the Army that takes scalps. This adds to their terrifying reputation and has earned them the nickname Skinners.

I had never seen Poppy in his Alacrán uniform before, and

the initial sight was somewhat terrifying. But looking beyond the bloody uniform, I saw that the white powder on his face smoothed the lines and made him look younger, like the Poppy I had seen at Bilskinir House, when Udo and I had accidentally gone back in Bilskinir's history. The loops of the crimson wig reminded me of the skeins of that younger Poppy's hair, which had been long and coppery rather than short and silvery. The younger Poppy had been beautiful; this Poppy would have almost been handsome if it weren't for all that bloody red.

Poppy said, "Here, let me blot your lip rouge; it's a bit too bright."

I dodged his outstretched napkin-waving arm and said, "I have to run out to the stables for a minute. I forgot to grain the horses."

"You should have remembered before you were dressed," Poppy said. "But go and hurry. The fly will be here any minute. You need a new pair of stays. You are about to explode out of the pair you are wearing."

"I know, Poppy," I said, feeling my face go hot. I grabbed my pelisse off the coatrack and threw it over my shoulders. I was suddenly regretting the low cut of my neckline. Maybe I could leave the pelisse on during the Ball. "I'll hurry."

I found Springheel Jack sitting on a hay bale, stiff as a board. Udo had been lucky the zombie powder had kept the dead outlaw going long enough to stash him in the barn, but now the powder had worn off and rigor mortis had set in. Udo had kindly wrapped a feed sack around Jack's head, but the parts of him that still showed—his neck and hands—looked waxy and livid. My arrival dispersed a merry band of buzzing flies that were hovering over him. Bonzo and Mouse hung their heads over their stall doors, complaining. For battle-hardened horses, they were certainly acting delicate.

Valefor flitted down from the shadows in the eaves. "You took forever, Flora Segunda. I thought any minute we would be discovered. The horses are unhappy. They don't like the smell."

I didn't blame them; I didn't like the smell, either—a meaty spoiled odor like the kitchen trash when no one has taken it out for a week. I held up my arm and sniffed deeply the laundry soap and bleach smells of my sleeve. To make my lie to Poppy less of a lie, I poured sweet feed into the horses' manger while I considered what to do. The horses left off their nervous complaining and started to gobble. This was actually their second ration of sweet feed today, and now they didn't care about the stinky outlaw stench.

"What are we going to do, Flora Segunda?" Valefor asked.

I looked at him hopefully. "I don't suppose you can move him, can you?"

"No. Not unless you give me some Anima, and I know, I know—I'm not asking, just saying. Udo's shirt was something, but not enough."

Having been down that road with Valefor before, I had no desire to set foot on it again. I would have to move him myself.

"Any idea how long it takes for the rigor to wear off?" I asked.

"Days, I think," Valefor answered. "I remember when Aeyptia Fyrdraaca hid in a gunpowder cask during a game of hide-and-seek. She cheated, silly duck, by using a Concealment Sigil, but her air ran out, and when we found her a week later, she was as stiff as a yaller dog's spine. We had to bury her in that barrel; she was stuck tight as a tick. See what happens to people who cheat?"

"Forget Cousin What's-her-name. Jack can't stay here until he softens up. I have to get him going somehow. Do you think more zombie powder would work even if he's already dead?"

Valefor said in alarm, "I don't want a revenant shuffling around my grounds, Flora. Once my henhouse got infested by ghouls; they ate all my chickens before I realized what was going on and put the whammy on them. That's how I lost Gallo de Cielo. Oh, he was a champion fighter—you should have seen his spur. Anyway, where would we move him where he won't keep spoiling?"

"To the Casa de Hielo. No one ever goes there, and that

should keep the flies and the smell down. Maybe by the time we come home, he'll have softened up again and Udo can get him out of here."

Valefor was, of course, outraged at my suggestion that we stow Jack in the old icehouse. He began to rave about the pristine quality of his ice, the purity of his spring water, and the absolute necessity of avoiding contamination by decaying outlaws. But he didn't offer a better idea, so I ignored him and hauled the wheelbarrow out of the hay shed.

I don't know how much Springheel Jack weighed in life, but the term *deadweight* now rang true. Even if I hadn't been hampered by yards of poofy skirt and those squeezy tight stays, I would have had a hard time levering him up off the hay bale and into the wheelbarrow. But the worst of it was that although the dead outlaw was rigid, he was also weirdly squishy. My fingers left deep indentations in his flesh. He was sloshy, too, as though his insides were turning to mush, which I suppose they were. The whole thing was horrible; my breakfast kept threatening to splash upward, but I commanded it to stay down. Rangers don't puke, at least not in the line of duty.

"Focus your Will," Valefor said encouragingly. "Heave-ho. Put your back into it."

I let off heaving and stood up, wiping sweat off my face and trying to flap the hay off my skirts. Maybe it would be better to just leave Springheel Jack until I returned from the Ball and Udo could help me. I couldn't go to the Ball looking like a soggy mess. But I couldn't risk leaving Springheel Jack in the stables. Poppy was sure to check the horses before he went to bed. And the smell was going to get worse long before it got better. What if it started to drift? What if the wind came up? What if the horses started to fuss again?

"If I was myself, I could just whisk him away, no problem," Valefor chirped.

"If wishes were fishes, then beggars would never go ride," I answered. *For every vampire*, said Nini Mo, *there is a kind of stake*. There's always a solution, you just have to think.

I thought, and then pushed the wheelbarrow as close as I could to the hay bale. Perhaps if I just gave Jack a good push, he would topple over into the barrow. I grabbed an empty feed sack so I didn't have to touch the squishy outlaw with my bare hands again, then pushed. He barely budged. Surely he couldn't weigh that much? Maybe it was the boots—I pushed again, grunting and gasping.

That wasn't going to work. I needed a rapid dose of strength and energy, and I knew of only one way to get it: a Stamina Sigil. A Stamina Sigil is rather advanced; it takes two Gramatica Words, not one—just a phrase, not an entire sentence. I'd never tried that complex a sigil. But the two Words were ones that I knew and could pronounce perfectly separately, so, surely, putting them together would be no problem. Plus, if I could fight off the Loliga's tentacle and conjure up an Ominous Apparition, I could certainly manage a little Stamina.

"I'd hurry if I were you," Valefor advised. "He's not getting any lighter and you are not getting any earlier."

I stood on one foot and laced my hands together in the Evocative Gesture. Took a deep breath and closed my eyes, envisioning the Words as little glowy glyphs inside my eyelids. The glyphs became so bright that they seemed to fill the inside of my skull with a brilliant coldfire glow.

I opened my eyes and the Words flew out of my mouth in a buzzing rush: "⧉⊹⩘ ⯬⊞⊞!"

The Words flitted around each other, twisting and turning, and came together to form one Brightly Shining Word. It darted toward me, and reflexively I reached out to snatch it from the air. For a moment the Word buzzed so strongly inside my closed hand that I almost let it go. Then suddenly the buzzing stopped. I opened my hand, and there on my palm was a black ant the size of a glory.

"Nicely done, Flora Segunda," Valefor said, peering down. "Though I'm surprised at the form it took. Were you thinking about bugs?"

"I don't know." I felt vaguely disappointed. I didn't feel

strong and energetic at all. In fact, the force of the Gramatica
had left me feeling even more weak-kneed than before.

"Well, don't waste it, anyway. Come on, chop-chop. Down
it goes."

"You want me to eat it?"

The ant waved its antennae and crawled toward my thumb.

"How else is it going to get inside you? Come on, Flora,
hurry up! Hotspur is hollering."

I'd never eaten an ant before. You can buy fried grasshop-
pers at Woodward's Gardens; they are delicious, but they are
also dead. This ant was not. But I supposed it wasn't really
alive, either; it might look like an ant but it was really a sigil.

I popped the sigil in my mouth; for a second there was the
tickly sensation of little feet scrabbling on my tongue. Before I
could gag, I bit down, and an effervescent buzz filled my mouth
and exploded in a heady rush. Suddenly I felt terrific. Sparkly
and strong. Fabulous. As though I could single-handedly per-
form deeds of great daring, with one hand tied behind my back,
and on my tiptoes.

Now Springheel Jack was as light as a waffle. I picked him
up with one hand and dropped him into the wheelbarrow, his
legs sticking up in a horribly pathetic way. I threw a drop cloth
over them. With Valefor trailing behind me, I hefted the wheelbarrow as though it were filled with air, then trundled it out of
the stables and down the overgrown path toward the icehouse.

The Casa de Hielo is built in the fanciful shape of a little
gingerbread house, complete with gaily painted stone gumdrops
on the roof, marzipan trimming, and windowpanes resembling
red and green candy. When Poppy was crazy, we had used the
icehouse by necessity; there's an icebox in the kitchen, but after
Poppy threatened the iceman with an ice pick, the company refused to deliver anymore. It had been a huge hassle hauling the
ice to the main house—who do you think had done the hauling,
and without benefit of a Stamina Sigil, too? But now that Poppy
was sane, we got ice deliveries regularly, and had abandoned the
Casa de Hielo again.

"Hotspur is really hollering now," Valefor said. "You'd better hurry faster."

I hurried faster. Inside the little building, a dashing stream bubbled up from the rock below and channeled into a deep stone trough. In the middle of the floor, a ringed hatch opened into the freezing ice cellar, dark and dank as hell's winter. Although the day outside was not particularly warm, inside the icehouse I could see my breath. I trundled the wheelbarrow into the room and let drop the handles. My palms burned, but I still felt pretty good.

"You aren't going to put him down in the ice cellar, are you?" Valefor said worriedly. "He'll spoil all my beautiful clean ice."

"It'll be cool enough in here, I warrant. We don't want him to freeze, just not stink like a dead fish."

"I thought you weren't going to do any more sigils, Flora. Not until you had more practice with Gramatica," Valefor said, watching as I finished stowing the outlaw, and then helping me to brush the straw and grass off my skirts before I rushed back toward the House.

"'Necessity is the mother of daring,' Nini Mo said."

"Huh," Valefor said, "I think you wanted to do it anyway, and just needed an excuse. I wish you wouldn't rely so much on Nini Mo, she wasn't quite—" As I reached the garden gate, Valefor disappeared in midsentence.

Poppy was standing at the top of the garden stairs, looking annoyed. "Where have you been? We are going to be late—and you have hay on your skirts."

"Mouse knocked me with his head," I lied. "I fell down. Sorry, Poppy."

"That Mouse—I hope you whacked him good. I told your mother we should get rid of him; he's a menace."

I followed Poppy to the Back Drive, where the barouche waited. Mamma never goes anywhere without outriders; Poppy and I alone didn't rate a full squad, only two privates, who were standing by their horses, smoking. Poppy handed me up into the

barouche and stuffed my skirts in after me. He climbed in and
the driver stuffed his skirts in after him. The driver slammed the
door, and then the coach rocked as he climbed up to his seat.

Off we went to the Warlord's Birthday Ball.

FOURTEEN

Saeta House. Snow. Sharks.

DURING THE RIDE TO Saeta House, Poppy peppered me with instructions, reminders, pointers, and orders. He seemed to have forgotten that I had earned an A-plus in Charm class and an A-minus in Deportment. Maybe I hadn't been out in society much, but that didn't mean that I didn't know how to act. *Manners make the ranger,* said Nini Mo.

But there was no point in protesting. Sober Poppy is not keen on contradiction, so I just nodded and mumbled *ayah* every little while. Despite myself, I felt nervous. Not for me—I knew I could behave—but for Poppy, who, despite his soberness, is still a bit of a loose cannon. He hadn't been out in public in a long time, and even then he had been supervised. Now I was supposed to be supervising him, but I couldn't watch him every minute.

You should always have a plan, said Nini Mo, *even if your plan is that you need a plan.* Well, right now that was my plan. But surely once I'd had a chance to reconnoiter, I'd come up with a better one.

The crush outside Saeta House was so great that we left the barouche and outriders a block away and legged it the rest of the way. You would think everyone in the City had been invited to the Birthday Ball. The Warlord is known for his generosity when it comes to hospitality. Every month he holds open house at Saeta House; anyone can show up, stand in line to shake the

Warlord's hand, and then go on to an all-you-can-eat-chile-con-carne buffet. For a puppet despot, he certainly worries about keeping his people happy.

"Don't let go," Poppy instructed me, holding out his hand. Though I am much too old to hold hands with my father, this seemed like a pretty wise move—if I lost Poppy in the mob, I'd never find him again. But his tight grip proved to be pointless, for we had no trouble getting through the crowd. In fact, people melted away from us as though we were emitting a noxious smell.

"It's Hotspur; keep your head down. You never know when he'll blow," I heard someone say, and then I realized the reason for our progress. People were afraid of Poppy. If he noticed this attention, he didn't show any outward sign. But he didn't let go of my hand, and his grip was crushing.

A militia guard was stationed at the bottom of marble stairs that led to Saeta's main portico. He waved us on, and upward we trudged. Poppy cannot walk very quickly on his bad leg, and so our progress was slow. I began to notice that the air was growing cooler, and my breath was like white steam. White flakes floated down, glittering in the lamplight. I held out my hand and caught a few of the flakes wisping through the white dusk: snow.

"Axacaya," Poppy gasped. He was leaning on me heavily. "He is a show-off."

"How can he make it snow?"

"There is no end to Axacaya's tricks," Poppy answered. "And he doesn't want us to forget that, either." He muttered something under his breath that, had he heard *me* muttering, would have gotten me in trouble for sure.

The receiving line was so long that it snaked out from underneath the portico, halfway down the steps. As we approached the end of the line, people began to whisper among themselves, and I knew: They were whispering about us. It's bad enough that Poppy is Poppy and has such a reputation, but why did he have to wear the bloody Alacrán uniform? He's retired on disability; there's no reason for him to kit up at all. He could have worn civilians. There were other uniforms in line, but they were all black-coats, and all officers who fight with paper, not guns. Poppy was the only Skinner present, and the only officer of the line. He stood out.

". . . killed and scalped five civilians at . . ."

". . . personally executed two deserters at Gehenna . . ."

". . . beat a horse-thief so bad he died . . ."

Poppy ignored the muttering. I tried to ignore it, too, but the words felt like hot cinders in my eyes, which were suddenly watering in a most unrangery way.

". . . Butcher Brakespeare, that bitch—"

This got Poppy's attention. His head swiveled toward the large man standing behind us, wearing a yellow-and-green checked velvet ditto suit and a purple plug hat. The man wilted under Poppy's icy green gaze and dropped out of line, in such a hurry that he slipped and slid the rest of the way down.

The whispering stopped.

As we got closer to the top of the stairs, the air grew chillier, and the steps grew slick with snow and ice. By the time we reached the portico, my leg muscles burned, and thanks to those blasted stays, I was feeling a bit faint. My hem was wet and soggy. My summer-weight pelisse wasn't doing much to keep out the cold, so I was freezing, also. If Mamma had been with us, we would have swept to the front of the line, but I didn't want to suggest we do anything that would make us stand out any more than we already were.

We finally made it through Arch of the Warlord's Glorious Conquest and into the Courtyard of the Warlord's Glorious Incarnations. Past the Warlord's Reflection Pool, now shimmering with ice, and by the enormous statues along the Courtyard's walls, each representing the Warlord at a different age. FLORIAN, YOUTHFUL AND PROUD. FLORIAN, ENSLAVED BUT UNTAMED. FLORIAN, TRIUMPHANTLY FREE. FLORIAN, THE CONQUEROR OF CALIFA. The line moved slowly enough that I had time to read all the inscriptions and study all the sculptures.

They were colossal, but not very well done. Indeed, FLORIAN, DEFENDER OF THE REPUBLIC looked like he was in urgent need of a potty. But the statues provided a good distraction from my growing nervousness.

The Receiving Hall was, blessedly, warmer. The walls, floor, and ceiling are glass, and behind them, swimming slowly and hungrily, is a *huge* great white shark—the Warlord's totem. The effect is very creepy. The shark drifts around in the gloomy water like a famished white ghost, and even though it's on the other side of a glass wall, it is close enough to make your skin crawl. I guess Saeta House's denizen, Furfur, is not going to let the glass crack and the water—and shark—pour out, but still, it's hard not to be worried. (There are stories that the Warlord feeds the shark with prisoners from the Califa City Gaol, but surely those are just stories.) The whole effect is to make you feel overawed and off balance, which is probably the idea. Anyway, because of the shark, the Receiving Hall was not icy; wiping my nose on my sleeve, I was glad of that.

First we made courtesy to Conde Rezaca, the Warlord's Chief of Staff. Poppy's bad leg and bad arm limited his courtesy to a sweeping flourish of his good arm and a sort of half bow, neither of which a proper courtesy made. The Conde Rezaca accepted Poppy's effort with a courtesy of his own, Acknowledging Heroic Style, and then slapped Poppy on the back and asked him to join the poker party he had planned for later in the evening. Poppy didn't exactly accept the invitation, but he didn't decline, either. *Sometimes,* Nini Mo said, *being politic also means being vague.*

Then on to the Infante Electo, Second Heir to the Republic. Electo's handshake was clammy, and even in the murky slithery light, his eyes had that empty look that comes from smoking too much hash. The Warlord is old, but he's still handsome in an old lion sort of way. Electo didn't look like a young lion; he looked like someone who wanted only a dark room and another reefer.

"Goddess save us from Electo," Poppy muttered to me as we

moved on. "If the Warlord's hammer should ever fall to him, it will be the end of the Republic."

And then we were at the Warlord, who didn't wait for us to come abreast of him, but rather stumped forward to meet us, smiling broadly. He was resplendent in an acrid orange kilt and an eggshell blue frock coat that opened over a weskit embroidered with gold suns. A sharkskin cape hunched over his shoulders. His one shoe had a huge diamond-studded buckle on it and a bright red heel. His purple wig was what they call a hedgehog: short and spiky. The entire outfit was a bit too colorful for my taste, but I'm sure Udo would have approved.

"Well, now, Colonel Fyrdraaca," the Warlord said heartily. "I'm right well glad to see you out and about. It has been too long."

"Your Grace is kind," said Poppy, making his fluttering, waving courtesy. "Please accept birthday greetings from the House of Fyrdraaca."

"Like a fine wine, I age well, don't you think?" The Warlord bellowed, and Poppy and I nodded our agreement. "How do you like our winter landscape? Axacaya thought it up. Bracing cold is so much more refreshing than heat. Don't you agree?"

"I do, Your Grace," Poppy said. "I have always preferred a *chilly* climate to a hot one."

"I am glad to hear it, Rev," the Warlord said approvingly, and I realized that their exchange had a double meaning. The Huitzil Empire is a desert land, hot and dry; Califa is usually cold and foggy. The Warlord was really asking if Poppy was loyal to Califa. Poppy had answered, of course, that he was. Now that I thought about it, I realized that the Birthday Ball's wintery theme was probably a dig at the Birdies.

"And little Madama Fyrdraaca." The Warlord advanced upon me, and while I tried to make the courtesy Owed to a Liege Lord, he swept me into a beery hug. "Do you prefer warm or cold?"

"Cold, of course, Your Grace," I said, sharkskin scratching my nose. "Too much sun is bad for your skin." For an old geezer with only one leg, the Warlord was awfully handsy; I squirmed but couldn't seem to escape.

"She's a chip off the ol' block, Reverdy." The Warlord grinned, then released me so suddenly I almost fell. "You should be proud."

As I staggered back to Poppy's side, I saw he had casually rested his hand on his pistol. He was smiling. A tiny shiver flitted down my spine; I knew that smile from Drunken Poppy days, when it usually heralded no good. Obviously, the Warlord knew this smile, as well, and that's why he had let me go.

"Your Grace is very kind," Poppy said.

"Well, well, we are glad you have come, both of you, and hope that you enjoy the party," the Warlord said, turning to the next person. We were dismissed.

The people in the receiving line are, of course, arranged in order of importance, and so with the Warlord, we should have been done. Poppy's grip on my arm became crushing, and when I followed his glare I saw why.

There was one person still ahead: the Ambassador from the Huitzil Empire.

FIFTEEN

Jade Masks.
An Unfriendly Face.
Cracked Ice.

THE BIRDIES LEAVE US mostly alone. The Peace Accord out-lines how we must behave, and the Infanta Sylvanna, First Heir to the Republic and Lord Axacaya's wife, lives in Ciudad Ana-huatl, the capital of the Huitzil Empire, as a hostage to the Warlord's good behavior. There's no point in causing trouble; the Huitzils would crush us like bugs the minute we got uppity. Even though the Warlord is still nominally in charge, there's no doubt that Califa is a client state.

The Ambassador from Anahuatl City is the one official Birdie in the Republic. He acts as a kind of duenna; he doesn't interfere unless there's a reason to, and of course Mamma makes sure that there is no reason. But he's there, and watchful, just in case. Normally, the Ambassador stays on the Birdie hacienda across the Bay. I had never seen him in real life.

The Ambassador was resplendent in a feathered cape, which fell from his shoulders to trail on the floor like a peacock's tail, wrapping his entire body in a sheath of glittering iridescence. Powerful Birdies always cover their faces from their inferiors, and so the Ambassador wore a jade mask carved to look like a stylized grimacing animal—a bear maybe, or perhaps a dog. The marble floor around him was dry and free of snow. But a shadow flitted behind him: the white shark, flicking back and forth slowly.

"Colonel Fyrdraaca," the Ambassador said. Behind the eye-holes of his jade mask was the vague suggestion of blue. "We have not met in many years."

"I would we did not meet now," Poppy said. He didn't make any courtesy, just glared.

"You appear much more well than our last visit, Colonel. I am glad of that." The Ambassador's voice was sibilant, like a snake's hiss. The Birdie language is naturally full of whispering sounds, and his accent echoed that. The overwhelming smell of lilies drifted from him, but underneath that eye-watering perfume was something else: the nose-wrinkling smell of decaying flesh.

"My accommodations now are more healthful." Poppy's grip was so hard that I had to clench my teeth to keep from squeaking in pain.

"I am sorry you did not care for our hospitality," the Ambassador said. "Perhaps some day you will allow us to host you again and see if we cannot do better the second time."

The hand the Ambassador held out to me was wrinkly and slack, skin spotted with black patches, nails discolored and yellow. Poppy was holding my right hand, and I was glad that he did not let go so I did not have to accept the handshake. Instead, I dipped my knees in the courtesy Respect Offered to a Foreign Dignitary.

I looked directly at the Ambassador, and the jade mask seemed to shimmer as though it were made of cloth instead of rock. Then the mask disappeared completely. His face gleamed wetly, bare white sinews and bare red muscles. His eyes floated like marbles in fleshless sockets, and his teeth grinned like yellow tombstones in his lipless mouth.

A Flayed Priest! They sacrifice their skin to the Hummingbird god, and then rely on magick to keep their flesh moist and living. My tum flipped and flopped; this was worse than Axacaya's eagle-headed guards, the Quetzals. They were monstrous, but at least they were not disgusting.

Next to me, Poppy still quivered. He and the Ambassador

stared at each other. Any minute Poppy was going to explode and attack the Ambassador and end up in gaol, and what was Mamma going to say? *Bullies,* said Nini Mo, *want to make you cry. Laugh instead, and ruin their day.*

"I hope Your Grace is enjoying the weather," I said quickly. "The cool weather is so good for the *skin*." My head felt almost light with fear, but my mouth seemed to be operating on its own and, for once, had something clever to say.

The Ambassador stared at me. The flicker was gone; now I saw only mask. His expression did not change, but Poppy's grip slackened a bit. I wanted to hold my own against that marble-eyed glare, but I could not. Feeling my face flush, I looked away.

The Ambassador said to Poppy, "Your daughter is quite the wit. What was her name? I misremember." I suspected he did not misremember at all. "Flora, isn't it? But then, wasn't the other one Flora, too? How clever of you, Reverdy. If at first you don't succeed—try again."

"Fyrdraacas never ever give up. Never ever," I said, horrified to hear the sound of my own voice.

The Ambassador looked down at me; the eyeholes of his mask were dark and shadowy. This time I refused to look away, and I pressed my lips together to keep them from trembling. The bare bloodshot orbs stared at me. How could he sleep at night, never able to close his eyes, for the lack of eyelids? Perhaps he did not sleep, ever. I imagined him staring into the Abyss with those naked eyes and could barely keep from shivering.

"Not wit, but insolence," the Ambassador said. "We know how to deal with insolent women in Anahuatl City, don't we, Reverdy?" I guessed he was referring to the Butcher Brakespeare's execution.

Two red spots burned through Poppy's white-face pancake and his eyes had gone a tornado black. He tried to drop my hand, but fearful of what he would do once his gun hand was free, I refused to let go, squeezing my grip with all my strength. The Ambassador's jade lips grinned at us.

The Warlord's totem saved us from what would surely have made the front page of all the news rags. The glass behind the Ambassador thudded, and we all jumped. The shark hammered its nose against the barrier again, jagged teeth snapping. The Ambassador jerked away, and then, before the shark could hit the wall again, the Warlord himself pushed his way through the pile behind us and dropped an enormous arm over Poppy's shoulders.

"Stop that hammering!" the Warlord ordered the shark. "You'll have your dinner soon enough." The shark flicked its tail and withdrew into the darkness.

"Well, well." The Warlord leaned so that Poppy almost buckled under his weight but was effectively now under his control. "I am well done with Receiving and need to wet the old whistle. Come now, Rev, let's see if we can scare up a dram or two. You will excuse us, Sieur Xholto, eh?"

"Of course," the Ambassador said. He bowed his head, his topknot (a wig of someone else's hair) bobbing. "I look to see you again, Colonel Fyrdraaca."

"In court—" Poppy began, but the Warlord interrupted. "Come, come. We are holding up the line, and my thirst don't quench itself, you know. By your leave, Your Holiness." The Warlord hauled us away; for an old one-legged geezer his grip was pretty strong.

"Pigface on a Pogostick, Reverdy. Why the hell did you come?" the Warlord said, as soon as we were away.

"He wasn't on the list," Poppy protested. "I didn't know he'd be here."

"Ayah so, he decided to come at the last minute," the Warlord said dolefully. "I think we're going to have a chat later about that blasted riot. I wish Buck hadn't left. He gives me the creepies."

"He doesn't frighten me."

"You are the only man in Califa not afraid of him, then. Come on, let's get you a drink. I'm parched myself; you've no idea what thirsty work it is, being nice to people you'd rather pop. There's a poker game setting up; you've always been a real razor with the cards, come on and play . . ."

The Warlord steered Poppy onward. I followed, forgotten, through a long passageway painted with scenes of the Warlord's escape from the Virreina of Huitzil's slave pens, into the Rotunda.

The last time I had been in Saeta House's Rotunda was a year ago, when I had accompanied Mamma to the swearing-in ceremony of Benica Barracks's graduating class of officers. Then, the Rotunda had been all marble and gilt, bathed in sunlight streaming from the oculus set high in the lofty dome. The marble stairs leading to the upper balcony had been covered with plush red carpet. The cadets stood in orderly rows upon the red swirled marble floor as they had waited to climb those stairs, kneel at the Warlord's feet, and swear him loyalty, before receiving their insignia and commissions from Mamma.

Now the Rotunda had been transformed into a wintry glade. Trees sprang from the Rotunda floor, their boughs heavy with snow, and every surface was rounded in blanketing whiteness. Luminescent icicles dangled from the dome, casting a pearly blue glow over the assembled throng. White flakes drifted down, glistening and glittering in the dim light. Directly under the now icy oculus, the marble had frozen over to form a skating pond, and upon this glossy surface, people twirled and glided, some more skillfully than others. Was this winter scene real or an illusion? I could not tell, but either way it was a testament to Lord Axacaya's power. I was impressed.

I craned my neck, trying to spot Lord Axacaya in the crowd, but I did not see him. As soon as I could decently duck away from the Warlord and Poppy, I would go in search. In the meantime, I followed them through the crowd, which fell back to let them pass, murmuring birthday greetings to the Warlord, who acknowledged each compliment with a wave.

At the edge of the icy pond, the Warlord halted. "Now, Hotspur, you and I shall go and play poker, and Madama Flora here— Hi, hi, my darling!" In response to his waves, a figure twirled away from the other skaters, coming to an ice-crunching stop at the edge of the pond.

The last person in Califa that I wanted to see: the Zu-Zu. She gave me a slightly sour look and then turned a brilliant sugar-sweet smile upon the Warlord.

"Ave, Papi!"

"Here, now, my darling Odelie shall take charge of young Flora here. They shall have more fun together than hanging with the oldsters, don't you think, Hotspur? Odelie, I present to you Flora Fyrdraaca. Flora, my granddaughter, Odelie Abenfarax ov Kanaketa. She's been away at school, my darling, and just now come home. I hope you shall make her welcome, Flora."

The Warlord's granddaughter! I had read in the society column of the *Califa Police Gazette* that Odelie Abenfarax had recently returned from school in Anahuatl City, but I hadn't connected the Zu-Zu with that girl. That explained her stuck-up attitude and the reverence everyone showed her. The Warlord's granddaughter, indeed.

"We've met, Papi," said the Zu-Zu, now turning that poison-sugar smile upon me. "Good evening, Flora."

"Good evening, Your Grace," I answered back, equally as poison sweet. "It is delightful to see you again."

The Warlord looked pleased. "Well, then, you are friends already. Come, Reverdy, I'm dying for that drink."

Poppy looked anguished at the thought of leaving me, but the Warlord ignored the look and, with one last wave, marched him off. That left me standing there with the Zu-Zu, wishing I was at the bottom of the Bay of Califa. Actually—wishing *she* was at the bottom of the Bay of Califa.

"Where's darling Udo?" the Zu-Zu asked. She was still dressed completely in black; her coat was of black astrakhan, and a black fur puffball perched upon her black lacquered head. In deference, I suppose, to the festive occasion, her lip rouge was red, not black, but that was the only touch of color. She looked elegant and adult, and extremely superior—the skant.

"He's at home," I answered. Her stays fit just fine; her waist looked to be about twelve inches around. But her face was flat, catlike, and her cheekbones too sharp. She wasn't that pretty, really—just extremely well dressed.

"Pity. He's so sweet. Will you skate?"

I hadn't been on ice skates since I was five. I would clomp about and the Zu-Zu would swoop by me and make me look like a fool. And anyway, I was not going to waste my time skating. I needed to ditch the Zu-Zu and find Lord Axacaya.

"I find skating to be a tremendous bore," I answered. "I shall be happy to leave you to it, madama."

The Zu-Zu smiled at me graciously. "Oh no. Papi said we should have fun. Let us find some refreshments. I can tell just by looking at you that you enjoy eating." I felt my face flush. Skanky bint!

The Zu-Zu stepped off the ice and a servant knelt to unbuckle her skates. She fluffed out her skirts, which were knee-length and very puffy. Behind her the phalanx of Boy Toys formed up: all as black-and-white as she, equally glamorous. All dark, brooding, and mysterious, just the kind of boy I can't stand, and exactly the opposite of Udo. Perhaps that's what she liked about him: the novelty. The Boy Toys abandoned their skates higgledy-piggledy, apparently not worried that someone might trip over the discarded blades and cut their throat. Too bad that someone wasn't the Zu-Zu.

"Are you at Sanctuary School?" the Zu-Zu asked as the servant tied her shoe ribbon. She kicked at him. "Not so floppy, dolt."

"Ayah. I have that honor."

"I would have been, but Papi said I should go to school in Anahuatl City. He is concerned for my safety. I am the only grandchild, you know."

I felt sorry for the Warlord if this was the best he could do as far as grandchildren went. The Zu-Zu's grandmother was the famous actress Odelie Crabtree, who had been the Warlord's favorite leman until the Warlady had her poisoned. Her mother was the Infanta Ondina, a useless flibbertigibbet, whose only contribution to Califa was helping to keep the economy going with enormous shopping sprees. Once the Senate had to have a special session to vote for extra funds to pay her shoe bill. Obviously, the Zu-Zu hadn't fallen too far from her mamma's shoe tree.

As we left the pond, the Boy Toys fell in behind us, blocking my hope of backing out into a quick exit. The Zu-Zu announced, "I shall be Warlady someday."

And presumptuous, too! There were four people between the Zu-Zu and the Warlord's ceremonial hammer. One of Nini Mo's sayings popped into mind, and I said, "'Bacon shrinks when it cooks,' Nini Mo said. 'There's never as much as you hope.'"

"Well, I don't know what that means, exactly, Flora, but I can see that you know quite a bit about bacon, so I will take your word for it." The Zu-Zu smiled and flipped open her fan, which was, of course, made of white ivory and stretched with black silk.

Now, there I could easily best her. I unsheathed my own fan deliberately, so that she could clearly see the chased silver splendor of the fan case, and then snapped the fan open. In the dim wintery light, the blue silk shimmered like bright sunlit water. My fan was twice as long as the Zu-Zu's and yards more magnificent.

The Zu-Zu frowned. "I do like your dress, Flora. It's so youthful and girlish. It reminds me of a dress I had when I was just a tot—wherever did you get it?"

"My dressmaker. He is a wonder, but he's very select and private."

"I don't wonder," the Zu-Zu answered. "I would wish to remain anonymous, as well, if such were my handiwork."

"Silent and secret," I said sweetly, inclining my head in the courtesy Responding to Rudeness with Grace. Before the Zu-Zu or the Boy Toys could react to my insolence, I turned my back on the Zu-Zu (a terrible insult to her rank) and sailed away.

Reconnoiter before you plan, said Nini Mo, and while I had been enduring the Zu-Zu's insults, I had also been looking around. No sign of Lord Axacaya in the splendidly dressed throngs, and Poppy and the Warlord had disappeared completely.

Beyond the ice pond was a gleaming wooden dance floor. The Califa National Band, a mixture of acoustic servitors and human musicians, was assembled on the balcony high above. On the other side of the Rotunda, the Warlord was stumping down the Grand Staircase, the wispy Infante Electo trailing behind him. Behind him came a knot of equerries—and behind *them* Lord Axacaya. Among the elaborate hairstyles and poofy hats, his plain silver-streaked head stood out.

The Califa National Band struck up a fanfare. The Warlord waved and the guests began to clap and cheer. The dancing was about to begin.

Suddenly I knew exactly what to do.

SIXTEEN

The Califa Reel. Clumsy Partners. Lord Axacaya.

TRADITIONALLY, every grand ball opens with the Califa Reel. The Califa Reel is verso-baile, which is to say that instead of pairing off with one partner, the dancers form two lines across from each other. The first set is danced with the person opposite, and before each subsequent set, the dancers change partners by moving one position to the left. The Reel is a hideously complicated dance, with lots of of bouncing, leaping, turns, and bows, but at Sanctuary we spent an entire term in Dance class learning nothing else, and so now I can dance it in my sleep.

There are five partner changes in the Califa Reel. If I got in the line opposite Lord Axacaya, within five people of him or less, then I should be sure to dance one set with him. And while we were dancing, I could tell him about the Loliga. Surely he must know about the Loliga already—but if he didn't, I'd gain points for telling him. And if he did, I hoped I'd gain points for initiative. Either way, I'd win.

The fanfare died away and the Warlord's booming voice called for everyone to form up for the Reel. I started pushing. Everyone else was pushing, too, trying to make sure they got good positions—the closer to the Warlord the better—but my need was greater than mere status and so I pushed the hardest. By the time the band struck up the opening bars, I was wedged between a skeletal man in a purple-and-yellow-striped lounge suit and a round woman wearing what appeared to be a chicken on her head. I glanced down the line: I was properly opposite Lord Axacaya, who had taken his place immediately to the left of the Warlord, but I had miscounted. I was six positions away from him.

As the dancers began to make their courtesies, I backed out of my place, ducked behind the Chicken Hat Lady, and squeezed between her and the man next to her. The Chicken Hat Lady protested, but I pretended not to see her, made a hasty courtesy to the dancer opposite, and grabbed his outstretched hands.

To the jovial rhythms of the music, my partner—a woman with sweaty hands, who was going to leave marks on my silk dress, darn her—and I bobbed and weaved, twirled and jumped, curtsied and kicked. The Califa Reel is a strenuous dance; I was already breathing heavily, and of course my tight stays didn't help, either. I sucked in as best I could and, as I twirled my partner, looked down the bouncing line and saw that the Warlord was gone. I guess the Califa Reel is pretty hard to dance with one leg, and he had done part of the first set for politeness's sake before retreating. He had been replaced by someone overshadowed by a large green hat.

Glad I was that Archangel Bob had drilled us so hard in the Califa Reel—I didn't have to think about the steps at all. I just let my feet follow the music and concentrated on not breathing like a steam engine. The set finished and I switched the sweaty woman for a shrimpy kid, now one partner closer to Lord Axacaya.

"Your face is as red as a cranberry," the ankle biter remarked, as I swung him up into a little hop.

"Aren't you up past your bedtime, little mister?" I asked him. In response, he stuck out a purple-streaked tongue. He was too small to swing me up, so I had to hop on my own while he pawed my waist with grubby hands. I ignored him for the rest of the set and then switched him for a heavy man with puggy eyes, who kept trying to peer down my neckline. Let him

look; the next switch would put me square in front of Lord Axacaya, who was already whirling and twirling next to me, close
enough that I could smell the deliciously dark woodsy scent of
Birdie ceremonial incense.

As I danced, I snuck glances at Lord Axacaya. Pigface, he
was beautiful, even more than I had remembered: the long
spiraling silver-blond hair, the perfectly shaped lips accented
by the jade butterfly lip-plug. The muscular chest covered in
intricate tattoos; the equally muscular arms, also inked. Despite the chill, he wore only a knee-length feathered kilt, iridescently blue and green, which swung low around his hips; a
jaguar skin hung over his shoulders, capelike, so that the poor
cat's head dangled against his broad chest. And his intense
eyes, completely black, iris and sclera both, a deep shiny blackness that made him seem inhuman and remote. And yet gorgeously glamorous.

My tummy fluttered in a very spoony way and I quelled it. I
needed to stay focused and calm.

The Pug-Eyed Man swung me one last time. I floated outward on a groove of music, hands outstretched, and Lord Axacaya caught my grip and pulled me into his arms. He radiated
heat like the summer sun, but the sudden flush I felt was due to
more than just that or the exertion of the dance.

Lord Axacaya gazed down at me, distantly, with no recognition in those voidlike eyes, and my stomach flipped—had he
forgotten? But as I made my courtesy and he bowed his own
head, he smiled.

"Madama Flora! What a pleasant surprise!" he said. "I had
not expected to see you here."

"Ave, Your Grace," I said. We twirled and then matched our
steps together. My eyes were about level with the burnished
bronze of his chest, and the sorry eyes of the jaguar head. I
looked down toward my feet; Lord Axacaya's feathery kilt
drooped alarmingly around his hips, below the taunt line of his
belly. I hastily went back to looking at the jaguar head. Now,

this close, his delicious smell was almost overwhelming, and my head felt as light and airy as a balloon.

"My condolences on your family loss," he said, and for a moment I was confused, then realized he was talking about Idden. Something about the way he said loss made it sound quite permanent. "I am sorry that General Fyrdraaca is not here tonight, but I must say that if your presence is due to her absence, then perhaps I am not so sorry after all."

"Thank you, Your Grace." Why did my voice sound so squeaky? And I couldn't think of an equally charming response. Archangel Bob says that when you are at a loss for words, you should compliment. "I like your winter."

We hopped and Lord Axacaya said, "Thank you. I thought it would be an entertaining novelty. I am so rarely cold that I enjoy the sensation when I can get it. Not everyone likes the chill, though. Do you prefer warm weather?"

"No, Your Grace. The snow is beautiful." My response might not be charming but at least it made it clear where my allegiances lay.

"I'm glad to hear it," he said, and the little butterfly lip-plug twinkled as he smiled.

The fatigue of the dance fell from me; I felt as floaty as air, weightless and feathery, elated and happy, caught up in our perfect synchronization. As he twirled me again, his hand on my lower back was firm and pressing; I couldn't put a step wrong, his pressure completed me, as natural as breathing. A wispy strand of his hair blew across my face, and I shivered at its tingly touch. I wondered how I had ever been afraid of him, and this absence of fear made me bold. The set would be over soon and I would lose my chance.

"Your Grace, I must speak with you. It's about the earthquakes . . ."

"Ayah, so?" he murmured encouragingly.

"I think I have discovered their source."

"Ayah, so?" His tone didn't change but his gaze sharpened.

"Can I speak with you more privately later?"

Now he was leaning down, so I could whisper and he could still hear me. A lock of his hair brushed my cheek, feeling like coiled silk.

"The Loliga," I whispered.

I heard the sharp intake of his breath. "What do you know of the Loliga?"

"A tentacle came out of the potty at—" I realized perhaps I shouldn't admit *where* the tentacle had attacked me, and hastily adjusted my words. "A tentacle attacked me. I think it belonged to the Loliga—it's still under the City—at Bilskinir Baths."

The other dancers had changed partners, but Lord Axacaya still held my hands. We were holding up the dance and people on either side of us were muttering.

"I will find you later," he whispered, and then swung me free. I floated away and turned my head to follow him. Lord Axacaya was apologizing to his new partner. A hard grip fastened on my hands and then jerked me around, almost wrenching my arms out of their sockets.

The protest that had sprung to my lips stuck there when I turned to face my new partner.

Udo.

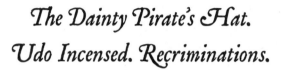

SEVENTEEN

The Dainty Pirate's Hat.
Udo Incensed. Recriminations.

I SHOULD HAVE recognized the hat; it was the monstrous green bicorn that the Dainty Pirate had sent Udo as a thank you gift when we'd tried to save his life. The Dainty Pirate shared Udo's over-the-top style sense, and the hat really was too much. Everyone was staring at him.

"You almost broke my arm!"

"You were holding the dance up," he said. "You and the Warlord's honey-boy."

"What does that mean?" I glared at him.

Udo shrugged and twirled, his skirts twisting like a whirlpool about his knees. He seemed to have recovered completely from his wound. In fact, he looked so great that I couldn't help but feel a pang. Clearly he had not suffered over his wardrobe as I had. His emerald-green frock coat had yards of gold lace swirled on his dishtowel-sized cuffs and his wide lapels. Diamonds twinkled in the buttons of his black silk weskit, and his kilts were long and flowing. He'd gone easy on the maquillage, and this made him look much more mature than usual.

"What are you doing here?" I demanded. "How did you get in?"

He looked down at me scornfully. "What? Only *Fyrdraacas* are good enough to attend the Warlord's Birthday Ball?"

"That's not what I meant. You have to be on the guest list and I know you weren't on the guest list."

"I guess I can get into the Warlord's Birthday Ball if I want to. I don't have to cadge an invite like *some* people. You aren't the only one with resources, Flora." He jerked me again as we twirled, and I realized he was angry. Not just angry—furious.

"What is wrong with you, Udo?"

"Ha! I wondered why you were in such a hurry, Flora! You just wanted to dump me and get to the party!"

"Udo!" What *was* his problem? I had never seen him this angry before, and he was completely misrepresenting everything.

"How could you let him do it?" Udo demanded.

"Who do what?"

"Valefor!" Udo hissed. "Your stupid snapperhead servitor. You knew this meant a lot to me, Flora, but you didn't care, did you? If it's not Flora's idea, then Flora doesn't care."

"What are you talking about?"

"Springheel Jack!" Udo shouted. Fortunately, the music was loud and so I'm pretty sure no one heard him.

"Shush—keep your voice down. What about Springheel Jack? I put him on ice in the Casa de Hielo. What else could I do with him? He was starting to smell."

Udo swung me and didn't let go. I flew in an arc, my feet scrabbling on the snowy floor. Then he yanked me hard, completely out of the line, even though the set wasn't quite finished. I tried to squirm out of his grip, but he is taller and stronger and wouldn't let go.

"What the hell is wrong with you, Udo? Let go of me!" I whacked at him with my free hand, but onward he pulled. Now people were staring at both of us. It seemed better to go with him than to make a scene, so I quit fighting. But as soon as we were alone, Udo was going to get it.

We rushed through people watching the Reel, past the Grand Staircase, and into the long gallery behind. Tall wooden doors, each topped with a glassy-green transom, punctuated the marble walls. Tea-leaf patterns of snow swirled and blew along the marble floors. The gallery was dim, and each alcove we rushed by contained a spoony couple. The last alcove was empty. Udo dragged me inside. I hit him hard with my fan and he let me go.

"You are acting like someone in a cheap melodrama, Udo Landaðon!"

"Oh, ayah?" he asked. "Do you think so?"

"Yes, I do. What is up with you? Why are you so worked up about your precious outlaw? I saved him for you, didn't I? Put him on ice until you could—"

"Valefor!" Udo shouted. There was a harsh tone to his voice I'd never heard before. "I went to the icehouse and Jack was gone! Your stupid snapperheaded servitor ate him! Ate him!"

"Ate him? How could Valefor eat him?"

"How should I know? Cut him up into tiny pieces? Chewed on his bones? All I know is that Valefor ate him and he is gone! What am I going to do about my bounty now, Flora? After all the trouble I went to to get that outlaw, now—nothing! You Fyrdraacas don't care about anyone but yourselves!"

I flared up. "Now, hold on a minute, Sieur Landaðon. I didn't have a thing to do with Valefor eating any stupid outlaw, so you can't blame me for that! And if you want to talk about stupidity, then how about zombifying an outlaw and then getting into a gun battle on a public horsecar—"

Udo interrupted with something very mean, and I responded with something equally mean, which made Udo say even meaner things. I answered with meaner things of my own. Every tiny slight hurt and annoyance of our entire lives came pouring out.

"—it took me three weeks to wash the green ink out of my hair—"

"—ate all the roses off my birthday cake—"

"—so I got a double F-minus in Composing—"

"—feed my pet turtle and it died—"

"—bossing me around like you are the Goddess Califa and I'm just your Boy Toy—"

"—and you left me standing there *alone* to go off with that skanky stick-insect girl!"

"—bossy, obnoxious, egotistical, bratty—"

"—annoying, whiny, vain—"

Udo stared at me. I stared back. My lip was quivering, and I hoped he realized it was from anger, not sorrow. The feather on his hat was quivering, probably for the same reason.

"Fine!" Udo said, finally. There was something extremely final about that *fine*.

"Fine!" I answered.

"I guess you don't need me, then."

"No, I guess I don't. Have a nice time with your scrawny little prune-faced girl."

"I will, madama. And you can enjoy your horrible family, and your drunken father, and your mealymouthed sister—"

WHACK!

My brain had sent a secret signal to my hand, which had raised itself and smacked Udo right across his rouged cheek. Udo's jaw was pretty hard—my palm stung. Even in the dim light, the red mark of my blow stood out on his white skin like a burn.

Now Udo's lips were also trembling. Without another word, he snapped around and rushed away, his rapid stride making his long skirts swirl. I caught a brief glimpse of sparkly red footwear, and then—adios, Udo.

I was no longer cold; instead, I felt as though I had a fever. I walked over to the bubbler, but the stream trickling from the dolphin-shaped spout was frozen. The water in the bubbler bowl was a thick rime of silvery blue ice, flat as a mirror. The cold drifting up from the ice felt good on my flushed face. Something wet and hot dripped down my chin and onto the ice. I wiped at my eyes with my glove, not caring if I smeared my eyeliner.

Udo. Oh, Udo.

A light flickered beneath the ice, and I thought I saw movement, a flash of luminescence deep down. Which was impossible, of course, as the bubbler was only about a foot deep. But it had a drain, didn't it? I peered under the bubbler bowl and saw a pipe not much bigger around than my arm disappearing into the wall. The ice flared pink and red, and I stepped away from it. Surely no tentacle could smash its way through solid ice? Could it? Or through a narrow drain? I wasn't going to stick around to see. I'd had enough histrionics for one night.

As the ice began to crack, I fled down the hallway. In the Grand Rotunda the music had stopped. The hushed crowd seemed to be focusing on the dance floor, and as I skirted the edge of the throng, I heard the shouting of a familiar voice. I pushed my way through the audience and discovered Poppy hollering at Lord Axacaya. His accusations were pretty loud, though not entirely coherent. Some bossy boiler had told Poppy about my dance with Lord Axacaya and now he was showering Lord Axacaya with dire threats. Only the restraining arms of the Warlord's bodyguards were keeping Poppy from carrying out some of those threats right then and there. Thankfully, a guard had snagged Poppy's gun out of his holster, and his war injuries made him easy to hold back.

While Poppy raved, Lord Axacaya glared at him through slitted eyes but made no response. Then the Warlord arrived, and Poppy, trying to flail his way out of the guards' grasp, almost popped him. I tried to fade back into the crowd, but Poppy saw me and somehow managed to throw off the guards and nab me. The Warlord was shouting, Poppy was shouting, the guards were shouting, I was shouting, and then a loud, sharp noise drowned us all out. My ears rang, and the frosty air was suddenly filled with the acrid smell of black powder.

"What the hell was that?" Florian bellowed.

"Someone just tried to shoot the Ambassador," Lord Axacaya said calmly.

EIGHTEEN

Poppy Rants. Locked. A Parrot.

WELL, THAT WAS IT for the Warlord's Birthday Ball. After the first few minutes of general panic, the Warlord's guards moved in and closed off all the exits to Saeta House, so as to make sure that the assassin (who I really, really hoped wasn't Idden) couldn't escape. The midnight supper (and the seating chart Mamma had slaved over) was scrapped. The Warlord told Poppy to go the hell home and stay there until he could behave, so we were allowed to leave through one of Saeta's back entrances. Poppy didn't seem at all concerned about the assassination attempt; he was fully fixated on my behavior with Lord Axacaya, and he ranted and raved about that all the way home.

My protest that I was an adult and therefore could dance with whomever I pleased was not well received. Neither was my claim that the partnership had been by chance and that I could hardly have refused in front of everyone to dance with Lord Axacaya and that Poppy was overreacting. Then I said nothing else, for fear of what else I might say—or do. I had had enough fighting for one night. I only wanted to get home, to the quiet of my room, to lie down upon my bed and die.

Once back at Crackpot, Poppy's ranting continued up the garden path and into the kitchen. The dogs, cowed by the tone of his voice, whisked away into the darkness as soon as the kitchen door was opened, those traitors.

"You still are under this roof, madama, and thus owe allegiance to this family, and Axacaya is no friend of ours. I will not have you consorting with him—in *any way*, do you understand?" Poppy said meaningfully. "It is a disgrace to this family."

A disgrace?! How could dancing with Lord Axacaya be disgraceful, after all that Poppy had put us through? Was *I* a convicted war criminal? Had *I* lost the First Flora? Was *I* a drunk and a lout? Did *I* just get the Fyrdraaca family's dirty laundry on the front page of the *Califa Police Gazette*? Well, the assassination attempt on the Huitzil Ambassador would probably be on page one, but surely we'd make page two.

If I stayed put one more minute I was going to explode. I would fall to Poppy's level, screaming and shouting, and I would be damned to the Abyss if I would fall that low. So I flung past him and tore upstairs. Poppy tried to follow but his lameness slowed him down, and I was safely in my room with the door locked by the time he got there.

"Open up, Flora!" Poppy yelled, pounding.

I sat down on my settee and folded my arms. Valefor, hovering over the wardrobe, looked petrified.

"I demand that you open the door!" Poppy roared.

"I demand that you drop dead," I whispered. "I demand that you go to *hell*!"

"Well then, madama, if you wish to stay in your room, you may stay in your room." Poppy said through the door. "You may stay until your mother returns from Fort Jones, and then we shall have a family discussion."

I continued to sit. My jaw was clenched so tightly that it ached as though someone had punched me. After a while I got up and tried to open the door. It was locked. I jiggled the handle and then pounded, but the door did not open and Poppy did not answer.

"What is wrong with him? What did you do?" Valefor asked.

"He saw me dancing with Lord Axacaya," I said. Pacing back and forth helped cool some of my agitation. So did throwing my shoes, which hit the wall with satisfying thumps. Valefor flitted back to the top of the wardrobe, out of the way. I kicked at my Catorcena trunk and got a spark of pain for my trouble, but that pain felt good—it only made me madder. I ripped the red poofy dress off and wadded it on the floor and then tore off the horrible stays. My ribs still hurt from the tentacle squeezing of the night before. I pressed my hand to the pain as I paced and was glad of how its throb fed my anger.

"Did you waste all your time dancing, or did you talk to him, too? I hope you got things settled," Valefor said. "I can't take another trembler. My roof is *creaking*."

I collapsed onto the settee in a miserable heap. We are all cursed, we Fyrdraacas. No matter what we do, we cannot escape it. We will never be free of anger—of fear—of despair.

"What did Lord Axacaya say when you told him about the Loliga?" Valefor persisted. He crawled down from the wardrobe and poked at me. For the first time since I had rushed into the room, I really looked at him, and I did not like what I saw.

Valefor was no longer a thin and wispy news-rag boy. No, indeed. It might be too much to say that he sparkled, but it wouldn't have been too far off to say that he twinkled. His white hair had darkened to deep damson plum, and his eyes were faceted amethyst jewels. When I poked him back, my finger hit solid flesh. Clearly, eating Springheel Jack had done Valefor a world of good.

"I saw Udo at the Ball, too, Valefor," I said, and poked him hard again. He grunted and jerked out of my reach. "And he was pretty wroth."

Valefor sniffed. "I don't see why. I was hungry and I couldn't let him stink up the icehouse, could I? There were beginning to be worms, Flora Segunda! Anyway, I did you all a favor!"

Well, I had to agree with him there. I wasn't too sorry that the decomposing outlaw was gone. Udo was mad, but at least I didn't have to move the body again. One less problem that I had to deal with. Tonight I really needed one less problem; I was at my utter limit of problems.

"I don't think Udo thinks you did him a favor, Valefor. Now he won't be able to get his bounty."

"Huh. I only ate the fleshy bits of Springheel Jack—they were no good to Udo, anyway, all stinky and rotting. I left him what really counts. Much less messy this way! He was a bit stringy, though, Jack. I used the last of the floss; you'll have to get more. I left the boots, didn't I?"

Now I realized that the sparkly red flash under Udo's hem had been Springheel Jack's sparkly red boots. Somehow this was not a cheerful realization. Springheel Jack probably didn't have very good hygiene. I hoped Udo had put on heavy socks.

"The boots are not going to get him the bounty."

"Of course they will," Valefor answered. "Those boots are famous. They are the source of Jack's power—no one else has boots like that but Springheel Jack, and he swore they would never come off his feet whilst he was alive. So if they are off his feet, then, he must be dead, no? Remember the case of Nobby Nack, the Gentleman Masher? The militia accepted as proof of his death—"

"That was a body part. Not a fashion accessory. An important body part. One you can't live without."

"There's plenty of precedent, Flora Segunda. Why, in *Marly Mack vs. the Republic of Califa,* the Chief Justice ruled that . . ."

I closed my eyes. Valefor's voice receded to a drone. My anger had burned out and now I felt exhausted and sick at heart. How could Udo say such mean things? We'd been best friends forever, and we'd had fights before but nothing like this. Never the kind of fight where you might never make up again. Never anything so final. Never anything that made me feel so sick inside.

And how could Poppy be so unfair? His good behavior was all a lie. He was like a bowl of rice pudding that had sat out too long. The cinnamon on top smells divine, but underneath the custard has curdled. Poppy would never really change.

And the Loliga. I had failed there, too. If it turned out that the earthquakes were being caused by the Loliga and she did turn the City into rubble, it would be all my fault.

I had gone to the Ball with such high hopes, and now I felt crushed and forlorn. The Fyrdraaca family was an endless pit. I would never get ahead and I would never escape. All my plans and all my hopes would forever come to naught. I rolled over and put my face to the settee, to drown Valefor out, and felt something soft against my cheek. The plushy pig. Now it looked sympathetic. I hugged it tightly to my chest and closed my eyes again. Drifted off into misery, hating Udo, hating Valefor, hating Springheel Jack, hating Poppy, and most of all hating myself.

A tap on the window and Valefor's sudden silence jolted me out of my daze. I sat up, still clutching the pig. Valefor flipped open the casement window. A blue-and-green parrot perched on the windowsill.

"Go away, bird," he said, making a shooing motion. "We don't want any."

The parrot fluttered up, then over Valefor's head and landed on the back of the settee, where it regarded me with bright beady blue eyes. Small green parrots live in the trees outside Saeta House. They are not native to Califa; long ago they escaped from a cage somewhere and then bred in the wild. But this parrot was as large as a housecat, and handsome, too, with blue-yellow feathers and a beautiful rounded coral beak.

"Don't you dare poo in my house, bird," Valefor said, "or I shall be having parrot pie for supper."

The parrot ignored him and extended a pink foot toward me. A small silver cylinder hung from its knobby ankle. I've seen messenger pigeons before, and for a while the Enthusiastics (Mamma's old regiment) had a messenger eagle named Old Reg, but a messenger parrot was a new one on me. Inside the cylinder was a rolled-up piece of paper.

"Who's it from?" Curious Val tried to grab, but I whisked the paper out of reach.

"Axacaya! Axacaya!" the parrot croaked.

A spark of excitement sizzled through me. At first glance, the paper appeared to be blank. But before I could take it over to the lantern to see if heat would reveal words, glittery pink coldfire letters began to scroll across the paper. The message was short and to the point:

Please meet me at the Potato Patch
at two o'clock tonight.
Wear your bathing costume.

I had just enough time to read the message twice before the coldfire letters began to run together, expanding outward. I dropped it as the page began to burn; with a sugar-scented puff it was gone, leaving not even ash behind.

"Parlor trick," Valefor said with a sniff. "I would have written it on the wall in letters of fire ten feet tall. That's the way to send a message. Not with a fat bird."

The parrot fluttered its wings impatiently, squawking, "Answer?"

"Tell him I'll be there."

"Ayah so, ayah so." The parrot launched back into the air. It circled once around Valefor, who shrieked and batted at it, and then zipped away through the open window.

Lord Axacaya did not hold Poppy's outburst against me, and he still took me seriously. Suddenly I felt a whole lot more cheerful.

"You can't go meeting Lord Axacaya in the middle of the night," Valefor protested. "It's scandalous. And besides, you are confined."

"'There's no prison that can hold me, not even death,'" I answered, getting up. "Didn't Nini Mo say that?"

Val sniffed. "Ayah, but she meant the Ultimate Ranger Dare—to escape death. Not escape being locked in. You aren't being menaced by ice hamsters, Flora Segunda—"

"Ice weasels; not ice hamsters." *Nini Mo vs. the Ice Weasels: the*

Ultimate Ranger Dare is the hardest of all the Nini Mo yellowbacks to find, and the most famous, of course. In it, Nini Mo drowns herself in an icy river to escape the clutches of the Ice Weasel gang and then, before she can cross the Abyss into true death, is brought back to life by Boy Hansgen. I've never managed to actually find a copy of the yellowback, but the event is recounted in her autobiography, *High Jinks in Low Places*, which I've read four times.

"Whatever—I don't care about Nini Mo—she was killed in a duel and no one has seen her since, so I guess that puts a lie to her trashy stories. I only care about you, Flora Segunda—and my House! What does Axacaya want? Oh, Flora, you should be careful. I don't trust him. He's never been a friend to our family. What if Hotspur finds out you are gone?"

It was almost midnight now. I had some time, but I'd be damned if I would spend it locked in my room like a recalcitrant bride in a sentimental novel. "I don't care if Poppy finds out I am gone. Let him think I am gone for good. Let him consider how it feels to lose *two* Floras."

I have a bathing dress, though I hadn't had occasion to wear it since last summer. When I dug it out of the bottom of my wardrobe, I discovered it was a bit moth-eaten and, when I huffed and puffed my way into it, was a wee bit small. Maybe more than a wee bit. The skirt barely came down to the middle of my thighs. The jersey across the chest was mighty strained. The wool smelled musty.

"You look like a sausage in a woolen casing," Valefor said. "Don't you wish now you'd laid off all those pancakes?"

"It's nothing to do with pancakes," I said. "I'm just growing, finally."

"Ayah, out instead of up."

"Shut up. I'd rather be round than look like a stick." I threw a smock over the bathing costume, drew on my last clean pair of socks, and buckled my boots. At least with the bathing costume there was no need for those hateful stays. I added my redingote, then my dispatch case, slung over my shoulder buckler style, and I was ready to go.

"What if Hotspur finds you gone?" Valefor followed me to the window.

"More trouble to him. He can explain to Mamma why I'm gone. Then there shall be no Fyrdraacas at all, and whose fault will that be?"

"What about me?" Valefor whined. "What should I do?"

"Eat him, too," I answered maliciously.

NINETEEN

Sneaking.
The Califa National Bank.
A Light.

MAYBE NO PRISON could hold Nini Mo, but there were plenty of prisons that I would have a hard time getting out of. Happily, my bedroom wasn't one of them. If Poppy thought that locking me in was going to keep me confined, he was in for a sad surprise. The climb from my window, down two stories to the garden, isn't hard. I've been able to do it since I was six years old. There's no real skill involved, just nerve and determination. And tonight I had plenty of both.

Ignoring Valefor's whines, I swung over the windowsill and balanced on the ledge, one arm wrapped around the firedragon-head rainspout. Valefor reluctantly pulled the window closed, and I scooted along the ledge until I reached the roof of the mudroom. Climbing across the roof is the trickiest part because it's small, slanty, and tiled, and those tiles can be pretty slickery. Plus, you must be superquiet because Mamma's window overlooks this roof, and you certainly don't want to make a noise that might inspire Mamma—or in this case Poppy—to look out that window.

Over the peak of the roof, and scoot down the other side—if you slip now, you'll end up in a huge mess of rosebushes; not that the thorns will bother you, because you'll already be hurting from the fifteen-foot drop. At the rain gutter, there's a very handy overhanging eucalyptus tree—just grab the fat branch, clamber down onto another fat branch, and then it's just a four-foot drop to the ground, or if that still seems too far, you can grab at the ivy that covers the mudroom and slide down that.

Sweet as chocolate.

Except when you get to the roof of the mudroom and glance down, and Poppy is sitting in the dark, on a chair right outside the back door, surrounded by sleeping dogs. I almost didn't see him in time; luckily for me, Flash snores like a miner. His snores made me pause, and then I smelled the stench of Poppy's cigarillo.

I retreated to my bedroom, where Valefor said with a sniff, "Well, it's not like you are the first Fyrdraaca to be confined—or to sneak out a window. Hotspur was confined for an entire year for setting the War Department on fire with an exploding cigar. Do you think he spent that time sitting in his room? He knows all the tricks."

I swore, and found that swearing did not improve my mood, but it didn't hurt it, either, so I did it again. Nini Mo said a good swear is like a good purge—it don't taste so good, but it sure does clear out your system. What was I going to do now? Maybe wait until Poppy was asleep? Go over the top of the roof? I'd never tried that before, but maybe I could do it.

Valefor, perhaps feeling a bit guilty for eating Springheel Jack, came to my rescue by suggesting that I try pressing on one of the fireplace tiles—the one painted with a rabbit. Though I was skeptical of Valefor's helpfulness, I had nothing to lose. So I pressed the tile and watched in amazement as one of the wooden wall panels swung open to reveal a dark, narrow set of stairs. These stairs led to a low door that opened near the Bog, which we haven't had to use for a very long time, thanks to Poppy's skills as a plumber. I couldn't believe I'd never known about this bolt-hole before, but it certainly came in handy now.

Once free, I turned on the skaddle, and by this skedaddling got to the intersection of the Slot, Geary, and Kearny—the intersection everyone calls the Potato Patch—only about five minutes past the rendezvous time. During the day, trying to get across this intersection is a fool's game: It's called the Potato Patch after the rough patch of ocean right outside the Oro Gate, the mouth of the Bay of Califa. Many a ship has gone down in the Potato Patch, done in by the shallow reef and the horrendous smack of the water.

The intersection of the Slot, Geary, and Kearny is just as dangerous. If a horsecar doesn't run you down, you could get squashed by a teamster hauling cargo, or some fancy man's barouche, or a whole herd of pigs being driven toward the China Bay pig-processing plant. If you avoid these dangers, the scrum of pedestrians can run right over you if you don't keep up with their hectic pace, and even if you do, you could still step into a rut and end up to your eyeballs in mud. During rush hour, a traffic signaler stands on an elevated pulpit high above the melee, trying to keep order, but the toot of his whistle is not much of a goad toward taming the ravenous traffic beast.

Tonight the Potato Patch was perfectly deserted. I could have lain down in the middle of the intersection and gone to sleep and been in no danger of anything other than getting my redingote extremely muddy. There was no sign of Lord Axacaya. For a second, I wondered if he had meant the real Potato Patch, but that seemed improbable—yet that might explain the bathing costume, but how on earth would I get out there? A rowboat? A surfboard? Dog-paddle?

A light rain was beginning to fall, so I crossed over Kearny Street, kicking up trash as I went—the Warlord should divert money from his cheese fund to the Sanitation Department— and took refuge under the overhanging portico of the Califa National Bank. From there I could lean against the locked iron grating and observe the intersection. *Better,* said Nini Mo, *for you to see them first, than for them to see you first.*

"Got a light?" said a voice out of nowhere.

I nearly elevated out of my skin. Despite the late hour, the gaslights in front of the bank were still lit, but the porch was in darkness. Still, I could have sworn no one had been standing there when I climbed up the steps.

I dropped my hand to the fan case (*Be discreet but be armed*, said Nini Mo) and pretended I hadn't heard. It was probably just a bum who had taken refuge for the night, but I sidled farther away, just in case he was a Stealie Boy.

"Got a *light*?" The bum was persistent, I had to give him that. He sidled closer. Now I could smell him: the ripe smell of rotting trash, and flesh in desperate need of some washcloth time. A particularly stewy stewbum.

"I don't smoke!"

"I didn't ask for a ciggie, now, did I, dolly? A light, *quiero un luz.*"

"I don't have any triggers, either."

"Not that kind of light," the voice said, annoyed. "A proper light. Pink and sparkly, sweet Current."

"I have no idea what you speak of, sieur." I knew he was asking for a coldfire spark, but he wasn't going to get it from me. If I sidled any farther, I'd run into the huge bronze turtle anchoring the portico's left. Where was Lord Axacaya? A cold feeling quivered over me. Maybe he had already come, not found me, and then left. But I hadn't been *that* late.

"You ain't gonna get onto the car without a light, dolly."

"I'm not a dolly. And I'm not waiting for the car. I'm waiting for a friend. A big friend. A very tall friend. She will be here any minute, and she don't like to be bothered by strangers."

"I'm just trying to be helpful, dolly, but you can have it the way you want it, with cherries on top if that's what girts your sword."

"I got a light!" another voice chirped. A bright pink wink of coldfire bloomed in the darkness, and I saw that not only was I not alone, but the portico was clustered thick with figures. The coldfire flicked out, but the afterimage of what it revealed continued to float before my eyes. Not people, but things. Entities. Praterhuman entities.

Some I recognized from the Entity Spotter, but not all. The stewbum asking for a light was not a stewbum at all, but a ghast, his flesh hanging precariously off his bones, slime trickling from his eye sockets. The scrawny greenish girl sitting next to him, puddling water, was an out-of-water nixie. I saw an ogre in a tuxedo reading the *Warlord's Wear Weekly,* a siren drinking from a takeaway cup, and a gryphon carrying three grocery sacks.

But the other entities were completely unknown to me. The guy next to the nixie could have passed for human except that he had two heads, one normal, and the other small and wizened, with blank bug-eyes and a slack mouth. The thing offering the light was covered in plush purple fur and had four eyes. Next to it wavered a diaphanous figure that seemed to be made of some sort of gauzy goo.

Only the realization that I would then become an even bigger target kept me from bolting. *Act cool if you want to stay cool,* Nini Mo advised. I tried to act cool, but my heart was near to boiling out of my chest. What were all these entities doing, standing around the portico of the Califa National Bank at two in the morning? Why were they not constrained? Magickal entities can only walk in the Waking World when they are called to do so by a magician, and even then they must suit their actions to the magician's Will. How were these entities looking so carefree?

I leaned against the giant bronze turtle and tried not to quiver, ready to rip open my fan at the first sign of trouble. Not that it would do much against this lot, but just clutching the cool steel ribs made me feel as though I was not completely helpless.

"I see the car lights!" the Ghoul hollered.

Finally, two little purple lights were crawling up the Slot—which was a bit odd because horsecar headlights are normally yellow. Maybe it was a new model. Whatever the case, I was very happy to see that the car was on its way; hopefully they'd all get on and leave me to wait for Lord Axacaya alone.

The Antler Dæmon said, "It's about time. I never waited so long. I'm gonna be late for my shift."

"The Current is slow to rise tonight," the Ghoul answered.

The darkness rustled about me as the entities went down the steps to queue up by the car sign. I was glad to see them go and even more glad that they were no longer paying attention to me. But a tall figure was making its way up the stairs. I shrank back against the portico and clutched the fan tightly. The figure crossed under the lamplight and was illuminated.

Axila Aguila, Lord Axacaya's Quetzal guard. Quetzals are the result of marriage between male eagles and women. From the neck down, Axila Aguila is shaped like an ordinary woman, but she has the head of an eagle. In the Huitzil Empire, the Quetzals are considered sacred creatures, but I find them extremely creepy. There's something very disconcerting about how they are neither human nor eagle, but a weird combination of both. It doesn't help that Axila Aguila's golden eyes are the eyes of a predator, pitiless and inhuman. I couldn't shake the feeling that any moment she might try to tear my throat out.

But tonight I was very glad to see her. She might be a danger, but she was a known danger.

"Ave, madama," I said. I made the courtesy An Unexpected Pleasure.

Axila opened her beak slightly and spoke: "Ave, Madama Fyrdraaca." Her voice was raspy and slightly accented. "Let us get in line. We do not want to miss the car. It only runs once tonight."

"Where's Lord Axacaya?"

"He will meet us. Come. The car will not wait." Another disconcerting thing about Axila Aguila is that an eagle's face doesn't change expression at all. I thought I detected a slight tinge of irritation in Axila's voice, but I couldn't be sure, and her face gave me no clues.

By now the horsecar had pulled up in front of the bank. It looked like no other horsecar that I had ever seen. In fact, it wasn't a horsecar at all.

It was a dragon.

TWENTY

The K Dragoncar.
Calculations. Up & Then Down.

Aᴜ I ɢᴏᴛ ᴏᴠᴇʀ my choking first look and took a less-choky second look, I realized the horsecar wasn't a real fire-breathing dragon. It was a trolley car that had been painted and papered to look like a dragon, and the illusion was powerful. Steam puffed out its whiskery snout, and purple headlamp eyes glowed out from under red spiky eyebrows. Four stubby legs pumped up and down, supporting a scaly blue and gold body. The dragoncar's rounded rooftop was ridged with triangular spikes, which grew smaller but no less sharp as the snaky body tapered into a long switchlike tail, which lashed back and forth, stirring up dust and trash.

"Come," the Quetzal said. "Let us board."

I hesitated. A row of small round windows marched down the dragoncar's side, through which I could see the silhouettes of riders—and I didn't like the look of those silhouettes at all. "What kind of car is it?"

Axila Aguila's eagle head could make no human expressions, but somehow I could still tell that the look she turned upon me said, *Are you an idiot?* She answered, "It's the K dragon-car."

There are four horsecar routes in the City. The B car goes out along the Gun Road to the Presidio. The N car goes across the Outlands to the Pacifica Playa. The R car goes up and down the Slot, from the Embarcadero ferry terminal to the foot of Twin Peaks. The Q car goes along the waterfront, from Black Point to China Basin. There is no K car of any kind, horse or dragon.

"Will you get on or not?" The driver leaned out of the door. "I can't hold up the route any longer. I'm off schedule as it is. The Current is sluggy tonight."

I stood alone in the middle of the Potato Patch as Axila boarded. Getting onto the car, filled with entities who might want to eat me, did not seem to be such a good idea. What if it was a trap?

"Hurry up!" the driver said impatiently. "You run me late!"

Would Nini Mo have been afraid to climb aboard? She would not have hesitated. Though it might be the last thing I ever did, I would not hesitate, either. I climbed up the steep step.

"Fare?" A crushed top hat sat askew on the driver's head, and an opera cape was draped over his bare muscular shoulders. He looked completely human, except that his skin was dark purple.

I looked to Axila for guidance, but she was making her way down the aisle. She had already paid, and I hadn't seen with what.

The driver refused my offer of a glory, with a shake of his head. I held out a diva. He shrugged that off as well. Heckling started to emanate from the other passengers. I offered two divas—no dice. I fished in my pockets. A chocolate bar? A needle-case? A button from one of my favorite red booties? Udo's cheek rouge? A paper-pin? All were rejected. In a minute, I was going to be rejected, too. The heckling was starting to turn personal.

"What do you want?" I finally asked, frustrated. My face felt as hot as a furnace.

"I don't need any of that. But I need an answer. That's the fare. An answer."

"What's the question?"

"What's the square root of thirty-six?" the driver asked, and he didn't look like he was joking.

"The square root of thirty-six? What kind of a fare is that?"

"It's my fare. Come on, now. Don't take all day. The Current falls, and we gotta go with it." Now the driver grinned. His teeth were glassy red; they glowed in his dark face, and they looked razor sharp. I had no idea what the square root of thirty-six was—in Math we'd covered square roots, but I freely admit that math is not my best subject. I'd memorized enough to pass the exam and then let all that memorization drain out of my brain. Who but accountants, gunners, and engineers needs math? At this moment, I did. And badly.

"Um, the square root of thirty-six," I said again, hoping to buy some time. Oh, how I wished I had paid more attention to Arch-Calculator Mox-Mox and his blackboard scrawls. Thankfully, before the driver could kick me off, I was saved by the kindness of a stranger. Out of the corner of my eye, I noticed that the minotaur sitting behind the driver had dropped her knitting and was wiggling her hands at me.

Not hands—fingers. Six fingers.

"The square root of thirty-six is six," I said quickly.

The driver snapped the door shut behind me. "All right, then. And I'll take that chocolate bar, too."

Relieved, I handed over the chocolate, promising myself that I would pay closer attention in Math. Clearly, a ranger should be prepared for anything—even on-the-fly mathematical calculations. The dragoncar lurched forward, almost throwing me into the minotaur's lap. I apologized, mouthed my thanks; she winked, and I careened down the narrow aisle toward the very back row of seats. There, I took the last seat, squeezing in between the Quetzal and an Apoplexia Dæmon, which causes men's heads to explode with anger. The Apoplexia had a jaculus perched on his shoulder; the lizard hissed at me as I sat down, flapping its tiny wings and almost putting my eye out with a flick of its arrowhead tail. I gave the Apoplexia a dirty look, but he didn't look up from his magazine. He was munching on a bag of pink sticklike snacks that I hoped only *looked* like human fingers.

The interior of the dragoncar was not much different from an ordinary horsecar's: swinging oil lamps, rickety wooden seats, wooden floor. It was the passengers that were extraordinary. Directly across from me, a vampyre was giving me the hairy eyeball. When I gave him the eyeball back, he licked his lips with a long black forked tongue, licky-licky, until I looked away.

Next to me, the Quetzal huffed. Her feathers were fluffed with damp, and this dampness communicated misery. She shook her head, fluffing further, and crossed her arms across her chest. She wasn't dressed for the weather; her tunic looked like it was made of thin cotton and her arms were bare.

"This city is too cold and wet," she said. "I do not like it. My feet are ice."

No wonder her feet were cold. They were bare, extremely muddy, ordinary human feet. The feet of the finger-munching Apoplexia were webbed like a duck's. The vampyre wore polished black boots.

"You need galoshes," I said. "Or at least waterproof boots."

The Quetzal leaned forward to inspect my feet. Having run out of other things to clean, Poppy had spent an entire day polishing and waterproofing every piece of footwear he could find in the house. Thanks to his industry with the bear grease, my boots were extremely watertight and my feet were toasty warm.

"Where do you get these boots?"

"Well, mine came from the Army-Navy store," I said, "but you could get them at the Emporium, too. Any dry goods store. Ask the clerk to waterproof them."

"I will go there tomorrow. This city is very wet."

I stifled a giggle at the image of Axila Aguila striding into the Army-Navy store, rifling through the racks of boots. I don't think about cruel, scary Quetzals getting wet or cold, but if half of Axila was human, she would not be immune to the weather. And she did come from the desert, too. She wasn't used to the damp.

The dragoncar turned off the Slot, and chugged its way along

Montgomery, past Saeta House—outside of which a few revelers were still straggling—and then stopped at the intersection of Montgomery and Califa.

"Kanaketa's Magick Shop!" the driver hollered, snapping the door open to let several passengers off.

I had never heard of Kanaketa's Magick Shop; in fact, I thought there were no magick shops left in the City, because the Birdies don't believe that anything relating to the Current should be bought or sold. When I had been trying to restore Valefor, that shop would have come in very handy. I'd have to remember the location and come back later to check it out.

The K dragoncar lurched forward, and in the next few minutes made several stops—always in the middle of an intersection. Never did the dragoncar stop at a corner or in the middle of a street, but always dead center in the crossroads. *The Eschata*, I recalled, had an entire chapter on the power that can be found where two pathways meet, an important nexus point. Some sigils can only be performed at a crossroads, and there is even a magickal guardian of the crossroads, whom the magician must summon—duh. I *was* an idiot.

"Is the driver Ronové, the Denizen of the Crossroads?" I whispered to Axila.

"Who else would he be?"

Her expression remained inscrutable, but I was sure I heard humor in her voice and maybe even saw a brief spark of amusement deep in her golden eyes.

The dragoncar turned off Montgomery, and was now chugging its way up Russa Hill, the third highest hill in the City. It's so steep that no horse or mule can get up it, not that teamsters hadn't tried. After many attempts ended up with crushed horses entangled in the wagon wreckage, the Warlord banned all four-wheeled traffic. If you want to get to the top, you must walk, a horrible shin-burning exercise. The buildings stop a quarter of the way up the hill, and few people have any reason to go all the way to the top. The only thing there is a heliograph station and it's off-limits to civilians.

But the dragoncar was having no problem making the grade, although we passengers had to grind our bottoms into our seats and hold tightly to the poles to keep from sliding. Being in the very back of the car suddenly didn't seem like such a prize; if gravity took over, the Quetzal and I would be crushed under a mighty heap of praterhuman weight. I held the pole with both hands and tried not to consider what would happen if the dragon lost its footing and slid back to the bottom of the hill—it was a long way down. But the dragon didn't lose its footing, and Axila and I were not crushed. The car chugged to the top of the hill and stopped.

"Leathertongue Fripperies and Falderas!" Ronové hollered.

Another place I had never heard of, and I've been to the top of Russa Hill. Long ago, when I was just a tot, Mamma had taken me to the heliograph station on one of her inspections. I had been fascinated by the mirrors and how each flash was answered by another far across the Bay in the Alameda Hills. To my childish eyes, it had seemed like magick. Now I realized it was just sunlight and glass.

The vampyre got off, and so did the medusa sitting next to him. Maybe they were together. I peered through the smudgy window, but the night was dark and the store lights weak. I couldn't see much except wide display windows filled with mannequins in assorted lingerie, including some very handsome stays—just the kind I needed. But I had the strong feeling that if I tried to come back later, Leathertongue Fripperies would be gone.

If going up one side of Russa Hill was bad, going down the other was awful. The dragoncar lurched forward and then dropped into a belly flop that turned into a scooch that turned into a horrible sweeping stomach-turning slide. Everyone and everything that hadn't grabbed tight was suddenly hurtling toward the front of the car. Screams mixed with shrieks, which mixed with roars, which competed with howls. I tried to brace myself in my seat, found myself slipping, reached out wildly, and then was wrenched back by a strong grip. Arms flailing, I grabbed back, threw my arms around Axila and held on for dear life.

The little jaculus tumbled by me, shrieking, and disappeared out the open window. The air was filled with a whirl of things: a garland of daisies, a large pink galosh, a fried chicken leg, a magazine. The swaying lamp hit a guy in the middle of his fish-eyed head and the car was plunged into darkness. Down, down we slid into black, the rush of air on my face making it hard to breathe. I closed my eyes and clenched my teeth; no power on Earth could make me let go of Axila. Pressing my face into feathers, I heard the *thumpety-thump* of her heart.

How long we fell, I don't know. An hour, a year, maybe longer. Maybe forever. And then suddenly our fall reversed itself. Instead of flinging forward, we were pressed back by a crushing sensation. The shrieking of the brakes reached a crescendo; my screams muffled into Axila's chest.

We stopped, suspended in mid-nothing. And then, with a crash that sent my teeth through my tongue, we thudded down and were still.

Or at least the K dragoncar was still. My tum was bobbing like a cork in a storm, and my head was awash with spiraling dizziness. My tongue throbbed and I swallowed the heavy taste of iron.

"Have you pain?" Axila asked. The dragoncar lurched forward.

"I'm all right," I said thickly. The fog had thickened to the consistency of custard; I couldn't see anything outside. But the dragoncar was now going bumpety-bump, which made me think we were on a corduroy road. There's only one corduroy road in the City: the China Basin Road, which leads to Woodward's Gardens, and then to points south.

"Where are we going?" I demanded. "And where is Lord Axacaya?"

"He will meet us there," the Quetzal said.

"Where?"

"Did he not say?"

"No."

"Do you not know?"

"No," I said, exasperated.

The Quetzal scratched her head with one long green-painted talonlike fingernail. "Not all that glitters proves to be worth the shine."

I was still trying to figure out what she meant when the dragoncar halted.

"Madama Rose's Flower Garden!" the driver hollered. "Last stop! All off!"

The Monkey's Grin.
A Swan Boat. Swimming.

WE CLAMBERED DOWN the dragoncar's rickety steps. Ronové gave a cheerful wave, and the door snapped shut behind us. The dragoncar disappeared into the fog, leaving us muffled in a miasma of grayness and standing before an enormous disembodied monkey head.

Not a real monkey's head, of course, but a two-story structure built to look like one. Now I knew where we were: Woodward's Gardens & Fun Fair. I've been to Woodward's a zillion times on Sanctuary field trips and for birthday parties; it has everything you could ever want as far as amusement goes: a zoo, fun-fair rides, an art gallery, and a giant open-air restaurant called Mag's Ham Bun. The last time I had been to Woodward's Gardens had been for Udo's Catorcena, when I had eaten too much pink popcorn and thrown up on the Loup de Loup, which fact Udo will never ever allow me to forget.

Udo!

"Are we meeting Lord Axacaya here?" I said to the Quetzal.

"Ayah."

"But Woodward's Gardens isn't open at night."

"Is that so?" Axila Aguila answered and pointed to the monkey head. It has large bulging eyes that glow a nauseating green, and its enormous mouth gapes open as though it is screaming with laughter. On the monkey's head, a crown of sputtering galvanic lights spells out FUN AND FROLIC. To enter Woodward's Gardens, you must step into the Monkey's Maw, as though you are being swallowed alive.

Normally the monkey looks as though he's having a pretty good time. Tonight, however, the gaping mouth looked as if it was screaming with horror, not fun, and the glowing eyes seemed to sparkle with rage. Cheerful things always look melancholy in the dark—but even so, there was something about the monkey's attitude that made my spine feel shivery. A short line of entities was queued up before the Monkey's Maw. Clearly, Woodward's was open for business.

"Come," the Quetzal said, and we got in line behind a fire elemental. The elemental was only about the height of Gesilher, Udo's six-year-old brother; his skin was a dark brick red, and his hair was on fire. Tiny flames licked at his temples, and a cowlick of acrid smoke drifted up from the top of his head. The line moved quickly, and we soon reached the front.

The gatekeeper was a boy in a ragged redingote, buttoned up against the night's chill. He didn't look more than two years old; he was sitting on a stool and his swinging feet didn't even touch the ground. His tiny red lips were distorted by the black cigarillo he was smoking, and a small top hat perched upon his white-blond curls. In other circumstances, he would have been adorable. Right now it seemed to me that anyone—anything—that cute had to be a trap.

He spoke to the Quetzal in Huitzil. She hissed back at him and he waved us on. Into the Maw we went, stepping over sharp wooden teeth onto a thick plush ruglike tongue. During the day, you can see the light at the end of the tunnel and know that you are not really being swallowed alive. But now, only darkness lay ahead and it was easy to imagine that we were on our way to the belly of the beast. Within a few steps, my eyes adjusted and I realized that the blackness was tinged with a diffused glow that was coming from Axila—and me, as well. I held up my hands and saw their outline gleaming pale pink. "I'm glowing."

I felt the movement of the Quetzal turning to me. "It is the Gramatica."

"What do you mean?"

But she didn't answer. Ahead, the darkness lifted into silver light. We were passing through a long gallery of mirrors, and Axila Aguila was walking so quickly I had to trot to keep up. I was only able to catch quick glimpses of myself, but these glimpses were not happy ones. Was I really that short? Had my eyeliner run that badly? I had two chins!

"Don't look to the left." The Quetzal grabbed my arm and pulled me along even faster. "It does not reflect true—it only magnifies your flaws until they seem monstrous. Don't look to the right—that shows only vanity."

Of course, I immediately looked to the right and was charmed by what I saw there. How bright my eyes and firm my chin, and what perfect ringlets my hair. How could I ever have felt ugly—

"Come! Come! Do not allow yourself to be caught!" Axila Aguila bundled me along. Suddenly the mirrors were gone and we were inside the Gardens.

During the day, the Gardens are bright with color and cheerful with the sounds of the sideshow music and children's screams of joy. Now everything was shadowy and hushed. Here and there a torch flared along the pathway, but the light seemed oddly pale and didn't travel far. I heard the distant sound of music, dissonant and out-of-key, mingling with high-pitched howls and screeches. Directly ahead, garish lights glittered above the treetops: the lights of the fun-fair and the midway. I didn't think I wanted to see who was on the rides or playing the games, and I *knew* I didn't want to see what kind of sideshows Madama Rose's offered.

"Flora, I am so glad you have come." Lord Axacaya co-alesced out of nowhere and drew me into a hot embrace. He clasped me closely to his chest; feathers tickled my nose, and a little quiver went down my spine. I was enveloped in the heady smell of incense, the dry heat of his skin. I inhaled deeply and deliciously.

"Are you all right? I'm sorry about that scene with Hotspur. It was most regrettable." He released me from the hug, alas, but continued to hold my hand, drawing me into a walk next to him.

Despite the darkness, I could see Lord Axacaya perfectly. The light that came from Axila and me was faint, hardly visible in the moonlight. But Lord Axacaya glowed as though lit from within. The tattoos on his arms, chest, and hands stood out like green tracings upon his luminescent skin. Even his hair shone like butter, yellow and rich. Now I understood what Axila had meant. My Gramatica vocabulary was limited, small, and thus, so was my glow. But Lord Axacaya's fluency in Gramatica made him brilliant. He just *had* to agree to teach me; I'd never find a better instructor.

"It wasn't your fault," I answered. "Poppy's the one who should be sorry."

Lord Axacaya said soothingly, "He did not hurt you, did he? You should not be left alone with him."

"I'm all right, really. Poppy wouldn't dare hurt me."

"Perhaps. Perhaps. I hope you are right. What a terrible situation—we shall discuss it more later. I'm sorry that I could not meet you earlier. I had to attend upon the Ambassador."

In my own woe, I had forgotten about the assassination attempt. "Is he dead?"

"No. It takes more than an assassin's bullet to kill the Ambassador—even a silver bullet won't do the trick. He was more annoyed than hurt."

"Did they catch the assassin?" I asked, hoping they had not. If the EI wasn't involved in this attempt, I'd eat my hat.

"Ayah," Lord Axacaya's answer sent a silver cold eddy through my blood. "He didn't get far—"

He! That was a relief. Not Idden, then, for sure. I was certain she was involved, but at least she wasn't caught.

Lord Axacaya continued: "I think he was hoping for martyrdom. Now he shall hope for a painless death. Ah well, seldom do we get exactly what we wish for. But never mind that, we have bigger fish to fry. The Current is about to crest, and we need that surge if we are to get where we are going."

"Where is that?"

"The Bilskinir Baths."

Triumph rushed through me. "To the Vertex there?"

Lord Axacaya glanced at me, and then laughed. "I should have known you would be informed, Flora. Ayah, Bilskinir Baths is the site of a Vertex, the most powerful Vertex in the City, and there we shall find what we seek. The Loliga. Clever girl."

We had reached the Circular Pond, which stands in the center of Woodward's Gardens. In the daytime you can rent a swan boat and pedal around the pond, feeding the koi that lurk in the murky water. A white shape drifted over to where we stood on the dock; I guess you could rent the swan boats at night, too. Axila Aguila was using a boat hook to reel the swan in.

But the Bilskinir Baths are on the other side of the City, and while it is true that there is no longer any way to get there except by water due to the unstable cliffs, I didn't see how a little swan boat would help us. Point Lobos is rocky and the surf is dangerous; the boat would be instantly crushed against the rocks.

Lord Axacaya must have seen my bewilderment, for he said soothingly, "It will all be clear soon, Flora."

He hadn't dropped my hand, and now he raised it to his lips. My knees felt extremely wiggly. I took a deep breath.

"I need you to trust me, Flora. It is easier to show you than try to explain. The journey is dangerous but necessary. And I promise I shall let nothing happen to you. Will you come with me?"

Think twice and act once, said Nini Mo, but I didn't have to think twice at all. Nini also said to go with your gut, and my gut said *go.* So did my heart, my liver, my lungs, every bit of me. A ranger never turns down an adventure. Nini Mo didn't say that, but it was true nonetheless.

"Ayah," I answered. "I'll come."

Behind us, I heard a noise that could have been a huff from the Quetzal, but I didn't turn around to check. Lord Axacaya was smiling down at me, and in the light of the torches, his eyes seemed almost the color of quicksilver. My heart was buzzing like a bee.

Lord Axacaya handed me into the swan boat and then climbed in. The Quetzal gave us a good shove off the dock, and off we went, pedaling madly across the silvery water to—where?

"The Current," Lord Axacaya said, "rises and falls, just as the tide does. It flows, just as water does. Hence, we in the Waking World so oft refer to it in liquid terms."

"Ayah," I puffed. Lord Axacaya was pedaling quite quickly and it was hard to keep up.

"The energy we call the Current can manifest in many forms, but it can also be channeled through water. The Current runs through the City much like an underground river. It is around us all the time, sometimes lightly, like a fog. Sometimes heavier, as a rain. And sometimes it floods."

He stopped pedaling and I did the same. From across the Pond came the sound of distant revelry. Somewhere a duck quacked and was answered by another. But the water was still and silent beneath us.

He continued. "There are three levels of human comprehension—"

"The Waking World, the Abyss, and Elsewhere," I said eagerly. "Life, Death, and In Between."

"Ayah, so. The Current flows through all three. There are places in the City where the Current bubbles close to the surface of the Waking World," Lord Axacaya said, "and manifests as water, mingles with water. Sometimes even appears to *be* water."

Poppy had once made me jump from the roof of the Folly into the Sunken Puddle, and he had said that the water was the Current. At the time, I had thought he was talking crazy, but maybe I had been wrong.

Lord Axacaya continued: "In these places, which are known as Wells, it is possible to enter the Current and to swim through it, swim along it, to follow the Current as it flows. If we pedaled to the ruins of Bilskinir Baths, that is all we would see: ruins. But we want more than that." Lord Axacaya stood up so suddenly that the swan rocked alarmingly and I clutched at the side of the boat. He unclasped his feathered cape, let it slither down, and jumped into the water. He surfaced almost immediately, shaking his head, and swam back over to the boat, grabbing hold of its side. Again, the boat surged alarmingly, the swan-head listing.

"The water is very warm," Lord Axacaya said. "Come now, we have no time to waste. You can swim, can't you?"

"Of course I can swim," I said. Orange and white flickered in the water's darkness; koi were nudging up against Lord Axacaya, who pushed them away with a sweeping arm.

"Then come—the Current will soon crest, and then begin to ebb. We must be in and out by then or we shall be stuck."

He ducked under the surface. I quickly pulled off my boots and socks, then bundled my pinafore into my redingote and stuffed them into my dispatch case. Without Lord Axacaya's furnace warmth so near, the night air was cold. I looked at the black water. Lord Axacaya had not resurfaced. I hesitated. The Loliga was at Bilskinir Baths and she'd tried to snatch me twice. The third time might be the charm. But Lord Axacaya was not going to take a coward as a student.

A keening howl echoed across the lake and suddenly I did not care to be left. Better jump in before he surfaced and noticed that I looked like a sausage in my bathing costume.

Dare, win, or disappear.

Clutching Poppy's ranger badge in one sweaty hand, I held my nose with the other. I closed my eyes and jumped.

TWENTY-TWO

Diving Down. Out of Air.
A Bit Too Deep.

AFTER THE COLD night air, the water felt oily and warm. I kicked back up to the surface, then shook my wet hair out of my eyes, trying not to think about the daytime murk of the pond and the zillions of ducks that had contributed to it. I clenched my lips tightly shut. If I swallowed any of that water, I'd be squirting for the next month. Curious koi bumped me until I splashed at them and they darted away.

The swan boat had drifted off. A dark shape bobbed near me. Lord Axacaya said, "Hold on to my hand, and don't let go. No matter what. I don't want to get separated; it might be hard to find each other again."

We splashed and found each other's hands. Even wet, his grip was hot.

"Are you afraid, Flora?"

"A little."

He laughed. "So am I. On the count of three, we will dive. It's a bit of a ways, so suck in as much air as you can."

He counted, I sucked, and then *three*—down he went, dragging me with him. I kept my eyes squeezed tightly shut, although it was probably too dark to see, anyway. Still, I didn't relish the thought of that dirty water scouring my eyeballs. Down, down we dove. Mamma had made me and Idden learn to swim in the icy water off the Pacifica Playa, and all those years of battling the riptides and surf have made me a strong swimmer. But Lord Axacaya was a strong swimmer, too, and I hardly had to do any work, just hang on to his hand and kick to keep the momentum up. Once my foot hit something, and cold fear jolted through me. I suddenly recalled reading in the CPG about an alligator escaping from Woodward's Zoological Exhibits, and then, of course, there was that grabby tentacle—

If you don't peer at the shadows, you won't see any ghosts, Nini Mo said. So I turned my focus to the swim and tried to think of nothing else. Kick, kick, kick. As we went deeper, coldness began to swirl through the warmth. The water grew thicker, as though it was congealing around us. Soon I felt as though I was swimming through jelly. I kicked harder, feeling my leg muscles burn, pushing deeper and deeper. Down, down we went. My ears popped.

And then I began to run out of air.

I pressed my lips together and tried not to snuffle out my nose, but the desire to breathe was becoming overwhelming. Pressure began to build in my head, pushing painfully against my ears. And still we continued down, down—even if I were to let go and turn back, it was too far. I'd never make it. The desire would be too strong—I would open my mouth—and suck in death. It dimly occurred to me that Lord Axacaya probably did not have small lungs and could swim much farther than I could on one breath.

Still we swam onward. The pressure became pain, and the pain became an urge so strong that I had to fight all my reflexes to keep from opening my mouth. With my free hand, I pinched my nose shut. My ears pounded and I couldn't help but exhale, feeling the bubbles bob off my face, but it didn't erase the desire to gasp. My lungs burned. I lagged, yanking on Lord Axacaya's grip, trying to turn my mind toward anything that could distract me from the instinct to breathe. But it's rather hard to distract yourself from the fact that you are suffocating.

Then Lord Axacaya twisted, and grabbed at my shoulders,

pulling me into him. Our legs tangling, his lips were against my lips, forcing my mouth open. Just as I gave in to the horrible need to gasp, he exhaled, pushing air from his lungs into mine. I sucked the air in deeply, and he twisted again, pulling away, and kicking strongly. Suddenly I felt buoyant and reenergized.

I opened my eyes and saw, instead of darkness, a rosy glow. Lord Axacaya floated next to me, a distorted silvery figure, his hair streaming behind him like seaweed. We hung in an immense nothingness, a hazy pink that seemed to extend forever. The emptiness of this huge Void was horrible—I felt very tiny, exposed, puny. Overwhelmed. A wave of vertigo rolled over me—Lord Axacaya was gone, I was alone, lost, dwindling to a tiny speck of insignificance. The glow winked out, flooding me with a smothering oppressive darkness. I couldn't feel my body, I couldn't move, I was adrift and alone—

Then I felt a brief brushing against me, and that touch brought me back to myself. I could feel my body again, my arms and legs flailing. The brush became a grip, the grip a tug—

Close your eyes and kick.

I closed my eyes and kicked. Kicked and kicked and kicked. Once again the water felt thin against my skin. My head broke the surface and I was gulping in air, stale and musty air, but air. I opened my eyes, and through the sting of salt water saw the blurry world and was relieved. I rolled onto my back and wheezed and panted, reveling in the sensation of inflatable lungs. Next to me, Lord Axacaya whipped his head back, tossing wet hair out of the way.

"Are you all right, Flora? It didn't occur to me that since you are so small perhaps the distance would be too great."

"I'm all right," I gasped.

"We will have to practice your breathing. You should be able to hold your breath for longer than that." Lord Axacaya swam to the edge of the pool and slithered up the side, then hauled me up after him. I sat panting and dripping on the cold wet tiles. Above, instead of a sweep of darkness, the sky glowed with a pink pallor that made everything seem sickly and pale.

In front of us a huge glass building loomed, long low wings stretching out from a central dome.

"You are shivering." Lord Axacaya crouched before me, his hair clinging to his shoulders like a sodden veil. "Here—"

He reached out with a long finger and touched my forehead. For a second, I felt the pressure of his touch on my skin, and the pressure bloomed into a warmth that suffused my body with a pleasant glow. I no longer felt cold and soggy, but snug and dry. When I followed Lord Axacaya's motion and stood up, I found that I *was* dry, my hair no longer drippy, my bathing costume no longer soppy.

"How did you do that without using Gramatica?" I asked.

"I did use Gramatica. You just didn't hear me. After a time, a magician no longer has to vocalize a Gramatica invocation; it is enough to think it. Come, *pequeña,* we are wasting the Current."

I followed Lord Axacaya across the front drive, over a set of horsecar tracks, and up to the arching entrance of the building, which the large carved sign over the doors identified as Bilskinir Baths. But I've been to the ruins of Bilskinir Baths and they didn't look like this at all. They are a twisted heap of fallen girders and blackened marble poised precariously over the cliffside, looking like they might, at any moment, collapse completely.

I said, "This is not a ruin."

"Ayah, so. Every place in the Waking World has a corresponding impression Elsewhere. This is the Bilskinir Baths Elsewhere—the revenant of the original. It is the culmination of all the energies that were ever concentrated on the Baths. A ghost, if you like."

"I thought only people could have ghosts. Don't only people have Anima?"

Lord Axacaya laughed. "It's a common misconception, *pequeña,* but you shall learn otherwise."

The enormous door, wide enough to admit a pushing throng of people, was closed. That didn't stop Lord Axacaya; he strode forward and walked right through it. I hesitated, for that door looked very real and very hard. Then I forced myself to move onward, trying not to flinch, closing my eyes just before I reached the point of impact. But there was no impact, just a waft of something soft on my skin, as though I passed through a curtain of gauze. When I opened my eyes, I was standing at the top of a magnificent marble staircase. At the bottom, dark water gleamed. And beyond that was a wide glass wall through which I could see the silvery shadow of the open ocean.

Lord Axacaya was already going down the marble stairs, and I hurried to catch up.

"Where is the denizen of Bilskinir Baths?"

"It's gone."

"Where did it go?"

"You are inquisitive, aren't you?" He sounded amused.

"I want to learn."

"So I see—watch that step."

I watched that step, and put my foot down into a bright spurt of pain. "Pigface Pogostick!"

"What's wrong?" Lord Axacaya turned back.

"I think I stepped on a piece of glass." He knelt, coldfire light blooming around his hands, casting his eyes into shadow and making his gold butterfly lip-plug glitter. He bent his head, and I saw, through the golden haze of his hair, the thin blue lines of a tattoo etched on his scalp. I tottered and put my hand on his shoulder to steady myself, and his skin was hot beneath my hand.

"It's just a little cut," Lord Axacaya smoothed one finger along the slice on my heel, tracing the thin line of blood and smoothing the pain away. The snake tattoo on his arm wiggled, as though it were a real snake coiled around his arm. I shivered at his tickle, which felt as flickery as a snake's tongue. He gently wiped the blood away with a hank of his hair, and I no longer felt pain or chill, but something much more fun.

"Is that better?" His face was so close I could see that his eyes were not completely black. In their depths a blue spark shone, tiny but bright. When I had met him once before in Elsewhere, his eyes had been bright blue, the color of the desert sky.

"Why are your eyes black?" I blurted.

"Shall I tell you?" he asked teasingly. "I think I shall, though few others know. Once, when I was not much older than you, I was burned alive."

"Burned alive!" My stomach flipped in horror. "But how, then, do you live?"

"The inferno I was cast into was made not of ordinary flames, but of a voracious coldfire. The coldfire did not consume me, though it settled into my flesh so that even today I can feel its heat. And it burned away my vision. I am blind, Flora."

"Blind! But how do you get around so well?"

"There are more ways to see than with your eyes, Flora. And now I see much more than I ever did when I had ordinary vision. It was a fair trade."

It didn't seem like much of a fair trade to me, at all. In fact, it was a horrible trade. I thought of never seeing the sunshine again, or Flynn's silly face, or the color purple. Surely no trade could possibly make up for that—could it? *You have to give to get*, said Nini Mo. Losing your sight wasn't a little thing—and yet, it had helped make Lord Axacaya the magician he was today. Powerful enough to be blind and yet to still see. And to hide this blindness from everyone. Maybe it *had* been a fair trade.

Lord Axacaya smoothed a lock of hair back from my face, and his touch made me shiver.

"The Art of Magick requires great sacrifices sometimes, Flora."

"Did it hurt?" I asked.

He released my foot and stood up. "Ayah, so it did. Come."

I followed Lord Axacaya down the stairs. It was hard to believe that he was blind. He moved so fluidly, so surely, with never a footstep wrong. But then, he'd said he could see more than I could. I really wanted to know what those visions were.

Every ten or so steps, the staircase leveled out into a wide landing. The hall was overrun with foliage; vines clung to the walls, thick with enormous flowers that filled the air with a heavy peppery fragrance. Trees grew along the edges of the stairs, their branches tangling overhead, so that the high ceiling was lost in a hazy lattice of leaves. The hot, wet air was hard to breathe.

Lord Axacaya said, "The Baths were destroyed before I came to Califa, so I never saw them when they were open. But they are glorious, aren't they?"

Glorious and also a bit overdone, I thought. Plus, too wet. My dryness was rapidly turning soggy again. Huge green eyes glittered on the landing ahead of us and I pulled close to Lord Axacaya, only to feel foolish when I realized that the glow came from the glass eyes of an enormous stuffed walrus. The walrus was perched on a rock, its mouth open in a roar, tusks gleaming.

I said, "But why have we come to the Elsewhere Baths? Why can't we just go to the ruins of the Baths themselves? Isn't the Loliga there?"

"She is, but she's hidden, guarded all around by various sigils, booby-trapped. Here, I can disable those sigils, so that I may visit her. I left the sigils undisturbed in the Waking World, to ensure that no one else might find her and try to meddle with her."

Ahead of us lay the enormous expanse of a pool, its surface black and flat. We reached the bottom of the staircase; the next step led directly into the water. A framework of metal struts arched over the expanse, supporting a high glass ceiling; directly across, the glass formed a transparent wall, and the edges of the pool lined up so perfectly with the ocean that they appeared to form one contiguous body of water. I stared at the ocean. There was something strange about it, and it took me a minute to realize that it too was flat, with not a ripple marring its stillness. And silent, too. No boom of surf, or thunder of waves. Silence as flat as the water's surface.

"The Salt Pool," Lord Axacaya said. "Bilskinir's glory. The true ocean is right there, but people preferred to bathe in a facsimile in which they were in no danger of being stung by jelly-fish or eaten by sharks. To stay in the shallows where they could not drown. Most people want to stay where it is safe."

"Most people are dull and boring," I said, and he turned toward me and smiled.

"Are you most people, Flora Fyrdraaca?"

"No," I said. "I'm bored all the time, and it's horrible. I don't want to spend the rest of my life being bored."

"Somehow I don't think there is any chance of that, *pequeña*. Anyway, the Salt Pool allowed people to believe they were being daring. See—" I followed Lord Axacaya's point. A long slide swooped down from the second-story gallery that overhung the south end of the Salt Pool. "And rope swings, too. And, of course, a denizen to fish you out if you ran into trouble." At the north end of the pool, a lifeguard hut was perched on stilts, but it looked forlorn and empty, the denizen long gone.

At the edge of the Pool, Lord Axacaya paused. "𝌀⊞ 𝌅🜚🜂🜄 𝌆🜍🝆!"

His Command flared like a star, Words twisting and turning around themselves, forming a long sparkling fuse of cold-fire. This fuse darted down and jacked into the water as neatly as a high diver, its glitter extinguished. The water again lay flat and black. Then, after a few seconds of stillness, the water began to churn, and the darkness swirled with an iridescent pearly light. The glow grew stronger, and the water began to froth and foam. A wave sloshed over the steps, wetting my feet, and I stepped back.

A huge blue eye, the size of a small wagon wheel, peered up at me.

TWENTY-THREE

Shifting Colors.
More Tentacles. A Threat.

I GASPED AND CLUTCHED at Lord Axacaya. I had not imagined that the Loliga was quite so enormous. Her body was easily as big as a barouche; her limbs—six short arms and two longer tentacles—stretched the length of three teams of horses. But other than her size, she looked exactly like the small squids that you see at the fish market. Those, though, lie dead and lifeless on a slab, their skin dull and gray. The Loliga's skin was translucently white, dappled with purple shadows, and her eye glowed.

"The Loliga," Lord Axacaya said. "An etheric egregore of the ninth order trapped into the form of a giant squid. Don't be afraid, Flora. She won't hurt you."

"She tried to grab me before," I protested.

"She will not harm you as long as I am here. She is sorry to have scared you—see how her skin flushes? That is her way of communicating. She is offering her friendship. Be sporting and offer her your friendship in return."

Never let them see you flinch, said Nini Mo. So I knelt down and reached out with a tentative hand. I expected the Loliga's skin to feel slimy, but instead it was satiny smooth. Lavender streaks bloomed under my fingers, then slowly shaded to amethyst.

"She is very sorry she tried to hurt you," Lord Axacaya said. I could feel his heat as he leaned over me, and a lock of his hair brushed my shoulder in a shivery way.

"How do you know what she is saying?"

"I spent many years looking for her and, when I found her, much time learning to communicate with her. Now we understand each other very well, the Loliga and I."

As he spoke, a long pearly tentacle enfolded out of the water and wiggled toward me. My nerve evaporated, and I scurried behind Lord Axacaya, putting him between me and those suckers.

"She will not hurt you, Flora. I promise. Come, accept her friendship." He tried to push me forward.

"She's trying to grab me!" Despite Lord Axacaya's reassurances, I had a very strong feeling that the Loliga didn't like me. Her tentacle was flushing a blackish purple—the angry shading of a bruise.

Lord Axacaya said soothingly, "No, she's not. Remember, I am here to protect you. I will never let anything happen to you, *pequeña.*"

I was still afraid, but I relented, not wanting him to think me a baby. I cringed as the tentacle touched my face, glided over my hair and shoulders. The caress was light and easy, however, and when the tentacle didn't try to grab me, I felt slightly reassured. The brilliant blue eye was staring at me, its color deep and vivid as a clear noontime sky. Suddenly my fear was subsumed by pity. I knew what it was like to be trapped, to feel abandoned and alone. It's a horrible feeling, and I wouldn't wish it on anyone.

The tentacle left me and undulated over to Lord Axacaya to gently pat his shoulder. Though the gesture made me uneasy— that tentacle was awful close to his neck, and I'd bet it could pop his head right off without much effort—he didn't flinch.

Lord Axacaya said, "The sigils that bind her are weakening, Flora. Not enough to free her, but enough to allow her to fight against them. Her reach extends into the City's Current, and the earthquakes that threaten the City are caused by her struggles. If she is not freed, she'll tear the City apart, destroy us all."

My triumph at being right that the Loliga was the cause of the City's rumblings was blotted out by the horrific images filling my head: the City in flames, in ruins; Mamma, Poppy, Udo, the silly dogs, crushed, squashed, burned, dead.

"You can't let her destroy the City! You have to free her! Undo the sigils or something!"

"The Loliga is trapped not by one sigil, but a series of sigils created and charged by Georgiana Segunda and then fused into one extremely strong Binding. Some of the small sigils have already unraveled. Others are fraying. But the fuse remains strong. The Loliga has slack enough to struggle, but not enough to escape."

"But couldn't you just undo a few more of the small sigils, enough to let the Loliga slip out? Nini Mo escaped from the Virreina of Huitzil's dungeon by using a sharpened toothbrush and an Intersection Sigil to cut through the bars of her cell and then squeeze through."

"Did she now?" Lord Axacaya answered. "If only it were that easy. The fuse remains strong. It would take a long time to untangle the sigils, and even longer to try to figure out the method Georgiana used to bond them together. We do not have that much time."

"Won't she stop struggling if she knows we are trying to help her?"

"She cannot wait. We cannot wait. The Loliga gestates—"

I broke in, astonished. "You mean she is pregnant? How can an egregore be pregnant?"

"Now is not the time, Flora, for a lecture in praterhuman reproduction habits. Let us just stipulate that the egregore was carrying a child when Georgiana trapped her—perhaps Georgiana didn't know, or maybe she did not care. Now the egregore—the Loliga—is close to the end of her term. Soon her labor pangs will begin. Her struggles will increase, grow uncontrollable. And those struggles will destroy the City, leave her and her child trapped forever in the wreckage of the City."

The poor Loliga! The poor little Loliga baby! I leaned down

again and patted her side. "We can't let that happen! But what can we do?"

"There is one hope. Georgiana used a Gramatica Word to fuse the sigil together. The problem is I don't know which Word she used; she was too clever, and disguised it too well. Every Gramatica Word has an antonym, an opposite. If I knew what Word she used, I would know its opposite, and use this knowledge to reverse the fuse, release the Loliga. And for this, I need your help."

Lord Axacaya needed *my* help? "But what can I do? I don't know anything at all."

"You know quite a bit, Flora. Don't sell yourself short. And in this case, it's not what you know. It's who you know."

"Who do I know?"

"Paimon, the denizen of Bilskinir House. As you know, all good adepts keep close records of their magickal workings. If we can get a look at Georgiana Haðraaða's *Diario,* I believe we'll find the answers we seek. But her *Diario* is at Bilskinir House, under Paimon's stewardship, and I fear that Paimon and I are not friends. I have tried to get him to allow me access to the *Diario.* But he has remained silent to my entreaties. Perhaps he thinks he is a strong enough denizen to stand firm, no matter what destruction the Loliga inflicts upon the rest of us. Or perhaps, with his family gone, he no longer cares if he is destroyed or not. I do not know. Anyway, he ignores me. But now the Goddess, may she consume us all, has sent me a solution. In the last fourteen years you are the only one Paimon has allowed entry into Bilskinir House."

"Me and Udo," I said, in fairness to Udo, even if he didn't deserve such kindness.

"But it was you to whom Paimon offered friendship. He helped you before; perhaps he will again. At least he will listen to you, which is more than I could get him to do. Will you ask him for help? It is our only hope."

The big blue eye still stared fixedly at me, still angry, but also full of entreaty. The poor egregore, lured and trapped, eventually forgotten and left to rot, unable to protect the new life within her. Fighting against her bonds, growing more and more desperate. And at last, destroying us all as she tried to bring forth the new life she had created.

Didn't Nini Mo say a ranger had a duty to free the oppressed? She wouldn't allow the Loliga to remain enslaved, and she wouldn't stand by and allow her City to be destroyed, along with everyone and everything she loved.

And although it probably wasn't exactly the best time to be thinking of myself, I couldn't help but consider my own ambitions. If I helped Lord Axacaya out now, he'd owe me one. If I impressed him with my initiative and daring, he would see I would make an extremely worthy pupil.

As though reading my mind (and maybe he was, in which case I should be more careful about my thoughts), Lord Axacaya said, "I know your ambitions, Flora. I know that you desire to be more than your family demands. In your own way, you are as trapped as the Loliga."

"It's not fair!" I said, looking at the Loliga lying watchful in the water. Maybe my cage wasn't as obvious as hers, but it was a cage just the same. "It's not fair at all!"

"You must follow your own Will. What is your Will, Flora?"

"It's my Will to be a ranger, not a soldier! And I want to learn Gramatica!" The words popped out. "Will you teach me?"

"Learning Gramatica is not something to be undertaken lightly. It gets into your blood, into your bones, into your Anima and changes it. You have seen the changes it has wrought on me."

"I'm not afraid. And I'm not a child. I understand the consequences. Will you teach me? Please?"

He didn't answer, and I was afraid I had gone too far. *But if you never ask, the answer will always be no,* Nini Mo said. In the pool, the Loliga's tentacles began to writhe, frothing the water into foam.

Then Lord Axacaya said, "I must consider the implication of such an alliance. When all this is over, we shall discuss it again. We do not have much time, Flora, a day or two only before her labor begins. We must act swiftly. Will you go to Bilskinir and ask Paimon for his help?"

"Ayah, I will," I said, and Lord Axacaya smiled and kissed my hand.

TWENTY-FOUR

Waffles. In Pig.
Judge Advocate General.

THE SWIM BACK FROM Bilskinir Baths seemed shorter, or maybe I was just more prepared. We didn't surface at Woodward's Gardens, but in the reflecting pool in the courtyard of Casa Mariposa, Lord Axacaya's house. A thin pink dawn was beginning to edge the sky. I grabbed a cab and made it back to Crackpot Hall and to my room, via Valefor's helpful hidden stairs, before full light. There, I crawled into bed and a sleep so deep and dark that I didn't even dream.

When I woke up, a plate of waffles and a pot of coffee, not quite cold, stood on my desk. My door was no longer locked, but I didn't think for a minute that Poppy had lifted my confinement. Still, at least now I could get to the potty, and I wasted no time in doing so. When I reached for the tooth polish, I realized that Mamma's toothbrush was back on the brush stand.

Mamma's boots were discarded at the threshold to her room, the pieces of her uniform were tangled on the floor, and her pistol lay on her bedside table. Her bed was strewn with snuggly dogs, who growled and shifted when I bounced up, but Mamma herself was invisible under a mound of blankets.

"Mamma! You're back!"

The blankets wiggled and surged as I poked and prodded, and then finally, Mamma's face emerged, "Ayah, I'm back, darling. Here, give me a kiss." She wrestled me into a squeezy embrace, and then didn't let me go, but settled back against the pillows. I buried my face in her neck, breathing in the familiar smell: lemon verbena, gunpowder, and ink. And today, the distant salt smell of the sea.

"Why are you back so soon? What happened?"

Mamma grimaced. "The Ambassador called me back. He's rather annoyed someone tried to kill him. He wants me to explain why."

"I'm sorry, Mamma." *But you saved yourself a big waste of time,* I thought.

She squeezed me. "It's all right, darling. Going to Fort Jones would have been a fool's errand, anyway. Idden is long gone. I wanted to see for myself, but it would have made no difference."

Guilt twanged at me. "I'm sure she's all right, wherever she is, Mamma. Idden's too mean to have anything happen to her."

"That's not a very nice thing to say, Flora." Mamma stroked my head.

"But I mean it as a compliment. Who would dare mess with Idden? She'd bite their hand off if they tried to grab her. I'm sure she's fine, Mamma, really. Don't worry." Darn Idden—couldn't she at least send Mamma a note saying she was alive?

"I hope you are right, Flora."

Despite her sadness, Mamma seemed in a mellow mood. Or maybe she was just sleepy. Either way, perhaps this was a good time to bring up Poppy's meltdown. *It is better,* said Nini Mo, *to let someone else give the bad news.* On the other hand, sometimes it is best to be first. "Mamma, at the Ball—"

"Your father already told me what happened, Flora."

"It wasn't my fault, Mamma, really. I could hardly—"

"We'll talk about it at breakfast, Flora. I need my coffee before I consider any further troubles. I'm exhausted. Ayah so?"

"Ayah so, Mamma," I said, kissing her forehead. She did look very tired, and a little sunburned, too. I noticed, for the first time, that thin lines of silver ran through her short blond hair. I was getting older, and Mamma was, too.

For some reason this thought made me sad.

POPPY DIDN'T SAY A WORD to me when I came into the kitchen and I didn't say a word back, for all I cared to say would get me in even deeper trouble. I sat down at the table and drank coffee; Poppy stood over the stove and fried bacon. Mamma came down a few minutes later, in a cloud of dogs.

"I'm starving," she announced, sitting at the table. "I think I could eat an entire side of bacon."

"You need to lay off the bacon, Buck," Poppy said. "You are getting a little tummy. You won't be able to get your weskit buttoned soon."

Mamma put her cup down and smiled. "This is just the start of my little tummy. Soon it will not be so little anymore."

I looked up from my waffles. Poppy's face had turned as white as an egg. "What do you mean, Buck?"

"I hope it's a boy this time, Hotspur. Then you will have some company in this nest of Fyrdraaca females."

Mamma and a baby! I sat there like a snapperhead, shocked into silence, my waffles abandoned. Of course, I knew that Poppy had moved back down into Mamma's room, and that she had begun closing her door at night, and making the dogs sleep in with me—but a baby! Mamma was fifty-one years old! Surely that's too old for a baby!

"When will this happen, Buck?" Poppy asked very quietly.

Mamma answered through a mouthful of waffle. "At the end of the summer."

"This is a great surprise."

"So the Goddess does love her jokes." Mamma smiled at Poppy, but he turned back to the stove, where the bacon was beginning to burn. He pulled the skillet off the fire, damped the burner, and put the bacon on a plate. He set the plate on the table and then, without another word, disappeared upstairs.

Mamma took a pile of bacon and passed the plate to me. I took two slices but didn't eat them. "Is Poppy mad?"

"No, darling, he's just surprised. You must remember that he was gone when you were born, and you were two years old before he came home. The last baby he remembers is your namesake. I am sure that he cannot help but think of her now."

The memory of what Valefor had told me about the birth of the First Flora dropped into my head: that Mamma had almost died, and only Val's intervention had saved her and Flora, as well. And that had been years ago; when Mamma had been young. She was no spring chicken now, and with Valefor banished he would not be able to intervene if things went bad.

Mamma said confidently, "But Hotspur will be happy, when he gets over the surprise. What do you think—girl or boy? Pass me another waffle; I'm starving. I forgot how hungry I get when I am in pig."

"Girl, of course," I said automatically, still thinking of all the horrible things that could go wrong. And thinking, too, of the Loliga, whose labor pains threatened to destroy us all. Lord Axacaya and I would not let that happen.

"This family already has had three girls. Four if you count me. Don't you think that it's time Poppy had some company?"

"Boys are troublesome and vain, Mamma. Look at Udo."

"I am thinking of Udo, such a handsome boy. Well, we shall get what the Goddess gives us, and we shall like it, too. Why do you look so worried, honey?"

"What if you should die, Mamma? It's not that easy having a baby."

Mamma laughed. "I guess I know how hard it is to have a baby, Flora. I'm not going to die. It's true I'm not so young, but I'm healthy as a horse, and no baby is going to break me. Never you fear. But listen, Flora—about Lord Axacaya, and your confinement—"

"Poppy is unreasonable! It wasn't my fault! And the scene he made—"

Mamma sighed. "And I know all about the scene—happily

the assassination attempt drove it off the front pages, but the CPG managed to find space for it on page two. I understand you could not snub Lord Axacaya; it would have been very bad protocol."

"So my confinement is lifted?" I asked hopefully.

"I'm sorry, Flora. I have to uphold your father. Even though it may seem unfair, it is true that you did speak extremely disrespectfully to him—let me finish. You know that Lord Axacaya is a sore subject with him, and he was only trying to protect you from what he perceived as a threat. Lord Axacaya is no friend to us, Flora. Can you blame Hotspur for being worried for your safety?"

I couldn't believe what I was hearing. Mamma can be many things, but she is almost always fair. And this was completely, totally, not fair. Not fair to me and certainly not fair to Lord Axacaya—Mamma had misjudged him. Hadn't he helped me when I needed help? Wasn't he worried only about the City and her safety? I burned to point all of this out, but, of course, I couldn't. Mamma still didn't know about my earlier brush with Anima Enervation, and I aimed to keep it that way.

"Lord Axacaya was very kind to me, Mamma. And when Poppy threatened him, he didn't raise his hand. Poppy was the one who acted badly."

"Lord Axacaya never strikes openly, Flora," Mamma said, "and I do not disagree that Hotspur overreacted."

I burst out, "How can you agree with me and yet still uphold Poppy? That doesn't make any sense."

"I agree that you could not avoid Lord Axacaya. But you had no call to argue with your father, and that is what he confined you for. And as he was right to take offense at that behavior, I see no reason why I should not confirm his sentence. You were extremely insolent and disrespectful. Can you deny that?"

"But—!"

"Do you deny it?"

"No—but I was no more disrespectful than Poppy was to me!"

"Hotspur's behavior is not the issue here. We are discussing your behavior, and at your own admittance you were disrespectful and insolent."

Now Mamma sounded more like the judge advocate general than a mother. Scratch Mamma and she bleeds Army black; she must always look at things in terms of regulations, even when governing her own family. I know Mamma well enough to know that if I argued with her now, I would only dig myself in deeper. But it wasn't fair!

"Please do not cause me extra trouble, Flora. I have enough as it is, what with Idden gone, and your father in mud with the Warlord. Not to mention riots and seditious editorials, and this Azota cult thing. I depend on you, Flora. Particularly now, with the baby."

My heart almost exploded with guilt. Mamma knows how to put the screws on. I was a few seconds away from bawling. That's how good Mamma is; she can get you to feel wrong about being right.

"However, I will," Mamma continued, "lighten the sentence from two weeks to one. And during the day, you may have the run of the House. You must only retreat to your room at night. You may also take your meals with us, if you like."

Thanks for a big fat load of nothing. I glared at Mamma, but she continued to eat her waffles—and mine—ignoring me. I felt sorry for that poor little baby, blissfully unaware of the awful fate awaiting it. It is horrible to be a Fyrdraaca.

TWENTY-FIVE

A Search. Band Practice. Udo In Heels.

VALEFOR WAS IN raptures about the baby. He twirled about my room, burbling about new blood, new life, new starts. Then he vanished into some distant part of Crackpot Hall to see if he could find the Fyrdraaca layette set. I couldn't argue with the new-life bit, nor with the new start, but it seemed to me that we were talking about the same old Fyrdraaca blood, and that was going to cancel out everything else. If Idden didn't reappear, would Mamma call the new kid Idden Segunda? Was that Mamma's goal—every time she lost a kid, she'd replace it with another? A terrible thought, I know, but now I was full of terrible thoughts.

Like what would happen if Lord Axacaya and I didn't free the Loliga. We'd all be squashed by falling rubble or burned up by fire. That would be it for all the Fyrdraacas, and maybe it would be a good thing, too. The Fyrdraaca line would end.

That was *too* terrible. No one else in the City deserved to be squashed. The City itself did not deserve to fall. And the Loliga deserved to be free. Would Nini Mo lie on her bed, thinking mean and evil things about her parents when there was a City to save?

No, of course not.

Lord Axacaya was counting on me. The City was counting on me, even if the City didn't know it. So I jerked myself out of my brood and tried to focus. I could still follow through with the plan I had made with Lord Axacaya. I would just sneak out again. I had agreed to meet him at midnight at the Lone Mountain Columbarium, which sits just outside the City limits on the Point Lobos Road. Together we would then ride out to Bilskinir House and I would ask Paimon very nicely to help save the City by giving me Georgiana Haðraaða's *Diario*. Or by telling me what was in it. Once Lord Axacaya knew what to do, he would do it. And once the City was saved, surely Lord Axacaya would be impressed enough with my bravery and force of character to agree to teach me Gramatica. I would have proven myself worthy of instruction.

Poppy never showed for my tactic lesson, so I spent the afternoon rereading *The Eschata* and practicing my knot tying. By six o'clock I was bored of knots and I was impatient, but I couldn't sneak out until after bedtime. Then, a stroke of luck.

Mamma had to go to Saeta House, and she took Poppy with her so he could apologize to the Warlord in person. A Formal Apology is long and tedious; it would take them at least four hours, and by the time they came home, I'd be in bed, of course—or at least so they would think. In the meantime, I was left alone, on my own recognizance, from which I did not hesitate to release myself the moment they were out the door. I left behind a closed bed door, and Valefor primed to provide a few diversionary snores, if necessary. As long as I was home by morning, they'd never know I had been gone.

I didn't have to meet Lord Axacaya for an hour or so, which gave me time to do something else first.

AT CASE TIGGER, I found a scene straight out of a yellowback terror novel. The front door was ajar and Case Tigger looked like it had been the scene of room-to-room fighting between several heavily armed factions. Udo's six younger brothers and sisters are constantly locked in a battle for supremacy. A battle that, today at least, appeared to be to the death.

I found Gesilher (age six) barricaded in the pantry, where

he had eaten an entire shelf of jam. There he was rolling about on the floor, sure he had been poisoned, though he was able to pause long enough between convulsions to tell me that Madama Landaðon and the Daddies had gone to Calistoga for three days, leaving Udo in charge, and that as soon as their barouche had turned the corner, Udo had scarpered, leaving the kids to their own devices.

These devices were thus: the Evil Twins, as everyone (even their parents) call Ulrik and Ulrika (eleven), had moved their fight for domination from the mental to the physical; the noxious Gunn-Brit (thirteen) was in the upstairs bathroom tinting her hair green; Ylva (five) had been taken hostage by Ulrik, who was hoping to trade her to Ulrika in return for rights over their favorite orange sweater. Moxley, I was relieved to hear, had gone with his parents—he's only six months old and not yet weaned.

I advised Ges to stay in the pantry until his parents returned—or he died of a surfeit of sugar, whichever came first. Dodged Ulrik and Ulrika's rubber arrow cross fire and made it out of Case Tigger alive. I had a sneaking suspicion I knew where Udo was.

At el Mono Real, this suspicion was confirmed. Bongo, the java-jerk, told me that Udo and the Zu-Zu had been in earlier for coffees, and when they left, they'd been headed back to band practice at her place. Of course, Bongo knew where the Zu-Zu lived because there is nothing about anyone who is cool that Bongo does not know. He scrawled me a map on the back of a takeaway menu.

The Zu-Zu lived in a narrow black house on a narrow black alley in LoHa, the supertrendy part of town where all the supertrendy people live. *The house is as tall and thin as she is,* I thought sourly as I rang the bell, then stood simmering on the black marble stoop. No one answered, so I rang again, banged on the heavy iron door, and then, just because it would make me feel better, kicked at it.

After about five minutes of hammering, the door swung

open, letting out a cloud of cigarillo smoke thick enough to choke a horse.

"Ayah?" The man who answered the door was as tall and pallid as the Zu-Zu, and wore a black velvet smoking jacket. Poppy at his absolute worst had never looked as bad as this guy; his aspect was both corpselike and stoned.

"I'm looking for Udo. Is he here?"

"Udo . . . um . . . who?" the man said, vaguely.

"Udo? Tall, blond, obnoxious taste in hats."

"Oh, ayah, Zu's little boy. Come on in. I saw him around once."

The inside of the house was as foggy as the Bay at midnight, but not nearly as fresh. I followed the Corpse into what I supposed was a parlor, although the clouds of smoke obscured most of the furniture. A group of equally zoned people sat in a circle on the floor playing knickety-knock with a squealing air elemental. They sat like black stones, flicking the poor little thing back and forth, oblivious to its distress.

"Udo?" I asked the Corpse, who'd thrown himself on a fainting sofa and begun puffing on a hookah that was not, I suspected, filled with tobacco.

The Corpse pointed vaguely toward the ceiling. "You look very sweet," he mumbled. "Why don't you come and sit on my lap?"

Ayah, right. I'd rather set myself on fire. I made my way back to the parlor door, not particularly caring if I kicked anyone on the way or not, but then I stopped. The elemental was making a mewling noise like a baby's cry. I went back to the circle and stood there, ignored, and when the elemental was flicked in my direction, I bent down and grabbed it.

The stoners just sat there, staring at nothing. The elemental crouched, shivering, in my hand; it looked like a little hedgehog—a hedgehog with translucent bat wings. Its little pointy nose wiggled anxiously.

"I'll let you go, but not until we are out of here, ayah so?" I whispered to it, not sure if it would understand. What do elementals speak, if they can speak at all? Gramatica, I guess. I did not know how to say anything comforting in Gramatica, so I hoped the creature would take friendliness from my tone. It scurried up my arm and nestled itself inside my coat pocket.

I went up the narrow stairs, jumping over empty bottles and discarded shoes that were strewn on the risers. The upstairs hallway was dim, the walls lined with huge black vases full of dead flowers and pictures of various cemetery-scapes. The first door opened to the filthiest bathroom I had ever seen; it was worse, far worse, than even the bathroom at the Poodle Dog. I hastily closed the door against the stench and hoped that the horrific image had not burned itself into my brain, ready to surface again in my nightmares. You'd think the Warlord's granddaughter would have a maid, but maybe she thought it was cool to be a mess.

The second door revealed a large brass bed piled with five snoring dogs, who were so lazy that they didn't bother to notice me. The wolfish dog closest to the door did open one yellow eye to see who was letting in the cold air, but then dropped the lid closed and went back to snoring. I realized it *was* a wolf and shut the door hastily.

The next door opened to the fluttering glitter of candlelight. At one end of the room stood a small stage, scattered with musical instruments: a drum kit, a banjo, a guitar. Califa's Lip Rouge were not practicing very hard; in front of the stage, they were lolling about on cushions, almost invisible in a fog of cigarillo smoke and incense.

"Udo!" I said sharply.

A tall shape rose from the shadowy sprawl. As Udo came into full view, I almost shrieked with horror. His gorgeous shiny golden hair, his greatest vanity and most cherished possession, was now a flattened jet black, hanging around his face in matted tendrils like limp strands of licorice.

"What did you do to your hair?! It looks horrible. Why did you do it?" Absurdly, I almost felt like crying.

"Zu says I look fabulous." He shook his head so the limp locks covered most of his face.

"Your parents are going to die when they see you," I said. "And speaking of your parents, I went by Case Tigger looking for you and the place is a war zone. Gesilher is locked in the pantry eating his weight in jam, and the Evil Twins are playing slave driver with the other kiddies. I'm not even sure Ylva is still alive. You are supposed to be there, in charge."

Udo waved his hand loftily. "It's not your problem, Flora. I can handle it." His breath smelled strongly of spice—boozy spice. And he towered over me, too; when I looked down, I saw why. He was still wearing Springheel Jack's red boots, and the heels of those boots were a full five inches high. I didn't see how he could even stand in them.

"What do you want, Flora?" The Zu-Zu coalesced out of the shadows like an Underfed Apparition. "We are busy in practice." She grabbed ahold of his arm, and he, in turn, slid his arm around her scrawny shoulders.

"I want conversation with Udo."

"Here I am; converse," Udo said impatiently.

"Privately." Before he could protest further, I yanked him away from the Zu-Zu and into a corner.

He shook off my grip, glowering, but didn't retreat. "What do you want, Flora? I thought we said all there was to say before."

"I'm sorry about Springheel Jack."

"Your blasted denizen ate him."

"Ayah, but he left the boots, the important part. You can still get the bounty on the boots. But I really don't think you should be wearing them."

"That's my business, not yours, Flora. You said you wanted nothing to do with me or my crazy schemes. So why don't you just go?"

"Springheel Jack clearly had some magickal powers, or he wouldn't have been able to bounce so far, or fast. You don't know what those boots can do. Listen to me. It's important."

"It's always important when Flora says it's important," Udo said. "Well, I got important time, too, and now ain't it. Go away, Flora."

While Udo and I had been talking, the Zu-Zu and her minions had somehow found enough energy to get up off their cushions and stumble to the stage. The hurdy-gurdy player turned his crank once, and the noise nearly deafened me. Califa's Lip Rouge's instruments were already charged; it takes a lot of Current and a lot of magickal juice to keep a band's instruments permanently infested with Amplification Dæmons. Someone in Califa's Lip Rouge was a pretty good magician. Surely not the Zu-Zu.

Without another word to me, Udo sprang away, leaping across the room in one giant bounce to join the band. He did a little shuffle, and my unease grew when I saw that the snake heads on each boot had come to life and were snapping and spitting.

"Take the boots off, Udo, and let's go. I don't have much time," I pleaded.

"She's in a hurry," said the Zu-Zu. "I'm sure she has many important places to go and many important things to do."

"Everything that Flora does is important, but nothing that anyone else does ever is." Udo took the tambourine the Zu-Zu handed him, and shook it mockingly at me.

Behind him, the rest of the band broke into a shuffling rhythm, the rat-ta-tat of the drums providing a steady backbeat to the banjo's twang. Anger flared in me. I should just give up and go. Let Udo have his fun. Yet I didn't like the way the light was glinting off those sparkly red boots, or the way Udo was suddenly cavorting and jumping in them. Udo's a good dancer, but he'd never been that energetic before.

"Play 'Fire Down Below!'" the Zu-Zu ordered.

The rhythm turned into the opening stanzas of the song, and Udo tapped out a few steps and gave a little twirl. A single spark flew as his left heel snapped down hard on the floor, and then another spark, from his right heel. As the tempo of the song picked up, so did Udo's tap dancing—and let me tell you, in all the years that I had known Udo I had never seen him tap-dance before.

"There's a fire all around, me kids—it's playing hide-and-seek," Udo sang.

"Hey, hey, hey, hey, ho!" the band chorused.

"It's trying to find a bunk, me kids, for to get some sleep."

"Hey, hey, hey, hey, ho!" The Boy Toys laughed and clapped as Udo leaped and twirled, his lank hair flying about him like rope. The sparks were growing larger with each strike of his boot heel, and the snake heads were snapping and hissing. Udo's face had gone taut with concentration, and sweat beaded his forehead. There was something familiar about his gestures, and the movements were so out of the ordinary for Udo that it took me a moment to recognize them.

Udo was preparing to Invoke.

But Udo didn't know how to Invoke anything.

"Udo! Stop!" I ran at the stage, but he was already a whirl of motion, gliding and jumping, leaping and bouncing, the clatter of the sparkly red heels louder than the drumming. The drumming grew louder and the sparks from the red boots brighter, sizzling wildly as they flew about the small room.

The song was no longer about a fire down below; Udo was now spitting out smoky, burning Gramatica Words that he couldn't possibly know on his own, and these Words were enveloping him in a whirling, whirring cocoon. The coldfire light was so bright that when I held up my arm to shield my eyes, they burned with a spotted afterglow.

The drums stopped. The music stopped. I peeked out from under my arm and saw only a bright roiling mass where Udo had stood. The cocoon began to shred and tear, great skeins of coldfire flinging about in the air, sizzling as they fell. A hand— Another hand— Two arms— The cocoon split down the middle and fell away, and there was Udo. He did another little jig, and the snake heads on his boot toes spit venom through gleaming fangs.

"I am myself again!" Udo crowed.

But plainly Udo was not himself at all. His features hadn't changed, and yet somehow he looked different. His head tilted at an unfamiliar angle, and the smile lurking around his lips was sardonic and cruel. Udo's eyes are light blue, the color of the summer sea. But now these blue eyes had turned an acrid, wolf-ish yellow. He no longer looked like Udo. He looked like a cruel, sadistic killer. He looked like Springheel Jack.

Horror flooded me as I realized the sparkly red boots *were* Springheel Jack. The flesh was merely a vessel. The boots were the true Will. They had enscorcelled Udo, possessed him. Changed him from a boy to an outlaw.

Nini Mo said, *Vanity is a silken scarf that gets caught in the wheel of your barouche and snaps your neck like a pretzel.* I think Udo had just proven that to be true, though with an entirely different fashion accessory.

Springheel Jack crowed, "Who then is the Jack of All Trades? The Jack-o'-Lantern, Jack Be Nimble, Jack in the Box? I am he, the Jack of Hearts, Jackhammer, the Jack Knife! Lum-berjack, Steeplejack, Bootjack, Dancejack, and Jack Dandy! Jackaroo—"

"Jackanapes!" I shouted. "Jack Pudding, Cheap Jack, Jack All, Jack Daw!"

Springheel Jack glared at me. The glare turned into an ugly, lascivious leer that made Udo's beautiful face look like a gar-goyle. Jack bounced. He landed with a thundering roar and the room shook. Another bounce, his hair flying behind him like an oily torn flag, brought him in front of me.

He enfolded me into an embrace of iron, and then, despite my squirms, kissed me with lips that were hard and wet. In the sentimental novels, when the villain sweeps the heroine into his arms, the heroine is quickly overcome by his burning kisses, by the strength of his ardor. Jack's kiss didn't burn; it felt as though he was trying to mash my lips into my skull.

"Ooof—" I pounded on whatever part of him I could reach, which didn't do a darn bit of good. I elevated my knee and gave

FLORA'S DARE503
him a good jab right where it counts, and he released me with a yelp. The Zu-Zu and her Boy Toys were laughing hysterically, though the situation had no humor in it at all.

"I'll remember that, girlie," Springheel Jack said ominously. Another bounce took him across the room, and then, with a crash, he jumped through the window.

Springheel Jack—Udo—was gone.

TWENTY-SIX

Shaking.
Another Parrot. Stealing.

BY THE TIME I GOT down the stairs and out on the street, there was no sign of Springheel Jack. Those sparkly red boots had lift; who knows where he had sprung away to? How high, how far, how fast—it didn't matter. What mattered was that he was gone.

What was I going to do now? I still had to meet Lord Axacaya, but I couldn't just let Udo bounce off into the night to commit mayhem, thievery, and terror. But how was I going to find him?

As if to remind me of the urgency of my first errand, the ground began to wiggle beneath my feet. I grabbed the front stoop banister and held on. This trembler was the biggest so far; the air filled with the screeching sound of shifting stone and wrenching wood. The house across the street had gorgeous planters hanging outside its windows; one by one they detached from the windowsills and crashed down, scattering dirt and flowers. The streetlamp flickered and went out. The ground buckled and heaved, cobblestones quivering like jelly. Shrieking people began to spill out of houses, staggering on the rolling ground as though they were drunk.

Maybe this was it—the last big quake. Maybe it was too late—the Sigil had weakened enough to let the Loliga extract her revenge. Mamma, Poppy, the mite in Mamma's tummy, silly Flynn—how would rickety Crackpot stand against this force? The elemental I had rescued was burrowing down my collar, tickling my neck, tiny claws catching on my skin. I held on to the iron railing with all my might, though it leaped under my grip like a bucking horse. I closed my eyes so that if the Zu-Zu's house fell on me I would not see it coming. The earthquake seemed to go on forever, but after a while, the trembling began to lessen, then ceased completely.

I opened my eyes. The air was boiling with dust, but through the cloud I saw that the City (or at least this part of it) still stood. Just barely. A giant crack had appeared in the middle of the street, and houses were listing like storm-damaged trees. A few doors down, an entire building had collapsed; it looked like a pile of toothpicks. I stood up, wiping dust from my face, tasting grit in my mouth. The Zu-Zu's house looked fine. Too bad.

The elemental launched itself out of my collar and disappeared into the dust cloud. It was getting out while the getting was good. Smart thing.

The temblor decided me. Udo would have to take his chances as Springheel Jack for a few hours. If the City fell around our ears, what would his sparkly red fashion disaster matter? The Landaðon kiddies were also on their own. I only hoped that Ulrik and Ulrika would put their feud aside in the face of disaster. I had to get to the Lone Mountain Columbarium and meet Lord Axacaya. The City was running out of time.

I ran up Fillman Street, toward the Lone Mountain jitney stop at Fillman and Turk, hoping the jitney was still running. As I ran, huffing and puffing in those stupid tight stays, I passed a whole lot of mess: screaming people, broken masonry, barking dogs, all nightmarish and shadowy in the light of broken street lamps—or, sometimes, just plain dark.

There was no sign of the jitney, and judging from the snarl of traffic, even if there was a jitney still running, it wouldn't be getting very far very fast. It was the same for cabs. I would have to walk.

I dodged up Turk. A woman pushed a baby carriage the size of a sixty-pound cannon; a man carried a rocking chair; another man led six dogs on a tandem lead, the dogs all pulling and jumping in different directions. I don't know where everyone thought they were going. When the earth is shaking, nowhere in the City is safe, but I guess people weren't thinking too straight—too scared to stay put. The only thing preventing the throngs from turning into a panicked mob were the City militia, who were out in force, keeping order with much whistle blowing and truncheon waving. But no gas gun. I guess Mamma had made good on her threat to have it confiscated.

I ducked between two guards and dashed by them, narrowly missing being run over by a fire squad barreling down the street, horns blowing, fire dogs barking. Another guard tried to grab me, but I dodged around him and kept going, ignoring his shouts and threats. Then I saw, fluttering over the crowd, a splotch of bright blue: Axacaya's parrot. I followed the parrot's flight path, shoving my way around a woman carrying a screaming baby, a cluster of howling schoolkids, another whacking militiaman. The parrot darted into an alley, and so did I.

The bird landed on the lip of a trash bin and cocked its brilliant head.

"Axa say go ahead without!" the parrot croaked.

"Go to Bilskinir without him?"

"Ayah," the parrot replied. "Quickly!"

It launched up and off into the darkness before I could ask it why, where, or—most importantly—how. Bilskinir House sits on the edge of the Pacifica Ocean, a full six miles from the City line. I doubted very much that the Point Lobos horsecar was running, and it would take me hours to walk out there, even if there was no traffic at all. But I had to get there, and quickly.

You gotta do what you gotta do, Nini Mo said.

What would Nini Mo do? She would beg, borrow, or steal transportation—anything to get where she needed to go. The first two options seemed unlikely to be successful in this hulla-baloo. That left the last.

So that's what I did: I stole a horse.

TWENTY-SEVEN

Horsejacking. Bilskinir House. Let Me In!

HORSEJACKING turned out to be surprisingly easy. I left the alley and jumped back into the flood of people streaming up Turk, with the idea of heading toward the horsecar barn at Turk and Division. If it was still standing, perhaps I could take advantage of the confusion to help myself to a ride. Getting through the panicked crowds was hard going—in fifteen minutes I barely made it half a block, and I was stepped on twice, almost run over once, and pushed, shoved, kicked, and yelled at many times. But then, as I reached the intersection, the Goddess granted me her favor.

Ahead of me, the hordes parted and a horse trotted straight toward me. It wore a saddle, but its reins were dragging, and by this I guessed that it had been tied up somewhere, jerked free during the earthquake, and bolted. Its head was bouncing nervously, and its eyes were rolling back and forth, trying to look everywhere at once. When the horse saw the fountain on the southwest corner of the intersection (a monument to some victory of the Warlord's), it rushed over and plunged its muzzle happily into the water. Carefully, slowly, I sidled up, slow and casual, and took hold of the bridle, coiling the reins around my hand.

No one shouted at my daring, and the horse didn't jerk away. Instead, it turned to me, nuzzling me somewhat gratefully. Horses feel better when they have company, and I can't say I blame them—you always feel braver with two. The horse ducked its head again, slurping more water, and when it was done, it turned an inquiring eye my direction as if to say *What now?*

The saddle was pretty fancy, of well-worn tooled leather, studded with conchos. The stirrups were too long, but I would have to wait until I got out of the crowd to shorten them. I used the rim of the fountain to mount up, and even then, I had to hop pretty high, for that horse was big—at least eighteen hands. The advantage of being mounted was immediately clear. People who weren't going to move for the 135 pounds of me were quicker to get out of the way of a thousand pounds of horse. Within a few minutes we had veered off Turk and started out the Lobos Road. The road was also clogged with people, but by the time we reached the Presidio crossroads, the way had cleared enough that I could give Sieur Caballo his head.

He took it and flew. The wind rushed through my hair and stung my face, the dark night a blur around me. My brain, which should have been on the future, was fixed on the past. Fixed on Udo. I was a total idiot—I should have seen the danger of Springheel Jack's boots earlier. When Valefor said that the boots were the source of Jack's power, I should have realized he meant it literally. The boots wore the man, not the other way around. When the boots had lost their host, they turned to the nearest replacement: Udo. They had beguiled him and turned his own weakness—vanity—against him. How could I have not seen that? No wonder Udo had been acting so strange. I should have realized he had not been himself.

But I couldn't do anything to help him, not yet. All I could do was hope that he wouldn't do anything foolish—rob the Califa National Bank or cut all his hair off, for example. And as soon as the City was safe, I would find him and figure out a way to get him unenscorcelled. Ayah, Udo had been a complete and total snapperhead, but I couldn't let Springheel Jack have him.

My brain churned with recrimination against myself, and

with fear that by the time the City was saved, it would be too late for Udo. And that maybe it was already too late for the City—that the Loliga was close to exacting her revenge. Round and round went these thoughts, and then, suddenly, we crested the edge of the Pacifica Playa and there, high over the Pacifica Ocean, was Bilskinir House, a black silhouette against the star-flecked sky.

The road to Bilskinir's front gate starts down on the Playa and then crawls up the cliff, and only at low tide is the foot of the road dry. Alas for me, when I arrived, the tide was high and the bottom of the road was flooded. By my watch, it was just one o'clock in the morning. I couldn't wait for low tide, whenever that might be. But from my previous dealings with Paimon, I knew he could control the weather around his House. Surely he could pull the tide back and let me in.

"Paimon!" I shouted. *"Paimon!"*

Sieur Caballo splashed along the tide line, toward the cause-way. He was lathered and thirsty, but I had nothing to water him with, poor boy. I petted his sweaty neck; he dipped his nose down into the surf and then tossed his head, snorting salt water. The wind was roaring straight off the ocean, blowing my hair in my eyes, and freezing my ears into lumps of ice. I flipped my collar up, which helped only my neck. But that was better than nothing.

"PAIMON! LET ME IN!" The wind and the pound of the surf tore my screams into shreds, tossed the pieces aloft into the night sky, where they were lost. The bulk of Bilskinir, rearing above me like a colossus, remained blank. Not a single light shone through its blackness. If I had not known that the hulking shadow was a House, it could easily be mistaken for a lofty rock formation. Where was Paimon?

The ocean began to slosh—waves wiggling not in a forward surge, but in a muddle, as though someone was stirring it with a giant laundry stick. A roaring rattle drowned out the ocean's pound, and Sieur Caballo shied suddenly, scrambling out of the surf and away from the cliff face. I almost slid off his back; my thigh muscles were whining with pain. Rocks scattered down the cliff, splashing into the water; first a few, and then a whole bunch. I hung on to the saddle horn as the horse bounced back onto the beach and shied down shifting sand. Then, suddenly, the aftershock was over. The ocean went back to its natural pounding; the sand blew only with the wind, and Sieur Caballo stood with his head hanging, somewhat abashed he had almost lost his cool. I patted his neck to show him that I didn't blame him one bit.

Now we stood at the bottom of Bilskinir's foundations, and the cliff reared sheer above us. When I looked straight up, the perspective listed, so that for one horrible moment it appeared the entire House was about to fall upon us. It remained completely dark and impenetrable.

"Paimon, please let me in," I mumbled. Still no answer.

There's always a back door, Nini Mo said. Bilskinir sat high above—if there was a back door, it had to be here, below, set in the House's foundations. And then I remembered the map I'd found in *The Eschata*—hadn't it said something about back doors? I dismounted and used Sieur Caballo's bulk as a shelter from the spray; I dug the map out of my dispatch case and opened it up, sparking an ignis light, so I could see it in the dark. The scale of the map was much larger than I had remembered it, large enough that Bilskinir House and its surroundings were rendered in pretty close detail—so close that even the individual tidal pools were marked.

"Back door, back door," I muttered, scanning the map—finding Avenue Bilskinir, Grand Gardens, Seal Rock, Point Lobos Road, and then: "The Haðraaða Gate (Bilskinir's Back Door)." According to the map, the entrance was on the south side of the cliff, not too far from where Avenue Bilskinir, the main drive, began.

A Direction Sigil is one of the simplest sigils there is (and one of the most important, too, for rangers always should know which way to go). It took me only a minute to charge a piece of driftwood with my desired terminus. I didn't remount, just tucked the reins under my arms. I'd done a pretty good job with the Direction Sigil—my Will to get inside Bilskinir was pretty darn strong—so I could hardly keep hold of the charged driftwood, it was pulling so hard. We clambered over slippery rocks, across sandy shoals, hugging the bottom of the cliff. Then, up ahead, a welcoming light glittered in the darkness. The charged driftwood jerked galvanically, flew out of my hands, and splashed into a tidal pool. No matter, I didn't need it now.

The source of the light turned out to be a small notch in the rocks. Warm air was curling out of the cleft, fragrant with the most delicious smell of fresh-baked cookies. Ginger cookies, if my nose knew ginger cookies, which it does, as they are my favorite. Who else would be baking cookies on such a blustery night but Paimon? On my last visit to Bilskinir, I had discovered that his savage and horrific appearance was merely the outward shell for a deeply domestic interior.

"I'm sorry I have to leave you, but you'll be all right," I said, patting the horse's nose. He nudged me doubtfully, but he would have to take care of himself. I pulled his bridle and saddle off, but he didn't immediately wander away, just stood there staring forlornly as I clutched my dispatch case to my chest and squeezed into the cleft.

Immediately, the roar of the wind and ocean ceased. The rocky walls were slick with water and claustrophobically narrow, but at least the air was warm. I couldn't see where the diffused light was coming from. Behind me I heard a sad whine from Sieur Caballo, who hadn't given up on me yet.

The passageway was twisty, and in some places so tight that I had to squeeze sideways to get through. But the smell of baking cookies carried me onward and provided a distraction from the unfortunate realization that if there was another earthquake, and Paimon could not hold his foundations firm, I would be squashed for sure. Normally I am not claustrophobic, but despite the increasing warmth of the air, I was soon in a cold sweat.

The light began to fade, and the passage became merely a crack. I took my dispatch case off, and swung it by its strap. I turned sideways so I could crab along in the dimness. Rock scraped my back, rock scraped my nose. The crack got thinner and thinner; for one blood-freezing moment, I thought I was stuck, wedged between the walls like a slice of cheese between two pieces of bread. Desperately, I sucked everything in and then—panic surging, clothing tearing—was through.

The passageway was still narrow, but at least I no longer had to walk sideways. The light was now so dim I could hardly see my hand in front of me. I had a collapsible lantern in my dispatch case but no room to dig the lantern out. I tried to ignite another ignis light, but my Will was starting to falter, and the resulting spark wasn't very bright. Still, it was better than nothing.

Maybe this wasn't really Bilskinir's Back Door. Maybe the map was wrong. Maybe this was just one of Bilskinir's air vents—I'd reach the end and find myself in Bilskinir's furnace. Or maybe Bilskinir's garbage chute. Or even—as an acrid smell began to cancel out the delicious cookie odor—one of Bilskinir's drains.

Save your fright for the campfire, Nini Mo said. Instead of thinking fearful thoughts, I should put all my energies into believing that the map had not led me astray. Just a little farther, and then, if I had to, I would turn back.

The passage began to narrow again, this time horizontally. First, I was stooping, then crouching, then bending, and then finally crawling along on all fours. Although the ground was sandy, it was still cold and damp, and scratchy on my hands and knees. Now I pushed my dispatch case before me, and soon I was on my tum, slithering like a worm, rock again scraping my back. My ignis light fluttered and gave out, and darkness descended, as heavy and oppressive as the rock pressing down upon me. I stopped crawling and rested my forehead on my dispatch case, sand grating on my cheek, then took a deep breath so as not to be overwhelmed with panic.

There is no way out but through. My knees and hands were sore, my shoulder sore, and I was out of breath. And terribly thirsty, too. I managed to get my dispatch case open, and fumbled for my flask. After a drink of water and a piece of chocolate, I felt better. Hadn't Nini Mo been in tighter squeezes? Had she given up? I could lie here in the darkness and die a worm, or keep going and do my duty. If I gave up now, died, or went back—Lord Axacaya would know me for a failure.

"For this we are rangers," I said, and my voice sounded weak and fearful.

"For this we are rangers!" I said again, and this time my voice sounded stronger, though still slightly wobbly.

"For this we are rangers!" Now my voice sounded powerful and bright, and I felt better. Worm, worm, worm, I went, and slowly the darkness began to lighten and the passageway widen a bit— not enough so that I could stand upright, but enough that I could get off my tum. A sonorous hum filled the passageway, and ahead of me, a silver light appeared. The hum grew louder, turned into a buzz, like a million cicadas rubbing their legs together. The air ahead began to sparkle and glow, as if each atom were on fire. When I swallowed, I tasted the Current. Then, a Vortex—a magickal portal—popped into existence, some five feet ahead.

The Vortex filled the passageway, whirling like a pinwheel with diamond-bright edges sharp enough to cut through the Waking World, to slice a door from here to somewhere else—who knows where? The Vortex whirled toward me: my bones began to vibrate, my teeth began to buzz. I was trapped like a bug in a rug. I ducked my head down, clutched my bag, and tried to brace myself. My hair grew stiff with static. A hot howling galvanic charge surrounded me—the dizzying sensation of falling—I opened my mouth to shriek, and sucked in water. Choked, and then . . .

TWENTY-EIGHT

Soggy. Swamped. The Mirror.

I CHOKED AND WHEEZED and choked again. Someone rolled me over on my face and thumped my back. Still choking. Another thump—this time really, really hard. I gagged, gurgled, upchucked a hot rush of water. I convulsed and spit, and coughed and spit, and convulsed and coughed again. But I was breathing.

A voice said, "Where the hell did you come from?"

Still gasping, I opened my eyes, saw a swampy marble floor and two bare feet. The feet were small and white and the toenails were chipped with red.

"You ruined my Working!" the voice said accusingly.

The white feet were attached to white ankles; the white ankles were attached to white calves, which disappeared into a giant shocking-pink skirt that was square and wide. Above the flat top of the skirt: a low-cut bodice, rounded cleavage, white shoulders, and a white neck surrounded by a stiff spiky lace ruff. And above—I would have shouted if I'd had the breath. My rescuer had the curvy body of a girl but the shaggy head of a black bear.

The Bear Girl's muzzle yawned, displaying very white sharp teeth. "Can you understand me?"

"Ayah. Where am I?" I sat up, ignoring the swimmingly dizzy feeling in my head, and saw in the flaring candlelight the pool from which I had been dragged. No, not a pool, but a perfectly round bathtub. Water had overflowed its rim and swamped the floor. Also swamped was the remnant of what clearly had been some sort of magickal Working: the pillar candles that ringed the bathtub were still burning, but the cornmeal sigils drawn on the floor had dissolved into a soggy mess. A pink plushy pig almost identical to my pink plushy pig sat upon the potty, which was as toweringly tall as a throne, gilded and carved.

"You ruined my fiking Working," the Bear Girl said. "I spent two whole weeks getting ready, fasting and gorging and purging. Then I had to wait until the Current was high enough and Paimon was busy elsewhere—and *him,* too—and you fiking ruined it all."

I clambered to my feet. My legs and knees felt wobbly, and a spike of pain was beginning to throb over my left eye, but I had to shake the weakness off and focus. My shoulders felt oddly light and I realized that I had lost my dispatch case. And my boots, too. And my redingote. And my stays had sprung open. I pulled them the rest of the way off—good riddance—and hastily tucked the ranger badge back into my chemise before the bear-headed girl noticed it.

Was I in Bilskinir? Who was this bear-headed girl with the foul mouth? In my muddled state, I couldn't remember seeing bear-human hybrids at Bilskinir before. A Vortex can go anywhere. I could be anywhere. All I knew for sure was that this bear-headed girl wasn't friendly.

"Well?" she demanded. "What the fike do you have to say?"

Play it close until you know the situation, said Nini Mo.

"That was one mighty big Vortex. What were you trying to do?" I coughed, trying to buy both time and information.

"I was trying to scry my future," the Bear Girl said loftily, "using a pool of the Current as my mirror. I had the Vortex open, and the Current was just starting to reflect when you popped out of the Vortex, and, fike, that was it. Where the fike did you come from? How the fike did you get into my bathtub?"

I might not know where I was, but I knew the Working she

was talking about. It's in chapter 52 of *The Eschata*, in the section labeled "Excruciatingly Dangerous: for Reference Only." In her notes, Nini warns that it's not such a good idea to know your future: Such knowledge will either paralyze you with fear or make you go mad with despair, depending on the nature of your fate. The Bear Girl was clearly reckless—and skilled, too. To create a Vortex of that size requires a tremendous amount of Will and Concentration, and making the Current reflect is even harder.

The Bear Girl bared her gleaming fangs. "Are you from the future? The Vortex was open to the Future when you came through."

I didn't answer. The bathroom was walled with mirrors, and these mirrors reflected back, in a fun-house sort of way, a whole slew of angry Bear Girls, and soggy Floras, sloshy tubs, flickering candles, and wrecked Workings. And something that was not reflected in multitudes, but only singularly: a little point of coldfire that had winked into existence over the bathtub.

I saw this coldfire spark in the mirror behind the Bear Girl, which meant that it was really behind me, but when I looked over my shoulder at the tub, there was no coldfire there. I looked back into the mirror. The light, which a moment ago had been a mere pinprick, was growing.

"Are you?" the girl persisted.

"Did you close your Vortex?" I asked.

She followed my glance, then let loose with a string of curses that could have fermented grape juice. "*Fike! Scit!* You made me forget to close the Vortex! FIKING SCIT!"

The light was the size of an orange now. A sudden gust of wind billowed from the mirror—the pillar candles fluttered and extinguished.

"Don't just stand there! Close it!" I had to shout over the sound of rushing air. How could air rush out of a mirror? Never mind—it was. The Vortex only existed in the mirror. How could something exist only in a reflection? Never mind—it did.

I could barely keep my eyes open against the wind. The

Vortex had grown to the size of a wheel—not a baby-cart wheel, but the wheel from a giant caisson for a giant gun, fully four feet across.

The Bear Girl waved her arms and shouted something in Gramatica, but the wind from the Vortex blew her sparkly Words back into her face and she staggered backward, choking on them. I put my hands up against my eyes, pushing my hair out of my face, and peered through my slitted fingers. There was movement within the Vortex—was I imagining that I could see something within this movement? Something that looked like a hairy finger, curved with a long curving talon? Somehow I knew to the very marrow of my bones that whomever that finger belonged to, it was Super Fantastic Bad News.

"CLOSE THE VORTEX!" I screamed at the Bear Girl.

The Bear Girl screamed back at me, "I TRIED! IT WON'T FIKING CLOSE! FIKE FIKE FIKE!"

The wind was pushing us backward; I staggered against the bathtub in a bright splash of pain; the Bear Girl fell against me. We clutched each other, for all the good that would do us. Out of the corner of my eye, I noticed the plushy pig still sitting, lordly, on his throne. His floppy ears were blowing back, but otherwise he looked unconcerned.

The Bear Girl was yelling something; I could barely hear her above the roar of the wind, but it sounded like "PIG PIG PIG!" I looked over the Bear Girl's shoulder—the one finger had become many fingers, an entire hand—no, two hands—grabbing at the edges of the Vortex, stretching it open so that the rest of the Superbad News could come through.

The wind pinned us into place; we were huddled up against the bathtub, which kept us from being flung against the far wall. All sound had been reduced to a solid roar, and I swear I could feel my flesh blowing off my bones, rippling like water.

Superbad News kicked at the mirror with one large splay-toed foot, and the glass shattered into a thousand flying pieces. I closed my eyes against the flying shards, and when I managed to open them again, a dæmon had stepped out of the mirror.

He was the exact color of swamp slime, greenish brown and glistening with ooze, with a toad-faced head, and a squat toad-like body—and, Pigface, did he smell bad, like rat-burger cheese, and blueberry poo-filled nappies, and rotting wet wool, and a hundred other horrible odors. I recognized him from *The Eschata Entity Spotter*: a tenth-level kakodæmon, whose stench can kill.

I tried very hard to breathe through my mouth. The Bear Girl wrenched out of my grip and hurled a bottle at him. It hit him in the head and doused him with blue bubble-bath—at least now he'd smell better—but it didn't stop him. Trailing stink, the kakodæmon sprang down from the sink, swiping at the Bear Girl with one gnarly hand. His clout hit its mark. I watched in horror as her head flew up and off, soaring through the air and landing with a splash in the bathtub. She collapsed like a rag doll.

A pink shape whizzed by me and hit the kakodæmon square on its bulbous nose, clinging there. The kakodæmon howled, scratching at his own face, his talons slicing deep lines into his cheeks, but the plushy Pig clung like a lamprey and would not be dislodged.

A Gramatica Word, thick and turgid as a black slug, squirmed out of the kakodæmon's mouth. It leeched onto the Pig, which let go of the kakodæmon's nose and dropped to the floor, where it and the Word began to writhe and roll. The kakodæmon, blood streaming from the gaping hole where his nose had been, staggered toward me.

"⟠⟐⟡ ⟐⟐⟡⟐!" The Gramatica Command shot out of my mouth, almost dislocating my jaw. Buzzing like a swarm of wasps, the Command hit the kakodæmon in his barrel chest and flung him backward, into the center of the Vortex. The Vortex snapped closed with a *pop* that almost turned every solid in my body to mush. My bones dissolved and I plopped to the ground in a heap.

After a while, the blankness began to resolve into a decidedly unpleasant soggy feeling. A while after that, the sog turned chilly; the marble floor was burning cold against my back, and something bright and painful was gouging my side: Broken mirror? Broken glass? Broken rib? I couldn't quite summon up enough interest to investigate further. A warm trickle pooled in my lips; I licked, and tasted blood. Somewhere a buzzer was ringing, insistently, or maybe it was a fly right by my ear; no, the buzzing was *in* my ears. I hoped the noise wasn't permanent, for if it was, it would drive me mad. I decided to get up. But it took a little while for my bones to harden up enough that I could rise, just as far as my knees.

From that not-so-lofty height, a horrific scene of destruction spread forth. All that remained of the Vortex was the cold-fire splattering the ceiling, the floor, the cracked mirror. Blackish water had sloshed from the tub, washing the marble floor with putrid-smelling liquid. One pillar candle still burned, defiantly; the others had melted into charred piles of glassy wax. Silver oozed down the wall where the mirror had been. The awful stench still hung on the air, but much less strongly.

The only thing in the room that had survived intact was the thronelike potty. The plushy Pig had resumed perching upon its closed lid, as though he had never left it. I gave him the hairy eyeball, but he did not return the look. Was his snout a little redder? Perhaps blushed with blood? Maybe it was a trick of the sputtering lamplight. I didn't plan on examining him more closely.

The Bear Girl had collapsed on the far side on the tub. All I could see were massive pink skirts, which looked rather like a fallen angel food cake. I crawled through the soggy cornmeal, which had solidified into a sort of wet dough, over the fallen candlesticks, trying to avoid the broken glass. Pulling myself up on the edge of the tub, I steeled myself. If I'd had the sense the Goddess Califa gave a duck, I'd have scarpered, but I had no sense, only the burning desire to *look*.

For this we are rangers, I whispered, as I looked down, expecting to see the Bear Girl's head bobbing in the water. Something hairy and black *was* floating there.

For this we are rangers, I repeated to myself, and reached gingerly down to fish the scalp out. It was limp and slimy—gaping eyeholes, gaping mouth. Then I realized, with bladder-weakening relief, that it wasn't a scalp at all.

It was an extremely realistic mask.

TWENTY-NINE

Masks. Nursie. Lies.

AT MY FEET, the shocking-pink silk skirts trembled and heaved into an upright position, revealing an extremely human head. The Girl clutched it, groaning and swearing.

I held out my hand, and she took it. Grunting, I managed to haul her to her feet, though I still felt weak and wobbly myself.

The Girl moaned and said a lot of words, all of them foul. The entire left side of her face was already turning purple, and she was going to have a magnificent black eye. She picked a piece of mirror up off the floor and peered into it, baring her tiny white teeth as though to make sure they were all there and her jaw still worked. "What the fike happened?"

"The kakodæmon whacked you, and then I kicked it back through the Vortex and closed it down." I didn't mention that I had no idea *how* I had kicked the kakodæmon or closed the Vortex down. *Always act like you expected it all along*, said Nini Mo. My mouth, tongue, and throat felt as though I'd just gulped down an entire pot of scalding-hot tea—just another pain to add to the rest.

"I look like a clown!" she complained. "Califa fike it! Ratsbane!"

"You look alive."

"I am alive," she said wonderingly. "I thought I was a goner, but I'm not. I'm still alive. Suck on that, you fiking kakodæmon!"

The Girl threw her head back and howled with laughter. I began to howl with laughter, too. We fell upon each other, clutching and howling, laughing so hard we were crying, so hard we could barely breathe. We staggered out of the bathroom, into the room beyond, which was cozy and warm with firelight, and collapsed on the sofa.

"I thought I was dead!" the Girl shrieked.

"I thought we were both dead!" I shrieked back.

"That was the ugliest pottlely pumpion I've ever seen in my life!"

"A weedy rude-growing clack dish!"

"A bootless rough-hewn whey-face!"

"Hope he likes his new *nose!*"

"He fiked with the wrong people!" she screamed, and in this case, I agreed with her language wholeheartedly. He had indeed fiked with the wrong people.

"Fike him!"

"And the Vortex he rode in on!" I shrieked back, and again we were speechless with laughter. There's nothing like barely escaping disaster to make you scream with joy. We laughed and rolled and howled and cried until our stomach muscles hurt, our eyes burned, our noses ran, and we were so out of breath that we could barely sputter.

The Girl staggered over to the rocker by the huge blue-tiled stove. She nudged the rocker with her foot. "Nursie! Make us some xocholattes."

The shadow in the rocker coalesced into a plump old woman, with a ruffled hat like a cabbage and little raisin eyes. A nursery servitor—a fragment of a domicilic denizen, created to care for children. I'd heard of them but (thanks to Mamma) never actually seen one. A smile creased Nursie's powdered cheeks, and she toddled over to the stove, where she began to potter around with a chocolate pot.

The room continued the childlike theme. It was small and snug and very cozy. On the rug by the tiled stove (tiles painted with animals), tin soldiers beseiged a towering dollhouse; the window seat was heaped with dolls and stuffed animals; and the book shelves were stacked with games, building sets, and kiddie books. The walls were papered with monkeys jumping on beds, and carved monkeys cavorted on the heavy wooden mantel and climbed up the chimneypiece.

And all this was very odd because the Girl was not a child; she looked at least fifteen, or even (based on her cleavage) sixteen. Her face was mostly obscured under smeared maquillage and bruises, but what I could see indicated she was cute in a round baby-doll way. Her hair had been tortured into three stiff braids and bundled together into a topknot, each braid a different color—red, black, gold. This hairstyle is worn only by the cadets at the Benica Barracks Military Academy. I was relieved to know I was still in the Waking World, but what was a Benica cadet doing in a nursery?

"Who are you?" I asked.

"Shush! We can't talk here—come on! Come *on*!" The Girl disappeared into the room beyond, which, when I followed her, was revealed to be a night nursery, dominated by an enormous bed. At each corner of the bed, a blue lacquered squid stood on its fluted tail, tentacles entwining upward to support a wooden canopy. The bed's blue curtains were closed; in the dim light they shimmered like a sheet of water. I was instantly jealous. I've always longed for a huge canopy bed—so cozy yet with room for you and all the dogs, and a heap of books besides. My bed is snug, but sometimes it feels just like the broom closet it once was.

The Girl hoisted herself up one of the squid columns. Clearly she had done this often, for she shimmied up it easily; at the top, she swung over the edge of the canopy and disappeared.

A rope slithered down from above and almost whacked me in the head—but if she could climb up one of those ten-foot-tall squids, I could, too. I jumped up, grabbed at a bulbous squid eye and started hauling, mentally thanking Archangel Bob for his insistence that I keep at Sanctuary's climbing wall until I could make it all the way to the top. Of course, then I hadn't been sore, burning, throbbing, and exhausted, but as Nini Mo said, *It's amazing what you can do when you have an audience.*

I made it to the top, slightly puffing. As I belly flopped over the canopy edge, I felt a slight galvanic tingle: I had just crossed some sort of Enclosure Sigil. The space between the top of the canopy and the ceiling was just enough to sit upright. The Girl was sitting cross-legged on a heap of blankets and pillows, with the plushy Pig—whom I could have sworn we had left in the bathroom—in her lap. What a supercool space, and so clever, too. My jealousy increased.

The Girl had lit a foul-smelling cigarillo, and now she said, through a puff of smoke, "Want one?"

While I waved her offer away, coughing, she continued: "We can talk here. I've got a Deafening Sigil set up. *He* can't hear us—it's safe. Look, you gotta help me—what's your name?"

"Flora. And would you quit blowing on me? That cigarillo smoke is almost as foul as the kakodæmon."

"That's the whole point, Flora. It drowns out the stench," the Girl said, but she quit blowing on me. "Look, Flora, I'm a prisoner here, and I need your help to escape."

"Where is here?" I interrupted. "Thanks to your Vortex I have no idea where I am."

"Bilskinir House," she said impatiently, and relief flooded through me. I was in the right place after all; the Vortex hadn't sucked me halfway across the world or to another locale entirely. "Hardhands is holding me prisoner—you gotta help me escape."

Hardhands! My heart, so recently buoyed with hope, sank like a fisherman's float in a storm. "You mean General Haðraaða?"

"Ayah, him, the cullionly"—and here the girl described General Haðraaða in terms that made her mouth need a good washing. "I'm his prisoner. He's locked me in this tower because I wouldn't obey him, and if he catches you here, you'll be his prisoner, too."

I listened, my heart sinking deeper and deeper. As far as I was concerned, Hardhands had been dead since before I was born, murdered by his malicious wife, the Butcher Brakespeare. A horrible feeling was starting to tingle up the back of my spine.

"What year is it?" I interrupted the girl's harangue.

"The fifth year of Florian's tyranny—may he soon drop into the rotten mouth of death," she answered.

I was born in the twenty-ninth year of the Warlord's reign. Which meant I was thirty-seven—no thirty-eight—years in the past. Pigface Psychopomp on a Pogostick! I was in the right place at the wrong time. My heart was past sinking. Now it was sunk. The last time I had visited Bilskinir I had briefly ended up in the wrong time, but not nearly so far back. That time Paimon had blamed me—said my Anima Enervation was making Bilskinir House unstable—but clearly Bilskinir House was unstable all on its own. It didn't need any help from me.

The Girl must have read the horror on my face, for she said avidly, "You *are* from the future!" The smoke puffed from her nose as she laughed. "My sigil worked! I am the crowned and conquering child, the girl with the most cake! Tell me my future."

"I don't know who you are!"

"Sidonia Romney Haðraaða," she answered impatiently. "But everyone calls me Tiny Doom."

"I've never heard of you!"

"But my sigil worked," she said, disappointed. "You should know."

"Worked! I was on a vital mission until I got sucked into the Vortex! You completely messed me up!"

"What kind of vital mission?" Tiny Doom demanded.

"I was trying to save the City from complete and utter annihilation."

"What kind of destruction?"

"Earthquakes. Look, I have to talk to Paimon immediately." He'd gotten me back to my proper place before; surely he could do it now.

Tiny Doom said fiercely, "You can't. If he finds out you are here, he'll want to know where you came from, and then it will come out about the Vortex and I'll be totally fiked. Hardhands has forbidden me to play in the Current. He'll murder me or worse! And you, as well."

"But how else am I going to get home and save the City?"

"Don't be a snapperhead. Your earthquakes are in the future. You've got no hurry now, unless the future you are talking about is in five minutes."

"Thirty-eight years," I corrected.

"Well, then, you've got plenty of time to figure it all out," Tiny Doom said calmly, and for one brief moment I felt much much better. The threat of the Loliga was far in the future. The moment ended when something else occurred to me.

"I can't wait thirty-eight years. I'll be ancient by then—over fifty. I have to get home now! I have to talk to Paimon!"

"Not on your fiking life," Tiny Doom said. "I have to get out of here, and if you alert yourself to Paimon, we'll both be stuck. Look, 'You got in, you can get back out again,' Nini says. In fact, that's who you want—Nini Mo. She'll know exactly what to do!"

Nini! Nini Mo! Tiny Doom's words sank in, and my heart began to buoy upward. Nini Mo was alive! The greatest ranger who ever lived was still alive! And she'd know how to get me back to my own time. Nini Mo!

Tiny Doom was still talking: ". . . so lucky that in the future they let kids your age be rangers! I have to fiking wait until I graduate from the Barracks before I can take the Ranger's Oath. Which is completely fiked since I've already spent two summers with the rangers—"

"You know Nini Mo?" I interrupted.

"Of course I do! I was detached to the Ranger Corps last summer, and when I graduate, I will be going into the Ranger Corps. Hardhands says he won't let me, but he can—" Tiny Doom suggested that he do something quite unappealing. I didn't care what Hardhands could do. My heart, previously so soggy, was about to explode with excitement. Nini Mo! Getting sucked through that stupid Vortex would be worth it if I got to meet Nini Mo. *Everything* would be worth it if I got to meet Nini Mo.

But first I needed Georgiana Segunda's *Diario*. I might be in the wrong time, but the *Diario* was still in reach. I'd come all this way, and I wasn't leaving without it. And suddenly I had a plan to get it.

"You are a Haðraaða?"

"Ayah," Tiny Doom said, somewhat belligerently. "So what?"

"Do you know about Georgiana Haðraaða's *Diario*?"

"Ayah, why?"

"That's what I came to Bilskinir for—I mean, when you sucked me into your Vortex, that's what I was looking for. Will you help me get it?"

"I can't let you have a Haðraaða heirloom. Particularly without knowing what you want it for."

"Nini sent me to get it." The lie rolled off my tongue. "She didn't tell me why she wanted it—just sent me on a mission. I don't ask questions of direct orders. I just follow them. Isn't that what rangers do?"

Tiny Doom stared at me, and so did the Pig sitting on her lap. I had the uncomfortable feeling that perhaps the Pig knew I was lying, but I hoped he couldn't tell her that I was. The lie was already twisting on my conscience, but *sometimes a small fib is the price you pay for a great victory,* Nini Mo said.

"Nini Mo from the future?"

"Ayah, so." I smiled what I hoped was a very sincere smile.

"Why didn't she just ask Hardhands for it?"

"Oh, she did," I said swiftly. "But he refused to give it to her—he's petty, you know—and so she sent me to sneak in and get it. Very deep cover, silent and secret, you know. She needs it to save the City."

"That sounds like Hardhands, the bootless whey face. Well, if I help you get the *Diario*, will you help me escape? Hardhands has me under a geas not to leave Bilskinir."

"But I don't know how to lift a geas."

"Who said you had to?" she said. "Here's the genius part. I can't leave under my own Will, but if I were your prisoner, I'd be leaving under your Will, and that would obviate the geas. It's not the Ultimate Ranger Dare, but it's a pretty clever plan. Hardhands never thought I'd be able to get anyone to help me; he can suck on that! Deal?"

I needed the *Diario* and I hoped to get to Nini Mo. If Tiny Doom was willing to help me, I could help her in return. Didn't Nini Mo say that the ranger who helps another ranger helps herself?

"Deal. Pinkie promise?"

"All right. Pinkie promise," Tiny Doom said. *"The ranger who helps another ranger helps herself."*

THIRTY

Tiny Doom. Planning. Hide!

TINY DOOM turned out to be by far the coolest person I had ever met. Not only had she spent two summers with the Ranger Corps, but she'd even participated in several ranger operations, some training (stealing the Redlegs Regiment's Colors) and others actual (which she couldn't give me any details on, citing mission secrecy). She'd been Nini Mo's aide-de-camp *and* her adjutant, eating and working by her side, sometimes sleeping on a cot outside her door.

Tiny Doom knew tons of Gramatica, too—far more than I did. Not only could she open a Vortex (though she clearly hadn't quite figured out how to close one) and get the Current to reflect, but she could command elementals and conjure retroactive enchantments. Tiny Doom had even enchanted Nursie so that she couldn't report back to Paimon. And she had embodied a Protection Sigil into the form of the pink plushy pig—fantastically clever, if you ask me, because who would ever suspect a pink plushy pig to be so powerful and strong? Superdeep cover—the best. I resolved that as soon as I got home, I would try to do the same with my own pink plushy pig—funny that we should have the same pig, so many years apart.

Tiny Doom had a huge wardrobe of gorgeous clothes, all of which fit her perfectly. She was kind enough to lend me some, including a pair of fabulous purple stays that actually fit me (how glorious to be supported and still be able to breathe!) and the most fabulous midnight-blue and shocking-pink frock coat—"You are too old to wear pinafores, Flora, throw that rag out!"—with kilts to match. Unlike the Zu-Zu and Udo, she knew that when it came to maquillage, less is more. By the time she was done with my face, you could hardly even tell I was wearing any maquillage—I just looked like me, only superbetter. She was even able to turn my bushy eyebrows into the most perfect little wings—a painful, tweezy transformation, but worth it. "Nini says," Tiny Doom said, "that if you look your best, people will think you are."

Even her nickname was cool—Tiny Doom. That was almost as good as Nini Mo. And yards better than the Zu-Zu, or Hotspur, or the Rock of Califa, or even the Dainty Pirate. By comparison, *Flora* sounded downright babyish. The only nickname I'd ever had was Tinks, which was fine when I was two, but not really rangery cool. I resolved to correct this lack as soon as possible.

Tiny Doom seemed to think I *was* rangery cool, even if I didn't have a cool nickname or know how to fix my eyebrows. She obviously thought I was already a ranger. It made me feel a little bit bad to let that lie continue, but I had no choice: I had to return with the book—not only did the fate of the City rest on me, but how would Lord Axacaya respect me if I returned home empty-handed? I was confident Nini Mo would know how to get me home.

How fabulous it was to be with someone who so completely agreed with you on everything. Unlike *some* people, Tiny Doom didn't argue with me or think my plan was stupid; *she* didn't constantly talk about her hair; *she* made no unkind comments when I had a third helping of blueberry buckle (conjured up by Nursie and so yummy delicious—I was starving). In fact, she had a fourth helping herself.

While we were gussying ourselves up and eating the buckle, Tiny Doom explained the circumstances by which she had become Hardhands's prisoner. As her braids indicated, she was in her third year at the Barracks, which is when you declare your regimental intentions. She'd declared for the Ranger Corps, but Hardhands, as Head of the House Haðraaða, had different ideas—Pigface, where had I heard *this* story before? He wanted her to go into his regiment, the Skinners—ugh! At least Mamma had never tried to force me there. When Tiny Doom had returned to Bilskinir for Hardhands's birthday celebration, he'd tried to force her to recant her choice. She'd refused, so he had disinherited her and then locked her up so that she couldn't tell anyone what he had done. *Anyone* in this case meant Nini Mo, "Who will never let him get away with this, believe me. When she finds out what he's done, there's gonna be trouble . . ."

Tiny Doom had many other things to say about Hardhands and his behavior, all unrepeatable. By the time she was done with her story, I was starting to feel rather glad to be a Fyrdraaca. Mamma is pretty tough, but I couldn't imagine her actually disinheriting me, or locking me in a tower forever. I wondered that Tiny Doom's parents let Hardhands treat her like that, but I suppose since he is the Head of their House, they had no choice. Poor Tiny Doom.

Tiny Doom told me all this as we hunkered down on the wooden canopy, waiting for the coast to be clear. Downstairs, Tiny Doom explained, Paimon was preparing for Hardhands's birthday party, which sounded as though it would (had already?) put the Warlord's birthday party to shame. The appointments were so lavish—chocolate fountains, flaming ice sculptures, etc.—that all of Paimon's focus went on them. (That explained why Tiny Doom was able to try to scry the future without gaining his attention—and why the kakodæmon had not rung his bell.) The party would culminate in a performance by Hardhands's band, and that would be our chance: Paimon's attention would be so focused on amplifying the band—"The Tygers of Wrath play really fiking loud," Tiny Doom said in disgust—that we would be able to snatch Georgiana Segunda's *Diario.* "It's buried with her, you know, and then we'll make our getaway—"

"Tiny Doom! Tiny Doom!" Nursie's voice interrupted.

"What?!" Tiny Doom said impatiently. She crawled across the blankets and peered over the edge of the canopy.

"He calls for you! The party is about to begin and you are required."

"Didn't you tell him I am sick?"

"I did, my dove, but he insisted."

"I'm really sick—puking. He doesn't want me puking on the Warlord, does he? Tell him that. Only nicely."

Nursie was insistent. "He is coming to see why you delay. Come down and I shall fix your hair and dress."

Tiny Doom jumped as though she'd just been barbed by a stingray. "Fike! He is on his way? Hardhands is on his way?"

"Ayah, so, my darling."

Tiny Doom looked at me wildly. "Fike! If Hardhands sees you, or the mess, we're screwed. Fike, you gotta hide—no, not here; he might hear you. The bathroom—get in the bathroom and lock the door so he can't get in!"

We scrambled down into the day nursery, where Tiny Doom pushed me into the bathroom. She didn't have to push me too hard. After all I'd heard about him, I had no desire to run into Hardhands in the flesh—I'd seen his corpse once, in the Cloakroom of the Abyss, and that glimpse was enough for me. Even dead, he was beautiful. But even dead he didn't look like someone you'd want to cross.

"Your face!" I hissed, as Tiny Doom started to close the door on me. I threw her the soggy bear mask and she yanked it on. Her skirts were still a deflated mess of crinkled shocking-pink satin and her feet were bare, but at least her shiner was hidden. *That* would be impossible to explain.

"Silent and secret!" she warned me, pausing in the doorway.

"Silent and secret!" I answered back. As soon as the door was shut, I locked it and leaned against it. The last surviving candle had gone out, but the bathroom was suffused from above with a soft night-light glow. The ceiling was a deep velvety blue, the nighttime sky twinkling with silvery stars and the comforting warm shine of a full moon. A few wisps of coldfire vapor eddied, left over from the Working. Pig had returned to his throne; I picked him up and squeezed him. He was soft and friendly, and very reassuring. I crept to the door, but I didn't need a glass to hear; every word was painfully audible.

". . . downstairs, ready to receive the guests," said a man's deep voice. He sounded annoyed.

"I cry your pardon, Your Grace," Tiny Doom answered. She sounded contrite. "I have a bad tummy. I did not think your guests would enjoy me much if I had a bad tummy. Things keep coming up."

"Tell Nursie to give you some of Madama Twanky's Sel-Ray Psalts. No one shall pay you that much attention, Tiny Doom— I have spent much time in making sure of *that*. But I still want you there, and I shall expect you downstairs in five minutes, with your brightest smile on. This is the first time that the Warlord has visited Bilskinir, and we wish to give him a good accounting and show him welcome."

"Ayah, sieur. I shall attend," Tiny Doom said sullenly.

Footsteps leaving, and then, just as I was about to unlock the door, Hardhands said, "What's that I smell? Have you been conjuring, Tiny Doom?"

"No. Of course not."

"I hope you do not take advantage of Paimon's distraction. But I fear—" Now the heavy footsteps were getting closer. "I have told you not to meddle in the Current. It is dangerous and you are inexperienced, and if the Warlord should discover that we have not abjured completely from the Art, it will not go down well."

"I have not," Tiny Doom repeated. "I haven't done anything—"

"Then why do I see coldfire seeping out from underneath the bathroom door?"

I glanced down and saw, with horror, that pink tendrils of coldfire were swirling around the floor and, apparently, wafting under the door. I grabbed the nearest towel and stuffed it against the gap, but of course, soggy cotton can't stop the flow of cold-fire.

"It's just steam from the bathtub," Tiny Doom said, which had to be about the lamest excuse I had ever heard. In almost no way do coldfire mist and steam look similar. At least she was trying. I swished my kilts back and forth, trying to dissipate the fumes.

The doorknob rattled.

"Why is the bathroom door locked?" Hardhands demanded.

I didn't hear Tiny Doom's reply, if she made one; I was too busy looking for a place to hide. The bathtub wasn't deep enough, and still full of Currenty water, anyway. Califa knew what would happen if I jumped in there.

"Is there someone inside? Who is in there?" The door thumped demandingly. "You in there—open the door before I get Paimon up here!"

"I'm getting out of the bath. Just a minute," I hollered. I snatched a towel up off the floor, threw it over my shoulders, and cracked the door wide enough to peer through. "Yes?"

"Who are you?" Hardhands asked. I could only see a sliver of him: the edge of a sangyn sleeve, a napkinlike cuff dripping with silver lace; a slice of sangyn frock coat, sangyn kilt and then jackboots, champagne shiny and beetle-black. "Come out where I can see you right this minute."

"I'm not dressed," I lied.

"Now! Or I'll smash the door in."

I hastily opened the door and slithered out, then slammed the door shut behind me, so that he shouldn't see the mess. I remembered well the expression on the corpse Hardhands—cold, stiff, and forbidding. That look was downright friendly compared with now. Mamma has a Look that can make colonels cry. I'll bet that Hardhands could make the Goddess Califa herself cry. He was certainly having that effect upon me.

He stepped forward, pushing me aside, and opened the bathroom door. He looked at the coldfire-stained walls, the broken mirror, the sloshy bath. He turned around and looked at me, fully dressed and draped in a towel. He looked at Pig, nestled in my arms. Of the three of us, Pig was spotless and, therefore, appeared blameless. He looked and looked and didn't say anything, and each second of his silence grew more and more ominous. My knees were starting to feel rather wobbly.

"Take off your mask," he demanded and Tiny Doom did so, glaring right back at him, her lips as thin as wire.

He looked at her battered face, back to me, and then he said, very quietly, "What is going on here?"

"A kakodæmon came up the drain," Tiny Doom said, but her lie didn't sound enthusiastic, and therefore not particularly convincing. "It almost ate me. Pig saved me. Us."

Hardhands turned his eyes slightly toward Pig, whose mouthless expression remained inscrutable. Somehow I had the feeling that Hardhands's Look was making no impression on Pig. He turned the Look back upon me. "Who are you?"

My mind went utterly blank. Who was I? Where was I? Why was I?

"Uh-uh," I stuttered.

"You stink of magick; I can smell the Gramatica in your blood; your blood is infested with Words. You don't belong here. Yet, there's something about you—" He stepped forward, sniffing, and gripped my face with one long white hand. His fingernails were painted a glittering silvery black, and a huge intaglio signet ring glittered on his forefinger. His grip was tight and pinchy, and strangely galvanic, too, as though the Current flowed through it. The urge to babble came on suddenly, but before I could give into it, Tiny Doom burst out wildly, "It was all her fault! Her idea! She thought we should try to scry the future on the Current—she opened a Vortex! I told her not to, but she did!"

I wrenched my face out of his grip and protested, "I did not! I did no such thing! I don't know what she is talking about!"

"She did!" Tiny Doom said, almost hysterically.

Pernicious villain!

"Paimon," Hardhands said in a quiet voice, so soft that it was almost a whisper. Upon my shoulders came a sudden crushing grip that I didn't dare try to squirm out of, remembering only too vividly the needlelike qualities of Paimon's long fingernails.

"How did she get in here?" Hardhands asked.

"She is not on the guest list," Paimon answered. He was still behind me, and he didn't sound very friendly.

"I invited her," Tiny Doom said, pointing accusingly. "But she tricked me: She said she was my friend, but she just wanted to get to Bilskinir's power! She opened the Vortex! I tried to stop her, but she kicked me in the nose!"

My babbling protests were ignored, and Paimon's grip grew painfully grippy. Though I twisted and turned, I could not wrench myself free.

"Dispose of her," Hardhands said. "I don't have time for this. I have guests to attend to, and you, madama"—and here he turned his iceberg gaze upon Tiny Doom—"I want you downstairs in five minutes. We shall discuss this later, after the party."

Before I could say more, or try to escape, or protest further, or blame it all on Tiny Doom, or threaten Hardhands, or beg for mercy, or do anything at all to save myself, Paimon had swung me aloft as though I weighed no more than a pancake. Pig bounced out of my arms and flew through the air, ears flapping, to Tiny Doom, who clutched him to her chest.

"Liar!" I shouted at Tiny Doom, as Paimon bore me off. "Snapperhead!"

The worst thing that can ever happen to a ranger had now happened to me.

I was caught.

THIRTY-ONE

Treachery. Pleading. Tamales.

D<small>OWN</small>, <small>DOWN</small>, Paimon and I went, down a twisty turny staircase so narrow it was a wonder that his massive bulk could squeeze through. He had hefted me over his shoulder like a sack of corn, and the head bobbing, along with the twisty turning, was making my tum slosh alarmingly. Surely Paimon wouldn't harm me, would he? He was my friend, wasn't he? In the future he was my friend. Here and now, he was Hardhands's servant, and bound to obey him. *Dispose of her*, Hardhands had said. What exactly did he mean by that?

"Paimon!" I said, my voice sputtering in time to the bouncing. *Clip-clop* went his hooves on the wooden steps—such dainty hooves upon which to balance such monstrousness. "Paimon, don't you know me?"

"Alas, to my sorrow, I do, madama."

"Then you know I meant no harm."

"Is that true? What a mess you have created. It shall take me days to get all the coldfire scrubbed away. And your Vortex tore a giant hole in my integrity. Who knows what might have come through. I could have been destroyed."

"But it wasn't my Vortex. I didn't have anything to do with it. It was *her* Vortex. Tiny Doom. She just blamed it on me! It wasn't my fault!" I must admit that a bit of blubbering may have crept into my voice, but then I did have quite a bit to blubber about, didn't I? And I was exhausted, and out-of-place, and in a world of hurt. Who could blame me for feeling so woeful?

We were still going down. Either Bilskinir's Nursery was in a tower as high as the sky, or we were headed for Bilskinir's basement, and I hardly dared consider how far *down* that might be. Or what might be lurking there. Down, down. The wooden steps turned to a wooden floor. Down, down. Flowery carpet bloomed upon the wooden floor. More down, and then the wooden floor turned to sterile white tile.

Paimon turned me over and set me on my feet to face him. I had forgotten how monstrous his visage was: the blue electrified mustachios, the long curving tusks, the enormous fringy ears, the blue wrinkly snout. And the Look he was giving me made Hardhands's earlier Look seem friendly by comparison. My skin flamed, blushing red with guilt. I tried to smile, but my lips felt numb.

We had stopped in a huge kitchen like none I had seen before. Everything about it was blinding white: the tile floor, the cabinets, the countertops. Rectangles of glowing light hovered high above us, casting a cold glow. I was reminded queasily of the destination of last year's science field trip: the Califa City Morgue. Bilskinir's kitchen smelled like charred meat instead of quicklime, but the overall effect was similar. Even the massive oven, a flat black rectangle set into one flat white wall, was horribly reminiscent of the morgue's crematory oven.

A long white slab ran the length of the room. A bowl of masa sat on the slab. Blood streaked the slab's surface, congealing in puddles around scattered pieces of hacked meat.

Big pieces of hacked meat, raw and well-marbled.

Next to the hacked meat was a Flora-sized stockpot.

Five seconds before, I would have thought that I could not possibly be any more terrified. Now I was numb.

Dispose of her! said Hardhands.

Paimon will eat you! said Tiny Doom.

"Give me your socks," Paimon ordered. I took them off, hopping on one foot and then the other, and then handed them to him. He held the soggy wool between two sharp fingernails and his tusks glinted with disapproval.

"Someone has not done a very good job mending your heels," Paimon said. He hung the socks over the handle of the huge iron door of the oven, then pressed on a flat white wall tile. It swung open to reveal shelves. He took a mortar and pestle from a shelf and filled it full of spice, which he then proceeded to grind. The rich smell of cocoa and black pepper filled the air. Cocoa and black pepper—Birdie spices—used to make ceremonial tamales, with centers filled with meat.

Human meat.

"I tried to keep you out, madama," Paimon said, as he ground away. "For your safety and for mine. But you would not heed my cautions. Just as before, you cause instability."

I protested, "But I didn't mean to end up here. I mean, I did mean to end up in Bilskinir—but not in this time. Tiny Doom caught me in her Working."

"How so?"

I took his interest as a good sign. Surely if he was going to make me into tamales, he'd hack me up and get on with it.

"Well, I was trying to get in through Bilskinir's Back Door and—"

Before I could react, Paimon picked me up and sat me down on the white slab next to the bowls. Now I could see that one held tamale masa; in the other, corn husks soaked.

"Go on, madama. I am interested in your explanation."

I stuttered, "Her Vortex—she—she opened a V-Vortex—it snagged me."

"What was the purpose of this Vortex?"

"She was trying to scry the future in the Current."

Paimon coiled one long blue mustachio around one long blue finger, tugging at the corkscrew so it bobbed like a spring. He said thoughtfully, "Well, that explains it somewhat."

"Huh?"

"Tiny Doom was trying to scry the future in the Current, but in the Current already, as she didn't know, *was* the future—

you. So, the Current offered you up as the answer to her question, but she didn't understand it. It is not enough to be told the future; you must know what it means. General Haðraaða has told Tiny Doom time and time again that she must not delve into the Current. But she doesn't listen. She doesn't understand the dangers; she is far too rash. She—"

I didn't wait around to hear any more about Tiny Doom—whose nickname was suddenly a lot more clear to me. Taking advantage of Paimon's distraction, I hurtled myself down and bolted. I skittered across the slippery tiles, expecting any second that needle-sharp claws would catch me and rend me to pieces. Which, of course, they did—the catching part, that is. Paimon swooped down and scooped me up. I twisted hard in his grasp, kicking him squarely where it should have counted, but that seemed to hurt my toes more than it hurt him. He did not relinquish me. My view was now restricted, but I thought I saw a pink plushy snout peering around the edge of the glistening white enamel table. Paimon swung me around and the view was gone.

"Please, don't eat me, Paimon! If you just send me home, I promise I'll never bother you again. Please, pretty please, wonderful Paimon! *Don't eat me!*" I howled in a most unranger-like fashion.

"I am sorry, madama, but my instructions are clear, and I can not violate them. I am bound to follow my orders. There is naught that you or I can do but take this as cheerfully as possible."

As a ranger should, I intended to make a good death when it came my turn, but as far as I was concerned, tonight was not a good time to die. I writhed and kicked, bit and scratched, but my struggles had no effect upon Paimon at all. He tucked me under one arm, and suddenly I found myself as limp as a noodle, unable to move. But at least I was not immediately going to the butcher's block. Instead, he carried me to the far end of the kitchen and opened a large metal door. Frigid air gusted out.

The room was small, round, and lined with hooks, from

which drooped a whole lot of dead birds, glassy-eyed, feathers
limp. Pigeons, pheasants, turkeys. A huge animal hung from a
meat hook in the center of the room; skinned, headless, limbs
removed. Its tendons glistened whitely, the muscles sickly red,
and a slick of blood pooled on the floor underneath it. In my
terror, it looked vaguely human. An empty meat hook dangled
next to it. Tiny Doom's coat was no protection against the cold;
already my teeth were chattering.

Out of the tamale, onto the meat hook.

"Paimon," I moaned.

"I'm sorry, madama." But instead of reaching for the meat
hook, Paimon bent down and yanked on a large iron ring set
into the floor. The ring pulled up a piece of the floor to reveal a
dark, round hole: an oubliette.

Well, it was better than the meat hook, that was for sure.

"Down you go, Flora," Paimon said.

"Paimon, haven't we been friends, and—"

He looked at me sorrowfully. "Madama, this hurts me more
than it hurts you."

Somehow I doubted *that*. "If you will just let me go, then I
promise to be good and I'll never bug you again, and no harm
will be done—Hardhands will never know. Please, darling Paimon?"

"I cannot. Not now. But later I shall return for you."

"How much later?" I asked hopefully, thinking I could probably manage an hour or two before I froze to death. I could wait
a couple of hours; didn't I have thirty-eight years before I had
to be back?

"When there is a new Head of the House."

"When will that be?"

"Twenty-three years."

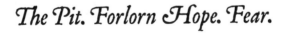

THIRTY-TWO

The Pit. Forlorn Hope. Fear.

I SAT WOEFULLY in the darkness for a long time. Once again all my plans had gone awry. I had failed in my mission. My lies had been useless. I'd been caught. All this made me feel very bad, but worst of all: I felt totally crushed by Tiny Doom's betrayal. She'd seemed so cool and tough, and then she'd folded at the first sign of pressure. No wonder Hardhands had been able to keep her locked up—she might talk big, but *she'd* never be a ranger.

Rangers stick.

Rangers also don't sit around woefully when they are caught. Did Nini Mo sit around sulking when she was captured by the Arivaipas, who planned to roast her like a pumpkin? No, she did not. The first duty of a ranger who is caught is to escape. Sulking would not help me achieve this goal. So, I swallowed my sulky crushed feelings and cupped my hands in front of me (or the best approximation of in front of me, for it was awfully dark).

"⸲⸵⧖⸱⧫ ⬳⸱'⸳⸴!"

A little blue lick of light glimmered in my palms and sputtered out; my Will was weak with fear. Well, I *wasn't* going to spend twenty-three years in this hole, so I needed to get over that fear, and quick. I thought about all the stuff I had to do— figure out how to get home, and then save the City. Lord Axacaya was waiting for me. The coldfire flame flickered a bit, and then died again.

Nini Mo! I'd escape and find her. She'd know how to get me home, and she'd make Hardhands give me the *Diario* and we'd all be saved. This time the flame lasted a few seconds, but then it, too, faded.

Udo. I had to get out of this stupid hole to save Udo. He might have left me in the lurch, but I was not going to return the favor. Rangers stick. I thought about *that* again, and the flicker flared into a little blue ball of Ignis Light. When I took my hands away, it bobbed gently in front of me, shedding a happy little cerulean glow. I was glad enough to see it; already the heavy black weight of the surrounding darkness had begun to weigh heavily upon me.

Now the oubliette's well-like wall was visible, at least thirty feet high and slick as marble. No handholds there. The floor was made of the same flat white tiles as the kitchen—so, no digging—and was ice-cold on my bare feet. Paimon had drawn the rope and basket up after me, of course, so no hope there. But the light also revealed a wonderfully familiar object: my dispatch case, which I had lost in the Vortex. Where Paimon had found it, or why he had left it for me, I couldn't guess, but I was grateful he had. All my supplies were still inside: my extra bars of chocolate, two boxes of triggers wrapped in oil cloth, an extra pair of socks, my cutlery kit, my collapsible lantern, my pen case, my penknife, my flask, and, most important: *The Eschata*. I lit the lantern, ate a bar of chocolate, put on the dry socks, and felt much better. *You'd be amazed*, said Nini Mo, *how much dry socks matter.*

Then I tried to make myself comfortable on the cold floor and reread the chapter in *The Eschata* entitled "Escape." Surely the answer to my exit must be there. Indeed, *The Eschata* offered many escape techniques. If I had some grape yeast and flour, I could make a smoke bomb to create a diversion—but I had neither grape yeast nor flour, and no need for a diversion. If I had six feet of hemp rope and a heavy weight, I could have perhaps swung the rope up, caught it above, and climbed out of the oubliette. But I had neither rope nor weight, neither, for that matter, did I have room to swing.

No prison can hold me, said Nini Mo. There had to be a way. If I couldn't get out via ordinary measures, perhaps something extraordinary would do the trick. I flipped beyond the practical escape methods to the impractical—the purely magickal. But here, too, I was hampered by lack of ingredients. I had thought my ranger kit was pretty well kitted out, but now I saw I was woefully undersupplied. I lacked various wacky ingredients: a hand of glory, powdered centipede gall, a fuzzy lemon popstick. That eliminated the Pogo Sigil (jumping), the Diaphanous Sigil (floating), and the Gummy Sigil (sticking). With a tin can, a string, and an Amplification Sigil, I could create a telegraph and wire Nini Mo for help. I had string, but no tin can.

Left then were sigils that required no special ingredients, other than the magician's Will and Gramatica Vocabulary that I did not have: a Transubstantiation Sigil (turn myself into a bird and fly out), a Vapid Sigil (turn myself into a fog and waft out), a Translocation Sigil (jump from one point to another). Once again I cursed my lack of Gramatica skills. If I were fluent—or even knew enough just to get by—well, all this would be easy.

A bubble of panic popped up my throat, and I tried to swallow it back down. I wasn't sure how long I had been in the oubliette, but the distant thudding that had started up not long ago was surely the sound of a bass guitar. The Tygers of Wrath must have begun their set. Paimon's attention would be fully engaged there, so the time for me to act was now.

Rangers don't waste time wishing for what they don't have; they use what they've got. What did I have? I had a satchel full of useless stuff—I had nothing. Fear bubbled again, almost choking me. Fear—I had plenty of fear, enough fear to swamp the Dainty Pirate's ship, enough fear to turn me into a gibbering mindless fool.

Enough fear to amplify a Gramatica Word?

A good magician can take a small Gramatica Word and amplify its meaning by applying a Catalyst to it. There are two kinds of Catalysts—Inhibitory Catalysts and Excitory Catalysts.

An Inhibitory Catalyst is any method that involves the negative of something, like burying yourself alive, or withholding food, or poking yourself with a needle. Pain and deprivation are the footholds of an Inhibitory Catalyst—anything that leads to Not Enough. Not enough food, not enough air, not enough light.

An Excitory Catalyst is any method that involves the positive of something—dancing frantically, falling in love, eating lots of chocolate. Happiness and joy are the handmaids of an Excitory Catalyst—anything that leads to Too Much. Too much love, too much food, too much light.

These Catalysts can be used to amplify a sigil, make it bigger, better, stronger. Or it can stretch the meaning of a Gramatica Word, make it last longer, go further.

In *Nini Mo vs. the Xocholatte Rustlers*, Nini Mo used an Excitory Catalyst (too much chocolate) to amplify the Gramatica Words *jump* and *space* to create a Translocation Sigil that catapulted her from the vat of boiling chocolate she had been plunged into, at the Rustlers' secret chocolate factory, to the local sheriff's office. After organizing a posse, she returned to the factory and arrested all the rustlers, who were later hung. (They take chocolate rustling seriously in Arivaipa Territory, as well they should.)

The Gramatica Word *out* was in *The Eschata*'s glossary. It's a four-syllable Gramatica Word, and I've only ever managed three-syllable Words, but you have to start someplace. With an Inhibitory Catalyst, I could make my fear work for me rather than against me, use it to Amplify the Gramatica, use the Amplified Word to Charge a Location Sigil, and then use *that* to jump myself out of this blasted oubliette. Tiny Doom had said that Georgiana Segunda had been buried with the *Diario*. From my previous visit to Bilskinir, I knew that the Haðraaða dead are kept in a crypt deep in Bilskinir's depths. If I could jump directly from the oubliette to the Cloakroom of the Abyss, as the crypt is called, I could grab the *Diario* and escape Bilskinir before the band finished playing. Then find Nini Mo. She'd know what to do from there, how to get me home again.

The other option was to sit in the oubliette for the next twenty-three years. Translocation Sigils are extremely dangerous. Done wrong you could easily end up stuck inside a wall or, even worse, half stuck inside a wall. Or even worse than that, half merged with another person: four legs, four arms, two heads.

But if you don't try, you are bound to fail for sure, said Nini Mo. *She* wouldn't sit in an oubliette for twenty-three years.

The claustrophobic darkness lurking just beyond the flickering, fading light of my lantern, its candle already down to a stub; the creeping fear that Paimon might come back for a snack; the skin-crawling horror of that headless carcass on the meat hook—as far as an Inhibitory Catalyst went, I was more than halfway there.

I fished my notebook out of my pack, and a pencil, too, which I sharpened with my little penknife, then wrote *The Cloakroom of the Abyss* over and over and over again until the paper was covered with an unreadable scrawling pattern. A powerful adept, of course, doesn't need a physical object to use as a focal point of her sigil, but I am not a powerful adept, and I wanted to be sure to get where I wanted to go. After I folded the paper into a small arrow shape, the signifier of a Direction Sigil, I was ready.

I blew out the light, and the darkness oozed around me, as thick as mud and almost as stifling. I crouched down, clutching the Sigil, and allowed my imagination to run free into horrible scary thoughts, and it didn't take much, let me tell you, to get me lathered. I have a *very* vivid imagination. All I had to do was think about Paimon's sharp teeth and the row of sharp shiny knives hanging in his spotless kitchen, and I began to shake.

My imagination had help, too. The darkness that sur-rounded me felt not ordinary pitch-black, but thick and old, as though years without the leavening of light had soured it and congealed it down, like when you leave the coffee pot on the stove and come back to find mud where your espresso should be. Sluggish and tired, but still with a spark of life—and curiosity. Although I knew perfectly well there was no wind, the dark seemed to move about me, stirring my hair and caressing my face with airy fingers.

Whispering voices surrounded me, and I knew that the darkness now stretched around me endlessly. It was an enor-mous Void full of horrible, hungry things, drawn to me like a moth to the flame, looking for tender young flesh, tender young Will, to snack upon. Chittering sounds, inhuman and diaboli-cal. Claustrophobia bore down on me, the weight of the dark-ness crushing me. I have no idea how long I sat there, gasping for breath. An hour, a day, an eternity of darkness, with the grasping greedy creatures of the Abyss getting closer and closer. Something brushed my hair. I began to hyperventilate; I couldn't breathe; panic overwhelmed me and I let out an enor-mously huge shriek, then another and another.

In my fist, my sweaty grip had condensed the Sigil into a little ball, which was now glowing with coldfire flare. The heat of it spread slowly up my arm, into my body, down my legs, up my chest, until it reached my head and exploded into a giant pulsing ball of staticky pressure. Now was the time.

"▓▒░▚▜▞!" I shouted.

The world shifted sideways, then whirled like a merry-go-round. For a moment, all my organs seemed to scramble and jump inside my skin, which was prickling and stinging as though I were engulfed in a cloud of extremely hungry mosquitoes.

I felt myself rise, and then drop. I landed hard, the impact shooting all the air out of my lungs and momentarily stunning me. I gurgled, lungs inflating, gasping. When I opened my eyes, I saw I was still in the oubliette.

When I tried to turn my head, I couldn't—my hair was

caught on something. I reached up, and when I realized why I was stuck, I had to fight down the urge to upchuck. The Sigil had worked after all . . . partially.

The hair on the left side of my head was now embedded in the wall.

THIRTY-THREE

Bad Hair. A Key.
An Unhappy Realization.

STILL FEELING QUEASY over my close call, I used my knife to cut my hair free. Needless to say, I was not going to attempt that trick again, though now my fear was such that an Inhibitory Catalyst would be mighty easy indeed. At least I had only lost hair. I could have lost a finger, or a hand—or worse.

Twenty-three years wasn't that long, was it? I wouldn't even be forty. Or I could try to persuade Paimon to free me the next time he visited me. I could take a nap and maybe I'd have another idea. Or I could just give up, curl into a little ball, and cry—

"Are you still down there, Flora?" a voice shouted hollowly.

High above me, Tiny Doom was backlit by a sputtering lantern. Something twisty fell down and almost whacked me on the head: Pig, with a rope tied around his waist.

I grabbed at him as he swung; he felt soft and cuddly in my arms. "What do you want?" I hollered back. "Come to gloat over your treachery?"

"Don't be a fiking snapperhead. I hope you are good at rope climbing, because I couldn't smuggle a ladder in. Come on, chop-chop . . . I can only confuse Paimon for so long."

Now, I didn't trust Tiny Doom further than I could kick

her (and oh, how I would like to kick her), but I wasn't going to stay down in this oubliette just to spite her, either. I would let her help me escape the oubliette and then I'd escape her.

"I can't climb and carry Pig, too!" I shouted.

"Never mind Pig, he'll bring himself up. Come on, hurry!"

When finally I hauled my puffing self over the edge, Tiny Doom announced, "If we'd been under fire, I'd probably be dead and you sure as fike would be. You fiking took long enough."

"I wouldn't have been down there in the first place if it hadn't been for you, pernicious traitor!" I gasped, rubbing my burning hands over my thighs.

"You didn't think I was going to leave you to Paimon, did you?" Tiny Doom sounded surprised. She'd changed into a supercool fringed buckskin jacket and a black leather kilt. Black paint was smeared on her face, obscuring her bruises and making her eyes look as bright as blue coals. A black knit cap had been pulled over her tricolor hair. "Here—I brought you some boots."

I caught the boots she tossed at me: purple, with jet buttons and sharp silver spurs. They were supercute, but they were not going to distract me from my ire. "You told him it was all my fault! What else was I supposed to believe? Paimon almost ate me!"

"Oh, Paimon wasn't really going to eat you—he's a vegetarian. I'm sorry about putting the juice on you, but we couldn't both be caught, could we? Who would rescue us both? I had to put Hardhands off the track somehow. I can't believe you thought I was really trying to do you in." She looked wounded.

"What else was I supposed to believe?" I sat down on a large crate marked CRAYFISH and put the boots on.

"Rangers are supposed to trust each other," she said, and a tiny feeling of badness began to wiggle inside me, for she was right, of course. Rangers do trust each other. And while I would have rather rescued myself than have been rescued by her, *It doesn't matter who rescues you, as long as you are rescued,* Nini Mo said.

"Sorry," I said. "But you sounded pretty sincere."

"Well, I had to, didn't I? To make them believe me. If Hardhands had thought I was lying, we'd both have been totally fiked. Anyway, I'm sorry it took so long to get down to rescue you. I had to go downstairs with Hardhands and make fiking nice-nice, and as soon as the Tygers started their show, I came down to get you. Hey—what happened to your hair?"

"I had an accident," I hedged. I didn't really want to admit my failure to her.

"What kind of accident?" She sniffed. "You smell of a Catalyst. What happened?"

"I tried to use an Inhibitory Catalyst to Amplify a Directional Sigil into a Translocation Sigil."

"Are you fiking me? That's one of the most dangerous Sigils ever. You could have ended up embedded in a wall somewhere."

"Well, it almost worked. I did translocate a little. But I must have said the Word wrong."

"That's a hard one; it's got that weird click in it. Still, you gotta lot of fiking nerve, Flora. I don't know if I would try that one, no matter how fiked I was. You are crazy—and I mean that nicely. Come on, let's get a move on; I'm freezing, and the Tygers are into their second set—they'll be done soon. We gotta get the *Diario* and get the fike out of here." Tiny Doom stowed Pig in her knapsack, and I followed her to the door of the meat locker.

"The door's locked," I said, rattling the handle.

"Ayah, so, but I have the key! See?"

After fishing in her cuff-pocket, Tiny Doom displayed a small porcelain jar, the kind that tooth powder comes in. In fact, it was a tooth-powder jar; MADAMA TWANKY'S OLD JUBI-LEE TOOTH POLISH, it said on the lid in black letters. *Give Your*

Teeth the Old Hurrah! Mamma's favorite brand, but I think it tastes like cod oil, plus it burns your gums.

She unscrewed the lid, then shook the jar out over her palm. A small round ring fell out.

"It's a ring," I said.

"It's the Key to Bilskinir," Tiny Doom said. "It's made from the hair of every Haðraaða who has ever lived."

That sounded rather disgusting to me, but she seemed pretty proud of it. She held up the ring so I could peer more closely at it. When I did, I saw that the ring was indeed made of strands of hair: blond, red, gray, black, brown, white, gold, and bright blue. The hair had been braided into one plait, and then somehow the ends of the plait had been fused to create the ring.

"Where'd you get it?" I asked.

"I found it when I was going through Hardhands's underwear drawer. It will open any lock in Bilskinir. I was going to use it to help me escape, but then Hardhands put me under that geas not to leave Bilskinir, so even if I unlocked the door, I couldn't go through. But it still comes in handy sometimes."

"Doesn't Hardhands miss it?"

Tiny Doom grinned. "He hasn't noticed it's gone yet. And by the time he does, I expect to be far from here."

She slid the ring on her index finger and then pressed the tip of her finger to the surface of the meat locker door. "The Ostium."

The door swung open, and we stepped through into a round room not much bigger than a closet. Its windowless walls were draped in heavy tapestries, blue embroidered with silver. And it only had one door—the door we had come in by, which as I turned, slammed shut behind us.

"The Ostium," Tiny Doom said. "Bilskinir's Secret Center. All doors in Bilskinir lead to this room and this door leads to all of Bilskinir's rooms—if you have the Key. Lucky we have a key, huh? Now, listen, before we go on, everyone should be watching the show, but we have to be super-low-key careful, anyway. Lucky for us it's a masked ball, so put this on."

I caught what she tossed at me: a rubbery mask.

"It's a chipmunk," I said, when I had stretched the mask out. Not just any chipmunk, but a grotesquely cute bug-eyed chipmunk with a skull-like grin and cheeks as red and round as tomatoes.

"Sorry, I was in a hurry and I grabbed the first mask I could find," she said impatiently. "Here, switch with me, then, if you are too delicate to be a chipmunk."

We switched, and I tugged on the bear mask, which was a bit soggy and smelled of wet fur, but at least it wasn't a rodent. The eyeholes were large, and I could see surprisingly well.

Tiny Doom, now grotesquely cute, pressed the tip of her index finger against the surface of the door and said, "The Ballroom of the Battle of Califa."

The door swung open and she made a little *follow me* gesture. We stepped out of the Ostium into the Ballroom.

Now the music was louder, a pulsating throb counterpointed by the rattling of the pictures on the wall, the porcelain in its cases, the glass in the windows. The Ballroom was empty of people but scattered with the debris of dancing: dropped fans, lost ribbons, stray garters, abandoned hankies. The fire had died down in the enormous fireplace that filled one entire wall; the long expanse of glass doors opposite were open to the night's darkness and a fresh cool breeze.

Above the fireplace hung a huge portrait of a woman sitting in a tree swing. A sweeping black hat perched upon her wild red hair; she clutched a small terrier pup to the breast of her dark blue riding jacket, and her bare feet rested on the wide back of a mastiff the same color as her hair. The top branches of the tree were on fire, the green leaves consumed by livid orange and red flames, and behind, the sky seethed with black clouds and lightning.

"Georgiana Segunda," Tiny Doom said. "She was a crush, Grandmamma. A real stunner." She was making a beeline for the fireplace. Following her, I tripped over a discarded shoe, twisting my ankle and muffling a curse. Tiny Doom turned to glare at me.

"What you do, Tiny Doom?" a small grating voice said, and we both froze. The voice came from the buffet. There, lying in the middle of an enormous tray of shrimp, looking bloated and picking his teeth, was a merman the size of a small house cat. A familiar merman. In fact, the exact same water elemental who, on my previous visit to Bilskinir House, had tried to persuade Udo and me that Paimon was going to eat us for dinner, thus inspiring us to flee from Paimon like giant idiotic snapperheads. Alfonzo something-or-other.

"*Quien es su amiga?*" Alfonzo asked. His fancy black jacket was smeared with shrimp sauce. He flipped his frilly red tail and ate another shrimp, without bothering to peel it.

Tiny Doom gave me a pointed look meaning *keep yer yip shut* and said, "Think you've had enough shrimp, Alfonzo?"

"Think you've had enough lip, *chica*?" Alfonzo said. "You are supposed to be watching the show—*muy bueno*—not wandering about causing trouble. *El jefe* will be—" His voice vanished suddenly as Tiny Doom slapped the bowl of shrimp sauce over him.

"ꗞꗞꗞ!" she said. The inside of the bowl filled briefly with bluish vapor, and when the vapor cleared, there was Alfonzo, coated with sauce, snoring.

"What did you do?" I asked, slightly in awe of how quickly all this had happened. Tiny Doom certainly didn't hesitate much; she decided and she acted.

"Put him into a little snooze. He's a fiking sneak, Alfonzo is, one of Hardhands's little snitches. You can bet that he'd be off like a shot to tattle. Well, the little pumpion can tattle to my darling husband all he wants when he wakes up—by then we'll be long gone. Come on."

We were almost to the glass doors when her words sank in. *Darling husband.*

I skidded to a halt. Hardhands was Tiny Doom's husband. As far as I had ever heard, Hardhands only had one wife, Cyrenacia Brakespeare—

Awful understanding turned my blood to water.

Tiny Doom was the Butcher Brakespeare.

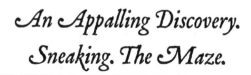

THIRTY-FOUR

An Appalling Discovery.
Sneaking. The Maze.

OF COURSE Tiny Doom wasn't the Butcher Brakespeare yet. Right now, in this time, she was just a kid, slightly older than me, already rather sour. But she was going to grow up and become the Butcher Brakespeare, whose crimes were legendary and almost too long to list. Forgery, murder, treachery, treason, necromancy, grand theft—she'd done it all. If the Birdies hadn't executed her, the Warlord would have; they just saved him the trouble.

The Butcher Brakespeare, she whose memory was now a rallying point for all who wished to see the City descend into chaos and mayhem. And Poppy's long-lost lover, whom he'd been mourning for as long as I could remember, unable to break away from her spell, whom he had loved more than Mamma, than Idden, than me. Whose death had made him mad and drunken—

"Come on! Hurry up!" The Butcher hissed, and I followed her, because I wasn't sure what else to do. Clearly, ranger or not, I shouldn't trust her. Yet, I needed her help, and for that I *had* to trust her. For the moment.

We reached the safety of the glass doors and passed into the cool night air. After discarding our masks by throwing them into a fountain, we crossed the dark expanse of Bilskinir's Great Lawn, scattering the huddling sheep, and went into the trees beyond. The pathway was narrow, barely a path at all, the ground rough with roots, the way thick with slappy tree branches. No one had come this way in a very long time, I wagered.

"This isn't the way to the Cloakroom of the Abyss," I said. Maybe she wasn't leading me to the Cloakroom at all, but into a trap. No, that was stupid. Why would she rescue me just to trick me?

She held a branch back for me so I could slip by. "Who said we were going to the Cloakroom of the Abyss?"

"Didn't you say that the *Diario* was buried with Georgiana Segunda?"

"Ayah, but I never said Georgiana was buried in the Cloakroom." She put her finger to her lips. "Silent and secret."

So, silent and secretly, we crept along, and as we went, I kept sneaking glances at the Butcher out of the corner of my eye. It was awfully hard to reconcile this ordinary girl with the notorious Butcher Brakespeare, she who they called Azota, the Whip, for her habit of flogging people who didn't agree with her. This girl was crabby and a bit hateful (at least as far as Hardhands was concerned), but otherwise was actually pretty cool. And certainly brave and intrepid. But she couldn't compare to Mamma, who is a hundred times more beautiful, and braver and stronger, too. Clearly, the Butcher had somehow enscorcelled Poppy—maybe even used a sigil on him. Otherwise, his preferring the Butcher over Mamma just didn't make any sense.

The Butcher had been trying to scry her future—but she wouldn't want to know. *Sometimes it's better to be blissful and ignorant,* said Nini Mo. Never more so in this case. She might be happy to know she would get her revenge on Hardhands, but she certainly had nothing else to look forward to. She was never going to be a ranger. Now I saw exactly why Nini Mo had counseled against trying to discover your future: How would you go on if it was only bad?

The Butcher was a dark shape before me. She muttered "⁂⊗⯊⧫⊐ ⯑⥐↯⩘!"and an Ignis Light flared, turning the branches above into the darkened arch of a tunnel. The roaring pound of the surf grew louder. The Butcher stopped suddenly, and I careened into her, grabbing on to her as I did. I fell back, pulling her with me, and landed hard on my hinder, the Butcher *oof*ing on top of me.

"Thanks," she said, pulling herself up. "Fike, I think I just lost a year off my life."

I pulled myself up and looked beyond her; my stomach dropped into the very bottom of my boots. The path had vanished. We were standing on the edge of a cliff, before a void of air. Below us, waves beat angrily upon the jagged rocks. We were, I guessed, looking north, for we had a magnificent view of the Gate, the silvery flow of the water moving from the freedom of the open ocean to the captivity of the Bay. Lights gleamed on the dark land rising up on either side of the Gate: Fort Point and Fort Gun. Ahead of us, the Potato Patch surged and foamed. A tiny light twinkled: the Chicken Point lighthouse, on the other side of the Gate.

The Butcher was shouting at me, but the buffeting wind and the water's thunder tore her words away. I leaned forward and her lips were warm against my ear; her breath smelled of applejack and tobacco.

"My mother jumped off this cliff!"

I jerked back. The more I was around the Haðraaða family the more ordinary and happy my own family seemed. Murder, suicide, madness: It seemed there was no vice that the Haðraaðas had not dabbled in. Perhaps it was a good thing that the family line had died out. The Fyrdaacas are sometimes insane, and often high-strung. They sometimes die in foolish accidents, and they occasionally murder someone—but they do not murder each other, nor do they murder themselves. No wonder the Butcher had turned out the way she did. Blood will win out, no matter what.

The path had not actually disappeared. It had merely turned to follow the cliff top, and so did we, carefully, for one misstep would terminate us and the expedition both. It was slippery, sweaty going, but at least we had the Butcher's coldfire light to guide us, and the light of the moon riding high above us. We grabbed at the branches and trunks of the stunted pine trees that were encroaching upon the pathway, and our feet dislodged rocks that spun out over empty air and disappeared into the foam below. Finally, the path turned back into thick brush, and I was glad to exchange the chance of slippery death for the surety of slappy branches.

Then the branches were gone, the path was gone, and we stood on smooth manicured grass. A perfectly manicured hedge stood before us, as solid as a wall. Its tightly woven branches reared up, impenetrable.

"The Great Maze," the Butcher said. "Georgiana Segunda's tomb is in the middle of it."

"You didn't tell me there was a maze!"

"Grandmamma was the Pontifexa of Califa. Did you think she'd just have a tomb like anybody else? A slab and a bunch of flowers? A welcome mat for any grave robber? A bier upon which she'd lie like a side of meat?"

"The other Haðraaðas do—"

"Grandmamma is special! Anyway, don't fret. I am a Haðraaða; of course, I know the way." And with that, the Butcher plunged ahead, and it was follow or be left behind. I followed, and soon discovered that, well, of *course* the Butcher knew the way, for it was marked clearly with fluorescent blazes at every turn. You'd have to be blind not to be able to follow the markings, and it made me wonder why you would have a maze at all if you were going to point the way to the center.

The hedges were a tight squeeze, and the branches prickled as we pushed through them. Paimon had not been attending to his gardening duty here, because in some places the branches had almost grown together and obscured the way altogether. But we sucked it in and pushed, and ignored the scratching, and on we went, through the twists and turns. Sometimes the pathway sloped down, sometimes up. Sometimes we passed intersections I could have sworn we had passed through before, but the blaze had moved: Before it had indicated right, now left.

Califa, I was tired. What I wouldn't give for a nice long nap. Or, barring that, a ginormous-huge coffee. *You can sleep when you are dead*, said Nini Mo, and the Butcher didn't show any signs of fatigue, so I forced myself to stumble on after her, lifting leaden feet smartly and stifling my yawns.

"How far is it to the middle?" I asked, after it seemed as though we'd been walking for hours. "Are you sure we aren't lost? We keep passing the same intersections."

"You just think that—that's part of the maze's magick," the Butcher said. "Anyway, we're almost there. Smell that?"

I sniffed deeply. I *did* smell something, something earthy and spicy, something that on the top smelled rather like ginger cookies but underneath had the unpleasant metallic tang of decay.

"Funeral incense and death," the Butcher said. "Pig's favorite smell."

Pig was riding in the Butcher's knapsack; as she moved in front of me, I could just see the pink tip of his snout sticking out from under the top flap. A few more twists and turns, and then suddenly the hedge fell away. Before us, in the clearing, sat a huge black object.

Georgiana Haðraaða's tomb.

THIRTY-FIVE

Georgiana's Tomb. Toby. Run!

A BLACK OBSIDIAN plinth sat in the middle of the grassy clearing. Upon the plinth sat a massive black sarcophagus. Upon *that* sat a stone pillow painted to look like red satin. Upon *that* sat a pudgy wirehaired terrier. Remembering the Haðraaða corpses in the Cloakroom of the Abyss, I was willing to bet that although this terrier looked asleep, it was actually dead.

"The *Diario* is inside the sarcophagus," the Butcher said. "With Grandmamma."

Before, I had decried the Haðraaða habit of exhibiting their corpses in the open air. Now, looking at that colossal marble lid that surely weighed a colossal heavy weight, I rather thought that the open-air habit was a pretty good one.

"How we are going to get that lid off?" I said, aware that a bit of a whine was creeping into my voice but not caring. Every time I thought things would be smooth sailing, the water got rough again. No one said rangering would be easy, but this was getting ridiculous.

"Oh, that's easy," the Butcher said. "We'll just invoke some leverage, and Pig will help." She popped Pig out of her knapsack and held him up. He looked about as strong as a bowl of blancmange. In fact, he seemed the very definition of flabby. But then, he had almost eaten that kakodæmon, so he had to be stronger than he looked. She tossed him, and he landed with a *plop* on top of the sarcophagus.

The Butcher clambered up on the plinth. She balanced on the narrow edge and extended a hand down to me, which I ignored, because it wasn't that high up—only about four feet or so. I hopped and huffed and pulled myself up, the marble cold against my skin. The plinth made a tablelike support for the sarcophagus, which was shaped very much like a tea caddy.

"Be careful," the Butcher warned, as I puffed my way up next to her. "Toby bites. At least he used to. High-strung little fiker."

Toby, I assumed, was the terrier. He did look high-strung; his lips were drawn back from his tiny teeth in a sort of shark-like grin, and his ears were flat against his skull. The Butcher reached out gingerly and poked at his side, and when he didn't move a muscle, she grabbed him around his salamilike middle and offered him to me.

"What am I supposed to do with him?" I asked. His fur looked a little moth-eaten and his eyes glinted in a rather malicious way. I didn't like the look of those nubby sharp teeth.

"Just put him aside, there at the end of the plinth," she instructed, and I did so, wiping my hands on my kilts. Toby's fur was rough and greasy. Yuck.

A tiny keyhole glinted just below the rim of the sarcophagus's lid.

"Will the Key open it?"

The Butcher grinned. "Ayah, so. It sure is coming in mighty handy, eh?"

"What were you doing in Hardhands's underwear drawer?"

"I was looking for stuff to kip. It drives Hardhands nuts, the way his things keep disappearing, but he thinks it is Paimon's bad housekeeping. He doesn't ever consider *me,* the nook!"

Her tone was scornful, but it suddenly flashed upon me that this scorn might just be a mask. When I was in sixth grade, there was a kid named Tiro Ram who was always pinching me and calling me names; once, he even threw an inky pen into my hair during Historical Inquiry class. I thought he hated me, but Mamma explained (after she came back from Sanctuary, where she'd been discussing with the Holy Mistress of Heaven why I had punched Tiro Ram right in the grape) that he really liked me but was just showing it in a stupid way because he was embarrassed. I had been skeptical, of course, but that spring Tiro Ram had asked me to the Spring Dance, so I guess Mamma had been right. (But I went to the Spring Dance with Udo, because Fyrdraacas neither forgive nor forget.) The Butcher's attitude toward Hardhands was pretty negative, but perhaps that was hiding her true feelings, in which case I felt even more sorry for her. And I wish she'd stuck with him, and left Poppy alone.

"Now, look, Flora, I've been thinking," the Butcher said, making no move to open the lock.

"Ayah?" I said warily. Whenever people say they've been thinking, they have never been thinking anything good.

"Maybe you never heard of me in the future, but surely you've heard of Hardhands. He's a great hero. The Warlord's Fist."

"Hmmm?" I said evasively.

"Tell me what happens to him. I gotta know."

"That wasn't part of our deal."

"It is now. Tell me, or you are on your own to finish that mission."

"That's not very rangery of you!" I said indignantly. "You can't change a pinkie promise!" Now her true colors were coming out—trying to change a pinkie promise!

"I don't care. I have got to know. Tell me. And the truth, too, don't make anything up, like I can see you trying to do. Ranger's honor. Please."

"Nini Mo said it's not good to know the future."

"I don't give a fike what Nini says," the Butcher said fiercely. "I want to know what *you* say. You said you never heard of me; does that mean Hardhands kills me?"

I didn't know what to tell her. If I told her the truth, she'd be devastated. But if I lied, she'd go forward unprepared. She might grow up to be a traitor and a killer, but now she was going out on a limb for me, and didn't that deserve something? "I don't know . . ."

"Tell me: Is Hardhands dead?"

Surely that couldn't hurt. "Ayah."

"Well, that's something. Does he die happily in his bed?"

"No." My blood went cold as I realized that earlier I had told her that Hardhands was still alive—that he had refused to help Nini Mo. Pigface, what if she noticed my slip? *You gotta keep your lies straight,* Nini Mo said.

But the Butcher was so pleased at the thought of Hardhands dead that she swallowed my lie without question. "Ah, that's good news. Tell me how. Was it painful?"

"Very painful," I said, desperate to get on with it. "Excruciating."

"But how?" she persisted.

I cast about for the most painful, embarrassing thing I could think of. "A rat crawled up the pot, bit him on the hinder, and the wound festered. Satisfied?"

"Oh yes," she answered, clearly delighted with my lie.

The Butcher pressed her index finger, still encircled with the Bilskinir Key, against the tiny keyhole on the sarcophagus's lip. The lock clicked as its tumblers turned over. The hasp popped open, and the Butcher flipped it up. She grinned at me, triumphantly. "Come on, put some back into it."

We braced ourselves as best as we could—which wasn't very good at all, with the ledge being so narrow—and grasped the edge of the sarcophagus. We heaved. And heaved. And heaved. Pushed and grunted, and grunted and pushed. All the blood rushed to my head in a dull pounding swell; my hands burned and my muscles screamed. The lid did not lift.

"Put yer back in it," the Butcher said through gritted teeth. Under the smeared black, her face had turned tomato red.

"I am," I gritted back. My hands slid off the marble, and I

almost lost my balance. The Butcher grabbed me just as I began to fall, and I steadied myself in her grip.

"On the count of three," she said.

"Maybe we need a lever?"

"I felt it move. Let's try again. One, two, three."

Again we heaved and strained, and this time I felt the marble move slightly. I closed my eyes, put my back into it, and felt another little movement. Another grunting push, and—the lid flew up so smoothly and easily that the Butcher and I both almost tumbled in. This time I recovered first, and grabbed her before she ended up flat on her face.

Inside the sarcophagus was a plain black wooden box, nailed shut. Green chalk marks were scrawled across the lid, but they were faded and impossible to read. A funeral prayer probably, or maybe a Protection Sigil. From somewhere on her person, the Butcher produced an extremely large knife and began to pry up nail heads. I dug my penknife out of my dispatch case and did the same. The air inside the sarcophagus was stale with old perfume and a musty, decaying smell, which was making me mighty uneasy. I was beginning to get the strong feeling that Georgiana Segunda was not so fresh. But when I voiced that worry to the Butcher, she scoffed at my squeamishness and I let it go. If she could take the stench, so could I.

After several broken fingernails (me) and spurts of horrific swearing (the Butcher), we had all the nails out and the lid loosened.

"Ready?" the Butcher asked. It was hard to tell under the black paint, but I thought she did look a bit green about the edges. Ha!

"Ayah."

But still we hesitated, staring at each other. Georgiana may be disgusting, I told myself, but she was dead. She couldn't hurt us. The Butcher must have been thinking along the same lines, for she said, "'Never flinch,' Nini says," and I think she was trying to persuade herself as much as me.

"Dare, win, or . . . ," I responded.

"Disappear!" we chorused together.

We heaved up and over. The lid flew right out of our hands, then hit the ground with an appalling thunder. If Paimon didn't hear *that*, he was stone-cold deaf. Or absolutely knackered from providing The Tygers of Wrath's galvanic juice. I'd take either one, as long as it kept him away.

I looked down into the coffin. And there was Georgiana Haðraaða, covered with a thin funeral drape, lying on a bed of red springy stuff—her hair, which either had been extremely long or kept growing after she died. The hair spilled out from underneath the funeral drape, filling the coffin almost to over-flowing.

The other Haðraaða dead had looked merely asleep, their flesh still firm, their clothes still bright, as though they were only waiting for the dinner bell to wake them. Georgiana Segunda's funeral drape was almost transparent, and it could not hide the sunken cheeks, the livid, twisted mark around her neck, the deep sockets of her eyes. She wore the Pontifexa's tiara, a thin band of silver from which sprang two blue-and-green enamel feathers, one on either side of her forehead, like antennae.

"Paimon should be punished for allowing Grandmamma to look so bad," the Butcher said. "She wouldn't be happy. She was very careful to always look her best."

"Gorgeousness ends at the grave," I said, which is what Mamma said to Udo once, when he had told her that he was go-ing to die young and leave an exquisite corpse.

"Not for Haðraaðas," the Butcher said. "He killed her, you know, Hardhands, the fiking rat's bane."

"I thought Georgiana Segunda killed herself rather than submit to the Warlord," I answered. The Butcher shot me a poisonous look.

"Who gave the City to Florian? *He* did. Hardhands. He gave her no choice. Better to kill yourself than to submit. There's no honor in submission."

"Better to retreat and regroup than to rout," I said. "Didn't Nini Mo say?"

Another poisonous look. "I never heard Nini say such a thing; I don't think she ever would. Grandmamma hung herself from the Tree of Woe, with her dressing-gown sash, but it was Hardhands's betrayal that made her do it. So he killed her. And he would kill me if he got a chance, but he's not going to get it."

Much as I hated to admit it, I was starting to feel a twinge of pity for the Butcher. No matter how annoying they were, I did have my family, and the dogs, and the horses, and my friends. Who did she have? A servitor nurse and a servitor plushy Pig. A murderous husband. And she was not going to live happily ever after.

The Butcher carefully drew back the funeral drape. Georgiana's clawlike hands were folded on her chest, her spindly fingers wrapped around a small black book: her *Diario*. Finally! A hopeful, triumphant feeling washed over me. There was the object of all my efforts, within my grasp. With Nini Mo's help, I would return to Lord Axacaya—*Lo, the Conquering Hero Comes!*—and he would be proud of me, and together we would save the City.

Suddenly, jarringly, the Pontifexa's thick black lashes fluttered open, and her hands trembled. Her eyes shone like glassy marbles, and their whites were not white at all, but a muddy brown. Her throat spasmed, and she gasped as though she were choking, then swallowed hard.

"Tiny Doom," Georgiana Segunda said thickly. Her tongue protruded wormlike from her bloody lips. She opened and closed her mouth a couple of times, as though to make sure that her jaw still worked.

The Butcher and I were transfixed on our precarious perch, hardly able to move for horror. Or at least, I was hardly able to move. The Butcher looked less horrified, more strangely joyful.

"Grandmamma!" she cried.

"Help me up, my darling," Georgiana Segunda croaked.

The Butcher gingerly reached out and took the Pontifexa's arms. The Pontifexa's eyes rolled wildly, and then they stared straight ahead. As she sat up, the *Diario* slid toward me. I grabbed it and slid it inside my dispatch case. Neither Georgiana Segunda nor the Butcher noticed.

Georgiana Segunda turned her head slowly in my direction, and the diamonds on her tiara jiggled. The enamel feathers now looked black, insectile, like the antennae of a cockroach. Mold crept down her cheeks, like greenish blush, and beneath it, her skin was mottled black and gray. But the Butcher didn't seem to mind. She hugged the Pontifexa, her hands leaving red marks on Georgiana's bare shoulders. Georgiana Segunda tried to raise her arms, but they wiggled, bonelessly, and fell away.

"Grandmamma, he stole my House from me!" the Butcher complained.

The Pontifexa answered slowly, "Who stole it, darling?"

"Hardhands! He stole my House."

"Shame on you for letting him."

The Butcher looked taken aback; I guess she expected sympathy. "But I was only a kid. How could I stop him?"

The Pontifexa coughed, gratingly, and a little trickle of white oozed out of her mouth—a fat wiggly worm. It fell onto her neck and then disappeared into her cleavage. I swallowed hard.

"A Haðraaða doesn't make excuses," the Pontifexa slurred.

"But—"

"Kiss me, darling girl, I'm feeling slippery again. Can I see you?"

The Butcher leaned forward, but her grandmother flapped a limp hand at her. "Not you, Tiny Doom. The other girl, the last one. Kiss me, darling girl."

I did not want to touch those dead lips, puffy and black. "Uh—"

"Kiss her, Flora," the Butcher said urgently. "She needs our strength."

Indeed, the Pontifexa was already looking more wobbly, as though her bones were dissolving and she would soon collapse into a puddle of empty skin. But I did not want to kiss her—now that I had the *Diario* I just wanted to scarper.

Then, at a sudden bright pulse of pain, I jerked back. As fast as a striking snake, the Pontifexa had bitten my arm. I jumped down, landing on the marble floor with a heavy bone-jarring jolt. That was nothing compared to the throbbing in my arm; the Pontifexa's sharp teeth had sheared through two layers of clothing to reach flesh.

"Grandmamma!" the Butcher protested. "That was mean."

The Pontifexa grinned at her, a trickle of blood—*my* blood—dripping from the corner of her mouth. Her wormy tongue licked her lips, and she closed her eyes, savoring my blood. When the Pontifexa opened her eyes, they had changed to red—even the sclera—and when she spoke, her voice was much clearer. "I'm so glad that you came to see me, darlings. So glad you thought to let me out. I've been trapped for so long."

"What do you mean, Grandmamma? Are you stuck in the Abyss?" the Butcher asked. She was still up on the plinth, awfully close to the Pontifexa's sharp teeth. Too close.

"No, my darling. My flesh is my tomb. And this box has been my trap. But now you have let me out, my bungalow baby-doll. And I am hungry."

The Butcher was slow on the uptake, but I immediately realized what that meant. Georgiana Segunda was a ghoul. Her Anima remained trapped in her corpse, in a kind of living death. I couldn't imagine a worse fate. Your body decaying while your mind stayed active. Lying like that for years, stuck in a coffin, while the worms nibbled at you and your entrails congealed into goo—it made me sick just thinking about it. Unlike zombies, ghouls have Will and Aptitude; they are not mindless animated corpses. They know what is happening to them. And they are ravenously hungry, always craving human flesh.

And what else was there for Georgiana to eat here but us?

"Butcher—I mean Tiny Doom—I think we should get out of here," I said urgently. The Butcher ignored me, still staring at her ghoulish grandmamma.

"Grandmamma, can we help you?" she asked.

"I am hungry and I want to eat," Georgiana said, and reached out one long bony arm. The Butcher remained transfixed. I ran forward and yanked her boot; she tumbled off the plinth, landing heavily on me, and then rolled to her feet, protesting.

"*Come on!*" I shouted. "Tiny Doom, RUN!"

Georgiana was standing, her red hair falling about her like some wiry galvanic cape. "Come to me, my little poppet!"

"But Grandmamma!" the Butcher wailed. I grabbed her arm. Georgiana's movements were jerky, but swiftness made up for the lack of grace. She clambered down the side of the sarcophagus, spiderlike. In a blur of motion, she was almost upon us, clawlike hands outstretched, mouth a gaping maw of rotting black teeth.

THIRTY-SIX

Trapped!
A Burrow. Desperate Measures.

WE RAN LIKE jackrabbits out of the clearing and into the maze. I was huffing and puffing; I should sign up for track at Sanctuary and work on my wind. The Butcher's wind was fine. She sprinted like a trooper doing triple-time with an entire company of Flayed Riders behind her, quickly outpacing me.

Though our drumming feet made too much noise to hear the sounds of pursuit behind us, I knew that Georgiana was hot on our heels. She was hungry, and we were fresh and sweet; who knows when she'd again have the chance for such a yummy snack?

Up ahead the maze forked; the Butcher had already torn down the right-hand path, even though the blaze indicated we should go left. I tried unsuccessfully to grab her, but she threw me off, kept going. I followed, not wanting to be left behind, even if we were going the wrong way.

"Darling girls..." The mournful cry echoed unnervingly close behind us. I tripped on a root, and the Butcher hauled me back onto my feet. We hit a dead end, turned around in a jumble, and made it back to the junction before Georgiana did. We plunged down the other pathway—but now she sounded much closer.

"Pig!" I puffed. "Set him on her!"

"I don't want him to hurt her," the Butcher puffed back.

"She wants to *eat* us!"

"She's my grandmother!"

"She's a *ghoul*!"

"It's not her fault! To the right!"

Behind us now, we could hear the shuffling slither of Georgiana's robes, the wet slap of her feet. "Baby dolls, a little nibble. I promise you, just a tiny nibble . . ."

The moans were getting closer, as was the stench of disintegration, strong enough that even the funeral incense couldn't hide it. We turned a corner and ran down a long leafy passageway. I looked over my shoulder and saw the shuffling shape of Georgiana, bony arms outstretched, her hair crackling and writhing around her head. She was gnashing her blackened teeth, which, though wobbly, looked more than sharp enough to shred our flesh.

"Darling lonely only," Georgiana slurred. She was fast, only a few feet behind us now, close enough that I could smell— could taste—the rancid puff of her breath as she wheezed air in and out of her lungs, not to breathe, of course, but to speak.

The Butcher sped up and pulled me with her, my lungs turning to painful bellows.

We turned another corner, and then another, and then saw up ahead—a dead end. If we doubled back now, we'd run straight into Georgiana. She hadn't caught up with us yet, but she was going to soon. *Oh Nini Mo, help us now, please.*

"Fike! Fike!" the Butcher gasped. "We are fiked. Completely fiked!"

"Language!" I panted. I noticed that near the ground some of the branches in the maze wall were bent enough to make a small opening. I slapped at the branches and discovered a burrow just big enough for the two of us. Quickly, we slithered inside.

We lay in the burrow, hardly daring to breath, and listened to Georgiana stagger by, muttering. The burrow smelled strongly of coyote, which hopefully would mask the smell of us. My heart was pounding so hard that it seemed as though my blood would pump right out of my ears. The Butcher pressed tightly against me, trembling, her quivery breathing echoing in my ear, her breath damp on my hair. Her presence was comforting. At least I wasn't in this alone. Also, she was closer to the opening, so she'd get eaten first. Gradually, the sounds of Georgiana's progress grew fainter. *A near escape*, said Nini Mo, *is better than no escape at all.*

"I need a cigarillo," the Butcher whispered, after a long, long time.

"I need to pee," I whispered back.

"What do we do? We have to free her from the ruin of her body. Send her on through the Abyss. We can't leave her like this." The Butcher sounded anguished.

"We'll have to call Paimon; he'll know what to do."

"I can't," she moaned. "Hardhands will kill me. He'll kill us both if he knows that we opened the tomb. He made her like this! He hated her, and he made her into a ghoul. We have to do something!"

"But what can we do?"

"You must know some sigil or something that will free her. You are a ranger—*do something!*" the Butcher hissed. No longer was she so cocky; now she was looking to me for a plan, and I was realizing the downside to lying through your teeth. What if you came to a point when you needed to prove yourself and could not? For a while Georgiana's crashing had been distant, but now it was starting to sound closer again, and the stench of the ghoul was growing stronger.

"Look, she'll be back any minute and she'll find us," I said. "And how can we help her if she eats us? Nini will know what to do. We've got to get out of here, and Nini will help us. Didn't she dispatch an entire crew of ghouls in *Nini Mo vs. the Meatpacking Sausage Makers?*"

Of course, Nini Mo had dispatched the ghouls by putting them through their own meat grinder, but I hoped that the Butcher was so freaked that she wouldn't remember that detail.

"Bungalow baby dolls!"

The branches above us shook. We froze. The Butcher's clutch became viselike. The stench of the grave was overwhelming—I gagged, clenching my teeth, feeling my blueberry buckle burn in the back of my throat. If I puked now, we'd be lost. Next to me, the Butcher gurgled; I slapped a hand over her mouth, pressing down hard. Then the air lifted, and the noise of breaking branches began to move off again.

Never before had I felt less like a ranger. No ranger would ever have allowed herself to be trapped like this, her back against the wall, unable to escape. A ranger would come up with a plan to escape, use what she had.

"Do you still have that Direction Sigil?" the Butcher hissed.

"Ayah, but it didn't work before."

"You didn't do it right. You must have mispronounced the Word. Let me see the Sigil."

I squirmed, loosening the Butcher's grip enough to pull the Sigil out of my pocket. Its coldfire glow was dim, but it was there.

The Butcher squeezed me encouragingly. "Look, I'll say the Word this time. You focus your fear."

I didn't need to focus my fear; my fear was already pretty darn focused on exactly what would happen if the Sigil went wrong. I'd rather take my chances with the ghoul than end up all the way inside a wall. "It's too dangerous. Remember what happened to my hair!"

"We're cool, Flora. The Key controls movement in Bilskinir. It won't work without a door, but the Direction Sigil is a kind of door. Together, the Key and the Sigil will combine into a Translocation Sigil that will get us the fike out of here! There's no chance it will go wrong!"

While we were whispering back and forth, the ghoulish noises had been getting closer again. Now that the stench of the grave was growing stronger, suddenly I felt as though maybe I would rather take my chances with the Sigil; surely if I ended up in the middle of a wall or floor or piece of furniture, I'd die instantly. And that was better than being chewed to death.

"Get us out of here, then!"

"Focus your fear!"

The Butcher covered my hands with hers, so that the Sigil was tight within our combined grip. The Butcher's hands were hot and sweaty, but then so, too, were mine. I didn't need to use my imagination to conjure up visions of horrific monsters about to snatch me up and rend my flesh from my bones. Not when I could hear the horrific monster, crashing around me, crying out, "Oh sweetness, where have you gone?" As I focused all this panic and fear upon the Sigil, the familiar buzz began to spread through me, stronger than before. The Butcher's hands ground into mine, cracking the bones. Pigface, she was strong, and her grip was hard, fierce, and galvanic.

The heat of the Sigil reached my head and again the world began to tilt and whirl. A great drumming filled my chest—my heartbeat and the Butcher's, thrumming together. I could see the brilliant glow of her Anima—blue and gold, tinged with black—even through my closed eyelids. Then the Butcher's grip loosened, pulled away, and she let out an almighty shriek. I opened my eyes to see her squirming and kicking in Georgiana's grip.

"Oh, my bright-haired child of sunset," Georgiana cackled. "How lovely you smell."

With my free hand, I grabbed one of the Butcher's kicking boots, trying to pull her away, but the ghoul was too strong. I needed both hands, yet I didn't dare drop the Sigil; if it activated when I wasn't touching it, it would go and leave me behind. And if the Sigil activated while Georgiana, the Butcher, and I were still linked, we'd all end up in the Cloakroom of the Abyss, which would be no escape at all. I pulled harder on the Butcher's boot, but it was no use. The ghoul had the strength of a starving creature who knew her next meal was nigh. In my hand, the Sigil was crackling and spitting.

"FLORA!"

"Say the Word!" I screamed.

"⛩🖐🐟👹🎏" the Butcher shrieked.

I let go of her boot.
And she—
The ghoul—
I—
Gone.

THIRTY-SEVEN

The Cloakroom of the Abyss.
Azota. Tent City.

*T*HE BRIEF SENSATION of falling surrounded me, and I landed hard, the impact shooting all the air out of my lungs and momentarily stunning me. I gurgled, lungs inflating, gasping. When the sparkly darkness lifted, I discovered I was lying on top of a man dressed in old-timey plate mail, the ridges of his armor digging painfully into my arms and legs. The man looked as though he were asleep, but he was not. The man was Albany Bilskinir, the husband of Georgiana Primera Haðraaða, and he'd been dead for years and years.

I was in the Cloakroom of the Abyss. The Translocation Sigil had worked, though it wasn't going to work again. The Sigil had burned up, leaving behind a throbbing scorch mark in my palm. There was no sign of the Butcher or Georgiana Segunda.

Other families dispose of their dead decently, bodies carefully wrapped and placed into holes or burned up on funeral pyres and placed in large pots. But the Haðraaða Family is not so tidy. The walls of the Cloakroom of the Abyss are lined with alcoves, stacked four levels high. Each alcove contains a catafalque, and upon each catafalque rests a Haðraaða corpse, perfectly preserved.

The Cloakroom is silent, except for the distant pulse of the sea, lit only by wavery greenish light that seems to be coming from the green marble itself. This light is dim and fluttery, and in it the corpses lie on their marvelously carved catafalques perfectly preserved. From my previous visit to Bilskinir, I knew this perfection was merely an illusion. Under the disguising Glamours, the bodies bear hideous marks of death: childbirth, dog bite, hanging, arrow to the throat.

I knew where I was, but *when* was I? When I climbed down from Albany Bilskinir's bier, I beheld the answer: There, in the middle of the room, stood Hardhands's shiplike catafalque, draped in sail-like red curtains. Hardhands was dead and I was home. I had no idea why the Sigil had taken me not only to the right place, but also to the right time, but I didn't care. *Don't look a gift mule in the mouth*, said Nini Mo.

Of the six alcoves at floor level, five contain Haðraaðas, but the sixth, I remembered from before, is empty. The mermaid figurehead at the prow of Hardhands's catafalque seemed to be watching me as I staggered over to that empty alcove. As I approached, the inscription on the lintel lit up: CYRENACIA SIDONIA ROMNEY BRAKESPEARE OV HAÐRAADA. When Tiny Doom had told me her name, she had left out the most important bits—the parts I would have recognized: Cyrenacia Brakespeare. An ivory-handled whip lay on the plinth, its lash made from a long vivid red braid: Poppy's hair, sheared as a sign of mourning. By the time the Birdies got done with her, there was nothing left to bury.

I stood there, looking at the whip. I knew Tiny Doom had survived the ghoulish Georgiana and had lived to die another day, but I still felt terrible for abandoning her, what seemed like only minutes ago. She'd come back for me, but I'd left her behind. Rangers never abandon a comrade.

I still could not reconcile Tiny Doom and the Butcher Brakespeare—the girl she'd been, the woman she'd become. But I couldn't think of her as the Butcher anymore, only as Tiny Doom. Whatever monster she grew up to be, she hadn't been a monster then. She'd been pretty darn cool, brave and faithful, clever and quick. And I'd lied to her and left her in the lurch.

"I'm sorry, Tiny Doom," I said, the dead silence muting my voice and making my apology sound insignificant, which, of course, it was.

And I was sorry about something else, too: Now I would never meet Nini Mo. To have been so close and yet too far was extremely disappointing. On the other hand, Nini Mo probably would not have been impressed with the way I'd treated my comrade, so maybe it was just as well.

But I couldn't waste any more time thinking about my failures. I had to get the *Diario* to Lord Axacaya. I had no idea how much time had passed since I had entered Bilskinir; perhaps it was already too late.

So I scarpered, quickly and quietly. As I had no intention of giving the *Diario* back, it seemed wise to leave before Paimon found me. But while making my way out of Bilskinir, no sign of Paimon did I see. The House felt strangely lifeless. Perhaps his power was fading at last, and the thought made me sad. Paimon deserved better.

Bilskinir's front gate, small and wooden, was closed. A huge bulk loomed on the other side, and my heart surged with gladness when I saw the whiskery nose and the chocolate eyes. The tide must have dropped, allowing Sieur Caballo to climb to the top of the causeway and wait for me. I had succeeded in my goal, despite all—time mix-up, oubliette, ghouls, Tiny Doom's foul cigarillos—and I should have felt triumphant. But I felt like hell, like every bone in my body had been pounded into mash, my blood replaced with thick gelatin and my sinews with rusty wire. If there hadn't been a rock to climb upon, I doubt if I could have mounted Sieur Caballo. He could smell my urgency; as soon I was seated, he took off down the causeway, which, happily, was dry.

Below us, the Pacifica Playa was now scattered with tents and shebangs. My heart thudded. Were these just refugees paranoid about future earth shakings, or all who were left after the Final Upheaval? My heart thudded faster: Thin tendrils of black smoke were trailing above the Loma Linda hills. Maybe I was too late—maybe the Loliga's labor had already begun and the City had succumbed to her convulsions.

Hope is free, said Nini Mo.

I hoped, hoped, hoped, that I was not too late.

People were straggling down the Lobos Road, some on foot, carrying baskets, babies, dogs. Others pushed wheelbarrows piled high with household goods. A dogcart carrying two small children, one holding a chicken whose plumage reminded me unaccountably of Alfonzo the merman. Two mules pulling a wagon full of turnips. Two black-and-white collies herding a small huddle of sheep.

Everyone was coming from the City. I seemed to be the only one heading toward it.

Please, Califa, do not let me be too late.

I urged Sieur Caballo into a trot. We crossed the Great Sandy Bank, also scattered with shebangs, and turned onto the City Road. We passed the Bella Union Saloon, which was doing a rip-roaring business; I guess people think it's better to face disaster drunk than sober. A man staggered out from behind a wagon, the front of his kilt falling open, and tried to grab at Sieur Caballo's head, but he shied away and took off at a full gallop.

By the time we approached the Portal Pass, I was lathered in sweaty fear. At the top of the pass, you can see all the way across the City, across the blue sweep of the Bay, to the distant hazy hills of Alameda. What would that vista show now? Smoking ruins? A hurricane of fire? I clenched the reins and bit my lip, feeling as though I might, at any moment, puke that chocolate and buckle I had eaten so many years ago.

Halfway up the grade, a squad of soldiers roared up from behind and passed us. The guidon proclaimed them to be from the Dandies. They looked tough and purposeful, and I felt a surge of relief—no matter what else, the Army was standing firm. I put heels to Sieur Caballo, and we followed in their dusty wake. As we crested the pass, my dread grew so strong that I felt as though I might faint.

But there, spread out before me, was the City intact. Smudgy with smoke, but intact. I was not too late. I pulled Sieur Caballo to a stop. If I squinted, I could pick out the second-tallest hill in the City: Crackpot Hill. If I squinted even more, I could see the very tippy-top of Poppy's Eyrie, and then, higher than that, a flutter—so small that I had to supply its color with my imagination: purple. Mamma's colors. Crackpot Hall was fine.

I was not too late.

Giddy with happiness, I leaned over and kissed the spot between Sieur Caballo's ears. "Remind me, when I see him next, to give Valefor a big wet one, too," I said. His ears flickered, and he tossed his head, pawing at the ground.

THIRTY-EIGHT

Tortillas. The Diario. Nap Time.

CASA MARIPOSA, Lord Axacaya's house, is built in the Birdie style, which means that from the street it looks unassuming, its front facade a long white expanse of windowless whitewashed walls. I left Sieur Caballo at the public water trough outside and made my way through Mariposa's open gate and into the main courtyard, which I had seen before only by moonlight, when I had come to Mariposa to ask Lord Axacaya's help in curing my Anima Enervation. In the daylight, the Courtyard was even more splendid, awash in flowers: violently purple bougainvilleas, yolk-colored marigolds, crimson rosebushes. Iridescent blue-green parrots darted over my head, and the air was flecked with butterflies: green and gold, white and red, some as small as gnats, others nearly as big as the parrots.

Casa Mariposa has no Butler, but Lord Axacaya does have a praterhuman steward called Sitri, who was now coming toward me. Sitri has the head of a camel and a human body, but this combination is not as weirdly horrible as the eagle-human Quetzals, maybe because his camel eyes looked so sad.

"Ave, Madama Fyrdraaca." Sitri bowed deeply. "Welcome to Casa Mariposa."

He offered me a stirrup cup, and after brushing away the butterflies swarming around it, I drank: deliciously cold hibiscus lemonade. "Thank you. My horse is outside," I said, handing him back the glass. "Could someone bring him in, brush him down, and feed him? He hasn't eaten in a while. And check his hooves for stones?"

Sitri nodded morosely. "It shall be done. Come. Lord Axacaya awaits you."

As we passed down the long passage, I caught a glimpse of myself in a mirror. I didn't look too bad. Tiny Doom's stays fit so much better than my old ones, and her frock coat was splendid—so old-fashioned it was almost stylish. Sure, my hair was a mess, and my eyeliner had blurred into black shadows, but I looked rather rough and sexy, like someone who was too busy to worry about how she looked, but always looked pretty good naturally.

Axila Aguila coalesced out of the shadows and joined us. She nodded at Sitri, who vanished.

"You took a long time," she said. "At Bilskinir."

"Longer than you might think." Little sparkles of anticipation were twinkling in my tum as I followed her down the hallway and across another courtyard. Now that I knew that Crackpot Hall still stood, and I had accomplished my mission, and everything was going to be cool—I felt pretty good, actually. A monkey chattered in a jacaranda tree, and jewel-colored birds clustered on the edge of an elaborate cactus-shaped fountain. But there was a long jagged crack in the plaster of one of the walls, plaster chunks on the sidewalk, and the ground under the citrus trees was littered with fallen oranges and lemons, filling the air with the pungent scent of rotting fruit. *Don't count your money until you have left the gambling hell*, said Nini Mo. We weren't safe yet.

"Lord Axacaya was concerned. He feared that perhaps you had gotten lost. Or that Paimon had not been welcoming."

"Well, I had a few difficulties, but overall, a piece of cake."

The Quetzal swiveled her head toward me, even as she continued to walk. The golden eyes gleamed. "I am glad to hear that, Flora."

"Flora!" Before I could respond to Lord Axacaya's call, I was enfolded in a burning hot embrace. He squeezed me until I was breathless, and briefly swung me up off the ground. Then, laughing, he released me. "I'm sorry, *pequeña*! But I am so glad to see you. I was extremely worried." Today he was dressed plainly in a white kilt. No features or ornaments other than his brilliant blue tattoos. But still, he was beautiful and his smile was like the sun.

"No problem at all," I said, laughing with him.

"Come—you must be starving. Let us eat, and then you shall tell me everything." He led me through a long gallery, its walls vividly painted with a mural depicting a Birdie sacrifice: a jade-masked priest brandishing an obsidian knife, four eagle-headed priests restraining a screaming figure. In the sunshine slanting through the slatted *latilla* ceiling, the mural was garishly lifelike. Lord Axacaya brought me to a small round room beyond the gallery, with whitewashed walls that were perfectly plain. The only furniture was a low wooden table, surrounded by brightly colored pillows.

A delicious warmth wafted from the brazier in the center of the table. A griddle stone had been placed on the brazier, and a bubbling pot sat at one end, whistling the most delicious spicy smell. We sat across from each other, and Sitri, who had silently followed us, placed an earthenware bowl and horn spoon before each of us. While Sitri ladled the pozole, Lord Axacaya began to pat our tortillas. Making tortillas without a press isn't easy; believe me, the grade I got in Elementary Cookery is proof of that. But Lord Axacaya seemed to have the trick down, and the tortillas were delicious, tasting of dusty corn and charred lime and the warmth of the fire.

Sitri had filled my bowl, and now a rich spicy fragrance drifted up, wonderfully steamy. The pozole was fat with swollen hominy and chunks of tender pork. Its warmth—heat and spice—spilled down my throat, into my vast empty tum, and then pulsated into my collapsed veins, filling them with goodness and light.

Lord Axacaya kept passing down the tortillas, and whenever

my bowl was empty, Sitri filled it again, and again, and again. The hole in my tummy was not as deep as I had thought; it took a while of slurping and chewing, but eventually it was full. I did manage to drink the xocholatte that Sitri finally set in front of me, but then I felt both sleepy and in need to loosen my (Tiny Doom's) stays.

"Now, tell me everything," Lord Axacaya said, and so I lay back upon the pillows and told him everything. He listened, occasionally sipping from his own xocholatte. Midway through my recitation, I felt a waft of cool air on my back, and though I didn't turn to look, I knew that the Quetzal had joined us. Lord Axacaya seemed pleased with my story; though he looked suitably concerned during the dark and scary parts of my tale, toward the end, his smile grew large and proud.

"That is a tale fit for a hero, Flora," he said, when I had finished and was rewetting my dry mouth with a gulp of hot spiced wine. "I am impressed with how well you handled the situation. And all the unexpected contingencies. And most of all, how you stood up to the Butcher Brakespeare and bent her to your Will. She was very tricky, and I am proud you could match her. Not many can say that. Shall we see the *Diario* now?"

My face had grown hot with blushes, alas, as Lord Axacaya spoke, and I felt marvelously pleased with myself. I reached into my dispatch case and withdrew the *Diario* with a flourish. But when I offered it to Lord Axacaya, he didn't take it.

"You should do the honors, Flora," Lord Axacaya said. "After all, you took all the risk. You should take all the glory. Open it."

So I did. Georgiana's *Diario* looked very ordinary, like the kind of notebook I use at Sanctuary School. The lined pages were covered in dense handwriting, with hardly a white spot left; even the margins had been written in. Her handwriting, thankfully, was easy to read, a beautiful scrolling copperplate hand done in vivid peacock blue, as neat and tidy as Mamma's best clerk. Each entry was laid out on a single page, with the title of the Working, the date, and notes.

"Look for an entry dated around 1380," Lord Axacaya suggested.

I flipped through the pages. The earliest entries were for very simple magickal sigils; Georgiana must have started out small and then worked her way up to bigger things. Much bigger things.

"Here it is!" I read out loud: " 'On the capture and confinement of a ninth-level etheric egregore: The most difficult and dangerous Working I have ever undertaken. It was a hard fight, but I triumphed in the end. The egregore is now confined within the form of a squid and at my command will menace the City, or even destroy it, if I so require. The Council tried to undo the Working, of course, tried and failed. To make sure the Working will not weaken, I have used the power of the Haðraaða bloodline to fuse the Sigils together. This power, of course, is embodied by the Head of the House Haðraaða. As long as our House prospers, as long as the House stands, the Working shall remain strong. Only when the last Haðraaða is dead, when there is no longer a Head of our House and the great Word of our Family falls silent, can the Working be abrogated. Only then can the cage that holds the Loliga be opened. Of course the Council does not know this; they only see a Working they cannot break. And so they wisely kneel in obedience to me.'

"That's all it says. She doesn't give any specifics about the Sigil itself—the technique she used, or the Gramatica Word. This isn't very helpful at all!"

All that trouble, and here we were, back at square one. I'd lied and cheated and abandoned Tiny Doom all for nothing. My disappointment was tinged with panic at the realization that the City wasn't saved after all. "What are we going to do!"

"Calm down, *chiquita*. The book tells us exactly what we need to know." Lord Axacaya had lit a cigarillo, and now he was blowing smoke rings up into the shadows of the ceiling. "Read it again and then tell me what it says about the Working."

I went back to the page and, after rereading the paragraph,

said, "She bound the Sigils into the Working with the power of the Haðraaða family."

Lord Axacaya nodded. "Ayah so. Georgiana Segunda was clever. It's very difficult to break a Working that has been tied to a bloodline, particularly a bloodline as powerful as the Haðraaðas. The family is dead, and yet Bilskinir House remains strong. What else?"

"As long as the Haðraaða family prospers, the Working remains strong. So is it because the Haðraaða family no longer prospers that some of the Sigils have weakened?"

"Ayah so. What else?"

"Well, she says that until the Word of the Family falls silent, the Working can't be abrogated, undone. The cage won't open until the last Haðraaða is dead, when there is no longer a Head of the House. I guess by *cage,* she means the Working."

"Ayah so."

"But there are no more Haðraaðas. And there is no Head of the House Haðraaða anymore. So shouldn't the Loliga have gone free?"

"One would think so." Lord Axacaya was smiling, slightly, the same smile that Mamma gets when she knows the answer and is waiting to find out if you do, too.

"Does Paimon count? Is he the Head of the House Haðraaða now?"

"Paimon is an immaculate egregore. He is not a Haðraaða, he only serves the family, his interests allied with theirs. It's the blood that counts. He cannot be the Head of the House."

"Maybe she means *House* literally—'as long as the House stands.' That could be Bilskinir, the House Haðraaða."

"No, she means the family itself, its members. She's speaking in symbols." Lord Axacaya was still smiling. He must think I was an idiot.

I took another sip of my wine. It was good, sweet and spicy. What did Arch-Calculator Mox-Mox always say about word problems? Break down the components and figure them out one at a time. I read through the paragraph again, thinking, and suddenly it was obvious.

"They aren't all dead! There must be a Haðraaða living somewhere!"

Lord Axacaya grinned. "That's it exactly! I knew you'd figure it out."

"That's why the Loliga isn't free! There is still a Haðraaða alive! He's the Head of the House."

"Or she."

My earlier disappointment had changed to excitement. Maybe we could all be saved yet. "But how shall we find this Haðraaða? Do you think Paimon would know? I didn't see him at Bilskinir this time, but I could go back and find him. He must know who his own Head is!"

"From what you have told me, Paimon knows. But I have sent messengers, in various guises, here and Elsewhere, and still he does not respond. You say you did not see him when you were leaving Bilskinir this last time. I think he must have been badly damaged in the earthquake. Though he appears strong from the outside, fourteen years of abandonment have taken their toll. We can expect no help from him. We must identify this person on our own."

"But where will we start? He could be *anywhere*! And we are running out of time; you said so yourself!" Something else occurred to me, something rather unhappy. "If the Loliga is to be free, then he's going to have to die, this person. I don't think he's going to like that idea very much. Maybe he even knows already and that's why he is hiding."

"Don't you worry about that, *pequeña*. I think he—or she—will understand how important it is to save the City."

"But we don't have much time. How are we ever going to find him?"

"Never fear, darling. I have had my suspicions for a while, *pequeña,* and now, with the help of the *Diario,* you have confirmed them. I know who the Head of the House Haðraaða is."

"You do? Who is it? How do you know?" I sat up, almost sloshing wine on Georgiana's *Diario* in my excitement.

"Soon, soon! There is much yet to do, and you look exhausted. We are almost done, and you must rest."

"I'm all right, really!" But I ruined my protestations by yawning tremendously. A great wave of slugginess was beginning to wash over me, swamping my excitement with torpor. My dinner suddenly weighed heavily in my tum. A nap did sound like a nice idea. A very short nap. Just enough to take the edge off . . . But I didn't have time for a nap . . .

"Look at how you can barely keep your eyes open," Lord Axacaya teased me. And it was true. In a delicious haze, I felt Lord Axacaya lift me up as though I were a baby, the slick smoothness of his skin, water-bottle hot. His lips pressed to my forehead. A little galvanic buzz passed from him to me, which left me feeling listless and warm, as relaxed as a wet noodle. The rhythm of his gait was as soothing as a rocker, and he was humming, deep in his chest, the sound a soothing burr. Within seconds I was asleep.

THIRTY-NINE

Drugged. Suckered. Appalled.

Sparks of pain brought me out of my happy dreams of sunlit warmth and Lord Axacaya's hot embraces. I groaned and wiggled, but the sparks only got more painful. Not sparks, pinches. Extremely pinchy pinches. A gust of cold air blew over me, and I protested.

"Get up, Flora! Get up right now!" Idden stood over me, tossing aside my covers.

"Lemme alone, Idden, I'm sleepin'."

"You're drugged is what you are, Tinks. Come on." She yanked on my arms, and despite myself, I sat up, blinking. My head felt like marbles were rolling around inside it, clanging against my skull. Idden thrust a flask against my lips and sloshed it until I opened my mouth and drank, then sputtered. Ice-cold unsweetened coffee.

"Come on, snap to it. We gotta get out of here!" Idden said urgently. "Shake it off. Get dressed." I stared at her blearily; she flapped a wad of clothing at me. Looking down, I saw I was only wearing my chemise, and I hoped fervently that Lord Axacaya had had nothing to do with *that*. (Well, most of me hoped so, that is.)

"What are you doing here, Idden?"

"Saving your bacon, Tinks."

Then her earlier words sank in. "What do you mean *drugged*?"

"The tortillas! They had a Knockout Sigil mixed into them."

"But why would he drug me?" I asked, still bewildered.

"To keep you from freaking when you find out he's planning on killing you, that's why!" She threw the clothes at me and began to shove my boots on my feet.

"Are you crazy?" Now I was awake and staring at Idden incredulously. She was dressed à la Birdie, in a white pleated kilt and a feathery cape. When I squinted, the familiar lines of her face shimmered and then vanished beneath the outline of an eagle head.

"And why are you wearing a Glamour that makes you look like a Quetzal?"

"Look, I'll explain it all to you later, but we got to split now. Firemonkey and Cyrus are set to create a diversion in about three minutes, and we gotta be ready to take advantage of it. Come on, Tinks—move!"

"I can't leave," I protested. "I have to help Lord Axacaya save the City."

"Freeing the Loliga won't save the City," Idden said. "Freeing the Loliga will only mean that everyone in the City will continue to be a Birdie slave."

"How do you know about the Loliga?"

"It's not important. What is important is that the only way to free the City is to allow it to be destroyed."

"You're insane, Idden." I snatched my stays away from her, trying to put them on as she dragged me toward the window. "Let go of me. What's wrong with you? Idden!"

"I hope you are still good at climbing, Tinks."

"*Stop!* Tell me what's going on, and *don't call me Tinks.*" I twisted out of her grasp. "Are you crazy? What the fike is wrong with you?"

Idden said slowly and clearly, "The tortillas were drugged. Axacaya is going to sacrifice you to his Butterfly goddess. You can stand around and wait for that to happen, or scarper with me. Your choice."

"Where did you get such a crazy idea, Idden? That's insane! Lord Axacaya and I—"

"We have our sources, Flora. Impeccable sources."

"Well, your source is full of hoo."

"Don't be an idiot and trust him, Flora. He's playing you. You've got him all wrong."

"No, Idden, *you've* got *him* all wrong—you and Mamma both. Lord Axacaya is only trying the save the City, and so am I. And you—"

Idden pushed me so hard I had to climb out the window or fall. So climb I did, grabbing on to a tree branch, oranges hitting me in the face. I let go and landed awkwardly, almost squashing a flock of chickens, which fluttered out of my way, protesting mightily. Idden landed gracefully behind me. She hadn't bothered with the tree, just jumped, the show-off. "This way, Flora!"

I didn't go that way. I dodged the well in the courtyard, trampled through an herb bed—the air filled with the pungent smell of cilantro—ducked under the water ollas dangling from the porch roof, and into the door just beyond them.

"Flora!" Idden was right behind me, but I didn't look back. Mariposa's *cocina* was sunny and warm, full of the delicious smell of cooking beans; an *abuela* sat before the fire, mixing masa. She looked up, startled, as I careened by her and out the other door. Then down a whitewashed hallway, Idden still behind me, and into the Main Courtyard, fragrant with orange and lemon trees, and colorful with purple bougainvillea and red geraniums. Past an astonished-looking Sitri in the Receiving Gallery and into Lord Axacaya's conjuring room, where I found him sitting cross-legged, grinding away at a *comal.*

"Axa! Axa!" I puffed.

He put aside the *comal,* filled with some sort of a red paste, and stood. "What's wrong, *pequeña?*"

"Are you going to murder me? She said you were going to murder me!"

"Calm down, *pequeña,* calm down. Of course I'm not going to murder you." Lord Axacaya led me to a stone stool carved in the shape of a rabbit, and I plopped down, full of wheezy relief. Idden had vanished—her vitriol against Lord Axacaya stopped at actually facing him. He sat next to me and slid his arm around my shoulders. I leaned against him, feeling the press of his warm body against mine.

"I knew she was crazy," I said. "She is happy to think the worst of everyone, especially you."

"That's an unfortunate talent some people have," Lord Axacaya answered. "But, Flora, do you not agree that the City must be saved at all cost?"

I nodded. His other hand was now on my knee and I could feel the heat even through my kilt, and it was making me feel squirmy in an extremely delightful way. "Sometimes sacrifices are required, *pequeña.* What is the life of one person compared with the lives of thousands?"

"What do you mean?"

Now his hand was rubbing my knee. I crossed my ankles and hoped he could not see me blush.

"I mean that it is too late to rebind the Loliga. She grew too strong for that long ago. She must be released. And her release will require a sacrifice. The life of one person for the lives of many. Is that not a sacrifice worth making?"

I remembered now something Nini Mo had said: *Trust your gut in everything but love.* It wasn't love I was feeling now, but something brighter and even less trustworthy. And under that feeling was something even stronger: a terrible wormy wiggle of fear.

"But only the death of Head of the House Haðraaða will free the Loliga," I said.

The worm was growing into a snake, coiling around my internal organs, getting ready to squeeze.

"But that is you, *pequeña.* Surely you know that by now!" Lord Axacaya smiled, and his hand did not move away.

The snake squeezed. "But I'm a Fyrdraaca!"

"Half of you is. But the other half is Haðraaða, and that's the half that counts."

"But Poppy and Mamma—they are Fyrdraacas—"

"Ah, *pequeña*, General Fydraaca is not your mother. Did you never wonder? You are the cuckoo's egg, hidden in another's nest. The Butcher Brakespeare is your true mother, and through her you are the Head of the House Haðraaða."

Now I was paralyzed. I heard his words, but I didn't understand them. How could I be a Haðraaða? How could the Butcher Brakespeare be my mother? Mamma—

"Get your hands off my sister!"

Idden stood in the door. She had let the Glamour drop completely; her face was flat and grim, and never had she looked more like Mamma. In one hand, she dangled my dispatch case. Her other hand held a gun, pointing steadily at Lord Axacaya. Mamma's own service revolver, which she had carried as a shavetail back in the day. She'd given it to Idden when she'd been promoted to captain.

Idden stepped into the room, and behind her, the doorway filled with shadowy feathery forms: the Quetzals. They were blocking her exit, but Idden made no indication she knew it.

"Well, now," Lord Axacaya said, "speaking of cuckoos. Ave, Madama Fyrdraaca Primera. I see you have been busy skulking around, pretending to be someone that you are not."

"Get your hands off my sister or I will shoot you. Flora, come here."

Lord Axacaya's hands fell away from me, but I did not move. I could not move. Axacaya's words were still spinning in my brain. *The Butcher Brakespeare is your true mother. You are the Head of the House Haðraaða.*

Axacaya was saying, "Come now, madama. I know we do not share the same politics, but surely you share my desire to save the City from catastrophe."

"First, don't you presume to tell me what we share—which is nothing! The City can be ground to rubble for all I care; better to die free than live as slaves! Second, Flora is no Haðraaða."

"Look at her," Lord Axacaya answered. "You knew Butcher Brakespeare."

"Don't call her that!" Idden said, fiercely. "She was no butcher!"

"You knew her. You were what, ten years old when she died? Surely you remember her well. Can you not see her in Flora's face? The resemblance is striking."

Idden took another step into the room. As she looked at me, her expression grew more agonized, but she answered, "She looks like Poppy! She has Poppy's nose!"

Lord Axacaya laughed. "And the Haðraaða eyes! Don't be a fool, Idden. Would I risk something like this if I wasn't sure? The City of Califa is at stake, and the lives of its citizens, too. I would not act unless I was absolutely sure—and I am. Why else would the Loliga attack Flora? Why else would Paimon allow her access to Bilskinir House? Why else would she be able to enter Bilskinir through its back door? But the final proof lies with Georgiana's *Diario*. Only a Haðraaða can read that book. To anyone else the pages would be blank."

His words fell like blows upon me. The *Diario*. I had risked my life for that book, cheated, lied, stole, abandoned my friends, and all to seal my own doom? I didn't believe it. I refused to believe *him*.

Could he be right? How could he be right? There had to be another explanation. To believe him would mean that Mamma and Poppy had lied to me all these years—and I couldn't believe that. It was impossible.

"It's not true! I am a Fyrdraaca!" I cried.

The look he gave me in return was full of pity, and so was his voice. "I am sorry, Flora, but it is true."

Idden spat. "I don't care. Even so, you can't have her! You Birdies already took one of my sisters. You can't have the other."

"It is a great honor to be called upon to sacrifice one's self for the greater good. Without sacrifice, the rain does not fall, the sun does not shine. Not all are so lucky to be so called."

Idden said viciously, "So you say now, but when it was your turn to give your life up to your stupid Butterfly goddess, you didn't hesitate to run."

Now Axacaya stood up, his face no longer beautiful, but distorted with rage. He raised one hand and Idden fired. The noise pierced my paralysis and I jerked to my feet. Idden grabbed at me as I went by, but I ran around her. From outside came more shots, and the Quetzals in the doorway scattered. I tore by them, dodging their fluttering attempts to catch me. Through the courtyard I ran, between flowerpots, around the fountain. I felt the sweep of wings at my back and knew it was Axila Aguila; at any moment I would feel her claws on me, but I kept running. A loud shriek echoed behind me. I risked a glance and saw Axila Aguila struggling to free herself from a net. Firemonkey dropped out of an orange tree and shouted cheerfully, "Run, Flora, run!"

I ran.

Outside Mariposa's gate, Sieur Caballo still stood at the water trough; the snapperheaded Sitri hadn't taken care of him at all. Poor boy, he was probably starving. I owed him buckets of oats and a good currying. More explosions echoed behind me, and the people in the street began to run toward Mariposa. I clambered up on Sieur Caballo and we went the other direction.

FORTY

Home. Udo. A Dustup.

As soon as I came through the bolt-hole secret passageway into my bedroom, Valefor leaped on me, chattering about the earthquake. His roof had almost caved in, his foundation had sunk three feet, his orange trees had fallen over, his swimming pool overflowed. I brushed him aside and tore downstairs, beat my way through the maelstrom of dogs, but found no Poppy, no Mamma. It would, of course, stand to reason that the one time I needed Mamma the most, she wasn't around. Actually, *whenever* I needed Mamma, she wasn't around. The more I thought about this, the angrier I became. Valefor, behind me, now demanded to know where I had been, and why, and how long, and who, and how . . .

I halted my frantic search in the kitchen. The fire was dead, and the stovepipe had fallen onto the kitchen table, soot mixing with spilled sugar and salt.

"Val, who am I?"

"What do you mean?"

"Who am I?"

"Flora Fyrdraaca ov Fyrdraaca, of course." Valefor sounded bewildered. "Why? Who else would you be?"

"Are you sure? Absolutely sure?"

"I think so." Valefor's wrinkle of bewilderment turned into a frown. "I mean, for a Fyrdraaca, you've always seemed a bit thin in Will, but I guess I know a Fyrdraaca when I taste her. Were you not born here, like the rest of the Fyrdraacas?"

"I wasn't born here!" I wailed. "I wasn't born at Crackpot Hall."

Valefor recoiled. "You weren't born here?"

"No! I was born by the side of the Shasta Road in the middle of the Trinity Campaign. They had to halt the whole army for six hours while Mamma had me, and the next day, she won the Battle of the Cedars. I'm even mentioned in the Official Records of the Proceedings of the Glorious War!" This fact, which had always made me feel special—to be the only Fyrdraaca not born at Crackpot Hall—now seemed ominous.

"That does seem strange, Flora, and now that you mention it, you are the first Fyrdraaca I can remember who doesn't have green eyes. Even I had green eyes once."

My blue eyes were another thing Mamma always said made me special. Mamma's eyes were green, and Poppy's eyes were green, and Idden's eyes were green. But Tiny Doom's eyes were blue. How could Tiny Doom have grown up to become my mother? She couldn't be! Lord Axacaya was wrong. I was not a Haðraaða. I was a Fyrdraaca. I had the Fyrdraaca nose, the Fyrdraaca hair, the Fyrdraaca black heart. So what if I had blue eyes?

"Where's Mamma? Where's Poppy?"

"If you'd given me one moment, I could have told you. Buck is at the Post, directing the earthquake relief, and I don't know where Hotspur is. After the quake, he rushed out of here as though on fire—he didn't even bother to check on us, or the dogs, or anything. Just bolted. I doubt we'll see him again."

I sat down at the kitchen table. My throat had sprouted a lump the size of a potato, and all the tears that I had refused to let out earlier were trying to trickle down my nose. I sniffed hard and rubbed my face on my sleeve—Tiny Doom's sleeve. Could Mamma have lied to me all these years?

"What is wrong with you, Flora? And where have you been? I almost collapsed while you were gone, and you don't even ask how I am. Have you been with Axacaya all this time?" Valefor peered at me, worriedly. "You didn't kiss him or anything, did you?"

"What?! Are you crazy?" Once, the thought of kissing Lord Axacaya had been delightful. Now I wanted to retch.

"Well, you were awful spoony about him, Flora. It's a fair question. And he's known to like the young girls. You are just his flavor—"

"Shut up! *Shut up!*"

Val, looking hurt, floated up toward the ceiling, where he swung idly upon the light fixture, his feet barely missing the top of my head. As I had escaped Mariposa House, my only thought had been to get home to Crackpot Hall, and to Mamma. And now I was home, and Mamma wasn't.

Valefor said worriedly, "You look pale, Flora. Do you want some soup? I could make you soup."

I refused Valefor's offer of soup, of sandwies, of back rub, of waffles, of hot water. Of muffins, soft slippers, bacon—

"Bacon? Is there bacon?" Bacon sounded awfully good all of a sudden.

"Well, there is if you go to the store and get some."

"You are a waste of time, Valefor."

Upstairs in my room, I sat on my settee, clutched Pig, and cried like a baby. Something warm and slippery nuzzled my hand—Flynn's wet nose. His worried eyes looked up at me. Mamma had lied to me. And Poppy, had he lied? Or did he even know? He was in prison when I was born, and he didn't come home until I was two years old. But Tiny Doom had also been in prison. How could I have been born by the side of a road in the Trinity Mountains when Tiny Doom was in prison thousands of miles away? Obviously, that was a lie, too.

In my heart, I knew it had to be true. How else could I have entered Bilskinir through its Back Door—a way open only to a Haðraaða? How else could I have read Georgiana Segunda's *Diario*? Why else would the Loliga have tried so hard to snatch me?

But . . . Mamma! I howled and howled. After a while I could do nothing but lie half on the settee, half off, my knees going numb and my head pounding. I was still clutching Pig, and he felt warm and soft in my arms. I sat up and wiped my nose on my sleeve. How could I have been such a snapperhead and fallen to Lord Axacaya's flattery? It's an old story—the darkly glamorous man and the silly young girl. I should have known all along that he was playing me. Stupid girl. Stupid, stupid girl.

Flynnie, faithful wonderful Flynnie, leaped up onto the settee, squirming into my lap. I let go of Pig to clutch Flynn's furry warmth and let him slobber on my face, licking the salty tears away. Then, the lamp fixture jingled, the floor creaked, and a puff of plaster fell from the ceiling. Another fiking temblor. We sat on the settee until it passed, and then Flynnie jumped down and rushed off, to check on the other dogs, I guess. The quake reminded me what was really at stake.

So I had been a snapperhead. That was my personal sorrow. But the Loliga was a public sorrow, and just as much a danger now as she had been before. *Suck it up*, Flora, *and get on with it.* If I was the last Haðraaða, then the City's salvation was up to me. I didn't know how to free the Loliga without dying, but maybe I could figure out how to renew the Sigils that bound her, and insulate the City from her. I still felt sorry for her travails, but the City had to come first.

I sat up and wiped my eyes, which now felt stiff and salty, and blew my nose on my sleeve. And that's when I realized the thumping noise I had thought was my head aching in time with my heartbeart was actually coming from the window. A white face was peering through the glass, waving a fist.

Udo! Oh, delicious, delightful, fantastic, handsome, charming, darling Udo! I flew to the window and threw the latch open, and he leaned in over the sill, grinning.

"Did you feel that? I fair near thought it would shake me from my tree, like an unripe apple, for I was not ready to drop!"

"Oh, Udo, I'm so glad to see you! Are you all right? When

you leaped away in the boots like that, I thought you were gone for good."

"Oh, I'm as dandy as candy, as sweet as morning. Never better than the day I was born!"

"I missed you, Udo. I'm sorry I was such a snapperhead."

Udo's hair had been bleached back, not quite its normal butterscotch color, but no longer flat pitch-black. I clutched that head and the head protested, "Let me get inside, sweetie, and then we shall get down to it, I swear. I'm powerfully eager."

I let go of him, and he slithered all the way into the room. I swear he had gotten taller since I had seen him last; his length was longer and his shoulders wider. And then I saw his feet, sparkling red, and my heart froze. He was still wearing the red sparkly boots.

Not Udo.

Springheel Jack.

We moved at the same time, me lunging for the door, Springheel Jack lunging for me. Alas, he hit me before I hit the door, like a wave hits the rocks, thunderously. I went down, and the ringing was so loud that I couldn't see anything but the dark explosion that filled my head. Then the blackness wore off to pinkness and that wore off to the hot taste of copper in my mouth, and that turned into Jack's menacing voice whispering something quite ugly in my ear.

I kicked, of course to no avail, and I twisted, equally as futile. The heat in my head was nothing compared to the cold fear in my stomach or the regrets that were suddenly passing through my mind like a rush of icy water. I regretted Udo's vanity, I regretted my hubris, I regretted Valefor's hunger, I regretted—I twisted hard, kicking something soft and squishy. Jack roared like a bear and swung his fist, and down I went, into darkness.

Furious.
Lip Rouge. Bungalow Baby Doll.

I WOKE UP TO A woozy head and a towering, burning rage. My mouth tasted like a fire elemental had died in it. My head throbbed as though an earth elemental had died in it. Compared with my fury, however, the pain and foul flavor were nothing.

I was sick and tired of being manhandled, panhandled, pushed around, set up, tricked, played for a snapperhead. Drugged, bopped on the head, sucked into Vortices, dropped into oubliettes. *Fool me once*, said Nini Mo, *shame on you. Fool me twice, and I'll kick you in the head.* I would have done some serious kicking, but when I tried to move my legs, I discovered they were bound. Bound tightly and tingling—asleep. My hands were bound too, with something slick and satiny, my dressing-gown sash, probably. I opened my eyes and saw, through the throbby pain, that I was inside my bed alcove. From the other side of the shut door, I could hear banging and a low humming song. Springheel Jack.

"Valefor," I whispered. *"Valefor!"*

Val materialized almost immediately, wringing his hands. "Oh, Flora Segunda, that awful Springheel Jack is going through all your drawers. Oh, Flora Segunda, what are we going to do? He's going to steal my silver, I know it, I just know it. What shall we do?"

"You shall untie me first," I said, "and then we shall see."

Out in my room, Jack was singing a little song, whose verses burned my ears with their nastiness, but whose chorus went something like "Who then is the Jack of All Trades? The Jack-o'-Lantern, Jack Be Nimble, Jack in the Box? I am! I am! I am *he*!"

"What are you going to do?" Valefor whispered. He untied me; I shook my legs, trying to get the feeling back, then reached up and flipped the lock on the inside of the door. I had no doubt that Jack could break the door if he wanted to, but I was done with making it easy. Let him work for it this time.

"I'm going to take care of Springheel Jack and then I'm going to save the City."

"And how shall you take care of Jack? He won't take the boots off himself. In fact, maybe he can't take the boots off at all now. There's a narrow window, you know. The boots are growing on to him. Once they've got him completely, they can only be removed in death. I think you'd better play it safe and just kill—owww!"

My pinch shut Valefor up; he stared at me through luminous pouty eyes but said not another word. Maybe it *was* too late. Perhaps the boots had already taken permanent hold. But for the moment, I would remain hopeful.

"Sweetie-pie! I think you are awake in there. Are you ready for me, darling love?" Udo's voice but not Udo's words, nor Udo's tone, either. He could never sound that smarmy or malicious.

"Are you ready for me?" I asked. "I may be small but I have sharp teeth."

Jack laughed. "A biter. Oh, bring on those pearly choppers, sweetie pie, for I do love the crunch." The door rattled. "Open the door willingly, lovey, and it shall hurt much less."

"I wager that if you want it, you'll have to fight for it," I answered. "And it will taste more dear that you had to bleed to get it." As I spoke, I was scrabbling through the bed, looking for something I had tossed there what seemed like so long ago, but really only . . . yesterday? Last night? How the last few days had blurred.

"You tease me. I am he, the Jack of Hearts, Jackhammer, the Jack Knife, Lumberjack, Steeplejack, Bootjack, Dancejack, and Jack Dandy! Jackaroo, Jack of All Trades—"

"And I'm Nini Mo's favorite mule, Evil Murdoch," I muttered. I found Udo's coat at the bottom of the bed, now stiff with dried blood. And in its tail pocket, exactly what I wanted: the tin of Sonoran Zombie Powder. Now, what had I done with Udo's lip rouge?

"Flora?" Valefor whispered in a voice so tiny I could barely hear him.

"What?" Ah, there was the lip rouge in my pocket.

"I think maybe really I should just go. I'm sure I'm no help here."

"Valefor, I need your help," I said, ominously. "Do you want Springheel Jack stealing your silver?"

Valefor whined, "I'm already down to only four salad forks. What on earth could you all have done with my salad forks? I used to have place settings for four hundred; I can't afford to lose any—"

I grabbed him and wrenched his collar so our faces were only inches apart. Consuming the corpse of Springheel Jack had done him a lot of good; he still felt pretty solid and his eyes were bright. "Look," I said. "I need your help, so suck it up. More than your silver is at stake here, and since you started this whole thing by eating Jack and getting Udo into an uproar, you owe it to him. You owe it to *me*."

"But, Flora Segunda, you were the—*oowfff.*" Twisting someone's collar until they choke really is an effective way of shutting them up.

"Got it, Valefor?" I let go.

His eyes glittered. "I got it."

I told him the rest of the battle plan, and he vanished from the alcove to take up position. I applied the lip rouge, good and heavy. When I was done my mouth looked wet and red, as though I had been drinking blood. I hoped that Jack liked ladies in red. Then I flipped the lock and slid the door open.

Springheel Jack was sprawled on my settee, looking mighty comfy, my chocolate stash well-smeared about his face. He might have taken over Udo's body but not his table manners, that was for sure. Jack was wearing all of my jewelry, including my Sanguine Day tiara, and several of my scarves; this should have made him look silly. Actually, he looked glamorously menacing. The giant red boots were planted firmly on my coffee table; they sparkled and gleamed, and the little snake heads on each toe snapped and hissed. Pigface, they were the ugliest shoes I had ever seen.

Now, face-to-face, I would have known that he was not Udo even if the boots had been hidden. He might *look* like Udo, but Udo never looked so hard and calculating and cold.

I wanted my Udo back. I *needed* Udo back.

As he slurped the chocolate, Jack was humming his little song about how fabulous he was, and all the fabulous (obscene, actually) things he was going to do to me. Well, we'd see about that.

"Hey, Jackanapes," I said, loudly. "Get your feet off my table. You'll leave a mark."

"Well, here's my dollymop!" Jack said, not moving his feet. Behind him, way up high on top of my closet, Valefor winked into existence and gave me a little encouraging wave.

I said, "And here's Cheap Jack, Jack O'Light—"

Jack launched off the sofa, bounced off the coffee table—his head narrowly missing the ceiling—and landed almost on top of me. I refused to give way, and he loomed over me menacingly, tossing mussed hair out of his eyes: a familiar gesture in an unfamiliar context. Udo is tall, but add the extra five inches of boot heels and Jack was enormous; I barely came up to the middle of his chest. Well, it takes more than heels to give you height; the taller they are, the harder they fall. Still, my insides quivered a bit when Jack turned his ruthless gaze upon me, but I held on to the thought that Udo was in there *somewhere*, and relying on me to get him out. I refused to look away, but out of the corner of my eye I noticed that he held a knife in his hand.

"What did you say, sweetie?" Jack purred.

"More jakes than Jacks, I think. Jack Dangle, too, no doubt."

He roared: "I am he, the Jack of Hearts, Jackhammer, the Jack Knife! Lumberjack, Steeplejack, Bootjack, Dancejack, and Jack Dandy! Jackaroo, Jack of All Trades!"

"And I am the Bungalow Baby Doll," I answered. "I am the Fleet Footed Fancy Girl. I am the Red Haired Daughter of Midnight. And I've got a giftie for you."

Jack struck like a snake. The striking I had anticipated, but not the speed. Before I could dance out of his way, I was caught, one arm twisted behind me, hands pinned, and the knife against my throat. In stories, the knife blade is always described as cold, but this one was strangely warm. The edge was so sharp that it didn't hurt a bit, although the pressure was hard against my skin.

"You have brought me a giftie, little lolly," Jack whispered in my ear. "A sweet and tender giftie, and I shall thank your bones for it when I am done with you." His voice, low and scratchy, had nothing of Udo in it, and neither did the gleaming eyes looking hungrily down at me. A trickle of fear ran down my spine, turning my feet to ice. Perhaps I was too late, perhaps Udo was gone for good, and perhaps I was about to be gone for good, too.

For a moment I could not move my lips, and then I swallowed hard and whispered back, "Such a sweet giftie I bring to you willingly, Jack of Hearts."

"And what is that, dollie?" he purred, licking my ear, and the disgusting slurping feeling hardened my resolve.

I purred back, "Why a kiss as sweet as summer, hot as heaven, red as love."

"The kiss does look as red as love, and it hasn't even left your mouth yet," Jack said, and blessedly he took the knife away from my throat. I twisted around and snuggled my arms up over his neck, trying not to breathe through my nose, for he smelled very strongly of cheap rose water. Blah!

He leaned down eagerly, and I stretched up equally eagerly—although in my case it was to get the whole thing over with. The ground began to quiver beneath our feet, but we ignored the temblor. Our lips met, as light as snow, and with their touch, he was mine.

FORTY-TWO

Brute Force. Siege. Poppy.

THE GREAT OUTLAW was felled by the oldest trick in the book: poisoned lip rouge. Well, maybe not exactly poisoned, but some of Udo's Sonoran Zombie Powder mashed into some of Udo's lip rouge. Add a heavy layer of hair pomade to the lips as a buffer: One smackeroo and Jack is your obedient mindless drone. *My* obedient mindless drone.

As soon as I stepped back, Valefor swooped down from the closet, pillowcase in hand, and dropped it over the outlaw's head. We tied the pillowcase off and bound Jack's hands with my curtain tiebacks. I gave him a good shove in the middle of the chest; he tipped back on his heels, teetering precariously. Another good shove, and—*Timber!*—down he went. Jack hit the floor with a thunderous shake, and then lay still. Pigface, was *that* gonna hurt later. Oh, well.

Jack might now be vacant, prone, and drooling, but the snake heads on his boots were still spitty; they hissed and snapped each time I tried to get close to the boots.

"You could try mesmerizing them with flute music," Valefor offered. "Can you play the flute, Flora Segunda? How about an ocarina?"

"I don't need a flute or a blasted ocarina when I've got this." I whacked each head with the fire-iron until they dangled limply. I knelt at Jack's feet. "Wish me luck."

"Luck!" he said. "You deserve some after all this. You are the unluckiest person I've ever known, Flora Segunda."

"Shut up!" I grabbed a stacked red heel with each hand and pulled.

And pulled.

And pulled.

The boots did not come off. In fact, all I succeeded in doing was to drag Udo along the floor, work myself up into a sweat, and almost pop a vein in my forehead. And still the boots did not come off.

I was not too late. I would not be too late.

I turned around and straddled Udo's leg, facing his head, and grasped the left boot.

Pulled.

Tugged.

Yanked.

Pulled harder.

Tugged harder.

Yanked until I thought every muscle in my body would twang like a broken guitar string from the strain. The blood rushed to my head. My hands began to burn.

"I think it's too late," Valefor said.

"It's not too late," I puffed.

"You are gonna have to cut his feet off. It's the only way to save him."

"Shut up!" I let the boots drop and rubbed my burning hands on my kilt.

"He can get wooden ones. He'll never notice the difference. I knew an admiral once who lost both his legs below the knee from a cannonball, and he had the most cunningly carved feet, shaped like boats, so he could walk across water—"

I turned my face to the ceiling and let out a horrible howl, a howl that came from the very bottom of my soul, tore my throat, and rattled my teeth. A howl that made me feel much, much better afterward.

"What in Califa's name was that, Flora? They'll hear you across the Abyss!"

"It was that or punch you in the nose, Valefor. Aren't you glad I decided to scream instead? Now shut up and take his shoulders. I'm going to pull and you are going to hold him. Hold him hard, don't let him go."

"Maybe we should try squirting soap—that works with rings."

For once Valefor had a decent idea; I ran and got the soap, mixed it with water from my washbasin, and we poured it into the boots as best we could. I wasn't sure it would do anything but get them wet and us slippery, but anything was worth a try.

"You have to know when to fold your cards, Flora Segunda," Valefor said. "Didn't Nini Mo say that?"

"Shut up and take his shoulders. If you let go, Valefor, I will pop you. Let's try one at a time."

"Wrap the boot in a towel, it will help your grip," Val advised, taking Udo's shoulders. I did as he suggested, and then took a deep breath and pulled and pulled and pulled and puuuuuuuuuuuuuulled. The boot moved slightly, and began to slide.

"I can . . . barely . . . hold . . . him."

"Don't . . . let go . . . I . . . feel . . . it . . . moving."

A quarter inch. A half inch. Success gave me a second wind, and again I put my back into it, feeling every sinew in my body go as taut as violin strings. The boot slid another inch; now I could see the top of Udo's sock. Almost there . . .

Behind me, through my grunting, I heard a door fling open. Valefor let go of Udo and I fell flat on my face, narrowly missing the edge of my desk.

"Valefor, you fiking snapperhead!" I rolled over. Poppy stood in my doorway, looking at me, looking at Valefor, looking at Springheel Jack. And looking not the least bit surprised at what he was seeing. A rifle was slung over Poppy's shoulder—his bad shoulder—and a pistol was tucked into his belt. He wore an extremely battered buckskin jacket, obviously field gear, for it had

Army-issue buttons and a major's gilt boards on the shoulders.
The Skinner scars on his cheeks had been touched with black
war-paint, bringing them into high relief against his white face.
He looked grim as death.

"Poppy, I . . . uh . . ."

"You have to get out of here, Flora," Poppy said calmly. "Axacaya's Birdie friends just rammed through the main gate.
They'll be here any minute."

Valefor blinked out and then back in again. "They're tram-
pling my rosebushes! What do they want, Flora Segunda?"

"I guess they want me." I had never thought that Axacaya
would dare try to steal me from Crackpot by force. I felt sick—I
had never even thought that by coming home I might be putting my entire family in danger.

"Well, he may want you, but he's not going to get you,"
Poppy said. "Not if I have anything to say about it. But you'd
better chop-chop, Flora. I set the dogs on the Birdies, and a few
other little surprises, too, but I wager you should make your
exit."

"I can hide in the Bibliotheca. He'll never find me there."

Valefor howled, "I am violate. There is no part of me he
cannot enter. I can't hold him back. See what happens! If I were
myself, he wouldn't dare to enter—"

"Take it up with Buck another time, Valefor," Poppy said.
"I'll hold him off, Flora, for as long as I can, but you need to get
the hell out of here. Get to the Presidio; get to Buck. Even Axacaya won't dare follow you onto the Post." He leaned over,
pulled me to my feet, and began to hustle me toward the fireplace. "You'll have to use the bolt-hole, which, yes, I know about.
Your horse is waiting at the bottom of the Straight-up Stairs. I
think you should get going, honey."

"They are in my kitchen," Valefor wailed. He disappeared,
the snapperhead, no doubt to hide somewhere until the fuss
was over.

Poppy pressed on the rabbit-painted tile and the panel
sprang open. "Flora, if I don't see you again—"

"Don't see me—" I clung to Poppy's good arm. "What do you mean, not see you?"

"Remember always that I love you, even if sometimes that love seems pretty paltry. I'm sorry I couldn't do better." Poppy clutched me; his pistol butt dug into my chest. I smelled his sandalwood soap and the mellow scent of tobacco and wood-fire. He kissed the top of my head and pressed something into my hand: a Madama Twanky's Tooth Polish tin. Tiny Doom's container for the key to Bilskinir. "Here—I think this is yours."

"Poppy, who am I?"

"You are my daughter and a Fyrdraaca." He pushed me back, so he could look me square in the face. "And you are, apparently, a Haðraaða—"

"Why didn't you tell me, Poppy?!"

"You look so much like her—you *are* so much like her. I should have known all along; I would have, if I had been paying attention. But, well, I've been distracted these last few years. Listen to me. Your mother—"

The door, which Poppy had bolted behind him, crashed open in a hail of splinters. Axila Aguila stood in the doorway, saying, "My apologies, Colonel Fyrdraaca, but—"

Poppy turned around, pushing me away. The rifle was now in his hands. He fired. Red feathers puffed into the air. He jacked the lever and fired again. Another puff of red feathers and the Quetzal crumpled to the ground.

"*Go!*" Poppy hissed, jacking again, and not taking his eyes off the door.

I went.

FORTY-THREE

Running. Ambling. Bouncing.

$\mathcal{A}$T THE BOTTOM of the bolt-hole stairs, I stopped to reconnoiter. From above: gunfire (Poppy's last stand?) and distant shouting, coming from upstairs, not outside. With a muffled thump, something rolled out of the darkness and landed at my feet. The ice water receded from my veins when I saw it was Pig.

I snatched him up, riding him on my hip like a toddler. He felt heavy and reassuring in my arms. When I cracked the door open and peered out cautiously, I saw a serene afternoon garden. So, I ran, without cover, because there wasn't any, across the yard and into the tangled bushes of the Gardens Beyond. Once, these gardens had been perfectly manicured, pruned, and organized, thanks to Valefor. Now they were an overgrown, tangled mess, for which I was grateful. I might be leaving a trail that a blind gazehound could track, but at least I had gained some cover.

I hustled by the Bog and tore through the Pet Cemetery, by the Casa de Hielo. I didn't think anyone was following me, but I couldn't hear much other than my labored breathing and the war-drum thump of my heart. Still, I didn't look back. I just kept going, glad, so very glad, that I was still wearing Tiny Doom's stays so I wouldn't expire from breathlessness after about the sixth step. My dead mother had done me a favor after all.

As I reached the top of the Straight-up Stairs, a horrible shriek tore through the air, and for a moment it seemed as though a huge cloud had blotted out the sun. But the sky was a cloudless, flat blue. Poppy? Valefor? I teetered on the top step, wanting to go back, but also—*coward!*—wanting to put miles between me and Lord Axacaya's Birdies.

But whatever had happened behind me I could do nothing about now, so that decided me. I flew down the steps as though my feet had wings, and thank the Goddess Califa I didn't stumble once—it was an awfully long way to the bottom. My heart bounced, Pig bounced, I bounced, but I didn't fall. I reached the bottom in record time, my calves grinding in pain, and saw, as I tore through the gate, Sieur Caballo waiting in the alley. He'd been eating someone's geraniums, and now he looked up, nickering through a mouthful of purple blossoms.

I flung myself onto Sieur Caballo's back as a red streak bounded down the last step and squeezed through the gate— Flynnie! Hot on his tail was a bouncing, lumbering shape: Springheel Jack. The pillowcase was gone from his head, and his arms and legs had been untied—by Poppy probably, who had not realized that Udo wasn't quite himself. His eyes looked like red-tinged fried eggs, and his smeared eyeliner made his eye sockets look like holes. He was drooling. Damn him! Well, at least he was still zombified and would follow my command. The last thing I needed now was Springheel Jack.

"Come on, Udo—Jack—whoever you are," I said, and he obediently bounced up onto the horse behind me and put limp arms around my waist. I wiped his chin with my sleeve so he wouldn't drool into my hair, and we took off, Flynn dashing behind us.

The fastest way to the Presidio from Crackpot is straight out the Post Road, but of course the fastest way is also the most obvious. As cool as it might have been to go flogging through the streets, scattering people and clattering hooves, it also would have been predictable and easy to follow. So instead, we went a long, roundabout way, ambling along slowly, trying to blend in.

Each moment, I expected to see wings above me, hear the incoming shriek of a diving eagle. *Play it easy,* said Nini Mo. *Try to look unimportant.* I was so easy, I was shaking. And Pigface, was I trying to look unimportant. But I must have succeeded, because no one paid any attention to us, not even the City militia that pounded past us at one point. *They* were easy and important—they never looked at us once.

At Abenfarax Boulevard and Turk Street, a rider drew alongside me, another fell in behind me, and another jostled in front: more City militia. I sucked in my breath and tried to quell my panic, before realizing the rider next to me, swathed in a captain's cloak, was Idden.

"Ave, Flora. Pig. Udo. Keep moving. Look unconcerned."

"Are you all right? How did you get away from Axacaya?"

"We have our ways. Don't you worry."

"Have you been following me all this time?"

"You don't cover your tracks very well, Tinks. Anyone could follow you. We've had you in our sites for a long time—Poppy, too."

"Poppy's been following me, too?" Now I felt like a complete snapperhead. Being able to cover your tracks is basic rangering. I hadn't even managed that.

"What's up with you, Udo?" Idden asked. He didn't answer, of course, so I told her, briefly, and she rolled her eyes, said, "Oh, Udo," and then no more. We rode in silence for a while, and now that I had a moment to think, my thoughts were not happy.

"I left Poppy fighting off the Quetzals. They stormed Crackpot Hall."

Idden grinned wolfishly. "Don't worry about Hotspur, he's more than a match for a bunch of mangy birds." She thrust something at me: my dispatch case.

"Idden," I said, dolefully. "I was a total snapperhead. I let Axacaya suck me in. I believed him."

"Don't be a pinhead, Flora. Axacaya's tricky. You aren't the first to be caught by him."

No, I thought, *but I wager when I'm done with him, though it may take the rest of my life, he's gonna wish he'd caught someone else.*

"But he was right about me being a Haðraaða. Why did Mamma never tell me?"

"To keep you alive, snapperhead. Do you think for a minute the Birdies would have let you live if they'd thought you had any connection to Azota?"

"But Buck could have told me she wasn't my mother. Owww—why'd you whack me?"

Idden said fiercely, "Because Buck *is* your mother, Flora! Love counts as much as blood. And Buck loves you and has done everything she can to protect you. Don't you dare forget it. We'll talk about it more later; this isn't the time and place. You can feel sorry for yourself when you're home free. Right now you need to focus."

Idden was right. *That day, that sorrow,* said Nini Mo.

Several times our journey was punctuated by temblors that reminded me of my current sorrow. I might be momentarily in the clear, but the Loliga still threatened the City. I didn't want to have to die in order to save her. Surely Mamma would not let me die; Mamma would come up with another plan. Mamma would know what to do.

At last we reached the edge of the City and turned onto Goat Hollow Track, the rough road used by the Outland Dairy Company to move their herds from the dairy in the Outside Lands to their pastures near Cow Hollow Lagoon. For about a mile, the track skirts along the edge of the Presidio; it's an excellent shortcut, and one that not many know about. The sun disappeared behind a fog bank—typical Califa summer weather—and a chill wind began to blow. The track is narrow and rough, and we went slowly, single file, the outrider moving ahead, the file-closer falling back.

A few more miles and we would be inside the Presidio gates. I wasn't sure what I would say to Mamma, but I knew, despite all, I would be mighty glad to see her indeed. And she was not going to be happy when she heard that Axacaya had invaded

Crackpot. He was going to be very sorry he had messed with the Fyrdraaca family. Mamma would take care of him, and take care of me, and take care of the City.

The road dipped between two sand dunes—at least now we were screened from the biting, sandy wind—and then twisted around a scrubby pine tree and turned behind one of the dunes. We turned that corner, and there was our outrider, lying on the ground like a broken doll, his clothes oozing red. Axila Aguila stood in the road, wiping blood from her beak with the hem of her cloak. Apparently it takes more than bullets to kill a Quetzal. (Oh, Poppy!) Three other Quetzals stood behind her, obsidian knives in their hands.

"Get out of our way," Idden hollered, and drew her pistol.

"I cannot," the Quetzal said. "Flora must come with us."

"The hell with you," Idden said. "And the hell with Axacaya. Fike you both. And your stupid Birdie Virriena, too. You got one of my sisters already. You cannot have this one." She spurred her horse and tried to ride down Axila Aguila, who leaped, wings fluttering, out of the way at the last minute. Another Quetzal soared into the air and made a grab for Sieur Caballo's head; he pulled back, half-rearing, and lashed out with his front hooves. *Crack* went the sound of metal on eagle skull and the Quetzal went down, but so, too, did Udo, sliding off Sieur Caballo's back, to lie in a motionless heap.

"Run, Flora, run!" Idden screamed, wheeling around for another charge, as a Quetzal jumped at her. She shot him point-blank in the head, but he fell forward and managed to pull her off her horse. Barely missing being trampled, they rolled and thrashed on the ground. Flynn had the other Quetzal; he was snarling and tearing and leaping at her throat. Flynnie is thin, but he's wiry.

Udo still lay sprawled. I couldn't leave him behind, but before I could reach him, Axila Aguila landed before me with her arms outstretched, her wings unfurled, the obsidian knife gleaming—Pigface, I hadn't known she could really fly. Blood still dripped from her beak, staining her tunic. Screeching, she lunged. Sieur Caballo, who had tolerated a lot, couldn't quite manage this. He jumped sideways, and his twisting motion caught me unprepared—I dumped right off his back and landed heavily, winded. The horse and Axila kept fighting, wings flapping and hooves slashing, both of them shrieking.

I heaved to my feet. Udo still lay on the ground, only now a Quetzal leaned over him, screeching.

"Udo!" I screamed, but my voice was lost in the din. I ran at the Quetzal, grabbed at its wings, yanking feathers. The Birdie turned on me, razor beak snapping at my nose. I recoiled and the Birdie lunged again.

"Pig! Pig!" I screamed. A weight launched off my back and flew pinkly toward the Quetzal. The Quetzal screeched again—in pain this time—as it grappled with Pig's pink fury.

"Get up, Udo! Get up!" I pleaded, shaking him.

He staggered up. I grabbed at his shoulders and jumped. It had been a while since Udo had given me a piggyback ride, but somewhere deep in that zombified outlaw-infested brain, he recognized my action and locked his arms around my legs, supporting me.

Axila Aguila sprang up, abandoning Sieur Caballo, her wings ripping the air as she flew aloft, preparing to dive.

"Jump, jump!" I screamed. Udo made a tiny little hop.

"Higher!"

This time we soared up as though we'd been shot from a cannon. My stomach lurched alarmingly, and I clutched Udo with all my might. We landed with a thump some feet from where we had started, out of Axila's reach. She pulled up just before she hit the ground and wheeled around, coming at us another time. The boots lifted us out of her reach, one bounce ahead, but we couldn't keep up jumping around like hot corn in a skillet while Axila tried to peck us to death.

Don't wait to be cornered, Nini Mo said. *Turn and bite.*

I could hear the snapping of her wings as they cleaved the air, could almost feel the breeze of their strokes.

"Around—turn around and then jump over her!" I whispered

in Udo's ear. Udo hit the ground, swiveled, and jumped again. As we did so, I leaned over and kicked at the Quetzal. My kick was weak but lucky, catching her in the wing. Feathers flew and she shrieked, wheeling down.

I felt a brief pang as we soared by her again, and then reached out with the pistol that I had wiggled out of Udo's holster, and buffaloed her on the side of the head with the pistol butt. She collapsed, and I saw by the angle of her head that she was not likely to get up again—ever.

Idden staggered toward me; her face was a mask of blood, and a knife hilt protruded from her shoulder. "Go, Flora! I ain't planning on dying for nothing! GO!"

"Idden . . ." I leaned over Udo's shoulder, reaching out my hand. For a moment, our fingers touched, and then she pulled back and pushed Udo hard. Those boots gave him lift—each stride was several feet long and several feet high, and the faster we went, the higher the bounce, until it seemed as though we were flying. I wrapped my arms around Udo's neck and held on, hoping that his iron grip wouldn't slacken.

When we burst out of the Goat Track onto the Point Lobos Road, I screamed for him to go left, toward Bilskinir House. I couldn't go back to Crackpot Hall, and Axacaya would only follow me to the Post; the Army might keep him out, but for how long and at what cost? Too much blood had been spilled already. Bilskinir House was my only hope.

A red streak ran alongside us: Flynnie, tongue lolling, legs moving so fast that it looked as though he was suspended in midair. I don't know how he could keep up with Jack, but somehow he did. Plushy pink clung to Flynn's back—Pig, riding him hard. I risked a glance over my shoulder, but the road behind us was clear. I doubted it would remain that way for long. So far Axacaya had relied on his servants to do his dirty work—now his servants were done. Surely he'd come after me himself. He was not going to give up until he had me. But I was determined that he would *not* have me.

Udo bounded down the Point Lobos Road, bouncing over

refugees and carts, and hit the Playa at full tilt, scattering people, dogs, children, chickens. Ahead, Bilskinir was invisible behind a soggy billow of fog. The wind blew my hair in my face, blinding me, and when I managed to brush it away, I realized that Udo was following Flynn and Pig, who had burst out ahead of us. Flynnie was arrowing not toward the causeway, but to the base of Bilskinir cliff.

"Udo! The road! The road!" I shouted. We were going at full speed; if we hit that rock, we'd smash into pieces. Flynn was practically a blur—snapperdog!

"Udo! Stop, Udo! Flynn—stop! No, Flynn, no! Pig!" I screamed, and the words were torn from my mouth, shredded by the wind. We rode into the shadow of the cliff, as dark as night. But ahead was a flicker of lamplight. A carved arch sprang into focus, its mouth blazing with light, as though someone had just unrolled a canvas scenery cloth. Through this arch we bounced and then whizzed through a tunnel, into daylight. Ahead of us was Bilskinir's long driveway, lined with yellowing trees.

Udo made one last little bounce and stopped. I slid off, and collapsed onto the soft grass. Flynn threw himself down beside me, panting. Pig flew toward me, and I caught him before he could hit me in the face. Udo continued to bounce gently nearby. He didn't look winded, but Pigface, his hair was a mess. Anyway, he was safe. Flynn was safe. I was safe.

"Well, Pig," I said, trying to sound ranger cool. "I guess we're home."

He did not answer.

FORTY-FOUR

Safe. Clean Towels. A Letter.

THE SKY ABOVE Bilskinir was faded, the shade of denim, and strange gray clouds, spidery and torn, blew across its wide expanse. Drops of rain spit on me as I trudged across the Great Lawn, whose grass needed cutting. The sheep huddled under an oak tree at the far end of the Lawn, bleating miserably, and a cutting wind was blowing. The flowers alongside the approach to the massive front door drooped listlessly, their colors washed out. A slight air of abandonment hung over everything.

But I knew Paimon was still around. If he'd been gone, I would know that, too. And I knew why his attention was elsewhere. Lord Axacaya was trying to get in, and Paimon was keeping him out.

After I had fallen off Udo, I had lain in the grass for a long time, staring up at the slate-gray sky, thinking of many things, none of them happy or good. It would say more of me if I admitted that I was finally rousted by concern for Udo, or Flynn, or Idden and Poppy, but alas, it was my squeezy bladder that forced me to get up. That, and the rough tongue that was slurping over my face, and returned each time I pushed it away: Flynnie.

Now Flynn trotted ahead, looking pleased, his tail waving like a fringy red flag. Udo had vanished; I'd go find him, but the bathroom had to come first.

As I mounted the wide stairs leading to Bilskinir's front door, a small twinge of excitement sparked through my larger feeling of despair. Could this gorgeous House really be all mine? The bronze doorknob was the size of my head and shaped like a crab. I opened the Madama Twanky Tooth Polish tin and shook the key to Bilskinir out. When I slid the ring on my finger it fit perfectly.

"The Ostium," I said, touching the doorknob.

The door opened and Flynn darted inside. Outside, the sky was now the shade of a damson plum, and an eddy of chill air blew inside, ruffling the tapestries. The door slammed, and Flynn jumped in surprise. From the Ostium I could get to any room in Bilskinir, but I only needed one room: a bathroom.

"A potty, please," I said, again putting the Key to the lock.

The potty continued the oceanic theme; the bathtub was shaped like a giant seashell, the sink was a smaller shell, and the deep blue walls were covered in gleaming gold designs: fish, seals, otters, whales—and a giant Loliga. The potty seat was warm and the towels on the towel rack were fluffy and smelled of lemon. Flynn jumped into the tub and nuzzled the dolphin-shaped faucet, so I turned the tap until water trickled out and he began to drink noisily.

I couldn't help but contrast this glorious bathroom with Crackpot's poor little dank loo. Without Valefor at full power, our loo is shabby. The porcelain in the tub is scratched; the water pipes gurgle alarmingly, spewing icy water one minute and boiling water the next. The mirror above the sink is streaked with green, the silver flaking away, and no amount of scrubbing can get the mold off the ceiling. All my life Idden has regaled me with tales of the cleanliness of Crackpot Hall's towels, back before Valefor had been banished. The luscious softness of them, the fluffy absorbency. Without Valefor, the threadbare towels were dingy, not much better than paint rags.

Now I had a seemingly endless supply of wonderfully clean, soft towels, each as large as a garrison flag. Not just soft and clean, but warm, too. And hot water that gushed from the gold dolphin's mouth into a tub shaped like an open oyster shell, water that frothed up into lavender-scented bubbles. And potty paper as soft as cotton, and a potty seat that warmed my hinder, and a flush chain that didn't tangle, and plumbing that didn't roar like the pipe was about to explode. Yet I would have traded it all for Crackpot's raggy bath towels, Crackpot's broken potty seat, and Crackpot's tepid water.

A ranger plays the hand she is dealt, not the hand she wishes she were dealt, said Nini Mo. The fish mirror showed a girl with messy red hair, and Bilskinir blue eyes. She didn't look like the Head of the House Haðraaða. She didn't look like much at all. But she was going to have to do, because she was all there was.

The room outside the potty glowed in the lamplight like a giant red gumdrop. I recognized it immediately: the Bedchamber of Downward Dreaming, a crimson chamber that continued the oceanic motif. On the walls silver fish, eels, and squid swam through a crimson red ocean, and the bed was shaped like a giant open clamshell. The bedroom of the Head of the House Haðraaða. The room Paimon had locked Udo and me into on our first visit to Bilskinir. Now I realized he had been trying to tell me something—but, darn it, why hadn't he been more clear? It could have saved us all a ton of hassle.

The delicious smell of coffee filled the room. The polychrome mermaid draped over the chimneypiece seemed to watch me with amused eyes as I reached for the pot sitting on the small stove next to the fireplace. But when I tried to pour, instead of liquid, a ruffly shape rolled out, flipped, and became the merman Alfonzo. He yanked on the bottom of his double-breasted tunic, straightening it, and made a deep Courtesy: *Welcome Home.*

"Ave, madama!"

"Where is Paimon?"

"Keeping Axacaya out—we are under siege, you know. Axacaya trying to get in, but he got no chance, *ladrón*! We are the strongest house in the City, even now. He'll have to try harder!

Paimon says he'll see you soon, but in the meantime, I am to say that there is a letter for you in the Closet by the fireplace. I must go help in the defense! *Hasta la vista!*"

With a flap of his frondlike tail, Alfonzo vanished. I saw the thin outline of a door on the red wallpaper next to the fireplace. The door was papered over and had no doorknob, so it was almost invisible. But as I approached, it swung open to reveal a room filled with drawers and cupboards, from the distant ceiling to the floor. I pulled on a drawer; inside were several dozen pairs of neatly rolled socks. Another drawer held neatly folded undershirts. The first cupboard I opened contained an array of uniform jackets: regular Army black sackcoat, Skinner sangyn frock, a dark green old-timey Army peacoat.

In the middle of the room sat a large trunk with an elaborate red-leather cover, torn in some places and held down with brass rivets. I crouched in front of it; the brass plaque over the lock-plate had CSRB carved on it. Tiny Doom's Catorcena trunk. The hasp lock was open. Inside, on top of a layer of buckskin, was a folded and sealed paper upon which was written spiky faded blue letters.

To Nyana Haðraaða ov Fyrdraaca

I rocked back on my heels and sat on the cold marble floor, holding the letter in my hand—which, I noted from a calm point somewhere away from my body, was shaking like a leaf. This calm point outside of myself saw clearly the muzzy, messy girl, staring at a piece of paper as though it were a snake about to bite her. Mesmerized, waiting for the strike, unable to pull away.

Nyana Haðraaða ov Fyrdraaca.

Nyana. My real name was Nyana? Not a second Flora after all, but named for the greatest ranger ever. *Nyana.* A tiny shaft of consolation rang through me. Not a replacement for, but in honor of.

I broke the seal and unfolded the paper:

Dear Nyana,

That is what I'm calling you, after Nini Mo, though obviously Buck is going to change your name to keep you hidden.

Does this not burn? I've been through a lot of horrible things recently—prison, trial, etc.—but I have to say that of all the burning horrible things, this is by far the burning horriblest. Once, I got hit in the side with a fifty-caliber bullet, which Taylor, my lieutenant at the time, had to fish out with a chopstick he sterilized with his own piss. That hurt. It really, really hurt, and when it was all over, all I got as a prize was a mushy piece of metal and an infection that almost killed me. But that didn't hurt half as much as getting you from inside to outside; toward the end, I would have been glad if someone had shot me with a fifty-caliber bullet just to take my mind off the pain. But no one did, and eventually you decided to join the rest of the world, feet first, and I got my prize, the best prize in the whole wide world. That's not what burns. What burns is that I can't keep you, my darling baby.

Also burning: that the only time we ever had together, neither of us knew, and so spent frivolously trying to steal crap and put Hardhands's nose out of joint when we could have been having quality mother-daughter time. Oh, and thanks for leaving me in the lurch like that, with ghoulish Grandmamma nipping at my heels. She got a toe or two, but obviously I got all of her in the end. I was pretty pissed at you, but now I know that while I was skylarking, you were on urgent business, and so I forgive you. But don't do it again.

(Also, thank you for the lie about Hardhands's expiration via rat bite. For many years it was a great consolation to me.)

I can't keep you, darling baby girl. They will catch me, and they'll kill me, but they won't catch you, not if I let you go. And so I'm letting you go, to Buck, who will love you like her own child, who will protect you and care for you and someday tell you about me. And hopefully you won't hate me for abandoning you or hate Buck for lying to you. And don't blame your father at all. He knows nothing of this; it seemed best to keep him blissfully ignorant and thus blameless should anything go wrong. I write this now as though Hotspur survives prison, as though he makes it home to Crackpot. I have to believe that he will. Losing him would be as bad as losing you. I can go to my death content if I can go believing that both of you still live.

So that's my problem. Now on to yours. Yes, I know all about your problem, and if you are reading this, I'm figuring that you must still be looking for a solution. How did I figure it out? Well, it took a lot of doing and scrying, and reading entrails, but one thing Nini taught me is that if you really want to find something out and keep looking and asking, eventually you'll look in the right place and ask the right question. And end up with an answer. So now I shall pass the answer on to you.

But, baby doll, don't be mad—I'm going to have to be elliptical and obtuse with my advice. You are cursing me now, I can tell, but "better to be cautious than caught," Nini says. On the small chance that Axacaya, that bastard, overpowers Paimon, or overpowers you (believe me, once you get to know him, Axacaya's charm is rather thin), and he is reading this instead of you, well, I'm not going to make it any easier for him. (And if you are reading this, Axacaya, I've got a special surprise planned for you, don't you worry.) Anyway, remember the Key to Bilskinir? And remember where I said I got it? Well, if you look there, I think you shall find the solution to your problem. I hope you have a good memory. Mine has never been too sharp, but Hotspur never forgets anything, so with luck, you take after him, not me.

I sure hope you do remember, as the safety of the City relies upon it. That's all I can do. The rest is up to you,

Nyana. Fyrdraacas are known for their courage, Haðraaðas for their cunning, and Brakespeares for their stubbornness. All three together is a potent combination. During our little escapade together, I remember thinking you were bratty and arrogant, but also that you had sand and spirit and were extremely good in a pinch. And being good in a pinch is the best kind of person to be. Being bratty and arrogant isn't so bad, either. Sometimes that is what it takes.

By now I expect you've heard some pretty awful things about me. I have a feeling that my reputation, which has never been that good, won't improve after I'm dead. Well, I've done a lot of things that are neither glamorous nor generous and I'm not going to apologize for them. But I will say that I thought long and hard before I did them, and I truly believed there was no other way. If that is evil, then I'm guilty as the Birdies charged, and deserve whatever I'm going to get. But I hope that you'll understand and not think too badly of me.

That's all the time I have. It would be impossible to let you go if I didn't know you were going to a better mother than I could have ever been. And it consoles me, too, that the misery is all mine: having never known me as your mother, you'll never miss me. But I'll miss you, darling baby doll, until the moment I die.

Dare, win, or disappear.

Gyrenacia Sidonia
Brakespeare ov Haðraaða

Post Script 1: Paimon will send you Pig; trust them both.

Post Script 2: Tell Hotspur I love him.

Post Script 3: Tell Buck thank you.

Post Script 4: Tell Axacaya that I'm coming for him.

FORTY-FIVE

Bad Memory. A Deal. Drawers.

THREE TIMES I reread that letter, and the papers grew more and more damp with each reading due to my sweaty hands and a few errant tears I refused to allow to develop into full bawling.

I had left Tiny Doom in the lurch, but she had not left me. She had done everything in her power to keep me safe. She had died so I might live. And she had named me after Nini Mo, who would surely not just sit there, sniveling, when the fate of Califa hung in the balance. I snorted up my tears and read the letter once more, this time focusing on the part about my "problem." The other stuff would have to wait.

Of course I remembered her telling me she had stolen the Key from Hardhands. But I did not remember where she told me she had stolen it *from*.

Pigface Psychopomp on a Pogostick! I should be able to remember. *She* remembered, and after years and years. For me, it had only happened last night. How could I forget so soon? But so much had happened since then, and so lightning fast, that my memory was a blur of rushing, running, swearing, fighting, running, screaming, et cetera. Some of the details—such as exactly where Tiny Doom had gotten that stupid Key—had fallen through the cracks.

"Thanks for nothing, Mother." I threw the letter down in

disgust and picked up the ferrotype that had been lying beneath it. Inside the elaborate hard rubber case was the silvery image of a woman I recognized clearly as Tiny Doom, older but just as furious-looking, holding a lacy bundle that I guessed was probably me. A dog sat at her feet, its head blurred by movement.

Underneath the ferrotype lay Tiny Doom's super-cool buckskin jacket. It was a bit tight across the shoulders but otherwise fit perfectly. A loud thump in the bedroom jerked me out of further inspection of the trunk's contents.

"Paimon?" There was no answer, but I knew it wasn't Paimon. There was another thump and the tinkle of breaking glass. I picked up the iron from the shirt-folding table; it wasn't hot, of course, but it was heavy. I crept on little mouse feet to the open door of the Closet. The thumping noise was closer now, and rhythmic. I peered around the edge of the door and saw glittering red sparkles and wild blond hair.

Udo. Who had, I judged from the shards of glass on the carpet, just sprung through the bedroom window. Now he bobbed silently in the middle of the room; by this I knew he was still zombified. I set down the iron and grabbed a heavy cloak from the clothespress, using it to corral him the way you use a towel to capture a cat, but much easier, because he didn't howl, spit, or claw. The snake heads on the boots had sluggishly awoken, and they did hiss at me a little, but that's all.

Now that I had Udo corralled, I realized I should leave him for later, deal with the boots when I had more time. But I needed him more than I had ever needed him before—for courage and company and because he would understand. I needed him and I wanted him, and I was going to have him. Boots be damned.

Before Axacaya's attack on Crackpot had sent me fleeing, Valefor and I had *almost* removed those stupid boots with a lavish application of soap. I closed my mind to the possibility that the boots had permanently adhered to Udo's giant gunboats, and decided that a little more slipperiness might do the trick. But what was more slippery than soap? A jar of Madama

Twanky's No-See-Um Vanishing Cream stood on the vanity; it was goopy, but there wasn't enough to do both boots, and the consistency was too viscous. I needed something that I could pour.

Next to the Vanishing Cream stood a bottle of Madama Twanky's Bear Oil. FOR A GROWLING GOOD COIFFURE proclaimed the angel on the label. I would be satisfied with a growling good success; never mind the coiffure. When I unstoppered the bottle, the rancid smell of long-dead bear wafted up. *Yuck!* Whatever perfume had masked the oil's origins had long since evaporated. Well, I had no time to be dainty, nor to dart out to the chemist for a fresh bottle. Udo would just have to be stenchy.

I had to sit on his legs and press down with all my weight, but finally I got a good grip on the boot and poured. As much stinky bear oil got on me as went in the boot, and when I was done, I was slippery and stenchy, too. Paimon wasn't going to be happy when he saw his nice carpet sodden with oil, but then wasn't it really my nice carpet, too?

Despite the slipperiness, the boots wouldn't budge. Maybe it was too late. No, I refused to give in to too late.

"Now, listen to me, Boots, Jack, whatever you are," I said threateningly, leaning down to glare at the snakes. "I'm done playing games here. You can't have Udo. Let go of him!"

The right snake's head drooped, but the left head peered up at me through slitty eyes and hissed, tongue flickering. Udo's body didn't move, but his mouth opened slightly and a rough voice said, "Must bounce . . ."

"That's fine," I said. "You can bounce all you want, but you can't use Udo to do it. I'll help you find someone else, but only if you let go of Udo."

" . . . young and strong . . . ," Jack croaked. "Beautiful blue-eyed boy . . ."

"Ayah so, but think about it: His parents are going to be looking, and when they find you, they'll take you back to Case Tigger and ground you. You'll have to deal with all Udo's evil siblings, and think of all the homework you'll have to do. That wouldn't be much fun for an outlaw, would it? Babysitting and homework? Come on, you can do better than that! I'll help you find a much better avatar—an orphan who doesn't have to go to school anymore, perhaps. Someone even taller and more good-looking. An actor, maybe?"

". . . trust, dollymop. Tricked us before . . ."

"I only tricked you because you were trying to get me. I swear to you that I am not tricking you now. I'll swear on—I'll swear on my mother's grave. How about that? And anyway, this is my final offer. If you don't let Udo go, I'm going to put your feet in the fire and we'll see how you like it all toasty and warm. So you can either do it my way and I'll help you out, or you can do it your own way and burn. Whatcha think?" Not a nice threat, but I was no longer a nice person. I had knocked Axila Aguila in the head and killed her; what then was a little torture by fire? Clearly I was my mother's daughter.

"Swear!" Jack whispered. One of Udo's pinkies wiggled. I hooked it with mine and shook, then I wiped my hands on the carpet. Grasping toe and heel, I pulled. For a second, the boot resisted.

"You swore," I said. My hands started to slip, and then—just like that—the boot popped off. The second one came even easier, as though it were filled with butter instead of Udo's meaty foot—Udo's meaty, smelly foot, for obviously he hadn't changed his socks for quite some time, even before he started bouncing. I hoped he'd at least gotten around to changing his drawers.

Drawers!

Underwear!

And just like that, I remembered where Tiny Doom had found the Key: Hardhands's underwear drawer. Finally, some part of Udo's escapade had proved useful.

Udo moaned and thrashed. Just in case the boots had left a little Jackness behind, I sat on his chest and said, "Udo, is that you?"

"Flora?" Udo groaned. "Why are you sitting on me?"

"Is it you, Udo?"

"Wha'? Wha'?" He struggled to sit up, and I got off his chest and let him. Sieur Vanity was going to kick when he saw himself in a mirror; he looked like an entire cavalry company had ridden over him. "What happened? Pigface, my head is splitting like a rotten tomato. And what's that horrible smell?"

"Are you sure it's you, Udo?"

"Pigface, who the hell else would it be?"

"What did I give you for your tenth birthday?"

"How the hell do I know? Hey, ain't this the Bedchamber of Downward Dreaming—how the hell did I get here? Hey! Where'd you get those duds? That jacket is killer—and what happened to your hair?"

I didn't need to hear any more. Obviously, Udo was Udo again. I grabbed him in the biggest squeezy hug. He caught me and squeezed back, and we were both laughing with relief, hugging and clutching, and suddenly we were clutching and kissing. Not just practice kissing, but real kissing, the kind that makes your blood bubble and your knees weak, and your heart feel as though it might explode.

Gradually, I dimly realized that the shaking of the floors and walls was not inside me but, rather, outside me.

"Udo, let go. The earth is shaking."

"I know I'm good, baby," he said, nuzzling my neck.

"UDO!"

We crawled across the heaving floor, into the Closet and under the ironing table, which would surely protect us from anything short of Bilskinir actually falling in. And surely Bilskinir could not fall in? Could it? Paimon would not let it. He was the most powerful denizen in the City. But then, the very fact that this temblor was affecting Bilskinir at all was worrisome; maybe Axacaya's attacks had weakened Paimon too much and this earthquake would be the final blow.

"It's not fair," Udo said. "I don't want to die smelling so bad. Though after that kiss, at least I would die happy. Smelly but happy."

"We aren't going to die," I answered, though I wasn't so sure. I closed my eyes and held on to Udo's hand. The furniture jiggled and the walls creaked and cracked, but nothing actually fell in or over or off.

When the temblor finally calmed, I slithered out from under the table and gave Udo a quick rundown of everything he had missed while he had been gallivanting around as Springheel Jack (a short and sweet rundown, minus some of the more embarrassing bits). He said, "That is *so* cool!"

"What, the part about where I have to die?" I asked sarcastically.

"You have your own House! You are always complaining about being a Fyrdraaca. And now you find out you are not a Fyrdraaca after all! Buck can never tell you what to do again! How blissful to be you! And look at all these clothes! Divine!"

"Fat lot of good it does me to not be a Fyrdraaca now! Ayah, so I have my own House, but the City is going to be torn apart by a giant magickal squid, unless I *die*!"

Udo said, "Don't shout, Flora. Of course you aren't going to die. Didn't Tiny Doom say that she had the answer to your problem?"

"So she said. But why should I trust her?"

"Come on, Flora. She wouldn't have left this letter with the clue for you if she didn't care. Rangers don't give up. Come on— but first, kiss me again." He made a grab for me, but I twisted away.

"Kiss yourself, Udo. We don't have time for this. We have to find Hardhands's underwear drawer."

Udo followed me out from under the ironing table and was immediately dumbstruck by the sartorial glories surrounding us.

"The thing that will save my life is in one of these drawers," I said.

"What thing is that?"

"I don't know. When we find Hardhands's underwear drawer I'll know."

"That's a lot of drawers," Udo said in dismay.

Udo was right; there must have been a zillion drawers in the Closet, all shapes and sizes, long and wide, short and narrow, tall, tiny, medium, round, oval. The walls that weren't covered in drawers were covered in closets, cupboards, recesses, and alcoves.

But which one was Hardhands's underwear drawer? Surely, after all this time—he'd been dead fourteen years—Paimon would have cleaned his underwear drawer out? Given them away to charity or something? But also surely, Tiny Doom—my mother—would have put my answer in a place she was certain would be safe all this time. And the size of the room and the number of storage places in it made *me* certain that every item of clothing ever worn by any Haðraaða must be right here.

"This is going to take some time," Udo agreed. "And I thought I had a lot of clothes. This is crazy; I am superjealous. Maybe I can find something that fits me. I can't stand these rags. I need a bath, too."

"After. Right now, look. Let's split up and try to be systematic about it."

Udo took the left side and I took the right, and we started yanking. Drawers full of scarlet gloves; cerulean gloves; cerise, amarillo, lavender, fuchsia, tan, and black gloves. Gauntlets. Mitts. Mittens. Hair ribbons. Waist ribbons. Shoe ribbons. Queue ribbons. Queue bags. Nightgowns. Nightcaps. Day caps. Dressing gowns. Sack coats. Shirts. Blouses. Sweaters. Polonaises. Baby dresses. Nappie covers. The Haðraaða family had been hot for clothes. There was even a closet for magickal garments: a Holocaust Cape, a Greatcoat of Impenetrability, Seven-league Boots, a pointy hat that obviously did something (though that something was unclear, and I wouldn't let Udo put the hat on to find out).

I said, "Even if we find a drawer full of underwear, how are we going to be sure that it's Hardhands's underwear? There's years worth of stuff in here; I don't think Paimon ever got rid of a single item of clothing that any Haðraaða ever wore. Look at these."

I held up a teeny-tiny pair of red velvet shoes, taken from a drawer filled with teeny-tiny shoes, all neatly lined up and covered with tissue paper.

"They are cute—oooh, but look at these." Udo held up a pair of azure silk stockings with embroidered dragons curling up the calves. "Aren't they gorgeous? Can I have them?"

"You have to ask Paimon."

"But you are the Head of the House. So that makes them yours. Come on, I think they'll fit me perfectly."

"Sure, fine, whatever, keep looking."

The more drawers we pulled that did not contain any underwear, the more panicky I became until—

"How do you like these?" From his perch on the top of a ladder, Udo waved a pair of red satin drawers like a flag. "I am the champion. King of all I survey. The most fabulous boy in the world. Udo saves the day!"

"How do you know those are Hardhands's?"

"They are monogrammed: B-M-H-B," he said. "Banastre Micajah Haðraaða ov Brakespeare."

Excitedly, I pulled the other ladder over, and together we rooted through the drawer, scattering underwear everywhere. Hardhands had flamboyant taste. His underwear came in every color and style, but that was all that was in the drawer: underwear and nothing more.

"It's not here. There's nothing in here but underwear!" I said. *"Blast it!"*

I scrambled down the ladder and gave it a good kick, even though none of this was the ladder's fault, poor thing. "Do you think he might have had *two* underwear drawers? Or maybe this isn't really his underwear drawer—just his underwear that was moved from somewhere else."

"Hold your horsies, Flora." Udo yanked the drawer all the way out, climbed down, and showered garish undies on the floor. As he started to throw the drawer aside, I saw a flash of white on its bottom.

"Hold your own horsies—what's that?"

The flash of white was an envelope, partially tucked into one of the joints. It was sealed with lumpy red wax, and on the outside was written: *I knew you'd remember!*

Using the stem of my earring, I slit the top of the envelope open and withdrew a thin booklet. Nini Mo, Coyote Queen: *Nini Mo vs. the Ice Weasels, or the Ultimate Ranger Dare.*

FORTY-SIX

Paimon. Attack. Last Words.

So, THANKS TO Tiny Doom—and Nini Mo—I now had a plan. A drastic plan. But a plan. However, before Udo and I put that plan into action, I needed to make sure there were no alternatives. That it was our only chance. I needed to talk to Paimon.

I went alone. Somehow I knew that only the Head of the House should enter the Butler's bedroom. So Udo stayed to clean himself up and I went to the Ostium to find Paimon.

You'd think that such an elegant denizen would have an elegant bedroom, with gold-painted furniture, and gold-crusted mirrors, and gold-fringed velvet drapes. But the Ostium opened into a small cozy room, not much bigger than my bedroom at Crackpot Hall. Paimon's furniture was plain wood, his curtains flowered flannel. He had only one mirror, and his ginormous bed took up most of the space.

Paimon lay tucked into that ginormous bed, his mustachios trailing over the nubby blue blanket pulled up to this chin, a blue wool nightcap perched upon his enormous head. A water bottle lay on his tummy, and a puffy gray cat sat at his feet, giving me an unblinking hairy eyeball. The first time I had seen Paimon's face unobstructed by his hat, the monstrousness of his visage—the tusks, the huge round eyes, the fringy floppy ears—had terrified me. Now I thought the blue curling mustachios rather dashing, and those spaniel ears darling. His eyes were so kind and such a pretty shade of blue that it seemed crazy that I had ever thought him ugly, or strange, or horrible.

"How do you feel, Paimon?"

"A bit weak, madama," he answered, and his voice did sound raspy. "I cry your pardon for not meeting you personally, but it is taking all my remaining strength to keep the House together and Lord Axacaya out."

"How is it going?"

"Axacaya is trying, but I have held firm. I can hold him for a while longer, but it is very tiring to try to keep him out, as well as keep the House firm. I may not be able to do so indefinitely. The Loliga's labor has begun."

"I know. We are running out of time. I know what to do, Paimon, but before I do it, I just want to be sure that is the only solution. Is there no way for me to simply strengthen Georgiana Segunda's Working?"

"I am sorry, Madama Haðraaða, but it is too late. Even a great magician would need time to strengthen the Sigils. And, alas—"

"I'm not a great magician. I know, I know. But, Paimon, why didn't you tell me before what was going on? I mean, I was here, and you could have said something. It would have saved me a lot of trouble. Saved us all a lot of trouble."

Paimon looked at me woefully. "Ayah so, perhaps, but it was not my place, madama. I only serve the family; I cannot interfere directly in family matters. I did what I could, but, I fear I only made matters worse by the way I handled the situation when you were affected by the Anima Enervation. When I sent you to Lord Axacaya those months ago, I thought that revealing your connection to Bilskinir House would make him think twice about harming you for fear of alienating this House further. Instead, I gave him a clue to your identity. I did not realize that the situation with the Loliga was deteriorating so quickly. I am sorry. I should have been more careful. I can only excuse myself by saying that my long isolation had me out of touch with events within the City."

"Well, we all make mistakes, Paimon. I can hardly blame anyone for screwing up, when I think about my record. All that doesn't matter anymore. What matters is that I have to free the Loliga, and there's only one way to do that."

Paimon closed his eyes and shuddered deeply. His ears quivered. I heard the distant sound of thunder, and then a bright purple light filled the room. I ran to the window; the sky was a roil of yellow-white clouds, like raw scrambled eggs. As I watched, a bolt of galvanic black lightning split the egg-sky and hit the sheep-sheltering oak tree, which disappeared into a burst of black smoke and flickering flames. The sheep burst out of the smoke cloud and ran, bleating, across the grass, which now lay flattened.

Paimon moaned, and I rushed back over to the bed. "Paimon, Paimon, are you all right?"

He didn't answer, and I didn't know what to do. Make him a cold compress? Shake him? Get him a drink? The cat stared at me disdainfully. *When in doubt, wait and see*, said Nini Mo. After a few seconds, Paimon's fringed blue eyes opened, and his tusks lifted as he grinned weakly.

"I cry your pardon. Axacaya, but he didn't get in. Not this time."

"Can I get you something, Paimon? Do you want some Anima? Will that help you?"

He said weakly, "You can help me best, Madama Haðraaða, by taking care of the Loliga."

"Don't you worry about that. Can you keep Axacaya busy until I get into place? Once he gets a sniff of me, I wager he'll leave you alone and will come my way. He wants me. I'm sorry I made you vulnerable to him, Paimon."

"Perhaps our policy of allowing you to remain in ignorance was not the best, but there's no point in stepping in spilled paint. The Haðraaða family has a private entrance to the Baths. You may access it via the Ostium. Alfonzo shall go with you to assist if you require it."

At the sound of his name, the merman crawled out of the

water jug, flapped his feathery koi-tail, and adjusted his jacket before bowing briefly.

Paimon continued, "You already have the Key. I can offer you nothing else."

I glanced down at my left hand, where the Key still encircled my index finger. It itched horribly, I guessed because it was made of hair. I hoped I didn't have to wear it all the time from here on out; the scratching would drive me mad. But for now, I'd just have to try to stand it.

"Thanks, Paimon." He enveloped my hand in his own massive hand, which made mine look pudgy and doll-like in comparison. He squeezed his grip and a galvanic flare went from him to me, a nicely energetic glow, like the buzz of strong coffee.

"Be careful, Flora."

"Dare, win, or disappear," I said, and went off to die.

FORTY-SEVEN

The Baited Hook.
The Cold Plunge.

WHEN UDO AND I tried to open the Ostium into Bilskinir Baths, the door opened an inch and no more. On the other side, rubble held the door closed. It took several minutes of pushing and straining before we could force it open any more, and even then we only managed a few more inches. But it would be enough to squeeze through.

"I will check the way," Alfonzo said, and zipped through the crack.

Udo and I looked at each other. While I'd been talking to Paimon, Udo had raided the Closet, and now he was dressed splendidly in a purple frock coat well-festooned with gold braid, and a red-and-purple wool kilt. The Greatcoat of Impenetrability he had found while raiding the Closet was draped over his arm. He had also raided the maquillage, but he'd applied it with a light hand (he surely hadn't learned *that* from Jack) and looked subtly, handsomely enhanced, not garishly painted. He looked less childish. Grown-up.

"It's a good plan, Flora," he said. "Nini Mo couldn't have come up with better."

"She came up with this one," I pointed out, for indeed our plan was entirely lifted from *Nini Mo vs. the Ice Weasels*, except for the very first part.

"Then that makes it the best plan ever," Udo said confidently, but he looked pale. He should have used more rouge after all.

"You won't be late, will you?"

"I will be right on time. Never fear."

Alfonzo peeked around the door. "It is clear, *hija*! Come along!"

"Dare, win, or disappear," I said, but before I could squeeze through the gap, Udo grabbed my wrist.

"First, now we've come to the part where the heroine gives the hero a big wet one and she promises to plight her troth if they come back alive. So plight me, baby!"

My stomach flipped over. "What are you saying, Udo?"

He looked dead serious. "Will you walk with me? Be my girl?"

For one heart-pausing moment, I had thought he meant something else. Something a whole lot more serious. Now I was thankful (disappointed?) he had not. "What about the Zu-Zu?"

"Aww, her. Kid stuff. What is glamour compared to stalwartness?"

"Are you saying I'm not glamorous? The best I can do is be stalwart?"

"That's not what I meant!"

"That's what you said!"

"What I meant to say, Flora, is that I love you. No, don't say anything, forget I asked. Come on."

"Udo! Wait a minute!" But Udo had already put on the Greatcoat of Impenetrability and vanished. "Udo! Come back here!" I hissed, but he didn't return. Blast Udo—of all the times to be romantic.

"This way!" Alfonzo appeared before me, waving in excitement. "This way! He is coming!"

The Bilskinir Baths were now a disaster of twisted steel, piled rubble, crushed marble. It was hard to believe that this had once been a place of fun and frolic.

I followed, picking my way through the rubble, hoping that

Udo was being careful. Wouldn't it be hilarious if the whole thing was ended by me and Udo both getting crushed by a falling marble slab? Or skidding on a loose piece of rubble and banging our brains out on a broken statue? *The Goddess does love her jokes,* Nini Mo said.

Well, today she'd have to find something else to laugh about, because I managed to climb my way to the Cold Plunge without killing myself. And since I didn't hear any sounds of falling or landing, I assumed that Udo was all right, as well. So far, so good; the easiest part of our plan was done.

The Cold Plunge was a blind white eye set in a sweeping expanse of dark blue cracked mosaic. Thankfully for our plan the Plunge was intact, surrounded by rubble but free of debris itself. That would have been another joke, if I'd arrived to find the Cold Plunge thawed. Why anyone would want to swim in water that frigid was beyond me—the Pacifica is too cold for me. But there is supposed to be a health benefit from jumping into cold water, then flinging oneself out to jump in the super-hot water of the Hot Plunge. Well, we'd see about that.

"Good luck, Madama Haðraaða," Alfonzo said. "And I crave your pardon for the little joke I played upon you before, pretending you were a snack. I do hope you shall forgive me."

He bent in a low courtesy, Abasing Before a Goddess, and I said, "You are forgiven, and you should get going, before Axacaya shows."

"*Besos!*" Alfonzo said, and zipped.

Something brushed in front of my vision; it was wispy, like cobwebs. I waved at the air with my hand but didn't feel anything. Then the blur came again and I realized it wasn't outside of my vision but inside, in my head, a quiet touch.

Axacaya, trying to rifle through my thoughts in a most rude manner. I let despair and fear well up inside me: *Poor pitiful me, to die so young, to be betrayed by my own mamma, why had the goddess picked on me, it wasn't fair, it wasn't fair.* A sob choked me and I wiped at the snivelly tears now trailing down my cheeks. Axacaya's touch withdrew, satisfied, no doubt, that I was a harmless mooncalf.

"Flora, brave girl." He was behind me.

"I don't want to die," I said, not turning around.

"We all must die eventually."

"But I've hardly even lived."

"The Goddess plans for us all, and we shall not question her plans," Axacaya answered, and I turned to look at him. A ray of sun arrowed through the gloom, touched him with gold. But now I found that his beauty had no power to move me. Now I knew that while his face was fair, his heart was false, and his glamour an illusion. Facing him, my feigned fear vanished in a surge of fury. He was smiling at me so kindly and gently; he thought I was a real sucker. Well, we'd see who the sucker was soon enough.

"I am sorry that it has to be this way, *pequeña,* truly I am. But sometimes we must sacrifice for the greater good. And is not the City, your family, the greater good?"

"I know you are right, Your Grace. I know. Will you help me, Your Holiness? I know that I must die; it's the only way to save the City, and the City is more important than me. But I'm afraid." The quiver in my voice was from nervousness, but I'm sure he thought it was fear.

"There's nothing to be afraid of, *pequeña.* Of course, I will help you. Death is not an end, it is a new beginning. We must all face Death eventually, and embrace her."

"I know, Your Grace. Still, I am afraid, but I don't want anything to happen to Buck, and Hotspur, or my friends. If I have to die to save them, then I will do it." Now I was stalwart, but a little teary.

"Brave girl. The courage must be the Fyrdraaca in you, but the pragmatism is all Haðraaða. I would have thought that the combination would be fatally flawed. But I must say, Flora, the two strains seem to temper each other in a most positive way. It is a pity that your career must be cut so short. You have potential."

The ground swelled under our feet, and the ice squeaked and cracked. I said quickly, "But, Your Grace, later I read Georgiana's *Diario* all the way through. If the Sigil cannot be strengthened, it is not enough for the last Haðraaða to simply die. Georgiana was clever. She didn't want to lose her advantage just because some Haðraaða fell off a horse, or was killed in a duel, or ate a bad oyster. Or that someone tried assassination. So she added a stipulation."

"Which was?" Axacaya had come closer and now loomed over me, but I stood my ground.

Here came the big fat lie. I turned my face into a horrified grimace and said, "That the death must be by drowning."

Axacaya smiled, his lip plug winking. "Clever. And appropriate. Well, there's no shortage of water here. I think we can accommodate you."

My internal organs stopped quivering. He had bought it! Praise Nini Mo, he had bought it! I flung myself forward, and he caught me with a surprised grunt, as I wailed, "But I'm afraid to die. I don't want to drown—dreadful noise in my ears, gasping for breath. Please help me, Your Holiness, help me make it easier, please."

"Now, now," Axacaya said soothingly. "I shall give you an easy death, Flora. Let that be my gift to you. It is the least I can do to award your bravery."

I looked up at him in the most sickeningly sweet fashion I could manage, fluttered my eyelashes, and pursed my lips into my cutest wistful pout. *Wait for it, Udo, wait for it!* "Oh, thank you, Your Holiness, thank you."

Lord Axacaya spoke a Gramatica Word. As it crackled from his lips, I felt the heat of it whiz by my head, and then heard the snap of ice breaking.

"This water is ice cold, my darling. So cold, you will feel nothing. It will be like falling into a deep sleep. Painless and easy."

"Oh, thank you, Your Grace. I knew you would not fail me. And—I almost forgot, Your Holiness—Tiny Doom left me a letter. There was a message in it for you."

"Really? Dear Azota. What did she say?" He sounded pleased that the woman he had betrayed still thought of him, even as she had died. He probably thought that was a compliment.

She said keep your stinking hands off my daughter, I thought, but I said, breathlessly, "She said to tell you that she is coming for you."

While Axacaya had been holding me, I had finagled my arms up and around his neck, and now I grabbed two great sheaves of his hair and pulled his head down. Surprised by my sudden grip, he barely flinched when I kissed him. Indeed, he started to kiss me back—yucky tongue—and then he stiffened.

I let go and sprang back. Axacaya stood there, looking extremely surprised. His lips were stained bright red by my zombified lip rouge. His eyes wobbled in their sockets, and his head bobbed. Fike, he was fighting it. The only thing magickal about Jack had been his boots; they were strong but no match for the powder. But Axacaya was an adept, and there hadn't been much of the powder left—apparently not enough.

A good ranger, Nini Mo said, *always has a fail-safe.* Mine was Udo and his Greatcoat of Impenetrability, and his legendary bowling arm, which had led the Sanctuary bowling league to victory on more than one occasion. Axacaya took one jerky step toward me, and his lips struggled to pronounce a Gramatica Word that would no doubt negate the zombie powder.

"Hit him, Udo!" I shouted. "Hit him hard!"

Thanks to the Greatcoat, I saw neither Udo nor the blow, but Lord Axacaya staggered and half turned, and then staggered again, as Udo hit him another time. The lacrosse stick (taken from a case of sporting equipment in one of Bilskinir's hallways) made a wet thunking noise, and Lord Axacaya went down. He did not get back up again.

Get it over with, Mamma always says. Axacaya lay crumbled on the rubble, darkness slicking his hair. I couldn't see Udo, but I could hear him shouting my name. I tore at the lacings on my boots, kicking them off, and flung my dispatch case aside. Udo appeared before me, breathless and disheveled. I thrust the buckskin jacket at him; he took it, saying, "Flora, are you sure?"

"Ayah."

I took one last look at his face, and before I could lose my nerve, turned around and jumped into the Cold Plunge. For a moment I felt only the slap of impact, but then, like a knife through my entrails, the cold cut in. I rolled, floundering, my bones feeling like they were splintering. Teeth chattering, I bit my lip and the hot spurt of blood was only a tiny spark in the giant void of coldness.

"Flora!" Dimly, I heard Udo shouting. "Flora!"

Axacaya had lied, of course; freezing to death was not easy, like falling asleep. Instead, it felt as though my flesh was being cut in ribbons with a razor blade. I tried to give in, to let go, but the instinct to live would not let me quit flailing.

"Is . . . he . . . still . . . down?" I gasped. My tongue could barely move, but my teeth were chattering like crickets. Udo's warm grip fastened onto my head, and his voice echoed from somewhere in the freezing void. "He's down and he ain't getting back up again. I'll see you in a few minutes, Flora. Don't go far—"

His words faded to noise that faded into freezing cold. Pressure on my head, pushing down hard. Sputtering, I went under the ice, and my chattering thoughts of Mamma, Poppy, Idden, Flynnie, even silly Valefor, cracked and fell away.

FORTY-EIGHT

In the Current.

I LOOK UPWARD and see the body of a girl drifting in the center of a black circle. Her arms and legs are outstretched, lifeless, and red hair wafts like seaweed around her slack blue face. Her eyes, frosted white marbles, stare down at me blankly. Her head jerks suddenly and her limbs flail; someone is hauling her up out of the water. Her feet are the last to disappear, red socks winking.

Good-bye, Waking World.

Rolling over, I jackknife down, swimming through a rocky tunnel, its walls bristling with lavender and emerald sea urchins, encrusted with crimson coral. I emerge from the tunnel into a shadowy green world. Flat strands of kelp rise from the seabed, tangle on the surface above my head. Narrow silvery fish dart through the kelp forest, their pink bellies flashing as they pass through the shafts of sunlight that stream down from above. The landscape is peaceful and calm, and I am springy and buoyant, as though a heavy weight has been lifted from me. Now that I am dead, I have been released from the prison of my physical body. I do not need to breathe; I cannot drown. Reveling in my freedom, I drift boneless in the water.

Not water, but the Current.

This underwater world is an illusion. My body is dead, but my Anima survives, and it is translating Elsewhere into images

I recognize and understand. I know the salmon are really elementals, the kelp is really ætheric energy, the coral is really fragments of old sigils, broken and encased with time. But the illusion is beautiful and I wish with all my Will that I could enjoy it, drift through the Current forever, give in to its pull, allow it to carry me away.

But I cannot.

I must find the Loliga—make sure she has been freed from her prison. Afterward, perhaps there will be time to play. *You can't enjoy the lemonade until you've squeezed the lemons*, says Nini Mo.

So I glide through the Current like an otter or a dolphin, though when I look down at myself, I see that my Anima has retained the familiar Flora form. I am disappointed; I would rather be an otter or a dolphin, but I remain trapped as myself. The seabed slopes and drops away, and I leave the sunlit shallows, the kelp forest, the salmon, the coral reef, behind. I swim through a brief twilight and into a darkness pinpricked with firefly phosphorescent lights. As I draw near them, the lights coalesce into fantastic creatures, strangely luminescent, transparent glowing ghosts against the Current's darkness. A shoal of jellylike creatures, fat as blancmanges, each trailing a plume of glassy filaments. A cloud of tiny crimson shrimp, sparking like embers. A long gleaming strand, thicker than my waist, its length strung with glowing pearls. A sinuous gunmetal-gray eel with bulbous crimson eyes and fangs protruding so far that it cannot close its jaws, with a long fleshy lure, pulsating with a lemon-yellow light, protruding from its forehead tip.

Downward I go, through water that is not water. Axacaya and I had only skimmed the surface when we visited the Loliga. Now, I go deeper, much deeper. The glowing entities grow fewer, and eventually I sail through the velvet blackness alone. Ahead of me, the Current will drop down into the Abyss. If I venture too far, I will not be able to return to the Waking World.

But I do not need to go that far. Soon, the form of a building rears out of the darkness. The Bilskinir Baths, drowned.

No, not really the Bilskinir Baths. The Loliga's prison. Georgiana's Working.

This version of the Bilskinir Baths is a hundred times larger than its Waking World counterpart. It towers over me like an enormous underwater mountain; below, its foundations are invisible. Like the Working it represents, the building is crumbling. Its walls are crusted with glowing green lichen, and pieces of the facade have fallen away. The marble statues in the pediment above the main doors are missing limbs, their faces pitted with wormholes.

The Baths look abandoned. But I know that someone—something—is still inside.

Directly ahead, I can see the Baths' main entrance. The doors are closed and I know they are locked. But I wear the Key on my finger. I can open the doors, allow the Loliga to go free.

As I arrow forward, I feel a brief tug, as though something is trying to pull me back. My Will prickles uneasily. But when I look behind me, I see only darkness. I swim a few feet further and feel the tug again. Again, I see only darkness behind me, but something is there. I can sense its malevolence, its hunger, its anger.

"⸲⟐⫫ ⬌ '⟋Ɏ⋏⋀⋀!"

The Word emerges from my mouth in the shape of a glowing pink bubble. The bubble bobs in the Current, but its light is too weak to illuminate very far. I flick the bubble with my finger, and it pops, momentarily flooding the darkness with a brilliant pink light.

Revealed in that light is a monstrous shape: a nightmarish creature, half octopus, half spider crab. The horror has long spiny legs, segmented like an insect's, springing from an oozy shapeless body. Its bulbous eyes protrude on sluglike stalks. The creature is a deep dark pulsating black, which had kept me from seeing it in the darkness. It radiates evil. And though it looks different from the last time I saw it, I recognize it instantly: The kakodæmon that Tiny Doom and I had vanquished in the Waking World. Somehow it has found me in the Current, and I do not think it has come to wish me well.

I flee toward the Bilskinir Baths' doors. The Working may be crumbling, but it is still relatively secure. If it can hold the Loliga in, surely it can keep the kakodæmon out. I put every ounce of my Will into my flight. I have no lungs to wheeze, no muscles to burn; I am not hampered by heavy flesh. But I can only go so fast, and the kakodæmon is quickly closing the distance between us.

My Will turns molten. If the kakodæmon gets me now, it will consume me completely—I will be worse than dead; I will cease to exist completely. The kakodæmon catapults over me, legs scrabbling, body inflating; now it is between me and the doors. Its bulbous eyes glow with hate. Its mantle flares open, umbrellalike; deep within the fleshy core is a sucking round mouth, which gapes wide to reveal a circle of horrifically humanlike teeth. I dart away just as the mantle snaps shut, trying to trap me inside. Before it can reinflate, I dive over the kakodæmon, brushing one of its arms as I do so. The arm, though spiny, is covered with soft black fur. At the touch, pain surges through me and I falter. A heavy dark gooey feeling begins to lap at my edges.

Now I am sluggish. I see those snappy shoe-peg teeth and try to dodge them, but I am too slow. The kakodæmon rears back, preparing to pounce, and then suddenly its mantle collapses. A furry shape has attached to one of the kakodæmon's arms and is chewing on it like Flynn chews a stick.

I try to dart away, but move slowly. The kakodæmon jerks its arm out of the Coyote's mouth—Coyote? Can coyotes even swim? This one can, in a graceful effortless dog paddle. Legs held close to its body, using its plumed tail like a rudder, the Coyote circles around the kakodæmon, jaws snapping at its flailing limbs. The kakodæmon retreats a few feet; the Coyote sails toward me and rams me with its long nose. I fly backward and hit the Bilskinir Baths' door. On my finger, the Key sizzles. I bang on the surface of the doors with my fists, and they fly open. I am sucked inside. I get a last glimpse of the kakodæmon bearing down upon the Coyote, and then doors slam shut behind me.

I am inside Georgiana's Working. Inside the Loliga's prison.

But I am no longer light and airy. I have landed on the floor of the lobby in a heap, and when I clamber to my feet, I find I am once again firm on the ground. The walls of the Working drip with Current, and Current puddles on the cracked marble floor, but the Current that fills the Working is so thin, it feels just like air. After being so buoyant, it is a real drag to suddenly feel so heavy again.

The doors rattle and jump on their hinges; the kakodæmon must have overpowered the Coyote and now its attention is back on me. The Baths echo with a high-pitched wailing. The walls vibrate, gusting plaster; chunks of marble plummet down from above; the tile beneath me heaves and buckles. I careen down the marble stairs. Ahead, where the Pacifica should be, is only darkness. Above, where the sky should shine through the glass ceiling, is only darkness.

A woman crouches in the bottom of the Salt Pool, now drained of Current. She clutches her immensely swollen belly, screaming.

I vault into the Pool and find that though the Current inside the Working is thin, it is strong enough to support my jump. I land lightly and run toward the woman. Even crouching, she's very tall; my head barely comes up to the middle of her giant tummy. I grab her hands, just as she lets out another shriek. An enormous wave of pain rolls out of her and into me, the worst pain I have ever felt in my life, a huge horrible squeezing sheet of pain that seems to go on forever.

And then is suddenly gone.

The woman has let go of my hands and unsteadily risen to her feet, towering over me. Her red hair lies in slicks around her puffy face, and blood stands out on her lip where she has bitten it. The ragged remains of her blue silk gown are dripping with sweat. A gold collar encircles her neck; it is fastened to a long golden chain that is bolted to the floor. She looks exactly like the portrait of Georgiana Segunda, but I know she is not Georgiana Segunda.

"Haðraaða bitch!" the Loliga cries. I dodge the curse just in time; when it hits the wall behind me, it explodes into a choking black cloud. She staggers toward me and then is stopped short by the length of the chain. "Free me!"

"But I thought my death would free you!"

"Your death freed me from the form of that monster, but no more!" the Loliga shouts, and then she screams again. The ground heaves and rolls, and a fissure opens up almost under my feet. I jump back, struggling to keep my footing.

I have been calm so far; death and immersion in the Current had taken the edge off my lively anxieties. Now, at the sound of the Loliga's screams, at the chaos around me, those anxieties come flooding back. It's all I can do to keep from screaming frantically myself. Here, deep in Elsewhere, the Loliga's screams are tearing at the Working; higher above, her struggles are rippling through the City's Current like a tidal wave. And in the Waking World, they are tearing the City apart.

"*Stop!*" I shout.

The Loliga's scream abruptly stops, and she stares at me with enormous blue eyes.

"Look, I will free you and get you out of here, but you have to stop screaming. You are destroying the City."

"I don't care about your stupid City. It deserves to be destroyed." She gasps, clutching at her middle.

"If the City is destroyed, then I won't have any reason to free you."

The Loliga lunges at me, but I have been careful to stay out of her reach. I say, "If you hurt me, I won't be able to help you."

"You are not helping me now." A shadow passes over the Loliga's face, but she doesn't scream again.

"Look, madama, I died to free you—how is that not helping?"

The Loliga says scornfully, "Am I not still imprisoned?" Then she tosses her head back, neck straining, mouth opening silently. She pants and gasps, but she doesn't scream.

I had expected to see the egregore still in squid form; I am shocked by the Loliga's shape. She looks like an ordinary human woman. A human woman in labor. Does this mean she will give birth like a human woman? I know nothing about delivering babies, magickal or otherwise. I do not *want* to know anything about delivering babies, magickal or otherwise.

As soon as her spasm passes, I say, "I will unchain you, but you must promise not to hurt me. Then you can go, ayah?"

The Loliga bites her lip, nods. I stand on tippy-toe and she bends forward so that I can reach the collar around her neck. Her skin is as smooth as porcelain, tinted with lavender. I gently push her matted hair away from the collar, which I touch with my index finger, still encircled by the Key. The collar wavers, shimmers, and vanishes. As I am doing this, I notice a faint odor. It is not the Loliga; she smells of salt and fish. This smell is ripe and muddy, the kind of smell that makes your mouth taste bad. I sense movement above us. I look up, and there is the kakodæmon peering down through a hole in the glass ceiling. It sticks one long arm through, probing.

The Loliga sees the kakodæmon, too, and spits out, "A kakodæmon. Scum."

The hole is too small for the kakodæmon to get through, but it's picking at the glass, as though trying to make it big enough to slip through. I can't wait and see if it succeeds. I had hoped that if I opened the doors for her, the Loliga could leave the Working on her own. But she can barely walk; clearly, she needs my help. The bottom of the empty pool is wet and slippery. I put my arm around the Loliga's waist and together we stagger toward the stairs that lead to the pool deck. I can't help but keep glancing up, and see that the kakodæmon has left off its picking and is following us, skittering from girder to girder.

Don't look back, Nini Mo says, and so I try to forget about the kakodæmon, to concentrate on not buckling under the weight of the Loliga. Still, I know by the stench floating down that the kakodæmon is keeping pace with us. Fear prickles me; I try to ignore it.

Our progress is not rapid. The Loliga staggers a few feet, and then falters. I urge her on, she staggers another few feet, and falters again.

"It's close—" She pants. "It hurts!"

"We are almost there." I point up the stairs. "Look. There's the door."

"I cannot go that way!" the Loliga cries. She collapses into a heap. "I cannot go through that door!"

"But it's the only way out!"

"Georgiana put me under a geas not to go through that door. I thought you knew another way."

The Loliga begins to scream and thrash, drumming her heels on the floor. The tile cracks under her blows; the air around her sparks. In the Waking World, the City is falling down. And I am powerless to do anything about it.

My Will begins to bubble with panic. Fike Georgiana! She had not mentioned the geas in her *Diario*. I have done the one thing I know how to do: die. I had thought that would be enough. I don't know how to do anything else. I have no idea how to tear the Working down. I have no idea how to lift a geas . . .

But, thanks to Tiny Doom, I know how to get around one.

The Loliga's eyes are rolling wildly, and when I lean over, she strikes out at me. I grab her hands, trying to ignore the pain that pulses through her grip.

"Shhhuushhh . . ." I hum soothingly, the same hum that Mamma would use on Poppy to calm him down, a tuneless little hum that she would do for me when the monster under the bed (not nearly as horrific as the kakodæmon) tried to get me. The hum vibrates in my chest, up through my hands, into the Loliga, and she begins to calm down.

I say firmly and calmly, "Listen. Georgiana put you under a geas not to go through that door. But a geas affects your Will only, not mine. Understand?"

The Loliga nods weakly.

"So, you can leave through that door under my Will, if I make you go with me. But you gotta get up!"

Somehow I manage to hoist the Loliga to her feet, and we climb the last few steps. The stench is growing. I look up to see the kakodæmon is still shadowing us. Only a few more feet and we shall reach the door. When I glance up again, the kakodæmon vanishes—gone ahead to wait for us. If we go out that door, we will walk directly into its grasp and be consumed.

We are trapped, just as I was trapped before—in the oubliette, by the ghoul. I had tried to spring myself from those traps and failed. I had been freed because of someone else's efforts, not my own. I had abandoned my comrade to save myself. I will not abandon the Loliga.

"The baby's coming!" the Loliga howls, and flings me off, falls against the door, falls down. Her back arches, her arms flail. Under the blue gown, her belly ripples. Her howls are shattering the ceiling; glass twinkles down like a sparkly sharp rain. I lean over her, trying to protect her from the rain, try to grab her hands, try to hold her, heave her to her feet. But she's frantic now, past reason, gone far beyond me, and I cannot get a grip on her. Her elbow rams my chin, and even though I have no blood to taste, my mouth fills with an iron tang. I have to get the Loliga out of here. Maybe I can distract the kakodæmon long enough to allow her to escape. Then maybe I can escape myself. And if not, at least she will be free and the City saved.

I am trying one last time to heave her to her feet, when the kakodæmon's stench almost overwhelms me. I look up to see it fall through the ceiling, land upon a piece of broken marble, scrabble toward us on skittering legs. It is now between us and the door. The kakodæmon rears up, inflating its mantle, exposing the moist gash of its mouth, those horrible square yellow teeth. I throw myself upon the Loliga; our heads knock together in a bright burst of pain.

Right behind that burst of pain comes my panic. I can't fight the kakodæmon and protect the Loliga at the same time; I can't protect the Loliga and help her, too. We have to get out of here now. Instantly. If there was ever a time for a Translocation Sigil, this was it.

But what would happen if the Sigil went wrong? Where would we end up? In the Abyss? The Loliga would be free, but I would never be able to return to the Waking World. What if I said the Word wrong? That would be a calamity in the Waking World. In the Current it could be catastrophic. We could be instantly destroyed, and because our destruction would occur within Georgiana's Working and this Working is tied to the City's Current, the City could be destroyed, as well.

Panic runs through me like rushing water, quick and cold, threatening to drown me, and bobbing along in the rush is one thought: If I don't try, we shall be destroyed for sure. The Loliga's back is arching like a bow; her mouth is open, but no sound is coming out. The kakodæmon is poised above us, pincers reaching down to cram us into those snapping teeth.

Now, or don't bother, says Nini Mo.

I lean over the Loliga and suck in all her pain, her fear, her anger; mix it with my pain, my fear, my anger. Those emotions run together, flood me with a huge pressure that grows stronger, stronger, stronger! No time to create a Direction Sigil; I don't need a Direction Sigil. An image of the Cloakroom of the Abyss pops into my head and I fasten on that image—hold it within my Will.

The mantle begins to come down, enveloping us. Before it can touch us, I scream: "🜂🜍🜔🜚🜅🜊!"

The pressure that has been building in me explodes. I am dwindling, dissolving, shrinking. My consciousness is swirling, twirling, as though I am spiraling down a giant drain. I am poured into darkness, where I float, diffused and formless. Images flash through me: the Loliga's human form disintegrating into a huge ball of coldfire light, a color I have never seen before, rich and deep. With a flash, the light splits in two and vanishes, leaving shimmering streaks behind. The streaks fade, and the edges of the Void begin to whirl and spin, catching me in their dizzying movement. I blur, the Void blurs, and then—

FORTY-NINE

The Cloakroom of the Abyss, Again. A Coyote. Hot Water.

Gasping, I surge up out of blackness. My vision swims around me, the world wavering, and then springs into focus. I splash to the edge of the pool and hang there, gasping, before hauling myself up out of the water into a familiar room: the Cloakroom of the Abyss. Familiar, but not the same as when I had last seen it. Hardhands's catafalque has vanished; taking its place, the pool from which I have just crawled. In the dim wavery light, the water looks as flat and black as ink.

The Translocation Sigil—*my* Translocation Sigil—worked. We had escaped the kakodæmon. The Loliga and her child are gone. Free.

I am wrung out, exhausted, weak. I sit on the edge of the pool, dripping, shivering in the cool air. The crypt is absolutely silent. The alcoves are empty, biers bare. No sign of any Hað↓raaða corpses. There is only one dead Haðraaða here: me.

Surely by now Udo should have fished me out of the Cold Plunge, yanked me back to the Waking World. But instead here I am, where all dead Haðraaðas end up, apparently. Maybe it is too late; I had been dead too long and now dead I would stay. This fear is muted by exhaustion, so I just sit there at the edge of the pool, too tired to try to figure out what to do next.

The water begins to churn and froth. I remember the kakodæmon, and alarm overcomes my weakness. I scramble up and take drippy refuge in one of the alcoves. In the pool, something is poking up out of the whip-creamy froth: a black nose, a long snout, a flat head, two tufted ears. The Coyote paddles furiously; I run forward and grab its ruff. Paws catch at the pool's edge; I pull, and we both fall over backward onto the icy marble floor.

The Coyote had escaped the kakodæmon after all. It scrabbles to its feet and shakes itself hard, hurtling diamondlike droplets through the air. Its fur shimmers, ruff flutters, fur flies—dissolves—and the Coyote is gone. In its place stands a laughing woman. She stamps her bare feet, tosses her magenta hair back and forth. Extends her arms, twirling, the fringe on her buckskin jacket whirling with her, and says, "Woo, that was fun!"

I sit on the cold marble floor, in a puddle of water, amazed.

"Sit there in that water, you just might get a cold. Catch the ague and die!" The woman slicks her hair back behind her ears, gold thumb-rings glinting. She is already completely dry. "Come on, girlie, get up!"

Still I sit, gaping at her like a broken window. Because I know who she is, and yet I can't believe it is really her. I've seen her image a thousand times: the buckskin jacket, the bare feet, the magenta hair, the wide red mouth.

Nini Mo. The Coyote Queen. The greatest ranger of them all.

"Sorry about that back there," Nini Mo says. "I thought I had that squirt licked. I let down my guard. A silly old kakodæmon, and the bugger surprised me. Aw, I tell you, I'm getting too old for this kind of thing."

"You are Nini Mo!" I blurt.

"So I've heard." She grins at me. Her smile is electric. It makes me want to smile, too.

Instead, I say, "But aren't you dead?"

"You are dead, too, my dolly. Though I hear you aren't planning to stay that way."

"What are you doing here? Didn't you cross the Abyss?"

"And miss all the fun? Tiny Doom asked me to give you a hand, herself being unable to, ya know. Or give you a paw, I guess you could say. Maybe a fang or two. Not that you needed much help from me, dolly. Your mamma's girlie, you are! And you got sand, my dolly, to try the Ultimate Ranger Dare. More sand than I ever had, that's for sure."

"Huh?"

Nini Mo has extended her hand to me; I take it and she pulls me up. Her skin is warm and the rich dirt smell of patchouli drifts from her. "I only made the dare up, baby doll. I never actually did it!"

"But what about *Nini Mo vs. the Ice Weasels*?"

"Oh, baby doll, lies all. Infamous lies. I never actually did any of those sportive tricks that they ascribe to me. Horse hoo, completely. Did you think they were all true? You and Tiny Doom—so gullible both!"

Now I am stunned with disappointment. I *had* thought the Coyote Queen yellowbacks were true. Embellished and exaggerated, yes, but otherwise true. She is saying they were lies? My great plan is based on a lie? If Nini Mo couldn't escape from death, how could I? No wonder I am still dead.

Nini Mo sees my disappointment. She slips her arm around my shoulders and squeezes. "Don't look so long in the face. You got to keep the truth safe behind a bodyguard of lies. I know how much mystique matters. The Coyote Queen books were just my cover; you know, they were flash. I couldn't hardly let everyone know what I was really up to, now, could I?"

"But how could they all be lies?"

"The secret center is true, baby doll. Cut the crap and the rest is good. It's like sleight of hand. Pretend to give into the embrace and then hit 'em as hard as you can. Like you did with Axacaya. Ah, I wish I had seen the look on his face—thinking he was so sweet, but he fell for an old trick: the lure and the drop. He should have expected that a kiss from a Haðraaða would be a real knockout!" She laughs, and I do, too, because now that I think about it, it really had been quite funny.

Nini cuts our laughter short. "Now, darling, I'd love to chat longer, but you got to get back, baby doll. You've been gone long enough as it is, but I want to have a few words before you go."

She turns me until I face her directly. She isn't smiling anymore. Her eyes are the exact color of dark chocolate, and her skin the color of strong coffee thinned slightly with condensed milk.

"Do you still wanna be a ranger?" she asks.

I start to say, yes of course, and then stop. Do I still want to be a ranger? Suddenly I do not know.

"Fun sneaking around being all important, no?" Nini says. "Not so fun being thrown into an oubliette to die, or getting shot at, or kicking people in the head and breaking their necks, hmm?"

"I don't think I'd make a very good ranger," I say. "I kinda messed everything up."

"Hmmm?"

"Well, I let Axacaya sucker me totally, and I left Tiny Doom to the ghoul, and I never noticed that Idden was tailing me, and I killed Axila Aguila. I didn't mean to, but I did."

Nini waves her hand. "All a ranger cares about, Flora, is getting the job done. A ranger will lie, steal, cheat, kill—whatever it takes to complete the mission. That's all that matters. The rest does not signify. You freed the Loliga, and saved the City. You got the job done."

"But I put Poppy in danger, and Idden, too. I let Axacaya attack our house. I was totally gullible."

"Ayah, you were gullible, but I'll warrant you won't be in the future, ayah?"

I say fervently, "No fear of that. But, Poppy, and Idden, and Udo—"

Nini Mo presses her fingers to my lips, cutting me off. "You aren't the Queen of the World, responsible for everyone else. Let them have their own Wills."

"But—"

The fingers press harder, painfully. "Listen to me, Flora.

Even the Goddess Califa ain't infallible; elsewise why would she have created such a fallible world? Don't flatter yourself that you are better than she. That'll come back to bite you for sure."

"But—"

"No *buts*!" Nini cries. "You and your mamma—always arguing! No argument! You gotta go back, or you're gonna have to stay here, and that is not part of the plan. I wish we had more time; it's a drag to hit and run like this, but there it is."

Behind us steam is rising from the pool's surface, the water bubbles. Nini is still talking. "You got sand, dolly. Your mamma had sand; you take after her, and I am proud to have you as a namesake. Don't give up on being a ranger, Nyana. The time is coming when Califa—when the Waking World—is going to need girls with sand. Anyway, it's too late."

"What do you mean it's too late? Because I'm dead?"

"No, silly girl. It's too late to back down now. You know too much. You've seen too much."

All the friendliness suddenly drains from Nini Mo's face and is replaced with a look I know only too well. Duty and determination. A little wiggle of fear slithers through me.

"You have to finish what you start, Nyana," Nini Mo says. "Magick is a game, ayah so, but it's a game with very real consequences. It's a game you don't want to lose. You've been meddling, not only in the Current, but in the City's affairs. You have made claims—claims to being a ranger, claims to being a Haðraaða—"

"I am a Haðraaða," I say dolefully.

"Maybe so, but don't claim what you can't hold. Do you understand? It's your Will to choose, but choices have consequences. Do you understand?"

I nod, though I do not fully understand. But I do understand the look on her face. It's a look that says, *I will be very unhappy if you do not agree with me*. I have the strong feeling that making Nini Mo very unhappy would not be a good idea.

"You are with us or against us. Ayah so?"

"I am with you," I answer fervently, for how could I ever be against Nini Mo?

She is smiling again, her face open and bright. "Well, then, I'm glad that's settled! Now, let's see . . . I guess I should send you off with a few words of wisdom—you know, from a dead ranger to a living one. Um . . . What can I say?" Nini purses her lips and rolls her eyes, considering. Then she laughs. "Of course! The best advice I was ever given, now I pass on to you. Never pass up a chance to pee. Adios, baby doll!"

"Wait—" I grab her hand and hold on. "What do I do?"

"The best you can, baby doll. The best you can!"

And with that, Nini Mo yanks from my grip and gives me a good hard shove. I wheel backward and fall into the pool. The water is slick and warm. When I bob to the surface, paddling, Nini Mo is leaning over the edge, splashing at me.

She cries, "Also, you should eat chocolate every day! And always wash your face before you go to bed! And never trust a fish—"

The water begins to churn around me, and it is boiling hot. I open my mouth to scream and the scalding water roars down my throat, scorching me into silence. The pain is excruciating. The edges of my vision begin to char. Distantly, I hear Nini Mo still yelling advice. A wave of fire rises up over me and burns me into blackness.

FIFTY

Home. Still the Same. Lessons.

IN THE TIME BETWEEN when Nini Mo pushed me into the pool in the Cloakroom of the Abyss and when I awoke, alive, in my own bed at Crackpot Hall, lots of exciting things happened. Before, I would have been wild at being cut out of all the fun, left out of the adventure. Now, I didn't really mind. I'd had enough excitement.

Udo, brimming with heroics, was more than happy to tell me what I had missed. With dramatic detail he related how he had fished me from the Cold Plunge and then dumped me into the Hot Plunge, which had, just as planned, shocked my frozen heart back to life. Then he bundled me out of Bilskinir Baths as they had collapsed around us—a final collapse into absolute rubble. I missed this daring hair's breadth escape, being alive but not yet conscious, and also burning up with fever. Then, even more heroically, Udo (with some help from Sieur Caballo, who had apparently followed our flight to Bilskinir and loitered around, hoping we would reappear) had fought his way through fire, flooding, alarms, debris, and looters, to Crackpot Hall. There he delivered me to Poppy, who thankfully had not been killed in the fight with the Quetzals.

The chaos was due to one final upheaval, which dropped the China Basin back into the Bay, flattened dozens of buildings, most of them South of the Slot, where architecture tends to be makeshift and rickety, and realigned the Navy Yard shoreline. I missed all that and the small tidal wave that luckily did not do too much damage, although it washed away part of the Pacifica Playa and, unfortunately, some of the people who had taken refuge there. I missed every water source in the City suddenly spewing forth spoiled squid-meat sludge. And Mamma declaring martial law and ordering looters to be shot on sight, putting the militia on fire detail. And the previously mentioned fires, alarms, and everything else. These calamities were great, but they were not complete, nor permanent. The City was spared total destruction.

And Lord Axacaya, having somehow recovered from Udo's head-bopping and my Zombie Powder, had escaped from the Bilskinir Baths himself and was taking all the credit for this miracle. Well, he was welcome to it, as far as I was concerned.

While all these exciting things were happening, I lay in my bed, burning up with a fever that almost killed me a second and final time. After a week, the fever broke, and I had no energy to do anything but lie in bed with the windows wide open, trying to stay cool. I still felt hot, as though the heat from the boiling water was lodged in my bones, still flickered in my veins. My death seemed distant and dreamlike, as though it had happened ages ago, or to someone else entirely. I could barely remember the details—the Loliga, the kakodæmon, Nini Mo.

Poppy brought me iced tea, and ice cream, bubble drinks, and cold watermelon. He opened all the windows in Crackpot so a breeze would blow through my room, and refilled my ice pack when it melted. He asked how I was feeling and if I wanted another pillow. But he didn't say anything at all about what happened—the attack by the Quetzals, or our discovery I was only half a Fyrdraaca, or how Udo had brought me home half dead.

And I didn't bring up any of this stuff, either. I didn't

think much about it, not about being an idiot regarding Axacaya, or about how Mamma had lied to me all my life, or about
how I was the Head of the House Haðraaða, or how I had
freed the Loliga, or had finally met Nini Mo. I lay on my bed,
empty.

Mamma came in and out—she was superbusy with the
martial law and everything—bringing me candy, yellowbacks,
fruit, flowers, newspapers. Her weskit was already strained
across her belly, and her face was puffy—from the baby, I
guessed. She didn't say anything about anything, either, and
whether this was because she was avoiding subjects or didn't
actually know what I had been up to, I wasn't sure. I couldn't
tell whether Poppy had told her everything or nothing. Before,
I had thought that when I saw Mamma I would not be able to
contain myself, that I would burst with righteous anger and
indignation. But I guess dying had sucked all the anger and indignation right out of me, because when I looked at her, I
didn't feel a thing.

Not one tiny thing.

Udo, still full of heroic puffery, had apparently forgotten
about his disgraceful behavior with Springheel Jack's boots, or
his infatuation with the Zu-Zu. He didn't mention our kisses or
his proposal we go steady. But he brought me flowers, and yellowbacks, and more flowers, and a giant box of bacon-bit truf-
fles (my favorite kind and hideously expensive—how it must
have hurt to dig so deep into his wallet . . .). While I theoreti-
cally appreciated the effort, I rather wished he'd leave me
alone.

Valefor popped in when no one else was looking and regaled
me with a long whine about the damage Crackpot Hall had sus-
tained during the Upheaval—a long list of cracks, sinks, buckles, and topples. When I closed my eyes, his whine became a
buzz that was almost soothing. Also soothing, the heavy weight
of Pig in my arms, and Flynn lying across my feet.

And once I woke up to see a parrot perched on my windowsill, staring at me. It fluttered away when I roused enough to lob

a boot at it. Axacaya, I knew, checking up on me. After that I made Val close and lock the windows.

Even Idden came to see me once, sneaking in through the bolt-hole when everyone else was in bed. She and her comrades had escaped the Quetzals somehow—she was vague on the details—but with Axacaya the Crowned Hero, the City was too hot for the IE. They were temporarily relocating to another locale—she was vague on those details, too—but she would be in touch later. "It isn't over yet," she said ominously, and I just nodded, because as far as I was concerned, it was all over. I was done. I had had enough excitement to last me a thousand years. Despite what I had told Nini Mo, all my desire to be a ranger, to be a hero, to be anything at all, had been frozen and burned away.

I just wanted to be left alone.

THIS ALL ENDED when Poppy came in one morning, pulled open my curtains, whacked the bed door, and said, "Get up!" When I didn't, only rolled over and put my face to the wall, he whacked the door again and again until I sprang out of bed, full of rage.

"What do you want!? Leave me alone!"

"Breakfast is in ten minutes, Flora," Poppy said. "It's time to get up. You've only got a week of holiday left and we are way behind in your studies. It's time to get back to real life. You've got a lot of work to do."

Before I could reply using Tiny Doom's favorite word, he had set my stack of clean laundry on my settee and left. I knew that if I went back to bed, he'd just come back in and make a lot more noise, and if I locked the door to keep him out, he'd just pound on that. And anyway, I discovered that for the first time in a long time, I was hungry. A delicious smell of bacon was wafting in the air, and my stomach rumbled. So I put on Tiny Doom's buckskin jacket over my nightgown and went downstairs.

In the kitchen, Poppy was flipping sourdough pancakes. I

could tell that he recognized the jacket, but he made no comment. Valefor sat at the kitchen table, guzzling hot chocolate. He looked up at me as I came in, and smiled a cocoa-rimmed smile.

"What are you doing here?" I asked.

"Hotspur said I could come down, Flora Segunda—"

"Don't call me that!" I sat down at the table and poured myself some coffee.

Valefor looked surprised. "But it's your name."

"No, it's not. My name is Nyana, not Flora."

Still flipping pancakes, Poppy said mildly, "Shall we call you Nyana then? Everyone will wonder why the change."

I didn't feel up to explaining any further, so I said, "Ayah, well, then, I'll be Nyana disguised as Flora, but I won't be Flora Segunda. Just plain Flora. You'd better remember that, Valefor."

"I'll try," Valefor muttered. "Nyana! *That* certainly explains a lot."

I ignored him and said to Poppy, "What if Mamma sees Valefor?"

"Hung for a sheep as well as for a lamb," Poppy said, setting a plate of pancakes in front of me. I poured ginger syrup and began to wolf. If Poppy wanted to take on Mamma—let him. It was of no account to me.

Poppy sat down across from me. "Now, let's have a little palaver. I've told Valefor that he can come down, as long as he behaves himself and keeps out of Buck's way."

"I will, I will!" Valefor said happily.

"You'd better be careful with him, Poppy. He bites," I said.

"I don't think he'll bite me, will you, Valefor?"

"No, of course not, Hotspur, I would never," Valefor agreed. "What Buck doesn't know can't hurt us, ayah."

"Did you tell Mamma what happened, Poppy?" I still wasn't sure if I wanted to know, but I supposed I'd better. I hadn't decided which was worse—that she didn't know, or that she did and hadn't said anything about it to me. Perhaps we were going to ignore everything; we are good, Fyrdraacas are, at ignoring things.

"No. I didn't want to upset her."

Ayah, ignoring. What did Haðraaðas do when they had family problems? Murder each other, I guessed.

"But Axacaya broke into our House! He tried to kill Flora!" Valefor protested.

Poppy replied, "Oh, I haven't forgotten any of that, no fear. But if Buck finds out about his trespass and what he tried to do to Flora, she might do something rash."

Poppy worried about someone doing something rash—what a joke.

"And that would ruin everything," he continued. "Never fear, I'll take care of Axacaya, but let's let him cool down a bit, think he's out of the woods. They take the blow harder when they don't see it coming." And then Poppy turned the conversation toward something else, and that was it. Subject closed. I thought of many things I wanted to say, but Poppy's matter-of-fact tone when he said he would take care of Axacaya had been chilling, and it didn't invite further comment.

After breakfast, on Poppy's orders, I cleaned my room, folded a whole bunch of threadbare towels, helped Poppy carry the groceries in, and gave the dogs baths. All of this put me in an extremely bad mood. What was the point? I'd saved the City, come back from the dead, found out I was the Head of the House Haðraaða and I was still doing chores? Still hopping to Poppy's tune? Still the same old Flora? Flora Segunda?

Since I had woken up from the fever, I had felt full of nothing. Now I was full of horrible thoughts—of running away to Bilskinir House, where no one could push me around. But as furious as I was, the thought of going to Bilskinir made my insides curl; I just couldn't face that yet. I could run away to some other place where no one had ever heard of the Haðↄ raaðas *or* the Fyrdraacas. Idden had scarpered, why couldn't I? But where could I go alone? How would I live? What would I do?

I remembered what Nini Mo had said: *Success is all that counts.* By that measure I had been successful: I had saved the City, saved the Loliga, saved Udo. But despite all these successes, I felt like a failure. Nini Mo's stories were all lies. I had failed in my attempt to find a Gramatica teacher. And I had been completely fooled by Axacaya. I was a gullible, idiotic fool.

Still in this awful mood, thinking these awful thoughts, I finally joined Poppy in the parlor for our lesson. Valefor was in the kitchen, happily polishing silver, and the dogs were in the back garden, chasing ducks. The parlor table was covered with books; clearly this was going to be a long lesson.

"Howdy, Pig," Poppy said, when I sat down and put Pig on the chair next to me.

Pig didn't answer, just looked at Poppy expressionlessly.

"You aren't trying to tell me something, are you, Flora?" Poppy asked.

"What do you mean?"

"Bringing Pig to the party is like sitting down to play poker and putting your gun on the table. It sends a message."

"I just like his company." And I did. Even though he had shown no sign of life since Bilskinir, he made me feel safe.

"Pig's always been good in a pinch. Azota had a lot of Will. Her sigils stick."

At the mention of Tiny Doom's other nickname, a tiny needle ran through my heart. Poppy had never mentioned her to me before. When he had still been drunk and crazy, it didn't take much to set him off into catastrophic wailing. Was he going to erupt into a huge sorrowful meltdown?

He didn't. He just said, quite calmly, "I started to suspect it when you came to me on the day of your Catorcena and told me off. You sounded exactly like she did when she was calling me on my crap. Which she did quite often, me so often being full of crap. I knew I was right when Pig arrived. There is only one Pig. There was only one reason Paimon would send him to you."

I didn't know what to say, so I just stared at Poppy. He was sharpening a pencil, the long strokes of the knife curling up shreds of wood, not looking at me.

"You are probably pissed at your mother for not telling you. I was rather pissed myself. I still am, but actually, I suppose I can't blame Buck for feeling as though I was not a steady bet to keep a secret. I see her point—the fewer people who know, the better."

"Why? Why does it have to be a secret?" My voice sounded cracked and high.

"The Birdies believe in doing things thoroughly, Flora. It's not enough to condemn a prisoner and put her to death. If her crime is great enough, it pollutes her entire line, sours it. They didn't just sentence Azota to death; they sentenced her entire family. Which would have included you, if they'd known about you."

"But won't they know now?" I squeaked. "Won't Axacaya tell them?"

"Oh, I wager that he'll keep this to himself for a while, while he tries to figure out how to use it to his advantage. He may be a Birdie himself and under their protection, but that don't mean he's happy about it. He chafes. He'd like to be free of them as much as we would—only for entirely different reasons. I don't think he's going to blab."

"But what about his Quetzal guards? Aren't they loyal to the Birdies?" I felt a pang at the thought of Axila Aguila. She'd been trying to kill me, but that didn't make me feel any better.

"They'd blab, for sure, if any of them were alive to do so." Poppy smiled wolfishly and I didn't want to know any more. "Don't fret, Flora. The Birdies aren't going to get you. I'm not going to let them. Your mother—Buck—is not going to let them."

"But why didn't Mamma tell me?"

"I guess she thought she was protecting you."

"But I have the right to know. I should know. She should have told me."

"Ayah, that's true. And now you know. What are you going to do about it?"

"I don't know." I wanted to confront Mamma, but I was afraid. Afraid of what she would say when she realized that I had been gulled by Axacaya, that I had given him ammunition against our family, that I had meddled in the Current. Afraid that she would drop the pretense of being my mother, and then what? What if she had lied about loving me, too? Soon there would a new Fyrdraaca. A real Fyrdraaca. Once Mamma had that baby, would she need me anymore?

"Well, you think about it, and let me know. And that brings me to something else, Flora . . ."

Uh-oh—here it came, finally. Where Poppy lectured me about being a fool, and to forget about magick, forget about Gramatica, forget about being a ranger. Where Poppy got all grown-up and paternal and commanding-officer on me.

"The Current is dangerous and unpredictable. You can't muck around in it; it'll drag you in and drown you. And you are leaving tracks—traces—that any good magician will see. You have got to lie low, not send up signal flares letting everyone know where you are and what you are doing. Keep it cool, Flora, or Califa knows what'll come sniffing around. Ayah?"

Poppy telling *me* to be more discreet! I said angrily, "What do you know about magick, anyway, Poppy? Are you a ranger or not? What about that badge you gave me?"

"I'm a ranger in a manner of speaking. I wasn't trained as a ranger, but toward the end, they needed all the help they could get. Delicacy ain't my line, but I do know a few tricks. They recruited me, and I did what I could. So I guess you could call me a provisional ranger."

"Does Mamma know?"

Another wolfish grin. "No."

And then I could no longer contain that which had been most weighing on my mind, which seemed to have swelled in my brain until there was no room for anything else. "Don't you love Mamma, Poppy?"

"Of course I do, Flora."

"Then what about *her*?" I couldn't say her name. It seemed stupid to keep calling her Tiny Doom, and Azota didn't seem right, either, but I couldn't call her Mamma.

"You can love two people at the same time in different ways, Flora. Buck and I were affianced in childhood, for our families' sake. We did our duty and we married and loved each other. But Azota—" He broke off and looked down at the pencil he was twirling, round and round and round. "That was different. It didn't make any difference between Buck and me. Your mother—Buck—understood. And you must not listen to the lies the Birdies spread about Azota; she wasn't the monster they made her out to be. She was . . . difficult . . . but she wasn't a monster."

I waited for him to continue, but he just stared at the twirling pencil. There was much I still wanted to say: How could he not know about me? How did Tiny Doom smuggle me out? Where was I really born? How much magick did he know? How did he find out that Axacaya was after me? But the questions were stuck in my throat. We sat in silence for a few minutes, and he just kept twirling that pencil until I wanted to grab it out of his hand and stick it in his eye.

Finally, Poppy put the pencil down and said brightly, "Well, then, did you read chapter eight of Captain Kotz's *Customs of the Service for Non-Commissioned Officers* as I requested?"

"No."

"Well, I suppose it don't really matter. I never liked Kotz; he was the most stuck-up pumpion I've ever met. He preferred charges against me once for whistling too loudly on the front porch of Building Fifty-six. What a whey-faced prune. So, good-bye, Kotz." Poppy picked up the book and tossed it away; it landed on the sofa next to Flynn, who half jumped out of his skin.

"How about chapter nine of *Hardel's Tactics*?"

"No."

"Massey's *Gunner's Handbook*?"

"No."

"Chapter one of *The Morphology of Littoral Languages and Their Cognates*?"

"No." I'd never even heard of that book. What the fike was a littoral language?

"Well, it would have been amazing if you had, Flora. Valefor!"

"Ayah?" Valefor's disembodied voice answered querulously. "What do you want? You interrupted my spoon count and I shall have to start all over again now."

"Valefor," Poppy said quietly. "Would you please bring me Thornton's *Morphology* and Xing's *Didactic Grammar*?"

"They are proscribed, in my Special Collection—"

"Valefor."

With a thump, two fat books materialized on the table. "Anything else?" Valefor's still-disembodied voice asked, in a much nicer tone this time.

"No, thanks. Don't forget to polish the pickle forks."

"Ha!"

Poppy cleared the table, then pushed the top book toward me. It was as thick as two redboxes stacked on each other, and the elaborately tooled leather cover was locked with a gold hasp. A faint galvanic burr was coming from the book, low and steady, like the purr of a cat.

"I'm not fluent," Poppy was saying, "but I know enough to get you started. If you are going to muck about, you'd better know what you are doing. Be able to cover your tracks. If you are not with us, Flora, you are against us. I hope you will be with us."

I looked up at him, startled, remembering Nini Mo saying

the exact same thing. Poppy smiled faintly and nodded toward the book. I undid the hasp and heaved the book open to the title page, which at first appeared to be blank. Then tiny, sparkling glyphs began to scroll across the page.

Gramatica.

AFTER

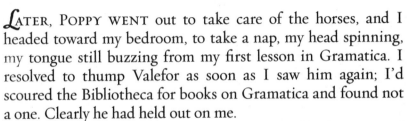

*L*ATER, POPPY WENT out to take care of the horses, and I headed toward my bedroom, to take a nap, my head spinning, my tongue still buzzing from my first lesson in Gramatica. I resolved to thump Valefor as soon as I saw him again; I'd scoured the Bibliotheca for books on Gramatica and found not a one. Clearly he had held out on me.

I met Udo on the stairs, leading a charge of barking excited dogs. He handed me a cake box—"from Arden's Cake-o-Rama, your favorite, chocolate chile with caramel frosting"—and escorted me to the kitchen. As I cut the cake, Udo got straight to the point. He wanted Springheel Jack's boots, which we had left at Bilskinir House. He wanted me to go back with him and get them.

Go back to Bilskinir! The delicious cake dried up in my mouth. I knew that someday I would have to go back to Bilskinir. But not today. Not tomorrow. Not for a long time.

"I can't, Udo."

"I want those boots, Flora. I went through a lot to get them, and they are mine. I remember everything that happened while I was Springheel Jack, though I sure wish I didn't, and I want something for all that pain. I *earned* them. I want that bounty. I need those boots." Udo was so upset that he didn't seem to notice or care that his pompadour was wilting. "I already went to

Bilskinir alone, but Paimon wouldn't let me in. He didn't even answer the door. He'll let *you* in. And you have to face the fact that it's your House sometime, Flora."

"Can we talk about something else, Udo?" My throat was starting to close up in panic.

"You do what you want, Flora. Ignore it, but I promise it won't go away. And I won't go away, either. I want those boots. You owe them to me after everything I've done for you. I'm just asking you this one small thing. Go with me to get the boots and then I don't care if you never go back to Bilskinir ever again. You owe me, Flora."

This I could not argue with. I owed him my life. He had stayed in Bilskinir Baths, as they crumbled around him, to make sure I returned to the Waking World. He had carried me from the ruins and gotten me safely home. Without Udo, I'd still be dead. Really dead. Dead forever. The least I could do was give him a pair of boots in return. True, I had promised Springheel Jack that I would find him a new avatar, but I owed Udo first. And promises made under duress aren't binding anyway, right?

Right.

WHEN WE REACHED Bilskinir House, it was shrouded in fog. We rode toward the base of the cliff, me on Sieur Caballo, Pig sitting before me, and Udo on Bonzo. As we approached the rocky foundation, the fog lifted briefly. Directly ahead, the Gateway of Munificence shimmered into existence. I now knew that this, not the little wooden gate at the top of the causeway, was Bilskinir's main entrance. The Gateway only manifests to the Head of the House Haðraaða; it is activated by the scratchy Key I wore around my finger. Or so Udo had informed me, having gotten this information from the entry on Bilskinir House in *The City in Shadow and Shade* guidebook. Now that I was not running (jumping) for my life, I had leisure to examine the Gateway as we approached it. Like the rest of Bilskinir, it was gigantically elegant: two enormous silver doors, polished to a blazing shine. The doors slid open at our approach, and before I lost my nerve, I spurred Sieur Caballo forward.

Briefly, we passed through darkness, and then almost immediately into warm sunshine. Down the Tunnel of Trees we jogged, onto the carpetlike grass of Bilskinir's Great Lawn. The sheep bleated a greeting and the dog pack flowed toward us, yodeling joyfully, Flynn dashing ahead to join them. The sky overhead looked like pale blue enamel, and the grass once again grew lush and thick, neatly cropped. The House gleamed sapphire-blue, its minarets, towers, buttresses, and gables glittering in the sunlight, which also made the windows look like hundreds of sparkling eyes watching us. Paimon's blue bulk, a tall figure standing on Bilskinir's wide front porch, was visible even at our distance.

I had thought I had already been about as afraid as I could ever be, before: when I had faced Axacaya and begged for my life; when I had told Mamma I would not go to the Barracks; when I had thought I might be trapped in the oubliette forever; when I had drowned in the Cold Plunge; when I had activated the Translocation Sigil. Those had been real fears, about real dangers. There was no danger here. And yet my fear lodged in my throat like a stone, making me shake.

Udo dismounted first and gave me his hand to help me down. I was glad, so glad, for Udo. He knew it, too, for he squeezed my hand tightly as we walked up the steps, and gave me a reassuring smile. Sieur Caballo followed Bonzo toward the stables.

At our approach, Paimon made the courtesy As a Servant to His Mistress, Respectfully but Without Servility. I returned the gesture As a Pupil to Her Teacher, with Honor and Respect and by the glint of his tusks, I think Paimon was pleased with my choice. He and Udo exchanged the courtesies To One Who Is Owed Great Thanks. Paimon nodded at Pig, who did not nod back.

"Come meet the rest of the family," Paimon said when all this flourishing, bowing, gesturing, and waving was done.

"The rest of the family?" I said. "I thought I was all that was left."

"Oh, no, madama, they are all here. Come. You shall see."

As Udo and I followed Paimon into the Hall of Expectant Expectations, Udo poked me in the side and hissed, "Don't forget the boots!"

The Hall of Expectant Expectations was not empty, as I had seen it before, but full of a buzzing throng of people, who fell into silence as they saw us. Suddenly I felt woefully underdressed. The waiting throng was fantastically arrayed in formal court-dress, their gorgeously bright outfits accented with glittering jewelry. And me in my old kilt and Tiny Doom's worn buckskin jacket. At least I had put on lip rouge and my hair was clean.

"The Head of the House Haðraaða," Paimon said grandly, bowing so low that his mustachios brushed the floor.

The crowd surged at me like a tidal wave. People were coming at me left and right, back and front. I was kissed, hugged, patted, squeezed, and twirled. Paimon couldn't keep up with the introductions; he was shooting names at me, rapid-fire, and they were flying right over my head. But one thing was clear: They were all Haðraaðas, literally hundreds of Haðraaðas, one after another. Where had they all come from? How had I not seen them before? And how could I be the *last* Haðraaða with all these Haðraaðas swarming me? Just as I was starting to feel light-headed from all the squeezing, the whirlwind parted. A familiar figure sailed forward. An imperious white head topped an imperious sangyn uniform—a Haðraaða I knew for an absolute fact was dead.

Hardhands.

"We've met, Paimon." Hardhands cut off Paimon's introduction. "Welcome to Bilskinir, almost-daughter." He ignored Pig, which was fine because Pig ignored him, as well.

"But you are dead!" I blurted, which probably wasn't the most polite thing to say, but I was feeling pretty overwhelmed. Next to me, Udo was uncharacteristically silent. I guess he was overwhelmed, too.

"Of course I am, girlie, or you shan't be here, in charge," Hardhands said scornfully. He might be dead, but he was still pretty stuck-up.

"What are you doing here if you are dead?" Udo asked, recovering.

"Ain't this my House?" Hardhands replied. "Why should I leave it just because I'm dead? I like it here."

Paimon interjected gently, "It is the custom of the Haðraaða family to rest within my environs, madama, even after death. You have seen the Cloakroom of the Abyss."

"But they didn't move then. I mean, they were all just lying there. Corpses!" I said. Hardhands was staring at me with an avid look that I didn't particularly like, as though I were a scrumptious cupcake and he had a craving for sugar. "Except the last time, when they weren't even there."

"Then, they were assisting me in the defense of Bilskinir House," Paimon answered. "Today, it is a special occasion, a new Head of the House, so of course the entire family is excited and animated. Normally the Animas are not so active. Georgiana Segunda was very concerned with family lineage; it was she who decided to use that as my underpinnings, the source of my continuing power, and so she spent much time tracking down the Anima of those Haðraaðas—and Bilskinirs—who had gone before us all, and bringing their Animas here, and containing them within my walls."

"You mean they are ghosts?" I asked, aghast. "Or reanimated corpses? Are they trapped in their bodies, like Georgiana Segunda was? That's horrible—"

"Ghosts!" Hardhands snorted. "Reanimated corpses! Listen to me, dolly—"

"Listen to you!" A voice behind him jeered, and he moved aside to allow entry to another familiar figure, who looked much, much better than I had last seen her: Georgiana Segunda. A ghoul no longer, she looked young and fresh. I realized now that we had the same color hair, coppery red, and just as curly, though her curls had been tamed into a mass of ringlets and mine were frizzy corkscrews. The enamel feathers of the Pontifexa crown on her white brow glimmered like dragonfly wings.

"Of course we are not trapped within our bodies like ghouls, dear Nyana," Georgiana Segunda said, with a pointed glance at Hardhands. "At least most of us are not. I intended that the energies of this family should always nurture both this House and Paimon, who has deigned to be our servant. So it was agreed that when a Haðraaða dies, his or her Anima joins the others, and together we are a well of strength that Paimon may draw from. This is how he survived all those years with no established living Head of the House. We nourished him in the interim while we waited for you."

"And you certainly did take your time!" Hardhands interjected. Georgiana Segunda whacked his arm with her fan—the fan Paimon had given me and with which I had fought off the Loliga's tentacle in the pisser of the Poodle Dog. Hardhands gave Georgiana a loving gaze, and did not look a bit abashed.

"Welcome to the family, Nyana," Georgiana Segunda said kindly. "You may kiss me."

She proffered a powdered cheek, and not knowing what else to do (and with the memory of Tiny Doom not so long ago—or, really, long ago—kissing that cheek, then filmed with mold), I kissed her. Her skin was smooth and soft and smelled like roses.

Georgiana Segunda said, "I am sorry that you had to deal with the Loliga, Nyana. Certainly, I never meant for things to work out the way they did. Tiny Doom should never have left you in the lurch that way—it was her responsibility to attend to the Loliga, and her responsibility to make sure that her daughter and heir knew her duties. But you acquitted yourself well, dear girl. You remind me of my dear mamma at that age; she also ascended at an early age, and was oft misjudged. Sweet as a bon-bon on the outside, but bite down and inside is an iron filling."

"Hell on your teeth," Hardhands remarked, and again was whacked with the fan.

Georgiana continued, "I think you shall do well, my dear.

Come, now—we haven't much time and I don't feel like wasting it blathering. Let us dance! You, Udo, dear sweet boyish morsel, dance with me."

Udo gallantly offered his arm to Georgiana Segunda and she swept him out to where the floor had suddenly cleared. Music burst out, and the rest of the Haðraaðas flung themselves into partnerships and began to hop about, extremely energetically for a horde of reanimated corpses and disembodied spirits.

"Shall we dance, little bon-bon?" Hardhands asked. He swung his arm low in a courtesy, but I shook my head. I still had the feeling that even though he wasn't a ghoul, he might snap at me if he had the chance. Hardhands took my refusal with an incredulous lift of one long black eyebrow and stalked away, the tails of his sangyn kilts swishing behind him with a reptilian hiss.

The dance floor was a crush of the Haðraaða dead. Those with bodies were so animated and forceful that you would hardly know, unless you squinted, they were dead. Those without bodies were ethereal and transparent, yet they, too, maintained their personalities. They knew who they were. Their Anima remained strong.

All the Haðraaðas were here.

All, I realized, but one.

Tiny Doom.

Her catafalque in the Cloakroom of the Abyss was empty; thanks to the Birdies there had been no body to bring home. But the Birdies couldn't touch her Anima; they could kill her body but they couldn't extinguish her soul. She had to be here somewhere. Everywhere I lo oked there were Haðraaðas, dancing, laughing, eating, talking. Standing in line at the buffet; laughing at each other's jokes; feeding the dogs nibbles; dancing the mazurka; threatening each other with umbrellas; toasting each other with punch glasses. Paimon had vanished; perhaps he was refilling the canapés, or retrieving Springheel Jack's boots. And I didn't see Tiny Doom anywhere.

"Where is she, Pig?" I asked. He didn't answer.

Then, I heard her voice in my head, as clear as if she were standing beside me. So clear, in fact, that I turned and looked, but there was no one there.

The Ultimate fiking Ranger Dare, baby.

And with a sick excitement, I realized that there was only one reason that Tiny Doom would not be here, celebrating my ascension with the rest of the Haðraaða family.

She wasn't dead.

Chatting with
Ysabeau Wilce

QUESTION: *The two main female influences on Flora—Mamma and Nini Mo—are strong, resourceful, and courageous women. Do you think Flora realizes that she has these characteristics as well?*

YSABEAU WILCE: I think Flora *aspires* to have these characteristics, but often feels that she fails to live up to the examples that Nini and Buck offer. She's trying, though! Sometimes she succeeds, sometimes she fails, but the important thing is that she does try! *Dare, Win, or Disappear!* as Nini Mo might say.

Q: *In contrast to most of the images teenage girls see in the media today, Flora is not a fashion victim and does not obsess over her weight. In contrast, her best friend Udo Landaðon is far more interested in fashion than she is. Do you think their relationship provides an opportunity to discuss gender and its construction?*

YW: Insofar as Flora and Udo are concerned, I wasn't trying to make a particular statement about the gendered construction of clothing. Udo's character just happened to be clothes-mad—I didn't plan on making him that way! In Califa, vanity is not a gendered vice—which is to say that men can be as vain as women, dress just as floridly, and be just as hair obsessed: e.g., Udo and the Dainty Pirate. Prior to the end of the eighteenth century, men's clothing was just as gaudy and fashion aware as women's, and it was this time that I wanted to evoke in Califa. Another major difference between the way that people dress in Califa versus the way we dress today (at least in the Western world), is that in Califa both men and women wear skirts. Why? Because I thought it would be cool!

I *am* extremely interested in the history of fashion, which is why I have tried to be rather specific in my descriptions of the clothing worn in *Flora Segunda*. Characters' clothing choices help to reveal their motivations and agendas. After all, clothing says a lot about people; it both reveals and disguises. Lord Axacaya, for example, continues to wear traditional Huitzil clothing—what does this say about him? Buck mostly appears in uniform, which is a kind of disguise, but she doesn't always wear garments appropriate to her rank—what does this say about her? Flora has to make her own dress for her Catorcena—her ability to do so says something about her maturity and readiness to be considered an adult.

Q: *Flora's initial impressions of Valefor, Lord Axacaya, Paimon, and even Poppy turn out to be wrong. Do you think Flora's tendency to jump to conclusions before she has all the facts serves as a warning to readers to think before making judgments about people and situations?*

YW: First impressions are important, but it's always good to reevaluate and keep an open mind. Flora is learning that life can be supercomplicated, and there's often more than one side to a story. However, I'm not sure that in our world we need to be so suspicious of everyone! Flora happens to live in a particularly political and tumultuous time and place, but most of us have much more prosaic lives and can take people more at face value.

Q: *Califa was the setting in "Metal More Attractive," one of your earlier short stories. With that piece and* Flora Segunda, *you're creating the history of Califa. Do you think history can play a role in works of fiction?*

YW: I think creating a sense of history is pretty important in fantasy worlds, because it helps to both anchor the setting and also make it seem more realistic. For fantasy to work well, it still has to have a kind of logic to it, and having realistic details help to make the fantastic elements easier to swallow. Keeping some details realistic also helps the reader to relate to the world and its inhabitants. As a historian, I'm fascinated by patterns and connections; history is made of interlocking events and motivations that are often only understood much later. I like to play with those connections; set the character loose, let them plot and scheme and see what happens. It makes the creative process seem like a little chess game, and much more entertaining than if I plan everything out myself!

Q: *Your short fiction has been widely acclaimed and has appeared in popular science fiction and fantasy magazines such as* The Magazine of Fantasy & Science Fiction *and* Asimov's Science Fiction. *What are the differences, if any, between writing a novel and a work of short fiction?*
YW: I find it easier to write novels. My short stories are always very long. I need the space to develop characterization and action. The most important element of fiction to me is characterization; I'm quite happy to have no plot, or an extremely slow plot, if the characters are compelling! But most people do require some action to move forward, and I find it hard to squeeze both character and action into a small word count.

Q: *The book has playful, descriptive language—choco sandwies and Stealie Girl, for example—sprinkled throughout the text. As well, there are a number of Spanish-sounding words such as Catorcena and Califa. Are you interested in how language is constructed and how it's influenced by culture?*
YW: Since I'm not really a linguist, I can't say much about language construction. But I am interested in how language is an expression of culture and also how it functions as a way to enforce group identity. Army slang, for example, is all about creating a sense of esprit de corps within a group of people whose only commonality is that they belong to the same army. Language can be quite powerful; obviously, I'm not the first writer

to explore that topic, nor the first to create a magickal system that hinges upon language. But since language really is a form of magick, I figured that there was room for one more on that boat, and thus climbed aboard! Language exposes us; our word choices tell the world who we are and what we believe, and sometimes even why. And of course, for a writer, language is all there is—it's the only way to communicate with the reader—words are all you have, so you must make sure each word is the right word, and make it count.

Q: *The type of stories you write can be considered speculative fiction. How do you feel about categorization of your work? Which writers or genres did you read when you were younger? Who do you read now?*
ΥW: All fiction is speculative, of course. And all fiction is fantastic by its very nature—even fiction that pretends to be realistic. Specific categorizations, I think, are more meaningful to booksellers and reviewers than they are to writers. I just write what I write; I don't worry about the details.

When I was younger my favorite books, and therefore biggest influences, were probably T. H. White's *The Once and Future King,* Shakespeare's *Hamlet,* Gene Wolfe's *The Shadow of the Torturer,* and all the Icelandic sagas. I also read tons and tons of popular history which also hugely influenced me. I pretty much read everything I could get my hands on, and graduated out of children's fiction at a pretty early age.

Modern writers/books I adore include Dorothy Dunnett, whose books are so complicated and rich with details and melodrama; George MacDonald Fraser's hilariously bawdy Flashman books; Elizabeth Hand, who writes lushly descriptive novels about obsessive artists and terrifyingly beautiful dystopian futures; Paul Park's gorgeous Starbridge novels, as well as his latest series, *The Princess of Roumania;* and Stephen King, who is, in my opinion, *the* great American novelist of the twentieth century!

Specific young adult writers I love include Diana Wynne

Jones; Tove Jansson; Tanith Lee; Joan Aiken; Ursula K. Le Guin; Daniel Pinkwater; and T. H. White, just to name a few.

Q: When can readers expect to read more of Flora's fantastic adventures?
*Y*W: As soon as Flora gets out of bed and gets going!